I0639619

# TRUSTICE JEFFRIES:

# FEAR INT* DARKNESS

## TAYLOR DYE

SAMANEDNA

FEAR INTO DARKNESS

Copyright © 2016 by Taylor Dye

Cover Art and Design by Najla Qamber Designs
najlaqamberdesigns.com

All rights reserved.
No part of this publication may be used or reproduced in any manner, in
any form, or by any means, without the consent and written permission
of the publisher.

ISBN-13 978-0692598320
ISBN-10 0692598324

Samanedna Publishers
samanedna.com

This story is a work of fiction. Any references to real people, events,
establishments, organizations, or locales are intended only to lend the
story a sense of reality and authenticity and are used fictitiously. All other
names, characters, places, and all dialogue and incidents contained
therein, are the product of the author's imagination.

*Previous Titles by Taylor Dye*

THE INTERMEDIARIES: BEAT & CASE
THE INTERMEDIARIES: REDEMPTION

*To all of those who live in fear...they say the first step is always the hardest.*
*Take it anyway.*

# CHAPTERS

# FEAR INTO DARKNESS

# 1.

# Arrivals

TRUST POINTED TO A PLACE near the top of the small sheet of paper. He then watched as the cheery girl looked where he had indicated.

*Trustice Jeffries*

"Oh, Trustice Jeffries!"

The girl looked up at him again, her bright eyes meeting his blue ones.

"You're the deaf student, right?" she asked in a lowered, slightly conspiratorial tone. Trust could see, though not hear, the difference.

He smiled back at her.

"I just remember them telling us your name," the girl continued, taking the small printout and placing it neatly in a pile along with the rest on her welcome table. A handcrafted banner—*Welcome to Weaver Hall*—in showy, colorful lettering adorned the front edge of the table, reaching down to the floor.

"Your name is very—"

She stopped speaking abruptly, and Trust noticed her jovial expression waver as her thoughts shifted.

"Can you understand what I'm saying?"

Trust smiled again, inclining his head.

"You're reading my lips?" the girl asked, her voice and face conveying her astonishment.

Trust gestured with his hands.

*Yes, I'm reading your lips. But isn't there a key you need to give me, or…*

"Is that sign language?" the girl asked excitedly. "That's amazing! What does it mean?"

"Hey, T-Dawg! What'd I miss?"

Trust glanced to his right as he noticed a figure approach from the corner of his vision. Kyler waltzed into the lobby through the open doors, a duffel bag slung across his body and a small, filled-to-the-brim-with-stuff trash bin secured under his other arm. Tufts of blond hair framed the sides of his face, with most of the rest tied in a careless bun or simply hanging loose in the back. A worn hat sat loosely on top.

Kyler shifted his gaze to the girl at the welcoming table.

"T-Dawg's not giving you any backtalk, is he?" he asked, inclining his head in Trust's direction. "Because if he is, feel free to slap him around a little—he's a marshmallow."

*T-Dawg?* Trust motioned.

The girl stared at Kyler, her expression glassy-eyed, before she shook herself out of the trance.

"Um, I'm sorry, what? No, I was just—"

"Argh, I'm sorry," Kyler said.

He fumbled the small trash bin briefly as he transferred it from one hip to the other while still supporting the duffel bag along his upper body. He then extended his now free hand across the table toward the girl.

"I'm Kyler-Scott," he introduced as the girl took his hand. "That's my first name, with a hyphen in there. My full name is Kyler-Scott Brooks. And I'm not deaf."

"Jessica," the girl responded, her bright smile returning full force. Kyler smiled back at her, inadvertently causing Jessica's heart to skip a beat. Suddenly, Kyler's smile vanished.

"Oh, my paper," he said, releasing Jessica's hand as he began to pat down one side of his body. He glanced over to Trust.

"Did you give her your slip already, T-Dawg?"

Before Trust could respond, Jessica answered, "Yes, he just gave it to me. I was telling him what a unique name—"

"I know I just had that thing!"

Kyler switched the trash can back to his other arm before looking to Trust.

"Here, T-Dawg. Hold this for a sec," he said, thrusting the bin full of knickknacks into Trust's chest, who let out a soft "oomph" in reply. Kyler continued to pat himself down, beginning near his feet and coming up to his chest before starting back down again. He paused at his kneecaps and looked up to find Trust snickering lightly. Kyler slowly raised himself to his full height, the answering smirk on his face fully sarcastic.

"Okay, thief," Kyler said. "That was a good one. Now go ahead and hand it over so we don't have any trouble."

The blond-haired boy extended his hand, palm up, his fingers beckoning.

Still smiling, Trust shook his head and held both arms out—one hand still gripping the miniature trash can—indicating he had nothing to hide. Kyler eyed him with suspicion before shifting his gaze to Jessica, who also held an amused smile on her face.

"Jessica," Kyler started, glancing at Trust again, "since you're in charge here, I would like to report a robbery, and I believe I can ID the perp. He's standing right in front—"

"Ugh, Kyler," a girl said as she stepped into the entrance hall carrying a large rubber bin, "you're still out here? What, did you get caught trying to smuggle in some contraband? And it's not even the first day of school yet."

Kyler glanced to Jessica quickly.

"That's my sister," he explained, "and, of course, she's joking about the contraband."

He looked back to his sister and smirked.

"She knows I would never get caught."

"Seriously," the younger girl, who looked to be about high-school-aged, said. "Are you just hanging out here or are you planning to actually move into the lobby? This thing's heavy."

Trust got the girl's attention.

*Jessica hasn't given me the key to our room yet,* he signed while balancing the trash can between his chest and upper arm. *Probably because your dim-witted brother "lost" his check-in paper. And he keeps calling me T-Dawg.*

"Uhh, T-Dawg," Kyler said, "I'm standing right here. I can totally see what you said."

"Who's T-Dawg?" the girl asked.

"He's T-Dawg," Kyler said, pointing.

*I'm NOT T-Dawg,* Trust returned.

Meanwhile, Kyler's younger sister continued to look at Trust.

"Why are you even bothering to hold that stupid trash can while you are just standing there, signing?" she asked.

Trust shrugged.

*Why are you still holding that box?* he asked.

The girl rolled her eyes, dismissing him, before she turned to Kyler. Looking him over, she rolled her eyes again.

"What's that mysterious sheet of paper sticking out of the side of your hat there?"

"What?"

On impulse, Kyler glanced upward, as though he would be able to see what she was talking about, before reaching up to take his hat off. The slip of paper began to flit lightly to the ground before Trust caught it in mid-flight. He glanced at the slip quickly before handing it to Kyler, who was fitting the worn white cap back onto his unkempt mass of hair.

Trust was smirking again.

"Okay, Mr. Magic Man," Kyler said, taking the slip while sneering at Trust's smug expression, "that was a neat trick, because I have no idea how that got up there."

Beside him, his sister scoffed again.

"I saw you put it under your hat before you got out of the car," she asserted.

Kyler shook his head, a look of skepticism lining his features as he handed the slip over to an apparently amused Jessica.

"Excuse her. She's only entering the eleventh grade," he explained, mumbling loudly. "I find it easiest to just agree with whatever she says, even when it makes no sense. Otherwise, she has the tendency to turn into an absolute—"

He stumbled forward as his sister shoved him with the container she was holding. Trust laughed openly as he watched the typical brother-sister exchange.

"Michelle Brooks, what have I said about beating up on your older brother?" a maternal voice announced from the doorway of the lobby.

The four teenagers turned to see Sherry Brooks in the entranceway, her eyebrow arched in the way only experienced mothers seemed to be able to convey.

Kyler snickered. "Looks like someone's about to be given a stern talking-to."

"Oh, please, Kyler," Mrs. Brooks scolded, "because we all know you probably deserved it."

Behind the welcome table, Jessica shook her head, laughing.

"I think I could watch this all day," she said.

TRUST LEANED AGAINST THE STORAGE bin he had just hoisted onto his bare mattress and watched the others in the room speak.

The seventh-floor dorm room he would be sharing with Kyler for the next school year had turned out to be not as small as he imagined. There was more than enough space for the two identical beds that lined opposite walls of the room, with more space along the back wall to fit a futon or some other such piece of furniture if they were so inclined. The currently sparse room held only its barest, pre-furnished items at the moment—beds, desks, chairs, floor-to-wall wardrobe, and, of course, his and Kyler's boxes and containers. Since Trust had been expecting a room barely big enough for one person, he was more than satisfied with the assigned quarters.

He then snapped to attention as he noticed his mother motioning to him. The others in the room were also looking in his direction.

"We're trying to decide where to go eat," Sonja Jeffries voiced and gestured at the same time. "What do you have a taste for?"

Trust performed a simple, fluid motion with his hands, twirling his pinky fingers away from each other.

"And how did I know you were going to say that?" Mrs. Jeffries asked, though a faint smile hinted at her cinnamon-hued features.

"Spaghetti sounds all right to me," Kyler declared. "All that moving, I think I've worked up a little bit of an appetite, and some old-fashioned Italian carbos should do just the trick."

"Anything sounds all right to you," Michelle, his sister, commented. Kyler shrugged.

"Well then, if no one has any objections," Tom Brooks, the patriarch of the Brooks clan, said, "Eye-talian it is."

"Eye-talian," Kyler scoffed as he mimicked his dad's pronunciation of the word. "It's a soft 'I,' Dad. I know that and I haven't even officially started my college edu-ma-cation yet."

Trust and the others chuckled, Trust more from the smug, know-it-all expression on his friend's face.

"Soft 'I'? I'll show you soft 'I,'" Mr. Brooks said, and with that, he grabbed at Kyler quickly, securing his son in a headlock before he could dodge out of the way. Even though Kyler himself was pretty tall—and still growing—his barrel-chested father still had about six inches on him.

"Mr....Mr. Jeffries!" Kyler strangled out weakly as he tried to pry his father's thick arms loose.

"Sorry, guy," Tyson Jeffries responded, chuckling deeply. "My hands are tied."

As he said this, he shrugged his shoulders, his palms facing upward. He then looked over to his own son.

*Your friend is crying like a little girl over there,* he signed, smirking.

*I'm glad I can't hear it,* Trust replied. *That seems like it would sound pretty terrible.*

*Your father means "little child,"* Mrs. Jeffries corrected, eyeing her husband.

*Sorry,* Mr. Jeffries corrected, *I must have gotten the signs mistaken.*

Mrs. Jeffries smiled in acceptance and looked away.

*Not really,* Mr. Jeffries then motioned quickly when he thought his wife was not looking, which caused Trust to laugh lightly. Mrs. Jeffries, who, in fact, had been paying attention, elbowed her husband in the stomach, which then caused Trust to laugh slightly harder.

"I hope I'm not interrupting anything?" a voice called out from the doorway, which caused Mr. Brooks to finally release his son's head and the others to glance toward the entrance. Trust turned as he noticed the room's interest had suddenly and simultaneously shifted toward the doorway.

The young man appeared to be a few years older than Trust and Kyler—probably a junior or senior—with a longish, wavy mop of brown hair and a faded gray *Stolen Property of UCC* T-shirt, the *Stolen* crossed out. He looked as though he could just as easily be at home beachside with a surfboard as he was on a college campus, and his easy, sheepish smile suggested that he might not have anticipated as many expectant gazes directed at him from inside the room.

"Sorry," he apologized, "I just wanted to introduce myself. My name is Holden, and I'm the R—"

"Wait, wait, don't tell me," Kyler interjected quickly. "You're the RA."

He gestured the older boy inside the dorm room and extended his hand. Trust shifted his glances between the two boys and his mother, who was signing the interplay for him.

"Man, I am just too good," Kyler went on, shaking Holden's hand. "I'm Trustice Jeffries—Trust for short—and I'm—"

He was halted abruptly as Michelle smacked him on the back of the head.

"Um, *ow*," Kyler said, glancing toward his younger sister and rubbing the back of his head with his free hand.

"His name is Kyler-Scott, actually," Michelle explained to a wide-eyed, yet smiling, Holden. "I would suggest you memorize his face and general physical appearance as soon as humanly possible, because whenever anything should go wrong around here, I would strongly advise that Kyler be your first, and probably only, suspect."

"Michelle," Mrs. Brooks admonished.

"I'm just trying to do my good deed for the day, Mom," Michelle responded, turning to her mother and smiling kindly. The Brooks and Jeffries parents both laughed.

"A troublemaker, eh?" Holden said, looking from Michelle to Kyler. "Thanks for the heads-up. Welcome to UCC, Kyler-Scott. And since we don't allow cross-gender cohabitation in the dorms on campus, I'm going to guess that you're Trustice."

Holden stood in front of Trust and stretched out his hand, which Trust received, nodding.

"Is this okay—me speaking like this?" Holden asked. "Dr. Duncan told us—the RAs, I mean—that you would be able to read our mouths as we talked as long as we were facing you, so I just want to make sure I'm not doing anything wrong."

Trust waved him off before he started to speak with his hands.

*It's fine. If I don't understand something, I'll let you know, or I'll have my assistant, Kyler, take care of it.*

Kyler interpreted for Trust nearly as fast as Trust signed, adding a "Dude, that's so not funny" for Trust's benefit as the others, including Holden, laughed.

"Actually," Holden offered, "when I first heard you were coming, and they said you could read lips, I tried to watch TV on mute. Seriously, that's, like, the hardest thing ever, trying to figure out what everyone was saying. I have no idea how you do it—it must be like a superpower or something."

Holden then looked to the others in the room.

"I can already tell this is going to be a fun and interesting year. Definitely full of surprises."

He then introduced himself to the rest of the Jeffries and Brooks families.

"I just wanted to meet everybody and tell Kyler-Scott and Trustice that there will be an introductory hall meeting at six o'clock tonight out in the TV room. I don't like saying anything is mandatory—this is college, after all—but if you were to go to any hall meeting this year, this would definitely be the one."

"That means it's mandatory, guy," Mr. Brooks said, playfully thumping Kyler's old baseball cap. The Jeffrieses were busy conveying a similar message to Trust.

"I'll get out of your way, then," Holden said, beginning to back toward the door. "It was nice meeting everyone."

He then glanced to Trust and Kyler.

"And I'm sure I'll be seeing you two at the meeting tonight. Otherwise, I'll have to call your parents."

As Holden departed, Kyler called after him, "Hey, Holden! My sister wants your number!"

Michelle and Mr. Brooks both thumped Kyler at the same time, with Michelle adding a few more on his shoulder for good measure.

THE ITALIAN RESTAURANT WAS LOCATED just off UCC's rural campus. The interior was cozy and dimly lit, without giving off a feeling of constriction. As the two families were being led to their table in the restaurant, Kyler-Scott hugged his arms around Trust's and Michelle's shoulders.

"When..." he started to croon in dramatic eloquence, "the...moon hits your eye like a big pizza pie, that's—"

"Oh, shut up, you big dope," Michelle said, shrugging her brother's arm off. "Do you have to start singing that every time we eat Italian?"

"Eating Italian always gets me in the mood to sing it," Kyler said, grinning. "Anyway, I know you're going to miss it when you're back at home eating at Napoli's and I'm not around."

Kyler then turned to Trust, who had not been paying attention.

"Meanwhile," he continued so Trust could read his lips, "I'll be up here serenading my best bud."

Confusion came across the deaf teen's features as the party sat down at their table.

Michelle signed to Trust, *He is so annoying.*

Trust gazed back at her with a straight face.

*And so are you,* Michelle added.

Trust grinned.

"That hostess sure did smile a lot at you two," Tom said, glancing between Trust and Kyler. "And I would guess she goes to the university."

Tyson Jeffries chuckled.

"So, you noticed that too, Tom?" he asked. "I thought it was just me."

"Huh?" Kyler asked in bafflement before turning around in the leather booth to look back the way they had come. "What? Where?"

*Maybe she just smiles a lot,* Trust motioned. *Was Kyler singing again?*

Michelle scoffed.

"It definitely wasn't because of his singing," she said.

Then her face brightened as she noticed someone approaching.

"Oh, here she comes again."

Grinning excitedly, Kyler looked up—only to be met by their male server. Kyler's smile faltered noticeably. He looked toward his younger sister in annoyance as the others at the table laughed.

"That's really not funny, dear sister," he intoned in an empty voice.

"I feel like I just arrived at the tail end of a joke," the server said, smiling uncertainly.

Michelle returned his smile.

"Yeah, and you were the punch line," she said. "But don't worry. It was in a good way. *Very* good."

Michelle's final words held a slightly suggestive tone, and Kyler made a face.

"Eww. Okay, sis, new rule. You're not allowed to talk to guys anymore while I'm around. It creeps me out."

Everyone ordered, with both Kyler and Trust asking for their usual standby, spaghetti, Kyler's with extra sauce.

"Too old, Miss Brooks," Tom said, looking at his daughter, his wry grin a not-so-subtle hint as the college-aged waiter—who had introduced himself as Riley—left the table with their drink and food orders.

"What are you going on about now, Tom?" Sherry asked, though everyone at the table, including Sherry—and including Trust—understood exactly what Tom Riley was "going on about."

"I'm not going on about anything," Tom replied.

"Oh, really? And just after that little comment about the hostess, you want to say something?"

Sherry turned to Sonja Jeffries.

"Anything to add, Sonj?"

"Oh, I would be more than happy to, Sherry," Sonja replied.

Her smile was dangerously alluring—like a shark's.

"Wait," Tom said. "I didn't say I condoned that hostess's actions, or vice versa, if that had been the case. I only commented on it. And actually, Sherry, I don't see why—"

"Give it up, Tom," Tyson coughed loudly in an effort to warn his friend of the trap he was falling into. "Give it up."

Meanwhile, Kyler nudged Trust in his side. When Trust's eyes turned to him, Kyler nodded back to the looming dialogue across from them, as if to signal, *Watch this*. Trust chuckled. Michelle was also listening, her quirked eyebrow illustrating clearly which side of the debate she would fall on.

"Honey," Sonja said, turning to her husband, "would you care to remind our good friend here of our age difference?"

"Hmm, no, not really. Hey, Kyler, Trust, what were you two planning after—"

"And here are your drinks," Riley announced as he lowered his tray full of filled glasses to a more manageable level. "Let's see, a water here—"

"Good, you're back," Sherry said as the waiter continued to give out the drink orders. "We have a few questions we would like to ask you—if you don't mind, that is."

"We?" Tyson echoed. "I don't think—ow."

Eyes turned to Trust's father as he was elbowed in his ribs by his wife. Trust's gaze was a split second behind everyone else's, though he was quickly able to surmise what had happened. Sherry returned to the young waiter.

"Of course, ma'am," Riley replied, his eyebrows raised slightly. "Is it something concerning your order?"

"No, no, that's fine. Actually, this may be a little personal, so please, feel free not to answer or simply walk away. We were wondering, how—"

"I'll double your tip if you walk away right now," Tyson said, quickly and loudly, before receiving a very sharp, very troublesome, glare from his wife.

"Uh oh," Riley said, glancing from Tyson back to Sherry. "That bad, huh?"

"Not even close to that bad, Riley, I assure you," Sherry declared. "Could you tell us how old you are? I assume you are a student at the university."

Riley nodded.

"Yes, ma'am. I will be a junior this year. I'm twenty, but I'll be twenty-one in November. That wasn't really that hard a question."

Michelle sighed adoringly, causing both Kyler and Tom to give her an extended look.

"And please, tell me if I'm out of line here," Sherry continued, "but are you single?"

"Whoa," Kyler declared.

"Oh, dear God," Tom uttered.

"I'll triple your tip," Tyson urged. "Just please, feel free to walk away now. Like, right now."

A faint smile came across the waiter's lips.

"Actually, I have a boyfriend."

A pause.

Instantly, the two families followed Trust's example—though for obviously different reasons—by going silent. All eyes remained focused on Riley. The young waiter stood still, waiting, his faint smile still evident.

Sherry was the first to speak.

"I—uh...that's..."

From his position in the circular booth, Tyson raised himself awkwardly, offering his hand. Riley took it and they shook.

"That took some courage, Riley," he acknowledged. "Back in my day, well—let's just say, that took some courage. Consider that tip times three yours. My hat's off to you, son."

"And I apologize for being so flippant," Sherry said, regaining her ability to articulate. "It was completely out of line, and we were having what I would now call a ridiculous discussion, and—"

"It's really okay, ma'am," Riley assured her. "No worries. It was my choice to say it, and I have no problems with what others think about it, though if everyone's reaction was as accommodating—and as gracious—as you guys', I would probably start off by saying I'm gay while I'm listing off the specials for the day."

"Yeah, you probably should have done that for my sister," Kyler said, gesturing to Michelle. "That way you could have put her out of her misery early."

Riley laughed as Kyler was hit under the table by his exasperated younger sister.

After he left, the table again fell quiet, each person mulling over their own thoughts.

This time, Trust was first.

*Well, this is already turning out to be an interesting year.*

*Trust,* his mother said and signed, looking at him in stern warning.

However, the word of caution fell to the relieved laughs Trust observed from the rest of the table.

# 2.
# Hall Meeting

AS HOLDEN, THE RESIDENT ADVISOR, had stated previously, the hall meeting for the seventh floor, Central Wing, of Weaver Hall started promptly at six o'clock that evening in the TV room. The room held various handmade welcome signs and informational banners, adorning what looked to be freshly painted lime-green walls. An ample scattering of chairs, couches, and beanbags littered the carpeted portion, while a few tables—handy for both school-related and non-school-related activities—held space on the side that was bare floor. A large television was suspended against the far wall on the carpeted side, currently turned off.

"Okay, okay, okay," Holden said, standing in front of the TV, clapping, and then rubbing his hands together. "Welcome, everybody. Welcome to Weaver Hall. Welcome to your dream school, the University of Centre City. Welcome to the beginning of the next chapter of your lives. I say that this is the next chapter because I'm sure that your high school valedictorian told you in his or her speech that graduating high school was the ending of the last chapter. We don't happen to have any high school valedictorians in this group, do we?"

He looked around the room, as did some of the freshman students, and spotted the raised hand of one seemingly hesitant boy.

"Hey, it's cool...John, right?" Holden said, to which the boy lowered his hand and nodded with a quiet "Yeah."

"Yeah, it's cool, man," Holden went on. "I was just going to say that I hated those stuck-up valedictorians if there weren't any in here, but since there is one, I can tell the truth. I actually love those kind-hearted, gifted, super-talented valedictorians. But, to be completely honest, I was valedictorian of my high school class, so I may be just a tad biased."

Holden glanced to John again as he received a few soft chuckles from the room.

"Did you say anything in your graduation speech about new chapters, or old chapters, or books, or novels, or anything like that?"

"Um...I actually went the 'one door closes, another door opens' route," John replied.

More chuckles.

"Hah, I so did that, too!" Holden acknowledged. "We'll have to compare speech notes after this meeting. But speaking of meetings, let's get the paperwork out of the way."

He held up a binder. More were stacked beside him on the floor.

"General dormitory guidelines, mishmash, interesting facts, and all-around hoo-ha. Now, this shouldn't take long to go through, and I'm definitely not going to read every word, but I think it is pretty important that everyone know exactly what's what, because I guarantee you that by the end of the school year, each of you—and probably me also—will need a certain, particular tidbit of information that is easily found in this notebook. So, without further ado, let me pass this baby around..."

Their review of the *Weaver Hall Dormitory Diagnostics Manual* took twenty-one minutes, including questions directly related to the material contained therein. Sitting directly in front of Holden as he spoke, Trust was able to follow along easily. His eyes roved between the RA and the binder he held. In addition, Holden cleverly reframed the questions he was asked into his answers, which provided Trust reprieve from either guessing the question, turning his head back and forth in an attempt to follow the exchange, or calling on Kyler's assistance beside him. He was unsure if Holden's method was due to his presence or if it was the way the boy normally answered questions. In any case, it was useful.

"All right," Holden said, closing his booklet and glancing around to the twenty or so freshman boys and girls in his care. "That's that. But before I conclude this summit, I want to open it up to any questions or concerns that you have, whether they involve Weaver Hall policies specifically, or Centre City and university living in general. If no one has any questions, then I'll let you guys and gals run free, get dinner, get arrested—whatever your plans are for your first night on campus. Just remember, I'll be coming around in the next few weeks for the first room check, so try to keep it in some way tidy until then. And, of course, you guys are always welcome to stop by my room anytime—day or night—with whatever you want to talk about. That's what RAs are here for. All right, to anyone with a question, fire away."

No one left. Nevertheless, the mood in the room became less official and more relaxed, as a few of the students began whispering amongst themselves.

"Really?" Holden asked. "Nobody leaving? Okay, that must mean everyone is dying to ask me a question. That's cool. I've got all day. Heck, I've got all year. All right, who's going first?"

Kyler quickly raised his hand, with Trust immediately turning to his friend, a slight expression of surprise on his face. Seemingly unconscious of his movements, Kyler began to sign as he spoke.

"Concerning the use of alcoholic beverages—"

Some of the other freshmen in attendance began to laugh before Kyler had gotten even midway through his thought. Trust shook his head. Holden, standing and looking down toward Kyler, smirked.

"—is it acceptable if—theoretically, let's say—an aforementioned alcoholic beverage somehow, mysteriously, wound up in your possession, and since you're twenty-one, I presume..."

Kyler trailed off, beckoning with his eyes, voice, and hands for Holden to confirm his presumption. Still smirking, Holden shook his head.

"Nah, I won't be twenty-one for a couple more months, so it would be just as illegal for me as it would be for you. But please, continue with your question. I'm interested to see just how much worse your completely ridiculous theory can get."

"Aww, man!" Kyler moaned dramatically. "You're not twenty-one? Well, there goes that plan. But, on the other hand, let's just say that—theoretically—when you do turn twenty-one, that you, somehow—accidently, mind you—*hey!*"

Trust's elbow was strong enough to send Kyler toppling off the beanbag he was lounging on and onto the carpet, his loosely fitted ball cap toppling off his head in the process. His floormates laughed as Kyler, now lying sprawled facedown on the ground, blindly reached for his fallen cap, finally capturing it and putting it—backward—on top of his mane of dirty-blond hair once more. Only after his hat was back in place did he lift his face, and then his body, off the carpet, half throwing, half rolling himself back onto the beanbag.

Meanwhile, Trust—with the RA's focus on him—mimed taking a drink, and then pointed to Kyler on the floor, shaking his head, a wry smile crossing his lips.

"Oh, so he doesn't even drink and he's already trying to start trouble?" Holden asked, looking from Trust, who nodded sagely, to Kyler, who was brushing himself off as he got comfortable in his cushiony seat once more.

When Kyler finally met the RA's glance again, Holden commented, "Your sister was right. I am going to have to watch out for you."

Holden then looked to the rest of the room.

"Okay, everybody. This is Kyler-Scott."

He looked to Kyler.

"Stand up, Kyler-Scott, so everyone can get a good look at you."

"Um, that's okay. I really—"

Kyler cut himself off as he caught sight of Holden's gaze.

"Okay, okay," Kyler relented, standing. "You don't have to tell me twice."

The teenager then turned and faced the group of students in the common room. He extended his arms up and to his side, his head tilted back and his eyes closed, his fingers on both hands displaying the peace sign.

"This is Kyler-Scott," Holden started again, "and—"

"That's all one name," Kyler murmured, opening his eyes briefly and peeking over at Holden. "I go by Kyler."

He tilted his head back and quickly closed his eyes again.

"To be clear, that's his first name. Kyler-hyphen-Scott," announced Holden. "But he also goes by the alias of Kyler. It's important—"

"I also go by Ky-Ky," Kyler muttered. "Or K-Scotty. Or KS—"

"It's important," Holden repeated, louder this time in order to drown out Kyler's murmurs, "that everyone in here is able to identify him in case any of you have reason to fill out a police report. I'm going to need everyone's help watching this guy, as I'm sure he will be our main troublemaker. So, if anything goes wrong and you guys blame it on Kyler here, I'll admit it right now—I'm probably going to believe you."

Kyler jerked his head, looking to Holden in alarm.

"Hey. No. Wait. What?"

From his place, still seated, Trust chuckled, leaning back in his seat.

Holden smiled at Kyler in feigned civility, and then looked around the room again.

"Okay. Now who has a serious question for me?"

Kyler hastily took his place on the beanbag chair. Trust glanced to him.

*You are an idiot*, he signed. *Way to go.*

Kyler grinned cheekily.

*I try my best,* he responded.

Trust turned back to Holden at the front of the room. Someone must have been asking a question, as the RA appeared to be listening intently, his focus directed somewhere behind Trust.

He then looked ready to respond.

"So, yes, the Freesef Society," Holden answered. "As all of you become more familiar with Centre City and more involved in all of the goings-on on and off campus, I'm sure you will run across some rumblings of what Marcie is talking about, if you haven't already—this supposed secret club or group called the Freesef Society."

Trust could not make out "Marcie" as Holden spoke the name, as he had never encountered someone saying the name aloud before.

"As far as I know," Holden continued, "much of what you will hear is a myth. It's like the haunted house in the neighborhood—some people believe that ghosts and spirits live there, and others don't believe in ghosts and spirits at all, much less living in the stupid, old house at the top of the hill. So, is the house haunted? Depends on who you ask. There's nothing that I would be able to say that would absolutely convince you that it is or isn't haunted, just like there's nothing I can say that could absolutely convince you that this society is or isn't real. But I'm telling you, here and now, that the Freesef Society is a legend and it no longer exists. If you are already convinced otherwise, however, then you're probably going to ignore what I just said. Get it?"

As Holden began to listen again, Trust turned around in his chair to see who was asking the question. Yet a quick glance of the rest of his hall mates revealed no one talking. Trust turned back to the front, and he felt a nudge at his side. He looked to Kyler.

*Marcie*—Kyler spelled out the name—*is the one with the crazy pigtails. She is wearing a black tank top over a green fishnet shirt. She just asked how the rumor got started about this Freesef Society*—Kyler spelled this name as well, since he did not know any sign for it—*and Holden is saying that the club used to exist, but I guess they disbanded a long time ago. Now you are caught up.*

Kyler then motioned to Holden, who was still speaking.

"—and they were dissolved at that time. Again, as far as I know, the group has not been officially revived, though a few groups have tried to adopt the name. One new club tried last year—I remember hearing about it—but I think there must be rules against it or something, as all the groups either come up with a different name or they don't even become an official club.

"And also, to clear this up, even when the Freesef Society existed, it was hardly a secret organization. As far as I know, it was a normal club, just like the hundreds that you can join on campus now. It was actually a pretty popular club, too—I think they had to start limiting membership, it was getting so big. But, like I said, they're gone now, and have been for a while. Maybe it started out as a joke or something, that someone was starting the Freesef Society in secret, and then it just snowballed into this secret society story—I don't know. It's an interesting anecdote, though, which is why it probably keeps cropping up every year, twenty or thirty-plus years after the fact."

Holden shrugged, as though visibly ending his long response with a question mark, before gesturing again to what Trust assumed was another hand. However, Holden's attention was then redirected toward the door to the common room.

"Hold that thought for a second, Amanda," Holden said.

He then pointed to the door.

"This lovely man who now graces our doorstep is the RD—the resident director—of Weaver Hall..."

Trust again failed to comprehend the name that came from Holden's lips, though he thought the first part looked kind of like *Dmitri*.

"He's pretty much like the housing manager and the RAs' RA, but you guys can go talk to him, too, if you need anything. If you see him lurking around, no need to call campus police—even though, I admit, he does look a little shady."

Trust then observed Holden laughing at something the resident director said in response, before Holden gave a "hang on" sign again, walking past Trust and navigating his way through the collection of students, heading for the doorway. His back was now toward Trust and the other freshmen in the seventh floor common room, and his body completely shielded Trust's view of the RD's face. Trust looked to Kyler.

"Don't even ask me how to spell that guy's name, 'cause I don't know," Kyler said and signed at the same time, with Trust concentrating on his friend's mouth. "It's foreign. Russian or something, I don't know."

Kyler grinned playfully.

"Slovakian?" he asked. "Ukrainian? Lithuanian? Polytiishronobiamism?"

Trust, watching Kyler's hands flick around randomly with the final word, shook his head, his expression deadpan.

*Nice try.*

"Oh, so you've never heard of Polytiishronobia?" Kyler inquired.

*Spell it,* Trust signed.

Kyler was about to respond, but a tap on his shoulder halted him. He noticed Trust's eyes already shifted in the visitor's direction. Kyler turned around.

"Hi."

It was Marcie, the girl who had asked about the Freesef club.

"My name is Marcie. Sorry if I was interrupting, but..."

Her eyes flickered between Kyler and Trust, her interest and curiosity obvious.

"...was that sign language you two were using?"

"Why, yes it was, Marcie," Kyler said and signed, both saying aloud and motioning Marcie's name again for Trust's benefit. Trust grinned.

"Actually," Kyler went on, "if you were looking just now, that last word was just a made-up gesture—I like to keep my friend here on his toes—but before that, and this that I'm doing now, is true-blue Kyler-Scott Brooks Sign Language. I, of course, invented the whole thing. I'm Kyler."

Trust rolled his eyes, shaking his head but still smirking as Kyler shook hands with Marcie, who laughed. When Marcie's eyes turned to him, Trust glanced quickly around the room again, now noticing that most of the room was glancing toward them.

He bent down, picking up the notebook at his feet. He had long since gotten into the habit of having some paper and a writing utensil close at hand, for times he would need to "speak" without the use of signing. Quickly, he jotted something down in the notebook.

Kyler was smiling, amused to be observing a display he had witnessed and been a part of numerous times before.

Trust then turned the notebook around, holding it so Marcie could see what he had written. Kyler also snuck a peek.

There, in neat script:

> *Nice to meet you, Marcie. I'm Trustice Jeffries.*
> *Don't listen to anything that comes out of my friend's mouth.*
> *You will soon learn that he is an idiot.*

Marcie laughed.

Kyler turned to Trust.

"Dude," he said.

Trust understood, grinning.

## 3.
## Night on the Town

AFTER HAVING FINISHED DINNER AND completing the experience of arranging the dorm room they would both be inhabiting the rest of the school year, Trust and Kyler were on the Centre Line, Centre City and the surrounding areas' well-admired public bus system.

Technically, the rural campus of UCC was on the outskirts of Centre City proper. The downtown nightlife of Centre City was where Trust and Kyler were now headed, however, having been convinced by Marcie and her boyfriend, Paxson—a floor mate of the three in Weaver Hall, but not along the Central Wing—of a few hotspots they should all check out. Their bus soon departed the rural grounds en route for the cityscape less than ten minutes away.

Trust, Kyler, Marcie, and Pax, as he typically went by, were each dressed in much the same way they had been throughout the long day, including Kyler's haphazard ponytail-bun arrangement that captured only about half of his head of blond hair, leaving the other half spilling about randomly under his still present baseball cap. Marcie's pigtails were only slightly more eye-catching—not long enough to flow down to her shoulders, but not too short as to poke straight up off her head.

Trustice, however, had on lightly tinted sunglasses, which shaded his blue eyes.

"Wait," Paxson said. "So, not only are your eyes blue, but they glow in the dark? Like a cat?"

Even though the natural light outside the bus windows was quickly fading toward the palette of sunset, and thereafter to evening darkness, the interior of the city bus was well lit. Still, Kyler had persuaded Trust to leave behind his notebook to write on, instead volunteering to interpret for him. For both of them, it was a common practice, and one that neither minded.

*Pretty much,* Trust signed as Kyler spoke the words aloud. *The doctor that I go to back home says there is an extra membrane over my eyes that reflects light in the darkness. It is easier to wear sunglasses or cover my eyes than always having to explain why my eyes are always glowing, or scaring somebody, both of which happen when I forget. But it's not a big deal. It would probably be best if you didn't tell anybody else about it.*

"No problem," Paxson said, "but if you really think that's not a big deal, you're so wrong. That's, like, the coolest thing ever. You could be, like, a superhero or something, you know?"

Trust released a short chuckle.

*Yeah, the guy with the shiny eyes. I'm sure that would help me catch a lot of evildoers.*

"Or," Kyler put in after he finished translating, "you could *be* one of the evildoers. Like once, during Halloween, he scared the holy crap out of this old lady who was always trying to scare us. She had left her porch light off on purpose, but then Trust took off the mask he was wearing, and 'ahh!' You should have seen her; it was the funniest thing ever."

Trust sighed melodramatically.

*She didn't even give us any candy that time.*

"Yeah," Kyler said, "she just slammed the door in our faces! We were, like, seven years old!"

Kyler looked to Trust.

"I still think she thought you were some kind of devil child for a few weeks after that. You totally got to her."

*I am the devil,* Trust motioned, raising his hands eerily, his imitation of a ghost.

The others laughed.

"Aww, but you seem so nice," Marcie said in a sweet tone. "And with those blue eyes, how could she confuse you for a demon?"

"Please," Kyler answered before Trust was able to respond. "You've only known him for a few hours. Give it a week, and then ask yourself that question again."

*I think you're confusing my behavior with yours,* Trust gestured. *You're the one the RA warned everyone to watch out for.*

"Yep, that's true," Marcie acknowledged once Kyler translated. "He didn't say anything about Trust. You're the one we're supposed to keep an eye on."

"Pax," Kyler said in a singsong voice, "aren't you going to step in with your woman mouthing off to me like this?"

"Uh oh," Paxson intoned. He swiftly averted his eyes.

"Excuse me?" Marcie asked, a hint of indignation—faked or otherwise—evident in her voice. Though Trust was not able to hear it, he could clearly see it in her expression. He glanced to Kyler.

*You're on your own, dude,* he signed, before also looking away in the same inconspicuous direction that Paxson gazed.

Paxson suddenly jerked his head, taking a look at the scene outside the bus windows.

"Oh, this is our stop coming up."

He then reached for the overhanging cable that would signal to the bus driver their desire to disembark. Through the bus's public address intercom system, everyone but Trust heard an electronic bell tone sound, followed by a mechanized female voice stating, "This bus will soon be stopping. Please watch your step when disembarking. Thank you for riding with us today."

"Ooh, you are so lucky," Marcie said, poking her finger into Kyler's chest. "Saved by the bell."

"Ow. That actually kind of hurt," Kyler responded, rubbing at the spot Marcie's finger had just vacated.

"Ow nothing," Marcie said. "Just be glad Pax is here. I don't like showing my bad side with him around."

"Really," Paxson said. "When did you start that?"

He and the others started to laugh, but quickly stopped when met with Marcie's glare.

The bus slowed to a stop at a busy street corner. While the group of freshmen, along with a few others, stepped off the bus at its back exit, other people streamed onto the bus using the front entrance. They had stopped in front of a restaurant, and Paxson ushered the group past it, down the street.

The restaurant appeared to be a good representation of the entire area as far as Trust could see—festive lights hanging from the restaurant's awnings, the entire curbside property awash with vibrant—though not entirely overwhelming—colors and people, including what looked to be several UCC students milling about, enjoying the merry atmosphere. Tall suspended lamps bordering the street shone brightly, easily illuminating the downtown area. Overall, the scene was dazzling to the senses.

Trust followed the rest of the group, with Kyler beside him and slightly ahead, so he could recognize when someone was speaking—or, more accurately, so he could recognize when he was expected to comprehend what was said and possibly respond. Being outdoors in the evening hours, the lighting, adequate for the most part, did fade and dim in some areas, such as behind towering buildings or near looming trees. Anyone attempting to pay attention to such an intricate detail as word-forming on a person's mouth would face sure difficulty in those more shadowed areas.

As long as the speaker was looking in Trust's direction, however, he had no such challenge.

"This club is called Centre Diamond," Paxson explained, walking backward as Marcie, Kyler, and Trust continued to stroll ahead, Trust receiving a clear view of Paxson's face. "Funny name, right? My older brother brought me here last year when he came to visit. He said you have to be eighteen or above to get in, and, of course, I was still in high school at the time. But I guess my brother knew somebody, or knew somebody who knew somebody, or whatever. Anyway, it's pretty cool, almost like an upscale-lounge-slash-Studio-54 kind of feel, even though I don't really know what Studio 54 is. It's mostly a younger crowd going up to twenties or thirties, with maybe some upper thirties and forties mixed in to class it up even more."

"So, in conclusion, what you're saying is that the girls in this place will be as hot as Marcie?" Kyler asked, signing at the same time.

Marcie looked at him.

"If only you could be so lucky," she remarked, to which Kyler, Trust, and Paxson laughed.

"I like that you're dreaming big, dude," Paxson said. "And you never know. Since you look like you just stepped out of some Abercrombie & Fitch catalog, you might just—"

"Ugh, don't even say it," Marcie declared, before remembering that one of her new friends may not have realized she was speaking. She turned her head again, noticing that Kyler, who was grinning, was already signing her response. She looked to Trust.

"His ego's already big enough, don't you think?" she said.

*You're about eighteen years too late to worry about that,* Trust

36

motioned.

"Hey, hey," Kyler said, after expressing Trust's reply aloud. "Who are you guys to decide how big an ego I should have? My ego, my rules."

Marcie rolled her eyes. Soon thereafter, the foursome approached the sleek-looking building Paxson had called Centre Diamond.

"All right!" Paxson said excitedly. "This is it! I don't really remember this line, though."

A line of awaiting club goers—a long line—stretched away from the doors of Centre Diamond and continued down the sidewalk. It was an accurate representation of the clientele Paxson had earlier spoken about—a mixture of college-aged and slightly older, with groupings of even older adults who were dressed to see and be seen. No one in line looked a day over forty, possibly a testament to fashionable appearances more than actual age.

Paxson was ready to lead the troupe toward the presumed back of the waiting line when he heard a shout.

"Pax! Paxson Haynes?"

Trust observed Paxson stop and turn as though he had heard something. Trust promptly turned and looked in the same direction, quickly noticing one of the club's doormen gesturing in their direction.

"It's Pax, right? You're Dolphin's kid brother?"

The bouncer was tall—taller than Kyler, who was probably the tallest amongst the group—and burly, though not massively so. He wore a tight, black short-sleeved shirt and black pants, the dark brown skin on his bald head reflecting the lights adorning and surrounding the Centre Diamond entrance.

Paxson nodded, though Trust could detect a slight hesitance in the gesture. Apparently, the bouncer detected the same hesitance, and laughed.

"So," he said, "you comin' in or what?"

"Don't we have to wait in line?" Marcie asked, glancing from Paxson to the guard, and then to the long queue.

The bald-headed bouncer shook his head, smiling. He also had a large earring in one ear, which winked in the light as his head moved.

"Not if you're with him, you don't," he replied, hooking his thumb toward a surprised, and somewhat perplexed, Paxson.

"You mean we're on the list?" Kyler asked, excitement creeping into his voice.

The guard turned to him.

"'The list'?" he echoed. "What list? You've never been to a club like this before, have you? You want to be on the list? Fine, you're on the list."

"Ahh, sweet!" Kyler said. "I've never known somebody who was actually on the list."

"I'm not really sure I understand how—" Paxson started, before the guard cut in.

"So, you and your crew comin' in, Pax? Or do you want the experience of waiting in line? Personally, I think the line is a little overrated."

He then motioned toward the entrance.

Paxson looked to Marcie, and then shrugged.

"I guess, since we're on the list," Paxson reasoned, "we're going in."

"All right!" Kyler exclaimed. "So this is how it feels to be on the list, eh?"

"What the heck are you kids talking about," the bouncer mumbled, mostly to himself, as he began to stamp the group's hands, which would notify Centre Diamond staff, particularly in the bar area, that the party was underage and thus not allowed to drink. The bouncer then began to shepherd them inside the building, past the two other guards who continued to work the line of waiting patrons.

"One warning: don't even try to sneak a drink through unless it's a soda," the guard declared. He then looked at Kyler. "Particularly you. I would almost think you've had a sip or two already."

*We haven't even been in Centre City for a full day yet and you're already cultivating a bad reputation that is beginning to precede you,* Trust signed to his friend, who smirked sheepishly.

The bouncer looked to Trust with added interest.

"Whoa. That's sign language, right? You're deaf? Well, at least you won't have any problems hearing people over the music."

Trust gave a thumbs-up in response, adding, which Kyler spoke aloud, "He says, 'Yeah. Being deaf seems to come in handy sometimes.'"

The guard then waved them toward another set of doors.

"The next time you hear from Dolphin," he said, pointing at Paxson, "tell him I said what's up."

He then turned, heading back to the throng of people still outside waiting.

38

The freshman group was in what looked to be a darkened vestibule, the sounds of the club already apparent just ahead of them. What the others could hear, Trust could feel—the faint vibrations of fervent sound.

"Um, so, what was that?" Marcie asked in the dimly lit interior, not making a motion toward the door but instead looking toward Paxson.

"That, Marcie," Kyler said, "was the distinguished power of being on the list. We are in the presence of royalty, and we didn't even know it."

He then glanced to Trust.

"Dude, we are so totally ballin' right now."

Trust, who had no problem seeing Kyler's mouth moving in the darkened reception area, gave his friend an exasperated look.

The pulsations of the club were getting more intense as the group moved farther inward. From previous experience, Trust knew the sounds causing the vibrations he felt must be particularly loud, as they came from the closed doors the group was now standing in front of. His gaze shifted to Paxson when he noticed the boy speaking.

"I guess Dolphin has stronger connections here than I thought," Paxson said, "and he must have told someone that I was starting at UCC this year.

"Dolphin is my older brother," he directed to Kyler and Trust. "Randolph is his real name, but I started calling him Dolphin when I was little, and the name stuck."

He had to speak louder because of the blaring, though muffled, music and activity coming from the other side of the door. Trust, of course, could not hear Paxson's adjustment. He could, however, see it.

"He graduated from UCC a few years ago. He's in the Army now, training to be in Special Forces, but when he was a student here, or whenever he is in town to visit, he usually stops by and—"

The double doors the foursome was standing in front of unexpectedly opened, with another security guard holding the door and looking out at them, his eyes quickly scanning the students' faces until he came to Paxson's. At the opening of the door, the wave of sound was overwhelming, almost knocking the group over. For Trust, it felt like a sudden burst of air had been thrust toward his body.

"You're Pax, right?" the guard practically yelled, to which Paxson, squinting against the sounds of the club, nodded.

Meanwhile, Trust and Kyler leaned around the guard's wide shoulders and looked into the nightclub, captivated by the lights, dancing, movement, and commotion all around.

"You guys coming in or what? People don't usually just chill in the entryway."

"Yeah! All right!" Paxson shouted. He looked to Marcie, Trust, and Kyler.

"Welcome to Centre Diamond!"

The group entered, filing past the security guard, with Kyler quickly signing to Trust the bouncer's parting words of "Stay away from the alcohol!" since Trust had not been looking. They were immediately swallowed up by the Centre Diamond throng as they each tried to abruptly acclimate themselves to the frenetic atmosphere. With Paxson clutching Marcie's hand, the party slowly weaved their way through the dancing, gyrating, seemingly pulsating bodies, toward the large, circular bar area near the center of the floor. Trust's head swerved left and right, forward and back, quickly as he moved ahead, taking in the extravagant sights that Centre Diamond presented. He observed the others all doing the same.

The sights, such as they were, did not disappoint.

After what seemed an inordinate amount of time, the group reached the elevated bar area, which also included several booths and tables—both for those who desired to sit and those who wished to remain standing. Over the bar, above the heads of the bartenders, a facsimile of a large diamond slowly revolved. The diamond was made up of large monitors, which displayed various alternating live video feeds of the club from an assortment of vantage points—shots and angles of the dance floor, the bar, the second level of the club, or the elevated DJ booth.

"Man, this is crazy!" Kyler exclaimed.

Due to some invisible engineering marvel, the sounds of the pulsating music were effectively funneled away from the bar, allowing for conversations at a more reasonable volume—or as reasonable as could be expected in a jam-packed nightclub. The group continued to glance around as they gathered at one of the few available tables. This one had high-backed stools, so each of them quickly perched themselves high, resting their arms on the back of their chair or on the high table they circled around.

"I know," Paxson replied to Kyler. "It was like this when I came before, but they changed the lights. The color pattern is different."

He gestured around the club's interior, across the walls, and around the upper level, where, above stylishly arched molding, tones of neon blue were visible, shining up toward the ceiling. In fact, the entire club had a bluish aura, with varied ornamentations and settings throughout the building bathed in similar coloring, such as spotlights on the dance floors, the bar area, and the DJ booth. Above the main dance floor, a glass dome, also tinted blue, replaced the ceiling and permitted those below a view of the night sky.

"You remember those pictures I sent you?" Paxson asked, glancing to Marcie, who nodded. He then looked back to Trust and Kyler. "Everything was this cool orange color last time. They must switch it every once in a while."

Even with the frenzied atmosphere on the dance floor—which was less intense around the bar, but still evident—Trust felt someone approaching from behind. He looked back, becoming the first among the group to spot the server. His eyes quickly took in her features before centering on her mouth.

"Anybody care for anything to drink?" she asked, making her presence known to the others moments after Trust had noticed her. Her eyes came to Paxson.

"Hey, you!" she said in warm greeting. "I thought I heard them say you came in."

"Mariana, what's happening?" Paxson asked, his eyes alight with recognition. "I can't believe you even remember me. But wait. Who told you I came in? And how does everyone here seem to know who I am?"

The pretty server laughed. It counted as one of those times Trust wished he were able to hear.

"Well, first off," Mariana said, "I don't know if you've ever heard of them, but they have invented these things called radio headsets."

She indicated to the side of her head, turning slightly so everyone at the table could see the small earpiece placed into the innermost curve of her ear.

"And everyone knows who you are," she continued, "because your brother talks about you and the rest of his family nonstop when he is in here—not to mention the time you graced us with your presence, though technically, I don't see how they allowed you through the door, since you were underage and didn't have a college ID. So of course we know you, and since Dolphin also showed us pics of your mom and dad, we would all probably recognize them, too, if they walked in."

"Now, before I say anything else, aren't you going to introduce me to your little posse here?"

"Oh, yeah," Paxson said.

He turned to Marcie, who was sitting beside him.

"I don't know if you remember, but this is Marcie, my girl—"

"Your girlfriend?" Mariana finished, a slightly incredulous expression on her face. "The one you showed us last year? Wow, Pax, I am impressed. I honestly thought that was a stock photo or something."

"Ooh," Kyler coughed. "Burn."

Mariana and Marcie exchanged greetings.

"And this one," Paxson went on, unfazed, gesturing to Kyler, "is Kyler-Scott—that's his first name, with a hyphen, mind you—but he goes by Kyler—"

"Or K. Scotty Nice-Nice," Kyler said, reaching over the table to shake the server's hand. "That one's for when I'm out in the streets, you know, doin' my thang."

From the way Kyler's mouth formed when he uttered the ridiculous "doin' my thang," Trust deciphered the slang immediately, as he had seen his friend use the phrase numerous times before. Behind his tinted shades, his eyes rolled.

As Kyler and the server shook, Mariana twisted his hand slightly, displaying the stamp he and the others had received when they first entered Centre Diamond.

"Oh, I heard about you over the radio, too," Mariana intoned. "They warned us that they were unsure if you had already been drinking before you came in."

The others laughed. Trust smiled.

"And who's this handsome guy who's been staring at my mouth like he wants to kiss me?"

For a moment, Trust did not make the connection that Mariana was referring to him, only "seeing" her question without fully comprehending what she meant. Also, since she was not directly looking at him as she spoke, he could just as easily assume—

"This, quote, 'handsome guy,' unquote," Kyler introduced, gesturing toward Trust and pulling him out of his contemplation, "and yes, he probably does want to kiss you, is—"

Kyler's words halted in his throat as he caught Trust's murderous glare.

"His name is Trustice," a grinning Marcie picked up. "Trust for short."

Mariana looked from Marcie and—for the first time since she arrived at the table—met Trust's gaze.

"Trustice? That's a very interesting name. I like it."

*Thank you,* Trust signed, smiling. *I think you are beautiful.*

Kyler leaned forward.

"He says thank you, and he thinks that you are very mmmph—"

Trust brought his hand to Kyler's mouth. He could feel Kyler still attempting to speak.

"Mnnmph mmm...mmm mmphm mmph..."

Trust quickly glanced around the table for hints as to whether Kyler had finished the thought before he had silenced him. He felt some relief to see that Marcie and Paxson were laughing, presumably at his methods for getting his friend to shut up.

He then looked to Mariana.

For Trust, the smile on her face was almost too alluring to look at directly. Feeling dazed, Trust slowly brought his hand away from Kyler's now-stilled mouth.

"So, I'm guessing you're deaf," she said, looking at him, "and/or you can't talk. Or maybe you just don't like to?"

Mariana then raised her hands.

*Hello, T-R-U-S-T-I-C-E. My name is M-A-R-I-A-N-A.*

Trust grinned, his eyes widening in surprise.

"I only know some basic signs," she explained. "That's about as complicated a sentence as I can make."

*Still, that is very good,* Trust signed.

He then quickly turned to Kyler to make sure he translated correctly.

"He says you look very good," Kyler said, smiling cheekily.

Trust looked at him in annoyance, and then shook his head.

"You don't think I look very good?" Mariana asked when Trust's eyes shifted back to her. She was also smiling.

Trust struck his palm against his forehead a few times before looking toward Marcie and Paxson. He gestured for one—or both—of them to start talking immediately. Paxson laughed.

"Okay, okay," Paxson said. "I'll bite. Hey, I forgot to mention it to you guys. Not only is Mariana a bartender and a server, she's, like, the co-owner of this club."

Kyler jerked in his chair.

"Wow, really? Co-owner? Is that even legal? Aren't you, like, a student, though? Man, you must be raking in some serious scratch."

Mariana laughed before looking to Paxson.

"That's so wrong and you know it. My dad owns Centre Diamond. I'm quite a few steps below that."

"Still," Kyler said, "that makes you what? President? Vice-president? CFO, whatever that means?"

"Chief financial officer, and still no," Mariana replied, continuing to laugh at Kyler's attempts. "And anyway, I graduated years ago, so no, I'm not a student. Thanks for puffing up my ego, though."

Kyler glanced to Trust.

"Dude," he said, barely loud enough for the others to make out, "she's pretty *and* she knows what CFO stands for. You should definitely ask her out, like, right now."

Mariana turned to look at Trust as well, who was back to gazing at her mouth. He quickly realized what he was doing, looking up into her eyes once more.

*Sorry,* he gestured, and Kyler translated aloud. *I am not trying to be rude or creepy or anything, but—*

Mariana interrupted, waving off the apology before Kyler—or Trust— could finish. She pointed toward Trust's glasses.

"Those are some cool-looking shades you're wearing. Can I try them on?"

Then, before Trust could respond, she reached up, slowly tugging the glasses away from his face. His eyes gradually came into view.

"Oh, wow," Mariana breathed, her voice softer than before. "Your eyes. They're so...they're..."

Trust, accustomed to the reactions to the way his eyes appeared in the dark, instinctively lowered his gaze, his head tilted slightly downward, only peeking up as Mariana's lips moved. Out of the corner of his vision, he saw both Marcie and Paxson edge forward, attempting to get a better look. He turned in their direction.

"Wow," Marcie said. "That is amazing."

"That is so ridiculously *cool*, dude," Paxson acknowledged, grinning. "It's like your eyes are reflecting the blue in the club. They're, like, dancing in the light or something."

Trust felt a nudge from where Kyler was sitting. He turned to him.

However, Kyler seemed distracted. He was looking away from Trust, toward an area of the dance floor. Trust glanced in that direction, and, not spotting anything immediately out of the ordinary, looked back to Kyler.

*Holy crap, dude,* Kyler signed without turning around. It was one of the many slang phrasings Kyler and Trust had developed on their own, which Trust had indeed termed Kyler-Scott Brooks Sign Language.

KSBSL for short.

After a brief moment of Kyler continuing to look out into the crowds on the dance floor, Trust regained his attention.

*What is it? What did you see?*

Kyler looked away to the floor yet again, confirming to Trust that his friend was definitely distracted.

"Uh, hey, everybody," Kyler announced, gaining the others' attention. "I'll be back in a minute. I think I just...I'll be back. In a minute."

Still looking toward a particular spot amongst the crowd, Kyler hopped from his stool to the floor. As he passed behind Trust's chair in order to head for the short set of stairs leading down to the dance floor, he tapped Trust a few times on the shoulder. Trust looked at him.

*I'll be back in a minute,* Kyler signed, his eyes shifting between Trust and the crowd.

*I gathered that the second time you said it,* Trust replied.

Mariana, Marcie, and Paxson watched as Kyler departed.

"Be careful!" Mariana teased after him, though, since her back was turned toward Trust, he had no idea she had spoken.

Marcie looked to him.

"And where the heck is he running off to?" she asked.

Trust shrugged, and then lifted his finger toward his ear, twirling it around quickly. It was a gesture the others easily understood.

"You can say that again," Paxson said, laughing.

Mariana prodded Trust lightly, bringing his shining, blue-tinged eyes back to her.

"So, do I look fly in these or what?" she asked, drawing laughs from Marcie and Paxson as she posed in a tough, not-to-be-messed-with stance, Trust's shades settled in front of her eyes.

"Super fly," Paxson acknowledged.

Trust mimed writing on a piece of paper.

"Here," Mariana said. "I've got just the thing."

She reached into one of her pockets, soon pulling out a small note pad with a pen attached. She handed it over.

Trust began to write, with Mariana glancing over to Marcie and Paxson with an inquiring expression. The young couple responded with shrugs.

Trust returned the pad to Mariana.

*You look better in those shades than I could ever hope to.*
*The only bad thing is I can't see your eyes now.*

He actually could, but Mariana chuckled lightly, which caused Trust to smile.

"Okay, Casanova. I think it's time you had these back now."

She pulled off the shades before slowly sliding them back onto Trust's face, eliminating the shimmering reflection coming off his eyes.

"What did he write?" Paxson asked, looking at Mariana. He then quickly looked to Trust. "What did you write?"

"Someone's nosy," Mariana said, smirking.

*I wrote that I hope you and I get a chance to run off into the sunset together,* Trust directed toward the other boy at the table.

"Wait! Write that down!" Paxson urged, motioning frantically to the note pad Mariana still clutched in her hands, before Trust waved him off, grinning and shaking his head.

"What did you say then? Did you curse me out? Okay, I'll remember that."

Both Marcie and Mariana laughed, with Marcie pushing Paxson playfully in his side.

"And what about you?" Paxson looked to Mariana as the young woman's laughter calmed. "Aren't you going to get in trouble for staying so long over here with us?"

"Oh, so you're getting tired of me, then?" Mariana retorted in a teasing tone. "For your information, I'm not on server duty right now—I'm just helping out one of the other girls, and since you haven't told me anything you wanted from the bar, I get to just hang out for a bit. And anyway, what is anyone going to say about it? I'm the co-owner, remember?"

"Fine, fine," Paxson conceded. "If my older brother taught me anything, it's to not make the co-owner of a place that serves alcohol unhappy."

Trust's attention suddenly wavered. As if by impulse, or perhaps because he had unconsciously noticed something, his eyes shifted away from Paxson to the slowly rotating television screens that hung above the bar.

At the same moment, the scene on the large display switched to yet another location.

Trust's gaze hurriedly swept the areas of the club, and he performed a near-complete three-sixty in his chair. He then glanced again around the circular bar counter toward the other side of the club, where the elevated DJ booth was located. Above the DJ, another gigantic display was perched on the wall, showing more live video of locations in and outside the Centre Diamond. The videos were interweaved with wavy, pulsing graphic overlays that seemed to mirror the rhythms of the music.

His eyes returned to those at the table.

"What's up?" Paxson asked as he saw Trust's gaze come to rest on him.

Trust then looked to Mariana's inquiring face. Putting his hands together in a sign of apology, he politely gestured toward her note pad again. She handed it over without hesitation, now curious as to Trust's intended action.

He wrote with his usual swiftness, after having relied so much on communicating with those not fluent in sign language through the written word. His handwriting, also through practice and repetition, remained clear and concise.

*Need to find Kyler.*

Trust handed the pad and pen back to Mariana, who read Trust's message.

"'Need to find Kyler,'" she said, before turning to Trust again. "Is something wrong?"

Trust was already sliding out of his chair. He held up one finger, hoping that his implication was understandable.

*I'll be back in a minute.*

A few seconds later, he was edging around the other club patrons who had found solace around the bar area, neatly sidestepping another server who was balancing a tray of drinks. Making it to the steps, he descended, once again becoming engulfed in the multitude of swaying bodies, just barely having enough room to find the way through. His eyes and head kept moving, never still, as he progressed in the general direction of the DJ platform, though he was forced into a more circuitous route, angling his way around people dancing—some close together, some gyrating wildly. Once more, he could feel the enthused, almost animalistic pulsation of the music throughout his body. Since he could not hear it, his mind was pressed to find another method to show him just how energizing the rhythm was.

As he moved through, someone grabbed at his arm. Trust quickly turned to look, his eyes instantly flowing up the stranger's arm, shoulder, neck, and to her face.

The girl smiled.

Inviting.

"Hi," she yelled over the music. "I want you to dance with me."

Trust read her glossy lips and smiled.

He turned, swiftly, gently grabbing the arm that clutched to him with both hands, his fingers lightly trailing down, almost ghosting across her skin to her palm. He enveloped her hand with both of his, and then bowed slightly. Still smiling, he raised himself back upright, taking one hand away from her delicate touch and holding up one finger again.

She seemed to understand.

"I'll be waiting," she called loudly, not knowing that Trust would not hear her no matter how strongly she shouted.

He continued moving, deftly dodging more dancers, ducking away just in time from an outrageously dressed gentleman attempting to perform a chaotic dance step that Trust had never witnessed before, his eyes continuing to search. As he neared the side of the DJ platform, he tried to visualize exactly where a camera would have to be positioned to show the brief glimpse—

There.

Kyler and another man had moved even farther away from the DJ booth since the time Trust had caught a hint of them on the display, having shifted toward a slight corner off the main dance floor area, but still in a spot where there were a few people congregated. With the blue-tinged lighting of the walls above them and all around, Kyler had his back facing the wall, his face toward Trust, though the other man—with his back to Trust and facing Kyler—was large, nearly preventing Kyler from seeing past him.

Nearly.

Kyler's and Trust's eyes met for a split moment, as Trust maintained his approach, easing past more people. Kyler immediately began to circle around, moving so that the man's attention continued to follow the college freshman as he spoke, but without becoming aware of Kyler's deliberate movements...

Suddenly, the man speaking to Kyler reached out, roughly pushing the teenager in his upper shoulder, Kyler recoiling slightly and putting his hands up in capitulation.

Trust started moving quicker. More urgently.

"...sorry, man," Kyler was saying. "It wasn't—"

Trust again lost his visual on Kyler's mouth as the boy continued to turn, but the man's mouth came into view.

"...think I'm playing? You think you can eye my girlfriend and now just run—"

The man stopped speaking as Trust appeared at Kyler's side, though his irritated expression intensified.

"What, so you called your fairy god-boyfriend over now or somethin'? You think I'm afraid of this chump? I can take both of you easily."

Trust glanced around as he and Kyler began to slowly pull each other back—Trust so Kyler would not get punched in the face on their first night in Centre City, Kyler for another reason entirely. The man—appearing to be as much as a decade older than the two of them—glanced between both teenagers heatedly.

"So, you gonna start something? Huh? You gonna start something? I can take both of you..."

The three of them were slowly, gradually backing onto the dance floor just in front of the DJ platform at a snail's pace, the crowd seeming to slowly but appropriately part as they moved. Trust also continued to look about, scanning the faces of the people surrounding them—most of whom were unaware of what was occurring—while still keeping a close watch on the man still stalking them.

"What, you punks tryin' to run away from me now? You try to disrespect me and my girl, and then..."

Trust's eyes flitted to Kyler, who he could see was still attempting to talk to the angered man. His gaze did not linger long enough to interpret his friend's words, but he could tell that Kyler was in peacemaking mode. Trust looked back to the man, all three of them maintaining their slow pace deeper onto the dance floor.

Contrary to whatever Kyler was saying, the man seemed to be working himself into a rage.

"I don't care, man! I don't care! You comin' on to my girlfriend and you're asking *me* to calm down? Me? I don't care—"

Trust spotted the bouncer approaching from behind the man.

The aggravated patron somehow sensed it, or the guard said something to give away his presence—Trust could not tell. As the guard reached for the man's arm, the man swung violently, bringing his elbow up and back, striking the guard in the middle of the face. The bouncer's arms shot up and he staggered back.

At the same time, the man lunged at Kyler, his fist cocked back, his face enraged as he roared.

Trust moved quickly, tugging Kyler away from the impending punch and then just as quickly letting him go. The man's charge was uncontrolled and blatantly overextended, as though he were putting all of his available energy into a single strike. As Kyler was pulled away, the man's fist began to follow, throwing him even more off-balance. In the same instance, Trust unleashed, throwing a lightning-fast punch that impacted near the bottom of the man's throat, just above his chest.

The man crumbled immediately.

Trust felt someone grab at him from behind.

Much faster than would be expected, Trust dipped his shoulders slightly and slunk away, turning in the same move, his hands poised, ready.

Another bouncer—the one from the closed double doors of the vestibule area of the club—held up his hands to show he meant no harm. In an instant, Trust surveyed the other faces surrounding him, looking for the faintest hint of additional threats.

Seeing none, he quickly relaxed and lowered his hands.

The music in the club continued to thump through his body. Every eye in the immediate vicinity was aimed toward him.

His eyes returned to Kyler, and, noticing that he was looking downward toward the fallen man, he followed his gaze.

The man was on his hands and knees, his body heaving visibly under the club lights, one arm clutching around his chest. From the tint of the club's lighting, the man and the floor all around were bathed in neon blue.

Trust's gaze returned to Kyler.

*He's panicking, trying to catch his breath,* Trust signed. *He'll be fine.*

As he finished gesturing, he observed a small commotion behind Kyler as someone attempted to push through the crowd, most of which was still dancing, ignorant to the unfolding events. The security guard who had first recognized Paxson and had let the group into Centre Diamond quickly emerged, followed closely by Mariana.

"Hey, what ha—"

The bouncer's mouth stopped moving as he took in the scene, his eyes lingering on the man still struggling for air on the ground.

"Jeez," he said, looking back up at Trust, and then to Kyler. "Someone want to explain why there's a guy flopping around on the dance floor?"

"What happened?" Mariana asked, yelling above the noise. "Is everyone o—"

By then, Paxson and Marcie had also joined the group in the small, open circle on the dance floor, but that was not who Mariana looked toward now.

"Mike! Are you—oh, my—you're going to the hospital. You're bleeding everywhere. Don't even try to argue with me."

Mike, the bouncer who had been hit in the face by the man now on the ground, was now standing beside Trust.

"Okay," Mike obliged, holding his nose while attempting to tilt his face upward, knowing not to argue. "But not before I personally escort this idiot out of here."

He motioned down to the man.

"He caught me with his elbow before I could reach for him, so at the very least, I want to make sure he gets outside safe and sound."

Mariana gazed at the bouncer for a brief moment.

"Then the hospital," she said. "And Trevor goes with you."

Mike started to reach for the man, who was still on the ground.

*Tell him to tell the guy not to hold his chest like that,* Trust signaled to Kyler. *The pain won't go away until he stops holding it.*

Kyler relayed the information to the bouncer.

"Will do," Mike said, jerking the man roughly to his feet. The man let out an agonized groan as Mike yanked at his arms.

Kyler, Paxson, Marcie, Mariana, and the other bouncer grimaced at the man's yell.

Trust grimaced because of the distressed look on the man's face.

Mike the bouncer did not grimace at all.

"Oh, you said *don't* put pressure on his chest," he said, smirking. "That's my bad."

He then "escorted" the man through the throngs of people on the floor, the other guard who had staffed the foyer entrance leading the way.

The rest of the group, still lingering on the blue-shaded, seemingly pulsating dance floor, looked to one another, the blaring music enveloping them.

Trust, catching Mariana's gaze, brought his hand to his heart briefly. Even with the darkened, blue-tinged luminance of the club, Mariana could make out the show of apology on Trust's face. Though she was not entirely familiar with the gesture he had used, the sentiment was still clear.

*I'm sorry.*

Mariana smiled, causing Trust to smile as well.

THE FIRST BOUNCER—WHOM THE group had finally learned was named Jayson—looked at them as they made their way back to the front doors of the club.

"Now, you guys are sure you don't want to stay?" he asked. "Like Mariana said, you are all more than welcome. The problem was the other guy, not you."

"Eh," Kyler intoned, "I don't want to attract any more jerks that I would have to lay out in front of everybody. It's not a good look for me in the streets. But if Pax here doesn't forsake us, I wouldn't mind coming back sooner rather than later."

"Are you kidding?" Paxson declared. "No way are you going to be getting rid of me that quickly. I'm going to follow you two everywhere now. You guys are freaking amazing."

Jayson paused before the doors that would lead the group outside once again.

"I'm not so sure Mariana was talking about you anyway, guy," he commented, grinning lightly and looking at Kyler. "Just the rest of you. I was right before—you attract trouble. You're a troublemaker."

"Seriously?" Kyler asked, looking around at the others. "Why is everyone saying that today?"

Meanwhile, Jayson glanced to Trust.

"Hey, think about what I said before, all right? I mean, it's no pressure or anything—only if you want to do it. But with what your friend said and how that guy looked gasping for air on the ground, I think you would fit on the security team easily. I mean, you may have to rein in those death blows a little"—he chuckled—"but, other than that, I'm sure it would be no problem. And to top it off, you would be seeing a lot more of a certain owner's daughter."

Trust flinched faintly, glancing toward the others—who, thankfully, were not listening—before returning to Jayson. Jayson chuckled again before extending his hand. Trust took it, and the two shook.

"Hey, Pax," Jayson called to Paxson, beginning to turn back toward the route he had just walked with the group, "remember to tell your brother I said what's up. Nice meeting all of you."

Paxson pushed and held open the door as the four freshmen filtered out. They noticed that the line of those waiting to get in had not lessened. If anything, it might have grown longer.

They began to walk back the way they had originally come. The downtown nightlife was still young, the streets and city blocks still teeming with people out for entertainment, with many attractions within walking distance and more than enough distractions to while away the evening in exciting, extravagant fashion.

"So, that was Centre Diamond, the place I was telling you guys about," Paxson stated in a casual tone, to which Marcie and Kyler soon fell into each other, laughing.

Trust, not able to catch Paxson's inflection, looked puzzled, wondering why the others were amused at what seemed to be an innocent statement of fact.

"Did you really only hit that guy once?" Marcie asked, looking at Trust, still laughing. "He looked like he had just run fifty miles, gulping for breath like that."

"Yep," Kyler grunted with a casual arrogance before Trust could respond. "My fists of fury have been known to bring more than one grown man to his knees with a single blow. It's a burden, but I have learned to live with it."

The teenager then started to shadowbox, ducking, dodging, and punching out at an invisible opponent. Trust shook his head in resignation, which the others noticed. They laughed.

*Sorry for getting you guys mixed up in that,* Trust signed, and Kyler—fortunately, this time—translated accurately. *I definitely don't want you to think I'm that guy who goes around punching people, because I'm not. But—*

Marcie waved Trust off, causing him to stop his gesturing.

"Are you kidding me?" she said. "Stop apologizing, Trust! You didn't even do anything wrong. You deserve a medal."

*Still,* Trust returned, *I owe you one. This doesn't seem like how this night was supposed to go. And you really didn't have to leave. You could have stayed.*

He then looked pointedly to Kyler.

*You, too,* he signed. *You didn't have to leave.*

"Of course we didn't have to leave," Paxson answered. "And neither did you, by the way—Mariana said so, and she's the owner—but I'm thinking it's going to be much more fun if we all stick together. Anyway, it's going to take all of us to watch out for Kyler just in case he is about to get beaten up again. You covered for him this time, Trust. Marcie, you're up next."

"Good," Marcie replied, grinning. "I'm in the mood to bust some heads."

"That's not funny," Kyler said. "You're assuming there's going to be people just waiting in line to beat me up."

Marcie looked at him.

"All I want to know," Paxson went on, "is did you at least get the girl's number?"

At that, Kyler seemed to choke on his own tongue in his surprise, coughing suddenly.

"What?" he managed to wheeze. "Girl?"

*I hope she was really—and I mean* really*—pretty,* Trust motioned.

Kyler finally got a hold of himself.

"You mean as pretty as Mariana?" he returned after interpreting his words.

"Ooh, that's a burn," Paxson said playfully.

Trust shook his head, the edges of his lips creeping upward in a faint smile.

*I don't know what you're thinking anyway,* Trust signed. *What's the point? Even if she was pretty, she's no Marcie.*

"Oh, pa-lease, not even close," Kyler agreed, reaching out in an attempt to pull Marcie into a hug.

Paxson quickly shielded her, hugging her tight to his body.

"Hey, no one better lay a finger on my Marcie," he warned.

Kyler and Trust ignored him. Both boys displayed expressions of longing—Kyler making smooching sounds—as they continued to reach for Marcie. Marcie and Paxson laughed as they tried to fend the other boys off.

To the many that passed by them on the downtown walkway, it was a curious, if not amusing, sight.

# 4.
## Saturday Morning

TRUST'S SURROUNDINGS BEGAN TO SHAKE *rhythmically. He looked around, glancing to the trees, and then to the sky, noticing the same subtle but persistent tremor. Though it would normally seem unusual, for some reason, Trust did not find himself surprised.*

*The vibrations seemed familiar. And yet he was powerless to stop them.*

*He then looked down, toward his own body, raising his hands.*

*There, he observed the problem.*

*In fact, the world around him was not shaking at all.*

*He was.*

His body motionless, Trust's eyes snapped open, instantly focusing on the phone that lay close to his head. The cell phone's many lights were on and flashing, and the phone itself was visibly vibrating, which seemed to be causing Trust's head to subtly vibrate as well.

The cell phone was his alarm clock. He reached up through the bed sheets with his hand and grasped the phone, nimbly pressing one of the buttons on its side. He had been using the phone—or one quite similar to it—for long enough that he would have been able to silence it without looking.

Still not yet shifting the rest of his body, Trust swung his eyes over to the other side of the room.

For a moment—a split second—he was stunned, before he calmed himself.

A dirty-blond mess of hair was all that was visible peeking out from under the covers in the far bed, and, for that split second, Trust thought it was a girl.

However, he quickly realized it was just Kyler in his usual deep, chaotic snooze.

Trust then raised the cell phone a little so he could see its face.

Nine a.m.

He got up.

Fifteen minutes later, he was ready to leave for his planned destination, the Sylvia J. Rose Fitness Center—much more commonly referred to as simply "North Gym"—the fitness complex open to the students and faculty on UCC's rural campus. Conveniently, it was less than five minutes' walking distance from where he now stood in his dorm room.

Trust laid a handwritten note on Kyler's desk, telling his friend to meet him at the gym when he woke up. Trust knew that the message might very well end up unnecessary, since Kyler's sleeping habits were completely topsy-turvy. He could wake up in the next few minutes, fully refreshed—or he could remain unconscious for hours more. It was anyone's guess, and Trust had long since given up guessing.

Just before leaving, Trust turned around again and crept closer to Kyler's bed, the huddled form wholly hidden underneath the bedcovers, except for the array of hair. Trust slowly, carefully reached out, poking the form in what he presumed to be a shoulder.

No response.

Another poke, a little harder.

Finally, movement. A face, mostly concealed behind the same mane of blond strands, slowly appeared. Trust chuckled lightly, shaking his head, before he turned away.

Even if it was not yet nine thirty in the morning—not dreadfully early, but nowhere near late in the day—it was a Saturday morning in a college dormitory, and Trust passed by no one until he was outside Weaver Hall. Outdoors, the sun was bright and the sky was clear, hinting at a perfect, if not hot, day ahead. Trust skirted a parking lot and an open field, upon which there were people gathered, setting up tented canopies and tables, most likely for some student-welcoming event held later in the day. Most of the University of Centre City upperclassmen students would be moving in throughout this day and the next, so the campus grounds would inevitably become busier as the hours ticked by.

After venturing up a short but deceptively steep hill, Trust climbed the steps in front of the North Gym, walking under a short awning before entering through a modern archway. Inside, the complex's design was sleek and state of the art, with different portions devoted to different recreational activities—from cardio to weightlifting, indoor squash courts, and an open space for yoga and other aerobic exercises—all within the cavernous edifice. The walls, floors, and equipment throughout were colored in black and varying shades of gold, the school colors of UCC.

Trust scanned his student ID card across the turnstile display scanner, permitting him full access to the fitness center. He passed through the cardio area, filled with treadmills, step climbers, row machines, stationary bikes, and the like. Some were already in use by other weekend risers. Then came the weight-training section, which was also scarcely occupied with a few fellow students. Mirrors ran almost the entire length of the area.

The back half of the complex held the gymnasium, complete with basketball courts and a boxing ring, along with other training equipment, such as heavy bags, speed bags, and human-shaped mannequins. This was the area that drew Trust in for this morning visit.

Two students—a boy and a girl—played a casual game of one-on-one at one of the eight basketball hoops, and from the looks of it, the girl appeared to be winning without much effort. The eight hoops were situated to create separate playing courts with a goal on each end, the court lengths not quite measuring regulation size, but providing more than enough room for a freewheeling, open-floor basketball contest from end to end. Other than the two students—and now Trust—the gym was empty at this still-early-on-a-college-campus hour.

Reaching the training section of the gym, Trust examined the generous supply with intrigued eyes. The bags and other equipment appeared slightly worn with use, yet they maintained good condition.

He gave one of the heavy bags a sudden one-two jab combination, his power light, but noticeable. The bag responded appropriately, giving ever so slightly with his quick strikes, but quickly springing back into form, as though it had not been touched.

Trust then moved to the boxing ring. It, too, had a vaguely scuffed but still perfectly usable look. The canvas flooring gave slightly as he pushed all of his weight down upon it. The give was faint, but Trust felt it.

He moved back to the punching bags.

TRUST HAD HARDLY BEGUN TO perspire as he circled around the bag again, his head, his hands, his entire body constantly moving, ducking, dodging against an imagined opponent, the cadenced, muffled sound of his unrelenting strikes, as always, unnoticed by him. As he moved, he detected someone motioning for his attention from up inside the ring. Surprised, Trust halted his circling, looking up toward what looked to be a slightly older boy.

"Didn't you hear what I said?" the boy asked.

Trust observed a few other boys—six total—along the edge of the ring, all looking toward him. A couple of the boys were standing on the ring apron, casually poised against the ropes, while the rest stood, like Trust, on the gym floor.

Trust's eyes returned to the only boy in the ring. He gestured to his ear, shaking his head.

Over his lifetime, he had found that this rudimentary sign was typically easy to comprehend for both hearing and hearing-impaired populations alike.

"What are you, deaf or something?" Trust watched the boy ask.

Trust leaned against the punching bag he had been pummeling. He grinned up at the boy, giving him a thumbs-up sign.

A few of the others surrounding the ring, along with the boy inside it, each showed a look of astonishment. Trust walked over to the small pile he had brought with him to the gym, quickly retrieving a stack of note cards and a pen. He then moved to the edge of the ring, palming the top card in the stack—which already had his writing on it—and passing it up to the boy who had been addressing him. The boy reached down to meet Trust's hand halfway. As the older boy took the card, Trust glanced over to another boy standing close by.

Trust nodded in greeting.

The boy smirked, nodding in return and saying, "What's up?"

Trust shifted his eyes back to the ring. The boy inside the ropes, now grinning, handed the note card back to Trust.

"Trust is really your name?" he asked.

Trust nodded, glancing around to the others in the group again, noting that all eyes were on to him and the boy in the ring.

"Cool," the boy said loudly. "Trust? That's a cool name. My name's

Jeremy. Anyway, I was just asking you if you wanted to spar with me a little bit."

As Jeremy finished speaking, Trust spotted a student on the far side of the ring. Though Trust could not hear the sound, he knew the boy was chuckling, amused at something that was being said. Another quick glance around identified similar reactions.

Trust looked down to the cards in his hand, produced the third one in the stack, and handed it up to Jeremy.

Jeremy read the note, and then tilted his head back, laughing.

"How could you possibly know that I was talking loud?" he asked, his head coming back down to where Trust could read his lips.

Trust swiftly wrote out his response on one of the blank note cards.

*It's a common reaction. Your friends gave you away.*

"So I guess that's happened to you before, eh?" Jeremy asked, handing the two note cards back to Trust. "Sorry about that. I didn't even realize I was doing it, but—"

His head turned to the side as he halted his speech. Trust's eyes shifted in the same direction, though by the time he pinpointed who had interrupted, the other boy had already finished speaking. Trust could not see what Jeremy said in response, though he dismissed the boy with a wave of his arm.

"Don't listen to him. He's a troll," Jeremy explained, motioning in the other boy's direction again, though Trust had no idea what he was supposed to not be "listening" to.

"Anyway, so how about it, Trust? A little hand-to-hand? You seem like you have an idea of what you're doing on that heavy bag. Let's see what you can do inside the ring."

Trust wrote something else down on the note card.

*You sure?*

Jeremy smirked.

"Ooh, getting a little nervous?"

The older boy reached down, gesturing with his fingers for Trust to grab his hand so he could pull him up to ring level. Trust grinned faintly, meeting the gazes of a few of the other boys encircling the ring, before he seized Jeremy's hand. As Jeremy helped him up, Trust could feel the older boy's strength. His grip was unexpected.

*This might be interesting,* Trust thought.

Ducking under the ropes, Trust moved to a corner, placing his cards and pen on the ring floor just in front of the turnbuckle, out of the way. Then, with a second thought, he grabbed them both again.

*Do you need to warm up? Are we using just open hands?*

"Don't worry about me," Jeremy remarked, grinning. "I was just out there lifting. And open-handed sounds good. Wouldn't want to damage that pretty face for all the ladies, right? You're a freshman?"

Trust nodded, replacing his writing tools to the spot in front of the turnbuckle. The boys who had been standing on the gym floor pulled themselves up, gaining a better vantage point for the upcoming show.

Trust took subtle note of it.

"I can tell," Jeremy went on as Trust approached him again. "You've got that freshman look."

Jeremy smirked again.

"Like you don't know what you've just gotten yourself into," he finished.

Trust smirked as well.

The two boys began to circle each other in the ring in much the same pace Trust had been revolving around the heavy bag minutes earlier. Jeremy had his hands up in a traditional fighter's stance, his fingers lightly curled, but not enough to form a fist. Trust's hands remained relaxed, down by his sides, his movements smooth and assured, the shoes that he wore light and bouncy on the apron. His eyes remained, unwavering, on Jeremy's, waiting for indication.

Also, in his peripheral sightlines, Trust stayed aware of the positions of the other boys lining the ropes.

Very interesting.

Jeremy feinted forward, as if readying for a quick strike.

Trust, still circling, did not even flinch. He smirked again.

"Oh, okay then, tough guy," Jeremy said, smirking as well.

The two of them continued to move around each other, and then— Jeremy came forward quickly, striking out as he did so.

Trust leaned away in the same instant, out of Jeremy's reach. His eyes remained on Jeremy's.

Jeremy resumed his fighting stance briefly before he reached again.

Trust, still moving, ducked his head away while keeping the same, circling pace with his feet.

Jeremy stopped, extending his arm once more. Quickly.

Trust dodged it.

Another jab.

Trust leaned away.

Another, opposite hand.

Trust evaded again, reversing his direction.

"Come on, put up your hands."

A smile tugged faintly at the corner of Trust's lips. He backed away, his circling steps becoming slightly larger, Jeremy advancing with him as both boys crossed to the opposite side of the ring. As Trust's retreat began to slow, Jeremy continued forward, keeping pace.

*He's light on his feet*, Trust mused. *An athlete, maybe for the school.*

Jeremy's movements were not of the plodding, uncertain pace of someone foreign to the art of fighting. The older boy reached out again, his arm shooting out even quicker than his previous attempts, and with a bit more force. Trust dodged once more, his head moving just ahead of Jeremy's hand, and then leaning out of reach.

Jeremy rapidly extended his opposite hand, and Trust ducked slightly this time, moving forward faintly. As Jeremy's strike glanced over, Trust reached up swiftly, lightly making contact with Jeremy's cheek.

Though the impact was soft enough, Trust could not hear the faint, but distinct—

*Smack.*

Jeremy's head turned with the contact, more from shock than from the light touch of Trust's fingers. Shifting back, he worked his jaw for a brief moment before looking to Trust again, who once more stood just out of arm's reach.

Trust was smiling.

"Oooh," echoed a few of the boys looking on. Trust could see their mouths take on the recognizable "O" contour of surprise and amazement—but, of course, he heard no sound.

A couple of the onlookers then snickered.

"Okay," Jeremy stated quietly. "All right."

He raised his hands again.

His grin had reemerged, though its present incarnation was slightly different from before.

Slightly off.

Trust took a step back in preparation.

Jeremy took a step forward, and the two boys were at it again.

"Put your hands up, Trust."

Jeremy jabbed again, and again his hand glanced across nothing but air.

Another reach.

And another evasion, Trust leaning his body away almost before the attempt even came.

Trust began to pace away again so as to not be trapped too close to the ropes, but Jeremy quickly, expertly cut him off.

Jeremy reached out again.

Trust again eluded it. He sensed his back nearing the turnbuckle.

Another attempted strike from Jeremy, this one somewhat arcing in its path, though still swift. Trust dodged it, and again ducked as another jab—this one straight on—breezed by.

Instantly, Trust struck again, once more catching Jeremy on the same side the older boy's hand reached from, and tagging the exact same spot on his face, though this time it was on the opposite cheek.

*Smack.*

It was that same smacking sound.

"Oooh, he got you again, man," someone said.

Trust did not notice, and Jeremy did not bother turning to see who had spoken.

Jeremy reached yet again. Trust was now backed into the corner—

—but he leaned away, finally putting his hands up in a protective posture.

Jeremy struck.

This time, Trust neatly parried Jeremy's hand away before it could reach his face. The unexpected deflection overextended Jeremy's arm slightly, and Trust promptly reached out again.

*Smack.*

As he was hit, Jeremy tried to strike back with his already extended hand, bringing it up so the back of his hand came first. Trust dodged under, and then reached out swiftly, catching the older boy on the side of his chin, just beside his mouth.

The *smack* sound was slightly dulled.

Abruptly, Jeremy reached out with both hands, one an instant after the other.

Trust moved under the first, and grabbed the second, pushing Jeremy's hand down and away, and then, moving just slightly to the side—there was hardly any room, as Jeremy had him cornered—he tagged Jeremy again. Jeremy came back with the hand that had been deflected, this time bringing it in hard and fast, Trust dodging out of the way once more, under the hand, and then sliding past the thin opening Jeremy's aggressive reach had created, while at the same time lifting his lead hand up again and striking Jeremy in the same spot he had targeted earlier.

Out of the corner, Trust backed away nimbly—he almost appeared to dance, the way his shoes deftly touched the ground and then instantly rose up again—leaving Jeremy facing toward the turnbuckle still, as though Trust were still cornered.

Trust watched as Jeremy pounded his hands on the ropes in frustration.

What Trust could not observe was Jeremy's loud curse.

Trust's attention fleetingly shifted to the boys along the apron again.

They were laughing.

Trust returned his gaze to Jeremy. The older boy gripped the two top ropes that fed into the turnbuckle, the muscles in his arms tensing, before he kicked at the stack of note cards that Trust had laid down.

He then turned. Trust looked at him with mild irritation, but Jeremy was not meeting his gaze. Trust had trouble reading Jeremy's moving mouth in that moment, but from the older boy's expression, the words he could not hear did not seem at all good-humored.

Jeremy then faced Trust again, advancing with purpose.

His earlier, easygoing grin was now noticeably absent.

"Put up your hands."

Trust slowly backed away, making the "time-out" signal.

"I said put up your hands!"

Trust glanced over again. One of the other boys was hanging over the rope.

"Get him, J! Don't let him punk you like that, dude!"

Still backing away, Trust returned his eyes to Jeremy, realizing that the boy was advancing hurriedly, nearly breaking into a jog.

"Come on!" Jeremy hissed. Trust could barely make it out through gritted teeth.

Trust kept pulling back, beginning to circle around the ring again, but Jeremy followed aggressively.

*Maybe we should stop*— Trust began to sign.

"You better put your hands up," Jeremy interrupted mid-gesture.

While still moving, the upperclassman reached out quickly, though with Trust continuing to move away, the attempt at contact was not close. Nevertheless, Trust leaned even farther out of reach, continuing to circle.

Finally, Jeremy caught on again, cutting off Trust's retreat.

"Come on! Put your hands up!"

Jeremy took a few more swipes, Trust ducking and dodging at each attempt, as Jeremy continued to advance, this time confining Trust along the ropes. Trust raised his hands, again in a defensive stance.

Jeremy extended again, his hand coming in fast.

Trust knocked it away easily.

Another attempt—

—and another parry by Trust. Jeremy's swings were swifter now, more forceful, more aggressive.

He came with a quick one-two combo, one hand extending, almost instantly followed by the other. Trust deflected the first attempt, and then leaned his weight back against the ropes behind him, the rope flexing back and allowing him to evade Jeremy's second strike. In nearly the same instant, Trust reached out as well, yet again coming over Jeremy's extended arm and hitting him lightly on his now reddened cheek. Immediately, Trust leaned back again as Jeremy swung in response.

On that attempt, Trust saw that Jeremy's fist appeared to have closed.

Jeremy then lunged forward, his oncoming swing bringing with it considerably more power than what either boy had utilized thus far in the contest.

Quickly glimpsing toward the boy, and an instant before he shirked out of the way, Trust detected the frustration—and perhaps even anger—on Jeremy's features.

Also, out of the corner of his vision, Trust spotted another boy who stood along the ring's edge, reaching out—

—toward him.

Evading Jeremy's lunge, Trust sidestepped, freeing himself from Jeremy's confinement...but, at the same time, turning nimbly on his feet, bending away and barely avoiding the other boy's grasp, while also bringing his own arm away from his body, immediately and swiftly impacting the boy through the opening in the ropes along the side of his midsection.

Trust had pulled the punch, not putting a lot of energy into the hit. Still, it was a stinger, and it had the desired effect.

"Ahhh!" the boy cried out, grabbing his side and half jumping, half crumbling off the ring apron as Trust backed quickly away.

Trust again assessed the positions of Jeremy and the other boys.

Jeremy, not even noticing the exchange between Trust and the other boy—the movements had been so quick—was turning and beginning to advance on Trust again.

Trust also saw another boy ducking under the ropes and climbing into the ring.

Trust's hands now remained upright, though his stance was adjusted, becoming more natural.

More aggressive.

However, he watched as Jeremy's steps faltered, the upperclassman spotting the other boy entering the ring.

"What are—"

The first two words on Jeremy's lips were all Trust could take note of before his gaze shifted to the other boy, who was already closer to him than Jeremy was and approaching quickly.

"Hey, that was my boy, you—"

Trust recognized the curse hurled in his direction, and he sidestepped in the same moment as the boy swung, the two movements almost looking synchronized. The boy, punching out with a closed fist, fully intended to do damage. Trust also sighted the other boys suddenly stepping through the ropes and entering the boxing ring, about to outnumber him five to one. Trust glanced quickly to his side again, assessing—

Kyler.

"Hey! Hey! Stop! Stop! Wait! Hold it!"

Kyler had also made his way into the ring, unnoticed by Trust until that moment, coming to stand in front of his friend, facing the other boys with his hands up, palms opened and facing outward. Trust could not see what Kyler was saying anymore, but his body language was clear enough.

Then, sighting the boy who had whiffed on his punch moments before rounding to return again, Trust began to move in response. Kyler, however, must have seen the boy's advance in the same moment, because he jumped ahead of Trust, keeping a hand on his friend to hold him back, while holding his other hand up to stop the other boy in his tracks.

"Wait! Hang on! Hang on! Just listen! Just listen to me for a second, all right?"

Trust watched as the approaching boys halted their advancements, though the boy who had missed his chance at hitting Trust was breathing heavily, huffing in frustration. Meanwhile, Jeremy pushed and shoved his way to the front of the group, fuming, before he turned back to look at the others.

"What are you guys doing? Huh? What are you in the ring for?"

The boy who had come after Trust looked at Jeremy heatedly.

"You didn't just see what this guy did to Joey?" he spat. "He was just playing around, and this guy caught him with a cheap—"

Not drawing any unnecessary attention, Trust tapped Kyler on his side. Trust's face conveyed his unspoken question, as he was in a poor position to read either of the speakers' mouths.

"I'll recap it later," Kyler whispered.

"Dude, didn't you hear me?" Jeremy was saying. "I don't care! Get out of the ring! Get out of the—"

Kyler turned to look at Trust again.

"This dude's cursing a lot," he muttered, "and now, the other guy's cursing back at him. It's a curse-fest."

Slowly, but soon enough, the other boys slunk out of the ring. Most of them, particularly the boy who had tried to punch Trust, shot heated looks in Trust's direction. The boy Trust had struck on the ring apron— who had not gotten into the ring—left as well, attempting to act as though he were no worse for wear, though anyone could see he was still favoring his side. After watching them leave, Trust turned to Jeremy, who had stayed behind.

"Hey, man," Kyler started in a placating tone. "We don't want any trouble—"

Jeremy ignored him, gazing at Trust.

"So, what, you're gonna hit my friends with cheap shots now? Is that it?"

Trust looked back to the boy, his brow furrowed in annoyance.

*He tried to hit me when you had me on the ropes—* he started to sign, forgetting for the moment that Jeremy would not understand any of it, and not knowing if Kyler would translate.

Jeremy, however, waved him off.

"Forget it. Whatever. I don't care."

Trust nudged Kyler and gestured again. Kyler raised his eyebrows, and then looked to Jeremy.

"He says you threw a punch, too, and that's against the rules."

Kyler then glanced to Trust again.

"What rules?" he asked.

"What? No, I didn't!" Jeremy declared, taking a step closer, Trust now well within his reach.

"Come on, man," Kyler tried again, sensing something was about to happen.

"I didn't throw a punch!" Jeremy stated again.

Then he swung. It was open-handed.

And, without taking his eyes off Jeremy's, Trust caught the boy's hand just before it reached his face.

"Trust, look out!"

Kyler ducked out of the way. His reaction was drastically late, however. Had Jeremy been aiming for him, he would have been slapped square on the cheek.

With his hand and wrist still enclosed in Trust's firm grip, Jeremy looked at the deaf teenager for an extended moment.

Then he grinned.

"Are you freaking kidding me?" Jeremy said with some surprise.

Trust released his hand.

"I got close that time, though," Jeremy boasted.

*Only because I let you,* Trust returned.

Kyler translated, and Jeremy laughed.

"Ha! Yeah, okay."

The older boy then turned, walking to the ropes without another word, soon hopping to the gymnasium floor below. Trust and Kyler watched from inside the ring as Jeremy went around to the corner where he had kicked off Trust's pen and note cards. There he picked up both, tidying the stack and returning them to where Trust had placed them in front of the turnbuckle. He then winked at Trust before sauntering off, beginning to cross the now deserted basketball courts.

"Hey!" Kyler yelled, Trust's eyes shifting to him as he noticed Kyler's hands cup his mouth to amplify his shout.

Jeremy paused and turned around, looking back to the boxing ring curiously.

"I don't know what you did, but I did see your friend throw that punch! Tell him he owes me!"

Kyler's voice echoed across the cavernous space.

"For what?" Jeremy called back.

"For saving his face!"

Jeremy laughed again, and, turning away, threw up a "peace out" sign.

Kyler looked to Trust, grinning, and was met with a questioning look.

"What?" Kyler asked, chuckling.

*Was that necessary?* Trust gestured.

"Hey, it was just a little warning," Kyler responded and signed at the same time. "And anyway, you should be thanking me for saving the day—once again, I might add."

Trust's expression turned incredulous.

*Really? Are you serious? Did I look like a damsel in distress to you?*

"I wasn't talking about saving you. I saved them from you. I'm a real hero."

Trust rolled his eyes. He then started to back toward the corner where his note cards were, still facing Kyler.

*So, I guess you got my note to meet me here?*

"Note? What note? Oh, you mean that scrap of paper on my desk? Nah, I threw that away without even looking at it. I thought it was trash. I just remembered you said yesterday you were coming here to test this place out."

*So, you came to work out, then?*

"Heh, that's funny. I know you can't hear it, but my stomach is seriously talking to me right now. It keeps saying 'Feed me! Feed me!' in this weird, creepy voice. I think it's trying to tell me that I'm hungry or something. You can fill me in on the rumble you almost had with the Jets and the Sharks while we get something to eat."

# 5.
## Disability Services

ON MONDAY, A DAY BEFORE the official start of classes, Trust arrived at Disability Services—Adams Hall—for his scheduled appointment. Adams Hall mirrored the framework of the neighboring University of Centre City administrative buildings, easily confusable if not for the sign placed on the property's well-maintained front lawn.

The grounds of the rural campus exhibited more life on this day then at any other time since Trust had moved into his dormitory. Everyone and anyone who had some sort of interest in the goings-on of the university seemed to be represented, milling about in some capacity, making final preparations for tomorrow. Other students were taking advantage of their final free day before they were enveloped in the educational obligations that brought them to campus in the first place, walking, hanging out, or joining in on one of the impromptu Frisbee or soccer games.

Trust left the pleasant day outdoors, entering the clean and modern-looking interior of the administrative building. If he had not known better, he could have just as easily been entering a corporation headquarters. A deceptively long walk straight ahead found him approaching the large receptionist desk.

Trust had visited Adams Hall more than a few times during his visits to UCC before—and after—he had officially become one of its students, but this was his first time seeing this particular receptionist.

Because, of course, he would have remembered seeing *her*.

She was very pretty.

Prettier than that, Trust thought. He grinned faintly, betraying his inner musings.

71

The young receptionist—perhaps an upperclassman, perhaps even a graduate student—displayed a welcoming smile as Trust drew near, causing Trust to grin a little more, even though he tried to stop himself.

He was glad Kyler was busy, not able to come with him on this appointment. If he had glimpsed Trust's face in that moment, he would have never heard—seen—the end of it.

"Hi."

Trust's eyes shifted slightly to the receptionist's lips as she started to speak.

"You're Trustice Jeffries, right?"

Trust's eyes expanded in surprise. Nodding, he started to reach into his pocket, fishing for his note cards. Normally, he would have had them out and ready, but on this occasion, he had been distracted...

*Are you surprised that I know your name?*

The receptionist's hands signed gracefully, causing Trust's eyes to widen even more. He removed his hand from his pocket.

*Not as surprised as I am that you know what I'm saying right now*, he replied.

The receptionist's smile turned playful.

*Just for you,* she gestured, grinning.

*Fantastic. Will you marry me?*

The receptionist laughed, with Trust—as he had with Mariana at the Centre Diamond nightclub—wishing that he could hear her at that moment.

*Wow, you are so shy,* she signed. *Proposing to me, and you don't even know my name?*

Trust grinned.

*You haven't said no.*

The receptionist laughed softly again. She started to reach for the phone on her desk, but before picking it up...

*I can already tell that the girls on campus are going to be in trouble. Let me notify Dr. Duncan that you are here.*

Trust waited while the receptionist glanced down to press a few buttons on the telephone console. The phone to her ear, her eyes then came up again.

*You know you still haven't said no, right?* Trust gestured, resulting in the young woman smiling once again. *Should we schedule a wedding date now, or...*

He held his hands up, as though waiting for her to fill in the rest of the sentence. A moment later, he observed the subtle reaction on the woman's face that told him someone had answered her call.

"Yes, sir, he is here. Should I send him back?—

"Yes, sir?—

"Yes, si—I mean, yes, Clarke."

*Dr. Duncan said you could go back to his office now. He said you would probably remember how to get there?*

Trust's hands were in his pockets, and he rocked back and forth on his heels, smiling at the woman seated before him. He looked as though he had no intention of responding to her question, or heading toward Dr. Duncan's office.

Just rocking, back and forth.

Smiling.

*What?* motioned the receptionist, smiling in spite of her question.

Trust continued to coolly sway, hands tucked away.

*You sure know how to use those pretty eyes to your advantage, don't you?* the young woman signed. *Now, do you remember how to get to Dr. Duncan's office, or should I give you directions? It's like a maze back there, you know...*

The woman, smiling still, finally shook her head as she realized Trust was not going to respond.

He continued to rock back and forth.

He continued to smile innocently.

*I think my boyfriend—fiancé, actually—would have a few questions for me if I said I would marry you.*

Finally, Trust removed his hands from his pockets.

*Then it would probably be a good idea not to tell him,* he offered, still grinning. *Maybe you'd like to look into my eyes some more and—*

The young woman behind the desk picked up a small sheaf of papers and waved them at Trust in dismissal. Trust's smile remained on his face as he backed away quickly from the desk with his hands up, beginning to edge around the counter to the hallways and maze of administrative corridors beyond.

*I hope you know where you're going,* she then gestured as she put the papers down again, *because now you've lost the privilege of me telling you the way!*

Even with the exclamation in her gestures, she was still smiling.

Still retreating from her and now on the side of her desk that led deeper into the building's interior, the receptionist's eyes turning and following his movements, Trust moved his hands through the air effortlessly.

*I think I can manage. If I get lost, though, it only gives me an excuse to come back to see you again.*

In fact, Trust nearly did get lost, but just before he decided he would need to retrace his steps, he saw the familiarly simple, handwritten placard to Dr. Clarke Duncan's office just to the side of an opened doorway. Adams Hall, in fact, housed many other university services besides Disability Services, and so the occasional disoriented visitor was not wholly uncommon.

Dr. Clarke Duncan, a wizened but very lively man, was the chief disabilities administrator of UCC. He was among the first administrators Trust had encountered during his initial visit to the school, and the man's spirited attitude was contagious, soon enough having both Trust and his parents—who had traveled with him—enraptured in his obviously exaggerated tales of his life and times at the university. The administrator had kept in touch with Trust throughout his decision-making process on choosing a college, and he remained a chief reason why Trust chose UCC.

Kyler, who had already been strongly considering the university, having been offered a baseball scholarship and tagging along on the visit with his own family, had also struck up a near-instant kinship with the old professor and administrator. The two could seemingly talk nonstop for hours, so for Trust, his best friend's appreciation of the man certainly did not hurt matters.

On top of his other large responsibilities, Dr. Duncan was also Trust's academic advisor, as he was to some of the other impaired students who so expressed interest in his services. The role of academic advising was another full-time occupation in itself, but Dr. Duncan seemed able to juggle his multiple hats fluidly.

The animated old man apparently had no need for sleep.

Inside the office, the administrator was facing a large corkboard occupied with papers and handwritten notes, on the opposite side that the doorway entered. Trust, seeing the man distracted, knocked on the already opened door as he poked his head in.

Dr. Duncan whirled about quickly, as though thoroughly surprised.

His face then brightened.

*Ah, Mr. Trustice Jeffries! Come in, come in! It's so good to see you!*

Trust took on his own look of astonishment as he entered.

*Since when do you know how to sign?* Trust gestured.

"Oh, I'm great, Mr. Jeffries, just great. Couldn't be better, couldn't be better. Come on, come on, have a seat here. Let me just clear some of this out of the way…"

As Dr. Duncan removed a stack of books and papers that had been placed on one of the chairs facing the desk, Trust grinned, shaking his head. He realized the administrator had had no clue what Trust had signed back in response, only guessing—and guessing incorrectly, at that.

"Welcome, welcome," the administrator continued, making sure to remain facing Trust's direction, while at the same time searching for somewhere to place the pile of materials he still had in his hands. Finally, as Trust sat down, the old man simply dropped them to the floor. Trust watched in amazement as the stack miraculously remained upright, seemingly in no danger of toppling over.

"My apologies for the mess, Trustice, my sincere apologies. I clean this office every week—every week, mind you—but I think it just prefers to remain in disarray. That's chaos theory at work, Trustice. Did you know that chaos theory isn't even a theory at all? It's a postulation. A small—very small—but important difference, Trustice."

Trust shook his head, knowing the old man was speaking nonsense, but the administrator continued.

"So, what brings you to my fair neck of the woods, Mr. Jeffries, hmm? Oh, yes! Of course, of course! Your appointment!

"But first, tell me, Trustice, what did you think of my signing abilities just now? Unfortunately, what you saw is all that I know at the moment, as I am very much a novice, even with as much as I have been exposed to it over the years. Miss Sharpshire, at the front desk, was patient enough to take a moment of her time to impart to me that little tidbit. I bet I had you fooled, eh? Yes, I could see it on your face. Did you happen to meet Miss Sharpshire at the front desk? Very pleasant young lady, very pleasant. She is a graduate student here at the university, though in what, at this very moment, I cannot recall. Very smart, Miss Sharpshire is, and she knows sign language! She is the one who taught me that little morsel that I showed you before. Now, shall we get on with it?

"But first, what in the world took you so long to get here? It seems I got off the phone with Miss Sharpshire thirty minutes ago, with her informing me that you had arrived. Did you get lost, Trustice? Did you? There is really no shame in it. I've wandered about this campus for over forty years and I am still unable to make my way to my very own office half the time..."

Trust, thoroughly amused, sat in his chair and watched.

"Now, let me show you this interesting little contraption here," the administrator said, Trust following with his eyes as the old man retrieved what looked to be a small, wireless microphone. His desktop computer was already turned, and Trust had shifted his chair's position, after having reviewed the slate of classes he would be taking for the upcoming semester, and now Trust watched Dr. Duncan open up another program.

Instantly, a blank page materialized.

After a moment, when nothing else happened, Trust glanced back to the older man, who was fidgeting with the tiny microphone and mumbling to himself.

"And I just have to attach this thing right here, and—how do I even turn this thing on again? Should be coming automatically...ah, there it goes!"

As the man looked up, Trust was able to decipher his final words. He then followed Dr. Duncan's gaze to the computer display.

> **Dr. C. Duncan:** "And I just have to attach this thing right here, and—how do I even turn this thing on again? Should be coming automatically...ah, there it goes!"

Trust's eyes shifted again to the man behind the desk. Dr. Duncan smirked, wiggling his eyebrows, before quickly directing Trust's attention back to the screen.

Another entry for **Dr. C. Duncan** appeared, the words becoming visible on the screen not at once, but at a usual speaking rate of speed.

> **Dr. C. Duncan:** "Voice-to-text messaging! Isn't it magnificent? Incredible, I say! Just incredible! Here, you can use my keyboard to type."

Trust, reading along on the screen, turned an instant later, taking the offered wireless keyboard. As he began, he observed the **Unknown** tag announce his presence.

> **Unknown:** You know voice-to-text wasn't invented yesterday, right?

> **Dr. C. Duncan:** "Ah, I almost forgot. This is Trustice, by the way. Um, TalkText, Trustice is typing."

Trust saw the **Unknown** tag switch to **Trustice (?)**.

> **Dr. C. Duncan:** "Yes, correct. 'Trustice is typing' is correct."

The question mark following Trust's name disappeared. Trust looked over to Dr. Duncan again.

"Quite ingenious, wouldn't you say?" the admin said. "TalkText is the name of the application. This is what I was telling you and your parents about last time. This is what your professors will be equipped with during lectures—"

Trust's eyes shifted once more to the computer screen, where he picked up the older man's dialogue.

> **Dr. C. Duncan:** "...equipped with during lectures, so you will be able to follow along without worrying about glancing away or looking down to write notes. Now, if you break contact, or if the professor turns away from you, you will still be able to get everything. See, look at me right now!"

Trust found Dr. Duncan standing and facing his corkboard again, his back completely turned to Trust. Trust returned to the screen.

> **Dr. C. Duncan:** "Now, you won't have to worry if the professor's back is turned, or if he or she is looking away, or looking down as they are talking. And I can also—"

Trust's attention went to the administrator again as he started to move from around the desk, still with his back turned toward Trust, as though ignoring him. Trust could not tell whether or not Dr. Duncan was still speaking, or—

> **Dr. C. Duncan:** "And I can also go wherever I want in the classroom, all with my back facing you, and continue to drone on and on about absolutely whatever I wish, and you will still be able to know what I'm saying as long as this microphone is active. And since you said you have your own laptop, I will give you the drive that installs this program. You, being able to read lips as well as you do, are already well ahead of the curve, as you probably know, so this is almost an issue of convenience for you. Every instructor on campus has been educated on how to use this program by yours truly and Dr. Reid from the School of Engineering, so they will be ready when you or the other students who will be issued this program are in their class. Any questions?"

Having made a circuit around his office, the admin returned to his desk, Trust's eyes switching occasionally between the man and the computer screen. The voice-to-text application seemed quite advanced, having not made a single error during his discourse, the words and sentences appearing on the page as though he were watching them emerge from the man's lips. As Dr. Duncan had said, it was more a program of convenience rather than necessity for Trust, but it was definitely appreciated, making Trust's chore of "listening" significantly easier.

Trust began to type again.

> **Trustice:** What if I have a question? In high school, I could just write my question on a note card and either someone else would ask it or the teacher would come over and read it.

As Dr. Duncan was sitting directly in front of him again, Trust took his eyes off the screen and looked to the older man.

"Yes, and unfortunately," he replied, "that will pretty much be the same for right now, although you never know what the Engineering School at this university will come up with next. I, in fact, raised that very same concern, but they don't have a suitable solution as of yet. Instead of writing the questions down, however, you will be able to type them. You can use your computer's voice program—most laptops these days have it, I believe. I remember you telling me before that you would rather not have an interpreter in class with you, so I won't even mention that—but, oh, I just did, didn't I?"

Trust arched an eyebrow, grinning faintly.

"Well, in any event, that is still an option as well—at any point during the year—should you change your mind. And, as far as I'm aware, you and your friend—what was the dear boy's name? Trevor? Clarence? Petey? I am completely drawing a blank here..."

Trust, smiling, gestured to the desktop screen.

**Trustice:** Kyler.

"Yes, right! Kyler is the name! Kyler will be in a few of your classes this semester, will he not? I do seem to recall him saying that he was put under a similar servitude during your high school years, so that should not be—"

Trust was pointing to the screen again.

**Trustice:** That was his idea! I never once asked him to do that, for the same reason I would never want an interpreter sitting—

**Dr. C. Duncan:** "Ha ha ha ha!"

Trust glanced toward the man after seeing the interruption materialize on the screen.

"I understand, dear boy, I understand completely!" Dr. Duncan responded as he tried to restrain his amusement. "Just having a little bit of fun. Now, any other questions about this program? No? Excellent!"

BACK AT THE RECEPTIONIST'S DESK in the entrance wing of Adams Hall, the young woman—the woman Dr. Duncan had referred to as Miss Sharpshire—was on the phone, facing away from the direction of the hallways that led deeper into the building. Soon, however, she was released from her call, her attention drifting to a few unfilled order forms on her desk—

—and then a subtle movement at her side drew her notice.

Her eyes widened slightly, and then she smiled as she saw Trust grinning at her.

*Well, hello again,* she signed. *I didn't even hear you walk up.*

Trust's grin became slightly wider.

*That's interesting,* he returned, *because I never heard you say no.*

"You're absolutely insane," the receptionist said, though her ever-present smile nullified the remark.

*I'm not so sure you would hear me even if I did say it,* she continued.

*Of course not,* Trust replied. *I can't hear anything.*

The young woman laughed.

*You never told me your name,* Trust motioned.

"Kimberlee," she said.

Trust attempted to spell it back to her.

*Almost,* Kimberlee responded. *Mine is with an "E-E" at the end instead of a "Y." Don't ask me why, it was my dad's idea.*

Trust nodded in acknowledgement, smiling and then bowing slightly in a casual attempt at elegance.

*I will be sure to see you around, Miss Kimberlee Sharpshire.*

He purposefully emphasized the "Miss" designate.

# 6.

## The Night Before First Classes

"DUDE." PAXSON STARED AT KYLER blankly. "You're still thinking about that girl, aren't you?"

*You've got it bad, man,* Trust gestured.

He, Kyler, Paxson, and Marcie sat in a loose circle, Paxson and Marcie in chairs, Trust and Kyler lounging on their respective beds.

It was the evening before their first day of collegiate classes, and Kyler looked forlorn.

"Ugh, I know," he groaned. He then shoved his hands into his face, as though trying to wipe something out of his eyes.

"She's eating into my brain!" he whispered in exasperation.

Trust, although unable to hear his friend's voice, could still see the overly agonized expression.

"I can't get her out of my head. I can't sleep, I can't eat, I can't—"

"You can't eat?" Marcie cut in. "Um, dramatic much? We just finished eating not even thirty minutes ago, and you had three full plates of fried junk."

Paxson and Trust snickered.

*And you sleep like a dead man,* Trust added. *I'll be interested to see how you're going to get yourself out of bed for your eight o'clock classes.*

"Hey, I've never had problems getting up on time," Kyler said to Trust, pointing to him with assurance. "Perfect attendance in school since kindergarten, and no tardies. Top that, playboy!"

"But didn't you say you barely even saw her, though?" Paxson said. "That place was packed. You said you didn't even get close enough to speak to her. You don't know her name, and you barely know what she looks like."

Kyler leaned his head back, faintly thumping it against the wall.

"I saw her for, like, a grand total of five seconds," he said, "and four of those seconds were following the back of her head as I tried to catch up with her. But"—he now looked to Trust again—"if you hadn't been there, and that guy had clocked me, those five seconds—that one second that I saw her face—would have been worth it."

Kyler's gaze then turned to Marcie, and Trust's followed, the deaf teen noticing that Marcie's mouth and face had taken on the "Aww" formation he had seen in the few romantic comedies he would just as soon erase from his memory. He had no idea people actually did that in real life.

He looked back to his best friend.

*Okay, this whole thing is starting to scare me a little bit,* he signed. *I'm going to need you to snap out of it and turn back to normal, crazy Kyler.*

Kyler shrugged.

"I can't help it, dude. But know that the only reason I'm telling you—any of you—this much is because I'm pretty sure I'll never see her again."

Kyler's face then scrunched up as he began to sing.

Terribly.

*"Because...she was like...an angel to me..."*

Watching Kyler's face, Trust grimaced as though he had just tasted something foul. Marcie and Paxson both doubled up in laughter.

Kyler stopped singing.

"And anyway, I know you would probably be saying the same thing about Mariana if you didn't know she worked—"

Marcie jumped out of her seat, pointing.

"Aha! I knew it! I knew you liked her! I knew it!"

Trust's mouth hung open, partly in confusion, but mostly in shock.

"Oooh, an older chick," Paxson said, grinning slyly at Trust and then nodding. "Good eye."

"An older chick?" Marcie repeated, looking at Paxson. "She's, like, mid-twenties, tops. That's not even close to being old."

"Not old," Paxson corrected. "Older. Getting a hot older woman is on every guy's list of things to accomplish before he dies."

"But I'm a month older than you are," Marcie said.

Paxson looked at her, grinning and wiggling his eyebrows.

"And that's just one of the things that makes you so fantastic," he remarked.

Marcie rolled her eyes, but could not hide her grin. The young couple began to lean toward each other, obviously about to kiss, before Kyler interrupted.

"Ahem. Sorry, but weren't we just discussing Trust's humongous crush on Mariana from Centre Diamond?"

Trust motioned frantically.

*No! No! We were talking about your crush—*yours—*on a girl—*

"Actually," Paxson said, looking around Marcie toward Kyler, "weren't we discussing your humongous crush on a girl whose face you only saw for a second?"

Trust waved in Paxson's direction, indicating that everyone should listen to him.

"Knock, knock," a voice announced from the opened doorway.

Trust's attention shifted toward the door in the same moment as the others' in the room, though his signal had been the unexpected movement, not the new voice.

It was Holden, their resident advisor.

"Hey, guys," he started. "Sorry to interrupt, but—"

"Wait," Kyler said, leaning forward on his bed. "That door hasn't been open this whole time, has it?"

Holden glanced back to the doorway he had just walked through.

"Yeah...I mean, it was open just now," Holden explained, turning back around. "That's why I said, 'knock, knock.' I don't just go around saying that, you know. Anyway—"

"Oh, come on!" Kyler cried, sitting back on his bed again, and again knocking his head against the wall. He glanced toward Trust.

"Did you see anyone walk past that door while I was talking?" he asked.

Trust smirked.

*Why? Because you don't want anyone else to hear about your humongous crush on a mystery girl whose name you don't know?*

Kyler narrowed his eyes, and then displayed a smirk of his own.

*Maybe,* Kyler started, signing back, *it's because we were also talking about M-A-R-I—*

"Oomph!"

Kyler failed to finish spelling the girl's name before he was swiftly impacted in the face by a flying pillow.

"What the heck is going on with those two?" Holden inquired, looking to Paxson and Marcie.

Paxson chuckled.

"They don't want anyone to know about their—oomph!"

Paxson went down, the unexpected pillow knocking him out of his chair. He lay sprawled out on the floor at Holden's shoes.

Holden looked down at Paxson, and then to Marcie. Marcie just shrugged, arching an eyebrow.

"Ooookay," the RA said. "Well, I mainly wanted to tell this to you anyway, Marcie, since you were the one to bring up the Freesef Society at the hall meeting. Well—and I have no way of confirming this, at least not right now—but it seems as though there may have been an...altercation, I guess you could say. At least, that is what the girl allegedly told some people."

"A rape?" Marcie asked, looking at Holden in disbelief. "By altercation, you mean rape, right? How...I mean, you said—"

"Marcie."

Paxson had raised himself off the carpet and back onto his chair. He reached toward his girlfriend in consolation.

"Just calm down for a second, all right?" he went on softly. "We don't—"

"No, wait," Marcie said, shrugging away from Paxson's outstretched hand and standing up as she looked to Holden. "How did you hear about it?"

"Vicki, the RA on the all-girls side down the hall, just told me," Holden said. "Vicki doesn't believe the stories are true, but according to what she heard, it may have happened last night. It's like I said at the meeting, Marcie. If it's true, no one's ever going to know who did it, most likely, and I doubt the girl even knows. If she does know, she's not going to tell. She won't go to the police—no one will. And no one will ever know for sure if it actually happened at all.

"I remember my RA my freshman year saying that he knew for sure of one instance where a group of girls made up a whole story to reap whatever benefits they thought would come of it. It's crazy and twisted, I know, but it's a distinct possibility. There's some sort of cool factor there that I can't even try to understand, but there has to be some circles on campus that believe it. If no one, especially the girl involved, will admit anything to the police, if it's all played off as a joke or a rumor to try to get popular, then..."

Holden shrugged faintly, and then met the Marcie's eyes again.

"It's like it never happened. Another crazy story we can all tell each other, like I'm doing right now. It feeds the legend. And we're right back where we started until it happens again."

There was a moment of quiet in the room as Holden's words were absorbed.

"That sounds so...weird," Paxson finally said. "I mean, does campus police even know about those stories? Or Centre City police? The school administration? How can all of it continue—how can all of it keep happening—if everyone knows?"

"How can all of what keep happening?" Holden asked back. "What's happened? Who knows what?

"Let's say, hypothetically, the story that I heard is actually what happened. I hope it's not true, but let's just say for now that it did. A girl—most likely a freshman; it always is—was assaulted by members of this reformed underground Freesef Society. First, let's assume that it actually was the Freesef Society and not someone else. You probably heard when you were choosing colleges that UCC is ranked in, like, the top two or three among universities with the lowest rates of assaults on campus, including sexual assaults. It's so unusual that people jump to a legend like Freesef to explain it.

"You guys have to remember, I've been here two years already; this is my third. I've heard this same story a dozen times—more than that—just with different girls in the middle of it. This girl in particular, whoever she is, will not—*will not*—go to the police and report what happened. Not because she's afraid, mind you, but because she doesn't want to. To her, no crime has occurred. In her opinion, she was not hurt—not hurt in a way you or I would define it. She won't go to the police, or to another authority figure like a professor, or even the chancellor, and so nothing happens on that end, because no one ever hears about it, at least not from the source, the victim. Case closed.

"Now, we'll continue to assume this girl was assaulted by members of the Freesef Society. That club was disbarred. From what I've heard, it was partly because rumors like these started to circulate out in the open. Freesef hasn't existed in any physical, official capacity for a while. Ask every student on campus if they are, or have ever been, a member of Freesef. They will say no; some won't even know what you're talking about. Ask every student on campus if they are, or have ever been, a member of Freesef or any club even faintly resembling it, whatever club you can think of. It won't matter how you word it. 'She was assaulted by members of the Freesef Society,' someone could say. But where are those members? How do you find the club everyone denies? You don't. Case closed. Noticing a pattern?

"Now, let's assume one of us in here actually knows this girl. Maybe we heard her name through the gossip tree, or we heard it from a friend who knows the girl, or we even heard it directly from the girl's mouth. First off, the words she will not use when describing this encounter will be 'rape,' 'assault,' 'force,' or anything like that. You want to save her from herself and go to the police? What do you have? Oh, nothing? Case closed.

"I already know what you're thinking, so let's just go there. Let's assume this girl does use one of those words, or all of them, or something similar when she tells us the story of what happened. Let's say we then ask her if she's going to report it to the police. 'No.' Let's say we drag her, kicking and screaming, to the police station. The police will ask the questions, and the girl will deny. The police will ask the questions in a different way, the girl will deny in the same way. She has nothing to report; she will admit *nothing*. Case closed.

"Every avenue of pursuit will come up empty, every facet of the story that you hear about will be denied, or can be contradicted. What does it say that a nonexistent group, with no apparent members, is able to find and take advantage of numerous girls—over a period of *years*—who they know will not speak against them or go to the police? What does it say if you allege a crime has been committed and yet the alleged victim refutes it? What does it say if you confidently identify a 'victim'—in the true sense of the word—if said victim doesn't ask for, call, seek, or desire help? How do you point out a culprit if no one reports or has concrete knowledge of the crime? How do you find an offender if he or the group he belongs to doesn't exist? No victim, no offender, no crime. That is dividing by zero, guys, an impossible case to crack. And that brings us here, back to this room, with me telling you that something may have happened to a girl, but then again not really, but *maybe* it did, but it didn't. So, any questions?"

Holden slowly looked around the room, taking in the blank, impassive faces staring back at him.

"Dude," Kyler declared, speaking for everyone, "you've thought about this."

"Oh, man," Holden said, "that won't give you guys any nightmares, will it? You have school tomorrow, you know."

*I want to be just like you when I grow up*, Trust motioned.

Kyler relayed the sentiments, and Holden smirked.

"I've got no idea if I should take that as a compliment, or if you're being sarcastic."

"Yeah, you'll get used that," Kyler agreed. "He's like talking to a person void of emotion. You know, like a sociopath."

Trust looked over at his so-called "friend." Briefly, he searched around for his pillow before he realized that—

"Oomph."

Trust could not hear himself, but he felt the sound in his chest and throat as he was suddenly struck with something soft and billowy.

He also could not hear Kyler's guffaw, which was then followed by yet another "oomph," as Kyler was hit by another pillow, this one thrown by Marcie.

# 7.
# Allison

THE FIRST DAY, TUESDAY, WAS simply that—a first day. And a Tuesday. In eighteen years, Trust had seen his fair share.

However, the second day of classes brought with it the first gathering of Freshman Honors Seminar-Progressive, registration code FHS-5381, scheduled to meet every Monday, Wednesday, and alternate Friday in Room 611 of the Bocholis Building. Like a majority of the other classrooms in the Bocholis Building, Room 611 was relatively small as compared to the idealized collegiate classrooms and lecture halls, which UCC also housed plenty of. However, the atmosphere within the smaller rooms was more intimate, more familiar, effectively blurring the lines between class and hangout without crossing into total informality.

After all, it was still a classroom on a leading university campus.

But, then again, it was also the Bocholis Building.

Outside, the air was warm and slightly humid, a light drizzle having intermittently made itself known. By the time the faint raindrops ceased, everything and everyone it had touched was instantly dry again.

Inside, the academic halls were quietly bustling, and Trust and Kyler entered Room 611, each with a backpack slung over his shoulder, trailing and trailed by other freshmen who would be sitting in on the same seminar. Kyler, with Trust following him, approached the front row of desks, as had been their usual seating positions throughout their schooling years.

It wasn't that Trust necessarily needed to sit in the front row. In fact, he would have been able to see just as clearly from the very back of the room.

Trust made a detour toward the instructor's desk. He assumed that the older woman, blond hair streaked with silver, was Mrs. Forte, the instructor.

Having had three classes the previous day, and one class an hour earlier, Trust was well versed in the process he was about to initiate once again. The woman's gaze shifted away from the student she was speaking to as she noticed Trust's advance.

He already had the handwritten note in his grasp.

*Hello, Mrs. Forte.*
*My name is Trustice Jeffries, and I am deaf.*
*It is nice to meet you.*

Trust observed the woman's face as she scanned the card, seeing her expression brighten faintly when her gaze met his again. She handed the card back to Trust.

*Hello, Trustice.*

Surprise found Trust once more.

"My apologies, Mr. Jeffries," the woman said. "That's actually all I know of sign language, and I was just taught that little bit a few weeks ago. But anyway, welcome to Freshman Honors Seminar. I assume you understand what I am saying right now?"

Trust nodded.

"And you have the voice-to-text program, correct?"

Another nod.

"Excellent, then. I finally get an opportunity to use my microphone," Mrs. Forte said, smiling.

She then watched as Trust wrote something on one of his blank note cards.

*Your signing was very good, by the way.*

The professor laughed lightly.

"Oh, that's the way to get on your instructor's good side. I see you won't have much trouble adapting to the college life."

Trust dismissed himself and turned, heading toward the empty seat beside Kyler, though he quickly noticed his friend completely preoccupied, spellbound as he gazed toward the entrance of the classroom. Depositing his book bag on the desk, Trust turned to look as well.

A small cluster of girls, having apparently just entered the room, continued to converse amongst themselves beside the doorway, out of the path of other entering students.

Spotting no aliens, monsters, or giant, genetically mutated rats—the last of which Trust knew to be a fear of Kyler's—Trust looked to Kyler again. Kyler, as though finally sensing the eyes on him, looked up at Trust.

*Dude, that's her! That's her!* Kyler signed, his gesturing frantic and nearly enough to cause Trust to misinterpret. *The girl from the Centre Diamond! It's her! Red hair—*

Trust returned his gaze to the girls. He instantly picked out the redhead, but her back was turned, blocking a view of her face. However, she and the other girls looked ready to part ways.

And with that, Trust suddenly had an idea.

He turned back to Kyler again. The boy, whose blond mane was drawn up in his regularly haphazard bun-ponytail combo, all of it somewhat stuffed under his also familiar ball cap, seemed able to read his friend's mind.

"Hey," Kyler said in a hesitant, halting tone. "Hey, now. Whattayou—"

*Switch seats with me,* Trust motioned, lifting his book bag again. *Quick.*

Trust glanced toward the group of girls, and then back to Kyler.

"What?" Kyler asked, incredulous. "What are you talking—"

Then he realized what Trust was doing.

"Oooh, no," he intoned, stretching the phrase and shaking his head vehemently. "Nope. Uh-uh. Sit down, man. Nope."

Trust's eyes repeated their circuit again, from the girls—the red-haired one seemed about to turn in his and Kyler's direction—and then back to Kyler, who was still shaking his head and muttering a string of nonsense to himself that Trust could not read.

Trust caught his attention again.

*Get up, or I'm going to punch you in the groin right now,* he signed swiftly. *You know I'll do it!*

*No! Trust, are you crazy? Sit down! No, I'm not—*

*Get up, Kyler! Last chance! Here comes my fist!*

*Uh-uh. Nope! You just—*

Kyler's hands froze in midair, his eyes catching on something just over Trust's shoulder.

Trust smirked, feeling a presence arrive beside him. He turned slightly, the grin still on his face, and looked toward their visitor.

The red-haired girl's expression was amused, curious.

"Wow," she declared. "I'm sorry for interrupting you, and I don't mean to intrude, but was that actual sign language you both were using? Oh, wait. Can either of you understand what I'm saying?"

Trust nodded in the affirmative. He then waved in Kyler's direction, waiting for his friend to start speaking, though keeping his attention turned toward the girl.

After a moment, the girl looked from Kyler back to Trust, a faintly confused look coming onto her features.

Trust looked to Kyler.

Kyler still had the same stunned expression on his face. Still gawking at the girl.

Unmoving.

Frozen.

Trust glanced fleetingly toward the girl in apology before shifting back to Kyler. He waved his hand briefly in front of the boy's face.

No response.

Trust drew his hand back slowly, as though preparing for a punch. Then his hand shot forward. Just before he reached Kyler's face, Kyler blocked clumsily with his arm, startling at the same time. His eyes refocused as he looked toward Trust.

"Hey!" he said. "What was that for?"

Grinning still, Trust backed out of the way, motioning for the red-haired girl to take the desk he had just vacated.

"Really? Are you sure?" the girl asked. She looked at Trust, and then to Kyler.

Trust nodded again. Kyler seemed incapable of forming a sentence, gazing once again toward the girl with a dazed look. The girl looked back to Trust.

"Is he okay? He looks like he's about to fall out of his chair. Can he understand me?"

The desk on the other side of the red-haired girl's was available, so Trust laid his bag down on top of it, again beckoning toward the girl to take his earlier spot. As she settled in, he passed in front of her desk once more, twirling his finger around his ear and pointing to Kyler. He was yet to come across anyone who was unfamiliar with the gesture.

He stood in front of Kyler again. The teenager appeared hypnotized. Trust leaned toward Kyler's face. Kyler did not respond, his eyes continuing to follow the red-haired girl's movements.

Clap!

Trust brought his hands together inches away from Kyler's face. Kyler startled noticeably, his gaze refocusing.

"Huh? What are we talking about?" Kyler asked, clearly not aware of what was going on around him.

*If you're trying to win the award for creepiest guy alive, you're definitely doing a good job so far,* Trust signed.

He then gestured, in a rather obvious manner, to the girl now sitting beside Kyler, who was observing the interaction between the two of them with barely hidden amusement.

"Oh. Uh, yeah. Hey," Kyler said, finally returning to reality. "Oh, wait, did you say something? Did I say something? I'm not really sure—"

*Ask the girl her name, man.*

It was Allison. Allison Tyler.

As Kyler finished the introductions, Trust, grinning, began to head back to his desk, but something at the front of the class caught his attention.

The professor, Mrs. Forte, was gazing toward him, her eyebrows raised in question. Trust watched as she then mimed clapping her hands, shaking her head and looking at him, as though saying, "What was that all about?"

Trust, comprehending her message, bowed slightly and put his hands together.

*Sorry*, the gesture said.

Mrs. Forte quirked the corners of her mouth upward and rolled her eyes, though she appeared to accept.

Trust soon had his materials—which mainly meant his laptop—on his desk, the voice transcription program open and running.

"Oooh, that's the voice-to-text application," Allison observed, plainly interested as she leaned toward his desk. "I've heard about that. Does it work as well as they say it does?"

Trust leaned back, allowing her to fiddle with the program. Allison obviously knew what she was doing. Kyler, from one seat over, signaled for his attention.

*Hey. You clap in my face like that again, and I will pound you. And I was not being creepy.*

Trust responded with a blank expression. He then mimed punching himself in the face, his movements in slow motion, exaggerating the violent effects, and then pointed to Kyler.

*You try it,* Trust added, *and that's what will happen to you. And yes, you were being creepy. Outstandingly creepy.*

To top Trust, Kyler began to act out a vicious punch that in his wildest dreams he would never be able to land, before Allison happened to turn and glance at him, catching him midway through the act. Kyler froze, one cheek puffed out, his face contorted in a thoroughly unflattering position.

Trust laughed. When Allison quickly turned back in his direction, he abruptly cut himself off and faced forward in his seat, attempting to act as innocent as possible. He tried to restrain his smile, but it was proving difficult.

Allison appeared to notice. Without moving his head, Trust cut his eyes toward her.

"Has anyone ever told either of you that you're both totally crazy?" she expressed.

Trust looked over Allison to his roommate.

*See? It's like she knows you already. She thinks you're nuts.*

*Oh, shut your mouth, you—*

Trust's attention was diverted by Allison, who was pointing toward his computer.

**Mrs. Forte:** "Well, if the antics of Mr. Trustice Jeffries and his blond-haired friend on the front row have concluded, I think I will be ready to begin class."

Trust glanced fleetingly up from the screen toward the professor. Seeing her eyes trained on him, Trust looked quickly down to the screen again. He began to type, and then motioned for Allison to read the transcription aloud.

"The blond-haired—ahem, *boy*—"

Allison looked to Trust, who shrugged innocently.

"The blond-haired boy's name is Kyler-Scott Brooks."

"Ah, thank you, Trustice," Mrs. Forte replied. "I'm sure I will be calling both of your names many, many times throughout the semester, although perhaps not always for the right reasons. Now, if we can get started."

Trust peeked over at Kyler again. The "blond-haired boy" had a cross look on his face, and he quickly mimicked punching himself in the face again and discreetly pointing in Trust's direction.

There were disadvantages to sticking out and the professor knowing your name, especially so early in the semester.

# 8.
## Theft and Brycen Johns

THURSDAY AFTERNOON FOUND TRUST RETURNING from class, walking up the short stone staircase in front of Weaver Hall, and entering the lobby. At this time of day, the area was, as usual, empty—save for a single student.

And the police officer speaking with him.

Trust's steps slowed briefly, before he resumed his trek to the elevators. He had, for a moment, considered a sly attempt at reading the student's mouth—the police officer's back was turned—but Trust thought better of it at the last instant. His blatant staring would have been easy to spot.

In any case, from the body language of both the student and the campus officer, the student seemed not to be in any trouble.

Thirty seconds later, Trust arrived at the already opened doorway to his and Kyler's dorm room. Inside, Kyler was reclined upside down on his tidied bed, his legs and sneakered feet raised and leaning against the wall. On his left hand he wore a baseball glove, and as Trust walked into the room, Kyler extended his glove easily and caught a falling baseball. Paxson was also in the room, sitting in Kyler's chair.

Kyler's head tilted toward the door as Trust came in, even as he caught his baseball.

"Hey-oh!" Kyler greeted, Paxson also turning to see who had entered.

Trust gave a dramatic wave to both boys.

*Someone's getting arrested downstairs,* Trust signed casually as he shrugged off his backpack, allowing it to fall onto his bed.

"Aw, really?" Kyler replied. "They're taking him in? We were just talking about that."

It took Trust a few extra seconds to decipher what Kyler was saying due to the teenager's inverted positioning. Meanwhile, Kyler's gaze shifted to Paxson.

"Trust said that guy's getting arrested."

Paxson looked to Trust.

"Really? Are you serious? His computer was stolen. Why are they arresting him?"

Trust looked to Kyler again.

*I was just kidding. I don't think he's actually being arrested. The cop was talking to him when I went through the lobby. Saying he was being arrested just seemed more interesting.*

Upside down, Kyler gazed at Trust for a moment, giving him a blank stare.

Paxson looked from Kyler, to Trust, and back to Kyler again.

"What'd he say?" he asked. Then he grinned. "Ha! Did he just curse you out in sign language? Because that would be pretty funny if he did."

From his upended position, Kyler chucked the baseball in Trust's direction, which Trust caught easily, as though expecting it. Kyler then righted himself, his shoes making contact with the carpet before he scooted back again, his backside coming flush against the concrete wall. His hair was now hanging down freely, and he had to brush it out of his face.

"He was lying," Kyler said to Paxson. "He said he only saw—"

*Joking,* Trust corrected. *Not lying.*

"—the guy talking to campus police. He thought it would be hilarious if he lied to his friends and told us the guy was getting arrested."

"What?" Paxson said, a confused grin coming across his features.

He looked to Trust, and Trust shook his head in exasperation, gesturing to Paxson that he should ignore whatever Kyler was saying. Trust then turned around, retrieving his book bag and flipping the baseball without warning in Kyler's direction.

He did not need to see if Kyler caught the unexpected throw. Instead, he pulled out his computer and placed it on his desk.

"So, he was just down there talking to him?" Paxson asked as Trust faced them once more.

Trust nodded.

"Marcie knows him," Paxson explained. "I had never met him before, but apparently he's from Potomac Park—same as me and Marcie. Even went to our high school, although he's a year ahead of us. Marcie introduced me to him last weekend when she saw him moving in on one of the lower floors."

*You said Marcie knew him from high school, but you've never met him before?* Trust motioned, Kyler interpreting verbally as Trust's hands moved through the air. Kyler looked at Trust, grinning as he finished his movements.

"Don't even waste your time with what you're about to ask next," Kyler advised. "I already brought up the secret boyfriend theory."

Trust smirked. Paxson rolled his eyes.

"Marcie's right," Paxson said. "Both of you really are complete idiots."

"You see where I get it from," Kyler said, pointing at Trust. "He's a terrible influence."

*Don't even look over here, dude,* Trust rebutted. Both Kyler and Paxson laughed after Kyler translated.

*You said the guy's computer was stolen?* Trust asked. *Do you know how it happened?*

"That's what I overheard," Paxson stated. "I was down on his floor earlier, and I passed by his room. He and the officer were inside. Kyler came up here about five minutes before you did, and I guess Jeff and the cop had already moved down to the lobby by then."

"Remember what Holden said at the hall meeting?" Kyler reminded them. "I guess a college dorm is a target-rich environment when you think about it. Every room's probably going to have at least one computer, and then you add in the TVs and a whole bunch of other stuff on top of that."

*It's target-rich if you can gain access,* Trust signed. *Holden said it's usually someone on your hall that would be most likely to steal, and odds are they won't catch the person unless someone sees him with it. Was his computer the only thing that was stolen?*

Paxson shrugged.

"Don't know. I just heard about the computer when I went past. But when Marcie and I were down there and he was moving in, he'd already set up a TV, and it was pretty big, like forty inches. Not to mention his roommate, who probably has a computer, too."

"And the plot thickens," Kyler intoned, though Trust did not hear the mysterious inflection in his friend's tone.

Even so, both Trust and Paxson looked at him with skepticism. Trust then got Paxson's attention again.

*And what were you doing eavesdropping, anyway?* Trust gestured, smirking slightly.

"On occasion," Paxson responded, "I find myself suddenly walking slower than I normally do."

*Sneaky.*

To demonstrate, Paxson rose from his seat and began to pace the room, each of his footfalls becoming markedly slower and more protracted than the last. At the same time, his eyes seemingly found various things—invisible, suspended in midair, things—suddenly interesting. It was all a cunning attempt to mask his now excruciatingly leisurely gait.

*Very sneaky,* Trust amended. *You're a regular man of mystery.*

Paxson winked in what could be considered either a suave—or idiotic—manner.

"That's a little James Bond for ya," he remarked.

Trust laughed.

*I doubt James Bond would ever be seen looking that ridiculous.*

"Yeah," Kyler said after he finished translating. "I'm surprised the cop didn't notice you 'walking' past the doorway and arrest you for bad acting."

"Whatever," Paxson dismissed, though he could not prevent his grin. "You guys just don't appreciate covert skills when you see them."

*Yeah, that's a good word,* Trust returned. *Covert—as in, we can't even see them.*

Kyler laughed while Paxson shook his head.

*So, switching topics, am I still allowed to go to convocation with you? You know, since Allison is going, I wouldn't want to be a third wheel.*

Kyler, in the midst of slamming the baseball into his glove—in the way that those with a baseball and a baseball glove are prone to do—froze. His eyes fixed on Trust's.

Paxson looked between both boys, his curiosity piqued.

"Hey, what just happened? Man, Kyler, you looked like you just saw a gho—"

Paxson then lurched forward, and then back, as he juggled the baseball tossed in his direction, nearly dropping it, but hanging on. At the same time, Kyler swiftly shucked his glove, both hands now free.

*That's not funny, Trust,* he gestured frantically. *That is seriously not funny! You're coming! You invited her! You can't just invite her and leave me alone! You better come!*

Trust smirked.

*Why, Kyler, you seem a tad nervous. I mean, it's only the girl who you're crazy in love with and who you've only actually seen for a single class period, plus five seconds at a jam-packed night—*

Trust's attention shifted as he saw Paxson beginning to speak again.

"Come on, guys," Paxson pleaded. "Don't leave me out. I like tormenting Kyler just as much as the next guy."

Trust raised his eyebrows at Paxson, and then, slowly grinning, turned to Kyler again.

"Don't do it," Kyler warned, speaking again.

Trust, still watching Kyler, slowly and dramatically reached to his side, toward the blank computer screen onto which he could communicate with Paxson without going through a suddenly reluctant interpreter.

"Hey!" Kyler's voice grew louder and more frantic—as though it would make any difference to Trust. "You tell Pax and I will *murder you in this dorm room!*"

"Oooh," Paxson crooned. "Does this have anything to do with the girl Kyler's so obviously wrapped up in?"

While Trust was already looking at Paxson, Kyler turned and stared at him. Trust's face held amusement, while Kyler's held something considerably less than that.

"Whenever he starts reacting like that," Paxson explained, looking at Trust, "you've been talking about the girl from the club. My covert spy skills have picked it up. Her name's Allison, right?"

Trust scoffed, nearly choking on his laugh. Kyler, meanwhile, continued to look at Paxson, stunned. Paxson then met Kyler's gaze.

"Catch," he said, tossing the baseball in Kyler's direction.

Kyler still seemed dazed.

Trust's eyes widened.

Paxson's throw was well off target, heading directly for the closed window between Kyler's and Trust's beds.

"Oh, sh—" Paxson started.

Just in time, Kyler reached out, capturing the wayward toss inches before it could hit the glass—

—then, finding himself off-balance on the bed, he tumbled off, landing on the carpet.

Trust looked from his roommate's sneakers—which now lay on Trust's bed—up to his face.

Kyler slowly raised his hand, the baseball assuredly secured inside.

*Nice catch,* Trust signed.

It was not the first time he had signed such a message.

Kyler and Trust, both quiet, turned to look at Paxson. The other boy was blushing slightly, rubbing his hand along the back of his neck.

"So, uh...I guess I forgot to tell you guys that I was never really any good at sports."

"And you have the nerve to call yourself 007," Kyler said, once again in an upside-down position, this time on the dorm room floor.

Paxson could only shrug awkwardly.

FRIDAY BROUGHT AN END TO the first week of classes, though that did nothing to diminish the business of the day for either the students or the university staff. In between two of his classes conveniently scheduled hours apart, Trust had another appointment in Adams Hall with Dr. Duncan.

While the university grounds outside and around the building were busier and more populated than they were on Trust's last visit before classes had formally started, the interior of Adams Hall was just as tranquilly quiet and spacious as it was at the beginning of the week. Absent were the students hustling and bustling around, weaving and sprinting this way and that now that the university was officially open. The reception area held the ambiance of a museum—or, more accurately, an atrium—as was already hinted at by the building's airy and modern architectural design.

But Trust spotted something different.

Miss Kimberlee Sharpshire was not present.

In her seat was a boy, most likely a graduate student as well. His dark hair, highlighted with white streaks, was immediately eye-catching.

Trust noted the boy's eyes on him as soon as he walked through the entranceway.

"Aha!"

The deaf teenager's eyebrows ascended slightly.

*You're Trust, right? Trustice Jeffries? You have a one o'clock with Dr. Duncan?*

Trust arrived at the reception desk.

*Yes, that's right,* he signed. *I'm surprised so many people know sign language around here. How did you know who I was?*

*Those pretty blue eyes of yours, of course,* the boy motioned back. *I can see those things coming a mile away.*

Any slight, casual fidgeting occurring throughout Trust's body halted immediately, and his breathing froze in his chest. He looked at the young man stationed behind the desk, not able to hide his...

Surprise.

The older boy took in Trust's expression. He grinned widely, and then laughed outright.

*Oh my God!* he signed. *The look on your face right now! I promise, I'm not going to bite. In all seriousness, Kimberlee—the girl who's usually here—described some of the people I should expect to see, just in case they needed some assistance, and her description of you was...*—the boy made a smooching sound with his lips and fingers—*it was spot-on.*

The older boy then fell quiet as he observed the freshman, Trust attempting to hide his sudden discomfort. The receptionist was still grinning.

*Anyway, let me tell Clarke his one o'clock has arrived safe and sound.*

The thought crossed Trust's mind to flee then, while the opportunity presented itself. If Dr. Duncan was busy with something else when Trust reached his office, he would not mind sitting on the carpeted floor of the hallway outside his door.

He assumed it would not be any less comfortable than...whatever was going on here.

The boy hung up the phone, and then chuckled again, looking at Trust.

*If your skin were lighter,* he signed, *I'm sure you would be blushing. In any case, Clarke's ready for you, so I guess I'll let you go...for now.*

Trust's face brought another laugh from the boy behind the receptionist's desk.

"GOOD! GOOD! EXCELLENT!" DR. DUNCAN exclaimed. "Coming

from the School of Engineering, I should have known everything would run smoothly. Nevertheless, whenever we introduce something like this that I know students will be relying on, one can't help a sliver of worry presenting itself. Not to mention, it's only been one week, mind you, but...yes, ha ha! Excellent! I have heard comparable reports from some of the other students who are utilizing this voice-to-text program as well, and if you all have such good reviews for it, that is all I shall concern myself with.

"And remember, any problems or issues, my door, and my email, are always open. Speaking of which, I have completely forgotten to check my email. Completely forgotten! I can only pray you haven't sent me anything urgent in the past few days, Trustice?"

Trust, holding back his laugh while shaking his head, began to type on the senior administrator's wireless keyboard.

> **Trustice:** No. You have warned me before about your forgetfulness when checking your email—

> **Dr. C. Duncan:** "Yes, that's right!"

> **Trustice:** You have also told me to CC the receptionist desk with any email I send you, just in case.

"Right you are, boy! Right you are! I completely forgot I even mentioned that, but I am nevertheless very pleased that I did. And speaking of receptionists, I am sure you encountered Mr. Johns when you came in? I hope you weren't too thrown off by the new face. Miss Sharpshire recommended him, believe it or not. Just so you are aware, Mr. Johns will be staffing the desk when Miss Sharpshire is absent, and Miss Sharpshire will be here when Mr. Johns is absent, etcetera, etcetera. Who knows, you may come in on a particularly busy day and they are both at the desk...although today has been relatively busy, and by all accounts, Mr. Johns has handled the onslaught with due aplomb, I must say."

Trust drew Duncan's attention to the screen.

> **Trustice:** Is Miss Sharpshire sick?

"Sick? No, no, fortunately for us all. I believe she is attending a conference of some sort out of town today...yes, she is giving a presentation! That's right! She is giving a presentation on the ways handicapped children unconsciously learn to cope in public arenas. Brilliant mind that Miss Sharpshire has atop her shoulders, resoundingly brilliant. The same can be said for Mr. Johns at the front desk. He is studying, I believe...oh, shoot...ah, yes! Yes! Mr. Johns is studying in the field of psychological analysis. Exceptionally interesting work being done by both of them. And I should add, if you have any questions or concerns that I can't fully answer—which, I must say, is astoundingly possible, Trustice—you would do very well to ask one, or both, of them. I must warn you, Mr. Johns is a touch on the audacious side. The very opposite of myself, of course."

Trust could not hold back his laugh this time. He soon noticed the older man's attention shift to the flashing telephone on his desk.

Trust took the opportunity to glance around the large office, which was, as usual, packed with books, papers, pamphlets, and the like, concerning academia and otherwise. His gaze soon fell on the intriguing stack of books the administrator had earlier removed from the chair Trust currently sat in. Curiously, the heap appeared to be unchanged from his previous meeting, the exact same size and dimensions—the exact same appearance, with some books aligned somewhat off-center but still fixed firmly in the stack, and some angled sideways—

Trust's focus returned to the admin.

"Ah, that Mr. Johns does indeed run a tight ship. It seems my 1:45 engagement has arrived. Any other questions, Mr. Jeffries, before we part ways? Anything at all? Come now, don't be shy."

Rising to his feet, Trust only shook his head.

"Good Moses, boy!" Duncan remarked. "Do you work out? What is the phrase...lean and mean? Whatever you're doing, keep it up, Trustice, keep it up. Except if it's this steroid business I've heard about. I have to say, I don't very much follow the sporting world—only a recreational exhibition of squash or tennis now and again with the fair Mrs. Duncan if I can be sure my knees won't curse me later on—but..."

Trust continued to nod and back away as the old man went off on another tangent. This would be one of the times he would have to leave the office while his advisor was still speaking, chiefly because his advisor was not going to stop speaking anytime soon. The situation had not developed in their previous meeting, but it had happened during one of his trips to the UCC campus before he had become a student...and once or twice when he and his parents had conversed on the phone with the senior administrator...and once when...

"...but our athletic department does a fantastic job of giving our athletes every advantage without giving our athletes *unfair* advantage, and that is surely a delicate tightrope..."

More smiling, more subtle waving, more nodding, and more backing away by Trust, until, finally, he turned the corner, stepping out of the doorway.

"Until next time, Trustice!" the wizened administrator called, effectively to no one in particular, since Trust was no longer able to read his mouth. "I will be sure to tell Miss Sharpshire that you asked about her!"

BACK IN THE WIDE FOYER, Trust glanced over to "Mr. Johns'" grinning face and motioning hands.

*Oh, back so soon? I knew you couldn't resist.*

Trust gave the graduate student a smirk as he stopped at the desk.

*Dr. Duncan warned me about you,* Trust replied. *I know what you're doing. You can't scare me.*

The young man with the blond highlights seemed to crack up at Trust's admission.

*You mean you're not scared anymore,* he signed. *Admit it: I had you terrified when you first came in. I knew you would be an easy one. You thought I was ready to come over the desk.*

*You're a good actor,* Trust acknowledged. *You should tell me your name so I can watch out for you, though. All I have is Mr. Johns.*

*Oh, you want to know my name?* the young man signed, wiggling his eyebrows in not-so-subtle suggestion.

Trust rolled his eyes, though he could not restrain a chuckle. Meanwhile, the receptionist reached his arm across the partition that ringed the desk along all sides. The sleeves of the young man's dress shirt were rolled up to near his elbows, the swirl and intricate outline of a tattoo evident, reaching down out of the sleeve and stopping just short of his wrist.

"It's Brycen," he said as Trust shook his hand. "Brycen Johns."

Noticing Trust's faint uncertainty, Brycen released the deaf boy's hand, and then spelled out *B-R-Y-C-E-N*. He then said his name aloud again, and Trust copied the older boy's lip movements.

Brycen extended his hand again.

"So, would you like to hold hands some more, or..."

He laughed again as Trust abruptly dismissed him, quickly turning and making his way to the set of double doors that led him out of the building.

## 9.
## A Chancellor's Welcome

"AND NOW," THE VICE-CHANCELLOR, William Hunt, said into the microphones positioned on the lectern as he looked out toward the crowd in attendance, "I give you the chancellor of the University of Centre City, Dr. April Beverly."

The audience inside the Tiger Dome erupted into enthused applause as the ever-popular president of the university rose from her seat and made her way to the podium. From his place on the front row amidst the audience, Trust could easily distinguish Chancellor Beverly's face as she attempted to conceal a smile behind a professional façade.

As Trust clapped along with the rest in attendance, he looked to his right, grinning. Kyler quickly caught his gaze. Trust then pointedly looked past Kyler to the person on the other side.

His cheeky grin grew wider still, and then he glanced back to Kyler, the message clear.

The faint grin on Kyler's face vanished, replaced with faint suspicion, his eyes narrowing, framed by the rebellious strands of blond hair that hung down across his face.

Trust's smile brightened even more.

*Isn't it just the greatest thing ever to be able to meet up like this outside of class?* Trust gestured happily.

Allison was the student to the right of Kyler.

*That* Allison.

*Red-haired* Allison.

*Kyler's* Allison.

Trust looked past Kyler again. Still clapping, Allison finally seemed to sense Trust's gaze. She beamed in acknowledgement.

Gazing out from the podium, the chancellor attempted to wait out the raucous cheers. Trust watched as she glanced down to opened folder on the lectern, while still fighting to hide the appreciative smile that threatened to overwhelm her features. She finally looked up, into the audience again, and nodded slightly in salute.

"Thank you," she started, though it was nearly drowned out by the prevailing applause.

Trust, Kyler, Allison, and thousands of other Centre City students and staff were gathered in the large sports arena for the annual convocation ceremony held at the beginning of each school year.

"To begin," the chancellor spoke as the cheers finally diminished enough for her to be heard, "I would like to welcome—and welcome back—the students of the University of Centre City. It may sound odd for me to say this, but I am both appreciative and humbled that you all have chosen to come to Centre City, and I can guarantee that the administration, and the entire university, will do all that we can to make your residence as challenging, prosperous, and as beneficial to you as possible. I don't think you—or those who support you coming here—would have it any other way.

"I would also like to welcome the faculty..."

Trust's vantage point along the front row was so good, he hardly needed to stray from reading the chancellor's lips as they moved. Still, he did glance occasionally to the sign language interpreter standing on stage close by. Like Chancellor Beverly, the interpreter was projected onto a large screen suspended above the stage, on the chance that those needing her services were sitting in less than desirable seats. However, as the welcoming usher had become aware of Trust's deafness before he was even able to choose his own seat, he, Kyler, and Allison had been escorted to the first row. One could assume that audience members possessing similar types of handicaps would receive similar preferential treatment.

At least, that was what Trust's group had been told when Trust asked the question of the usher.

Trust looked to Kyler, getting his attention.

*This is so cool. It's like seeing the president give a speech or something. You remember when we met her when we came over the summer?*

*Heck yeah, dude,* Kyler replied, slipping in a little Kyler-Scott Brooks Sign Language along with conventional signs. *And she had those*

110

*bodyguards, too, like the Secret Service. I think that's one of them over there.*

Trust glanced to where Kyler indicated, noticing a man to the side, just off stage, stoic in bearing and dressed formally, if not a tad stuffily, in his suit. Glancing quickly to the opposite end of the stage, Trust spotted another man of similar appearance.

*Why would a school chancellor even need bodyguards?*

Kyler looked at him skeptically. He glanced over to the man again, and then back to Trust.

*Dude, you're not serious with that question, are you?*

Allison, noticing the slight disturbance as Trust's and Kyler's hands moved furtively but swiftly through the space of air in front of them, poked Kyler in his side. Kyler yelped.

Fortunately, he did not seem to attract much attention, the audience clapping again.

"You invite me to convocation," Allison whispered, "and then you two have your own animated conversation without me?"

Trust, seated on Kyler's other side, could not see what Kyler was saying, though with Allison's help and Kyler's visible hesitance, he did not need to.

"You sure do say you're sorry a lot," Allison said, grinning, Trust able to read her lips.

*You must be special,* Trust signed, though he knew Allison would not be able to understand. *He never tells me he's sorry.*

While Allison looked at him, Kyler, seeing the latter portion of Trust's comment, tried to send an elbow into his friend's torso. Trust saw it coming and parried it away easily.

"He just had a little smarty-pants comment," Kyler said in explanation to Allison. "Ignore him."

Trust, trying but still failing to gain a better view of Kyler's mouth, grinned anyway, knowing without a doubt that Kyler would not dare to translate his observations accurately.

"Consider yourself lucky you don't have to listen to what he's saying," Kyler went on, to which Allison put on a saddened face.

"Stop making fun of Trust," she said, looking to Trust an instant later with an apologetic expression.

Before Trust could respond, Kyler leaned in, breaking their eye contact.

"Oh, no," Kyler warned. "Don't let him see you feeling sorry for him, and don't look directly into his eyes. He will take advantage of it, big time. He's like a shark that way. Once he senses blood in the water—or in this case, sympathy—he'll—"

*Glad you got over being so tongue-tied,* Trust signed, turning Kyler to him, *but now I can't see what you're talking about.*

Allison was shaking her head, a disbelieving grin on her face.

Meanwhile, the chancellor's speech continued.

"Our goals, what we strive for at this university, are quite simple: to attract, mold, and send out individuals who know what it takes to strive for the very best version of themselves..."

"You guys have to tell me what you're saying when you do that," Allison remarked quietly. "You weren't talking about me, were you?"

Her soft grin informed both boys that she was not offended, simply curious. Kyler told her his and Trust's bodyguard exchange, vaguely gesturing again to the stoic, suited man visible offstage. Allison laughed quietly, lowering her head and covering her mouth so as to not cause a distraction.

"So you think those are bodyguards? Why would a university chancellor have use for bodyguards?"

Trust motioned triumphantly, pointing from himself to Kyler.

*That's what I said!*

"That's what he said," Kyler admitted, rolling his eyes. "But when we saw her on our visit, she was walking across campus, going somewhere— I don't know—but then she saw our group and stopped to talk. She had people with her just like that guy. I don't remember him, though. He wasn't there."

Kyler had started to sign as well as speak, so Trust was finally able to understand.

*They could just be part of her staff, smart guy,* Trust gestured, to which Kyler verbalized in whispered tones to Allison, Allison grinning at the "smart guy" reference.

*Or,* Trust went on, *they could be on the administration, like a vice-something of the university.*

"Yeah, the Vice-Assistant To Kicking Somebody's Face In If They Get Too Close To Her," Kyler said and signed back.

Trust saw Kyler's and Allison's eyes suddenly shift at the same moment, looking just off Trust's shoulder. He studied their eyes a brief moment, before his own eyes shifted—without moving his head—to the place he had spotted the second suited man.

The man was staring back at him, his face expressionless.

Trust subtly shifted his attention back to Kyler and Allison, now certain that the first "bodyguard," the one that Kyler had pointed out, was probably close by and eyeing the group as well. Seeing Kyler and Allison's frozen expressions, Trust could not help but snicker, though, lowering his head, he attempted to lessen the vibrations coming from his throat.

From his questions in earlier years to both his parents and to Kyler, he understood the strength of those vibrations were in direct correlation to the volume of his laugh.

Kyler elbowed him anyway.

## 10.

## Football Saturday

SATURDAY.

The Stadium at UCC was its name, and it was packed, filled to the highest walls with students, fans, supporters, onlookers, and the like.

The reverberations inside and around the stadium were deafening. Vibrant, spirited sights and spectacles in the stands and on the field; bright, lively colors on a vividly sunny day, stimulus all around, as was the intention...

Kyler had his chest painted. And his arms. And his face.

In fact, his entire upper body was decorated. Trust would have thought the idea absurdly ridiculous had he not been the one to help paint him.

Actually, Trust had thought the idea ridiculous anyway, particularly when a number of their dorm mates from the seventh floor of Weaver Hall painted themselves similarly and were now yelling at the top of their lungs, Paxson being one of them.

Instead of hearing it, Trust could feel the roar of the excited stadium as Centre City's defense held their ground, forcing the opposing team into what would surely be a punting situation. The sensation was a vibration seemingly emanating from within his body, not unlike what he had felt at the Centre Diamond nightclub, and not unlike the sensation whenever he was enveloped by thunderous noise.

Anticipating yet another excited shake from Paxson and Kyler seated behind him, Trust glanced back just as Kyler's hand reached his shoulder.

"Woo-hoo! Fourth down!" Kyler yelled.

Trust exhibited a thrilled grin of his own, giving his friend what had to be the thirtieth high five of the game so far, before facing forward again, the exaggerated expression diminishing just as quickly as it appeared, reverting to a more normal smile. He caught Allison's glance beside him and she laughed.

"But I don't understand!" she said. "What happened?"

Trust could tell Allison was almost shouting, as though the booming sounds of the stadium would be the reason he would have trouble hearing her.

*Our defense stopped their offense.*

he wrote in the notebook he had brought with him.

*We're about to get the ball back.*

"And that's a good thing, right?" she asked after reading off the page, her voice still loud.

Trust smirked at her and began to write again.

*You tell me.*

He then hooked his thumb toward Kyler, Paxson, and the fanatical cheering section behind them, their bare chests—some thin and scrawny, some round and soft, and some, like Kyler's, lean and muscular—adorned in black and gold and bizarre designs signifying nothing but a passionate, and perhaps obsessive, support for UCC. Their exuberant cheers were more than enough to indicate to Allison whether their team getting the ball back was indeed a "good thing."

Turning back, Allison looked to Trust, who was still grinning, his eyebrow arched. She then looked to Marcie, who sat on the other side of Trust.

"And this"—the crowd continuing to shout and scream around them, Allison gestured back briefly toward the other boys—"this is normal just because our school gets the ball back? Is it really that significant?"

Marcie leaned over, nearly falling into Trust's lap in the process.

"Um, have you met these guys?" she countered. "Exactly what part of their personalities would you say is normal?"

"That's a good point!" Allison yelled back, causing Trust and Marcie to laugh.

Trust's laugh was almost instantly interrupted as Kyler eagerly shook his shoulder from behind again. He looked back.

"Woo-hoo! Back on offense!"

Kyler's face was glowing with exuberance.

*And now you're just doing that to annoy me,* Trust signed.

Kyler laughed and reached toward Allison, who was still looking down to the field and bringing a drink closer to her lips—which Kyler failed to notice.

"Woo-hoo!" he exclaimed, hugging her shoulders.

Allison jumped but was somehow able to keep her drink from sloshing. She whirled about swiftly, her face, framed by her crimson hair, seemingly on fire now, catching Kyler midway through another cheer.

"Woo-ho—whoa! Wow. Sorry. Okay. Sorry. Wow."

He had caught sight of Allison's abruptly terrifying look. Trust, a silent observer to the entire scene, laughed and then turned, unwittingly—but fortunately for him—catching Paxson as he was about to surprise his girlfriend from behind in a similar manner. The shirtless boy began to shout.

"Woo—"

"Paxson Xavier Haynes, I swear if you grab me right now I will punch you incredibly hard in a place I know will hurt really bad!"

Marcie did not even look away from the action on the football field below.

Trust saw Paxson's eyes widen as his hands froze a very short distance away from Marcie's shoulders. After a moment, and with the same scared-stiff expression that graced Kyler's face, Paxson looked over to Trust.

Trust doubled over in laugher again. As he was laughing, he wrote in the notebook.

*Funniest ten seconds of my life.*

Still laughing, he showed it to the others. Marcie shoved him lightly, though she smiled as well. Paxson smirked, shaking his head. Allison issued an "It wasn't funny, Trust!" though she too displayed the tiniest trace of a grin.

*And you're an idiot,* Trust signed to Kyler. *As usual.*

*Me?* Kyler responded. *What did I do?*

*Scaring a girl is not really the best way to get her to like you.*

*Hey, now,* Kyler replied. *That is not—*

But Trust's attention was quickly diverted as Allison pulled on his arm.

"Trust, what's happening now? Is this good?"

She directed his eyes down to the field. In their ample-sized section of the stadium exclusively dedicated to the UCC students, the group was fairly high up relative to the field below. Still, their seats were excellent, providing a great view of the action.

*They're measuring where to put the ball. It means we're close*
*to a first down, which is good.*

As he glanced from Allison back to the field again, he watched as the referee signaled that UCC still had inches to go to gain the first down.

Second and inches.

On the faces of those nearby, Trust could see the slight groans and looks of disappointment. Not glancing back, he could imagine Kyler and the other painted students were expressing their own displeasure with a bit more fervor.

Even though it was only second down in a game midway through the first quarter, the students and fans of UCC football who filled the stadium took every action on the field quite seriously.

Unless they were like Allison, Trust thought, who didn't know enough about the game to take it so seriously.

Maybe that was a good thing.

Silent chaos surrounding him, Trust watched as the offense lined up for their next play.

*Our team, the ones with the ball, is probably going to run*
*here.*

He nudged Allison slightly, bringing her eyes to his words.

"Because it's only inches, right?" she asked.

Trust gave Allison a bright, expansive beam in response, his thumb raised in approval.

On the field, the center hiked the football between his legs to the quarterback, the quarterback then shuffling and turning backward in the same motion, preparing to hand the ball off to the running back jogging toward him. It was indeed a running play, and the opposing defense, anticipating, were already creeping toward the line of scrimmage, ready to stop the running back in his tracks—

—but the quarterback maintained his grip on the football, the halfback rushing past, and then, an instant later, slamming into the colliding chaos of limbs and bodies at the line. The quarterback backpedaled a few more strides, putting a bit more room between himself and the destruction in front of him, the opposing team seemingly only now realizing the run play was a fake, the quarterback looking downfield, his throwing arm extending back, and then propelling powerfully forward...

The crowd in the stadium seemed to hold their collective breath as the football sailed in its low-orbit arc, everyone's eyes following its flight path up, and then spiraling forward, nearly horizontal, then beginning its downward turn, heading for a player sprinting ahead across the trimmed grass of the field...

The stadium exploded in cheers as the sprinting receiver caught the ball, though Trust could not hear it.

He could, however, feel it without difficulty.

The receiver ran the remaining yards before reaching the end zone, the nearest defender—the player from the other team assigned to cover him on the play—nearly ten yards behind.

By now, Trust and the rest of the group—and the rest of the stadium—were standing, as much out of excitement for the sudden touchdown as it was to see over the heads of those excited spectators standing in the row in front of them. Allison's cheers were a split instant after the others', but she was soon jumping around, high-fiving with the rest, though she was careful to avoid jostling the drink still in her hand. Through the frenzied, animated pandemonium of the crowd, Trust's eyes shifted toward one of the scoreboards.

Displayed on the screen was a split scene, one half showing a replay of the touchdown throw and catch that was still only seconds old. The other half showed a previously recorded video of the student athletes—in casual, UCC athletic attire instead of football pads, helmets, and jerseys—who had orchestrated the play.

As the replay started yet again, the quarterback was shown, grinning and laughing, as key information was displayed—*Cooper Davidson, #10, 6' 2", junior, majoring in...*

Then, as the catch and race toward the end zone played out on the other half of the screen, the next player's video appeared.

Trust recognized the wide receiver instantly.

Dirty blond, almost brown, hair. Green eyes that seemed to pierce through the scoreboard. Sharp, full face. He was smirking confidently at the camera, throwing in a wink for good measure, as though he knew he had just scored a touchdown.

Trust turned around, nearly shoving a frenzied Kyler to get his attention. He then directed his friend's gaze toward the giant scoreboard, the wide receiver's face still brightly displayed, another smirk coming over the player's lips. It was as though the large, inorganic display of the athlete was overseeing Trust's and Kyler's reaction at that moment. The smirk was cocky, extremely confident, almost taunting. On the edge but not going quite so far as to be offensive.

*He look familiar?* Trust signed to Kyler, the spirited ruckus of the stadium still going on all around them.

"Oh, holy crap!"

Trust watched Kyler's mouth form the words as he continued to look toward the scoreboard. He turned back to Trust.

"Now I'm really glad I stopped you from pummeling that guy at the gym. I saved our school a touchdown!"

Beside him, Paxson—apparently not hearing all of what Kyler was saying, but clearly hearing the word "touchdown"—renewed his cheering, holding his hand up to Kyler for yet another high five.

"Woo-hoo! Yeah, touchdown!"

Trust looked again toward the scoreboard display.

*Jeremy Higgins, #23, 6', junior, majoring in Business Administration,* the scoreboard presented.

Jeremy Higgins, star wide receiver for the University of Centre City football team, was also Jeremy, the older boy Trust had encountered—and nearly come to blows with—in the fighting ring at the gym exactly one Saturday earlier.

On the scoreboard display, Jeremy flaunted that confident, telling smirk of his again.

# 11.
# The Party

LATER, HOURS AFTER EATING AND hours more after the opening football game of the season ended with Centre City victorious, a few hours after the sun had set but not even an hour after the gossip mill had reached Weaver Hall vis-à-vis an off-campus party—a party that some of the football team would also be attending—Trust and the others were on the Centre Line, winding their way through streets on the outskirts of town.

As it was a weekend night—Saturday night, to be exact, the first Saturday night since classes had commenced—the bus was a bit more crowded than what would be typically expected when compared to ridership during the evening hours of a weekday. Still, Trust's group had no problem commandeering seats at the back, with Kyler, ever the rebel, making his own accommodations. He was perched, seemingly uncomfortably, along the back of a short row of chairs, one of which was empty and available.

"You're so going to get in trouble," Paxson said. Though he was grinning faintly, his eyes flitted between Kyler and the front of the bus. "He's looking right at you."

*That's what I said,* Trust motioned. He, like everyone else on the bus, was sitting in a seat in the typical and proper fashion, though he was turned sideways so he could see everyone.

"Trust said that's what he said," Kyler said. "But what all of you fail to realize is that I am perfectly safe up here. See, I have trained my body to be able to sit—yahhh!"

The bus jolted suddenly, the driver fleetingly stomping on the brake and then accelerating again. Kyler, meanwhile, tumbled forward, rolling off his improvised seat, his upper body flopping onto Trust and his lower half landing awkwardly into the empty seat beside his deaf friend. He was partially sprawled on Trust's lap, his limbs askew.

Allison gasped as it happened. Paxson and Marcie laughed loudly. Trust was somewhere in between. Kyler seemed frozen, too stunned to move.

Trust looked down in his lap, meeting Kyler's gaze.

*How could you not see that coming?*

Kyler started to respond.

"Shut—"

"Apologies for that sudden jerk, everyone," a voice came over the bus's public address speakers. It was the bus driver. "Some thing in the road back there. Fortunately, nearly everyone was seated safely, or holding on to a safety bar. Otherwise, I'm sure there would be more people embarrassed right now than just the boy with the long blond hair in the back. Thank you for riding the Centre Line."

Trust, although not hearing the bus driver's announcement, observed the heads turn toward the front. He surmised that someone was speaking, though he could not identify the speaker, nor the speech being spoken.

Then every head turned back to Kyler.

Kyler, meanwhile, righted himself in the seat beside Trust.

"I'm okay!" he announced, raising his hands.

"Fantastic," the voice of the driver replied dryly.

*Who's talking?* Trust signaled. *Is it the bus driver?*

Paxson, not knowing for sure what Trust had just signed but guessing, said, "Kyler just got verbally roundhouse kicked by the bus driver over the intercom. Hilarious!"

As Kyler signed the driver's words from moments before, Trust laughed. His attention was then drawn to Marcie.

"Are you actually trying to get us kicked out of another party, Kyler? We haven't even made it into the door of this one yet."

"'Another party'?" Allison snickered. "You mean he's gotten you into trouble before? This I've got to hear."

The four other teenagers fell quiet, glancing at one another.

Then, Paxson, Marcie, and Trust doubled up in laughter once again.

Kyler maintained a cross look, though he blushed faintly. Allison, her grin still apparent, looked confused.

"What?" she asked, looking around at the others as the bus stopped, letting passengers off and on. "Did I say something? What did I say?"

Paxson, clearly amused, looked to Kyler.

"Really, man? Really? You haven't even told her yet?"

"Told me what?" Allison asked. "This is the first time I'm hearing about someone getting kicked out of a party."

When Allison glanced in his direction, Trust gestured to Paxson, suggesting he should answer.

"Technically, we didn't get kicked out," Paxson said. "We left voluntarily. But...oh, you tell it, Kyler. I'm just too tickled."

"'Tickled'?" Marcie repeated, laughing again.

All eyes turned to Kyler, his hair once more tied back in a disheveled half-ponytail, though on this outing, he was without his favorite ball cap.

"Oh, ha-ha, guys, it's not that funny," Kyler said. "In fact, I don't even know what you're—"

"Tell me, Kyler."

Trust did not have to hear Allison to interpret her tone of voice. She was giving Kyler a pointed look—head tilted slightly downward, her greenish eyes steady, slightly mischievous, directed straight ahead, the smallest hint of a smirk tugging at the corners of her mouth...

"Wait, before you tell the story," Paxson said, "why, exactly, were you lying on the back of the seats again?"

*It's his weird way of showing off,* Trust replied through his hands, though he knew Paxson would not understand. However, Kyler would. *Trying to impress a girl, perhaps?*

"I wasn't trying to impress...anyone."

The final syllable came out much quieter than the rest as Kyler realized he was speaking aloud. He glanced around at the others, his eyes wide.

Trust snorted and started to laugh, quickly joined by Paxson and Marcie again.

"Oh, poor Kyler," Marcie managed through her amusement.

"What?" Allison asked, looking around to the rest with pleading eyes. "I still don't understand what you guys are talking about! Please, tell me!"

The Centre Line bus continued on.

THE PARTY WAS BEING HELD in a house amidst a wooded area on the edge of Centre City proper. The closest bus stop was still a seven-minute walk to the party's front door, a detail that no one in Trust's group realized until the seven-minute walk was completed.

The multistoried colonial residence was somewhat isolated, set in a clearing with dark forestry in the near distance. The house's nearest neighbors would have been visible had it been daylight, but at night, the house, brightly alight with the action and extravagance of the ongoing party, appeared to be alone, seemingly the only house on the face of the earth at that moment.

The road in front of the house and edges of the yard were crowded with vehicles, with more than a few people seeming to prefer to be outside the house than in.

Trust was second-to-last amongst the group to enter the large house, with Kyler bringing up the rear. Trust's eyes surveyed the interior thoroughly, flicking around the rooms, his vision taking in even more than what his lack of hearing left out.

Upon coming inside, there was not a room on the lower level that was not at least partially congested with college-aged partygoers smiling, laughing, talking, shouting, drinking, or eating—enthused, hot, animated, dynamic, unrelenting, movement everywhere, everywhere movement. Trust could feel his body humming very slightly, almost as though it were set on a faint frequency, caused by an insistent, continual wave of loud and multiple voices, or, judging by the dancing of many in what could be deemed a living room area, loud music, or both. The humming was not as pronounced as it had been at the Centre Diamond, or the football game earlier in the day, but it was enough to be noticed.

Typical domestic furnishings, while sufficiently present in some rooms, were sufficiently absent in others. Trust could only assume it had all been moved out to make space for the throngs of people now in attendance—

He felt a light tug on his shoulder, somehow sensing the familiar touch as Kyler's. Turning, he glanced down at his phone.

Time had slipped past. He had already been at the party for over a half-hour.

"This place is crazy!"

Trust could tell Kyler was speaking loudly, nearly shouting.

*I wonder whose house this is,* Trust signed. *Not any pictures or anything.*

"I don't know. I think I heard someone say something about a frat house or clubhouse or something. Who knows?"

Kyler then gestured for Trust to follow him.

"Have you seen the kitchen yet? You gotta check out the layout in there!"

Before Kyler could turn around to lead the way, however, Trust aimed a curious look toward his roommate, and then to the cup in his hand. Kyler gazed back at him, already knowing what Trust was thinking.

"Soda. Anyway, it doesn't hurt to look. Once you see this, you'll understand what I'm talking about."

Trust trailed after Kyler as the pair made their way through the crowds of people, both boys issuing subtle up-nods and sly smiles to the guys and girls respectively that they passed by. In some places, such as the archways that connected the rooms, partiers were packed close enough so that incidental bumping was unavoidable, but Kyler—and then Trust, steps behind him—was able to slink their way through, Kyler expertly avoiding spilling his soda in the process.

The kitchen was large and spacious, actually a combination of both a dining room and food prep area, with the kitchen section seemingly built for a professional cook rather than a group of partying college students. The décor was spotless, the cabinet and wood paneling well maintained. An eye-catching L-shaped countertop effectively sectioned off the cooking area from the rest of the space, with an island countertop inside it, providing additional room for cooking—or, in its present case, a perfect display area for the many assorted beers, liquors, and other beverages on hand, most of them alcoholic. The ornate drink display was where Kyler led Trust.

"Take a look at this spread, dude!" Kyler said, waving to the impressive exhibit of bottles and cans, different sizes and different colors, most of them already open and empty. The assortment would not have been out of place behind the counter of any club or bar downtown.

*Impressive,* Trust signed back. *You should take a picture of this. Send it to your mom and dad. They'll be so jealous.*

125

"I already did," Kyler acknowledged, grinning and patting his pocket. "Not the sending part, though. That's just ridiculous."

He then waved Trust's attention forward again, where another boy was approaching from the other side of the island counter.

"So, you guys see any—hah, it's you again," the boy said, his smirk becoming wider as he recognized Kyler. "Change your mind and decide to go in for some liquid courage?"

Kyler grinned.

"Nah," he said. "I'm good."

He then gestured to Trust.

"My buddy here may want something, though."

Trust shot Kyler the same skeptical expression he had given him a minute earlier, before returning his eyes to the boy on the other side of the counter.

"Ah, cool, cool," the boy said, rubbing his hands together in anticipation, and then beckoned to Trust. "Let's hear it. Come on, I can fix anything you want."

Smirking faintly, Trust glanced to Kyler for an instant.

*So, is this guy the bartender or something? He looks the same age as us.*

He waited for Kyler to interpret his questions and Kyler did so, verbatim. A look of shock showed on the other boy's face for a moment as he looked from Kyler back to Trust.

"Whoa! Sign language? That's so awesome! Are you deaf, or is that just a labor-intensive way to meet chicks?"

Kyler scoffed.

"What? I'm not deaf. I can hear just fine."

"No, I meant—"

Trust quickly gestured again, the other boy falling quiet as he observed Trust's hands.

Without looking over, Kyler said, "Yes, I'm deaf."

He then took a sip from his drink.

"Huh?" the other boy said, looking back to Kyler. "No, I meant—"

"No, dude, I'm telling you. I'm not deaf," Kyler said.

Trust was signing again, and both Kyler and the boy behind the counter looked in his direction.

"You're an idiot," Kyler said.

"What?" the other boy said, his brow furrowing slightly.

"What?" Kyler asked.

More gestures from Trust.

"I said you're an idiot. A big idiot. You're an I-D-I-O-T," Kyler stated, before calmly taking another taste of his drink.

Trust was grinning, shaking his head.

"Oh, I get it," the other boy said. "You had me goin' for a second there."

Trust signed.

"I think he's onto us," Kyler said.

"Yeah, I'm onto you," the boy replied, grinning again.

"Would you believe we've almost gotten beat up doing that?" Kyler asked.

*You mean* you *have almost gotten beat up doing that,* Trust amended, which Kyler verbalized.

"Oh, I believe it," the boy said. "And if I wasn't ever so slightly buzzed right now, I probably would have come at one of you."

He glanced to Trust, and then to Kyler.

"Probably you. Your friend looks like he would be a tough go."

"You think you could take me?" Kyler asked. "You would be surprised."

The other boy looked to Trust again as Kyler flexed, and both shared a dubious look.

"Ah, shut up, man," Kyler intoned, catching Trust's expression and pushing him in the shoulder.

"So, what can I get ya?" the other boy asked, waving his hand around the assorted range of beverage choices again. "We've got it all, domestic and foreign, pretty much everything"—he picked up a bottle—"Paisley Lite, always a crowd favorite. Liquors, we've got rum, whiskey, spirits, gin, right on down the line. Bourbon, of course. Schnapps, we got ya. Dark Rose vodka. And this Mount Vernon Blanc has gotten some good reviews if you're into Singani. I've gotten a lot of people to try it out tonight, and—"

*Wow, you really are a bartender,* Trust signed.

The other boy laughed.

"Viticulture and Oenology and International Business Administration double major, but yeah, I'm also a bartender. I'm Wick, by the way."

He reached across the counter, shaking hands with Trust and Kyler.

"I bartend at Centre Diamond downtown," Wick continued. "Pretty popular place. So, come on, anything your heart desires, I can pretty much cook up right here."

With that, the boy gestured around the entire cooking area, and Trust made a grand display of studying the many cans and bottles, tapping his chin as though in deep analysis and blatantly ignoring Kyler's amused staring. Rising from his crouch to stand straight again, he met Wick's expectant, if not altogether eager, gaze.

*I'll have what he's having,* Trust finally signed.

Wick, noticing Trust gesture toward Kyler's cup, said, "Yeah, yeah. I can put it in a cup, but come on. Point something out. What do you want? Make me work a little."

Chuckling, Trust simply pointed to Kyler's drink again. Wick looked from Trust, to Kyler, and back to Trust.

"What? You want—aw, come on, man! After all that scrutinizing, all you want is a soda? You're killin' me, dude! You're really, really killin' me!"

"So, you work at Centre Diamond, eh?" Kyler said, grinning. "I guess that means you would know—"

Trust swiftly elbowed the boy in a sensitive area along his side, Kyler doubling over, while giving a sympathetic look to Wick. He waited for Kyler to meet his gaze again.

*Tell him he can mix up the different sodas if he wants. I don't want to stifle an artist's creativity. And you try that again, I'll lay you out on the floor.*

Wick brightened with Trust's message, though Kyler left out the last part, still rubbing his side.

"Now you're speaking my language. But, I have to know, do you actually want a specific type of taste, or do you just want something non-alcoholic? 'Cause if it's the second, it gives me more options to exercise such creativity."

Trust held up two fingers.

"The second option? Great! Comin' right up. I've actually got the perfect thing. I've been working on..."

As Wick turned to gather his ingredients, Trust looked to Kyler.

*Now, tell me. What are the chances this guy tries to slip in some alcohol anyway, and then tries to take advantage of me?*

Kyler, who had been taking another swallow of his drink, nearly coughed it up as he started to laugh.

"Dude, that almost came out of my nose!" he exclaimed.

"There you guys are!"

Kyler turned at the sudden sound of Allison's voice, causing Trust to turn as well.

"Hey, I was looking everywhere for you!"

Both Kyler and Allison said this at the same time, Allison being serious, and Kyler in an amusing manner, attempting to predict what Allison was about to say and succeeding.

"Ah, shut up," she said, hitting Kyler lightly.

Grinning, Kyler glanced to Trust.

He was met with another skeptical look.

*You're so obvious,* Trust signed.

"Ah, shut up," Kyler said.

Trust motioned toward Allison, indicating to Kyler that he should interpret what he had said. Allison caught the gesture, and she looked to Kyler.

"What?" she asked.

"Nothing," Kyler dismissed. "The ramblings of a madman talking about going on a serial-killing spree and all that nonsense."

"Um, pretty sure that's *not* what he said," Allison remarked, to which Trust smiled. "If he did, it probably would have looked more like this."

With an empty cup in one hand, Allison mimed a dramatic downward stabbing motion with the other. Then she clutched at her throat, her eyes bulging, seemingly choking herself.

Trust and Kyler both laughed.

*She's dark,* Trust signed to Kyler. *She's the total package, dude.*

Then, looking to Allison, though he knew she would not understand what he was signing, *That's a new sign. I'll have to remember it.*

Trust's chuckles were quickly shoved aside, however, as he detected something—a smell of some sort. It was floral, not too strong or over the top. Certainly some sort of perfume or fragrance, alluring, almost beckoning him to discover it. Before he could stop himself, he furtively glanced around, searching for its origin.

He spotted her before she spotted him. His eyes were trained on her as she finally met his gaze.

Curly, dark blond hair with fleeting streaks of auburn. A cute, attractive face, seemingly able to exhibit the most innocent, or most sensuous, of expressions. Trust could make out her eye color even from across the room—an intriguing hazel. An athletic figure, and full, pouty lips.

Trust had only been studying her for a few seconds before a fluttering motion to the side of his vision drew his focus to Kyler. Kyler directed him to the makeshift bar counter again, where Wick had returned with his newly concocted drink.

"Now, this drink is actually supposed to be in a glass for you to appreciate the full effect, but at least it will still taste good," Wick said. "Okay. Red grenadine syrup and a few dashes—shots, you could call them—of white sugar, hard powdered. Over that, two parts Coke, and more powdered sugar."

Wick held the cup up to eye level.

"If this were in a clear cup and we were looking at it straight on, this drink would look like the body of Mickey Mouse—you know, red pants, white buttons, white gloves, black top. Look it up if you don't believe me. I'm telling you, this drink is a work of art, guys. I was originally calling it the Mickey, but you can probably picture a few of the problems with that, so my boss down at Centre Diamond just said go with Mickey Mouse."

Grinning, obviously pleased with his presentation thus far, Wick extended his arm across the island counter, handing Trust the cup.

"Your boss, as in Mariana?" Kyler asked.

This time, he leaned away when Trust turned to him.

Wick's eyes widened in surprise.

"So you've been there. Come through again, first round's on me. You'll get a chance to see me in action."

Trust shot Kyler a look. Kyler grinned merrily.

"This is non-alcoholic, but that can be changed quite easily if you want," Wick explained, returning to the drink. "My only suggestion would be to stir it"—he pointed to the stirring straw he had also placed in the cup—"before you take a sip. It's really going to taste awful right now because all the ingredients are sep—"

The boy's eyes suddenly alighted to Allison, only just now sighting her.

"Ah, speaking of no alcohol, Sexy Red is back! How goes it, Sexy Red? Finally ready to take a shot with me?"

"The answer is still no," Allison replied, though she was grinning.

Watching the dialogue between them, Trust lifted the proffered Mickey Mouse concoction to his nose. It smelled like a fruity soda—very sweet, but overall, relatively harmless. He stirred the drink and started to take a sip.

The floral perfume was suddenly more apparent, though it still held its tantalizing allure. Without looking, Trust knew the girl had moved closer.

"Do you like it?"

Trust did not hear the question, of course. He glanced toward Wick, who was still in conversation with Allison and Kyler. He began to take another sip.

The floral scent was wafting, a warm cloud. Distinct, obvious, clear.

And the Mickey Mouse wasn't bad, Trust thought. Actually, it was pretty good. Though, with all the sugar, it was probably enough to—

As though on instinct, Trust's eyes flitted to his right just as he was raising the cup to his lips.

There.

Trust froze the cup right in front of his face, turning his head.

The attractive girl he had spotted moments before was now right beside him...and standing quite close. She was leaning in as though she were about to whisper something.

Their faces were very close, even though Trust was clearly taller than the girl. Trust's eyes darted down to the girl's lips, and not simply to catch the words that could be coming out of her mouth.

"...didn't hear me?" she asked.

It was obvious that she was speaking at a near whisper.

Trust's focus shifted faintly, minutely, from her lips to her eyes. He shook his head lightly.

"Oh. Wow," the girl breathed. "Your eyes. They're...so blue."

Trust smiled.

"I asked if you liked your drink."

*What drink*, Trust thought.

His and the girl's face seemed to have drifted slightly closer. To anyone observing, it would look like the two were having a particularly challenging time hearing each other.

Or, more likely, it would look like they were about to...

The girl turned her head at the last moment, jerking as though someone had called her name. Trust, his head not moving, studied her profile for a second longer, his expression contemplative. He then also turned.

Apparently, that was the correct move, as he was quickly met with the frat-boy bartender's bemused grin, his eyes shifting between Trust and the girl. Trust looked toward Kyler and Allison.

Kyler was grinning widely. Allison was eyeing Trust with the same curious smirk as Wick on the other side of the countertop.

Trust pointed to his ear and shook his head innocently, indicating that he had not heard what the group had just said.

Kyler burst out laughing.

"Ha! So now you want to play the deaf card, eh? How convenient for you."

Trust turned to look back at the girl, who was now looking at him with astonishment.

"You're deaf?" she asked.

Trust smiled and held up his free hand, his thumb and forefinger a few centimeters apart. He then reached into his pocket, quickly pulling out his small stack of note cards. Adeptly, he separated one from the bunch and handed it to her.

*I'm Trust, and yes, I am deaf.*

the card read in neat, elegant print. The girl looked at him after reading the card, a small, almost playful smile showing on her lips.

"Well, I guess that would explain it," she said, slowly giving the card back to him.

Her hand lingered.

Or perhaps he was reading a bit too much into a fleeting moment of contact.

Pocketing his cards again, Trust looked to the boy behind the counter.

*I think you're onto something with this Mickey Mouse. It's pretty good.*

Even with one hand holding his drink, Trust was able to get his point across to Kyler, who then interpreted the message to Wick.

"Thanks, man!"

Wick then looked to the girl.

"See, Jezzie? I told you it was good. You honestly think I would give you something that tasted butt-awful?"

Trust looked quickly to Kyler as he spelled the name.

J-E-Z-Z-I-E.

Jezzie.

"I didn't want to try it because you said you were 'experimenting,'" Jezzie charged. "Excuse me for not wanting to be one of your little white mice. And anyway, didn't you say it had no alcohol?"

"First off, I'm the only one who tastes it when it's going through the trial-and-error phase, babe. It will only touch your pretty lips when it's guaranteed to be at least good."

Wick then motioned to Trust's cup, which was already half-empty.

"Now, it has reached the level of great. And secondly, adding alcohol is the easy part. A little mix of whatever you want and you're good to go."

"What did you add to his?"

Jezzie looked to Trust.

"What does yours have, Trust?"

Trust began to shake his head before Wick answered for him.

"Nah. These three are going dry tonight. Matter of fact, I should've known you were all together even though you didn't get drinks at the same time. I think you're the only ones I've seen so far without alcohol."

Allison started to respond, but Trust looked to his right again.

"So, no alcohol, huh?" Jezzie observed, her eyebrows raised slightly. "Afraid of losing control?"

Trust eye's made the shift again from her full, pouty lips, up to her brown-green irises.

*Not even close,* he signed.

Though she would not understand his exact meaning, she would at least comprehend his shaking head. As he looked into her eyes, he smiled despite himself.

Jezzie returned his smirk with one of her own.

Then, seemingly out of nowhere, an arm slithered its way around Jezzie's shoulders and back, neatly drawing her toward another body.

Trust noticed Jezzie jump faintly at the unexpected contact, but then instantly relax as she realized who was clutching her.

Trust's eyes, meanwhile, swiftly shifted to the visitor.

Green eyes, glinting.

Faint stubble over the bottom half of his face.

And a recognizable, subtly cocky smirk.

Trust identified him immediately. Jeremy Higgins, UCC's star wide receiver. The same one he had identified on the giant football stadium scoreboard. The same upperclassman that had "sparred" with Trust exactly one week earlier.

And he was apparently confident enough to sling his arm around any girl he chose.

Unless Jezzie was not just "any" girl.

"Oh, I remember you," Jeremy declared, meeting Trust's gaze. "Truth, right? No, Just."

Trust did not respond, save for the corner of his mouth upticking ever so slightly.

With his arm still wrapped around her, Jezzie hit Jeremy in his chest. She was smiling, though.

"His name is Trust," she corrected, to which Jeremy gave a dramatic "Ahh."

"You two know each other?" she continued, her glance skirting between the two boys.

"We danced last week," Jeremy answered. "A little light sparring."

The football player then looked down to Jezzie.

"He's actually not too bad."

He then glanced back to Trust, the smirk returning full force.

"Not quite good enough to try stealing my girlfriend, though."

Trust and Jeremy locked eyes for an extended moment, Trust's gaze impassive, Jeremy's taunting, anticipatory.

"Don't start, Jeremy," Jezzie said, looking up at him. "You know I don't think it's funny when you talk like that."

Trust placed his now-empty cup down on the edge of the counter, noticing that Wick, the party's bartender, had disappeared again. A quick peek around turned up Allison and Kyler in their same positions, Paxson and Marcie having joined them. All were glancing toward him, Kyler mumbling something in Allison's ear.

Other eyes were also aimed in his direction. A few of the boys Trust recognized.

Hopefully, this would not turn into a problem.

Trust briefly looked back in Jezzie and Jeremy's direction and held up one finger. Then, turning back to Kyler, he gestured, *Do you mind?*

"What's up?" Kyler said, coming forward.

He glanced past Trust.

"We got a problem here?"

Trust cleared his throat in exasperation and rolled his eyes. He could not hear Jeremy's scoff.

"I'm just kidding," Kyler said.

He then looked past Trust again.

"Hey, you're Jeremy Higgins! And you're that guy we saw at the gym last week!"

Kyler extended his hand excitedly, and Jeremy had to release Jezzie to complete the handshake. The older boy looked slightly thrown off by the enthusiastic greeting.

"Oh, man. Great game today, dude," Kyler said. "Six catches, three touchdowns. You're awesome, man. You probably didn't notice, but I painted my chest and everything."

Jeremy, meanwhile, was eyeing Kyler with a curious air.

"Well, if he didn't, I definitely saw you," Marcie spoke up, "as much as I would have liked not to. I mean, with your chest out and everything."

She said the last part mockingly and looked to Allison, both girls sharing a knowing glance.

"Hey, I was there, too," Paxson added, nudging Marcie. "My chest was painted."

"You look familiar," Jeremy commented, still looking at Kyler.

"You don't remember me?" Kyler asked. "I was at the gym with Trust that day. You see, I stopped you from getting your head knocked off—"

"Ha!" Jeremy guffawed loudly. "Yeah...no. I think I know you from somewhere else..."

"So you did see me this afternoon," Kyler said. "I was the R in Centre—"

"You play baseball?"

"Yeah," Kyler replied.

*He's pretty good,* Trust signed.

"What?" Jeremy looked at Trust in confusion.

"He said I suck at baseball," Kyler said.

Trust rolled his eyes, shaking his head.

"Your name's Kyle, right? Kyle? Scott? No, Kyle...Kyler! Kyler-Scott Brooks."

*Your reputation precedes you again,* Trust signed. *Only this time, it's for a good thing.*

Jeremy looked to Trust in question, and then back to Kyler.

"You want to tell us what he's saying?"

Then, returning to Trust: "Didn't you have note cards last time?"

"You don't really want to know what he's saying right now," Kyler assured him. "He's using bad words to describe his relationship with my mother, which, frankly, I'm surprised at, since he's been to my house loads of times with nothing but nice things to say to her."

"Okay," Jeremy said, confusion still laced in the word, "whatever. Anyway, I heard one of the baseball coaches talking about you. You're supposedly, like, some sort of freshman phenom or something, right? He had some newspaper article with your picture in it."

"Wait. Are you on the baseball team, too?" Kyler asked. "'Cause we just had a thing yesterday, and I don't remember—"

"Oh, heck no," Jeremy scoffed. "I stick to football. A sport that, you know, real *men* play."

His smirk returned.

Kyler suddenly lunged forward, though Trust, already anticipating the ruse, easily blocked his path.

"You take that back, you son of a—"

Trust quickly placed a hand over Kyler's mouth. Allison's eyes widened at the sudden outburst, and Trust, noticing her reaction, shook his head, smiling gently.

"Really?" asked Jeremy with some surprise, though he had not flinched at Kyler's abrupt lunge toward him.

Kyler calmed down quickly, and Trust turned to look at Jeremy, having not been facing him before to see his comment.

*He does that every time someone talks bad about baseball. It's kind of a stupid joke he thinks is funny.*

"Yeah, I really have no clue what you're saying," Jeremy said.

This time, Kyler correctly interpreted what Trust had signed, before adding, "But it's not a joke. I'm...dead...serious."

With his red cup still in his hand, he aimed a menacing finger in Jeremy's direction, jabbing it toward him in emphasis. Jeremy stared at him for a moment, an amused expression covering his face, and then shifted his eyes to Trust, and then to Paxson and Marcie.

"Are all you freshmen this crazy?" he asked them.

Trust noted that Jeremy's arm had worked its way around Jezzie's shoulders again.

"I wouldn't know," Paxson answered smugly, breathing in a lungful of air. "Yep, I'm a junior. I know it doesn't look it, but..."

Everyone stared at him, including Marcie, her look incredulous.

"Sophomore?" he tried.

Marcie continued to give him the eye.

"Argh, all right, all right," he admitted. "Freshman."

"Guess that answers my question," Jeremy said. He looked down to Jezzie, who giggled.

"Well, if you're going to go by these three," Marcie said, gesturing to Trust, Kyler, and Paxson, "then that's a terrible sample group."

Jeremy grinned. Trust turned to Marcie.

*Me?* he gestured. He then waved to Kyler and Paxson. *Me...with them?*

"Just because you're the least crazy out of the three doesn't make you sane," Marcie explained.

Kyler grinned, looking at Trust.

"See?" he said. "Told ya you were a bad influence."

"Well, you guys are a barrel of laughs," Jeremy remarked, "but I came in here looking to get a refill"—he then looked directly at Trust—"and to find my girl."

The ghost of a smirk showed on Trust's lips.

Jeremy glanced to the island countertop full of the available drinking choices, and then looked to Jezzie.

"I thought Wick was standing there a second ago," he said. "He always hides the good stuff from me. I don't think he likes me very much."

"That doesn't seem very hard to do," Allison said under her breath, and not very softly.

Everyone in the loosely knitted circle looked toward the red-haired girl in some amazement, except for Trust, who only turned to the subject of everyone's attention a split second later.

*What happened?* Trust signaled to Kyler swiftly. *I missed it that time.*

"She said—" Kyler started.

"I said that if he treats other people the same way he's been acting toward you guys just now—like a stuck-up bully—then it's not hard to see why some people wouldn't like him much," Allison asserted further, bold and suddenly unafraid.

Trust now joined the others in surprise.

"Technically," Kyler tried again, "that's not *exactly* what you said before, but..."

Trust glanced to Jeremy.

The usual smirk was still etched across the football player's features, though now it seemed frozen in place, devoid of any of the characteristic cockiness. His attention remaining on Allison, he stepped forward slightly, almost as though shielding Jezzie from what he was about to do, his arm sliding off her shoulder again.

"Well, speaking of bullies," he started, his tone a touch lower, a touch more ominous than before, "have you guys heard about the Freesef Society yet?"

Jeremy's smirk had come alive again, the arrogance back as though it had never left, with a bit of roguishness added in.

"Apparently, there's this secret club that's a tough bunch to handle, not to mention practically untouchable, and I've heard their specialty is—"

"Jeremy, stop," Jezzie said, stepping forward also and hugging his arm. "Spreading stupid rumors and trying to scare—"

"I'm only trying to warn them, baby," Jeremy intoned, "since it seems freshman girls—and particularly freshman girls like you two—would probably be just the type to catch their eye. The university and the police—"

"Wait," Paxson interrupted. "What do you mean freshman girls like them? What does that mean?"

Jeremy looked to Paxson.

"I'm assuming this is your girlfriend?" he inquired, waving lightly to Marcie.

"Yeah?"

Jeremy shifted to Allison.

"And you are..."

His eyes shifted to Kyler, and then to Trust.

"I'm single," Allison answered before the wide receiver could voice his assumption.

Trust glanced fleetingly to Kyler, who suddenly avoided his gaze.

"Hmm," Jeremy said, looking from Allison to Kyler again. "Well, don't take this the wrong way, but neither of you"—his eyes flitted between the two freshman girls—"fell victim to the ugly stick, which seems to put you in the category of other girls who have come into a similar fate with the Freesef Society, shall we say."

"Jeremy," Jezzie warned again. Her voice held a slight edge, which Trust could detect by the tense movement of her mouth and the expression on her face.

"All I'm saying is that this so-called secret society—and the characteristics I see in the girls they have 'met'—follows a certain pattern, and you two seem to fall into that pattern pretty nicely. On the other hand, I've also heard that these girls wouldn't necessarily label themselves as victims, more like...hmm, I don't know...lottery winners. Maybe you two would fall into that category also?"

His leer was snobbish, arrogant.

Allison seemed momentarily stunned at his insinuation, as did Jezzie.

Marcie, however, expressed a different reaction. She took a quick step forward.

"You're an ass!"

Paxson grabbed at her from behind.

"Whoa, whoa, Marcie. Don't—"

"Let me go!"

She was physically struggling against Paxson's grasp. Jeremy backed off slightly, though his smirk was ever-present.

"That's it," Jezzie declared. "We're going home. You're outta control—"

"You can't tell me that guy isn't completely tanked out of his mind right now," Kyler whispered to Allison, somehow hoping to lessen the blow of Jeremy's words.

Trust, meanwhile, was looking intently at Jeremy Higgins.

All movement and ongoing effects of the house party were already taken into account, the numerous bodies rocking and swaying, moving this way and that, virtually all of them unaware of what was occurring in the kitchen just in front of the beverage counter, some people skirting past to get another drink, completely blind to the looming explosion. Jeremy's positioning had also been taken into account—in fact, from his arrival—as had Trust's own location, which he always did intrinsically. Trust was also aware of the other partiers loitering barely on the periphery, some who seemed to have more than a fleeting interest in their encounter.

He was like a computer—or, more precisely, a predator. All of this information and more was observed, an instant analysis of the immediate situation, his eyes not only detecting each person's movements, but also the—

And then he noticed the subtle, faint, slow sway. It was not for the first time.

Jezzie was correct in saying Jeremy was "out of control," perhaps more so than she understood.

Indeed, Jeremy Higgins was steadily losing control of himself. And with that, Trust disengaged, his combative senses already diminishing.

He quickly glanced to Kyler, who was already looking in his direction. Kyler was, most likely, aware of where Trust's mind had gone moments before.

*Something's going on here,* Trust signed swiftly. *Something's wrong. Ask Jezzie how much he's had to drink, or if he's had something else. Does he usually act like this at parties?*

"What?" Kyler asked. "You're serious?"

The group's attention, including Jeremy's, now shifted to Trust as he again motioned to Jezzie. Though Jeremy's arm was around his girlfriend once more, Trust could now see what he was doing, even if Jeremy himself did not quite realize it.

The boy was leaning on her, slightly, for support. He was off balance.

"Yeah, we get it already," Jeremy remarked. "You can talk with your—"

He seemed to lose his train of thought. Kyler started to speak.

"Hey, Trust thinks our good friend here may have had a little too much to drink."

He looked to Jezzie.

"Have you, by any chance, noticed how much he's been drinking? Is it possible he's high right now on something?"

Jezzie looked up to Jeremy, a flash of worry coming across her features. Jeremy, meanwhile, was looking at Kyler.

"What?" he asked. "I don't...I don't even..."

Trust and Kyler exchanged a glance as Jeremy once again struggled to articulate a coherent thought. Whatever he had consumed, it was taking effect quickly.

"Jeremy, are you all right?" Jezzie asked. "Are you feeling okay? Did you take something?"

She then looked to the four freshmen encircling them.

"He doesn't go near anything else besides alcohol. Not to mention, he would definitely be kicked off the football team if they ever caught him on anything."

Jezzie looked to Jeremy again. Jeremy was looking back at her, his

140

expression puzzled.

"Jeremy?" she said again.

Trust stepped toward the older boy, meeting the football player's gaze when Jeremy finally looked his way. The others watched as Trust's head bobbed and weaved slightly, his blue eyes remaining fixed on Jeremy's as he studied him. Jeremy attempted to follow the deaf teen's movements, his confusion still evident.

Trust glanced back to Kyler.

*I'm no doctor, dude, but he's either really drunk, or something else. Whatever it is, it's starting to affect him more and more as we've been standing here. Watch him, he's swaying. Have you seen—see? There he goes again.*

Though Jeremy's tilt was again subtle, he did have to shuffle forward slightly, as though trying to stay on his feet.

"Whoa, man," Paxson said after Kyler interpreted Trust's comments. "You may need to lie down or something."

"There's...I don't feel right," Jeremy muttered, seemingly to himself, barely loud enough to be heard over the general din of the party still going on. "I need...to get out of here."

"Maybe he should go to the hospital," Allison volunteered, her apparent dislike of the boy completely overridden by her concern.

Jeremy seemed to have forgotten about the conversation moments earlier as well. He gazed toward Allison with some confusion.

"Huh?"

"If you don't know what you've taken," Allison started, "the ER—"

Out of nowhere, Jeremy exploded.

"For what?" he shouted, his features suddenly very intense.

Allison startled back. Other people in the area glanced Jeremy's way. All three of the other boys—Trust, Kyler, and Paxson—stepped forward.

"Hey, Jeremy," Kyler said. "It's okay. Ease up, man."

Trust continued to study the older boy silently.

"That's it," Jezzie said, tugging on Jeremy's arm. "We need to go. I'm taking you to the apartment."

Surprisingly, Jeremy seemed to give in to Jezzie's pull without much resistance, the confused look enveloping his face again. He reached one of his hands up to wipe at his forehead, his brow furrowed. Both he and Jezzie started to turn away.

Trust gestured quickly toward Kyler, but Allison beat him to the punch.

"If he doesn't go to the hospital, give him water," she advised. "It will help flush whatever it is out of his system."

Jezzie turned back, still leading Jeremy through the crowd that had started to develop in the kitchen.

"Thanks," she said, looking at the group. "I'm so sorry about this. I promise, this is not the way he usually acts, no matter how drunk he is."

She seemed to lock on Trust's gaze.

"I really am sorry," she said again, turning away once more and leading Jeremy out. Jeremy glanced back a final time as well, the same bewildered, disorientated look on his face, the same drawn brow.

His familiar smirk was gone.

Trust watched the pair make their way through the other partiers, most not paying much attention to them, with Jezzie calling to someone to help her get Jeremy to her car. With their backs now turned to Trust, however, he had no idea she was speaking.

The five remaining freshmen, still standing in front of the drink counter, looked to one another.

"Well," Paxson began, making sure Trust was looking at him, "that is now the second party I've been to with you that you've sent a guy out of the building in worse shape than he was when he came in."

*I didn't—*

Paxson waved him off.

"I'm just kidding," he said, before covering his mouth, as though preparing to sneeze.

"Kinda," he added with his mouth covered.

Kyler could not help but snicker, while Trust looked on unawares.

"You guys said you'd met him before?" Marcie asked, looking at Trust and Kyler. "Was he that much of a jerk last time?"

"His jerkiness was of a much lower grade last week," Kyler replied. "Last week he was Diet Jerk. Jerk Lite. Jerk Zero."

*Last week he wasn't high, either,* Trust added, and Kyler spoke aloud. *Not to give him any excuses, but I'm not entirely sure that was Jeremy Higgins we were talking to just now.*

"I'm not sure if that's good or bad," Allison remarked.

Her face then abruptly changed to one of accusation.

"Hey, what does that mean, 'the second party you've sent a guy out in worse shape than he came in'?"

Trust looked at her, his face once again giving nothing away. He then looked to Kyler.

Kyler looked at him, and then turned to Paxson.

Paxson laughed, looking to Marcie.

Marcie was looking at Kyler, her hands on her hips.

Kyler looked back to Trust.

*Dude,* Trust signed. *This is getting old.*

# 12.
## Sunday Breakfast

ALLISON LED THE WAY TOWARD the entrance to Hollins Cafeteria, the main—and largest—dining hall on the UCC campus. It was late morning, another clear and sunny day with a smattering of clouds. The winds were light and the air was clean.

And the rural campus was quiet. Typical on a Sunday—Sunday morning, no less.

Trust, Kyler, and Allison were dressed for the occasion, Allison in a low crop top and shorts that showed off her long legs, her auburn hair tied into a high ponytail and tucked under a baseball cap. Trust and Kyler both wore athletic shorts that stretched past their knees and T-shirts.

Kyler was absent his usual ball cap, his hair untied and virtually unstyled, hanging in loose waves past his shoulders. Trust's hair, tightly curled and coal black in a small Afro, only needed intermittent maintenance, something that Trust often kidded Kyler about when the other boy tried and failed to control his lengthy mane of hair. This morning, Trust had spent all of twenty seconds on his head, fifteen of which occurred in the shower.

Add to the fact that Trust was already dressed in his second set of clothes of the day, having gone for his gym workout earlier. He had attempted to wake Kyler to see if he wanted to join him, but he was rebuffed. Along a similar vein, Trust and Kyler had attempted to get Paxson and Marcie to tag along on this, their Sunday morning trek to the cafeteria. They were rebuffed on both counts, with Paxson sending back an agonized *Noooooooooo* text message, and Marcie's fiery reply returning with a few choice expletives for what she considered "way too early" on a Sunday morning.

145

Trust had laughed when he received the replies. Kyler had, too, when he had finally woken up enough to read them.

"Lazy teenagers," he had chastised, his pale blue eyes still laced with sleep at the time.

The pathway clear, Trust leaped lithely up the steps rising to the cafeteria's entranceway, skipping ahead of the other two to open the first set of doors. He then bowed in elegant manner as they approached, his arm coming across his midsection as he bent over.

"Why, thank you so much, kind sir," Allison said in an airy, princess-like tenor, Trust's eyes peeking up as his head was lowered in order to see her reaction.

"Good work, old chap," Kyler declared, his voice taking on a Victorian quality. "I would pitch you a few pounds, but golly, I seem to have left my change purse in my other breeches!"

Allison chuckled.

She laughed outright when Trust sprang up just after Kyler had passed by, his hands swiftly landing on Kyler's head and aggressively mussing his hair.

"Argh!" Kyler cried as Trust and Allison laughed. "That's why I usually wear a hat."

"Really?" Allison replied.

"Heh, no, not really," Kyler said. "I just like wearing hats sometimes."

Trust finally released his head when the group passed through the second set of doors, entering into the foyer of the large cafeteria.

The Hollins Cafeteria was a grand, modern building both inside and out, a cathedral to university fine dining. Were it not for the multitude of tables, chairs, and numerous food stations, the refined interior space could just as easily be confused with a trendy hotel lobby. From either of the main front entrances, one had to pass in front of a short wall adorned with live plants and trees, before turning onto a gradual incline that led up to the cafeteria's main level, open and refreshingly spacious, with vast portions of the walls fashioned as floor-to-ceiling windows. The towering ceiling was also aesthetically constructed so as to provide those inside an unobstructed look toward the Centre City skies.

Not to be outdone by the architecture, the food selection was a magnificent affair, an experience unto itself. Present were the eating concourses housed in any university—and many high schools—buffet-style arrangements with cafeteria employees serving up provisions. But that was where any traditional similarities ended. Vibrant, colorful displays and placards graced the various stations, broadcasting the cornucopia of fare available. And a bountiful assortment it was, with quality equal to any five-star restaurant.

In short, Hollins Cafeteria was a far cry from any ordinary dining hall. It was certainly one of the reasons—however frivolous it at first seemed—why Trust, Kyler, and countless other students decided to come to the University of Centre City.

A few familiar faces greeted the group as Trust, Allison, and Kyler took their seats after choosing their food. The sprawling cafeteria was largely empty, though it would begin to fill after students finally emerged following their Saturday night escapades.

Brycen Johns, the graduate student and sometime receptionist in Adams Hall, was the first to get Trust's notice.

"Well, I knew you wouldn't be able to stay away," he said, "but really? Stalking me on a Sunday morning? That's a little overboard, Trustice."

Introductions were made. Holden, Trust and Kyler's resident assistant, grinned, looking between Brycen and Trust.

"Oh, so you already know each other?" he asked. "Fair warning, Trust—this guy's a live wire."

Trust threw up his hands, rolling his eyes.

*Now he tells me,* he signed.

Kyler and Brycen, both observing Trust's gestures, laughed. After verbalizing Trust's comment, Brycen shifted his eyes to a still-chuckling Kyler.

"Ah, another sign language connoisseur?" Brycen asked.

By then, Trust, Kyler, and Allison were all seated, Trust taking a chair near the end so he could see everyone's face without any extra effort.

"Pssh," Kyler scoffed. "I know more than he does."

Brycen glanced across the table toward the other familiar face and wiggled his eyebrows, tilting his head in Kyler and Trust's direction.

"I know," Riley said. "I've run into them before."

"Hey, what was that look?" Holden raised, gesturing between Riley and Brycen.

"I remember you," Kyler said, pointing his fork at Riley. "From Elizabeth's."

Kyler looked to Allison.

147

"Riley was our waiter at that Italian restaurant down the street the day we moved into the dorms. My sister has a crush on him."

Allison replied simply, "I can see why that could become the case."

Trust, Holden, and Brycen looked at her and then doubled up in laughter, having to temporarily pause their eating. Kyler fumbled and dropped his fork.

Allison shrugged.

"Wow, I like you already," Brycen said, still laughing. "It's like I always say, 'It's okay to window-shop, so long as you don't touch the merchandise.'"

Holden chuckled.

"Yeah, I've *never* heard you say that," he said.

"That's because you don't like to hear me talk about other guys," Brycen responded.

*It sounds like something you would say,* Trust motioned, *and I've only spoken to you for about a minute in total.*

Kyler translated for everyone else while Brycen laughed again.

"What's the joke?" Kyler said. "I don't even understand what's going on."

"In this case, it just means I'm taken," Riley said, smiling. "I told you I had a boyfriend, remember?"

Trust glanced to Brycen, who was grinning, his eyes directed across the table to Riley.

"You asked Riley if he had a boyfriend?" Holden asked Kyler. "Cool, dude. I didn't even know you were gay."

Trust burst out laughing.

"What?" Kyler sputtered, his voice rising an octave. "No, no! My sister—"

"So, you two are a couple?" Allison asked, looking between Riley and Brycen. "That's a shame. I never would have guessed, but I should have known. You're both too attractive."

This time Kyler nearly choked on his juice, flabbergasted once again, turning to look at Allison as the others laughed at his expense.

"W-what?"

"Your girlfriend's totally playing you right now," Riley remarked, chuckling.

"Girlfriend?"

"Girlfriend!"

Both Allison and Kyler spoke the word at the same time, Allison's tone surprised, Kyler's astonished.

Trust could not catch his breath, he was laughing so hard.

"You never mentioned you had such good-looking freshmen on your floor, Holden," Brycen said.

Allison, Riley, and Holden found that amusing, particularly when Trust's chortles turned to coughing as well.

Kyler turned to look at Trust.

*He just called you good-looking, dude,* he mouthed.

*Idiot,* Trust directed to his roommate. *He was talking about you, too.*

After the laughter of the others died down, Holden looked to the three freshmen.

"So, did you guys hear about what happened last night yet?"

"Last night?" Allison echoed, to which Holden nodded.

"Freesef strikes again," Riley said, not looking up from his food.

"I still don't really understand that, by the way," Brycen said. "I did my undergrad in Massachusetts, and I'm just starting to hear about this whole Freesef thing."

"Ironically, not understanding it is kind of the objective," Holden said.

His gaze turned to Allison.

"These guys probably already know the thread I'm going to take with this story, but have you heard of the Freesef Society?"

Allison's eyes flitted to Kyler and Trust briefly before returning to the RA. She nodded.

"Yeah. I had a bit of a crash course about them last night at a party."

"Last night?" Brycen repeated.

"Party?" Riley asked.

"Crash course?" Holden echoed. "What does that mean?"

"We had a...run-in, I guess you could say," Kyler clarified, not very well.

Holden's eyes widened.

"Are you serious?"

Trust was quick to assuage the RA's concern, swiftly shaking his head and waving his hands.

*No, no. Not like what you're thinking,* he then signaled, which Kyler voiced.

"You care to clue us in?" Holden asked.

"You go first," Kyler said.

Holden exhaled, shrugging.

"Not that much to tell right now," he started. "Like I said, it was only last night, supposedly. That's only nine hours ago, maybe a little more, maybe a little less. The rumor will get more traction today and tomorrow. But, allegedly, it was some girl—a freshman, of course—by Centre Village Commons, about a ten-minute drive from the city campus. It's student-preferred housing, and since freshmen aren't allowed to live off campus, I'm guessing it was at or near some party out there."

"Freshman girls, though," Brycen said, shaking his head in amazement. "I mean, it's always freshmen? How does whoever's doing this even know that these girls are freshmen? And how is it always the same story, the same formula step by step?"

"I'm telling you guys," Riley said after taking a sip of his orange juice, "I don't think it's real."

Trust, Kyler, and Allison looked to Riley, their expressions surprised.

"What do you mean?" Allison spoke up for the group.

"I mean like I said," Riley said, looking back at them. "I think it's just a story, a myth almost. I think it's all fake, though. Maybe these so-called 'victims' are the ones keeping the story alive once they hear about the Freesef Society when they get to UCC. By saying they were a victim, it gets them attention amongst their little circle of friends, and then their friends probably spread the story, which gets them popular, and so on.

"Or maybe it's a guy, or a group of guys, making up some story about a girl, I don't know. It doesn't really matter. The bottom line is, rape and sexual assault are serious crimes that get a lot of attention, particularly on college campuses, particularly on *this* college campus. The administration here prides itself on having a consistently low rate of sexual assaults on campus and sexual assaults involving university students in the city. We're, like, top five in the nation, is what they told us when I was a freshman—remember, Holden? And we're best overall when you factor in the large number of students that go here.

"If these stories we always hear about were true—about some secret group that consistently and flagrantly goes after a specific, vulnerable part of the student population—don't you think someone besides just the students would be talking about it? We get those campus alert messages when a crime has been reported. You think it's realistic that, out of all the alleged 'victims' this top-secret society that every student on campus knows about has supposedly assaulted, that none of them—*none*—would report it to the police? Not even one?

"And what about Chancellor Beverly? I know you guys"—Riley gestured to Trust, Kyler, and Allison—"have only been here a week and may not have had many chances to see and hear Beverly do her thing, but take it from me. She's goes hard, particularly when it comes to students. She's Centre City all the way. If she even got a whiff of some new Freesef Society...conspiracy, in which students were being repeatedly victimized, do you think she would just stand idly by and let it happen? No way, Jose! She'd probably go after the people involved herself, like Rambo, and she'd probably find them pretty quick."

"She spoke at a meeting with Disability Services before school started," Brycen said. "She's a good speaker. And you're right, she seems like she would be the first one to get tough if the situation called for it."

"And don't forget the university police. City police, too. The entire UCC faculty. Everyone's keeping it a secret? Why? That's why I think it's just a myth—something interesting to tell incoming freshmen. Then some girls take it too far to get some attention."

The others at the table were quiet for a moment.

*Makes sense*, Trust signed.

"Eh," Holden voiced uncertainly, "I don't know. I mean, what you're saying seems logical, but some of these stories just seem too...real, I guess. And then to hear these girls saying they won't go to the police or the administration because they are suddenly now part of the 'in' crowd—it just seems too authentic to be just a goof a group of girls make up once in a while. There's got to be more to it than that."

By now, the plates on the table were, for the most part, empty. Meanwhile, more students, and some adults—most likely administrators who found themselves on the Centre City rural campus this Sunday morning—were beginning to stream in at an increased frequency as the breakfast hours rolled on and lunchtime loomed in the near future.

Trust's hands glided nimbly through the air in front of him.

*In the Big Lie, there is always a certain force of credibility. The broad masses, in the primitive simplicity of their minds, more readily fall victims to the Big Lie than the small one. It would never come into their heads to fabricate colossal untruths, and they would not believe that others could have the impudence to distort the truth so infamously. Even though the facts which prove this to be so may be brought clearly to their*

151

*minds, they will still doubt and waver and continue to think that there may be some other explanation. For the grossly impudent lie always leaves traces behind, even after it has been nailed down.*

Brycen's eyebrows rose as he finished translating Trust's sentiment.

"So, we're quoting *Mein Kampf* now?" he asked. "Why didn't anybody tell me?"

Trust could only shrug.

"Well," Kyler said, bringing his hands down onto the tabletop with finality, "all this confusing gay/Freesef Society/Nazi fascism talk has gotten me hungry again. Who else is in the mood for seconds?"

Trust, his expression incredulous, glanced to Allison. The girl chuckled as she shook her head.

Kyler was standing, surveying the other people at the table.

"Really?" he questioned them all, before shifting his eyes back to Trust. "Dude, I know you're still hungry. You just finished at the gym. You're going to make me go up there alone?"

"I'll go with you," Riley spoke up, grinning, to which Brycen laughed.

*I'll be up there in a second,* Trust signed.

Kyler grinned and headed back toward the food.

"So, what about that run-in you guys had last night?" Holden asked.

Trust looked to Allison, indicating that she should speak.

"We went to—I guess it was a frat party—outside the city."

Trust nodded.

"It was a lot of people at this house that seemed to be on the edge of nowhere," she continued. "Some of the football players were even there. It was actually one of them who brought up the Freesef Society stuff— that was the first time I had heard of it."

"One of the players?" Riley asked. "Cool."

Allison shook her head.

"I don't know if 'cool' is the right word. The guy was drunk and probably high on who-knows-what. Trust thinks he might have been drugged. The guy was acting really weird, almost like he was trying to scare us with that Freesef stuff, something about we're just what they're looking for. Marcie was there, too, and—"

"Oh, crap," said Holden.

"—and frankly, if she and Paxson and Trust and Kyler weren't there, I would have left right then."

Trust was gesturing toward Brycen. The graduate student leaned forward.

"Jeremy Higgins? He was the guy?"

"Yeah, that's it," Allison said. "I forgot his name. I guess he plays...catcher?"

The others chuckled, except for Holden.

"Jeremy said that to you?" he asked. "I know him. He's usually pretty cool."

Trust looked at the RA expectantly. Before he could sign anything, however, the others at the table suddenly looked behind him, toward the food stations. He soon spotted what had caught their attention.

Kyler, with a plate already in his hand, was shouting across the cafeteria toward them. The distance was great, but Trust was still able to make out his lips.

"Dude, this lady's cooking cinnamon apple French toast up here!"

Trust turned back to the table, his eyebrow crooked upward, a smirk hinting at his lips.

*Boyfriend's calling*, teased Brycen, his hands moving swiftly.

Trust's face contorted more, as though he had just taken a huge bite from a particularly sour lemon. His subsequent hand gesture toward Brycen hardly needed to be interpreted for the others.

They all laughed.

## 13.
## Flashes on the Centre Line

HIS BACKPACK SLUNG LOOSELY ACROSS one shoulder, Trust followed the stream of students also exiting the Decatur Building, emerging onto the busy sidewalk in metropolitan Centre City in early afternoon hours. The sun was high in the sky, high enough not to be obscured by the tall buildings that lined the city streets, able to illuminate every section of typically shadowed real estate in dazzling sunlight. Some of the people outside—ranging from the casually dressed college students to more formally attired corporate employees—already wore sunglasses to shield their eyes from the harsh glare.

Pulling his own shades out, Trust followed suit.

The Arnie J. Decatur Building was a part of UCC's urban campus, which comprised several buildings intermixed with the many other non-university-affiliated structures making up the cityscape. Along with several institutional venues, there were also dormitory buildings downtown, offering students signed up for university housing—and anyone outside of freshman status—the choice between urban living and the slower, more controlled lifestyle of Centre City's rural campus grounds. Freshman students were not given the same option, as they were assigned a university dorm by the Housing Department and almost exclusively designated to the country campus.

From the Decatur Building, it was barely a two-minute walk to the bus stop, where the Centre Line bus would take Trust back to Weaver Hall on the rural campus, just outside the main city limits. The aforementioned bus eased to a halt at the stop just as Trust arrived, and with a wait of only seconds, he was on board, sitting near the back. Slipping off his sunglasses again, he glanced to his phone.

155

From stepping out of the Decatur Building to settling into his seat, two minutes and thirteen seconds had elapsed.

New world record, Trust mused, chuckling to himself.

The bus maneuvered away from the street curb, quickly becoming enveloped in the downtown traffic again. It was only moderately filled at this time of day, and empty seats were plainly noticeable along portions of the bus. The other riders were mostly students, though there were more than a few occupants healthily over conventional college age. The Centre Line transit system served the entirety of Centre City and surrounding towns. It was also a primary form of transportation—other than personal vehicles—in, out, and around the rural UCC grounds. As it maintained a partnership with the university, students rode the Centre Line free of charge, while other citizens frequenting Centre City paid a nominal fee.

In time, and after a few more intermediate stops as they began to leave the immediate surroundings of downtown, the traffic improved, the bus driver able to cruise more easily through the less congested roads. Outside Trust's window, the scenery gradually transformed, the large, towering structures made with brick, steel, and concrete transitioning into more open land, less expansive houses and shops, and greenery.

With stops included, the usual time between the Decatur Building bus stop and the stop near Weaver Hall was twenty minutes. Trust glanced across the bus aisle, toward the large window facing an empty row of chairs, and then looked forward, his eyes falling on an older woman in one of the aisle-facing seats at the front, her attention absorbed in a book.

Trust's eyes then flitted just beside her as a man stood. His action seemed rushed and unexpected as he sprang out of his seat.

The older woman with the book startled, looking up at the man.

The man immediately turned toward the bus driver. Trust could not tell what the man was saying, or if he was saying anything at all. The bus mirror, stretching the length of the driver's side, was blocked by the man's body, and since his back was turned, lipreading was impossible.

Trust started to look away, toward the window on the opposite side of the bus again, before his attention caught on a girl—most likely a student like himself—sitting midway down the length of the bus, rows ahead of him. Trust was only able to see the side of her face, her attention aimed at the goings-on at the front as well, her eyes noticeably widened.

Like a photograph, his glance and scrutiny of the girl only taking a millisecond, Trust's eyes swiveled toward the front again. The man was turning around.

The bus was pulling over onto the looser gravel along the side of the road.

"All right, listen up!" the man ordered. "Everyone's hands in the air!"

Even though he was nearly a full bus length away, Trust could read the agitated man's mouth clearly. Also clear was the fact that the man seemed to be shouting, which further emphasized his lip movements.

However, it was the handgun the man was wildly wielding that was attracting the most attention.

"I want everything in everyone's pockets! I want cell phones and wallets! I want your music players, your computer tablets, everything, in this bag! I only want to see your hands lowered when you're putting stuff into the bag!"

The man continued to wave the gun around as he spoke, the firearm briefly ghosting across each of the passengers on the bus. It passed over Trust's spot a few times, not pausing as it was brandished through the air.

"Let's make this quick!" the man instructed. "I don't want to—"

He abruptly turned toward the bus driver, the pistol now centered steadily on the driver's hat. Again, Trust was not able to see what the man was saying, though he could tell he was distressed. Abruptly, he pulled the bus driver out of his seat, shoving him to one of the open aisle-facing chairs at the front.

"And that goes for all of you!" the man said, turning to face the bus once again, while still keeping the driver in his peripheral vision, the gun again flashing around toward the other passengers. "No quick moves, no trying to call anyone, no running! I will shoot—put it down, and put your hands up! I will shoot you if you try to run, or you try to call for help. Start putting the stuff in the bag! Now!"

He was holding a black trash bag out toward the first person sitting just behind the driver's seat, glancing toward the bus driver still in an attempt to warn him off any further actions. The gun swung between the college girl currently holding the bag and dropping items into it, and the indiscriminate riders his furtive eyes searched out as he looked around.

"Let's go! Hurry up! Faster!"

The handgun flashed toward the opposite side, farther down the aisle.

"Keep your hands up, I said! That's the last time I'm going to say it! Next time someone looks like they're trying to do something stupid and I'll shoot you in the head! Don't test me!"

In his row toward the back, Trust—his hands still raised—was sliding away from the window and toward the aisle, getting ready to stand—

"Get up! Sit up straight!"

The man's attention had pivoted to another rider, his gun trained menacingly. He then turned to back to the nearest hostage.

"Let's go! Pass the bag quickly and put your hands back in the air!"

Trust slowly stood. Almost immediately, the gun swung in his direction, the man stepping back slightly. His eyes darted across the faces of the other commuters.

"Sit down! Now! Get back in your seat!" the man shouted vehemently.

Trust took on a look of confusion, shaking his head and gesturing toward his ears. He started moving up the aisle, very slowly.

"I said sit down!" the man yelled louder, his eyes continuing to flit around to the other occupants of the bus briefly before centering again on Trust.

Trust shook his head in uncertainty.

Still slowly moving forward.

"Hey, sit down, dude. Are you crazy?" another boy sitting near where Trust currently stood whispered fervently.

Trust, glimpsing the boy trying to get his attention from the corner of his eye, did not turn to look in his direction. He did, however, lower one of his hands, reaching slowly toward his pocket.

The man holding the gun took an aggressive step forward down the aisle toward Trust.

"Hey, stop moving! Stop moving now! Keep your hands in the air!"

Trust halted, but his hands went toward his ears again.

Then, he gestured.

*Do you understand me?*

"I said keep your hands up!"

The man then glanced quickly toward the rider presently holding the bag, which was slowly filling up.

"Keep going!" he ordered. "Put the stuff in the bag and pass it! I didn't say stop!"

Trust had slowly started to move forward again as the man's attention was temporarily—

"Hey, I said stop moving and sit down! I ain't saying it again!"

The man now gripped the gun with both hands, his widened, manic eyes aimed squarely on the deaf student.

"Sit down now! Right there!"

The gun was waved briefly to the row of seats to Trust's left, one of which—the seat closest to the window—was already occupied by a visibly frightened student. The boy's hands were straight up in the air, a phone gripped tightly in one palm.

Still acting bewildered, Trust pointed to the boy next to the window while still keeping his gaze toward the man with the gun.

"Sit down there!" the man repeated, his patience clearly wearing thin. This was an unexpected disturbance to his already shaky plan. His attention quickly turned away again to check the other passengers.

"Keep passing the bag! Stop stalling!"

The man's gaze returned to see Trust leaning across the row of seats, wrenching the cell phone out of the other student's raised hand.

"Hey! Hey! What are you doing?" the man said, taking a few quick steps toward Trust, who was still more than a few rows away.

Trust, the phone now in his grasp and his hands raised again, turned slowly back toward the man. He pointed to the boy still in his seat, who now seemed terrified of both the man with the gun and Trust. Trust then motioned toward the phone, and then offered it to the man.

"No, sit down, sit down!" the man ordered, motioning again to the seat, before once more sweeping the gun across the other faces on the bus.

"Keep your hands up now! I'm serious! I'm watching everyone!"

The man, who had been keeping up with the progress of the bag, was slowly edging closer to Trust. Trust began his measured approach again, again holding the cell phone out to the man.

"Hold it! Stop right there!" the man said, the gun trained on Trust's chest. "Okay. Do you understand what I am saying to you?"

Trust once more shook his head in confusion, lowering his arms to signal to his ears again.

"Keep...your...hands...up!" the man said in frustration. "Okay. Slowly,

slowly, come put the phone in the bag. Slowly."

He gestured in an embellished manner toward the trash bag that was nearing the row where Trust stood. The man had stopped moving alongside the bag, now having fallen a few rows behind its progress.

Trust gestured toward the bag.

The man nodded vehemently, indicating toward the bag again.

Trust slowly moved forward, his hands back in the air. The man mirrored the teenager's careful movements, fleetingly looking around and behind him toward the other passengers. The two reached the desired row at the same moment, Trust stopping at the row just behind, the man halting at the row ahead. The bag was held still by a woman sitting in the aisle seat. In her lap, the opened trash bag trembled as her hands shook in fear.

Trust gestured to the bag again.

"Put the phone in the bag," the man ordered, "and then sit down. Everyone, keep your hands up! I mean it, or I'm shooting this kid first!"

Trust edged forward, turning sideways slightly so as to be able to reach toward the bag. He glanced toward the man again, his face—he hoped—conveying some fear.

Inside, he only felt acutely aware.

"Don't try anything stu—"

As Trust was lowering his hand, the cell phone slipped from his fingers. He cleverly moved his body, and then his legs, in an attempt to slow the phone's descent before it hit the floor.

There were a few gasps through the relative stillness of the bus. With widened eyes, Trust looked to the man holding the gun a few feet from his face.

"Are you kidding me?" the man huffed in frustration.

After a cursory survey of the other riders, his frenzied gaze returned to Trust.

"Pick the phone up—slowly—and put it in the bag."

Trust slowly kneeled down toward the floor, one hand still raised in the air above his head, the man with the handgun edging slightly closer, the firearm drawing within inches of the deaf teen's head.

Trust's hand gripped the phone as the steel of the weapon came into contact with the hair on his head.

He paused.

"Now get up, and put the phone in the bag," the man growled.

Trust, his head turned down and away from the man's face, could not see his mouth move. Still, he sensed the man was speaking.

In the still, silent air of the bus, he could feel it.

He did not move. The pressure of the gun barrel on his head intensified.

"I said get up and—"

As Trust slowly started to rise, his head swayed forward slightly.

The gun barrel did not immediately follow his movements, the man apparently not expecting the shift.

His mistake.

Trust acted instantly. Pulling forward even more, the gun barrel was no longer aimed at his head as Trust shot his phone-filled hand abruptly upward, meeting the bottom of the man's wrist squarely. The blow forced the man's hand up, at the same time sharply driving his wrist into an upsetting angle, his fingers instantly splaying open as he began to lose his grip on the gun. Before the rush of pain could even register, however, Trust's other hand was pushing the man's arm higher still. He immediately began taking a dominant grip on the weapon where the man's had weakened a split instant before. Trust's first hand—the one that had landed the initial strike on the underside of the man's wrist—was already coming forward, aimed just under the still-stunned man's jaw.

His fist connected violently with the man's jawbone not even two seconds after he had started his move.

New world record.

The man's limp—and, most likely, fractured—hand slipped off the gun completely as he started to fall back, Trust clutching the weapon firmly. Tucking the cell phone still in his hand into his pocket, he moved forward as the man fell, not in an attempt to catch him, but readying himself for further action.

There was no need. The man hit the aisle floor, solidly, limply, like a stiff doll, his arms seemingly locked into place, his unprotected head striking against the floor of the city bus. The man—fortunately or unfortunately—did not feel it, already unconscious from Trust's punch before he hit the ground.

Crouching over the unresponsive man, Trust hurriedly checked for a pulse.

The man was dead to the world, but still absolutely alive.

Trust glanced up, looking around. All eyes were fixed on him, most of them conveying some degree of shock and panic.

Gesturing with his hands as he stood, he mimed binding his hands together and then pointed to the unconscious man lying on the floor.

There was a moment's hesitation from those on board. Trust began to mimic tying his wrists together again, but movement at the front caught his attention.

It was the bus driver.

"Duc-duct tape. I've got some duct..."

The man moved toward a cabinet panel near the driver's seat, away from Trust's view. Quickly he turned back, a hefty roll of industrial-strength duct tape in hand, Trust's attentive gaze on him the entire time. Trust could still sense the many eyes aimed toward him. He glanced around again.

He then stood as the bus driver approached.

As the man handed the roll of tape over, he looked around the interior of the bus as well.

"Is everybody all right?" he called out. "Does anyone need medical attention? Does anyone need to go to the hospital right now?"

He received no verbal reply in the affirmative, a few of those who were finally surfacing from the shock of what had just occurred shaking their heads faintly.

The individual on the bus requiring the most immediate medical attention did not have the wherewithal to speak.

"Okay, then," the bus driver breathed out. "Okay."

Trust, meanwhile, missed the entire exchange, busy performing his own operation on the unconscious man. The driver kneeled down, watching Trust finish tying the man's hands and ankles. Trust worked quickly, as though he had performed the same task before.

He could feel the bus driver's labored, adrenaline-fueled breathing and looked up. The driver gestured to the man on the ground.

"He isn't...uh...you know..."

Through with the tape, Trust gave the driver a brief, unruffled gaze as he returned the roll. He began to hand over the gun as well. Even though Trust was holding the gun by the barrel, his fingers nowhere near the trigger, the driver shrank away from the offering.

"Whoa, whoa, whoa. Watch where you point that thing, son."

If anything, the gun was aimed more toward Trust than anyone else on the bus, and the teenager looked at the driver in slight confusion. He then retracted the weapon, expertly engaging the release, the magazine falling out at the same time he pulled the slide, the bullet in the chamber springing out of the slide opening, Trust catching it nimbly in his hand. An instant later, the entire barrel was removed, the firing spring unattached.

He offered the disassembled, thoroughly disabled gun to the driver again. For a moment, the bus driver was motionless, astonished at Trust's proficiency with the weapon, reducing it to spare parts in seconds. He looked from the weapon sections to the boy, only responding when Trust again beckoned silently for him to take the firearm.

"All right, all right," the bus driver voiced, at last holding out his hands. He grimaced further as Trust gave him the pieces.

"Argh, I do not like guns."

He then returned to Trust.

"You're one ice-cold cucumber, you know that?"

Trust gave the man another look of puzzlement, and then motioned around for something to write with. In what was still only minutes after the tremendous turn of events, all eyes were still fully trained on Trust—and now, the bus driver. The riders who had not put their belongings in the trash bag searched for what Trust had motioned for.

Quickly, a loose sheet of paper and a pen were passed to him.

*My name is Trustice, and I am deaf. I am a student. I assume we are now way behind schedule. It is your decision as to whether you drive to the nearest police station or call the police to meet us somewhere along the route, and what to do with the other riders.*

*However, I would appreciate it if you didn't mention what I did to anyone outside the police.*

*I'll drag him to the back.*

The bus driver read over Trust's shoulder as he wrote. He lifted his cap slightly with one hand, scratching at his bald head.

"Okay, then. Well."

He glanced to Trust, who was looking back at him.

"All right. Let's do this."

The driver then looked back down toward the disassembled weapon in his hands, as if still uncertain what to do with it. He started walking to the front of the bus.

Then, he stopped.

"Hey, has anyone called the cops yet?"

Trust, not paying attention, grabbed the unconscious man's bound ankles and began to drag him back down the aisle toward the rear, where Trust had originally been sitting. As he started to pass one row, however, he did a double take as he recognized the rider.

Trust put the man's feet down again and retrieved the paper and pen he had borrowed. He wrote out a quick note, tearing off the piece and then grabbing the cell phone out of his pocket. He handed both over to the student sitting in the window seat.

*Sorry about that,* the message read. *Hope it still works all right.*

A few moments later, Trust had his answer. The other boy grinned faintly.

"It's all good, man," he said. "Thanks a lot."

Trust grinned, tipping his head slightly in a nod.

Suddenly, the other student's eyes darted to the man on the ground, Trust's gaze following.

Though the man's eyes were still closed, he had an agonized look on his face.

Trust picked up the man's ankles again, towing him toward the rear.


AS THE CENTRE LINE BUS pulled up at the next stop a few minutes later, two Centre City Police Department patrol cars were already waiting nearby, lights flashing. An officer came on board through the front entrance, while another cop went to the back exit doors to meet riders who were disembarking.

"You okay, Mr. Jackson? You remember me?"

Reuben Jackson, the bus driver, nodded, his lips curling faintly.

"Ben Ryan. The trainee with the lead foot."

Officer Ryan glanced down briefly to his pocket-sized notebook, hiding a slight grin of his own.

"Okay. Where is this guy?"

"He's in the back," Mr. Jackson answered, tilting his head toward the rear of the bus, the police officer following his indication and glancing back as well. "I think he's awake now—or semiconscious, at least. We got him trussed up like a Thanksgiving turkey back there, so he ain't moving until you're ready to take him out."

"All right," Ryan replied. "Here's the plan. We're going to secure him first, and then I've got some questions that I need to ask. Altogether, it shouldn't take too long. Now, you reported a firearm on board as well? I'll take that off your hands, if you don't mind."

"Oh, yeah, yeah," Mr. Jackson said, jumping into action and opening the cabinet door. "It's right in—"

"Allow me," Ryan declared, stopping the driver and reaching in.

He pulled out the disassembled barrel. Looking to the bus driver questioningly, the young officer reached in again, feeling and pulling out the rest of the weapon.

"Okay," he drew out, chuckling faintly. "When you said there was a gun, I thought you meant one that...you know. I'm guessing you did this, Mr. Jackson?"

Mr. Jackson was already shaking his head.

"I can hardly stand the things."

"Really? So, you didn't take it apart?"

"What? No...I mean, yeah, yeah. No."

"Mr. Jackson?"

"Huh?"

Ryan looked at the man.

"Okay," he said again, "we'll circle back to that one later. Any other firearms on board that you are aware of?"

"No, sir, officer."

Ryan turned to face the rest of the bus. Only a few passengers had opted to get off, and of those, all had been planning to disembark anyway, since it was their stop. The rest of the riders stayed put.

"Ladies and gentlemen, this will only take a few moments of your time, and we'll have you back on the road as soon as possible. Is anyone currently carrying a gun or any other weapon on their person? If so, please let me know now, so this process will go a whole lot quicker for the both of us."

After no one volunteered any such information, Ryan started down the aisle.

"All right, this will only take a moment, and then I and the other officer will get your contact information and schedule a more appropriate time to hear from you about what happened here. Excuse me..."

Ryan soon reached the man "trussed up like a Thanksgiving turkey." The man was sitting alone in a row, his hands—and, the officer quickly observed, his feet—roped tightly together with duct tape, the hooded jacket he wore askew, showing a thin undershirt. His mouth was also taped shut.

The expression visible on the man's face looked to be a combination of frustration and anguish.

From the bound man, the officer's eyes shifted to the row behind, which held the last passenger still on the bus, toward the closest passenger. The college-aged teenager looking back at him appeared harmless enough, though the boy's startling blue eyes—particularly in contrast with his African-American skin tone—was a look the young officer had never come across.

"Did you put this guy here?" Ryan inquired before he could stop himself, motioning to the tied man. "Did you do this?"

Trust took on an uncomprehending expression, gesturing to his ears. Then, as if just remembering, he reached into his book bag pocket, pulling out one of his cards. He handed it to the police officer.

*Hello.*
*My name is Trustice, and I am deaf.*

"Oh, okay. Sorry," Ryan said, nodding.

The imprisoned man turned around slightly in his seat, looking over his shoulder at the deaf boy.

Trust, catching his eye, grinned faintly.

166

# 14.
# Rory, Another Robbery

AFTERNOONS AT THE NORTH GYM were busier than the mornings.

In spite of that, however, Trustice Jeffries was alone in the boxing ring. To keep him company, he had pulled in one of the fighting dummies as well.

Trust's combat movements were swift, calculated, and precise. His punches and strikes toward the stationary mannequin—which was shaped as the torso, head, and shoulders of a human form with its hands raised—were lightning quick and growing quicker as he pushed himself to move more rapidly, his hands and arms becoming a blur of motion, the only evidence of his strikes the crack of impact and momentary recoil of the fighting mannequin as it reacted to the punishing effects of the blows. Trust circled and ducked about after each series of combinations, sometimes skirting completely around the dummy only to materialize on the other side, quickly striking out again and pummeling his target before it could know what hit it...if it had a brain. His cracks landed hard and at varying locations—rib cage, obliques, abdomen, upper chest, clavicle, shoulders, elbows, hands, neck, and, most brutally, the head, which caved in fleetingly after each violent strike, only to then pop back into shape again as though nothing had happened.

Any questions as to whether Trust's opponent would fare any differently had it been a live being instead of a mannequin were questions only the dummy would ask.

The answers were clear.

As Trust began to shift again a spilt second after shooting a roundhouse jolt to the mannequin's left temple, the fluttering movement of someone entering the ring captured his notice. He slowed and glanced over.

It was a girl, a young woman. She was not presently dressed in common gym attire, her jean shorts formfitting and showing ample leg and thigh, and her curly hair hanging in loose ringlets across her shoulders, slightly obscuring her face. Her shirt was relaxed and thin, suitable for the summer Centre City heat, as were her stylish sandals.

It was Jezzie from the party over a week earlier.

Jezzie, Jeremy's "girl."

Jezzie was effortlessly beautiful, and she was smirking.

Trust hoped his gulp went unnoticed.

"Well, fancy seeing you here," she commented teasingly, Trust obviously missing her tone, but seeing it plainly on her face. "Not sure I would have taken you as the MMA type, but since you have a bit less clothing on than the last time I saw you, I can see I was mistaken."

Starting to breathe slightly harder than usual from his exertions, Trust could not restrain himself as his eyebrow raised. He glanced down to his gym clothes. Athletic high-top sneakers, loose shorts that came down to his knees, a well-worn T-shirt, training gloves.

His gaze returned to the girl. She had stepped closer.

"Oh, don't look at me like that," she said, still smiling. "Just take it as a compliment. Don't read into it too deep."

Slipping off a glove, Trust held up a finger, beckoning Jezzie to wait while he retrieved his pen and note cards. He was writing something down on one of the cards as he returned.

*So, to what do I owe the honor?*

Jezzie looked up after reading the card, her flirtatious grin coming back full force.

"Um, maybe I came to ask you to teach me how to box?" she replied, tilting her head slightly.

Trust arched his eyebrow again, giving Jezzie a skeptical look. The girl feigned surprise.

"What? Is that so hard to believe?"

Trust eyed her for a moment before he wrote:

*No offense, but you're the kind of girl who provokes fights,*
*not the one that becomes involved in them.*

It was Jezzie's turn to raise an eyebrow, though her smile remained.

"Oh, that's good. You're good. And you're lucky you don't talk, because I would like to see if you had the guts to say that out loud to me."

Trust smiled, a light chuckle coming from his throat. He started writing again.

*Speaking of fights, how's Jeremy? I assume you both got home okay after that party?*

"Yeah. That's really why I came over here to talk to you. I'm here to meet one of my girlfriends, but I'm a little early and she's still in her spinning class. But yeah, Jeremy's fine now. I still don't really understand what happened, though. It was like you said, like he was drugged or high on something. It got a little worse after we got home. He was really sluggish and slow, and he kept saying he was dizzy. It was like he was roofied. I kept giving him water like your friend said, and he passed out. But, besides a hangover, he was back to normal the next day.

"And the weirdest thing about it is that he barely remembers the party. He doesn't remember talking to you guys, or even seeing you there. I don't know if it was just a weird mixture of drinks he had, or maybe even if he was slipped something...like I said, he's not the guy who experiments with different things—especially if it would keep him from being able to play football. He stays miles away from that kind of stuff. But, I mean...I don't know what else it could be..."

*Being drugged is possible, though then the question becomes why anyone would want to do that.*

Jezzie looked up from the card, biting her lower lip nervously. Whether she was aware of it or not, it was an oddly endearing gesture.

"Yeah, or maybe it could have been meant for someone else and he took it by mistake, or..."

Trust saw the shiver wind its way through Jezzie's body. She wrapped her arms around herself.

"I don't know," she went on. "I'm not sure I even want to know. And there's not much use in speculating. The whole thing's done with now, and I know Jeremy and I both will be watching to make sure it doesn't happen—"

Trust's eyes flitted away.

He spotted them as they slowly, leisurely, ambled toward the boxing ring he and Jezzie stood in. They acted unconcerned, joking about and lightly pushing each other as they passed by the busy basketball courts, but one too many glances toward the ring had caught Trust's notice, and now he observed that the group was indeed advancing toward them.

Trust's diverted attention must have alerted Jezzie. She turned around to look as well, following his gaze.

From his position—now standing slightly behind Jezzie relative to the group of boys approaching—Trust could not see what the girl said once she saw their approach, though she did put her hands on her hips, her body language tensing.

One boy, leading the pack, smirked wickedly as he ran the final steps before hopping onto the ring apron.

"Aw, we were just hanging out, Jez," the boy was saying to her. "A couple of the guys were already up here lifting weights. You having a problem with guys following you around?"

His eyes shifted to Trust.

"'Cause we'll handle it to make sure you're okay."

Trust's eyes went to Jezzie as she turned to look at him.

"Sorry, Trust," she said.

She then nodded toward the others.

"This is Rory and his merry band of rejects—I mean, friends. They're all friends of Jeremy's."

"Aw, Jez, really?" said another boy, who now stood on the ring apron as well. "We're not just Jeremy's friends; we're your friends, too."

Jezzie issued a mocking grin.

"Anyway, aren't you going to introduce us to your friend?" Rory inquired, his expression both inquisitive and amused.

Sooner than Jezzie could give him a reply, Trust nudged her to bring her attention to what he had already written.

*Tell him that I've met him before.*

Jezzie relayed the message, and Rory's eyes widened slightly in surprise.

"We're passing notes now?" Rory asked. "What is this, middle school?"

Trust grinned faintly. He wrote again.

*See? He wants to fight me now, and it's because of you.*

Jezzie shook her head, though Trust's statement brought a faint, and this time genuine, smile to her lips.

"Hello? Yeah, over here," Rory called out, waving his arms. "You going to tell us who your pen pal is or what?"

"His name is Trust," Jezzie answered. "He writes because he's deaf and I don't happen to be fluent in sign language."

Trust wrote another message.

*Will you also be signing up for sign language classes to go along with your fighting lessons?*

"Oh, I remember!" the boy standing beside Rory declared. "You were at the party the other week, right? After the first game? Yeah, I think I remember seeing you, but honestly, my memory is a little fuzzy about that night. I think I got pretty wasted."

The other boys laughed. Trust grinned again. No one was mentioning the incident that had occurred in the very ring they were all centered around, and Trust easily recalled half of the boys presently in attendance also being at hand then, including Rory.

*What's his name?*

"That's Oliver," Jezzie said. "Out of the whole group, he's probably the most human. And he's funny."

"Well, I'll definitely take that," Oliver said, bowing graciously as he leaned across the ring ropes.

"What's he writing?" Rory asked, motioning to Trust's cards.

Jezzie took one of the cards out of Trust's hands.

"Well, just now he wrote, 'What's his name?' to which you heard me answer, 'That's Oliver.' And then, before that, he wrote, 'Who's that annoyingly nosy guy with the hat? Ten bucks says he's going to ask you what I'm writing.'"

Trust shook his head, though one side of his mouth lifted in a grin.

"Oooh," voiced Oliver in appreciation, echoed by a few of the other boys still down on the floor. "That's a burn, Ror. She totally burned you."

"Whatever," Rory said, shoving Oliver slightly. His attention returned to Jezzie. "So, you coming with us or what? We're gonna go meet up with Jeremy and then get something to eat."

"Yeah...no. I'm meeting some friends here and then *we* are going to get something to eat."

"Uh-huh. Does Jeremy know?"

Jezzie looked at the boy in disbelief.

"Does Jere—argh!"

She rounded on Trust.

"Trust, please, *please* punch him in the face right now for thinking—or worse, for assuming—that I would need my boyfriend's permission to do absolutely anything!"

She returned to Rory.

"And yes, actually, Jeremy does know, because *I* told him yesterday what *I* was going to be doing."

Rory looked at Jezzie silently for a moment, one edge of his mouth ticking up slightly. He shrugged.

"Okay, suit yourself. I was just putting the offer out there. Didn't know you had plans already."

His eyes shifted back to Trust. He gazed at the freshman without speaking, as though sizing him up, or perhaps wondering what exactly Trust and Jezzie were doing together.

Trust, unmoved, returned his stare.

"What are we waiting for, Ror? Let's go, dude," one of the boys standing on the gym floor said.

Rory chuckled softly, darkly, his head tilting down just enough that he had to look up through his eyelashes. Trust, not able to hear his tone, had no trouble spotting the characteristics of snide amusement detailing the older boy's features.

At last breaking his gaze, Rory looked one last time at Jezzie.

"All right, Jez. I'll be sure to tell him I saw you."

Jezzie huffed, rolling her eyes and crossing her arms.

"Yeah. I'm sure it will be the first thing out of your mouth."

Rory laughed again, this time louder, before springing down from the ring apron, Oliver mirroring his movements. Oliver turned back to the ring, though, as the rest of the group started to depart.

"Good meetin' ya, Trust," he called out, gesturing to the deaf teenager. "Maybe I'll see you at the next shindig. Bring a wooden leg!"

His good-bye returned Rory's gaze to the fighting ring as well. Rory gave Trust a casual mock-salute, the smirk on his face eerily reminiscent of the one Jeremy Higgins typically displayed. Trust wondered fleetingly if Rory's version of the smirk was natural or practiced.

He smiled back at the other boy in return. His attention then turned back to Jezzie.

"Ugh, sometimes I just can't stand those guys," she said as she ran both hands through her hair.

Trust scribbled on one of the cards.

*And here I thought he only acted like that around me.*

Jezzie smiled.

"Nope, not even close," she intoned. "Rory's default switch is set to obnoxious."

She then reached into her pocket, pulling out her phone.

"And that would be Alyssa finally finishing with yoga."

She typed back a quick reply. When she looked back up, Trust was already holding out another card.

*See you next time. Glad to hear Jeremy turned out okay. Tell him his crazy freshman friends said hello.*

Jezzie smiled, her full, naturally pouty lips, as always, drawing Trust's eyes.

"I'll be sure to tell him," she said. "He'll be glad to hear it. See you around, Trust."

She delivered another tantalizing grin, and Trust watched her as she turned and started across the ring, reaching the ropes and climbing through, scaling down to the gym floor. She started to walk away, but quickly turned around again.

"Oh, I almost forgot! I wanted to apologize again for the things Jeremy said at that party, particularly to your friend—you know, the one with the red hair? I'm sure Jeremy would just as soon apologize to her himself—to all of you. He didn't even believe he said that stuff when I told him. But still, it's no excuse for saying it."

Writing as he walked, Trust came to the edge of the ring and leaned down, showing his reply to Jezzie.

*She's in one of my classes. I'll pass it along. Her name is Allison.*

The girl looked back at Trust, a gleam in her eye.

"She wouldn't happen to be your girlfriend, now would she?"

Trust stared at Jezzie a moment, his face showing the slightest, faintest trace of a smile.

He then shook his head slowly.

Jezzie smiled brighter, laughing.

"See you, Trust."

Trust gave her a small wave. As she began to make her way back through the gymnasium area, Trust spotted most of the other male eyes in the gymnasium shift toward her. On one of the basketball courts, one player was nearly beaned in the head, paying more attention to the passing girl than he was to the ongoing game.

Trust grinned, chuckling. He went to lay his pen and note cards down, before returning to the fighting dummy.

He was barely able to make one complete revolution around the mannequin, however, before he sensed someone else's presence.

This visitor was hardly a surprise.

Trust made a sudden cut to the left, dodging completely behind the mannequin. Now, facing his company, he pushed the dummy forward slightly.

The fighting mannequin came alive, suddenly on the attack.

Kyler put up his hands.

"Whatcha want, huh?" he challenged the dummy, dancing around on his feet. "Whatcha want?"

The boy swung out. Trust moved the mannequin to the side, avoiding the jab. Trust then laughed loudly.

"Oh, you're not even going to suck me into this," Kyler declared. "I'm not losing a fight to a dummy. No one could land a shot on that thing with you controlling it."

Grinning, Trust rose back to his full height, coming from around the mannequin.

*You'll never guess who you just missed,* he gestured before he began to take off his fighting gloves.

"Who?" Kyler asked. "Allison was here?"

Trust made a face.

*Wow,* he responded.

"What? Was it her? Shut up! Come on, who was it?"

*Jezzie.*

Kyler's eyes widened.

"Jezzie, as in Jezzie from the party Jezzie? Jezzie, as in Jeremy Higgins's girlfriend Jezzie? That Jezzie?"

*How many Jezzies do you know, man?*

Trust picked up the mannequin, preparing to move it out of the ring. He kept his eyes on Kyler.

"I'm just surprised, that's all."

Kyler then did a quick survey around the outside of the ring apron.

"Well," he continued, "I don't see anybody laid out, so I assume she came alone?"

*Yeah. A few of Jeremy's friends came in while we were talking, though. I recognized some of them.*

"Did you tell Jezzie you stopped a bus holdup and gave the bad guy a concussion?"

Kyler wiggled his eyebrows.

Trust made a face again.

*Remind me why I even told you about that?*

"Hey, I can't help it that it was on the news and I knew that was the bus you're usually on at that specific time. That's simple deductive reasoning, Watson. And..."

Both boys were standing outside the ring now, back on the gymnasium floor, Trust having returned the fighting dummy to its normal place against a far wall, and Kyler having retrieved Trust's writing utensils. Kyler leaned in closer, as though on the verge of telling Trust a secret.

"You know, girls dig the action hero," he whispered.

Trust motioned in wide, exaggerated movements, which was equivalent to a yell.

*Seriously, you're creeping me out!*


"UH OH, UH OH, UH oh."

Kyler was making nonsensical sounds as he messed around on his laptop while sitting at his desk, the four other freshmen lounging about the dorm room after dinner in Hollins Cafeteria.

"What in the world are you 'uh oh'-ing about?" Allison asked. She was seated on Kyler's bed.

Kyler turned from his laptop screen and glanced toward the redhead.

"Huh?" he asked.

"Huh?" Trust echoed perfectly.

Everyone in the room turned to Trust, who was sitting at his own desk, facing the room. It was the first time any of them had heard him speak—besides Kyler.

A moment later, they all doubled up in laughter.

"Oh, my...dude," Paxson managed through his laughs as he looked at the deaf teen. "That was awesome. You sound just like him—the same tone, everything. That's hilarious."

Reclined beside Paxson on Trust's bedspread, Marcie said, "Why am I so surprised that you can do that? Then again, I've heard you laugh before, so it shouldn't be so shocking."

*Shocking just happens to be my middle name,* Trust motioned, grinning, and Kyler interpreted.

The blond-haired boy then added, glancing back to his roommate, "And remind me to give my dear sister, Michelle, a charley horse for ever teaching you that."

Trust's smile grew wider.

"I'm almost ashamed to ask," Allison started, "and you don't have to answer, of course, but can you actually speak out loud? You know, verbalize with words?"

"What kind of crazy question is that?" Kyler asked, his attention turned back to his computer. "Of course I can speak out loud? What do you think I'm doing right n—oomph!"

A pillow from Allison silenced him.

"Oh, was that not directed to me?" Kyler asked.

*I can say a little bit,* Trust confirmed, *but I usually need to practice the words for a while in front of someone—usually Kyler—to make sure I'm saying it correctly. I have to remember how it feels and remember the way my mouth moves when I say it.*

"I usually go back and forth with him," Kyler continued, "saying the words *really slowly* so he can get the mouth and jaw movements right, and then he speeds it up to normal talking speed. Don't tell him I said this, but he's actually really good at articulating once he gets the words down. It just sometimes takes a long time because he doesn't have the audible feedback like the rest of us to realize what he's saying right or wrong."

*Thank you, Dr. Brooks.*

"Shut up," Kyler declared, smirking.

"Huh?" Trust voiced again.

This broke everyone into another round of laughter. Kyler then made a sound of surprise as he glanced back to his laptop, the others turning their heads.

"Another dorm room theft. This one was in Weaver again."

"Really?" Marcie said. "What floor?"

"Doesn't say," Kyler responded, continuing to read. "They think it's connected to three other thefts, though, including the other theft in this dorm."

He looked to Paxson and Marcie.

"Probably that upperclassman you knew from your old high school who had his computer stolen. There's a monetary reward for any information that leads to the location of the items stolen or the identity of the thieves."

On Kyler's bed, Allison reached into her pocket.

"I just got the alert on my phone," she remarked.

"I wonder who got their stuff stolen this time," Paxson mused. "Maybe I should start carrying my laptop and TV everywhere I go so I'm not leaving it in my room."

"Funny," Kyler said. "This email has a section called 'Preventive Tips,' and I don't see anything about hauling a TV around campus being the smart thing to do."

"Ah, see?" Paxson declared. "That means I'm one step ahead of the criminal mind."

He tapped his temple with his finger.

"More like two steps behind," Marcie intoned, to which the others laughed. "Think about how you would look trying to lug that thing everywhere you went—to class, to the cafeteria—"

"How he would look?" Kyler repeated. "He could just look at the television screen as he's carrying it around. Ha!"

He looked to Trust, grinning. Trust gave him a thumbs-down,

shaking his head.

"Argh, shut it," Kyler said as the others laughed. "That was set up perfectly, and I knocked it out of the park."

Allison was reading through the rest of the campus-wide email alert on her phone.

"It says that the other two thefts were in Duncan Hall and Gateway. I know where Duncan is, but I've never heard of Gateway. Where's that?"

"That's the housing for graduate students and married couples," Paxson replied. "It's on the city campus."

"So, they have all been places students live," Marcie said. "I'm sure that means something. And twice in this dorm."

"I know," Paxson whined. "Why do we get the least protected dorm? They've stolen from Weaver twice and haven't even touched some of the other dorms."

Trust remained still, his head and eyes shifting as he followed the conversation of the other four.

"That actually sounds kind of stupid of them," Kyler said. "Coming to Weaver twice, and so quickly after the first time? Higher chance of getting caught, I would think."

"And why only dorms?" Allison said. "Is it easier to steal things from dorm rooms than the campus store, or the computer labs, or from one of the department buildings like Engineering or Technology? I would think there are more chances to get caught in a residence hall, since there are always people around."

"The Case of the Dorm Room Robbers," Paxson said with an air of mystery.

Marcie rolled her eyes, though the corners of her lips upturned faintly.

"Oh, don't even start that again," she warned.

"All right, gang," Paxson declared. "We're on the case!"

The others looked at him skeptically. Trust tried to conceal a snicker.

"Huh?" Kyler asked.

*Sounds like something from Scooby-Doo,* Trust signed.

"Exactly!" Paxson exclaimed after Kyler verbalized the observation. Meanwhile, Marcie groaned, falling back onto Trust's bed, her arms spread out beside her.

"You watch *Scooby-Doo*?" Paxson asked, looking to Trust. The boy's eyes seemed to glimmer with excitement.

Trust shook his head.

*Not in a long time. It was the "All right, gang" that gave it away, though.*

"Oh, yeah," Kyler said after relaying Trust's comment. "The guy with the blond hair who wore the weird orange thing."

"Fred!" Paxson supplied, his enthusiasm for the classic show blatantly apparent. "So you guys have watched it before. Fantastic! I've got the complete box set in my room, and—"

Marcie sprang up into a sitting position again.

"You brought them? I haven't seen—"

"I hide them in the closet when I know you're coming," Paxson said. "I know you don't really like watching them that much anymore, and I guess that's all right, but—"

"You guess that's all right?" Marcie repeated incredulously. "What do you mean, you 'guess that's all right'? I've watched every single *Scooby-Doo* episode with you fifty times over, so much that I can still see them when I close my eyes, so excuse me if—"

Trust, Kyler, and Allison laughed as Paxson and Marcie bickered, before Trust got Kyler's attention again. He then gestured toward Allison, indicating that his next remark was directed toward her.

*She mentioned the School of Engineering earlier. Isn't that what she plans to major in? What's worth stealing there?*

## 15.
## The School of Engineering

THE FOLLOWING EVENING, FRIDAY, FOUND Trust and Kyler shepherded by Allison along a quiet and deserted corridor of the main building housing the School of Engineering—the Grayson E. Thomas Building. They were headed toward one of the many labs.

"Still," Kyler continued, "a lab class on Friday night? That sounds like a particularly horrifying form of student torture."

Trust grinned. Allison laughed.

"Well, it's no different from you having to go to a baseball practice on a Friday night. And anyway, we get to pick which lab we want to go to during the week. I just so happened to pick Friday this time...in here."

Departing from the wide, spotless, seemingly antiseptic corridor, Allison led the boys into a large room that, initially at least, appeared no different from any other science lab either had been in. There were a dozen or so students scattered about, along with a lone professor presently preoccupied on the laptop at the front of the room.

The similarities ended with the items at hand on the tables and workstations throughout the room. Intricate, ultra-modern-looking equipment out of a sci-fi movie caught the eyes of the boys, projects in varying degrees of completion littering tables, along with the tools and unfamiliar-looking paraphernalia most likely used to build them. The other students—Allison had mentioned that this lab was for freshmen taking advanced courses in mechanical engineering—worked either alone or paired with another, the intermittent sounds of precise technological craftsmanship ringing through the room. Kyler could hear the small, brief bursts of drilling and understated clacking of keys, along with sporadic beeps, buzzes, whirs, and pops. Trust could not hear the noises, but he could immediately spot their sources in the laboratory.

It was a shop class—a shop class set in the twenty-third century.

Trust's eyes returned to Allison as he finished scanning the activities of the room.

"Our lab subject is to devise and develop methods and innovations that would assist students otherwise handicapped in the classroom and around campus. That's what everyone's working on now, though we're also free to work on other project ideas we have so long as we don't neglect the primary assignment. One of the things I've been working on is over here."

Allison guided them to a lab table away from the door and past the professor's workspace, the young instructor not even looking up as they passed by.

"Holy jalapeño," Kyler remarked, "this is so cool. It's like the students run the class. Why can't all—or at least one—of my classes be like this?"

*Probably because students like you need adult supervision,* Trust countered.

Kyler rolled his eyes as he translated, to which Allison snickered.

"I have normal classes, too," she explained, "and, of course, we have the seminar with Professor Forte, so not all of my classes are like this either. Not even all of the engineering labs are like this. I guess this is what they do in the advanced labs."

*Told you,* Trust motioned. *She's a nerd, too. Total package.*

*Dude, no way,* Kyler returned. *That has to be against the rules of nature or something. You can't create nerds this beautiful.*

*Now why can't you tell her that?* Trust gestured wildly, becoming exasperated. *You don't think a girl would like to hear—*

Trust's focus was drawn away as Allison waved her hand to get his attention.

"Hello?" she called. "I'm right here. You guys do that a lot, you know. It's like your own secret clubhouse language."

She then chuckled lightly. Self-consciously.

"It makes me afraid you're talking about me."

Kyler's face immediately took on a sympathetic look.

"Oh, no! I mean, yeah, sure. I mean, sometimes, it is about you, I'll admit. But I promise—*promise*—it is never anything bad. Always complimentary."

*Kyler thinks you are a beautiful nerd,* Trust signed nonchalantly, as though Allison would understand.

Kyler remained quiet, not interpreting. Allison looked to him pointedly.

"Well?" she asked, waving to Trust. "Are you going to tell me what he said that time, or does he need to write it out? That was obviously directed to me."

Kyler glanced over to a smirking Trust.

*Yeah, tell her,* Trust motioned. *Tell her what you just told me. What could you possibly be afraid of?*

"Uhm..." Kyler started, his hand going up to the baseball cap on his head in what was clearly a sign of nervousness.

Fortunately, he was interrupted by a voice on the other side of the workstation.

"Yo, were you guys just using sign language?"

Both Kyler and Allison turned at the sound of the other boy's voice, Kyler's hand still clutching at his cap, Allison's arms still crossed in a sign of defiance. Trust had turned to look at the boy an instant before, when he detected the other student turning away from a microscope, which probably cost a year's tuition, and gazing in their direction. Under the microscope was a small bundle of loose wires, along with what looked to be a tiny circuit assembly.

"Yeah," Allison answered her lab mate, starting to walk around the table to the same side as the boy, "and before you say it, I was just going to—"

"Show him the EMR transcriber!" the boy interjected, reaching for a small device the size and shape of a cell phone. "Here, here."

"And if you had let me finish what I was saying," Allison remarked, "you would have heard me say that I was going to show them the—"

"The EMR transcriber, yeah, yeah!" the boy finished eagerly, grinning.

Allison waved Trust and Kyler over to their side of the workstation. While the other boy went back to the microscope, Allison handed Trust the device. As he studied it, he noticed a small, rounded protrusion on one end, almost as though the gadget had a built-in mini-flashlight. Trust turned it over in his hand before looking up.

"...one of the things Cortez and I have been working on for this lab project," Allison was saying. "It uses a low-wave infrared wide beam projected from the source lens to capture and digitize vocal or acoustic wavelength vibrations into digital feedback, which can then be electronically transcribed onto the display screen or remotely to the device of your choice. In essence, it is a portable low-wave electromagnetic vocal-synchronization transcriber."

Allison beamed expectantly as she looked to Trust and Kyler, awaiting their reactions. Trust and Kyler, in turn, stared back at her, their mouths hanging open slightly.

"Umm," Kyler finally attempted, "so it's magic, then?"

*Was she actually speaking English just now?* Trust signed. *I mean, I think I recognized some of the words, but...*

Cortez barked in laughter as Kyler interpreted Trust's comments.

"Are you the one in Allison's class who uses the voice-to-text application?" he then asked.

Trust nodded.

"Well, basically, this thing works similar to that, but instead of the person you're listening to wearing a microphone, you would just aim this at them and read what they're saying on the screen. The laser Allison mentioned would be able to be adjusted in order to concentrate on a specific person or a group of people at once, and what they were saying would just show up on the screen there—or to another device, like your laptop, if you wanted it to."

Trust and Kyler nodded and smiled, the understanding clear on their faces. Allison looked at them.

"But that's exactly what I said!" she declared.

"Meh."

Kyler shrugged.

"Cortez said it in non-Advanced Mechanical Engineering talk. You know, in a way regular humans can understand."

Allison stared at Kyler, her eyelids lowered slightly in a glare. Kyler grinned.

*Does this work?* Trust motioned, drawing the others back to him.

"Yes," Allison said.

"No," Cortez answered at the same time.

They then glanced to one another, before Cortez turned back to Trust.

"Technically, yes, *that* works," he clarified, "but it's a prototype. There's still a lot of bugs and issues to work out before anyone could ever use it for real, and we haven't been able to upload a complete vocabulary database yet, like you have on your transcription software. This EMR transcriber just has a very basic, skeletal version of it."

"That's why I was so interested in seeing your program that first day in Professor Forte's class," Allison added. "I had never actually seen it live before that. Cortez has way more experience with it than I do."

"And," Cortez said, nodding faintly toward the young-looking instructor still huddled over his computer at the front-center of the lab, seemingly unmoved and oblivious, "Dr. Reid is one of the creators of that application."

The four freshmen at the table turned to glance toward Dr. Reid. Trust could see the man's furrowed brow as he concentrated wholeheartedly on whatever was currently displayed on his computer screen.

*Not much of a talker,* Trust signed.

"Now, that's a funny one, coming from you," Kyler said.

Trust rolled his eyes.

"He doesn't talk much during the labs," Cortez said, speaking in a slightly lowered voice. "We all know what to do, so there's really no need. He's basically here if we have any questions, or the off chance something blows up."

Kyler's eyes lit up.

"Which doesn't happen," Allison added, looking at him.

"Much," Cortez mumbled. He then motioned back to the transcriber in Trust's hands.

"So, you wanna try it out? Here, just press and hold that tab over there to turn it on, and then...yeah, and then to activate it, we just programmed a shortcut, since it's a prototype. Just slide the icon over to the right..."

A moment later, with Kyler looking over his shoulder, Trust was pointing the device in Cortez's direction.

"Yo, yo, yo. See? Is it showing up? It's probably not going to display in clear sentences, but you'll get the idea."

Kyler read off the screen.

"Yo, yo, yo, and then the letter C with a question mark. Is it sho' nuff? Prob not going to diss play in clear sins, butta get Thea idea."

Both Trust and Kyler snickered.

"Awesome," Kyler added.

Allison gasped and rounded swiftly on Cortez, who was already laughing and shrinking away, anticipating her wrath. Allison lashed out anyway, slapping him on the shoulder, nearly causing him to juggle the tablet he had picked up.

"Whooah," he said, juggling the tablet.

"You loaded that stupid slang file while I went to get them, didn't you?"

Cortez continued to shield himself as Allison tried to hit him again.

"Okay, okay! You know we can just take it off," he said, still laughing. "It takes ten seconds, and then it's back to normal. Jeesh!"

Trust nudged Kyler and pointed to the transcriber's screen.

"Why isn't it writing out what you're saying now?" he asked.

"He rigged it," Allison replied, beckoning for Trust to hand over the device. "That message you saw was encoded to come up, probably once he said that 'Yo, yo, yo' stuff. It wasn't really deciphering his voice. I'm going to take out that preset right now."

Kyler pointed to something else on the table.

"Hey, what's that stick thing?"

While Allison fiddled with the transcriber, Cortez turned to the bar lying near the edge of the workspace.

"This?"

He picked it up.

"This isn't ours. Raul—he's in another lab this week—wanted me to look at this to see if there was any benefit to adding a CPU Zeniq relay—pretty much just a type of small computer chip—into this that could then be intrinsically controlled by the user. Try to guess what you think this is."

"It's a shower rod," Kyler said instantly.

Trust looked at him, squinting. He then gave his guess.

"Trust thinks it's one of those rods that would replace bone, like a prosthetic," Kyler said.

"You're both wrong," Cortez said, "although, Trust, yours is really not too far off. It's actually not a bad idea, especially with this composition."

Cortez touched something along the top portion of the rod. It instantly snapped open at the top, a T-shaped handle emerging, securing into place. Gripping the handle, Cortez pointed the rod downward, and, when he touched something else, the bottom portion extended out, quickly reaching the floor.

"It's a walking cane," Cortez stated, smiling at the expression on Trust's and Kyler's faces. He continued to manipulate the cane as he spoke.

"More like the walking cane's high-tech cousin. Raul said that an adjustable cane"—the T-bar handle transitioned again into an upside-down L—"isn't anything new, although I was like you guys when he first showed this to me"—he pressed yet another, seemingly undetectable button and brought the cane up into the air; the top section separated, and moments later extended into an identical cane, thus creating two, full-length staffs instead of one—"but it's made with something called light-metal granite—super strong, super hard, and super light. Perfect for anyone who needs a cane around campus, if not a bit overkill in terms of the materials used and what it could potentially do compared to what it would actually be used for. But, hey, still pretty cool, right?"

*This thing is like a weapon,* Trust signed, holding and weighing one of the full-sized canes in his hand, Kyler holding the other. *You remember those nunchucks?*

"That's always a problem," Allison said, hearing Kyler's translation as she returned to the group. "Everything that can be created to help people can also be used to hurt people, depending on the user. Like the EMR transcriber? Imagine how easy it would be to eavesdrop with that. Right now, its range is thirty-five feet, but with a few adaptations..."

*And you definitely weren't lying when you said the Dorm Room Robber should target this place,* Trust reasoned. *This is a goldmine.*

"But this is a far cry from a dorm room," Cortez said. "I'd like to see someone try to get in here and steal something. I heard these buildings have a pretty high-tech security system just for that reason."

"Trust and Kyler live in Weaver Hall," Allison said, looking to Cortez.

Cortez grimaced.

"Oh," he intoned. "I hope you guys are using protection."

Trust and Kyler looked to each other, each visibly trying hard to hold in a guffaw. They succeeded only for a few seconds before they fell into hysterics. Cortez started laughing as well, while Allison rolled her eyes.

"Why is it I always get stuck with the children?" she asked.

187

## 16.
## Another Run-In With Jeremy Higgins

KYLER AND TRUST SKIPPED UP the steps of Adams Hall, Kyler exuberantly leading the way. Trust stopped him just before they went through the second set of glass doors.

*Hey, you do anything to try to embarrass me in the next five minutes and I'll make you wish you were dead,* Trust warned, looking into his smirking friend's eyes. *Grown-up Kyler-Scott starting right now.*

Kyler stood at attention and saluted, his hair pinned back in his typical messy bun.

"Sir, yes, sir!"

Trust glared at him a moment longer.

*You know what, on second thought, just get out of here—*

But Kyler was already opening the door, entering the hall. Trust exhaled forcefully, then followed.

While Kyler's eyes immediately took in the open layout of the reception hall, Trust's gaze shot toward the receptionist's desk.

She was there. On the phone.

Kyler's eyes followed Trust's soon enough.

An instant later, he looked back at Trust and wiggled his eyebrows, grinning. Trust swiftly leaped ahead of the other boy as they walked, continuing to stride backward as Kyler moved forward, his back now facing the reception desk they were heading to.

*Hey. Hey! I'm warning you, Kyler. Believe me, they won't be able to find your body if you decide to do something stupid—*

Skirting around Trust, Kyler waved animatedly before his deaf friend could stop him.

"Yoo-hoo, Miss Sharpshire!" he called, his voice reverberating

189

throughout the lobby.

Trust hurried to catch up. As Kyler reached the front desk, he extended his hand across the countertop. Kimberlee, having completed the call, looked slightly surprised as she gave Kyler her hand, her gaze shifting between him and Trust.

"I'm Kyler-Scott Brooks, Trust's roommate and his best friend in the whole, wide world. I know everything about him. Go ahead; ask me to tell you an embarrassing story."

Kimberlee, still saying nothing, looked to Trust, amusement clear on her face.

*It's not true,* Trust gestured. *Don't listen to—*

Kyler laughed.

"Oh, Trustice Jeffries."

He turned back to Kimberlee.

"This guy. He is hilarious. Cracks me up all the time."

"So, you know sign language, Mr. Brooks?" Kimberlee asked. "You seemed to understand what your friend was trying to express there."

"Absolutely," Kyler signed and verbalized at the same time. "Who do you think had to teach him? And, by the way, Kyler is fine."

Kimberlee grinned at Trust.

"Have we moved on to the stage where you're introducing me to your friends now, Trust? When Brycen said you were asking about me, I was flattered, and now—"

Trust waved his hands in the air.

*Okay, okay! That's it! This has been so much fun, but I think my "friend" has some place to be that's not here.*

He grabbed for Kyler's shoulder, hoping to nudge the boy back toward the entrance. Kyler, however, gleefully ignored the hint.

*Don't you have some baseball meeting to go to?* Trust asked.

Kyler grinned.

"No way, dude. That's not until later tonight. I've got the whole afternoon to tag along with my best buddy. Anyway, I seem to remember you saying you wanted me to meet the super-hot recep—"

"Kyler."

Kyler stopped speaking. Kimberlee, behind her desk, turned to Trust, agape.

Trust's voice was low and clear, though slightly throaty from lack of use. The single word—one of the few over the years that he could speak on a somewhat regular basis—was remarkably articulate, clearer even than when non-deaf speakers pronounced Kyler's name.

*That was perfect,* Kyler gestured. *But I thought I was being a good wingman?*

Trust stared at him.

*How many times do I have to tell you that you're a terrible wingman? And anyway, Kimberlee knows sign language, so you might as well speak.*

Kyler turned to look at the young receptionist, smirking.

"Oooh, first names," he said, his eyebrows wiggling again.

Trust gazed at Kyler's profile, and then looked to Kimberlee.

*You see what I have to deal with here?* he signed.

"GOOD, GOOD," DR. DUNCAN SAID merrily, rising from his seat behind his desk and extending his hand. "So good to hear that you're coming along nicely, Trustice. So good to hear it. It warms my rickety heart to know that our students are able to adjust to university life so splendidly."

Trust couldn't help but grin at the senior administrator's quirky zeal. The freshman then held up a finger, indicating he had something else to say. He gestured to the keyboard again, which remained on his side of the desk.

The old man's face took on a look of misunderstanding before it swiftly brightened.

"Sorry? Oh, yes!"

He motioned to the computer keyboard as well.

"Please, please! Yes, of course!"

Trust began to type.

> **Trustice:** This is going to seem like a question out of left field, but I was wondering what you knew about the Freesef Society.

He looked up. Dr. Duncan's brow furrowed.

"Freesef Society?" he mumbled. "Freesef Society...why does that name sound so familiar? Freesef Society..."

> **Trustice:** Apparently, the Freesef Society was a student-run club here at UCC years ago. From what I understand, it has since been disbanded—

Detecting sudden movement, Trust glanced up to the old man quickly. Dr. Duncan held up a finger in delight, his wizened face animated again.

"Yes, yes! The Freesef Society. How could that slip my mind? I don't think I've heard the name in years! Yes, yes. Popular organization with the students, very popular. Well run, very well organized, and they had noteworthy financial sponsorship from donors outside the university as well. Yes, I actually worked with them a few times when they were active. One of their principal objectives, Trust, was volunteer work around campus and within the Centre City community, you understand, and I believe—yes, I worked with them on an undertaking relating to local financial assistance services amongst students here at UCC. Then we decided to open the venture citywide—that is where the Freesef Society's financial support came into play, you understand. As I recall, it was a successful enterprise. Still going strong, I believe. Well, yes"—the administrator chuckled—"very strong, as a matter of fact. I should know, seeing as how I am still on the Endeavor Group's board of directors."

Trust looked at Dr. Duncan in disbelief.

> **Trustice:** The Endeavor Group? You're not talking about that big building downtown, are you? The place that looks like the headquarters of a Fortune 500 company?

Dr. Duncan beamed.

"Ah, so you've heard of the Endeavor Group? Splendid! That's fantastic!"

> **Trustice:** Heard of it? From the outside, it looks like an investment bank or something. I've seen the Endeavor Group letters on the front of building, but I've never heard anyone mention them until you said it just now. I didn't even want to go inside—too intimidating.

"Oh, preposterous, Trust," Dr. Duncan huffed, "simply preposterous.

If anyone is to be welcomed into that behemoth of a building, it is you and fellow Centre City students, and those curious to learn what one teeny version of making a difference looks like."

**Trustice:** You and the Freesef Society did that?

"Oh, no, no," Dr. Duncan replied. "That building is only ten or so years old—quite new. The members of the Freesef Society were, for all intents and purposes, the Endeavor Group's first employees—or should I say, its first volunteers—selflessly laying the groundwork to give rise to that building you see today. They volunteered precious time—I know how you college students are with your free time: never enough!—handing out flyers and pamphlets, spreading the word of what we were trying to do and how we would go about doing it, holding meetings both on campus and around the city—grassroots, Trustice, grassroots! Exactly what idealistic college students are perfectly equipped to do, while jaded old-timers like myself are so crudely terrible at the same. And those students in the Freesef Society were the ones most able to bring those outside contributors to the cause in ways that other adults could not. So, actually, in point of fact, to answer your question correctly, yes. The Freesef Society did build that building, however indirectly it may seem to some, as they started construction long after the organization was disbanded."

**Trustice:** So what happened to them? It sounds like they did
a lot of good.

"Very much so, Trustice," Dr. Duncan agreed, his bushy white eyebrows crinkled in assent. "But I suppose—as is the case with anything else, no matter the subject, no matter the intentions, no matter the time in history—I suppose the Freesef Society simply ran its course, and thereafter, became its own hindrance.

"The Freesef Society helped to initiate the Endeavor Group and many other projects across campus and throughout the city. Nevertheless, in their latter years, the organization began to...devolve, turning into some underdeveloped social group instead of a volunteer organization with goals and ideals and a purpose. The latter form of the Freesef Society had no purpose—at least, not one that was sustainable. Those students who carried the torch in the early days moved on, graduated, slowly drifting further and further away through the years, to be replaced with others less...inspired. Less driven. Less idealistic. The group became more known for excessive partying and vapid celebrations, nothing more and quite a deal less. Their pecuniary support, however, continued unabated, which should have been further warning of dark clouds on the horizon line.

"I lost touch with the Freesef Society near the very end of their existence—perhaps a mistake on my part, though I don't know what I could have done to prevent its decline. I wonder if the group still being student-run at that time was still a good idea.

"There was some horrid affair at the end as well. Rape and criminal assault allegations, I believe. Multiple charges were filed, and then, somehow, they were quietly dismissed. I don't believe anything permanently scarring came to those charged, but that was the final page of the Freesef Society as a university-sanctioned organization. That was years ago now. I'm sure you were not even in elementary school when that occurred, Trustice, perhaps not even born yet. Actually, I'm surprised you even know the name."

**Trustice:** One of those things you hear on campus, I guess. Rumors, legends, etc.

"Of the good variety, I hope?" the older man asked.

Trust grimaced.

"Oh, dear. That figures. Well, whatever you hear about the Freesef Society, particularly in their decline, they were a good group—an exceptional student association—for their time. And I would know, since I was very much around and kicking back then. Very, very few others still roaming these hallowed university grounds can say the same. Those who were in the organization at that time, I've been privileged enough to keep in touch with a few of them through the years. They do great things, perhaps some of which you have even heard about. And that just goes to show you, the ideal cannot survive the people, the people survive the ideal. The people, Mr. Jeffries, the people!"

Trust smiled. He then thought of something else.

**Trustice:** You never said what your role was in the creation of the Endeavor Group.

"Me?" Dr. Duncan laughed. "I was but the designated orator, Trustice! Anything more than that, and I haven't the faintest idea."

AS HE TURNED THE CORNER, Trust was not surprised to notice Kyler absent in the open reception area.

He was surprised to see Jeremy Higgins, Rory, and a few of their friends at Kimberlee's desk, speaking with her.

Trust hesitated briefly, contemplating for an instant returning the way he had come and searching for another exit.

In the brief moment he hesitated, however, it just so happened that Jeremy chose the same moment to glance in his direction. Trust could see the other boy's mouth form into a barking laugh.

"Well, well, well," Jeremy said loudly, drawing the others'—including Kimberlee's—attention. "Here we go...again. Almost thirty thousand students enrolled at this school and I keep having the excellent luck of running into you. It's like you're everywhere I'm trying to be, dude!"

This, of course, brought a laugh from the other boys. Trust smiled as he approached.

"It's...Trunk, right?" Rory inquired. "I know it's something weird like Trunk or something."

Continuing to smile, Trust signed, *Not even close, asshole.*

A look toward Kimberlee behind her desk and he observed her eyes widening slightly at his gestures. Trust, meanwhile, reaching the desk, pulled a few cards out of his pocket.

"His name is Trust, actually," Kimberlee corrected, looking at Rory.

Rory smirked, and then shrugged, as though he had made an honest mistake.

"Yeah, Trust, right. I was close."

Trust, just then looking back up from what he had written on the note card, did not notice the exchange.

*Always a pleasure, Miss Kimberlee Sharpshire,* he motioned quickly, smiling at the graduate student before turning to show Jeremy the card.

*Nice seeing you and all your buddies again.*

He then started to step past the group, heading toward the front doors.

"Whoa, whoa." Jeremy chuckled.

He reached for Trust's arm, who froze immediately at the touch. His arm tensed into steel.

As he turned, Jeremy let go of his arm almost too quickly, though he seemed unaware that he had done so.

And he was still smiling.

"Come on," he said. "Leaving so soon? I feel like we don't get a chance to talk anymore."

From what Trust could observe, it seemed that everything the star wide receiver said brought a snicker from the rest of the group. The deaf teen maneuvered slightly, back around the group of boys so he could see Kimberlee again—and so that Kimberlee could see him.

*Do you mind interpreting for me? It will be quicker than writing it down.*

"Of course, Trust. Go ahead."

She gave him a reassuring smile.

Jeremy looked from Trust to Kimberlee.

"Really?" he asked, smirking, his eyebrows raised. "Since when do you know sign language?"

Kimberlee only smiled in response. She then looked toward Trust, translating his gestures.

"She fooled me, too, when I first learned about her talents. She's very sneaky."

After she finished speaking, Kimberlee gave Trust a look.

"And do you want me to *keep* interpreting for you?" she asked pointedly, an eyebrow arched. "Because you can go back to writing if you wish."

Trust grinned.

*My apologies,* he motioned, bowing slightly.

"Well, isn't this fun," Jeremy voiced.

Trust indicated to Jeremy again while looking at Kimberlee.

*I watched your game on the big screen in our dorm the other day. You guys were so close to winning. You, Jeremy, played really well, though. Ten catches—*

Jeremy interrupted Kimberlee while she was verbalizing Trust's motions.

"Cool, cool, thanks, appreciate it," he said, dismissing the praise. "Here's the thing—"

Kimberlee cleared her throat, and Trust saw Jeremy glance in her direction.

"Jeremy, do you really think it's a good idea to interrupt me while I'm speaking?" she asked, giving him a very similar look she had given Trust moments before.

The easy, cocky smirk Trust had grown accustomed to seeing—that slow, leisurely, smug uptick of one side of Jeremy's mouth—presented itself once more.

"My apologies," Jeremy said, unknowingly echoing Trust's phrase.

"Thank you," she said. She waved to Trust. "You may speak."

Jeremy's eyes—and his smirk—returned to Trust's own smile.

"So, here's the thing," he started again. "I heard a little rumor—just a little one—that you're becoming BFFs with my girl. You've met Jezzie, haven't you? Say it isn't so, Trust. Say you aren't becoming BFFs with my girlfriend! Please!"

At Jeremy's theatrical plea, complete with a dramatic tone and exaggerated gestures, the other boys cracked up, with Rory being the loudest among them. Trust looked intently at the curly-haired boy as the laughter started to die down. Rory's gaze flitted between Jeremy and Trust.

Then the laughter finally stopped. Trust continued to stare at Rory, his eyes narrowing just faintly enough, as though examining him.

The tension started to rise.

"Heh, what are you staring at, dude?" Rory said, chuckling again as he spoke.

Trust stared at him a moment longer.

Then he grinned. He turned to Kimberlee, waving to Jeremy again.

*Three guesses as to who told you that rumor,* he proposed.

Jeremy's smirk was ever-present.

"All right," he said. "Shoot."

"Your girlfriend," Kimberlee translated.

Jeremy began to chuckle.

"Actually," he said, "Jezzie told me after I brought it up, but she's not who I heard it from first. Try again."

Trust held up a finger to Kimberlee and scribbled something out on a card. He held it up so only Jeremy could see.

*I wasn't talking about Jezzie.*

Jeremy looked back up to Trust in question.

Trust's eyes shifted to Jeremy's left—toward Rory—and quickly back again. Jeremy looked to where Trust had indicated. He was frowning when he looked back to the deaf student.

"So, this is funny?" he said, the tone possessing an edge of irritation. "You think this is a joke?"

"What'd he write?" Rory asked. Jeremy ignored him.

*No, I think you and whoever told you that rumor—R-O-R-Y—*Trust signed the letters in exaggerated fashion—*are looking for a fight, and I'm not the guy, I assure you. You say Jezzie is your—*

"Hey," Rory said, cutting Kimberlee's translation off as he stepped forward. "Listen up, Trunk. You better keep my name out of your mouth. I don't know what you—"

"That's enough," Kimberlee said, standing up behind the reception desk, Rory halting his accusatory advance and looking toward her. "Are you guys actually serious? Jeremy, you, Rory, and the other boys can go back to Mrs. Thatcher's office. You're still a few minutes early, but I'm sure they will be able to find you something better to do than standing out here and bickering like little boys."

She looked around at all of them, including Trust.

"I've been around preschoolers who act more mature than you guys," she continued.

Rory and Jeremy were still fuming. Trust's face was completely devoid of emotion.

Kimberlee turned back to Jeremy and the others.

"Well?" she said. "What are you waiting for? Go."

She pointed away, down one of the hallways. The pack of boys began to slink off, Jeremy and Rory trailing the rest.

Rory shot Trust a heated look as he departed, Trust eyeing him back.

Jeremy did not even turn around.

Kimberlee shifted to Trust as the rest left, leaving the reception lobby quiet and empty again. Trust met her glance.

*Well?* Kimberlee signaled. *What do you have to say?*

Trust took a moment to respond.

*Are you going to send me to the principal's office now?*

Kimberlee attempted to uphold her stern façade, and she largely succeeded. She took her seat again.

*I'm starting to get the feeling that you may have visited the principal's office once or twice in the past,* she motioned. *You seem to have a bit of a temper, though you've gotten pretty good at hiding it.*

Trust started to grin faintly, looking down.

*Kyler, the guy I came in with, typically made sure I stayed out of trouble. On the other hand, that was always after he pulled me into trouble, but I guess it all balances out in the end.*

*He sounds like a good friend,* Kimberlee remarked.

Trust smiled and shrugged. He looked down at the countertop briefly before returning his eyes to the girl only a few years his senior.

*So,* he signed slowly, *I hope my earlier behavior does not dissuade you from entertaining our—*

"You may leave now, Trustice Jeffries," Kimberlee said aloud, giving Trust a doubtful look, her lips pursed but curling up slightly, her manicured eyebrows raised, one slightly higher than the other.

Trust looked at her for a moment, and then clutched at his chest.

*Ouch,* he signaled.

Kimberlee did not budge.

Trust began to back away from the desk, grinning.

*Think about it?* he signed swiftly.

*Go,* Kimberlee mouthed, though no sound emerged. However, her faint smile remained.

Trust smiled back before turning and jogging toward the front doors.

# 17.

# Genesis

ALLISON'S SHOES SANK EVER SO slightly with each step on the woodchip-covered trail. Lampposts along the edges of the trail illuminated her path, but the rest of her surroundings were shrouded in darkness. Beyond, the furtive shadow of trees and woodland loomed.

During the day, the walking trail was scenic and serene, with sunlight filtering through the woodland pines. At night, however, the setting adopted a more ominous look, though the lights lining the pathway helped to keep some of the more frightening undertones at bay.

Returning from another evening lab in the Thomas Building, Allison had her books clutched against her chest as she walked. In the three months since the beginning of the school year, she had become more than accustomed to the trail on the rural campus that conveniently traveled between the science quadrant, among which was the School of Engineering, and Mueller Hall, Allison's dorm, located relatively close by. And, with her familiarity, she was also accustomed to the ambiance of the trail at night, due to her frequent late evenings spent holed up in the labs working on her own projects.

On this night, the walking trail was again silent, the natural, nocturnal sounds of the woodland providing the sole soundtrack to her journey. The flanking light posts swathed their areas in a wide circle of dampened orange, the outermost fringes of the circles growing fainter and fainter still before becoming bright again in the next circle of light in the lamppost she approached. The shine did not penetrate very far into the woods, either, leaving the surrounding trees in silhouette.

She was twenty yards away from the end of the trail when she heard the first sound.

A faint chuckle. Or giggle, perhaps. Some sort of laughing.

On the trail it was slightly out of place, but not entirely unexpected on a college campus in the late evening.

Allison glanced around fleetingly, her red hair, appearing to glow with a faint halo around it in the orange-tinged light, whipping around as she attempted to locate the origin of the sound.

As swiftly as it started, the faint laughter ceased, her dampened footsteps becoming the loudest sounds on the trail once again.

Beyond the mouth of the trail, a corner portion of Mueller Hall was visible—though it appeared in shadow, which was unusual.

Allison's footsteps sped up slightly. She looked straight ahead, toward the ending of the trail, as she—

Another laugh. The same faint chuckle.

And some shuffling, coming from the woods.

Glancing to the side only briefly, Allison hurried the rest of the way through the trail, emerging at the rear of Mueller Hall in front of a small service lot where trash and recycle bins where located. She rushed down a short flight of steps, stepping into the lot, the trail and woodland behind her situated on a higher ground level than the rear of the dorm.

Typically, a light blazed over the back entrance. Tonight, the lights were out, bathing the small lot in darkness.

She arrived quickly, hurriedly, at the back door, her card key already out and in her hand. In the dark, her breaths were coming slightly heavier than usual.

Just as she was about to insert the card into the reader—

"Psssst."

She glanced back, but could not make anyone out in the—

She was suddenly grabbed from the opposite side, many hands at once, one covering her mouth, two, three, four or more grabbing at her middle, pulling her away from the doorway and along the side of the building, against the wall, many hands, many dark forms at once—

"Mmmmph! Mmmmph!"

They laughed quietly. Hands pulled at her shirt under her open coat, tugging it upward, more hands fighting against her the top of her pants, though her movements continued to jerk them away.

"Whatcha strugglin' for, girl?" one masked face asked, grinning, coming directly into Allison's line of sight.

"Mmmmph—"

"You know you want—aah!"

His yell was light as she bit down hard on the side of his hand that had slipped into her mouth.

Another of the assaulters grunted heavily as Allison's knee flailed, nailing him somewhere in the lower stomach. Her leg was briefly free.

"Hold her!" someone hissed. Male. Young, not old.

Her face was slammed against the concrete wall of the building, her neck strained as it was forced to turn.

An immediate, white-hot flash of pain. Numbness. Blood seeping from...somewhere.

More hands pulling, this time at the back of her jeans. Struggling, too tight.

Allison fought back, turning her face again.

"Mmmmph! Mmmmaaah! Help! Help me-whahhh!"

Her face smashed into the wall again.

A light suddenly blinked on at a window that had not been lit before. One of the masked boys happened to glance up.

He spat out a curse.

An arm was against Allison's throat while another hand covered her mouth.

She wrestled her left arm free—she swung, but missed, just grazing a head.

"We gotta go!" someone whispered urgently. First voice. Same boy.

Familiar? No.

Continued struggle. Jostling.

"Bitch."

Someone's hand started from her neck and yanked downward roughly. Her shirt tore. The hand scratched roughly against her breast and continued down, nearly ripping the shirt open completely. Allison was yanked forward, pulled down with the force. She stumbled.

The hands and bodies were immediately gone, as though vanishing into thin air. Footsteps...moving away...

"Hey, are you okay?"

A voice from above. Allison fell to her hands and knees, gasping. Sobbing.

And then screaming in frustration.

"Ahhhhhh!"

TRUST ROCKED WITH THE GENTLE motions of the Centre Line bus as it navigated the streets downtown. Though the interior of the bus was well lit, the bright lights that passed by outside flickered through like a strobe, flashing everything inside in different colors before just as quickly vanishing as the bus rumbled past.

With his tinted shades already concealing his eyes, Trust looked away from the window, to the floor, and then across the bus aisle.

He caught her looking at him an instant before she looked down, a small smile ghosting across her lips before brown hair fell across her face.

Trust grinned faintly, continuing to watch her, the oscillations of the bus swaying them this way and that. Trust waited for the girl to look up again.

It took a few moments.

She peeked through her hair.

Caught again.

Trust tilted his head slightly to the side, smirking.

The girl raised her head farther, a smile of her own tugging at the edges of her mouth. She was shy, or maybe a bit self-conscious...

She stuck her tongue out at him, like a child.

Surprise and disbelief shaded Trust's features.

Then he laughed.

Vibrating from his pocket broke the spell, and he turned to glance out the window again as he reached for his phone. The residuals of a smile still on his face, he looked down to the phone's display.

The smile evaporated at once.

He quickly looked out the window one more time, and then back to his phone.

Then he turned toward the girl across the aisle.

Back to reading the book in her hands, she looked up in his direction, as though sensing his gaze a second after he turned to her. The smile that began to appear on her face again just as quickly faded to a look of concern.

Trust was already moving. He held his phone out to her as he slid into the empty seat alongside.

**Kyler (9:16 PM):** Allison hurt. Arlington Memorial Hospital.
NOW.

"Arlington Memorial Hospital" was highlighted.

The girl seemed to understand what Trust was requesting.

"Arlington Memorial?"

She then pointed over her seat, toward the rear of the bus.

"It's back in the other direction, about eight, ten blocks from here."

Bowing slightly, he mouthed *thank you* as he took his phone back. He then sprang to his feet, nearly startling the girl with how gracefully and swiftly he moved, reaching out for the cord as he moved toward the rear exit.

The bus slowed, edging to the side of the street.

Trust leaped out before the doors had fully opened, surprising the groups of bystanders on the sidewalk with his sudden appearance. As his foot made contact with the walkway, he was already breaking into a run, dashing past a cluster of people his own age as he started back the way the girl had pointed, the way the bus had just come from.

*Allison hurt.*

It was nighttime in the city, but there were lights and people everywhere, movement and action, excitement and adrenaline. Unconsciously, Trust took it all in as he moved, his brain utilizing all his available senses to discard everything that was irrelevant and unnecessary like a high-powered computer, his instincts—and training—taking over as he darted and dodged around others on the sidewalk, his actions and reactions as though everyone else were standing still. Through his eyes, they might as well have been.

Through his eyes, the world had always been dramatically different.

He approached the first busy intersection. The crossing signal displayed DO NOT CROSS in bright, unmistakable red. People waited.

Trust skirted them, bounding into oncoming traffic.

Cars moving in slow motion...in reality, at that moment in time, it was impossible. Impossible for each and every car to suddenly and immediately slow to a crawl, in concert, the moment he stepped out into the street. But those who watched it happen with their own eyes, standing and staring, spellbound, waiting for the inevitable collision...

...If the cars did not actually slow down, what other possible explanation could there be?

That this crazy teenager was faster?

Trust was focused, fully zoned in. In the final lane before arriving on the opposite side of the street, he jumped, his hand coming out behind him as an oncoming car bore down on his position, his emergence on the road too sudden and unexpected for the driver to even contemplate slowing down in time...

The brief, fleeting contact with his hand served as an extra push, a boost perhaps unnecessary in hindsight, as the rest of his body had already cleared the crossing.

Some form of insurance, perhaps. A way to confirm to his brain, working at warp speed, that he had, indeed, cleared the intersection unharmed.

Trust did not even notice, every single movement automatic, without thought.

There were gasps and shouts that he did not hear. The eyes chasing after him as he ran, however, were identified, swiftly taken into his consciousness like a state-of-the-art tracking system only to be straight away thrust aside. The people watching him, who were out of his path, not doing anything to halt his running...unimportant.

If asked about it later, he would most likely not even remember them.

He bobbed and weaved through more pedestrians, still sprinting alarmingly fast through the crowds but able to avoid making contact with a single one. By the time those he evaded were able to react to his presence, he was already gone.

Three blocks, three intersections he ran through, not stopping, not pausing for a moment...four blocks...

*Arlington Memorial Hospital.*

At a corner, he vaulted onto a low wall, swiftly pulling himself up and over the railings at the top, landing on the covered walkway of a strip of stores elevated above the sidewalk. Up here, there were still people in his path, but much less than on street level. He raced down the walkway, those who saw him coming scrambling out of the way clutching their store bags. Trust rushed past, seemingly not giving them any notice. His breathing was only faintly labored.

The end of the strip mall, which spanned the equivalent of two city blocks, loomed ahead, protected by another metal railing that guarded against the drop down to the sidewalk.

He leaped, his feet on the top rail—

—and stopped in an instant, balancing, holding on to the rail below with both hands.

People, unaware, were walking on the sidewalk below.

He flipped around, still gripping the handrail, his feet now against the low wall. He pushed off, releasing his hold.

In the split second before he jumped, Trust had caught sight of the Centre City police officer standing farther down the sidewalk. The officer had most certainly noticed him.

But, unlike the officer, Trust just as quickly disregarded his presence.

The police officer was not as quick to turn a blind eye.

"Hey!"

Trust landed, rolled, and continued his sprint, already halfway through an open crosswalk, the traffic stopped at the red light. He cut around and through the others traversing the street.

*Allison hurt. Arlington Memorial Hospital.*

*NOW.*

"Hey, you! Police! Stop!"

Trust did not hear, of course. The officer gave chase. He was already well behind.

Trust hopped a small decorative fence, running past tables filled with people eating, ducking under—while still running—a tray of drinks held by a waiter. He then hopped the other side of the fence, back onto the main sidewalk.

The cop was still in pursuit—clumsily, his round body bumping pedestrians with much less agility than Trust had shown, nearly knocking over a young couple in his way. He was quickly losing sight of the runner, and he reached for his shoulder radio as he ran, his breathing already coming in gasps.

"Bravo 10...to Dispatch...In foot pursuit...east down Kivet...Kivet Drive...need backup...Black male, hoodie...black male, black hoodie...college-aged, wearing...wearing colored sunglasses...east on Kivet..."

Unknowingly, Trust was stretching the space between himself and the officer by a block and a half, and steadily growing. He could see a large complex of buildings ahead, set on a slight hill—presumably Arlington Memorial. He nimbly sidestepped a family, the father pulling his small daughter into him far too late, away from potential danger well after Trust had passed them by.

Just ahead of the hospital, Kivet Drive intercepted a major thoroughfare, Sky Boulevard, which was twelve lanes in total, six flowing each way with a large traffic island in the middle. Trust absorbed it all in an instant.

DO NOT CROSS in bright red, cars speeding past with no available openings to dart between.

Still hurrying, he turned, now heading north, parallel to the busy roadway. He glanced across to the other side again.

Definitely Arlington Memorial.

His attention came back to the oncoming traffic—

A police car's emergency lights suddenly blinked on.

There. Trust saw the break.

The quick adjustment in traffic flow was predictable as cars began to slow, attempting to give the patrol car room to go wherever it pleased.

Trust rushed in.

The first two lanes were right turns feeding into Kivet Drive, easily negotiated as the already slowing cars moved slower still with the flashing police car behind...then dashing down the roadway on the dotted white line...darting again, skirting past one car, then another, running, sprinting, leaping...

His conscious mind registered what he was doing only a second after it had already been done, his hand touching the cool surface.

He was crouching on the back of the stopped police car.

Still probing the traffic in the farthest left lanes before the center island, he moved to the front of the car, where the driver's-side door was opening.

In the middle of a busy Sky Boulevard.

The lanes directly adjacent to the police car were clearing, the cars on either side diverting to the outermost lanes...

Another opening. Trust leaped off the trunk hood.

"Hey! Sto—"

Trust tossed his phone as softly as possible toward the officer, who was just then stepping out of the car.

"Wha—"

The cop bobbled the phone, nearly dropping it, but Trust had already turned, crossing the final lane of traffic, reaching the island.

FOURTEEN SECONDS LATER, AFTER CROSSING the final six lanes headed northbound on Sky Boulevard, with the aid of stoplights and halted traffic, and scaling the small hill the hospital sat on, Trust rushed into the emergency room entrance, his steps slowing, and then stopping, as he stood just inside the wide lobby entrance area, his still-heightened awareness taking in the overly clean, professional setting. The sudden, full-tilt, ten-block tear through the city streets was beginning to catch up with him now that he had slowed down, though he attempted to control its onset with slow, deep breaths. He was not sure it would work.

All of the eyes in the waiting room—nurses, doctors, and awaiting patients alike—were fixed on him, most with some air of shock.

Still trying to control his breathing, he took his shades off, glancing down to the hoodie he was wearing before looking back up again. He then noticed the eyes had averted, now directed behind him.

Some had taken a step back.

Trust stilled his breathing again, his adrenaline returning. His eyes flitted down, and he faintly turned his head to the side...

"I said get down right now!" the officer ordered, flanked by two more policemen behind him, reaching out for Trust with one hand—

—his other hand aiming his gun.

Trust nimbly stepped forward and away as he turned, his hands up. The move caught the officer off-balance and he stumbled forward slightly, grabbing nothing but air. Trust took a few more steps back, his hands still raised, keeping space between himself and the officers.

"Get down now! Get on the ground!" the first officer shouted, both his hands back on his gun as he motioned a warning.

Trust's eyes went to the second officer behind him. He lowered one arm to point—

"Both hands up! Kneel down on the damn ground! This is your last—"

Trust's eyes shifted at the same time as heads turned toward a bank of elevators at the other end of the waiting area.

"—down! Stand down!" another officer declared as he approached, Trust recognizing him immediately. Kyler accompanied him, hurrying alongside.

"It's all right!" Officer Ben Ryan said. "He's with me. He's here for me."

Kyler and Trust exchanged glances.

*She's okay,* Kyler signed. Then, motioning toward the other officers, *Your fan club?*

Trust could only shrug his shoulders faintly, his arms still raised. The adrenaline was beginning to ebb again, so he once more concentrated on his breathing.

*She's okay.*

"He disobeyed direct commands from a law enforcement official!" the first officer charged, visibly irate, though he lowered his weapon. "I've got this under control, Ben!"

Kyler and Officer Ryan were beside Trust now.

"He's deaf," Kyler declared. "He can't understand a word you're saying."

Ryan glanced to the blond-haired boy.

"Lying to a police officer is a crime, kid," he intoned.

Trust cleared his throat, and when Kyler glanced in his direction, Trust gave him a pointed look, before gesturing faintly to Officer Ryan with a nod.

"You didn't let me finish," Kyler said. "I was going to say that he can't understand a word you're saying if he has his back turned to you or he's not looking at you while you're speaking. *That's* what I was going to say."

"Who are you?" the first officer demanded, looking at Kyler, and then to Ryan. "Who is this?"

"Sir, he's—"

"I'm his friend," Kyler interrupted, motioning to Trust. "We're roommates at UCC. One of our friends got hurt, and I texted Trust to come as soon as he could."

He looked to Trust again.

"Actually, he got here a lot sooner than I would have expected. Where you already downtown?"

"He's right, Wallace. I've got that text," the second officer acknowledged, the same one Trust had pointed to moments earlier, as he held up Trust's phone. "You're Kyler? Wallace, this kid threw me his phone when I was stopped on Sky after he jumped off my car—"

*"Jumped off your car?"* both Ryan and the first officer—Wallace—echoed in shock.

210

*Jumped off his car?* Kyler mouthed to Trust.

"Fortunately, everyone's all right," the cop remarked, "though he did cross twelve lanes of traffic like a complete madman."

"More than that," the third officer said from the back of the group. Where the second cop was tall, lanky, and seemed none the worse for wear, the third cop's lack of exercise was in evidence, as he was still attempting to catch his breath.

"I've been chasing him since...since Eighth Street...You should have seen this guy, Wally...He jumped off a wall...like Spider-Man or something...running through traffic and...dodging around people...It was..."

The officer then bent down, his hands on his knees, obviously struggling. While bent over, he pointed to Trust.

"He was already running...when I started after him...And look...he's not even...breathing hard...like I am..."

Kyler leaned over beside the cop.

"With all due respect, Mr. Officer Sir, I think you're having some sort of heart—"

"He's fine," Officer Ryan said, hauling Kyler back upright. "He gets out of breath easily."

"What?" the third officer managed. "What was...he going to say?"

"Damn it!" Wallace huffed. "Got us looking like the Keystone freakin' Cops out here! I'm through!"

He abruptly turned toward the doors, heading back out.

"Tubbs, Longley," he called over his shoulder, "you finish this up!"

"You got it," Longley, the second cop, mumbled under his breath, Wallace already out of earshot.

The rest of the hospital waiting area had already returned to normal, as though this were only one more in a steady stream of unusual occurrences they played host to each day.

"You can lower your hands now," Longley said to Trust.

"What was Wallace's problem?" Kyler asked.

He then nudged Ryan with his elbow.

"Tough times with his old lady?" he inquired, waggling his eyebrows. Ryan frowned.

*"Old lady?"* Trust signed. *What 1970s buddy-cop comedy did you just step out of?*

"That's Wallace O'Patrick for ya," the lanky Longley replied. "It's not a normal day if he isn't a bit grumpy about something. Or everything."

He turned to look at Trust again.

"And I know I speak for him in apologizing about him pointing his gun at you like that. It's part of his bark, which is a whole lot worse than his bite. I wouldn't worry about it too much."

Trust gave him a disbelieving look.

*He was pointing a gun at my face, but I shouldn't worry about it too much?* he motioned, Kyler interpreting aloud.

"Excuse me," Ryan intoned, quietly enough so that only their small group could hear, "but I seem to recall several accounts of you having a gun pointed in your face not too long ago and not being too shaken up about it."

Trust did not respond. Longley and Tubbs looked to each other and shrugged.

Longley returned to the young officer.

"Just to verify," he said, "you are vouching for this kid, Ben?"

Ryan nodded.

"I'm on the 10-32 reported from Mueller Hall on the rural campus, sir. Trustice Jeffries was alerted to the victim being taken here to Arlington by his friend, Kyler, and from what it sounds like, he jumped over buildings and ran through oncoming traffic to get here as soon as possible. In full disclosure, I have met Mr. Jeffries before, as he was one of the passengers held on that bus holdup on University Parkway a month ago, and I was one of the first officers on the scene."

The slender officer whistled lowly.

"I heard about that one," Longley remarked. "They overpowered the son of a gun and lashed him up like a Christmas tree on the hood of a car. Well, in any case, I'm satisfied. Cliff, you all set?"

The rotund officer was back to standing upright, having finally regained a regular flow of air in his lungs. He hiked up the pants under his ample waist.

"Sounds good to me," he said.

He looked to Trust.

"How about cutting down on the wall-jumping and traffic-running, all right? I think we both know this little adventure could have easily had a much different ending."

"Not to mention hopping on top of police cars," Longley added. "Believe me, Mr. Jeffries, you don't want to hop onto Wallace O'Patrick's squad car by mistake. He'll probably have an aneurism."

Trust bowed slightly, inclining his head in gratitude.

"Deaf, huh?" Longley said, before shaking his head in wonder. "Boy, the people you meet in this job."

"...AND I JUST GOT HERE a minute before you did," Kyler said.

Trust, Kyler, and Officer Ryan were on an elevator, heading up to the third floor.

"But then again," Kyler continued, "my late class is two blocks away, so I'm expected to get here quick. Where did you say you were coming from again?"

The elevator dinged. Ryan led them out onto the floor.

*I didn't say it a first time,* Trust replied. *How can I say it again?*

"Yeah, you're right," Kyler said. "Jumping off walls, dodging cars...where did you say you were coming from again?"

*What happened to Allison? Why is she here? Was there some type of accident in the labs? You're sure she's okay?*

The tidy, sterile corridor the three of them walked through was quiet, the nurse's station they passed presently vacant.

"I don't know what happened," Kyler answered. "When I got to her door, this guy"—he motioned to the police officer alongside them—"was coming out. He wouldn't—"

"I'm sorry," Officer Ryan spoke up, looking to Kyler as they walked. "'This guy'? You're referring to me?"

"Officer Ben Ryan of the esteemed Centre City Police Department—who you have seen in action before—wouldn't tell me what had happened, only that Allison was all right, that she was stable, conscious, and speaking, and that it is mostly bumps and bruises and a possible concussion. I don't know—"

"Aat!"

Ryan stopped Kyler, who had been reaching for the door handle to room 312. The officer then softly knocked on the closed door.

*Ask him what a 10-32 is,* Trust motioned as they stood, waiting.

Kyler looked to the cop.

"Trust wants to know what a 10-32—"

The door they were standing in front of opened partway, a young woman's head appearing.

Ryan's back was turned just enough so Trust could not see what he said.

The nurse, however, smiled.

"We haven't forgotten about you, Officer Ryan. It should be just a few more minutes, and then we'll be able to let you and your friends in."

"Kyler, are you still out there? I'm okay!"

The announcement from inside the room caused a reaction in Kyler, which Trust spotted.

"Trust is out here, too!" Kyler called back. "He almost got arrested! You're not going to believe it!"

The nurse chuckled softly as she shut the door again. Officer Ryan, meanwhile, gave Kyler a look. Kyler smirked.

"Don't think I didn't notice that little tête-à-tête there between you two, either," he said. "And what's a 10-32?"

"First off," Ryan said, "I don't think a tête-à-tête means what you think it does, and second, ten and thirty-two are numbers. Seeing as how you're allegedly a student at the University of Centre City, I would have thought you'd have learned that before now."

Kyler gave the policeman a sarcastic look, but Trust gripped the young officer's arm lightly and stared at him, communicating his seriousness. Ryan gazed back at him.

*Ask him what a 10-32 is again,* Trust signed, still meeting Ryan's stare.

Kyler did.

Officer Ryan continued to look at Trust for a moment before he spoke.

"How many lives—including your own—did you endanger trying to get here?"

Trust remained still, not reacting.

"And what about that bus holdup? I saw those security tapes. Do you have a death wish? "

Kyler looked between Trust and the young officer, before Officer Ryan turned to look at him again.

"Tell your friend that 10-32 is a CCPD radio code. I'm not going to tell you what it means, and I'd rather let the young lady in there tell you what happened if she wants you to know."

At that moment, the door opened again.

"You're free to come in now," the nurse said.

As she stepped aside, two more of the medical staff exited the room, each carrying a small bundle of equipment. Kyler slipped in as they came out.

A few more seconds...

*I hit the guy and tied him up. He had the death wish. I don't like threats made against me or people I know.*

Ryan's brow furrowed as he watched the deaf boy's hands move rapidly, suddenly.

"What?"

However, Trust was already heading into the room.

He stopped abruptly just inside the doorway.

Kyler was on the floor, kneeling beside Allison's bed. He appeared to be speaking, but with his back to the door, Trust had no idea.

What stopped him was Allison.

Heavy bruising along her face, neck, and arms, with small bandage strips covering multiple cuts and scratches. A black eye. She was turned toward Kyler as she lay on the bed, seemingly trying to placate him as she patted his hand.

Her eyes shifted, noticing Trust.

Trust's expression tightened.

Kyler, observing Allison's diverted attention, looked back over his shoulder.

*Stay calm,* Kyler mouthed silently.

*You stay calm,* Trust motioned back.

Officer Ryan came around Trust, heading to the foot of Allison's bed. He glanced toward Trust's face briefly before looking to the girl.

"I have some more questions for you, Miss Tyler," he said, "if you feel up to it."

His eyes then went to the nurse who remained in the room, the same one he had spoken to just minutes before, who was typing on a laptop positioned on a stand near the bed. The nurse looked up, glancing toward him, and then toward Allison.

"It's okay," Allison said. "I'm okay. Go ahead. And please, call me Allison."

And then, looking toward Trust again, "And after these questions, I want to hear about you almost getting arrested."

*Kyler, ask her who did this.*

*Stay calm, Trust.*

Trust set his jaw and looked from Kyler, to Allison, and then to Officer Ryan, who was looking back at him.

"You two wanna tell me what that was?" Ryan asked.

"Oh," Kyler said, "that was just one of Trust's typically sarcastic comebacks—"

"You're lying," Ryan said. "Again."

He looked to Allison.

"Are you okay with these two in the room while I ask you questions?"

"Yeah, it's okay," Allison said.

"What you two did," Ryan said, pulling his notebook out of his pocket, along with a small pencil, as he eyed Kyler, "just then, *that* was a tête-à-tête."

Kyler scrunched his face up comically.

"You really should use a recorder," Allison said, watching the cop with a faint smile. "Or your phone, at least."

"Oooh," Kyler said, grinning. "Was that a burn?"

The nurse chuckled, and Officer Ryan gave a feigned smile.

"Get out," he said, looking at Kyler.

"Okay, okay," Allison said, waving off Ryan's displeasure but wincing slightly. "On with the interview."

Trust noticed her grimace.

Ryan's pencil was poised over his note pad.

"Before I left, I was asking you about the voices you heard. You said they were all male?"

"Yes."

"Did you recognize any of them? Ever hear any of them before?"

Allison's brow furrowed briefly as she thought.

"No."

"Do you think you would be able to recognize any of the voices if you heard them again?"

Allison thought again.

"One spoke more than the others. I would remember him if I heard him again. I would remember the smile in his voice...like he was laughing."

"'The smile in his voice'?" Ryan repeated, looking away from his note pad. "Was his voice distinctive in some way?"

"I don't know. It's really hard to..."

She gestured to her face, the IV attached to her arm following her movement.

"You know when you hear someone begin a joke, or say something they think is cute or funny, and their lips turn up as they're talking? It's like you can almost hear them laughing before they actually laugh."

She turned toward Kyler.

"You do it," she observed. "A lot."

Kyler looked at her, his face deadpan.

"Wait. Did you just burn *me* now?"

Allison started to laugh, but then winced again. She twisted awkwardly on the bed, trying to get comfortable.

The nurse laid a hand lightly on her shoulder.

"Are you all right, sweetie?" she asked, her voice soothing, delicate. "Where does it hurt?"

"It's okay," Allison said, settling down. "It's just this bed…"

"And you know what they say about hospital beds," Kyler said.

He then caught the look on the nurse's face, her eyebrow raised.

"Nothing," he finished. "They really don't say anything about hospital beds. At all."

The nurse just shook her head, chuckling again.

"Stop," Allison said. "You're going to make me laugh. But you did it. Just now, during the 'You know what they say…' part? You had a smile in your voice."

Trust raised his hand slightly from his position near the doorway. Allison spotted him, and Kyler looked over his shoulder again.

"Oh, quiet, everyone, quiet. Trust has something to say."

This time, Allison pushed him.

"Aah." She winced.

"I don't think I've ever said this before," the nurse said, "but I really think you should try being a little less funny."

"I'm just in a zone right now," Kyler said. "I don't know what it is."

Trust moved toward Officer Ryan, motioning for his pencil and notebook.

"Forget your note cards?" Kyler asked, after waving to get Trust's attention.

*I don't carry them around* everywhere, Trust pointed out, before taking the articles Ryan held out to him.

"Ahh," Kyler said.

Trust was already writing and didn't see. He handed the pencil and paper back to the cop. Ryan glanced down, and then back to the deaf teen.

"What do you know about this?" he inquired.

Trust could tell that the man's voice had turned considerably softer.

"What?" Kyler said, standing from the floor. "What is it?"

*Ask him what he knows about what I just wrote,* Trust signed to him.

Kyler relayed the message before motioning back to Trust swiftly, *What did you write?*

*An urban legend,* Trust replied.

Ryan rubbed at the bottom of his face as he turned to Trust.

*How much do they know about this?* he mouthed.

"Hey, I know what you're doing," Kyler said. "I can read lips, too, you know."

*That was a lucky guess,* Trust signed, *and no, you can't.*

He turned back to Officer Ryan and nodded, motioning to Allison and Kyler, who were watching them.

The officer looked between all three teens, assessing, before looking over to the nurse, still typing away on the computer.

"Hailey."

The nurse stopped her typing, looking up.

"I'm not up on the procedures for nurses regarding confidentiality, but I think we are about to discuss something that I don't want to leave this room. If you have any concerns, feel free to leave now."


RIDING THE CENTRE LINE BACK to Weaver Hall later that night, Trust and Kyler sat next to each other, Kyler against the window, looking out, Trust looking down to his hands. It was now after ten, and though the downtown nightlife was still active, the bus was, at the moment, mostly empty.

Kyler turned to look at his friend. Trust had taken his shades back off once they were on the well-lit bus.

*You think it's true, don't you?* Kyler motioned. *You think that Freesef did this?*

Trust looked at him, and then looked down again, thinking. Kyler put his hand under Trust's chin and nudged it up, meeting deep, sky-blue eyes again.

*Hey,* Kyler signed. *Tell me what's going through your head.*

Trust sat back in his seat, rubbing a hand across his face.

*I was going to Centre Diamond,* he gestured quickly. *That's where I was going when I got your text. I was going to try to see Mariana again.*

"What?"

Trust could tell Kyler had shouted by the exaggerated motions of his mouth and his incredulous expression.

Also, the other passengers who turned to look gave it away.

*Indoor voice,* Trust advised.

*I knew it! I knew it! I told you you liked her. It was so completely obvious—*

*Somebody was stalking her,* Trust signed.

Kyler paused.

*Who? Mariana?*

*Allison,* Trust motioned. *How else would they know she was going to be there tonight? You heard what she said. All of the other classes in the Thomas Building were over. She stayed after, in the lab, which is not unusual for her. Someone would have to know she regularly leaves alone, after dark, after most of the other students are already gone. And they would know she uses that trail back to Mueller.*

*But didn't Holden say that the girls usually went along with it?* Kyler replied. *Like they almost wanted it to happen to them? Like they expected it?*

*Allison didn't go along with it,* Trust observed. *She fought back. It probably wasn't what they expected.*

*That's what I'm saying,* Kyler said.

They both stopped again. The bus was edging out of the city, into more natural landscape.

*And they took her phone.*

*Yeah,* Kyler agreed, *but the cop said they would call to try to locate it. They can track it down using the GPS. But whoever took it probably turned it off, like Allison said. Turned it off or took out the SIM card.*

*Would you know to take that out of a stolen phone?* Trust asked.

*No, but I don't know electronic stuff like she does,* Kyler replied.

*Maybe whoever took the phone won't either,* Trust added.

He thought for a moment.

*Right outside her dorm.*

*Yeah,* Kyler replied.

Another pause.

*I wonder what Holden's going to say?* signed Kyler.

*I wonder what Marcie's going to say,* Trust returned.

Kyler nodded, smirking faintly. But his smile slowly disappeared.

*What about you?* he asked.

*Nothing much we can do right now.*

Kyler let it go, though Trust had not really answered his question. He sat back in his seat, with Trust watching.

"Holy crap, I can't believe this. Safest school in America."

*When are you telling Holden?*

"We can find him as soon as we get back," Kyler said. "Then we can tell everyone at the same time. In fact..."

He reached into his pocket for his phone.

"I'll text Pax and Marcie to find him and meet us at the room."

The bus rumbled on. With a few more stops in between, they were about five minutes away from Weaver.

After typing the message, Kyler looked up to see Trust's hands moving again.

*I think back at the hospital would have been a good time to tell Allison you like her.*

"Um, sorry. Excuse me, guys."

Both boys directed their attention to another boy who took the seat directly in front of them.

"Hey, sorry to pry into your business and everything, but was that sign language you two were using?"

Kyler and Trust looked to each other.

BACK IN THEIR DORM ROOM on the seventh floor, Kyler and Trust both straddled chairs. Opposite them, Marcie and Paxson sat on Kyler's bed. Holden, the RA, leaned against the tall closet.

Their stunned silence seemed interminable.

"Please, please, *please* tell me you're joking," Marcie finally said. Her green eyes seemed to glint, her hair fashioned once more in several miniature pigtails, her attention shifting steadily between Kyler and Trust.

"I know, I know," Kyler said, running a hand through his hair. "When she called me, she told *me* not to come, just to tell you that she was okay, but I just texted Trust without even thinking, and—"

Marcie grabbed one of Kyler's pillows and flung it at him before he could react.

"I don't care about that!" she shouted.

Trust glanced toward their still-open door, and then to Holden. Holden nodded faintly and moved to close it.

"Tell me you are joking right now!" Marcie demanded.

Holden stopped another student passing by in the hall.

"If you hear anyone looking for me, tell them I'm in here," he said quietly.

He then shut the door.

Marcie hit Kyler with the pillow again, Kyler shrinking away.

"Allison was assaulted—nearly raped—outside Mueller Hall by the Freesef Society?" she asked.

"Marcie," Paxson said.

He grabbed at the pillow.

Marcie immediately let it go.

But she raised her fist, preparing to hit Kyler again.

"Marcie!" Paxson shouted.

Trust was already out of his seat; his chair turned over with his sudden movement as he blocked Marcie from lashing out again. Paxson hugged the girl around her middle and pulled her back onto the bed, falling on top of her. Paxson's face was turned away from Trust, so he could not see what the boy was doing. Nevertheless, whether by word or action, Marcie quickly started to calm.

Trust glanced to Kyler. The blond's eyes were wide, nearly circular.

"Is she okay?" asked Holden, now poised close to the bed.

Trust could not see Paxson's response. He looked to Kyler again.

*What did he say?*

*She's fine,* Kyler relayed. *He says she...does that sometimes.*

Both Marcie and Paxson sat up again, Paxson beginning to loosen his grip on her while still rubbing her back. Marcie looked up, seeing Kyler—

—and launched herself at him again before Paxson could grab her again.

This time, however, Trust noticed her shift in demeanor and did not intervene.

"Oh, Kyler! I am so, so sorry!"

Marcie slammed into the boy, and they both toppled over, onto Trust's bed just behind.

She hugged Kyler tightly. After a brief delay, Kyler patted her gingerly on the back.

"Um, no worries, Marcie," he intoned, eyeing Trust with a puzzled expression as he spoke. "I think we all want to punch a wall—or me—every once in a while."

Marcie laughed, though from the way she was positioned, Trust could just as easily infer that she was sobbing. He leaned over to get a closer look at her face.

When Marcie caught sight of Trust, she released Kyler and threw herself at him. Trust had his arms out, frozen as he stood there in between the two beds. He could feel Marcie speaking into his ear as she embraced him, but he could not see her face. Kyler rose into his eye line.

"She says she's sorry," he explained. "And that it was incredibly stupid of you to run through traffic."

*Duly noted,* Trust signed behind her back before Marcie released him.

"Oh, sorry, Trust," she said as she stepped back, Trust seeing her face again. "I completely forgot."

Holden cleared his throat, Trust following the glances of the others.

"Okay. So while I'm definitely going to want to discuss *this* later"—he pointed to Marcie, and then gestured vaguely about the room—"I would like to return to the initial topic. Namely, has Allison's RA been informed? If she hasn't, I need to tell them now."

Trust bent down to pick up his chair, but kept his eyes on Kyler.

"Yeah, she knows," Kyler answered. "She called her before she called me."

"And Allison's seriously all right?" Paxson asked.

"Bumps and bruises. A black eye. Minor concussion. She's sore. She fought them off long enough for someone inside Mueller to hear the commotion. Their intent seemed to be to...you know, but it didn't get that far."

"And you think it was Freesef?" Holden asked. "Why?"

Kyler looked to Trust.

*Doesn't it seem like it follows what we've been talking about?* Trust signed. *How they carried it out, the circumstances surrounding it, at least from what we know from Allison. But actually, now, thinking about it, I'm not so sure.*

Holden nodded, prompting Trust to continue.

*The problem is Allison. Allison was targeted. She is a victim, but she fought back. Police were called; there was an officer at the hospital already when I got there. From what you said, other girls wouldn't do that if the Freesef Society were behind it. They wouldn't fight back once they realized who it was and what was happening. They wouldn't have contacted the police to report a crime. Officer Ryan said the same thing you said, Holden—almost word for word. No cooperation from the girls who were alleged to be victims, so no way to look into a crime that the supposed victim says did not occur.*

*But Allison doesn't fit into that mold. From what you said, the Freesef Society should have—would have—known that, wouldn't they? They would not have gone after Allison if they thought she would fight back and call the police. So maybe it wasn't them. In any case, this isn't done yet.*

Trust looked at the others in the room as he finished. For a moment, no one said a word.

Paxson scratched at the side of his face, where a small amount of stubble was growing in.

"What if it was an accident?"

The others looked at him, waiting.

"What are the chances it was the Freesef Society, but Allison wasn't the intended target? What are the chances they attacked the wrong girl?"

# 18.

# The Day After

TRUST, KYLER, AND MARCIE WERE back at Arlington Memorial the next morning. Paxson was in class.

"So, can I ask what you talked to Holden about after you left our room last night, or am I in danger of getting smacked around again?" Kyler inquired as the group walked down the third-floor hall of the hospital. While the corridor last night had been virtually empty, it now hummed with activity, hospital and various medical personnel passing this way and that.

Marcie grimaced visibly.

"I really am sorry. Again," she said, looking over. "You're not scared of me now, are you?"

*Now?* Trust motioned. *You say that as though we weren't terrified of you before.*

Marcie shook her fist at Trust as the three of them snickered. The dimples appearing along the edges of Marcie's mouth made her look like a child.

Her smile then slowly disappeared.

"It's...I don't know, it's stupid, really."

They stopped in front of the closed door to room 312.

"I hate talking about it because it just sounds like I'm making up an excuse, but...Pax thinks I have trouble managing anger and that I need some type of functional outlet, like exercise. Or meditation."

Trust and Kyler watched as she rolled her eyes.

"I told him I think meditation would be a good way to *cause* my anger," she said.

*Don't knock it until you've tried it,* Trust advised.

After interpreting for Trust, Kyler reached for the door.

"You meditate?" Marcie asked, looking at Trust in astonishment.

*There are many more ways to meditate than the one you're probably thinking—*

Trust halted his hand motions when he spotted Kyler not watching, his roommate having walked inside the room. Trust glanced in.

He then leaned back, eyeing the room number again. His attention returned to the room, and he met Kyler's gaze. The blond-haired boy appeared suddenly uneasy.

*Hey, knock it off,* Trust signed. *They probably just moved her. Don't jump to conclusions.*

"Is there a reason we're staring at an empty room right now?" inquired Marcie. "I mean, it's nice and clean and everything, but—"

Kyler was already rushing out, coming through the doorway and passing by Trust and Marcie, and nearly colliding with a janitor rolling a mop bucket.

"Hey, where's the fire, Danny Boy?" the custodian declared, soapy water very close to sloshing over the rim of the bucket with the bump.

Trust's brow furrowed with the unusual reference. Meanwhile, Kyler steadied himself and the man.

"Sorry, I just..."

Kyler then pointed back into the empty room.

"Do you happen to know what happened to the girl in there?"

The janitor looked to Trust and Marcie, and then glanced past Kyler, into the room.

"Oooh, sorry, lad," he said. "You're a wee bit late this mornin', I'd say. The girl, she's gone. Didn't make it through the night, I'm afraid."

Kyler's face paled almost instantly, his eyes wide.

"What?" Marcie said, stepping forward. "That can't be right "

Trust was still having some difficulty. While the janitor appeared to be speaking English—Trust was able to pick out some of the words—the contortions of the man's lips were somewhat...off.

"What happened?" Marcie went on. "What do you mean she didn't make it—"

Trust observed the heads of his two friends—and the janitor—turn as they glanced down the hallway. Trust turned as well.

The nurse from last night—Hailey—was approaching them.

"Kian!" she called. "Kian!"

Trust turned his head quickly.

"What?" the custodian replied, his expression wrinkling as though he could not hear. "What? What?"

For Trust, the "What?" was easier to comprehend.

"Kian," Hailey said again.

She was now close enough to the group to speak normally. She turned to Trust, who was nearest.

"You're here to see Allison Tyler?" she posed. "From last night, right?"

Trust nodded, his eyebrows raised.

"I remember," she said.

Kyler stepped around Kian the janitor, rushing toward the nurse. He reached out his hand, seizing her upper arm.

"Allison...she's..."

"She's gone!" Kian bellowed, employees nearby turning to look at him. "What, you hard o' hearin', Danny Boy? She's gone!"

"Stop saying that!" Hailey said.

Her attention returned to a frantic Kyler.

"She's fine. Your friend is perfectly fine. She was discharged early this morning."

Kyler slunk off her, his hand sliding down Hailey's arm as he slowly fell to the hospital floor, the nurse continuing to hold on to him as she stooped down as well. Though he appeared to be muttering something, Trust was in no position to read his lips, Kyler's face turned away just enough.

"Yes, discharged by her mom and...uncle, I believe. She's gone. That's just what I said!" the janitor argued.

"You don't say 'She's gone' *in a hospital*, Kian," Hailey shot back from the floor as she rubbed Kyler's back.

Trust tilted his head back in realization. He had not caught on until just then what exactly Kian had been suggesting. Kyler's agonized response should have been a hint, but Trust had gotten used to overlooking some of his best friend's more melodramatic displays. Through the years he had known Kyler, there had been much more than a few.

He assisted the nurse in getting Kyler back on his feet.

"She's gone, she left, she was discharged," the custodian said. "They all mean the same thing, Hailey-Ann. Don't any of you speak any

English? If she was dead, I would have simply said she died."

Marcie looked at the man. He looked to be in his mid- to upper-thirties, with dark stubble peppering the lower half of his face.

"Actually," Marcie clarified, "those three things you said *don't* always mean the same thing."

Kian turned to her.

"Huh. I forgot you were standing there."

Trust started to sign, his eyes shifting between Kyler and the curious janitor.

*Did Allison leave any way to reach—*

"Is that boy having a seizure or something?" Kian asked.

Trust's hands stilled as he again looked to the custodian in confusion. He then returned to Kyler.

*What kind of accent does he have? I can barely understand a word he's saying.*

"Uh, I think it's Scottish or something?" Kyler guessed.

"Scottish?" Kian cried out. "I'll show you Scottish, you little...Dublin, Ireland, lad! Ever heard of it?"

Kyler shrank away at the outburst, stepping slightly behind Hailey.

"What the bloody 'ell are you doing?" Kian asked. "Hidin' behind a girl? Oh, if only your father could see you now..."

"Thank you for your assistance, Kian," Hailey said. "I'm sure you want to get back to work."

"She's gone, she's discharged," Kian tried again. "They both mean the same thing. Maybe I'll just be rude and not answer next time? Or maybe I'll just shake my head, hey?"

"If it's between those two," Marcie said, crossing her arms, "I would suggest the first."

Kian turned to the girl, giving her an amused look.

"Or maybe you can just direct them to a nurse," replied Hailey. "You know, like you usually do? You're always so gruff with visitors. What made you stop and talk to these three?"

"Danny Boy ran into me," Kian said, pointing to Kyler. "Anyway, I'm in a good mood. The Rovers won."

"This is you in a good mood?" Kyler gawked, still positioned slightly behind Hailey, though he stood nearly a foot taller than her. "What would have happened if the Rovers lost?"

Kian pointed again, causing Kyler to shrink back once more.

"You take that back! There's no way on the good Lord's green earth the Shamrock Rovers would lose to Shelbourne—"

"Okay," Hailey declared. "Thank you again, Kian, but I will take it from here."

She motioned for the three UCC students to follow her back down the hall.

"Miss Tyler's file is at the nurse's station. When she was discharged, we would have been given a number where she could be reached, and I remember her saying yesterday her phone had been stolen..."

As they moved down the hall again, Trust saw Marcie glance back to the janitor, who was departing in the other direction. She then turned forward again, noticing Trust's glance. She shook her head.

"Can you believe that guy?"



Trust went to the trail that night.

Darkness. Nearly pitch-black amongst the woodland and well off the illuminated walking trail.

He leaned back against a tree, completely, absolutely still. His breathing was shallow, very nearly nonexistent. He did not make a sound.

His eyes, glowing but concealed behind his tinted shades, took in the scene. He had long since learned that what he saw—his view of the world—was radically different than anyone else could possibly imagine.

The darkness might as well have been daylight. He could see everything—more than everything—including the miniscule, microscopic particles floating lazily in the air, particles that were very much invisible to everyone else in the daylight, much less at night. The tiny specks—from leaves, from the trees, from the ground, from his own body and clothing, from *everything*—glimmered in an orangish haze as they hovered, appearing like trillions of tiny embers or fireflies amidst a conflagration that did not exist. No special equipment was necessary, no radiation monitors.

He used to think everyone could see what he saw. That it was normal.

Trust refocused, moving his attention away from the minute specks and dots floating directly in front of his face.

The lit trail was presently vacant, but he could still distinguish the faded body signature of its most recent visitor, a male student who had walked past Trust's location unknowingly, heading for Mueller Hall and entering through the back entrance—the same entrance Allison had been destined for when she had been attacked. Now, nearly twenty-four hours later, Allison's signature was long gone from Trust's notice, completely diluted. Not that Trust had come out on this night to search for it.

The track from the boy who had passed minutes ago was only faintly present, nearly indiscernible against the infinite number of other particles Trust saw in the air.

Behind his shades, Trust's eyes glowed brightly.

The specks in the air shifted abruptly, and not from the wind.

Movement. Someone else was coming.

His eyes shifted. His body did not budge.

One, two, three. He could see them easily through the foliage, the shifting air having given him the initial indication.

The three of them were moving slowly, sneakily, carefully. They were not on the walkway, instead creeping through the forest, on the same side of the trail as Trust.

Trust turned his head quickly to the end of the trail, where it opened out at the back of Mueller. The back entrance was illuminated, the lights having been fixed.

He returned to the sneaking trio.

They were still a distance away. Trust did not recognize any of them, though all three were male. He presumed they were UCC students, all fitting the typical college-aged demographic.

He remained still. In the dark, in this dense wooded area off the woodchip trail, none of the boys would know Trust was there unless they were standing directly in front of him.

Or unless he made a sound.

"...never can tell what..."

One of the boys was speaking, but with his head turned downward, Trust could not make out every word.

The three of them passed behind a tall tree. Now, Trust could not distinguish any lip movement, but he could still see their bodies, glowing in that similar but softer orangish tint, even through the tree and undergrowth. They quickly emerged again.

"...about right here."

The group paused.

"...wrong, though."

Their heads did not stay facing Trust long enough for him to decipher complete sentences. Who knew what they were saying. They continued to talk—very quietly, Trust assumed. One was shaking slightly, with a hand covering his mouth, trying to hide his laughter.

Another, different shift in the air, distinct from the motions the three boys were causing. The particles floating along the trail pushed forward.

However, Trust, already looking in that direction, saw the approaching student just as quickly.

A girl. Blond. Cute. A couple of textbooks in her grasp, an oversized satchel—which, for some reason, she was not using—over her shoulder.

She was alone, seemingly without a care in the world. Almost skipping.

Apparently, the boys in the woods were not expecting her, still unaware of her presence. Trust watched their sudden change in behavior when they finally noticed. On the walking path, the girl had almost drawn even with their spot in the woods.

One of the boys quickly grabbed the one that was snickering. The first boy's face was insistent, intense. He did not utter a word. All three froze.

The girl must have heard something. Maybe a stray giggle, or perhaps a shuffled footstep. Her own footfalls faltered as she peeked toward the dark woodland, her gaze coming very near to the huddled boys.

Trust knew she could not tell that the three boys were staring directly at her.

After slowing for a split second, her pace quickened again.

And then, something completely idiotic. One of the boys, trying to stay still, must have lost his balance briefly. He took a stumbling step forward, and then froze again.

The girl definitely heard it. Having passed their position, she turned to look over her shoulder, but she staggered again, the books tumbling out of her clutch. She fell to her knees.

Her mouth was open. Trust assumed she must have cried out. His eyes shifted again.

Fortunately, the three boys were not budging from their position, apparently shocked that they were so close to being discovered.

The girl scrambled, quickly picking up her books.

Still, the boys remained frozen, watching.

The orange tinge to the scene filling Trust's eyes stemmed from the light emanating from the lampposts bordering the walking trail. The flashing specks in the air danced and leaped with the disturbance around the girl's hurried movements. Standing upright again, she now rushed along the trail, her feet sinking slightly into the woodchips with each step before she pushed off again, the chips then flying and scattering behind her as they were kicked up.

To Trust, it seemed as though tufts of smoke followed each footstep.

Soon, she was gone, emerging from the wooded trail at the back portion of Mueller Hall and disappearing inside.

Trust's attention turned back to the boys. They still had no clue they were not the only ones in the woods at that moment.

"...get outta here. That was too close."

Another of the boys muttered a curse. The trio began to creep back the way they had come, Trust watching them the entire way. He was able to observe them for much longer and much farther than a human being should have been able to.

TRUST STEPPED THROUGH THE DOOR. Kyler was twisting and gyrating in his chair, a controller in his hands, as he focused on the video game on the TV screen. The teenager immediately paused the game, briefly eyeing the bag in Trust's hand before moving up to his friend's eyes. Trust's shades were hooked to the collar of his shirt.

"Where did you go, all the way to Timbuktu to get ice cream sandwiches? I thought I was going to have to go get some myself."

Trust reached into the bag, pulled out a sandwich, and tossed it to Kyler, who caught it easily.

*You wouldn't have tried to come find me?*

"What's the point? We both know how that ends. I would get lost, and then you would have to come find *me*."

Trust smirked as Kyler bit into the ice cream. Trust threw the bag away and began opening his own package.

*Seriously, though. Where did you go?* Kyler signed.

He knew not to try to speak while he ate. No way would Trust be able to read his lips.

Trust smirked again, chuckling slightly.

*You remember how you were writhing on the ground when you thought something had happened to Allison at the hospital? That was funny.*

Kyler looked at him, his expression deadpan. Trust tried again.

*I took a walk. Get off my back, woman.*

"Where?"

Trust shrugged.

*Mueller.*

He took a bite.

Kyler, having just finished taking another taste from his own ice cream sandwich, slowly lowered the food from his mouth. He looked toward his best friend curiously.

"And what did you see, Sherlock?"

## 19.
## Dinner on Thanksgiving Day

EARLY THURSDAY AFTERNOON, TRUST AND Kyler accompanied Holden and a few others from Weaver Hall to a restaurant just off campus that specialized in made-from-scratch cooking—and lots of it. The mom-and-pop restaurant was fitting for this day in particular, and apparently, many seemed to agree, since the waiting list was so spectacularly long that customers had to call days in advance to reserve a table.

Fortunately, the group from Weaver Hall was already on the list, courtesy of both the University of Centre City and the Centre Towne Inn. The party was able to obtain a grouping of tables with no trouble.

It was Thanksgiving.

It was also Riley's birthday. The server from Trust and Kyler's first day in Centre City was tagging along.

"Boom, boom, boom," Kyler sang. "Twenty-one, twenty-one, twenty-one. So, where's the party gonna be? The booze, I can only hope, will be flowing freely."

Sitting across the table, Holden and Riley shot Kyler a dubious glare. Riley's hand, grasping a chicken wing, was frozen in midair. Beside Kyler, Trust just shook his head as he turned back to his heaping plate of food.

"Really, if I didn't know you any better, I would think you were already on the sauce," Holden stated.

"Wait," Riley said. "You mean this is him sober?"

*Sober, yes,* Trust motioned, and Kyler interpreted. *Sane? Eh...*

Trust shrugged.

"Yep," Riley said. "I can definitely see that."

"What can I say?" Kyler said. "I'm typically in a merry mood."

"Um-hmm."

Riley's expression was one of amusement as he took another bite of his chicken.

"So, your girlfriend's taking a break from you today?"

Kyler coughed, nearly choking. Trust and the others leaned away as a thin spray of mashed potatoes emerged, luckily all landing in—or, at least, around—Kyler's plate. Trust held up Kyler's water, which his friend took gratefully.

"That wasn't gross at all," Holden said.

Riley looked to Holden and Trust, confused.

"Her name's...umm, Allison, right? Allison? I don't get it. What did I say?"

"Not...my girlfriend," Kyler managed around gulps of water.

"She's back at home for Thanksgiving break," Holden explained.

He then looked to the two freshmen across the table.

Waiting.

"She said it's all right," Kyler said, his voice still raspy. "You can tell him."

Riley turned to Holden.

"What happened?"

"We should keep this quiet," Holden said. "It would probably be okay if you told Brycen since she met him already, but no one else. Allison, the girl you're talking about, was involved in an assault a few days ago. Monday. Monday night."

Riley inhaled sharply.

"Assault? Like a fight? A mugging?"

"That's kind of what it ended up as," Holden said, "though it seems like their intent may have been more...sexual."

Riley leaned forward.

"Rape?" he whispered urgently. "Someone tried to rape her? On campus?"

"Near the trail behind Mueller Hall," Holden said, nodding. "It was a group, but she fought them off long enough—and loud enough—for someone inside the dorm to hear and scare them away. She was taken to the hospital. Arlington. Scratches, bruises, a black eye, concussion—all relatively minor, but still."

"Yeah," Riley breathed. "Still."

*She left the hospital overnight,* Trust added. *We saw her there Monday night, and when we went back Tuesday morning, she had been discharged by her parents—her mom and her uncle, actually. We talked to her yesterday, though. She's okay, but she's more angry about what happened than anything. Her parents are making her stay at home this week. She'll be back on Monday.*

"And she's not my girlfriend," Kyler added after he finished voicing Trust's words.

"Not yet," Holden remarked, cutting his eyes to the freshman.

"Man," Riley said, "that's awful. What...How...Do the police know who did it? Does Allison know?"

*Don't get all worked up over it,* Trust signed. *She wouldn't want you to ruin your appetite on this Thanksgiving-birthday lunch-dinner thing we're doing.*

Riley balled up a napkin and lobbed it at Trust. Trust caught it.

"That would have worked a lot better if you'd have let that hit you in the face," Riley said.

Trust shrugged, smirking faintly.

"They were wearing ski masks," Kyler continued, "but Allison—who's not my girlfriend—thinks they were students. She said she would be able to pick out the voice of one of them if she heard it again."

*And they took her phone,* Trust signed.

"They can track those things," Holden observed, just before shoving a spoonful of creamed corn into his mouth.

"Who can track what things?"

The voice at the end of their table drew Kyler, Holden, and Riley's gazes. Trust, however, had already spotted the approaching visitor moments before.

It was Jeremy Higgins.

"Ahh, Jeremy. What's up, man?" Holden greeted, giving the star athlete a grin and a nod. "Your guys ready for the game tonight?"

"I'll let that question pass as rhetorical," Jeremy replied, his typical, self-assured smirk present and in full display.

He glanced quickly around the table, coming to a stop on Trust and Kyler. His eyes then returned to Holden.

"Dude, you know everybody," Jeremy remarked. "I should have guessed I would find you with these two at some point."

"These two?" Kyler echoed, feigning offense.

"Yeah, these are two of the troublemakers—I mean, freshmen—in my wing in Weaver Hall this year," Holden introduced. "And this is Riley. You remember him from our dorm freshman year, right? Today's his birthday."

Jeremy looked to Riley, his eyes lighting up slightly.

"Really?"

He then turned away, toward the rest of the room. Other customers were busy eating and talking, not paying him any attention.

"Hey, everyone!"

He motioned to Riley.

"Birthday boy over here!"

"Oh, God," Riley muttered, quickly leaning back in his chair and putting a hand over his face.

"Happy birthday!" the room announced as one, perfectly synchronized, as though they had practiced beforehand.

"Happy birthday, Jimmy!" Kyler exclaimed, well late.

"Happy birthday, Jimmy!" the rest of the room proclaimed.

The boys looked at Kyler.

"Now that," Kyler said, "was awesome."

"You can tell it's a roomful of regulars today," Holden remarked. "Otherwise, you two would have just been a couple of guys shouting for no reason."

*No worries,* Trust gestured, before hooking his thumb at Kyler. *He's used to being that guy.*

"Yep, I can definitely see that," Riley said for the second time.

"From what I've seen of him so far this year, I can definitely see it, too," Jeremy said.

He then looked around the table again.

"So what were you guys talking about when I came over? Who can track what?"

"Heh," Riley said, smirking. "Someone's nosy."

"Was it this one?"

Jeremy pointed to Trust.

"You getting tired of stalking my girlfriend so you want to track where she is now? Trrrr...Trust, right?"

Trust rolled his eyes.

*I feel like this is a conversation we've had before.*

"Yeah. Sounds familiar, doesn't it?"

*Now, just to be clear, are we talking about Jezzie or Rory?*

"Now," Kyler was translating, "just to be clear, are we talking about...well, that was just uncalled for."

*He started it,* Trust argued.

"What did he say?" inquired Jeremy.

"He made an inappropriate comment about my relationship with my sister this time," Kyler said, shaking his head. "I'll tell ya, the dirty thoughts that go through this guy's head..."

Jeremy looked doubtful.

"Do you even know sign language?"

"Not at all," Kyler said. "I'm mostly just guessing."

Holden cleared his throat, bringing Jeremy's focus away from the two freshmen briefly.

"So, I heard you met Trust and Kyler at a party at the beginning of the year. And I heard *you*"—Holden pointed to Jeremy—"pulled the Freesef card. On a bunch of freshman girls, no less."

Jeremy scoffed, and then chuckled.

"You would hear that," he replied. "You hear everything. Most of it, though, is probably straight garbage. But don't act like you don't get a kick out of telling those Freesef stories, too. They're like ghost stories; it's funny to see all these freshies start to shake."

"Funny?" Riley repeated, an eyebrow arching.

"Oh, come on," Jeremy said. "You can't honestly tell me those stories make even an ounce of sense. What was the first thing we did when we first heard about the Freesef Society when we were freshmen? We laughed our heads off! Dude, those stories are so ridiculous, the only reason we still tell them is for entertainment."

"You don't believe them, then?" Holden asked.

"Do I believe—"

Jeremy shook his head.

"You're really on a roll with these rhetorical questions today, aren't you?"

Meanwhile, Trust nudged Kyler just before he could take a sip of water.

*You should tell him about Allison. See what he says.*

Jeremy looked back to Holden and Riley.

"How can you stand that?" he said, waving to Trust and Kyler. "It's like they're in their own private club or something."

"You remember that party you saw us at, right?" Kyler asked. "After the first game? You were talking about the Freesef Society then, to our friends, two freshman girls. One had red hair, the other had...well, spiked-pigtail things."

He demonstrated, gesticulating around his head. Jeremy stared at him with an expression somewhere between bewilderment and hilarity.

"Vaguely," he replied after a moment's contemplation. Even his smirk hinted at his curiosity. "I remember you two there. Not so sure I remember a redhead and a girl with crazy pigtails. You're sure these weren't imaginary friends?"

"Quite sure. Holden and Riley have met them, and so—"

"Actually," Riley spoke up, "I only met Allison. I haven't met the girl with pigtails."

"That'll be an event," Holden remarked, and stuffed his face with a large, buttery roll. "She's one of my freshmen in Weaver, too, but she went home for break. Marcie's a riot. Literally."

"But you've met both of them," Kyler went on, still directing his words toward the football player. "You're having trouble remembering because you were high and drunk on who-knows-what—"

"Hey, calm down," Jeremy said, glancing around to see if anyone else had heard. "I didn't—"

"I mean, seriously, you were, like, *seriously* high on something. You were so high you almost fell out right in the middle of the floor—"

Jeremy quickly kneeled down, leaning in closer.

"Seriously, man. *Knock it off.* I know what party you're talking about, but...I don't know what happened there. I don't know if I took something I wasn't supposed to, or if I mixed something—"

"That redhead you met was raped Monday night."

Jeremy stared at Kyler for a few moments, his mouth hanging open, his eyes unmoving. The table was quiet.

Jeremy then glanced around toward the others—Riley, Holden, Trust—before completing the circuit back to Kyler.

He started to laugh quietly.

"Oh, this is one of those things, right?"

Kyler observed the older boy a moment before shaking his head slowly.

"No, this isn't one of those things," he replied. "It really isn't."

Still smiling softly, Jeremy shifted to the other side of the table.

"He's joking, right?"

"Afraid not," Holden said. "He is a jokester, but this one's for real."

Jeremy's eyes switched to Riley briefly. Riley nodded.

"They just told me," he explained. "That's what we were talking about when you came over."

Jeremy looked to Kyler.

"Seriously?"

"Yep."

The usual smirk was gone.

"Man."

He shook his head, his brow furrowed faintly.

"And you say I was going off about..."

He suddenly slammed his fist on the table crowded with piles of food and abruptly stood. Glasses, plates, and silverware clashed briefly as they bounced. Fortunately, nothing turned over.

"What's her name?" he asked. "Marcie?"

"Allison," Kyler supplied. "Allison Tyler."

Jeremy rapped his knuckle against the table and turned away brusquely. He was leaving.

"Wait, Jeremy," Holden said. "You okay?"

As the older boy's back was turned, Trust could not see his response. He glanced quickly to the RA.

"He said he's fine," Holden said.

"Allison's not here!" Kyler called.

Under the archway heading out of the room, Jeremy froze. He looked back to the table.

"She won't be back until Monday night," Kyler said.

Even from a distance away, Jeremy's clenched jaw was visible. Trust, Kyler, Holden, and Riley—and other onlookers in the room who had witnessed Jeremy's brief eruption at the table—watched as the boy turned away again, exiting.

Trust started to turn back, but another face popped into the entryway Jeremy had just vacated. It was one of the proprietors of the Centre Towne Inn, an older woman with white hair. Trust had learned earlier that she was also one of the main cooks.

"Who's the one in here with the birthday?" she asked.

All eyes shifted to Riley, who sighed heavily.

## 20.
## Allison's Return

ON MONDAY, TRUST AND KYLER waited for Allison's call notifying them that she had arrived back in Centre City. It came just after seven that evening in the form of a text message.

> **Allison (7:03 PM):** Hey, guys. I'm back. Could you meet me at the campus police station? We'll get something to eat afterward. I'm buying.

The text, coming into Trust's and Kyler's phones while the pair were lounging lazily in their room watching television, jolted Kyler instantly to his feet. Trust watched, not moving, as Kyler frantically tapped his phone and brought it to his ear.

He was facing Trust, allowing the deaf teen to read his lips as he spoke.

"Allison? What happ—"

He paused briefly.

"Yeah..."

Kyler's face showed a trace of puzzlement as he listened, continuing to meet Trust's cool gaze.

"But—"

He listened.

"But—"

He was interrupted again. Trust finally sat up from his bed, casually getting his shoes.

"But what I was going to say was—"

Tying his laces, Trust was shaking his head as he looked at Kyler.

Then when he was done...

*Tell her we'll be there soon, and then hang up the phone.*

Kyler ran a hand through his mane of hair.

"Trust said to tell you we're on our way and to hang up the phone."

Whatever Allison said on the other end of the line caused Kyler to purse his lips and roll his eyes in resignation.

"Yeah, I'm definitely *not* going to tell him that...Yeah, we'll be there in five minutes."

Kyler slowly drew the phone away from his ear, ending the call. He looked at it for a moment before meeting Trust's gaze again.

Before he could say anything, however, Trust's phone vibrated and flashed. He looked at it briefly before showing it to Kyler.

**Allison (7:05 PM):** Thanks, Trust. Can you please make sure Kyler doesn't have a panic attack before he gets here? I'm fine. Everything is fine.

Kyler looked from the phone back to Trust.

*Grab that tired, old hat of yours and let's go,* Trust signed. *And I'm for sure texting your sister about this, because I think you really like Allison—a lot—and you're terrifying me and yourself because you don't know what the heck you're doing and you don't know how to control it. After she finishes making fun of you, I'm sure Michelle will know what to do.*

Kyler could only look at him, frowning.

THE JOINT CENTRE CITY POLICE Department – University of Centre City Campus Police building was located next to the student union, up a neat, artfully arranged brick-laden walkway intersecting manicured patches of grass and flowerbeds, trees tactfully placed to provide ample shade and pleasing aesthetics. A water fountain was at the center of the courtyard, the statue of a police officer, poised and standing tall, water springing out of the base on each side of him like exploding fireworks. Night lighting from lampposts about the area provided a picturesque view even after the sun fell, the scene worthy of a postcard. The University of Centre City was well known for the charming look of its campus, and even the setting of its police station was no different.

Presently, however, a very recent cold spell—the first of the year—had swept through the city, so the water fountain was shut off. Postcard photographers and the like would have to wait patiently for the return of spring to capture the setting in full effect again.

Not to mention the grass, which was brown and dormant. The winter season was slowing approaching.

Trust was walking alongside Kyler up the brick path, head turned in his direction, when he spotted the lurking figure out of the corner of his vision. It was a man, somewhere on the lower end of middle age, standing just on the edge of a cone of illumination from a nearby lamp.

The man was standing so still, anyone else would have easily overlooked him.

*Don't make it obvious,* Trust signed. *See if you notice anything out of the ordinary to our right.*

Kyler halted immediately in his tracks and turned ninety degrees to his left, crouching slightly into a ready position. Trust stepped back quickly at the boy's abrupt movement.

Kyler then jumped again, facing away from the police building ahead, and then again, facing the direction Trust had told him to look in the first place. Kyler then hopped one more time, once again facing forward.

Trust was staring at him incredulously.

*There's a guy over there, standing in the shadows,* Kyler signed. *I think he's on his phone. He's in a suit—seems weird, but harmless.*

Both boys stood alone on the path leading up to the building. Trust continued to stare at Kyler.

*What?* Kyler motioned. *I had to make it look good. If I had just looked over when you said and he was watching us, it would have been obvious what I was doing.*

*Really?* Trust replied. *Did Pax teach you that move? I would so pay to see you two play a couple of spies in a movie.*

*I don't want to give anything away,* Kyler responded, *but we're in talks for just such a project as we speak. Pax is in, but my agent wants me to hold out for a bit more money on the back end, whatever that means.*

The boys started walking again, approaching the front entrance.

*Anyway, I saw what you wanted me to see, right?* Kyler gestured. *You wanted me to see that guy?*

He grinned.

*See? You make fun of me and Pax, but our covert abilities are fully honed.*

*Okay,* Trust raised, *what color shirt was that guy wearing?*

*White or cream-colored dress shirt with a dark blue or black suit jacket,* Kyler shot back effortlessly. *His pants are the same color as his jacket, and he has on...black dress shoes.*

Standing in front of the door to the building, Trust stopped and turned to the boy alongside him.

*Well, I should have known you would cheat. How are you even allowed in school with a photographic memory? You're cheating all the time.*

Kyler sniffed at the crisp November air.

*Smells like someone's grilling some hate-me-back ribs and hate chops with a side of hate on the cob. But I see you've already gotten yourself a plate.*

Trust laughed.

*That was a good one.*

In the front lobby, the boys spotted Officer Ben Ryan first, though they did not immediately recognize him. The young cop was without his uniform, dressed instead in boots, jeans, and a hooded sweatshirt, a white T-shirt peeking out beneath. His hair was cut short, but it was still long enough to become slightly disheveled at times, as it was now.

He looked like a typical college student. Perhaps the only reason Trust and Kyler recognized him at all was because Allison was sitting right beside him.

Trust looked toward Kyler fleetingly, wondering if he was thinking the same thing Trust was at that moment.

That Ben Ryan and Allison Tyler could be a couple, and looking at them, no one would think twice about it.

Ryan and Allison stood as Trust and Kyler came near. The lobby was quiet at the moment, a slow period in the night.

"She said you would be here in five minutes," Ryan remarked, eyeing the pair of them. "What, did you take a leisurely stroll around the city before deciding to drop by?"

Kyler glanced to his phone.

"It's been...exactly four minutes since we got your text," Kyler said, looking to Allison.

*It's that patented CCPD humor,* Trust stated, to which Ryan chuckled softly. *You'll grow fond of it in time, Kyler.*

"Well, hello to you, too, Trustice Jeffries," Ryan greeted.

*You started it,* Trust responded.

"Is it a good sign when a police officer can remember your full name without having to look it up?" Allison asked.

"No," Ryan said.

"Yes," said Kyler at the same time.

Everyone looked at him.

"I just said that because I knew you would say no," Kyler said.

"I probably need to remember your name, too," Ryan commented. "Okay, let's go to the back. There's a room open for us."

"You mean we're on the list for the police station, too?" Kyler declared. "Now, I don't think *that* is a good sign."

As they walked back, Trust studied Allison.

She appeared in good health. Visibly, there was scarcely any sign of the incident from a week ago. Her face was clear, alluring, and adorably pretty as usual, with only a few light, nearly nonexistent scratches remaining. No limp—not that Trust should have suspected she had one before. The bruising around her face and eye was gone, but she was wearing long sleeves—not strange, given the cool weather, but concealing any lingering evidence of the injuries Trust had seen in the hospital.

Allison caught sight of Trust's examination. Trust pointed at his head, then hers. The group entered into a small conference room, a table surrounded by chairs waiting for them.

"My head?" Allison asked. "Oh, I'm fine. My brain stopped leaking out of my ears days ago."

Trust grimaced.

"That was so not funny," Kyler intoned.

"Okay, bad joke," Allison said. "It was only a minor concussion, though. Very minor. If the genetically mutated guys on the football team can deal with them all the time, then so can I."

Ryan waved the teenagers into seats.

"Minor concussion or not," he began, "I want you to know we are all taking this very seriously, and we thank you, Miss Tyler, for doing the same. UCC—and all of Centre City—takes pride in being named as one of the safest universities in the country, so, like I mentioned before at the hospital, we won't slow down until we find who did this. I apologize for what you went through."

Allison started to open her mouth, but—

"It's no problem," Kyler said. "I have faith in the CCPD and the UCCCP and whatever other PDs and CPs are investigating this. I'm sure you all will get to the bottom of it."

Ryan leveled a glare in Kyler's direction.

*Any time you want to cuff him,* Trust indicated, *by all means, feel free.*

Allison looked to the two boys.

"I told Officer Ryan in the lobby that I've been thinking about what happened on Monday, about what I could remember. It was at least four of them, probably five or six. The others didn't say much—I think one of them cried out when I kicked him—but I still remember the first one, the main one, as clear as if it had happened five minutes ago. I can remember what he said; I can remember that smile in his voice as he spoke. I can see his eyes through the holes in the mask. Not the color; I guess it was too dark. But he was standing so close...there was a...a shadow. It's hard to explain, but I would know it if I saw those eyes again."

"The detective assigned to this investigation has already interviewed some of the people who were in Mueller Hall at the same time of the incident, including the student who looked out the window and called 911," Ryan said. "I sat in on that interview. Out of everyone, that student is the only person besides you to catch even a glimpse of the assailants, but it is still very little to go on—dark clothes, possibly wearing hoodies or some type of hat. This is probably the masks that you mention. The student saw three or four individuals fleeing the scene—it's possible there were more, as this student saw them just as they disappeared.

"I think the most significant note," Ryan went on, "was that the witness said the attackers escaped into the wooded area instead of directly onto the walking trail behind Mueller. Crime scene techs walked through the area the student specified, but they didn't find anything."

*What side of the trail did the group run into?*

"What?" Ryan asked, looking from Trust to Kyler.

*The student who called 911 said he or she saw them run into the wooded area beside the trail. There's woodland on both sides of the trail. I'm asking which side the witness saw the attackers run into. The woods on the left side? The right?*

Ryan looked at Trust.

"It would have been the student's left side, facing away from Mueller Hall and toward the trail. Why? Why does that matter?"

Kyler chuckled.

"Because he—"

He stopped suddenly. Trust looked at him, his eyebrow arched.

Ryan leaned forward.

"What?" he said.

"I was just—" Kyler started, before the cop quickly held up his hand.

"No."

He reached into the back pocket of his jeans, soon pulling out his notebook and pencil. Ryan placed them both on the table and slid them to Trust.

"I want you to write down what he"—he pointed to Kyler—"was about to say. I want to hear—see it in your own words."

*I was in the woods outside of Mueller Hall Tuesday night.*

Ryan stared at the message a moment longer than necessary, his expression transforming as he thought. He then brought his hands to his face, massaging his forehead.

"Who do you think you are?" he asked, looking up and meeting Trust's eyes again. "Some UC on transfer? Did I not get the memo?"

"What's UC?" Allison asked.

"Undercover cop," Kyler answered before Ryan was able to, Ryan glancing toward him again.

Trust was writing.

*I wanted to see the place at night. I didn't expect to find anything. Just watching.*

"You ever heard of disturbing a crime scene?"

Trust pointed to Kyler.

"Nothing was blocked off," Kyler said, interpreting for Trust once more. "There was no caution tape. Students were using that back entrance during the entire time I was out there. I could just as easily assume the police had already examined the scene during the day and opened it back up again, if they had bothered to block it off at all."

"You're making assumptions on how the police run their investigations now?"

"I said I *could* assume. Frankly, I would have been out there either way and no one would have known. And no one did until I told you about it just now."

Kyler then motioned to his friend.

"I just want to make sure everyone is aware this is still Trust speaking, by the way. I would like to keep my position as upstanding citizen for the CCPD intact."

Ryan pointed to the notebook.

"You wrote down, 'I didn't expect to find anything.' Does that mean you did find something?"

Kyler read aloud as Trust wrote.

> Three guys—boys, about my age, I would guess, maybe slightly older—came into the woods about ten minutes after I did. They were moving slowly and cautiously, probably so they wouldn't be heard by anyone walking along the trail. One girl almost discovered them anyway. She practically ran away and the boys left soon after that.

"And this was on Tuesday night?" Ryan inquired, to which Trust nodded.

"Describe the boys."

> I didn't recognize any of them; I haven't seen them before or since. I would assume they were students, or at least college-aged. They all had on normal clothing—jeans, long sleeves. Two of them had on jackets, I think, and one of them had on a hoodie, all dark colors—blues, browns, blacks, dark grays possibly. The two boys with jackets had dark hair, brown or black. Cut close, kind of like yours, one shorter, the other maybe a little longer. But they didn't have anything that said UCC.

"So, in theory, they could be from anywhere and not be UCC students at all," Ryan said. "Or they could just be unrelated to the incident with Miss Tyler."

He looked to Kyler again.

"And where were you during this? Did you know he was planning to go out there?"

Trust signed quickly.

"He says it wasn't planned," Kyler relayed. "Spur of the moment. And no, I didn't know anything about it until he got back to the dorm. He was originally supposed to be going to get ice cream sandwiches from Hollins Cafeteria, so I thought he would be gone for five minutes, maybe ten on the outside. It ended up being closer to thirty."

"And you didn't call him or anything?" Allison said, aghast. "Kyler, what if something had happened?"

Trust smirked.

*If I had a problem, Kyler would only be a liability. But if he had really, really gotten worried, yes, he would have texted and come looking, although in this case, I'm glad he didn't. Not to mention, unless he's sleeping, Kyler's kind of afraid of the dark.*

Officer Ryan and Allison gave Kyler questioning glances, and Kyler shrugged.

"See, now I really don't know how that's relevant to our discussion," he said. "And anyway, being afraid of the dark doesn't make me any less of a man."

"Yeah," Ryan said dubiously.

Trust was writing in the notebook again. He slipped it to Allison.

> *Don't let Kyler read this, but if there was even a second that he thought you were in trouble, he would be the first one out the door, no matter how dark it was. I would be right behind him.*

Ryan looked over Allison's shoulder as she read. Allison then glanced up to Trust.

"Can I hang on to this?" she asked.

Trust shrugged casually.

"What'd it say?" Kyler asked. "Why can't I read it?"

*It says being afraid of the dark doesn't make you any less of a man,* Trust signed to him, *but that luxurious blond hair you have probably doesn't help your argument.*

Fifteen minutes later, Trust, Kyler, and Allison were back in the front lobby. The reception area had grown busier while they had been gone, more uniformed officers crisscrossing the room, and more people sitting in chairs, waiting for assistance.

"So," Kyler said, "where are we eating? And you already offered to pay, so no take-backs."

"What was that in there about not being seen as less than a man?" Allison raised, arching an eyebrow.

"Oh, that's easy. You see, Allison, men are also smart, so when someone—"

*Hold on,* Trust motioned. *Stay in here for a second. I want to see if that guy is still hanging around outside.*

Trust left the two of them, going through the doors and venturing outside into the cool night air, pulling his phone out of his pocket at the same time. As he stood at the head of the brick walkway, he held the phone up in the air, waving it around as though searching for a signal...

The man was still in the same location, now sitting on a bench. He had his phone in his hands as well, apparently engrossed in whatever was displayed on the screen.

Trust did not look directly at him—he didn't even have to come close. His peripheral vision was more than enough, sharper, particularly at night, than most people's vision was head-on during the day. He lowered his phone and went back inside.

*He's still there, but I don't know. I'm not sure if we should be concerned or not.*

"What's going on?" Allison asked.

"Some well-dressed vagabond with a phone was hanging around outside, lurking in the shadows when me and Trust came in," Kyler explained. "He seemed a little shifty."

Allison's face took on a look of concern.

"Do you think he's here looking for me?"

Kyler and Trust exchanged a glance.

*Maybe we should—* Trust began.

"Will you two ninnies roll up your pantyhose and let's just go already?" Allison declared, her expression quickly changing to one of exasperation. "And just when I was about to thank you guys for treating me like normal and not like my parents..."

With that, she pushed past both boys, shoving the door open. Trust and Kyler trailed quickly behind her.

In the night, even with the illumination coming from the neighboring light poles around the courtyard, Trust saw everything in precise, brilliant display, like he always did, down to the microscopic specks floating in the air. Different from the light along the walking path at the rear of Mueller Hall, which had thrown the scene into a soft orange tone, the light in front of the campus police station must have been of a separate quality. The particles in the air glowed in a diverse array of colors, a sparkling rainbow radiance. The infinite number of specks in the air seemed to only enhance Trust's vision, his view still astonishingly clear, so dramatically unlike what Kyler and anyone else saw when observing the same scene at the same time.

It had taken Trust, Kyler, and their families a while to realize exactly how different Trust's sight really was.

Trust's eyes immediately shifted to the man on the bench—but the man was already standing, moving across the small courtyard in their direction.

Before Kyler and Allison could react to what he was doing, Trust was already moving behind them and around, putting himself in between Allison and the stranger as he came closer...

The man smiled, holding up his hands.

Trust stopped, looking at him quizzically. He then looked to Allison, who had stopped walking as well. Allison glanced to Trust, before following his gaze back to the approaching figure.

Her eyes widened in surprise.

And then she smiled, beaming.

"Uncle Smith? What are you doing here?"

The well-dressed man held his arms out in a welcoming gesture.

"I wanted to see my girl for a little bit longer. Am I going to get the third degree now?"

Allison ran over to him for a hug. Trust and Kyler looked to each other again.

*Uncle?* Kyler mouthed in disbelief.

The man released Allison, chuckling, and looked over to the boys. Trust had his shades on, and Kyler had his hat, but both were staring unabashedly.

"So," Uncle Smith said, glancing down to Allison again, "you took my advice and got yourself some bodyguards, eh?"

AT THE RESTAURANT, SMITH DID not look up from his menu as he remarked, "I saw what you did out there."

Trust, not looking at the man, did not realize he was being addressed. Kyler nudged him.

Uncle Smith looked like a young banking executive or Wall Street tycoon, if there was such a look—but with an edge. Dressed in a suit Trust had already told himself he would not dare to contemplate the value of, the man looked to be in his mid-thirties, forty at the most. In the light of Han, a posh Chinese restaurant in downtown Centre City, Smith's hair was a peculiar blend of brown and red, not as richly crimson as Allison's, but not fully brown either. His tailored suit showed he was trim, bordering on muscular but not at all bulky, his face sharp, cut, chiseled. He looked like a million bucks personified. To Trust, he also gave off the impression that he would have no problems handling himself in a dark alley if the situation arose.

That was the "edge."

Moreover, in the time between their initial encounter in front of the police building and sitting down in Han, Trust and Kyler had also learned that "Uncle Smith" was really not an uncle at all.

The Smith part of his name was accurate, though whether it was his first name or his last was still unspecified.

"Sorry," Smith said. "I've got to get used to that. I was just saying that I saw what you did out in front of the police station. You spotted me when you first went in, didn't you?"

*Did Kyler's covert spy technique give it away?* Trust asked.

"Actually, no. But, to be honest, I didn't know what the heck he was doing."

"Exactly!" Kyler exclaimed, almost too loudly in the elegant restaurant. "See, I told you. They should have me training spies. I'm just that good."

"Wait," Allison said, looking to Smith beside her. "You were already here when Trust and Kyler got to the station? How is that even possible? You were at the airport when I left."

Smith smirked. Allison dropped her menu on the table and turned to face the man fully.

"No! No, no, no! You're not here to babysit me, are you?" she pleaded. "I made you, Mom, and Dad promise not to do that!"

Trust and Kyler shared a look. It seemed as though they had been doing that a lot lately.

"Umm...nope," Smith said. "Don't remember it quite like that. Your parents said okay. I just smiled like I'm doing now."

"Argh!" Allison groaned.

"I'm sorry. Is this a bad time?"

The server was standing beside their table. She held a small computer tablet in her hands.

"Saved by the bell...No, I think we're ready," Smith said, the first part emerging as a mutter, though Trust was able to decipher the lip movements. "You can go around the table and save me for last."

He looked up, giving the attendant, whose name tag read Judy, a magnetic smile. Judy's flush was visible even under the intimate lighting of the restaurant.

After the orders were made and Smith cast another smile toward Judy, resulting in another blush as the server departed, he turned to see Allison staring at him again, with Trust and Kyler staring at them both.

"Oh," Smith said, "don't start—"

"Why do you always do that?" Allison interrupted.

"Do what?"

Kyler snickered.

Smith and Allison glanced to him, Allison's expression less than amused.

Kyler stopped snickering.

"Courtesy ensures prompt service," Smith answered, turning to the girl again, "not to mention the fact that she thought she was about to witness something juicy to tell her friends about with you on the verge of throwing a tantrum. Now she's forgotten all about it. And don't even try to pull the innocent card with me."

He gestured to Kyler and Trust across the table.

"Look at these two. Pretty good-looking guys, wouldn't you say? They know. *Oooh, Trustice, your eyes are so blue. Oooh, Kyler, I like your hair.*

Or whatever it is college girls say these days..."

"Creepy," sang Kyler, drawing a chuckle from Trust.

"Don't even get me started on you," Smith continued, now pointing at Allison. "I can only guess—and then shudder—about how many of the boys you have in the palm of your hand already at this school."

Trust looked to Kyler.

Kyler mimed punching himself in the face.

Allison shook her head at Smith before rolling her eyes.

*So, New Orleans,* Trust signed. *We've known you for four months, Allison Tyler. How did we miss knowing where you were from until now?*

"And the Big Easy, no less," Kyler added, nodding.

"Me?" Allison said, pointing to herself. "What about you two? I have no idea where you guys are from."

"We're from N'awlins, too!" Kyler said. "Oh, how have we managed to not run into each other in all this time?"

Allison just looked at him, her expression deadpan.

"Sheesh," Kyler said. "Tough crowd tonight."

"That's a good question, though," Smith said, leaning forward to rest his arms on the table. "Where are you two from? Al has told us a lot about you, but not that."

"Who's Al?" asked Kyler.

"I am," Allison said.

"Okay," said Kyler.

*We're from North Carolina,* Trust signed. *The coast. About a five-and-a-half-hour car ride from here.*

"The Outer Banks?" Smith mused. "Impressive. I've been through that area a few times in my day. Looks just like the postcards."

"It's a dump," Kyler declared, causing the man to chuckle. "I mean, if you like charming coastal island towns near the beach, I guess it's all right, but beaches are so late twentieth century."

"I like the beach," Allison said, brightening.

"Me too," said Kyler.

*Could you possibly sound any more pitiful?* Trust signed.

"No, I will not say that, Trustice Jeffries. Need I remind you that there's a lady present?"

Trust smirked.

"And you stayed at school over Thanksgiving break?" Smith said, looking at the boys. "How did your families feel about that?"

*His sister loved it,* Trust observed, gesturing to Kyler as the boy returned to interpreting. *His sister thinks we're annoying. Us? Annoying?* She's *annoying.*

Smith and Allison laughed.

"We decided to stay and attempt to fully immerse ourselves in Centre City during the first half of the year," explained Kyler. "You know, get down deep—*deep* deep—in the Centre City culture. Trust has never been to Centre City before, and I've only been up here once for a baseball tournament in middle school, and I barely got to see anything. And this is from us being only a state away. I'm surprised you even heard of UCC down in Louisiana. We'll go back home during Christmas, though."

Allison was giving Kyler a cheeky smile as she sipped her drink with a straw.

"You're surprised that we heard of the University of Centre City *down in Louisiana*? You sure you want to stick with that?"

"We've definitely heard about the football team this year," Smith said. "Who's that wide receiver you guys have? Higgins?"

Both Trust and Kyler spotted the trace of worry that came across Allison's features at the mention of Jeremy Higgins. Smith did not. He whistled quietly.

"Five receiving touchdowns and one rushing touchdown in that game on Thanksgiving Day. I heard he was good, but that guy's going to have every pro team fighting over him at the draft—that is, if he decides to declare."

*You sound like a football fan,* Trust noted. *Hang around us for a week and you'll probably meet him. We seem to run into him pretty regularly.*

"Good guy?" asked Smith.

Trust gave him an extended look.

"Yeah, I've seen his picture on TV," Smith said. "Cocky's about the impression I got."

Judy the waitress soon passed by their table for the fourth time since delivering their drinks, informing them that she would bring out their food as soon as it was ready, which should be shortly.

"Did you get the alert about the theft in Revere Hall?" Allison asked Trust and Kyler.

*On Black Friday,* Trust replied, nodding. *I figured it out. Somebody's getting their Christmas shopping done on the cheap.*

Allison feigned a laugh before saying, "I still can't believe the police don't even have any leads—"

"Sorry, Al," Smith cut in. "Trust, can I speak to you for a moment in private?"

Trust glanced to Kyler before shifting back to Smith.

"You'll only need to read my lips," the man assured him. "It'll be quick."

Trust shrugged loosely before beginning to slide out of the booth seat.

"Don't be long," Kyler voiced. "I'm sure Judy would be disappointed if Smith wasn't here when she passed by again."

Though Han was full and busy, the high-end and intimate atmosphere discouraged a bustling setting. If Trust had been able to hear, only the dull, low hum of quieted conversations would have been audible, occasionally punctuated by laughter or a briefly animated voice, the soft keys of a piano playing over the sound system hovering in the background. Smith led Trust to an area that was unattended and out of the way.

"Is this okay? Can you still understand me? I know it's kind of dark in here."

Standing before him, Trust nodded and waved his hand, dismissing the man's concerns.

"I'm not sure if you've picked up on it, but other than whatever she's told the police in front of you, Allison's going to stay away from what happened last Monday. Maintaining a calm façade, concealing the panic, you could say. She's good at it."

Trust nodded.

"But she's thinking about that night all the time, even when she's not talking about it. I've been around her her entire life; I was there when she was born. I can't understand what she's going through, of course, but I know how she thinks, how she manages. I know what's going through her head. And I wanted to thank you and Kyler."

Trust looked at the man, his face expressing slight confusion. Smith tucked his hands into his pockets.

"Allison wouldn't want me to say the things I'm saying now if she was listening, but like I said before, she's told us a lot about you and Kyler—more than she even realizes, I suspect. I'm not sure she's even aware she's talking about you two sometimes. Nevertheless, from everything that I hear, you sound like a couple of stand-up guys. Perhaps a little...eccentric at times, but hey, people say that about me, too, so I wouldn't think that is all so bad."

Trust continued to watch Smith intently.

"Allison told us—me and her parents—briefly, vaguely, of how you arrived at the hospital where she was transported. Just little fragments, before she caught herself and switched to something else. I think she's afraid of what her parents would think of you—or, more specifically, what her parents would think of her associating with someone who would even conceive of doing something like that. I don't have the whole story of what you did, but on the other hand, I don't think I need it. I've heard it involves running through traffic and being chased by police..."

He paused. Trust's expression did not alter.

"Yeah. Anyway, you're standing here now, which means you're not in jail or flattened on the street. Thanks for that."

Smith pulled out his phone. Seeing it, Trust did not immediately recognize the make or brand, but it was ultra-sleek and obviously state of the art. In the space of two seconds, Smith tapped and scrolled, handing the phone over to him.

It was a video showing the interior of a bus. Trust recognized the interior right away as one of the Centre Line transports.

His eyes lifted quickly to Smith. Smith was studying him.

The definition of the video was good, taken from the front of the bus and showing every seat, including that of the bus driver. Trust could see himself sitting at the back.

A man at the front of the bus abruptly stood.

Trust handed the phone back to Smith. The deaf teenager's face was inscrutable.

"I know what you're thinking," Smith acknowledged, "and you have to take my word for it when I tell you I have no ill intentions. However, I do want you to know that I know. The video was not obtained illegally, and you are the only one I plan to show it to. As far as I'm aware, no one else has seen what happened outside those on the bus and the officers involved—"

Trust's thoughts flashed to Officer Ryan.

"—and before you suspect it," Smith went on, "I did not acquire this copy from either of them. I won't go into it, but I will say that what I do for a living allows me access to people and things typically off-limits. I haven't mentioned what was on that video to anyone else—that includes Allison. And speaking of..."

Trust glanced away, following Smith's gaze and seeing the girl approach.

"The food is here," Allison said, looking between Trust and Smith. Her eyes settled on the older man.

"And stop hijacking my friends. I'm not dumb. I know what you're doing."

"You're absolutely not, and you absolutely don't," Smith said, smiling. "We're talking about guy stuff over here, stuff that Trustice will also need to impart to Kyler later. I went to college, too, you know, and I know what I'm talking about. This is stuff that I never want to hear about any boy telling you, ever."

Trust gestured back toward the table, Smith and Allison following his motions.

"It looks like Kyler is showing a dangerous amount of interest in that candle on the table," Smith observed. "You should go back and monitor him, Al, before he burns this place down. Trustice and I will be there in thirty seconds."

Allison glared at Smith briefly in unspoken challenge before she backed down.

"We're talking about this later," she intoned. She then turned on her heel, her fiery red hair whipping around behind her.

Once she was out of earshot, Smith said, "She's so much like her father it's not even funny."

He then turned back to Trust fully.

"Running through streets and busy highways, the episode on the Centre Line bus, the way you stepped in front of Allison when you didn't know who I was, and who knows what else you've done while you've been here, and before, in Wilmington. I still don't know that much about you, Trustice, but you seem like a good kid, and full of surprises. I'm glad you and Allison found each other, and Kyler, too. I just wanted you to take that from me without having to pay attention to Al's grief. And, like I said, I wanted you to know what I know."

He extended his hand, and the two of them shook.

"By the way," Smith added, "Kyler and Allison. Am I seeing what I think I'm seeing, or..."

Trust smirked as they started back toward the table where Allison and Kyler were waiting.

*And now you know what I know,* Trust signed, knowing that the man would not understand him.

AFTER DROPPING OFF TRUST AND Kyler at Weaver Hall, Smith pulled up to the curb outside Mueller. He had somehow managed to find a black, sleek, new-model SUV for his visit to Centre City, and he cut the engine, the soft purr of the vehicle silencing completely. The normal sounds of a weeknight on the rural campus were muffled inside the vehicle as the occasional students meandered past. Due to the later hour, the street-lit university grounds possessed a smooth, ambient quiet.

Smith's eyes shifted from the tinted front windshield to Allison, sitting in the front passenger seat.

"I'm going to be in town for a few days."

He noticed Allison tense.

"I'm not going to hover," he clarified quickly. "You won't even notice me. But I do have some other business to take care of, so you can just think of me as being here for something completely unrelated, which I am anyway."

"It's fine," Allison said.

From her lap, she looked up to the man.

"I just...I just don't want anyone to think I can't take care of myself. You know how much I had to go through with Mom and Dad just so I could come up here alone."

"I do know," Smith replied. "So does your mom, and your dad. But don't worry about them. We've all seen how much you've wanted this, how much work you put in. Everyone's going to try their best to stay out of your way and give you space. But you can't—after what happened— you can't expect it to be so quickly forgotten. I'm not a father, thank God—"

Allison smiled faintly.

"—but this is essentially every father's nightmare scenario. Fortunately, you were able to fight them off long enough—"

He exhaled noisily.

"I don't need to count off the ways in which it could have gone differently."

Allison nodded slowly.

"I understand," she said.

Smith gazed at the young girl, a smile beginning to edge across his lips.

"I know," he said. "Now get out. You've got a class at, what, nine in the morning? Besides, my night isn't quite over yet."

Allison looked at him, amused.

"How would you know I have a class at nine? I never told you my schedule."

"You mean that guess was right? Man, I'm good."

"Yeah, right," Allison said, chuckling as she opened the door.

She turned back around once she was on the sidewalk.

"You stay safe out in the big city, Uncle Smith. Don't do anything I wouldn't do."

"Please," Smith declared. "I do things you wouldn't do before you even have a chance to wake up in the morning."

Allison's nose wrinkled.

"I was alluding to exercise. You know, the thing you hate to do? Get your mind out of the gutter, young lady, before I call your parents."

Arriving back in her dorm room, Allison was met with a familiar face.

"Melody!" she said. "I'm surprised to see you here at this time of the night."

Her roommate, engrossed in the sheet music displayed on her laptop, jerked her head when she heard Allison's voice. Her hair, varying shades of black, brown, and purple, whirled about as she turned to look.

"Allison! You're back!"

"I'm back? You mean you came back to the room long enough to realize I was gone in the first place?"

Melody stuck out her tongue, though she laughed. Allison moved to her baggage, which she had left behind before her appointment at the police building with Officer Ryan.

"Seriously, I was worried," Melody said, "but I didn't want to call you over break and disturb you. But then I came in earlier and saw your bags and—yay!"

She clapped her hands excitedly and Allison snickered.

"My parents made me stay at home for the week," Allison explained. "But I should have called. Wait...I did call! You didn't answer!"

"Oops. I must have left my phone...somewhere again."

Allison laughed once more, shaking her head.

"But wait!"

Allison glanced up from unpacking her clothes, watching as Melody practically leaped out of her chair, heading toward the girls' shared closet space.

"The RA gave me these to give to you earlier today; they must have come before I stopped in. Thinking about it now, I don't know why I decided to put the flowers in the closet. I guess it's from hearing all this stuff about the Dorm Room Robber..."

Melody was clutching a beautiful bouquet of flowers, a colorful arrangement stemming from a small decorative vase. She held it out to Allison, who took it, her mouth hanging open in shock.

"I know!" Melody said, reading Allison's face. "How totally adorable is this? Even though they're not all roses, I guessing it has to be from a boy. I'm going to lock you in this room until you tell me about him, but first, read the card."

Allison was still moving dazedly as Melody motioned toward the envelope tucked carefully into the bouquet. Her roommate then lost patience, retrieving the card herself and handing it to her.

"But...there's no boy," Allison said faintly, mostly to herself, though it was still loud enough for Melody to hear. "Maybe it's from my parents. Or my uncle."

"Or a secret admirer," Melody said. "Ahh, unrequited love. Here, let me put these down while you open it. You're moving so slow, Allison!"

Melody took the flowers and placed them on Allison's desk. Allison finally opened the envelope. Melody tried to peek over Allison's shoulder.

"Money?" she voiced an instant later. "He sent you money?"

## 21.
## Almost Caught

*We ask that you please no longer pursue investigation. If you
accept, you will receive further compensation. We apologize
for the misunderstanding.*

The message from Allison's mysterious note flitted in and out of
Trust's thoughts as he nimbly skipped around the boxing ring in the
North Gym, his lightning-quick strikes on the fighting dummy producing
brief, thunderous pops as his gloved hands made impact. His early
afternoon class had been canceled, and with Kyler currently busy with an
off-season baseball workout along with the rest of the university team,
Trust had decided to return to the gym even after his customary
morning regimen.

We ask that you please—*Pop!*—no longer—*Pop! Pop!*—pursue
investigation—*Pop!*—If you accept—*Pop-pop!*—you will receive further
compensation—*Pop-pop-pop!*

Feinting, and then ducking away, he felt someone entering the ring
behind him. Trust stopped, turning around. The visitor was unexpected.

Smith.

The man was dressed for the occasion, with athletic shorts and a
sleeveless shirt. He was barefoot, his shoes left behind on the gym floor
below. Trust's shoes were off as well, his ankle-length socks remaining.

What Trust had guessed before was a trim body was actually a mild
understatement. Smith was ripped, obviously quite at home with some
sort of regular physical routine, whatever that was. Not only did he look
like he would be able to fend for himself in some nondescript dark alley,
he looked like he would relish it.

Trust was made aware quite often that his own body was nothing to sneeze at, but Smith looked straight out of an action movie.

"Now how did I know I would find you here?" Smith said, grinning.

Trust smiled faintly and held up a finger as he went to retrieve his note cards.

"So, you come prepared," said Smith when Trust returned.

*Kyler can't follow me around all the time. I didn't know you were still here.*

Smith shrugged.

"I told Allison on Monday I had other business to take care of in the area, which I do. But I think we have an unspoken understanding that I would be around, at least for a few days. I did promise her she wouldn't notice I was here, which, as far as I know, she hasn't. She certainly doesn't know I'm here with you. I know she's in class right now, but you weren't expecting to meet her here anytime soon, were you?"

Trust shook his head.

"Figures. I think the girl is allergic to gyms, unless they have a swimming pool."

*I hope I'm not out of turn, but Allison told you about the note?*

Smith nodded.

"She called me not even five minutes after I had dropped her off. I was there watching when an officer came to pick it up, but I didn't go in. I saw him bring out the flowers. 'We ask that you please no longer pursue investigation. We apologize for the misunderstanding.' And five hundred dollars, with an assurance for more if she cooperates."

Trust nodded, communicating that he knew the message. Smith studied the deaf boy for a moment, his hands on his hips.

"What do you think about it?"

Trust thought before writing.

*There's an urban legend around here about a secret group called the—*

Smith, reading along as Trust wrote, stopped him.

"The Freesef Society. I'm aware. I didn't want you to waste space writing that down."

Trust looked at the man, surprised.

*So it's real, then?*

"I'm sure we've both heard the same stories. Apparently, they've been floating around for a while, but I haven't had a reason to put much stock in any of it. You think differently?"

*Don't know. But if rumors are true, could be a possibility.*
*Allison's attackers?*

"I don't think Allison's case matches their usual behavior, if we're to believe the stories in the first place. The end result doesn't correlate, nor does the way they went about it, nor does where it happened, like they were almost begging to get caught. And then to pick a victim who was not only going to go to the police, but was going to fight back during the attack. These attackers weren't nearly as organized or prepared as the Freesef Society is alleged to be."

*And the note. "We apologize for the misunderstanding."*

"Doesn't sound like a roving gang of unruly college misfits, does it?"

*Perhaps that's the part that's organized. Ever heard of the*
*Endeavor Group?*

"I have."

Trust gave him a skeptical look.

*Who are you really? How do you know all this stuff? Me,*
*Freesef, Endeavor Group.*

"You think you can read my lips as we spar?"

Trust looked at him.

"You try to hit me first," Smith offered, "and I'll tell you what I can. I want to test my theory about you."

Trust stepped back, laying his cards down again in the corner, he and Smith soon getting into combative stances.

Then they started to move.

"I work in the security field," Smith began, backing and circling as Trust advanced and circled at the same time. "What I said on Monday about getting access to things typically off-limits—that's true. Sometimes that thing is something relatively small and seemingly unimportant, like a security video taken from inside a Centre Line bus that turns out to have an extraordinary story behind it. Other—"

Trust lashed out, faking one way and quickly going another while still moving forward. Smith was able to sidestep out of the way.

"Other times," he continued, "I may have to speak to a person—a very important person—who is unavailable to most others. A good deal of the time, my work brings me into contact with law enforcement agencies on various levels—local, state, federal. In all of those instances, such as obtaining that video, everything goes through appropriate channels. But I also like the times when I get to do things my way."

Trust looked at him pointedly before releasing a straight jab. Smith leaned away. On impulse, Trust went low, attempting a leg sweep. Smith hopped over it effortlessly, as though expecting it, Trust rising and dancing away.

Trust was smiling, as was Smith, as the two circled again.

"I was in the military in my younger years," Smith stated, "and then in college, briefly, before I went right into—"

Trust was instantly close again, shooting one, two, three strikes toward Smith's head, Smith parrying them all away. Trust spun and fell to the floor again, this time landing on his stomach, pushing himself back quickly under Smith's legs, his hands snatching Smith's ankles. The sudden force of Trust's pull tossed Smith forward, but the man corkscrewed his body in mid-flight and flipped around, landing on his feet and facing Trust's prone form again. Smith abruptly dropped to the ring floor as well, kicking a leg out ahead of him just as his body made contact with the ground. His foot was aimed directly at Trust's head, who was also still on the ground. Trust pushed himself off the ring floor completely, his body fully horizontal to the ground and suspended for a moment in the air, Smith's leg sweeping underneath him.

Trust landed, this time on his back, but immediately jolted himself up again to avoid Smith's foot coming back through, set to give a punishing blow. Trust's handspring landed him on the tips of his feet. He leaped into the air, as Smith had done earlier, to avoid Smith's kick for a third time. Smith rolled swiftly and stood at the end of the sweep.

The flurry of moves by both of them was astonishingly rapid, taking only seconds. Neither appeared to be breathing even moderately hard.

"That's what I thought," Smith said, standing a distance away from Trust and grinning again. "I knew you were going easy. I could tell."

Trust pointed to him subtly and gave a thumbs-up.

"Allison showed me that note you wrote at the police station."

Trust gazed at him, and Smith stared back as though waiting for a response.

"And now I'm dying to ask you where on earth you learned those moves."

Trust gestured toward Smith, beckoning him to speak first.

"Me? Military, from places and people that shall remain classified. And if you say that, I'll know you're lying. You're barely old enough to join up now, but I can tell you've been doing this for years."

Trust snapped his fingers, as if Smith had taken the words right out of his mouth.

Smith grinned.

Out of the corner of his eye, Trust saw a familiar flashing, just as Smith said, "I think that's your phone." Trust went to where it rested alongside his note cards.

It took him half a second to read the short message. He then started to gather his things. He motioned to Smith, who came closer. Trust showed him the text, from Kyler.

**Kyler (1:32 PM):** I almost caught the Dorm Room Robber in
front of our room!

LEAVING SMITH AT THE NORTH Gym, Trust arrived to an astonishing sight on the seventh floor of Weaver Hall. There were more students packed into the area than Trust had even seen on the floor at one time, the congestion increasing as Trust drew nearer to his room. He had to slither through the horde to get to the center of all the attention, in front of his and Kyler's doorway.

Kyler, along with Holden, was standing just outside the door, speaking to two University of Centre City Campus Police officers.

Kyler was clad only in a bath towel and slide sandals. His hair was still wet.

Unsurprisingly, a large majority of the spectators crowding the hall were female.

Kyler was the first to spot Trust.

"Dude!" he exclaimed. "I was *this* close to catching him! I was chasing him down the hall, but then I ran into a door and—"

*Are you charging money for this show,* Trust signed, *or is this a freebie?*

Kyler looked at him, completely baffled.

*You do know you're one unexpected breeze away from being completely naked, right?*

Kyler looked down.

"What, this? Dude, you know I should have a patent on securing towels. There's no way—"

Kyler was demonstrating the steadfastness of the towel on his waist by tugging on it this way and that, and the pack of girls surrounding them seemed to hold their breath as one as they waited for the inevitable.

"Okay," one cop, a female, declared.

She pointed back inside the dorm room.

"This obviously isn't going to work out here. You, me, your RA, and I'm assuming this is your roommate?"

Kyler, Trust, and Holden all nodded.

"I'll finish talking to you three in the room."

She then turned to the other officer.

"You can finish finding any other witnesses, hopefully without any more distraction."

"Yeah." The officer snorted. "We'll see about that. I think this crowd's out for blood."

Nevertheless, he started to turn to the spectating horde of females as the three boys were ushered into the dorm room.

"Okay, I want everyone who actually saw any of what happened to raise their hands high in the—"

The female officer closed the door, reducing her partner's directions to a muffled muttering. She turned back inside.

Kyler was seated in his desk chair. Trust and Holden were still standing.

"I've been with the campus police for six years," the officer remarked, "and we've had some pretty famous people visit this university. But I've never encountered a scene quite like that."

"They probably want to hear more about the Dorm Room Robber," Kyler said. "I still can't believe I almost had him."

The officer—Trust read her nametag as Mendez—looked at Kyler in complete disbelief, before looking to Trust and Holden. Trust looked to his roommate.

*Tell the officer exactly what I'm saying; don't leave anything out. As hard as it may be to believe, no, Kyler is not acting right now, and yes, on some things, he really is this naïve. But without even knowing what happened here, I would stand by whatever Kyler says as the truth. He's a terrible liar. You would be able to tell as soon as he tried.*

Kyler translated it, word for word, but then said, looking back to Trust, "But I don't get it. If they don't want to hear about the thief, then what the heck are all those people out there for?"

Blowing out a puff of air, Officer Mendez raised her notebook again, her pen ready.

"Let's start where you left off. You were walking from the bathroom back to your room, and you saw someone—a boy in blue jeans, the bottoms slightly frayed; black Nike Shox 3DXs; a dark blue hooded sweatshirt with what looked to be yellow cursive writing on the front bottom left-hand side; and an old blue baseball cap with a cursive *M* on the front, facing backward, the *M* outlined in blue and yellow. You saw this individual attempting to enter your room. Then..."

"Then," Kyler picked up, "I called out to him, like, 'Hey!'"

"That's when I first heard him," Holden said. "My room is a few doors down, and I had my door open."

"I said 'Hey!'" said Kyler, "but not hey like 'Hey! What are you doing?' but like 'Hey, what's up?' I probably should have said what's up; maybe I wouldn't have scared him off...but anyway. I called out 'Hey!' and he looked up quickly. He had something in his hand that he was sticking into the keyhole—it looked sort of like a key, but I don't think it was. I was too far away to see it clearly at the corner of the hall, and he was at the door. But the key-grip part of the key-thing was yellow. I do know that."

"You think you could identify the object if you saw—"

Officer Mendez's radio activated, interrupting her.

"Thirty-two, negative on that 10-30 so far."

Mendez's hand went to the mic on her shoulder.

"Thirty-two, ten-four.

"They haven't found anything," she then told the boys.

Trust assumed there were more officers in and around Weaver Hall, searching for the boy. Kyler must have described him earlier, before he had arrived.

"So, this key device. Do you think you would recognize it if—"

Kyler was shaking his head.

"It was about the same size of a key, and it definitely had some sort of yellow thing on the end, but I don't know. It was too small and I was too far away to make it out fully, and he put it back into his pocket so quick, I didn't get a closer look. Right when I called out to him and he saw me, he put the thing in his pocket and bolted down the hall. I called out 'Hey!' again—that hey was a 'Hey! Where do you think you're going?' type of hey. I think that's when it entered my mind that he could have been trying to get in the room to steal something. Maybe he was the Dorm Room Robber. So I chased after him. He only got an extra step or two when I started running...two steps, yeah."

"In a towel and sandals," Mendez pointed out, her voice still conveying some skepticism.

Kyler nodded.

"Well, I kicked off the sandals. If I had on regular shoes, and I hadn't run into that door, I definitely would have caught him. Easily."

"He's on UCC's baseball team," Holden told the officer, indicating to Kyler. "Varsity. Apparently, he's pretty fast."

*Not fast enough to beat me, though.*

"Not fast enough to beat you?" Kyler said. "What are you *talking about?* Dude, I can smoke you—"

"You started to chase him," Mendez prodded, eyeing Kyler.

"Yeah, I started to chase after him down this hallway, going that way."

Kyler gestured from left to right, pointing toward the door.

"He passed by Holden's door, still running, and I'm after him. I call out 'Hey!' again. I was barefoot—actually, that was stupid, I could have stepped on something. Fortunately, the cleaning staff—I guess it would be the cleaning staff...anyway, the carpet was clean. No shards of glass or anything. I had just gone by Holden's door when he stuck his head out and said, 'Kyler, what's going'—oh, crap!"

Kyler, in his seat, swiftly turned to Holden.

"I'm not going to get in trouble for running, am I? Dude, you know I wouldn't have even thought of doing that if—"

The junior resident assistant waved him off.

"Don't worry about it, Kyler. Extenuating circumstances. Anyway, I think the hallway dished out its own punishment with that door."

"Yeah," Kyler agreed. "So when Holden said, 'Kyler, what's going on?' I didn't even say anything. I'm really running, and the guy is at the end of the hall already, about to turn the corner on the girls' side."

"After he went past," Holden remarked, looking at Mendez, "I went after both of them, but I was jogging. Probably why I didn't get to the corner in time to see anything. Kyler and that other kid were in an all-out sprint."

"I turn the corner after this guy," Kyler recounted, fully animated, gesturing with his hands, but not in sign language. "I think he might've run into the wall or lost his balance or something. When I first see him as I turn the corner, he's still running, but he's just turning to face forward again. That's when I saw that yellow cursive whatever on the bottom corner of his hoodie, but I couldn't read it; I didn't see enough. His head was turned back—he must have seen me—and then he turned back around. I run past a couple of doors, and—bang! I didn't even see it coming. That closet door, *opening outward*—I haven't even noticed until now that those doors do that."

"I'm sure they'll be changing it," Holden said.

"I must have noticed it at the very last second as it came open. I started to fall back before I hit it—I guess it was instinct or something. I didn't smash into the door head-on and I had started to bring my hands up, so I ran into it with the rest of my body as I was leaning back. I didn't even hit my head that hard, and I fell on my butt."

Trust grimaced at the image.

*Are you all right?*

"My butt is just fine. Thanks for asking, buddy."

Trust sent him an emphatic gesture that did not need interpretation. The sentiment was clear.

"That's where I lost him," Kyler resumed. "It was completely my fault. I—"

Trust cleared his throat. Loudly.

"Yeah, I mean I know it wasn't actually my fault," Kyler said, "but I'm sitting there in the hallway. My head's down, on my knees, and my eyes are closed. For a few seconds, I shut down, completely. I can't hear anything. I don't move. Trust knows this story.

"When I was younger, in middle school, I was pitching, and one player came back at me with a hit that came *this close* to hitting me in the face. First time that had ever happened to me. I was scared to death, and to dodge it, I guess I fell on the mound, and I had started crying.

"Trust was at that game. My dad, one of the coaches, came out to the mound—I don't know how long I had been sitting out there. I was crying, but I wasn't moving. I was frozen. But my dad didn't tell me to get up, even though I hadn't actually been hit. He didn't tell me to shake it off. He said, 'Put your head down, close your eyes, and let go. Breathe. Relax.'

"The *sound* as I hit that closet door was a lot worse than it felt. It sounded like a gunshot. And I was already starting to fall back, off balance. I think the combination of it all shook me for a second. Luckily, my butt broke the fall. I don't know what happened to the boy, though. I mean, I assume he went down the stairs at the end of the hall, but I don't know. I lost him there."

A SHORT WHILE LATER, OFFICER Mendez had completed taking Kyler's and Holden's statements. Leaving the three boys in the room, the cop had gone back outside, where she was now conversing in low tones with her partner in the hallway, who had also returned.

Trust could tell they were speaking softly due to their body language, but Mendez had her back to the door.

However, it gave him a perfect, unhindered view of the other officer, who was taller and facing Mendez and the door.

"You hear that call? Downstairs, fourth floor."

"No word so far of anyone seeing our boy in the red hat. It's gonna be like finding a needle that may or may not be in this giant haystack."

"Nope. Nothing in the stairwell. They're gonna do another run-through, but what's the likelihood of this kid just going down a floor or two and getting out again to get on the elevator, or going down another set of stairs? Or maybe even hanging out in the building for a few more minutes to let the search run past? Once we lose him in the hall, he has options."

"I was thinking a sketch before from the way he can describe him. Or at least have him run through that suspect-rendering program. Kid's apparently got a crazy-good memory; we should be able to pin down a pretty specific depiction of this guy."

"The door was closed. Anyone could have shut it between then and now, though. Could've been a student, or—"

"*Inside* the closet? That would mean multiple people inside on the same robbery. We've been working on the theory of one on the inside and Red Hat lookout. You think we're lookin' at some type of gang or theft ring here?"

"Yeah, ask him. I'll go start on the report. Chuck and that new guy, Bellamy, are still over on the other wing. Sarge has Bellamy on-site for the possible hit on the Thomas Building tomorrow night. I'm with you; I think we need a couple more cars out there, but Sarge could be right. It may be a false call to draw us out of position."

"Yeah, I'll be outside."

Trust, now sitting as well, turned away as Mendez started to come back in. Kyler and Holden were talking, but he failed to pick up their conversation before both boys turned toward the doorway.

"One last question," Mendez said. "We have reason to believe a boy who commonly wears a red baseball cap may be involved as a possible lookout outside of the buildings where these thefts are taking place. Did you see anyone with a red hat when you arrived from your baseball practice?"

Kyler shook his head.

"I came in the back entrance. There wasn't anyone else back there."

The police officer nodded.

"And that may be how you stumbled on him so unexpectedly. If there's a chance the lookout knows what you look like, he wouldn't have been able to warn his friend if you came around the back."

*But weren't you in the shower?* Trust asked, looking to Kyler. *That would mean you'd been here more than a few minutes. Why would a thief wait so long to try to break in to our room?*

"You'll probably hear about it within the hour," Mendez replied once Kyler translated, "but there was a second robbery reported, downstairs. We just got the call while I was standing outside in the hallway, but from what we know so far, it seems to have occurred before this individual came upstairs to your room."

After informing Kyler that the police would be contacting him in the next few days to schedule an appointment with the department's sketch artist, Officer Mendez departed.

Paxson wandered in just as the cop was leaving, and his eyes followed the female officer's back before shifting inside the dorm room.

"Hey, what's the po-po at yo' do' fo'? Argh, Kyler! Is it so hard to put on some shorts and a T-shirt? This isn't some nudist holiday that I haven't heard about, is it?"

## 22.
## Jeremy Apologizes

*SO, YOU'RE SERIOUS?* TRUST MOTIONED. *You really want to do it?*

"Why would you not think I was serious?" Marcie questioned. "It's not going to be every week, of course. Just occasionally, every once in a while. It'll be like you said—a way to vent frustration. It'll be my form of meditation."

The group of freshmen were sitting at a table in Hollins Cafeteria, eating dinner. The dining hall was splendidly decorated with Christmas and winter-themed adornments. Lights, wreaths, bells, and ribbons hung along walls and banisters, and a mammoth, live Frasier fir stood in the center of the room, lit and covered in ornaments.

"Vent frustration?" Kyler joked. "And you don't think you'll need it more than 'once in a while'?"

Marcie gave him a sharp look.

"Maybe she should use you as the punching bag," Allison said.

Trust chuckled knowingly.

"Sounds like Allison could use some of these venting sessions, too," Paxson observed wryly before taking a bite of his steak.

Both Allison and Marcie turned to him.

"Oh, so you think we can *use* it?" Marcie challenged. "I guess we're just a couple of bratty, irritable girls, huh?"

"Huh? What?" Paxson said. "I didn't say anything. Uh-uh. I wasn't even talking just now."

Trust gestured quickly. Kyler translated with a low, rapid-fire delivery.

"The express opinions of Paxson Haynes are his and his alone. The other males at this table do not necessarily agree with his beliefs and are

277

in no way bound by them. Any allusion to the contrary is strictly discouraged."

*Kyler, why don't you tell the story again about how you were running naked through the halls chasing after one of the Dorm Room Robbers,* Trust added.

Marcie slammed her palm against her forehead.

"Jeez, I can't believe I missed that," she declared. "How did you manage to keep your towel on during all that again? Glue?"

She caught Paxson looking at her and she stuck her tongue out in adolescent fashion.

"The key is getting the top wet," Kyler explained. "It's really not that hard. I thought that's how everybody did it."

"So now they think it's more than one person stealing this stuff?" Allison asked. "Like a team?"

*Exactly like a team,* Trust replied. *And it would have to be a group of them if they were attempting two robberies on two different floors within minutes of each other. The boy Kyler was chasing wouldn't have had time to take whatever was stolen from the other room, stash it somewhere without anyone noticing or asking questions, and then come back to our room ready to steal more. Not only were there near-simultaneous attempts, which would suggest multiple people, but also multiple people on each attempt, because there's no way he would be able to carry everything he was stealing and get away so easily.*

"Not to mention lookouts," Paxson said. "I'll bet there's more than one. But really. A boy in a red hat? Who's stupid enough to wear that every single time?"

"What about that closet door?" Allison inquired, glancing over to Kyler, who was eating again. "Do they really think someone was hiding inside, waiting for you?"

Kyler shrugged as he swallowed.

"Trust saw the police talking about it. But I can tell you, the door definitely wasn't open when I started down the hall. And for it to just open out of nowhere like that? I mean, if you think about it, what else could it have been besides someone already waiting inside?"

*Which would mean a preplanned escape route,* Trust inserted. *They would have had to know the layout of Weaver Hall beforehand. The boy you ran after passed by two other staircases, not to mention the elevators, before he turned onto the girls' wing. Marcie and Pax know. He had to have been leading you that way for that reason. Who knows, maybe one of the robbers lives in our dorm. It would explain why so many of the thefts happen there.*

"And the plot thickens, gang," Paxson intoned. Marcie rolled her eyes. "On to the Mystery Machine!"

"And now they might try the Thomas Building," Kyler said. "I guess they're thinking the same thing as you, Allison. You'd probably make a good thief."

"Ehh," Marcie said. "She'd probably have to wear a hat or something. That red hair would be easy to spot."

"Fortunately, becoming a thief isn't something I'm all that drawn toward," Allison said, laughing.

"That's good to know."

Trust had already caught sight of Jeremy Higgins heading in their direction, but his voice apparently surprised the others at the table, who each jerked their eyes toward him.

Out of the corner of his vision, he saw Allison stiffen.

Marcie, however, leaned back in her seat, crossing her arms. She was glowering.

"Ugh, not you again. And here I was hoping I would never run into you anymore."

Jeremy put his hands up in surrender, though he shot a fleeting glance toward Kyler.

Trust noticed.

Kyler.

"Yeah, I guess I deserve that," Jeremy said, "even though I don't really remember why all that much. I just came to apologize and I'll get out of your way."

"Apologize?" Kyler asked, his eyes widened. "But Jeremy, whatever for?"

Everyone turned to him. Kyler's eyes flitted around to the others briefly, before he reached for his spoon.

*Bring it down a notch,* Trust signed subtly.

"At a party, at the beginning of the year, after our first football game," Jeremy went on, shifting away from Kyler again, "I was out of control. I don't...Believe me, I know it's not an excuse, but I said some things I don't remember now, things I know I didn't mean. I have no idea what I was thinking—in fact, that's just it. I wasn't."

His eyes were focused on Allison and Marcie.

"And then I heard about what happened from your friends over Thanksgiving"—Jeremy motioned to Trust and Kyler; crap, Trust thought—"and they told me what I said at the party, about how I was acting, and I...I screwed up, royally, and I know it. Jezzie, my girlfriend, told me the next day, but I don't know. I didn't really believe her, I guess. Anyway, I came over to say I really am sorry—to everyone, but particularly to Marcie and Allison—for my behavior that night. I've been called a jerk—and worse—before, but I'm not that guy you met. I've never...I haven't...I just wanted to say I'm sorry."

Trust looked to Allison and Marcie. Both girls seemed taken aback.

Trust was a little surprised himself. The apology actually seemed...sincere. Genuine.

"Well," Marcie said after a moment of silence, her tone softer than before, less harsh, "my dad is a big fan of the football team. And you. He talked about how you played during that Thanksgiving game the entire time I was at home during break."

She shrugged.

"So, I guess that's something."

"Holden's your RA, too, right?" Jeremy asked. "I've known him since middle school. He's got my number. If your folks come down for a game or something, I'd be happy to meet them. I can show your dad the locker room and stuff."

"I gotta say, it takes some guts to come out and apologize in front of everyone like that," Paxson said. "I guess you're not such a bad guy after all. Which is good, since you're such a good football player."

"Thanks. I try—most of the time, anyway. But I've actually gotta jet. Football meeting. Thanks for hearing me out."

Jeremy's eyes centered on Allison.

"I'm sorry again."

Allison nodded, seemingly dazed. Trust and Jeremy exchanged a brief glance, Trust nodding faintly, before the other boy departed, accompanied by two other football players who had been standing off to the side.

"Well, I guess it can turn out all right in the end," said Kyler, grinning.

*The peacemaker returns,* signed Trust.

"How...how did he..."

Allison hesitated, looking between Trust and Kyler.

"He...he wasn't referring to what I think he was referring to, was he?"

Kyler's grin evaporated.

"But..." he started, before he, too, wavered. He looked around the table before returning to Allison. "But I thought it—"

"Kyler, you told *him*? How...who..."

Allison, distressed, pushed away from the table abruptly. Kyler's eyes widened in alarm.

"Who said you could do that?" she declared loudly, her voice carrying over the din of the crowded dining hall.

Those at tables nearby turned to look. Kyler stood, but Allison was already storming away.

"Allison, wait! I—"

"No!" she cried, turning back briefly, her hair flying, her eyes wild.

Even from a fair distance away, Kyler recoiled at the outburst.

More people turned and stared.

Marcie stood as well.

"It's okay," she said. "I'll go with her."

Trust, Paxson, and Kyler, still standing, watched as Marcie hurried after Allison. Trust and Paxson then turned to Kyler.

Kyler, looking around and noticing the additional eyes in his direction, took his seat. He met the gaze of the two other boys at the table.

"What just happened?" he asked quietly. "I thought I was doing a good thing."

"You did, Kyler," Paxson said. "You did."

Kyler leaned back in his seat, closing his eyes and sighing.

## 23.
## Sneaking Into the Thomas Building

"I CAN'T BELIEVE WE'RE DOING this, dude! I *so* can't believe we're doing this!"

In the darkness of the woods on the edge of the clearing, Kyler crinkled his nose at Paxson, though he was smiling. Both boys were crouching, keeping as still as possible as they monitored the building in the middle distance.

"Well, you definitely get the award for weirdest reaction to sneaking through the woods at night," Kyler whispered back. He then turned his attention back to his phone.

WITHOUT A SOUND, TRUST PULLED himself up and over the edge of the roof, finding purchase on soft white gravel. He paused, just for a second, his body motionless as he took in the area.

On the rooftop of the Thomas Building, nothing moved.

He felt a faint vibration.

> **Kyler (9:18 PM):** Pax is about to pee his pants from excitement.

Trust scoffed softly before he started forward, keeping his profile low. The rooftop was in deep shadow, the lights closer to ground level not reaching high enough to pierce the darkness above. A crescent slice of the moon provided the only illumination.

For Trust, it might as well have been bright and sunny.

Actually, bright and sunny wasn't even this good.

He reached the access door and placed his hand on the doorknob. He started to turn—

—but the knob didn't. It was locked.

He looked again into the tiny, millimeters-wide crack of space between the edge of the door and the frame.

Nothing.

He didn't know whether to be happy, or apprehensive.

Leaning toward the latter, he reached into his pocket.

The locked door was a predictable delay. His apprehension would rise if it turned out to be the only one, because it would most likely mean that he had missed something.

"YOU SEE ANYONE?" PAXSON ASKED quietly as they slowly crept through the woodland, each step tested for firmness and the absence of fallen leaves ready to crackle or fallen twigs ready to snap.

"Nope," Kyler replied. "Not even the police. They can't have seriously not sent anyone out here if they thought something was going to happen."

As the boys moved to gain another vantage point of the engineering building, their eyes surveyed the calm landscape. Light posts around the Thomas Building and surrounding area cast a soft, antiseptic glow, but everything was still. Hushed.

*CLICK.*

Trust felt the sound through his tools. The telltale *click* of a suddenly unbolted lock. It was a familiar sensation. The sound would have been just as recognizable—and almost jarring amidst the silence of the rooftop—had he been able to hear it.

He then moved one of the small picks he used up to the upper corner of the doorframe, bit by bit beginning to edge his way across, peeking around and behind him fleetingly to make sure he was still the only—

There. He felt something.

A small break interrupted the natural surface of the frame. It was as

Trust guessed, but at the same time...it wasn't. Something was still off.

Keeping one hand up close to the frame, Trust reached into another pocket without looking, pulling out a small sheet of specialized adhesive. He tore off a piece, and, using his pick for something it wasn't entirely designed for, he fit and smoothed the adhesive over the break in the frame, covering the tiny opening completely.

There were six such openings in the doorframe—two at the top, two along the side, and two at the bottom. Trust located them all, covering each. It took about five minutes.

He opened the door slowly, making sure the adhesive remained in place. When the gap was wide enough for him to go through, he lingered halfway in, taking a closer look at the small breaks he had covered.

As suspected, they were laser pinholes.

And, as suspected, they were presently deactivated. Had they been on, and had Trust not covered the holes with the special adhesive, an alarm signal would have surely been triggered.

Security breach. Unauthorized opening. Rooftop access door.

And thus, the question.

Why was such a security measure disabled?

Trust slipped in silently, wondering.

**Trust (9:20 PM):** Inside. Security disabled on roof door. Don't know why. Anything unusual?

After hearing and spotting no vehicles in the immediate area, Kyler and Paxson darted across the road into the forestry on the other side.

"Trust said the security's off on the door to the roof," Kyler said quietly once they were under cover again. "He's inside now."

Paxson glanced back to the street.

"No security out here, either," he said. "Is he sure those officers were talking about *this* Thomas Building? Tonight? Maybe they meant the other Thomas Building next week."

Kyler suddenly turned on the boy, grabbing him by his shoulders.

"Get a hold of yourself, man!" he whispered urgently. "Are you losing your nerve, Pax? Are you cracking under the pressure? 'Cause if you don't think you can take it, if you don't have the stomach for this type of work, I need to know, and I need to know now, before you get us all kilt!"

He was shaking the boy lightly, and Paxson was gazing back at him in complete bemusement.

"What?"

Kyler let go and shrugged.

"I think I saw it in a movie," he said.

"Why did Trust even ask us to come out here with him?" asked Paxson. "We are *so* not the people for this. Next time, I'll tell him to ask Marcie."

**Kyler (9:23 PM):** Nothing out here so far, but still looking around. No police. We're at the front, across the street.

Trust was moving swiftly down the corridors, ensuring, as much as he could, that his movements were silent. He briefly looked into each windowed door that he passed.

Any security system that was present seemed to be off on the uppermost floor, and Trust imagined that would be the case for the entire building. Even the cameras, which Trust noticed along upper corners of the halls, appeared switched off.

This undertaking had the increasing potential of becoming one gigantic waste of time and energy, particularly since Trust hardly had a clue what he was looking for, or what he would do if he found whatever it was. *To see what we can see*, the reasoning he gave Kyler and Paxson to embark on this madcap adventure in the first place, was flimsy at best.

And the same reasoning would be purely idiotic if he was caught.

After checking the last classroom, he moved toward the stairwell, going down, to see what he could see on the lower floors.

"IT'S QUIET," PAXSON MURMURED IN a country drawl as he and Kyler continued to creep through the woods. "It's quiet, and it's too quiet— wait. Stop. Look."

The boys halted, both of them gazing across the street.

"Looks like a handicap van," Kyler observed. He raised his phone.

"Nice," said Paxson.

TRUST READ THE MESSAGE THAT accompanied the photo Kyler sent.

**Kyler (9:26 PM):** Suspicious? Still quiet. Don't see anyone,
but windows are blacked out.

The wheelchair-accessible van in the picture looked new, or at least recently washed, gleaming under the lights outside the building. It was parked in the loading bay, and as Kyler had expressed, its windows were tinted heavily, making it impossible to distinguish anything or anyone inside, particularly from across the street.

Trust texted a short reply.

**Trust (9:26 PM):** Y

Yes, he had received the message.

Or yes, the van did seem a little out of place.

The hallways throughout the Thomas Building were unlike any Trust had encountered before. As a majority of the lights were off, Trust's vision adapted in the way it uniquely did. However, where he expected to see particles floating about, following the flow of air, there was instead a very vague, very faint residue. It was hazy, slightly blurred, as though the particles had been vacuumed away and the faint residue remained. Still, Trust knew what was happening.

Reverse pressurization.

Whether it was from a specialized cleaning system, an unaffected security procedure, or simply the normal conditions found within the building, the air in the hallways and classrooms was being circulated and removed at an astonishingly efficient rate, not even giving the dust and trillions of specks usually found in the air a chance to settle. The air was clean, sterile, uncontaminated, unpolluted.

And yet Trust could spot no evidence of flowing air. If the air was circulating, why couldn't he see it? It was the first time he had ever had to ask himself the question.

But he was breathing perfectly fine. The phenomenon was intriguing, but probably not related to what he was doing there that night. Just something to ask about later.

He stepped back from another window—the classroom was dark, but for Trust, entirely observable. He started to turn the next corner and froze.

Trust identified the heat signature first, the boy's body fully alight in Trust's eyes before his vision instinctively fine-tuned itself. He then took in the boy's appearance—dark clothes and sneakers, obviously dressed for the chilly weather outside, with the hood of his sweatshirt pulled over his head. Incidentally, his style of dress was not too dissimilar from Trust's own clothing.

The boy was pushing a handcart, a tall, nondescript box set on top.

KYLER ALREADY HAD HIS PHONE out. He and Paxson watched as the campus police vehicle pulled to a quiet stop along the shoulder of the road, just short of the driveway that led to the loading bay, out of sight of the parked van. The police car's lights switched off, and it sat, silent. With its newest arrival, the vicinity surrounding the Thomas Building grew hushed once again.

> **Kyler (9:28 PM):** Police car pulled out front. Cop hasn't
> gotten out. Just sitting there.

"This just got real," Paxson intoned quietly.

The two boys continued to watch. At the moment, nothing was moving.

TRUST WASN'T MOVING, EITHER. APPARENTLY the boy farther down the hall had not heard Trust's incoming text message. As he had it set on silent and at the lowest possible vibration setting, Trust barely felt it.

He started forward again, tiptoeing around the corner, but immediately he paused once more along the wall as the boy stopped.

The boy turned his head slightly. In the shadows of the hall, Trust remained completely still.

He spotted something. Something in the boy's—

An earpiece. It was blinking. He was on the phone.

The boy rotated farther, turning completely, one hand staying on the cart handle. He was looking back toward the still-open door of the laboratory he had come out of, and he was speaking.

"...from the police? And he's just sitting..."

He turned away again.

"WHAT THE HECK?" PAXSON SAID, he and Kyler observing from their hidden position as the police officer stepped out of his patrol car and jogged—at a fairly quick clip—down the drive of the loading bay.

Kyler was texting the update.

> **Kyler (9:29 PM):** Officer looks about to check van. Jogging. May be about to head inside soon.

The cop had his gun and flashlight out, both aimed at the black van. Paxson and Kyler saw him draw closer, approaching the driver's side. He appeared to look in, his flashlight turning in multiple angles, before he stepped back. He was then moving around the front of the van again, still hurrying, reaching for his radio as he moved toward a door that led into the building. Because of their distance, the two boys in the woods could not make out what he was saying.

IT WAS OBVIOUS TO TRUST that Kyler was beginning to get nervous.

> **Kyler (9:29 PM):** The cop's coming in, still jogging. Don't know if he's been tipped off to something.

Replacing his phone, Trust took a careful step forward, remaining close to the wall.

The boy was still standing behind the handcart, presumably talking to whomever was in his ear. His body language, however, suggested that his plans were changing—

The hallway was suddenly awash with light, blindingly bright, before the lights were just as abruptly turned off again.

Even with his tinted shades, Trust was forced to close his eyes.

When he opened them, the boy had turned in his direction, and was now seemingly looking right at him.

A second elapsed before Trust burst out of the shadows.

The other boy seemed to freeze for a moment before he turned to run—and immediately slammed into the cart, almost tripping.

Trust's stride wavered ever so slightly as he noticed the tall box sway. A thought—a person—flashed through his mind.

The boy, regaining his equilibrium, started off again, scurrying away in a tear, his hood flying off his head and flapping off his sweatshirt in his haste.

Trust changed direction, his eyes now focused on the large box as it tilted, seemingly in slow motion—

—he lunged, falling to his knees and then turning onto his back, sliding along the polished floor—

—and caught it, the weight and downward momentum of the container forcing a sharp grunt from deep in his chest. His arms strained and tensed straight away, the heavy box coming close to crushing him.

He gritted harder and pressed the box up, and then lowered it back down again as he rolled from underneath, the box—and whatever was inside—quaking against the floor with a muffled *thud* and not the sharp *crash!* he feared would have occurred otherwise. Still on the ground, now lying on his stomach, Trust began to reach for his phone, but something caught his gaze and his eyes flitted to the wall in front of him again.

Similar to the pinholes along the roof access doorframe...

His eyes ran up the wall quickly, noting additional openings, before he rolled again, rising to his feet in the same motion.

The instant he stood, green beams of light shot out across the dark hallway in several directions, forming an immediate laser grid throughout the corridor stretching from the floor to the ceiling.

The security system had been activated.

Trust studied the static grid as he moved back against the wall in an open section. He then pulled out his phone. Multiple messages.

**Kyler (9:29 PM):** Another cop car. Something's happening.

**Kyler (9:30 PM):** Dude! Someone ran out and got into the

back of van! Have you seen anyone?
**Kyler (9:30 PM):** Another cop! Trust, get out.
**Kyler (9:30 PM):** Someone else just came out a different
door! They must be getting past the cops.

Trust deleted the messages and sent back quickly,

**Trust (9:31 PM):** Meet me back in room. Delete messages,
don't respond.

The shafts of light shooting from the walls and partitions held varying heights: one tier was ankle level, one at chest height, another near the top of his head, and more closer to the ceiling. There were also a series of beams extending lengthwise down the corridor, though they did not reach higher than Trust's knees and would be easily avoidable as long as Trust moved in a straight line—

—and he was already moving, trotting almost, quickly, ducking under and stepping over the beams at chest and ankle level in a deliberate, accelerated contortion, not at all dissimilar to navigating a moderately difficult obstacle course. However, he had a feeling he needed to hurry.

The whereabouts of the boy he had seen was now unknown to him— most likely one of the figures Kyler had spotted escaping to the van.

And now, the police—more than one, and more than two—inside the building, somewhere, probably on a lower floor, but perhaps gaining access to the security cameras and having now already caught sight of him—

He hurdled the remaining crisscrossing of lights and then sprinted deftly up the unprotected steps.

The lights on the floor he had just departed switched on suddenly.

HE REACHED THE TOP FLOOR, ducking and sidestepping through another green-tinged laser maze, before coming to the final, abbreviated staircase leading to the roof. His mind, zoned in and calculating quickly, stayed steps ahead of him.

The door.

To get out without the security system detecting his presence—since he had no overt indication that it had already—he would have to leave the adhesive on the doorframe. There was a chance—very slim, but still present—of a custodian, a maintenance worker, or even a random student stumbling across it...

Arriving, he opened the access door slowly, studying for a snag in the adhesive.

No problem. The adhesive was small, strong, and transparent. Even if one happened to look directly at them, they were difficult to distinguish.

Difficult, but not impossible.

Closing the door again, he was now outside, once more under the cool night sky, once more amidst a shadowy darkness, which, unlike inside the Grayson E. Thomas Building, gave canvas to an infinite number of tiny specks and shimmering sparkles floating everywhere and all around, altering his vision to one he had never been able to accurately describe. He also saw the strobe coming from one side of the building, the emergency lights of police vehicles filtering through the air. Fortunately, it was directly opposite from the side he had climbed up and would now climb down.

Nearly out. He checked his phone one last time.

No response from Kyler.

In this instance, he interpreted that as a good sign.

BACK IN TRUST AND KYLER'S dorm room, Paxson leaned back in his chair, running both hands through his hair.

"I can't believe we just did that, dude! I *so* can't believe we just did that!"

He then brought his hands back down to eye level.

"Look at me. I'm vibrating!"

Trust looked at the sheet of adhesive he had pulled from his pocket, a small corner section now absent, before placing it on his desk.

*Are you going to be all right?* he gestured to the boy, Kyler translating.

"Me?" Paxson questioned in disbelief. "*Me*? You! Oh, my...oh, my...I don't even know what to say. I'm...I'm speechless! I am without speech. I am literally without speech. Literally without speech."

*Really? Could have fooled me.*

Trust then looked to Kyler, who was perched on top of his desk.

*I don't understand how those guys could have slipped past the police. And you said one of them even came out of a door after a cop went in? How could they miss each other?*

Kyler swung his legs against his desk, looking like an overgrown kid, his long hair untied and continuously flopping in front of his face. He nodded, brushing his hair back again.

"Not right after," he said, "like fifteen, twenty seconds. But these people might be, like, real pros. I mean...I don't know, I was thinking they were just some students stealing stuff because they could, but maybe they actually know how to sneak around and evade police. You know, like you do."

"Picking locks, skirting laser security systems, dodging cars, evading police," Paxson listed excitedly. "And you knocked out that guy at the club at the beginning of the year. Dude. Who cares about the Dorm Room Robbers? Are you some type of mutant or superhero or something? I mean, I don't even know—"

*Please tell me he's not shouting right now,* Trust signed.

"He's not shouting," replied Kyler.

*He looks like he's shouting.*

"He's not. He's doing like this."

Kyler mimed a soundless tirade, beating his chest and waving his hands in the air crazily.

When he was done, Trust looked between the two boys.

*You're both, literally, the craziest people I have ever met. It's really not even close.*

"But it may be true," Kyler said after interpreting for Paxson. "About these robbers, I mean. And we're gonna have to come up with another name, since they've graduated from just residence halls. But, I mean, they are good, right? It's just bad luck on their part. They're obviously some sort of coordinated team, and they go in with a strategy, complete with escape scenarios, and they haven't gotten caught. Me almost catching one of them was a fluke, all the more so since I can remember everything about that kid without even breaking a sweat—"

"Yeah," Paxson interrupted, "and I think you're a mutant, too. Don't think you can get away with it, either. You, with your baseball talent and super memory and amazingly good looks—"

Kyler and Trust looked at him, Trust's eyebrows arched in surprise.

"Oh, I'm just repeating what I've heard," Paxson said, "but, yeah, let's rewind that back and act like I didn't say anything."

Kyler continued to stare at the boy before shaking his head, as though waking up from a daze.

"And tonight," he resumed, turning back to Trust as though nothing had happened, "from when you just so happened to catch the police talking about it, so we go out there on basically a hunch and you see another member of this gang. Besides the vague sighting of some mystery person in a red hat—which, like Pax said before, probably won't be happening anymore—we're the only two who have actually seen these people. They didn't take anything from our room, but they had already stolen from someone else's minutes before. We'll probably know tomorrow if they had time to lift something tonight before you and the cops spooked them."

*It's interesting,* Trust signed. *You saw two of them escape on ground level, the same level the police went in. One of them used the same door, and the police didn't notice? Or did they? The boy I saw was speaking into an earpiece, but how would a person outside help him avoid police indoors? I'm sure the only reason I wasn't spotted is because I went up to the roof. And that still doesn't include the cameras, especially when the alarm system came on.*

Paxson had taken the adhesive packet from Trust's desk and was now examining it closely.

"I thought you said you thought the cameras were off?" he asked.

*They looked like they were off when the security system was down, but I can't be sure. And maybe, when the grid activated, they—*

"How was the system activated in the first place? Some type of trigger? Something simple, like a light switch? And who activated it? The police? You, accidentally? The robbers? Someone else?"

Paxson was now holding the adhesive sheet toward the light, his head tilted up. Smirking at Kyler, Trust nodded toward Paxson.

*Detective Paxson Haynes, at your service.*

"It makes me seem like I know what I'm talking about if I'm studying something while asking questions," Paxson explained. "They do it all the time on—"

"On *Scooby-Doo*," Kyler finished, to which Trust snickered. "Yeah,

yeah. I think I've heard you say that before. And speaking of sounding like Marcie, do you think Al—"

Trust watched as Kyler's attention diverted abruptly toward Paxson, who had lowered the adhesive and was now reaching for his phone. He checked the display.

"Well, speak and she shall appear," he voiced, before tapping the screen. "Why, hello, Marcie-Mar. You're on speaker. Kyler was just making fun of you for watching *Scooby-Doo* with me."

Kyler signed Marcie's voice for Trust.

*But I just saw you two watching one of those episodes last night! How can he possibly make fun of me?*

"I wasn't going to rat him out to Trust, who's sitting here also," remarked Paxson, "but what you say is quite true."

*I wasn't invited to this?* Trust inquired.

"Hold on," Paxson said into the phone. "Trust is trying to get a word in edgewise."

*What does that even mean?* Kyler translated Marcie's comment for Trust before also saying aloud, "Paxson did invite you. You told us you had class, and then you went to the gym."

*You said you were just going to watch TV. You didn't say anything about* Scooby-Doo.

"Oh, so you'll skip another round at the gym to watch *Scooby-Doo*, but—"

Kyler then motioned to the phone, indicating Marcie was talking again.

*Okay, so it sounds like Trust is talking about Scooby-Doo also, which means nothing to me, which means I'm going to talk over him impolitely.*

"This is Kyler," Kyler said. "Have you seen Allison today?"

*Really? You don't think I can recognize your voice? And of course I've seen Allison. I'm in her room right now.*

"She's there? Can you tell her again that I'm sor—"

*Argh! Yes, for the 435th time in barely over twenty-four hours, I will tell Allison that you're sorry, and, for the 435th time, she will accept it, and for the 430th time, I will tell you to knock it off and stop avoiding her like a little boy. Can't you just tell her you like her already and get it over—*

"Marcie! Is she sit—"

*No, of course she's not sitting right here. I wouldn't do that to you...although I should. No, she had to go up to her RA's room.*

"What's in her RA's room?" Paxson asked.

*Her RA. And the police.*

"What?" Paxson and Kyler voiced in the same breath. Trust's eyebrows rose again.

*How's it going?*

"The police?" Kyler repeated.

*I'm the one who called. Do I get a chance to speak now?*

"What?"

*Are we done with your groveling and debating everyone's schedule of what time we can all get together to watch a cartoon dog who solves mysteries—which, I'll remind you,* Paxson has on disc so you can watch it anytime.

"What's Allison talking to the police for? Did something happen?"

There was an extended pause. Kyler and Paxson were looking at the phone in Paxson's hand. Trust was looking at Kyler and Paxson, his unflustered gaze shifting between the two of them.

*Allison received another stupid note from...whomever,* Kyler translated, before meeting Trust's eyes. *We just got back to her room less than five minutes ago, and the police were already here, talking to the RA. Apparently when whoever delivered it found that neither Allison nor her roommate were here, the RA accepted it, promising to give it to Allison. But I guess the RA already knew what to look out for from last time, and she called the cops. I barely know anything right now, and I'm just waiting for her to come back since her roommate, Melody, isn't here, but the note came with some type of gift. And more money. It's gotta be from the same people.*

Trust assumed Marcie had stopped speaking, and there was another break. The three boys looked at each other.

And then...

*But we can all talk about it later, whatever Allison feels like sharing. So, to change the subject, what have you boys been up to?*

## 24.
## The Peacemaker

TRUST LOBBED THE BASEBALL TO Kyler on the other side of the dorm room, and then gestured with his hands.

*Four point oh. Seriously, I'm not kidding. Explain to me again how having a super-duper, photographic, videographic memory where you never forget anything ever is not unfair when you're at school. I like hearing you tell this story.*

Kyler, replicating Trust's positioning by sitting on his own bed with his back against the side wall, mimed looking at his imaginary wristwatch.

*Is it hate o'clock already?* he signed back. *Don't get mad at me because I was born this way. I'm not the one who can watch the movement of the constellations at night or the sun during the day— literally. Really, who else do you know that can look directly at the sun without needing to blink after? And, by the way, what's your GPA right now?*

He tossed the baseball back to Trust.

*Way to change the subject,* Trust replied.

*Way to not answer my question,* Kyler shot back. *I already know you're at a 4.0, too, so there's no need in trying to dance around it.*

Trust tossed the ball.

*That's typically what happens when you have easy classes.*

*Oh, okay, with your U.S. Immigration 4000-level class,* Kyler signed. *I'm sure that excuse will work on some unsuspecting soul, but not the guy who knows your schedule. Give me some credit.*

Trust detected movement in the corner of his vision, and he turned toward the open doorway at the same time as a boy raised his hand to knock.

The visitor glanced up, noticing Trust's attention aimed at him.

"Oh, hey. Sorry. Are you Kyler?"

Trust grunted, loudly, waving the boy in—and, seemingly without looking, he caught the baseball hurled by Kyler.

Kyler leaned over the side of his bed, spotting the other boy as he entered. The boy had black hair, longish and naturally curling around his ears, along with the very faint shadow of a beard. He wore glasses and had on a University of Centre City long-sleeved shirt.

*I'm Trust,* Trust greeted as the visitor glanced toward him again, *but you seem to be looking for Kyler, the houseboy. That's him over there.*

The boy smirked as Kyler interpreted Trust's statement, Kyler then looking to his deaf roommate.

"Well now, that was just a little bit racist, wasn't it? You would be so mad if I said that to you."

*Nice try, but not really, since I've known you my entire life and I know you would be kidding just like I am. And racist? Need I direct you to a mirror, sir?*

"'Sir'? Now that *has to be* racist somehow, but let's not upset our guest."

Kyler turned to the boy, who had been following the remarkable exchange.

"So, I hear you ask for Kyler, ol' chap. What can I do you for?"

"Okay. Well, my name's Perry and—"

"I know, dude!" Kyler said. "Long time, no see!"

"Long time, no...uh, have we met before?"

*Don't entertain his antics,* Trust motioned. *That's how he sucks you in.*

"That is completely and utterly untrue," Kyler stated after translating. "Continue, Billy. Sorry for interrupting."

"Actually, it's Perry."

Kyler nodded.

"Right. Tristan."

"No, it's Per—"

"Your name's Kyler, too? So is mine!"

Trust was shaking his head. Perry motioned back toward the door.

"Uh, would it be better if I came back later, or..."

*I praise your optimism, thinking he'll be "normal" later. Better to push through now. Wade through the mud.*

"Well," Perry began, "me and my roommate stay downstairs on the fourth floor, and—"

"Anybody ever tell you you look like a young Clark Kent?" Kyler said. "Lift up your shirt. You have a cape on under there?"

"—and someone broke into our room and took our stuff a couple of days ago."

"Ahh, man," Kyler said, his tone instantly changing. "Sorry to hear that. Have you heard anything from the police yet?"

Perry shook his head. Trust nudged the chair out from under his desk, beckoning Perry to sit.

"That's actually what I came to talk to you guys about," the boy explained. "It's only been two days—I mean, I didn't expect them to solve the investigation and find everything in forty-eight hours—but I heard that you caught someone trying to break in to your room that day. You caught him before he could get in. Something about wearing only a towel?"

*It's a long story,* Trust signed.

"Not really," Kyler said. "I had just come out of the shower."

"Have the police said anything to you guys? I heard you saw one of the burglars."

Kyler nodded.

"I'm actually going to the police station in about...ten minutes to meet with a sketch artist. He's supposed to be really good. They said they're going to want me to look at some photos, too. But don't worry; if this guy is in the photos, I'm going to recognize him, and if he's not, the drawing that the artist makes is going to be just as good. I don't forget faces, and I saw his clearly."

*Can you tell us what they took from your room?* Trust inquired. *We would understand if you'd rather not talk about it.*

Perry shrugged faintly.

"Both mine and my roommate's—his name's Rob—both of our laptops. Rob had a big-screen from home, fifty inches—that's gone. I had a smaller TV on my desk, and it's still on my desk. Don't know why they didn't take that, but I'm certainly not complaining. They stole this cool little speaker setup that I had for my music player. Luckily I had my music and my tablet with me, so they didn't get that."

*Big TV, two laptops, music speakers,* Trust observed. *I still don't understand how they can just walk out with this stuff. All of that and no one notices, even with all the alerts we've had, and this is just the first half of the year. We even call them the Dorm Room Robbers, so it's not like people carrying TVs out of rooms should be something to overlook.*

"And the guy I saw didn't have a backpack or anything," Kyler said. "Unless he hid it all somewhere—or unless he had help, which is most likely—I don't know how he would have been able to sneak all that out when everyone's back was conveniently turned. And what if he'd gotten in this room? Was he planning to walk out carrying a TV in his bare hands? Surely someone would have noticed that. Can one person even carry a fifty-inch by themselves?"

Trust shifted back to Perry.

*Did the police ask you about the lookout? Someone in a red hat?*

"Yeah," replied Perry. "I didn't remember seeing anyone with a red hat, and if I did, I wasn't paying any attention to them at the time. Did you guys see anybody?"

Trust shook his head.

"I came in through the back, at the rear entrance," Kyler said. "No one was out there."

"Really, the back?" Perry said. "Was there a van or truck or anything? Any way they would be able to transport that stuff?"

Kyler shook his head. Perry blew out a puff of air.

"This is wild," he said. "I've never had anything stolen from me before. I've never been robbed. So of course it happens at the University of Centre City—the Safest University in the Country."

Trust's brow furrowed as he thought of something.

*What are the chances these people knew you weren't going to be in your room? Kyler's baseball workout ended earlier than expected, so it's possible these guys wouldn't have been prepared for him to come back when he did.*

A light of recognition came across Perry's features.

"Rob and I were both in class. You think there's a chance they may have known our schedules?"

"I don't know," Kyler said, looking to Trust. "Neither of us had class, and you just went to the gym on a whim. How would the robbers know you were going to do that, and be gone long enough that they would assume they wouldn't get caught?"

"Could they have been monitoring us?" Perry asked. "I don't know if you regularly go to the gym, but if there's a chance they've been watching and maybe picked up on a routine..."

Trust nodded, pointing to Perry.

Perry stood up.

"It's definitely something to think about. I have to go get ready for class, and it's almost time for your appointment at the station, right? I really just wanted to come meet you guys and see if you had heard anything new."

Kyler stood as well.

"I'll walk out with you. I'll find you with whatever I learn from the police. They're going to find out who did this and get your and your roommate's stuff back—I can feel it."

"I've heard that kind of thing is unlikely," Perry said, "but I'm definitely holding out hope."

Kyler looked toward Trust, who was still reclined on the bed.

"You're sure you don't want to come down to the station with me? Officer Mendez said it would only take about an hour. Hour and a half, tops."

*You're asking me if I want to sit beside you while a guy draws and then redraws a nose for an hour and a half. I should probably just stay here and get some work done so I can keep up with your 4.0 average.*

Perry looked to Kyler, his eyebrows raised. Kyler shook his head.

"Don't read into that GPA stuff. It's typically what happens when you have easy classes."

*Nice job stealing my line,* Trust noted. *And try not to mention our little escapade at the Thomas Building in front of campus police.*

"What a terrible thing to say about Perry's mother," Kyler said. "Frankly, I am offended. Come on; let's get out of here, Perry, before he says something else rude."

Trust shook his head, smirking.

"You guys should talk with Jeff on the third floor," Perry said. "Someone stole from his room at the beginning of the year. I think the police think it's the same group, the Dorm Room Robbers."

NOT TEN MINUTES AFTER KYLER and Perry had vacated the doorway, Trust identified movement out of the corner of his sightline once again.

An instant later, the lights in the dorm room, which were linked up to a button just outside the door, flickered on and off.

Trust was already scribbling something in his notebook, which lay alongside his laptop on his desk. Without looking up, he showed the notebook to Allison as she came in.

*I saw you before you even pressed the button.*

"I didn't want to startle you," she explained, grinning faintly.

*Startle? Remember, I'm a guy.*

"I should so hit you for that. What if your back had been turned?"

Trust pointed to the mirror positioned over the head of his bed, facing the doorway.

*I have my ways.*

He watched as Allison went to sit on his bed.
She sighed.
"Kyler's not here, I guess."

*Appointment with police sketch artist about attempted break-in. He'll hate he missed you.*

"Do you know how long he's supposed to be?"

*Just left 10 mins ago. Hour, maybe more.*

Allison blew out a puff of air and fell back onto the bedspread. A moment later Trust leaned over, showing her the notebook again.

*If you came to apologize to him, while considerate, it couldn't be more unnecessary coming from you.*

Still lying back, Allison looked at Trust.
"What do you mean?" she asked.
Trust arched an eyebrow.

*Exactly what I wrote.*

Allison rolled her eyes, chuckling softly.

"God, I know it's kind of weird, but I wish you could talk. Then you wouldn't be able to hide behind enigmatic phrasings that don't even answer my quest—"

"Al-le-son."

Allison, shocked, looked swiftly to Trust. Trust grinned.

He then went back to the notebook.

*Back at home, we call him "the peacemaker." It's just what he does.*

And then,

*You remember the note I showed you at the police station?*

She nodded.

*We all know how smart you are. If I could speak, you wouldn't have the excuse of not "understanding" me. You know what I'm talking about.*

*Eat dinner with us. I'll text Pax and Marcie.*

Allison smiled.

"So, you've been practicing my name? You're good, almost perfect. I like the way you make it sound."

*A certain someone's forcing me to learn. I'll have it down soon enough.*

"Al-le-son. Al-li-son. Al-lison."

THE GANG WAS BACK, EATING together in Hollins Cafeteria once more.

*If we were all standing right now,* Trust motioned, *we could have a group hug.*

"Good," Marcie remarked after Kyler's translation. "That would make it easier for me to punch you square in the face."

The others at the table looked at her, their eyebrows raised in surprise.

"Sorry," she said. "Ignore that. It's been one of those days. I almost overslept my first class and I haven't caught up yet."

*I'm ready to hit the gym whenever you are,* Trust signed. *Just say the word. I'm actually looking forward to it.*

"And don't worry," Paxson said, hugging Marcie with one arm as she sat alongside him. "We're done with classes for the day, so after this, we can just sit back and relax with Shaggy and Scoob. I wonder what kinds of hijinks they'll have up their sleeves this—"

"You want to start tonight?" Marcie said, looking toward Trust. The others laughed.

"You know what?" Kyler said, pointing a half-eaten drumstick at the rest of the group as he spoke. "I think I'll join you guys, if you don't mind. I've got some extra energy to burn."

"Extra energy, eh?" Allison said, grinning. "I can believe that. I've heard being a law-breaking trespasser can give you an adrenaline rush."

Kyler stopped chewing, looking up to Allison. He then pointed immediately to Trust.

"Him. He did it. It was Trust's idea. He asked me and Pax to go!"

Trust's face contorted into a look of disbelief.

*Well, at least we all know who wouldn't last three minutes in an interrogation room.*

"Especially if Allison's the one doing the interrogation," Paxson mumbled, snickering before catching an elbow from Marcie.

Trust spotted the sly comment, but apparently Kyler did not hear—or else he simply chose to ignore it.

"Oh, who are we kidding?" he declared. "The cat's out of the bag on this one. We already told most of the story to Marcie last night. It's just fair that everyone knows."

"That's just it," Allison replied. "I don't think *anyone* knows. I had a class and a lab in the Thomas Building today and no one even mentioned it—the attempted robbery, I mean. I would have thought I would have heard something, especially if anything was stolen. But nothing, and no campus alerts either. Maybe you and the police arrived before they could get anything out."

She looked to Trust, who shrugged as he tore off a bite of his food.

"How did you even get in without getting caught?" Marcie asked. "I've never been in there, but from the way Paxson was talking about lasers and whatever else, and from what Allison's mentioned, it seems like that would be one place on campus you shouldn't even think about breaking in to."

*Who says I haven't been caught?* Trust replied. *Perhaps I just haven't been caught yet. The police may have someone doing a sketch of me just like they did with Kyler. The cameras may have caught me. They could be looking for me as we speak.*

"You don't seem too concerned," Allison observed.

*I'm not. However, if they do come for me, I'm going to rat on this one so fast...*

He pointed to Kyler. But Paxson scoffed.

"He's being modest, guys, I'm telling you. I watched him climb up the side of a building. *The side of a building.* Stairs? Nope. Scaling pipes and cracks and crevices and stuff. No way a person who can do all that is going to be caught easily doing *anything.* It was incredible. And the lasers inside—*pew, pew, pew*—"

*You weren't even in there,* Trust signed. *I could have made all of that up.*

"Yeah? And what about that special adhesive stuff you used? Going in, you had a whole sheet of it, and then, back at the dorm, there was a section missing. *Missing.* What about that, Trust? Huh? What about *that*? Kyler, what's that stuff called again?"

"Polyurethane glass," Kyler supplied between chews.

"Poly-uranium! Whatcha got ta say now, Trust? What...cha...got...ta...say...now?"

Paxson struck his fist against the table with emphasis.

Trust simply stared back at the boy, unmoved.

*Please tell me he's not shouting all of this in the middle of a* crowded dining hall?

Translating to the others with his mouth full, Kyler then shook his head.

"He'sth noth. He'sth jus' doing lith thisth."

He pretended to pound the table with both hands again and again, his head thrashing about, appearing ferocious.

Grimacing, Trust leaned away, out of food-coming-out-of-Kyler's-mouth range. He then looked to Allison as she motioned for his attention.

"You have polyurethane glass? How? Did you buy it? Do you know how unbelievably expensive it is?"

*If you know how expensive it is,* Trust answered, *I guess you know what I was using it for.*

"To block the lasers," Paxson said. "*Pew, pew—*"

*I almost didn't need it, though. The alarm system was off when I went in—I assume the thieves disabled it somehow. But why was the building empty in the first place? It wasn't that late. Why were there not students or faculty staying late like Allison does sometimes? No custodians, nobody. It was mostly all dark except for a few auxiliary lights—until all the lights came on.*

"We weren't allowed to be there after hours yesterday," Allison said. "They didn't give a reason, and I didn't even think to ask."

"They didn't allow you to stay late," Paxson voiced dramatically as he pointed at Allison, "because they were planning a robbery. It's a conspiracy! By Jove, we've broken this case wide open, gang!"

Trust glanced to Marcie.

"You don't even have to say anything," she said. "But, you have to admit, it's strangely cute in a way."

*No, I don't,* Trust returned. *And no, it isn't.*

Marcie stuck her tongue out.

"So you used polyurethane glass to shield and reflect the beams around the rooftop door," Allison stated, "but is that the only place you had to use them? Didn't you"—she glanced to Paxson—"mention something about a laser grid?"

*The system must have reactivated after the thieves escaped and as the police entered. One of them had to set it off—I don't think it was me. It was right after I caught that box, and the boy could have been—*

"Box?"

"The burglar Trust saw was planning to steal something in a large box," Paxson said, "and then, when he heard the police were coming in and he saw Trust—*zoom!*—he started to split, and—*bam!*—he ran into the box, which started to fall. Trust, using his superhuman speed and catlike reflexes, got to the box just before it crashed to the ground, but the box was heavy, and he had to use his superhuman strength—*argh!*—to then push the box off of him before it crushed him."

Trust leaned across the table toward Paxson.

He then looked down to Paxson's food.

*Seriously, what are you on right now?*

"I really think it's this cheesecake!" Paxson whispered excitedly, his eyes dancing, wide and wildly animated. "Chocolate mousse, it said. I don't even—it's so sweet, my hair feels like it's standing straight up on my head! I can't control it!"

"I try to limit his sugar intake for just this reason," Marcie remarked, before looking over to the hyperactive boy. "Obviously, you see what happens when it gets out of control."

Kyler laughed.

"Dude, that's so cool. Paxson's a sugar freak!"

Trust sat back in his chair, still eyeing Paxson curiously.

*Anyway,* he started again, *the security system came back on, I guess, and that grid shot out just like you see in the movies. But it was easy to get through—too easy, I think. The beams were spaced out pretty wide—I don't think they were supposed to be visible. Had they been hidden, I certainly would have tripped the alarm, if I didn't anyway.*

*Maybe they already were invisible?* Kyler motioned back slyly, even as he interpreted Trust's observations for the rest of the table, no one else able to tell the difference.

Trust understood what Kyler was saying. He shrugged faintly.

"But if you used those poly-whatever things to get in," Marcie said, "how did you get out with the alarms back on?"

Trust pointed to her in affirmation, nodding.

*I had to leave them so I wouldn't risk disturbing the grid around the door. I want to go back before someone else finds them.*

"I doubt anyone would notice, or even be looking," Allison said, "particularly if they're as small as I imagine they are. But it'll be easy to get them back. Come with me tomorrow. I can be your cover in case someone asks questions. We'll just say we were going up to the roof to make out or something."

Kyler coughed, nearly spewing his drink.

Paxson burst out laughing.

"You're coming with us to the gym," Marcie said to Paxson with finality. "You need to burn off that sugar or you'll never get to sleep."

"I know," Paxson managed through his laughter, "but it was

just...you know when...I don't even..."

*Well, at least we all know who to keep away from sugar,* Trust signed.

Marcie just shook her head.

As the group was getting ready to leave Hollins Cafeteria, Trust motioned for Kyler and Allison to hang back. He looked to Allison.

*I probably shouldn't even bring it up, but I did notice we didn't talk about the second bribe you received. I don't know if that was intentional or not, but just know you can talk to any of us. And by us, I mean me or Marcie. You know, the normal ones.*

"So not funny," Kyler said lowly.

Allison smiled.

"Thanks, Trust. Believe me, I know I can come to you guys, but I'm fine, really. The police are handling it. One of the great things about being around you guys and not by myself is that you help me keep my mind off it. But really, thanks."

"And you know what else would keep your mind off it, right?" Kyler posed, grinning. "I seem to recall—quite clearly, I should say—a few mentions from your Uncle Smith when he took us to dinner about a certain, oh, how shall I say, disinterest in gyms?"

Allison started to back away.

"Actually, I was just going to let you go ahead and—aww, you can't do that! That's so unfair!"

She was met with two heartbreaking pouts.

## 25.
## Snowfall

AS ALLISON HAD GUESSED, TRUST'S retrieval of the polyurethane glass adhesives from the rooftop access door was effortless, since, during regular university hours, the Thomas Building hummed with activity, no one paying the two of them any mind.

"I think there was a lab that came up to the roof a few weeks ago," Allison mentioned as Trust detached the bits from the doorframe. "Drone testing."

During their outing, Trust had also raised the subject of the intriguing air conditioning system that he had observed during his late-night rendezvous with the burglars. Allison had turned to look at him, her face one of surprise, when she read the question off his note card.

"You're talking about the reverse over-pressurization? That's amazing! How could you even tell?"

More out of habit than anything else, Trust's response was vague.

*Empty building. No students. Felt the difference.*

Allison seemed to accept the answer, going on to explain that yes, the Thomas Building's air circulation and conditioning system was highly sophisticated, according to what she knew and had heard from casual discussions with professors. Its overarching purpose was, as Trust had witnessed firsthand, to intensely regulate the amount of dust and foreign particles throughout the building—especially in the labs and classrooms, where even a small trace could ruin the work being done.

Allison said that the system was almost certainly extremely expensive. It was a telling indicator of the importance placed on UCC's

309

School of Engineering. Trust left the Thomas Building impressed, and, more importantly, in possession of his special adhesive.

He also left even more intrigued by the building than when he went in.

BUT THAT EVENING BROUGHT WITH it an entirely different affair.

Chancellor Beverly's annual Disability Services dinner.

At the Centre Diamond club.

Along with the staff and personnel of Disability Services in Adams Hall, the students who utilized them—Trust included—were invited to dine with the chancellor at the semiformal but surprisingly ritzy event. Eight o'clock was the scheduled start time, with Chancellor Beverly slated to give a few opening remarks, followed by catered food served buffet style, with mingling and music provided by the Centre Diamond DJ during and after. The dinner was in recognition of Disability Services, but it was also an opportunity to allow everyone within arm's reach of the chancellor at least once during the school year.

Snow was expected at some point during the festivities, the first snowfall of the year.

Inside Centre Diamond, Chancellor April Beverly was speaking. She stood in front of the stage and elevated DJ platform without a podium, without a microphone, without a prepared speech folder. Like her convocation address, her image was broadcast on the large display above her head, along with Mrs. Pegees, who had also been one of the sign language interpreters during convocation.

"Again, I thank you all for joining me this evening," Beverly said. "On this, a night to recognize and celebrate not only the hardworking and capable staff of Disability Services, but also the students who we work for and strive to assist in any and every way we can. Far from an obligation, I like to think it is a calling, and a joy, that we as administrators share, and far from entitled, it is a gift that these shining students receive. I think this event shows that you are all a splendid example of what makes this university so special, a university that so many publications have called a 'glowing pinnacle of the highest learning.'"

She looked around, tables having been brought in on a portion of the club's dance floor between the stage and the circular bar area. The tables were now occupied with faces of Disability Services staff and students, all turned attentively in the chancellor's direction.

Beverly brought her hands together slowly in an almost reverent posture. A small smile ghosted across her lips.

"And now, we eat."

The tables erupted in cheers and applause, both for Beverly's speech, and the so very imminent expectation of dining. Clapping along with the others in attendance, Trust watched as Chancellor Beverly once again shook hands with the slightly shorter, significantly pudgier, and fashionably mustached man who had been standing just off to the side.

The owner of Centre Diamond, Pablo Eldorado.

Beside him...Mariana, just as strikingly beautiful as Trust recalled from his only other visit to the club nearly four months previous.

Four months, he thought, shaking his head faintly. Now, watching her shake hands with Beverly, it seemed more like four...

Brycen Johns nudged Trust in the side as they clapped.

"That girl up there is pretty hot, huh?" he said, unconsciously leaning in closer as he spoke, most likely forgetting that, with Trust, the noise level did not affect his hearing.

Trust raised his eyebrows.

Brycen laughed.

Tonight, Centre Diamond possessed a subdued holiday atmosphere. The colored lights around the club emitted gold and white, and decorations were enough to be recognizable with more than a passing glance, but just as easily fading back into the overall ambiance. The walls along the upper floor and the DJ booth were adorned with soft white Christmas lights, as were the buffet stations set up.

Trust finished piling another dish onto his already heaping plate when another familiar face came alongside him.

"Well, you clean up pretty nice for a freshman," Kimberlee Sharpshire said, her smile enchanting in the gentle lighting of the club.

Trust smirked, squinting slightly.

"Don't try to give me one of your smart-aleck responses," she said. "I can see you have your hands full."

They both made their way back to the round table they shared with Brycen and a few others.

Trust put his plate down on the tablecloth and motioned, *Just admit it. Not only do I clean up nice for a freshman, I clean up nice, period. I*

311

*would say you look nice, too, but I know you probably hear it every five minutes and I wouldn't want to follow everyone else.*

Kimberlee shook her head as she sat down, smiling.

"Oh, Trust. A girl never gets tired of hearing she looks nice, particularly from handsome boys. It seems you still have much to learn. But, then again, you're, what, eighteen?"

Trust sent her a sarcastic smirk as Kimberlee took a bite of her food.

*Every time I get you, you have to resort to the old-age card. How old is your imaginary—excuse me. How old is this fiancé who I've heard about but never met?*

"Oh, you haven't met Kimberlee's man?" Brycen interjected, catching a glimpse of Trust's signs as he took his seat, his plate of food in front of him. "Kimberlee's hunk o' man? Kimberlee's strong, chocolate, steaming hot cup of—"

*Yeah...I'm just going to turn this way and pretend I didn't understand a word of what you just said,* Trust gestured.

"If you think that's bad," Kimberlee said, smirking, "you should hear how he talks about you. Hide the children."

"It's like I tell Riley all the time," Brycen said. "It's okay to window-shop, so long as you don't touch the merchandise. Oh, and speak of the devil, look who decides to stroll in fashionably late."

Trust followed Brycen's gaze, Kimberlee turning to look as well.

Coming around the bar area on the other side of the buffet stations was a bald man dressed in a smart, yet casual, jacket and button-down shirt with jeans. He looked older than Trust but still quite young, somewhere in his mid- to late-twenties. The stud in his ear sparkled as he moved, matching the glint of his white teeth as he smiled, his eyes falling on Kimberlee.

Trust glanced to Brycen again.

"I saw him first," Brycen declared, smirking.

Trust rolled his eyes.

"Hey, Kim," the man said, Trust not able to distinguish the man's deep voice.

"So, you made it just in time to watch us enjoy your food after all," Kimberlee said, starting to stand before the man ushered her down again. The man then chuckled as he kissed Kimberlee on the forehead.

Trust stole another glance toward Brycen, missing whatever the man said next as he slipped into the empty seat alongside Kimberlee. Brycen was leaning forward on the table, grinning expectantly as he looked at the couple.

"Trustice Jeffries," Kimberlee announced, "I would like you to meet my 'imaginary' fiancé, Kendell Stewart. Kendell, this is Trustice. He prefers Trust."

Kendell stood up again, extending his hand across the table, Trust mirroring his movement. Kendell's charming, courteous smile caused Trust to grin even wider than he would have otherwise.

"Trust, the one you're always talking about, Trust?" he asked, glancing back toward Kimberlee but still keeping his face mostly turned to Trust. "Trust, the one that I think I might need to be jealous of? That Trust?"

Kimberlee bumped Kendell lightly as he and Trust took their seats again.

"Now you're just trying to embarrass me," she said.

"Don't worry, K," Brycen declared, looking at Kendell. He slung his arm around Trust's shoulder. "For the record, I will say that Trust is my date tonight, so your fiancé's going to have to go through me to get to him. I've got your back, man."

Both Kendell and Kimberlee laughed as Trust shot Brycen a look.

*You just tell me when you get to the punch line,* Trust signed to him. *Oh, wait. Did I miss it?*

Brycen grabbed his heart dramatically, as though he had been injured.

*You said he could watch us enjoy his food?* Trust directed to Kimberlee.

Kimberlee nodded as someone from another table came to greet Kendell.

"I'm sure you eat in Hollins Cafeteria a lot?" she asked.

*I'm sure just about everyone eats in Hollins a lot.*

She smirked and directed her fork toward Kendell.

"Meet one of the executive chefs. He's the one who supervised the preparation of all the food for tonight's dinner."

Trust looked down at his plate. The gargantuan pile of food he had when he first sat down was already mostly gone—all, seemingly, without him even realizing he had been eating. He looked back to Kimberlee.

*I didn't even know colleges had chefs. He doesn't happen to make chocolate mousse cheesecake, does he?*

Kimberlee's eyes sparkled.

"Ooh. His cheesecakes are amazing. Have you had it in Hollins?"

Trust feigned a glower.

*So he's perfect, then. Crap.*

A FEW MINUTES AFTER HE had completed his meal, Trust spotted Chancellor Beverly alone—a rare sight—eating a slice of one of the cakes that had been provided as dessert.

He had come prepared if he received the chance to talk to Beverly one on one.

That chance had abruptly arrived.

The chancellor smiled as Trust took the chair beside her.

April Beverly had light blond, almost platinum, hair cut right at shoulder length, styled straight to give her a professional air. Her pantsuit, even while sitting down, emanated posh taste, though Trust would never in a million years be able to guess the designer. In all, she was an attractive woman. Her authoritative appearance and bearing, however, served to overshadow her natural beauty. It seemed intentional.

"Don't tell me," she voiced before Trust could pull out a prepared note card. "I pride myself on this."

She studied him for a moment, taking another bite of her cake. She then pointed to him with her fork.

"You're...deaf? Trustice Jeffries."

Trust's eyebrows shot up. He scribbled on a blank card.

*That is impressive. I wouldn't expect the chancellor to know my name.*

"I try," she said, smirking lightly. "And I apologize in advance for not knowing sign language."

She began to glance around.

"Would it be easier if we had an interpreter? I'm sure you don't want to write—"

Her attention returned to Trust as he waved her off. This response had already been prepared.

*I'm used to writing. I would actually like to talk to you alone for a few minutes.*

"Nothing serious, I hope," she said, starting to take another bite.

*Actually, it is.*

Beverly paused, her fork poised in the air as she looked at Trust. She watched him slide across another card, this one also having already been written on, and completely covered, front and back. Picking it up and laying her fork down, she squinted at the writing slightly before reaching into her suit jacket and bringing out a pair of reading glasses.

"Look away while I put on my eyes."

Trust gave a soft smile before gesturing back to the card.

*I wonder how aware you are, Chancellor Beverly, of a series of unreported rapes and sexual assaults committed on this campus by a group called the Freesef Society. Seemingly every few months, a story circulates among the students of a freshman girl becoming a "victim" of one of these assaults. As the story goes, repeatedly, the girl does not report the incident to the police once she realizes it's the Freesef Society; it simply becomes a story to tell her friends, making her popular, and the rumor begins.*

*My friend was attacked behind Mueller Hall the Monday before Thanksgiving break. She was able to fight off multiple attackers and scream for help. The police are currently investigating, but have found nothing so far.*

*I do not know for sure if Freesef is involved. I do not know if the stories are true. But my friend was hospitalized, and unlike the other alleged victims, she is speaking up.*

*So I wonder how aware you are of these unreported events that we hear about anyway. I wonder if you've ever heard of the Freesef Society.*

315

*And I wonder what you would say to my friend, Allison, if she were standing here.*

The chancellor's eyes looked over the tops of her glasses, meeting Trust's gaze.

She then looked back down, reading the note again.

Then back up.

"Your friend is Allison Tyler."

Trust nodded.

"I am aware of what happened," Beverly stated. "I am kept informed of investigations as they relate to the university and its students, though I am not always as privy to the actual details of these investigations as I would like to be for privacy reasons.

"I was devastated when I first heard about your friend. I have been in touch with Allison, and her parents. The University of Centre City prides itself on its safety and community just as much as our academics and athletics, if not more so. I have unwavering faith that the police will get to the bottom of what happened, and anything this university can learn to prevent something like this from happening again, we will implement it promptly and effectively."

She waved the card, which she continued to hold in her hand.

"Your observations concerning these other possible girls, along with this group, the...Freesef Society, are troubling. It is the first I've heard of either. Your style is measured here, calculated, so I assume you already know what I'm about to ask. Do you have any evidence of these other assaults, or any evidence of this Freesef Society?"

Trust shook his head.

"I was not even aware we had an organization named the Freesef Society on campus. Who—"

"My apologies, ma'am."

A shorter man in a suit materialized at the table, coming from somewhere behind Trust. Studying him as Beverly's attention diverted, Trust instinctively assumed the man was some sort of administrator, or perhaps one of the chancellor's assistants. He certainly did not have the build to be a bodyguard.

His face was vaguely familiar. Trust had probably seen him in some official photo with Beverly.

"You have a call from Vice-Chancellor Britton," he announced.

"Tell him I'll call back."

She started to turn back to Trust.

"I'm sorry, ma'am, but I think you should take this one," the man said. "It sounds as though it might be time-sensitive."

The chancellor huffed.

"Every time he's on the phone, he says it's 'time-sensitive.' I'm not sure he understands the meaning of the phrase."

She looked to Trust.

"Excuse me, Trustice. I step off campus for an hour and the world comes tumbling down."

She took the proffered phone out of the man's hand as she stood, and started to move away. Trust noticed she had left the note card on the table, and he stood as well, reaching for it and turning to follow.

The aide intercepted him with a simple sidestep, holding his hand out.

"I'm sorry, son," the man said, Trust bristling at the word. "That's an important phone call she's on right now. The chancellor cannot be disturbed."

Frowning, Trust looked down to the man's hand, his palms up and outward, which had made contact with Trust when he had first started to move, and were still raised to block his path.

Trust's eyes returned to the man's face.

The aide lowered his hand, but then raised it again.

"Did you want me to give the chancellor that note?"

Trust glanced down to the card, and then back to the aide. He handed the card to him.

"My apologies again for the interruption."

The man then moved off to where Beverly was standing in a quiet corner. Trust watched the aide tuck the card neatly into his inner suit pocket. His eyes trailed after him for a moment before the deaf boy turned back—

—and straight into Mariana.

Trust inhaled slightly.

Mariana was smiling.

"So, you think you can grace us with your presence once only to disappear for four months?"

She then shook her head. Trust could not hear the "tsk, tsk" sound that she made.

Trust quickly grasped his cards.

*Wait. Before you get the wrong impression...*

Mariana looked at him silently, her eyebrows raised, a knowing smirk starting to present itself. Trust gazed back at her for a moment.

*You were supposed to interrupt me there. That's why I wrote the ellipsis.*

She smiled and then looked up toward the domed roof.

"It's snowing," she said.

Trust glanced up as well. The snow was indeed falling, clearly visible against the ambient glow of the metropolitan night outside the curved glass. Trust could see the dispersion of light, the small flakes shimmering like diamonds until they hit the pane or fell out of sight.

It was another stunning phenomenon he had learned that he alone could see. Nevertheless, his eyes seemed to reflect the view.

Still looking up, he smiled.

He felt a touch on his arm and shifted his glance down once more. Mariana's hand glided down to his.

"Come on. Let's take a walk around the block and make snow angels."

Trust started to raise the cards so he could reply, but Mariana would not let go of his hand.

"Nope. No chance for you to give me any backtalk. We're going."

*Wait a minute. Am I being kidnapped?*

The pair were walking down the presently empty sidewalk, the Centre Diamond club now behind them. Though the air was chilled, it was also still, tolerable during a slow stroll without worry for snow and tiny ice crystals whipping across their faces. Trust and Mariana donned coats, neither overly bulky, but still thick enough to combat the cold. The snow landed lightly atop their heads and shoulders, most of it dissolving on contact.

Instead of writing on his cards, Trust had typed on his phone.

"Oh, definitely. Because I'm physically capable of forcing you to come outside with me," Mariana replied.

Trust could see the milky brown of her eyes. They appeared to glimmer.

*You would be surprised what you're capable of.*

Mariana looked at him, her soft, enthralling smile never leaving her face.

"So, you think I'm actually capable of doing that? Be serious, Trust."

Smirking, Trust pointed to his phone again as they walked.

*You would be surprised what you're capable of.*

Laughing quietly, Mariana snatched the phone away from him and pointed it in his direction.

"Smile!"

Trust quickly hid his face with his hands. He then removed them, putting on a grotesque expression. Mariana laughed and took the picture anyway.

"Oh, I am *so* sending that one to my phone and uploading it to every social media site that I can think of!"

Trust pointed at her menacingly. Mariana smirked as she typed.

"Okay, or maybe I'll just keep it on my phone. But I'm still going to laugh every time I see it."

Trust beckoned for his phone back. He then moved quickly, aiming the camera at Mariana before she could anticipate it.

A snapshot of Mariana still looking down, away from the phone, having just handed it over, the traces of a playful grin still playing across her lips, her winter cap tilted ever so slightly downward.

Another shot, Mariana now beginning to look up, just to the side of the camera toward Trust's face, seemingly realizing what he was doing.

Another, Mariana looking directly into the camera, her eyes widening in surprise and her smile brightening as well, silky flakes of snow falling around her.

Another, Mariana reaching for the phone, her face now bright and animated, her mouth opening in exclamation, the merriment in her features obvious.

Trust retracted the phone as Mariana snatched at it, the forward momentum carrying her into his chest, Trust catching her. He was grinning, and he could feel her laughing as they both held on to the phone, unwilling to concede.

She looked up, still leaning in. He glanced down.

The sidewalk remained empty. The snow fell.

"Those pictures were unauthorized," she remarked, grinning. "I didn't give you permission to take those."

Trust arched his eyebrow. He slid the phone from between them, positioning it an arm's length away and directing it toward them. He glanced down to Mariana again.

"This picture is also unauthorized," she said.

Trust could tell from the subtler motions of her lips that her voice was softer. And she was still grinning.

Without looking, Trust snapped the picture, his eyes still on hers.

Then his attention shifted slightly.

Up the deserted walkway.

He thought he had noticed something before, but his attention had been focused on—

This time, Trust picked it out easily amidst the unmoving air and slowly falling snow, amidst the night and the chill. From that alley across the road, nearly half a block ahead...

He brought the phone back so he could type.

*Do you hear anything?*

Mariana's smile wavered.

"No...wait, what do you mean?"

The trillions of tiny glimmers and particles in the air, highlighted further by the descending snow, appeared almost like a sparkling dust cloud puffing out and away from the opening up the sidewalk. The heated air in contrast to the surrounding chill was distinguishable in Trust's eyes.

"Trust? Trust, what's wrong?"

He looked to her, and then to his phone again. Checking. Then, he typed.

*Wait here. I think something's happening in the alley up the street. Get your phone out. I'm going to text you.*

He looked at her for a moment, waiting for her nod, and then he moved, nimbly, lightly, jogging across the deserted street to the sidewalk on the other side. As he stepped, he took a photograph in his mind of his surroundings—all avenues of escape and entry, hidden or questionable areas, distances, heights, other bystanders, of which there were none. A mental topography.

After years of training and practice, it was now instinct.

Another glance back to Mariana as he slunk toward the mouth of the alley. She was watching him. Silently.

Eyes back ahead.

The disturbance—whatever it was—was still taking place, farther into the alley. The agitated, heated air continued to shift and move.

In isolation, given the circumstances, a larger animal rummaging for food was most likely. But the disturbance, the shifting air—it was too intense.

Multiple animals?

But Trust thought differently. He was easing into the excited mass of air now, nearing the corner that would lead into the alley. He could feel the subtle rise in temperature.

He slowed his movement further, soundlessly edging along the wall of the building. His phone was still in his hand.

Closer still.

One more glance toward Mariana.

He moved his head slowly, cautiously, to the corner.

A quick, fleeting glimpse.

He brought his head back. Pressed against the wall, his focus shifted quickly to his phone.

**Trust (8:13 PM):** Your car nearby?

Mariana's response was near immediate; she seemed to sense the urgency of the situation.

**Mariana (8:13 PM):** Yes.
**Trust (8:13 PM):** Bring it here, but first, count down from 5.

Then shout, hey!

Trust looked toward her, holding up his hand.

*Five...*

*Four...*

*Three...*

*Two...*

*One...*

He could see her shout, the "Hey!" rushing from her mouth. She then started to hurry back the way they had come...

Trust turned slightly, facing the alleyway again but not looking in. Waiting. His muscles were tensed, taut, arched.

The air shifted more, differently. Without having to look into the alley, without having to hear, he could tell that someone was approaching the opening quickly, the air shifting more, further agitated, further stirred—

What came next occurred in only a few seconds.

One eye.

Half a face.

A puff of air from the boy's—

Trust reached out, unbelievably fast, bringing the boy's face against the brick edge of the wall. Hard.

"Uhh!"

Trust drove the boy back in the same motion, one arm held under his throat and the other clutching the boy's shirt as he quickly steered him, deeper into the alley, the boy starting to stumble, obviously dazed from his impact against the wall, Trust keeping him on his feet and moving. Another hard shove finally sent the boy falling back against another body—

Trust had already swung his focus to the next person, the next target, nearest to him, but with his back turned, only just now beginning to react to Trust's presence—

Much too late.

Trust yanked back and down on the boy's hood. There was a tearing sound that Trust could not hear—though he felt the fabric give slightly—the boy falling back, jerked down by the sudden, forceful pull that briefly strangled him. He landed on his back, his feet flying out from underneath him.

A fleeting glimpse toward the huddled, sunken girl lying against the wall—

—and then Trust immediately reengaged, having never stopped moving. He kicked out and forward with both legs, leaving his feet, completely avoiding the girl, completely horizontal in the air above her, his hands anchoring his body to the ground as he struck the knees of another boy standing on the other side of the girl.

Kneecaps.

There was a crunching sound.

"Ahh!"

Trust, of course, heard neither.

He sprang back to a standing position almost as quickly as the boy registered the searing pain in his legs. The boy was already beginning to drop, crying out in agony. Trust assisted him, whipping the boy down by his head and shoulders, the boy slamming down to the concrete on his back as well, much like Trust did to the boy previous.

Another. Still moving. Someone was reaching out, swinging toward Trust, but Trust, already lower to the ground, rose up just slightly, delivering a stiff shoulder into the boy's midsection. The boy started to double over. Trust, standing quickly again, shoved the boy upright as well, sending him against the wall of the dark alley. A forearm was immediately shoved against the boy's throat.

Rory. Jeremy's friend. The boy's eyes were closed in a grimace.

Trust drove him into the wall again, stunning him, before he had to let go, another boy—the one Trust had shoved the first boy into—charging him, his head down. Trust caught him in a headlock but backpedaled—partly due to the boy's advancing momentum and partly of his own doing. After a few steps, he pivoted, and then turned again before bringing the boy down by his neck. He cradled the boy's head, not letting it hit the ground directly.

As they landed, Trust brought the boy's struggling body over, the boy's legs and feet flipping up in the air as though he were doing a handstand, before crashing down again to the cold surface. Trust himself turned over quickly, grasping the boy in a full-bodied choke hold, arms and legs tight, constricting.

Holding on to the boy, Trust surveyed the alley again.

Destruction.

The boy in his embrace was fading quickly.

Amidst the damage of the alleyway itself, four other boys lay in varying states of consciousness. One—the boy he had snatched down by the hood of his jacket—appeared fully out of it. The other three writhed on the ground in one form or another, their movements sluggish.

The girl was...

Trust let the fifth boy go, his body now limp, unconscious. He shrugged him off, standing again.

Even in the alley, the snow continued to fall.

Approaching the girl, he passed Rory, shooting him a quick, evaluative glance. The boy was curled up on the ground, his back against the alley wall. A small puddle of...something pooled near his mouth, some still dropping off his lips, obviously involuntarily expelled as a result of Trust's shoulder into his stomach.

Trust stopped in front of the girl, kneeling. Her clothes were ripped in places, including her shirt, and a second shirt underneath, her skin exposed to the wintry elements. She was wearing UCC sweatpants, but those were also slit and shoved down...

Trust moved his eyes back up.

Jezzie Delaney, her hair damp and matted, a dark red bruise already forming below her eye. She was looking up at him with a dazed, almost inattentive expression.

It was clear she was under the influence of something.

Trust turned to the alley opening. Mariana was already out of her car, which she had left idling along the curb, and was coming toward them.

Trust held up his hand.

Mariana halted immediately.

He looked to Jezzie again.

She was slow, but responsive enough to be able to meet his eyes.

He reached out toward her, slowly. She shrank back slightly, but when he made contact with her hand, she clutched it, her grip surprisingly tight.

He leaned forward, scooping her up, Jezzie seizing him. Trust looked into the alley one last time.

Five boys lay scattered on the ground.

The snow continued to fall.

Mariana hurried to open the rear door of her car.

"Oh, no; oh, no; oh, no. Is she hurt bad? We're going straight to the hospit—"

"No."

Trust could not hear Jezzie's voice, how hoarse and scratchy it sounded, how weary, how depleted. As he put her into the backseat, he felt Mariana gently grab his arm.

"We really need to take you to the hospital," Mariana said, looking at the girl. "You're hurt. You're bleeding. And if those boys—"

"Please..."

Jezzie was gripping Trust's hand again, and she squeezed it as she spoke.

"Please...Jeremy...take me..."

Trust looked at her, analyzing quickly, and then turned to look at Mariana, and then past her, toward the alley.

A few of the boys were slowly beginning to come around. Rory was attempting to push himself upward, leaning heavily against the wall, before slumping back down again, the grimace clear on his face.

Trust looked back to Mariana, catching the last of her words as she asked for Jeremy's address.

And the snow continued to fall.

MARIANA STOPPED THE CAR IN front of the tall building right in the middle of downtown Centre City.

The Millennium Complex.

The building was impressive, particularly at night, with specially positioned lighting that gave the structure a grand, almost majestic appearance. A wide set of stone stairs led up to the entrance, doors glinting with gold trim.

Luxury condominiums for the privileged and highest of high class in Centre City.

And, apparently, Jeremy Higgins.

The street and sidewalk in front of the building were quiet, even in the heart of downtown, only a five-minute drive from Centre Diamond club. The wintry weather was surely the cause.

Mariana ran around the car but Trust was already out, reaching back and then bracing himself as he carefully maneuvered Jezzie to the edge of the seat. He then helped her to stand on the cold sidewalk, his coat around her shoulders. He gazed at the girl now, allowing Jezzie to use him for support as Mariana started to run ahead, up the steps—

Trust watched as Jezzie's head turned in reaction, and Trust followed her stare.

Jeremy was rushing down, barefoot and shirtless, in basketball shorts.

"Jezzie! Jez! What happened?"

Trust recognized the string of curse words that surged freely from Jeremy's mouth, intermixing with his questions. The deaf teen moved out of the way as Jeremy leaped the last steps.

"What happened?" he asked.

He gingerly cupped Jezzie's face in his hands, his frantic eyes shifting to Trust.

"What happened?" he asked again. Demanded. Pleaded. His tone, his face, anxious.

Trust's eyes shifted to Mariana, who was still standing on the stone steps.

"Trust found her like this," she answered for him. "We don't...we wanted to take her to the hospital, but she didn't want to—"

Trust saw Jezzie's chapped lips moving.

"Please...just...upstairs...no hospital..."

Jeremy tilted his head up, bellowing another curse into the quiet night, puffs from his condensed breath visible.


MINUTES LATER, THE SCENE WAS still again. Trust and Mariana were both standing at the bottom of the steps outside the Millennium Complex.

He turned his head, looking at her. She was looking back at him, her expression unreadable.

He reached into his pocket for his phone.

*I hope you won't tell anyone what you saw in the alley.*

Mariana did not reply.

They began to move back to her car.

Suddenly, Mariana turned on him, immediately capturing his lips with hers.

Her lips were remarkably soft.

He opened his eyes as she slowly pulled away.

"I don't think you have an inkling of an idea the magnitude of what you did tonight," she whispered, her eyes roving slowly between his eyes and lips. "Whether you want people to know it or not."

She then crushed into him again. But this time, Trust was ready.

And all around them, the light, feathery flakes of snow continued to fall.

MARIANA DROVE TRUST BACK TO Weaver Hall. During the ride, Trust somehow had the presence of mind to ask if she was missed back at the club, but, smiling, the pretty girl only waved his concern away.

After the kiss, Trust was having a difficult time thinking straight.

He was touching and licking his lips unconsciously as he got out of her car, as he entered the residence hall, as he rode up the elevator to the seventh floor, as he stepped out, passing familiar faces who observed him with a mixture of curiosity, intrigue, and amusement. Trust returned their looks, not seeing any of them at all.

He arrived at his door, closed partway. Numbly, he nudged it open.

Kyler was in, sitting on the floor, looking up to the television with a video game controller in his hands. Paxson was there, too, sitting in a desk chair, also with a controller. Marcie and Allison were both sitting on Trust's bed.

They all turned toward the door as Trust entered.

Trust's gaze skirted across all of them, landing on Kyler last.

Kyler's eyebrows shot up. He grinned brightly.

"Dude!"

Then the grin slowly faded, his mouth hanging open limply. His brow furrowed as his gaze lowered.

"Dude? What is that on your shirt—"

Trust looked down.

For the first time, he noted the thin spray of blood splattered across a small section in the middle of his shirt.

## 26.
## Make It Rain

*CRACK!*

Trust could feel each impact as they reverberated through the air of the indoor cages, almost as though he could actually hear the sounds of multiple bats making contact with multiple baseballs.

*Crack!*

After years of accompanying Kyler to games and practices, the experience was effortlessly familiar, whether it was solid contact on the sweet spot of the bat, or the thin, wispy ricochet that would be fouled off in an official contest.

*Crack! Crack-crack!*

Multiple batters exercised and further perfected their swings again and again in separate batting cages in the state-of-the-art complex housed beneath the rows of seats in the baseball stadium, balls hurled at the players from remotely controlled machines over sixty feet away. The cavernous, basement-like space almost resembled a shooting gallery, and it was...of a slightly different variety.

*And you really believe Chancellor Beverly doesn't know anything about it?* Kyler gestured, attired in UCC-branded shorts and long sleeves, batting gloves covering his hands. *You don't think there's a chance she was just denying it?*

*You've met her,* Trust returned, sitting beside Kyler on a bench overlooking a few of the cages. *You've seen her speak. Not only do I not get the impression that she would even bother to lie—about anything, much less something serious like this—she seems like one who would shout from the highest building in Centre City that she would find every single one of the people involved in the assaults—if they even happened.*

*She doesn't strike me as the type to lie to a deaf kid.*

In the cage Kyler was assigned to, one of his upperclassmen teammates—Kyler being the sole freshman on the squad—sawed away at a steady series of baseballs launched in his direction.

*Crack! Crack! Crack!*

Trust recognized that the older boy was slamming each pitch directly on the sweet spot of his bat.

*And then Jezzie,* Kyler signed.

He shook his head.

*I know why you don't want to tell me who the guys were. I don't agree with it, but I get it.*

Trust looked at him, his eyebrows arched.

*Do you really?* he asked.

*Not even a little,* Kyler replied.

Trust smirked faintly.

*For one, she doesn't even want her own boyfriend to know. Whatever reasoning she has, we should respect it. Two, there's absolutely no logical reason why you or anyone else should be carrying around that information. If I told you the people but swore you not to do anything, where does that leave you? I'm not putting anyone else in that position. I don't want to be in that position. I wish Mariana hadn't been there, but I don't think she recognized Jezzie or anyone else.*

"Did *you* recognize any of them?" Kyler asked.

*I think your phone's ringing.*

Kyler scoffed, smirking.

"No, it isn't. I would hear—oh, hey, my phone's ringing."

He reached down to his bag, which was beside the bench.

*ESP?* he signed as he pulled out the device.

*You forgot a letter,* Trust signed back.

*N,* both boys motioned at the same time, laughing, as Kyler brought the phone to his ear.

"Yello," he greeted, and then, "No, it was just Trust telling one of his corny jokes again. I have to laugh every once in a while so I don't—

"Yeah. I mean, I can do it while I'm holding the phone against my shoulder, but why—

"I think Marcie's starting to rub off on you. I can tell her influence, and it's starting to scare me."

*Who are you trying to kid?* Trust signed. *That's Allison, right? You've* been scared of her from the start.

*Allison just found out that the Dorm Room Robber victim in Duncan Hall has been in one of her classes this whole time,* Kyler signed. *They talked a little bit about what happened.*

Trust watched him, a studious look on his face.

*Crack! Crack! Crack-crack!*

*Two TVs, one laptop,* Kyler continued. *One music player and entertainment system, and her roommate's DJ turntable system. No idea how or who. Happened in August; police think she was the first victim. It was someone else on her floor who first brought up the boy in the red hat. White, or possibly Asian, with straight black hair—that's all she really knows. The girl and her roommate were in class when the theft occurred. She had two classes and the roommate had one, so there was about an hour's worth of time when neither was in the room.*

*They know the schedule,* Trust motioned. *They have to. There's no other explanation.*

Kyler relayed Trust's sentiments to Allison while signing back, *But how? Watching us? Some sort of surveillance? Would it be possible for them to access our schedules online?*

Then...

"Okay, yeah. I've gotta get back in the batting cage anyway. Have fun in Bio-thingamajig-class-I-can't-pronounce-whatever. Later."

He ended the call.

*You're brilliant at playing stupid,* Trust signed. *Bio-thingamajig-class-I-can't-pronounce-whatever?*

"Who says I'm playing?" Kyler replied, grinning. "And aren't you glad I came up with that thingamajig sign? KSBSL strikes again."

*Whatever. But I think your perfect grade point average so far this year would say otherwise.*

Kyler rolled his eyes.

"Oh, here we go with that again."

Trust spotted the older player exiting the batting cage. In Trust's occasional ventures joining Kyler at UCC baseball-related activities so far this year, he had since learned the beefy first baseman's name was Trent Atkins, and he was a bona fide star in the sport, garnering national attention.

"You're up, Scott," Trent said. "Make it rain."

The "Scott" was reference to the latter half of Kyler-Scott's name.

Originally meant to be mildly derisive, a subtle form of freshman hazing, Kyler never received such instruction, embracing the designate and thus endearing him to Trent and the rest of the team even more.

Kyler stood, picking up his bat and pointing it at the senior.

"Oh, don't you worry, Atkins. I'll make it rain, all right. I'll make it rain so hard, you'll..."

Trent smirked, arching an eyebrow.

"Don't hurt yourself trying to think of a way to finish that, Scott," he said, turning away.

"I'll make it rain so hard, you'll think it's actually raining in here—and that would be impossible!" Kyler called to Trent's broad back.

Kyler looked to Trust. Trust was wrinkling his nose.

*Pee-yew. Something smells like garbage in here. I think it's your trash talk.*

Kyler feigned a grin before entering the batting cage, picking up the device that controlled the speed, frequency, and type of pitch that would be thrown at him.

Trust spotted someone else approaching. Like him, it was another non-baseballer, and, also like him, he seemed a welcome face in the inner sanctum of the baseball team.

Trust had encountered the same non-baseballer not even twenty-four hours before.

Jeremy turned away from greeting another athlete, finally coming across Trust's gaze. He continued to approach.

Inside the cage, Kyler had already lapsed into his zone, the rest of the world nonexistent as he readied for the machine's pitches.

Trust watched as the university's star wide receiver took the spot on the bench that Kyler had recently vacated.

But Jeremy said nothing. He sat, looking down at his hands.

Trust had brought his notebook.

*Jezzie?*

He saw the older boy read the name. Jeremy started to open his mouth, but his head was still aimed down and away, Trust not able to read his words.

He touched Jeremy on the shoulder, and Jeremy looked up.

"What? Oh, uh, sorry."

Trust could tell he was speaking softly, not meant to be overheard.

"I took her to Arlington Memorial after she fell asleep. She had wanted to take a shower before, but she could barely even make it to the...I didn't know what else to do. She *hates* hospitals—I'm sure that's why she told you not to go—but I'm past the point of caring. Not last night. Not now."

Jeremy's head had begun to lean downward again, as though he were reliving the night over again. Trust lowered his own head, following, before Jeremy caught himself and looked up again.

"She's still there," he explained. "In the hospital. They want to keep her a few days. She wants to hate me right now, but she knew I was going to take her. If she really didn't want to go, she would have just had you take her to her apartment."

Jeremy huffed. Trust continued to look at him.

"Sexual assault," Jeremy intoned. "No DNA. They used...some type of object. A bottle, or a rod or something, but it was just bruising on the outside. There was no..."

Trust nodded faintly. Jeremy looked him in the eyes.

"She won't tell me who. She won't tell me who did it."

Trust gazed at him. Wooden bats cracked as they collided with baseballs, and snippets of dialogue hummed through the air. But Trust and Jeremy seemed in their own world.

Trust motioned to his notebook. Jeremy followed along as he wrote.

*We got off on the wrong foot at the beginning of the year.*
*Sparring in the North Gym. The party after your first game. I*
*think we both jumped to conclusions about each other.*

*I hope you believe me when I tell you I have no ill will toward*
*you, especially after you apologized in front of everyone like*
*that in Hollins. I have no ulterior motives with Jezzie, and I*
*mean that.*

*And you're a REALLY good football player. Like Marcie said,*
*that must count for something.*

Trust could see Jeremy chuckle faintly out of the corner of his eye as he wrote.

*But before you ask the question, Jezzie doesn't want me to say anything about what happened—especially to you. I don't know why. I'm not really that experienced with couples or relationships, but I think her reasoning has everything to do with protecting you—either to keep whoever did it from doing something to you, or, more likely, to prevent you from doing something to them that would get you in trouble. You know Jezzie much better than I do, but I think it's best to trust her decision for now, and her reasons for doing so.*

*I do think she'll tell you the full story. Just give her some time.*

Jeremy pursed his lips, his cheeks hollowing. His eyes then met Trust's again.

"She had on someone's coat yesterday. Yours?"

Trust nodded.

"There was some blood on the—"

*Not Jezzie's.*

"Yours?"

Trust arched a dubious eyebrow.

Jeremy nodded ever so slightly, the faintest trace of a smile appearing on his lips.

"Well, at least you got a couple of shots in. It's at the cleaner's. I'll get it back to you."

*More than a couple. I think you would be proud.*

Jeremy's grin grew slightly wider, the beginnings of the smirk that Trust was now so accustomed to.

Both boys then looked toward the batting cage door, which was opening, Kyler sticking his head out. His blond hair streamed out from underneath the batter's helmet he wore.

"Hey, Trust, you—hey, it's Jeremy Higgins, my favorite athlete. Dude, I have all your trading cards."

"Favorite athlete?" Trent asked, ambling up again, a sports drink in his gloved hand.

"Favorite non-baseball athlete," Kyler clarified before rolling his eyes. "Man, Atkins, you are a sensitive one."

"Don't you just stand there on first base and wait for someone to throw the ball into that oversized glove you wear?" Jeremy directed at Trent, his patented smirk returning full force as he slapped Trent's hand. "You sure we need to stretch the definition of an athlete that far?"

Trent gave Jeremy a look.

Kyler coughed.

"Burn," he said.

He then held his bat out toward Trust.

"You want another go before Trent's up again? I've been making it rain so much in here my clothes are getting damp."

"And the award for Corniest Line Ever Uttered goes to..." Trent said, Jeremy laughing.

Trust stood, heading for the cage door. He missed the quick exchange that went on behind him.

"I've got ten he whiffs," Jeremy said.

Trent looked at him.

"You've never seen this kid swing before, have you?" he asked. "Look, Higgins. I know you, and I know taking all those shots to your head has probably rattled some stuff loose, so I'll do you a favor and not take that bet. Taking your money would be downright criminal right now."

Meanwhile, inside the cage, Kyler was unclasping his gloves to give to Trust, who already had on a helmet.

"So," Kyler said, his voice not able to carry out of the cage with the constant commotion of pitching machines, swinging bats, and general male bravado, "can I ask what you two sheilas were gossiping about? It looked serious."

*Go ahead and ask,* Trust signed back.

And then...

*Wait. Was that a bit of Australian slang you tried to slip in there?*

Kyler snickered, relinquishing the batting gloves and stepping out of the cage.

After he slipped the gloves on, Trust picked up the pitch control device, tuning it to the setting he desired. Then he put the device down.

The clock was ticking.

A couple of practice swings, reacquainting himself with the feel and weight of the bat in his grip.

He got into position, placing his feet, digging in, the bat seeming to flow and stream this way and that in a natural rhythm in the space above his head as he waved it, before raising it up to his shoulders, where it hovered slowly, back and forth...back and forth...back and forth...

A light near the pitching machine started blinking rapidly.

Then a solid green.

One second...

The machine emitted a slight puffing sound that Trust did not hear, a baseball materializing at a speed approaching ninety miles an hour.

Almost immediately, the ball seemed to slow down...way down...Trust gauging, reading, his grip tightening in anticipation...

And then the ball sped up again as he started to swing, faster, faster, faster...

*CRACK!*

He couldn't hear the hit, but he could certainly feel it.

Outside the cage, Trent looked to Jeremy again.

"This is the part where you would be handing over ten dollars."

Jeremy's eyes were wide.

"Holy—!"

## 27.
## Christmas In Adams Hall

THE NEXT DAY, TRUST FOUND himself in front of Adams Hall once again. The snow from a few days prior, which had carried on through the following morning, provided a thin layer of white across the grounds—not enough to impede the travel or the workings of the university and surrounding city, but enough to distinctly alter the vista of the collegiate landscape. Even with others milling about, going on with an otherwise normal day at school, the campus almost appeared to be sleeping, a distinct difference from what occurred during the warmer months when the university seemed alive and full of energy.

Regardless of the weather, however, the view was always enchanting.

Trust skipped up the short staircase, leaving footprints in the snow, and entered the building. Kimberlee was behind the receptionist's desk.

*It's like you live here or something,* Trust signed.

He placed two Christmas cards on the raised partition before sliding them closer to the graduate student. He pointed to them.

*This one's yours. That one's for Brycen—you can probably leave it here. I'm sure you'll see him again before I do.*

"Oh, Trust. You didn't have to do that. Thank you," Kimberlee said.

*Actually, you can just wait and—*

But she had already opened her card, beginning to read the inscription Trust had written himself.

Her inquisitive expression changed, her eyes widening, her eyebrows rising.

She brought a hand to her mouth.

*Don't,* Trust signed, attempting to divert her attention and failing. *Look, it's really not—*

337

Kimberlee reached for a tissue, her eyes welling up. Laying his arms down on the ledge, Trust put his head down, watching her.

"Kim...berlee."

She lifted her head in surprise, the tissue clutched in her hand, poised in midair.

Trust smiled gently.

"AND FINALLY, LAST BUT NOT least," Dr. Duncan intoned, Trust shifting his attention between the senior administrator's face and the computer screen, where the voice-to-text application was open and functioning in a minimized window, "Martial Arts 1010. Kobe McKenzie is the instructor—hmm, why have I not met him?—but I have heard things, Mr. Jeffries, I have heard things. An excellent instructor, just excellent. A little on the quiet side, so they say—*so they say*—but that shouldn't be any hindrance. I think you will do well in there. Tell me, do you have any experience, any at all, in the martial arts?"

Trust typed.

**Trustice:** Yes, I've done it before.

Technically, it was a true statement.

Dr. Duncan grinned excitedly, clapping his hands together.

"Well, good! Good! I'm sure you will have a leg up in an introductory class, then. I myself have never ventured into the realm of the martial artist, although, I must admit, I do have quite an affinity for it when I see it on film. The lovely Mrs. Duncan, on the other hand, is actually a practitioner of the art. She is a tenth-degree black belt—wait, is that a thing? I may have just made it up...anyway, she's been practicing it longer than you've been alive, Trustice!"

The wizened admin laughed, obviously tickled at the thought.

"In fact, she's been doing it longer than I've known her, and I've known her for over f—"

On the computer screen, the program transcribed the older man's clearing of his throat as a simple *ahem*.

"Well, on second thought, I am positively certain Mrs. Duncan would rather I not bring that particular number into the discussion, or I may fall victim to that aforementioned martial arts practice."

Trust nodded.

> **Trustice:** We can't have that. I don't want to see how this university functions without you.

"Oh, it will function just fine, don't you worry," Dr. Duncan said. "But have a look at this! I just derive such joy when a schedule comes together, and yours is looking quite good, quite good indeed. I am aware of your exceedingly outstanding academic record from your more formative years, so my goal for you is to have you challenged while still maintaining a sense of balance. We would do well to avoid the most stifling of curriculums, though even then, I would wager that you would do quite well in even that."

> **Trustice:** Miss Sharpshire at the front desk said you had a family matter to attend to the night of the Disability Services dinner. Everyone was asking about you.

Dr. Duncan grunted. If Trust could have heard it, he would have found it amusing.

"Miss Sharpshire certainly has a way with coming up with the most...aesthetically palatable of phrasings, which is a fantastic skill as you get older, mind you. But really, it was much ado about nothing. Mrs. Duncan's father—the most shrewd, petty, conniving, senile, nonsensical example of an almost-centuries-old father-in-law that I have ever come across, real or imagined—had another one of his bizarre adolescent temper tantrums, seeking some attention, so we had to go for a visit. We won't mention that Mrs. Duncan had three other siblings who also had to put their lives on hold for forty-eight hours to tend to his whims. We also won't mention that I ignorantly expressed a desire not to go visit him—to let him have his tantrum alone—but again, the tenth-degree black belt, you see.

"Nevertheless, I heard the gala was a delectable affair. Our lovely chancellor made an appearance, I presume."

> **Trustice:** I know in my head she is a university chancellor, but she almost seems like a celebrity. Or a politician.

Wherever she goes, whatever she says, people watch and listen.

"An absolutely riveting public speaker, and when she speaks, she almost always has something good to say, unlike yours truly. I could pontificate for two hours about...well, anything, and the lovely Mrs. Duncan will just smile and nod absently while everyone else will have since nodded off. It was a good day for the university, and the city, when Madam Beverly accepted our offer to become chancellor."

**Trustice:** I got a few minutes to speak with her. Has she been here long? I actually brought up rumors about the Freesef Society with her, and she—

**Dr. C. Duncan:** "The Freesef Society?"

Trust turned to look at him.

"Oh, Trust, the Freesef Society had dissolved long before April Beverly arrived at our doors. I would actually find it surprising if she were aware such an organization existed at all."

The deaf student shook his head.

**Trustice:** She wasn't. Apparently, she also wasn't aware of the rumors that circulate about them these days.

Movement captured Trust's attention once more. Dr. Duncan quirked his head, his bushy eyebrows expressing perplexity.

"Rumors? There are still rumors about the Freesef Society?"

An equally baffled look crossed Trust's face as well.

**Trustice:** Didn't we talk about this last time?

**Dr. C. Duncan:** "I don't recall..."

**Trustice:** According to rumors, along with what you mentioned before, the Freesef Society was officially disbanded but is now a secret organization on campus. Allegedly, its members have been known to target and assault select freshman girls, girls they somehow know beforehand can be persuaded not to go to the police. Apparently, these girls carry this "incident" as a badge of honor.

It could be argued that, were these events true, they may not even be illegal, since the girls seem to give consent, if not before, then perhaps during and almost certainly after the act. But it's just a rumor that surfaces from time to time. It could be nothing.

Trust turned to the administrator. The older man appeared frozen, his expression fixed into a look of surprise as he stared at the computer display. After an extended moment, his eyes shifted to Trust. Surprise had changed to concern.

"The Freesef Society?"

Trust could see that the man was speaking softly. A whisper.

"Please, tell me everything you know about these rumors. And you say you've told me this before? I had absolutely no idea. Leave nothing out. Everything that you can think of."

IT WAS OPPORTUNE THAT BOTH Trust and Dr. Duncan's schedules were clear, as Trust remained in the administrator's office an additional twenty minutes. When he emerged into the open reception area of Adams Hall again, he was deep in his own thoughts—so much so that he did not notice the movement until the last possible moment.

Kimberlee Sharpshire had come from around her desk and was now giving Trust a hug, Trust taken aback. As she released him, she pecked him gently on the cheek.

Trust's eyes were wide when the older girl met his gaze again.

"That Christmas card was so sweet. Thank you," she said.

The kiss on the cheek had snapped Trust out of his musing.

*Well, if I had known a simple card would be the thing that would make you profess your love to me, I assure you that I would—*

"And you don't even have to finish that thought," Kimberlee said. "I already know what you're going to say. You're such a guy."

Even through the scolding, however, she was smiling.

"Still," she said, "thank you for the card. Really. I'm sure Brycen will appreciate his as well."

*He won't try to kiss me, too, will he?* Trust asked as Kimberlee returned behind the desk.

She gave him a dubious look, scooting her chair up. Trust shook his head.

*Of course he will,* he motioned in a resigned manner.

Kimberlee laughed.

Trust then jerked his head, a look of annoyance flashing briefly.

*What is it?* Kimberlee signed.

*I had another question I just remembered I wanted to ask Dr. Duncan,* Trust replied, looking toward the corridor he had just come from. *But actually, you may be able to answer better than he can. Who has access to a student's schedule besides a student and his academic advisor?*

Kimberlee thought briefly.

"Well, a student can grant permission to anyone if he or she provides the password to their account, along with their username..."

Trust nodded and motioned, *Yes, but besides that. Is there anyone else, even other administrators, who would be able to access schedules without having to ask for the student's password? I assume the staff in Student Services could access the accounts independently, for instance, if a student had some type of issue.*

But Kimberlee shook her head.

"I strongly doubt it," she said. "They would still need to know your username and password to gain access to your account, which is the only site I'm aware of with your full class schedule. Student Services would be able to reset your password, of course, but the student would notice when they tried to log in again. Professors can see their rosters for each class, but they wouldn't be able to access another instructor's roster without permission. I can't think of any other way someone would be able to access the contents of an account without actually knowing the student's password and username."

*Fantastic,* Trust signed.

Kimberlee arched an eyebrow.

"Fantastic?"

*You've heard about the string of robberies on campus in the dorms?* She nodded.

*My roommate, Kyler—you remember him—*Kimberlee smiled—*Yeah.*

*Well, he caught someone trying to break in to our room the other day. The police think it's the same robbers. We've talked to two other people who were robbed also, and they were all in class at the time it happened, which would suggest the thieves knew their schedules. But the thing is, when they tried to break into our room, Kyler was at a baseball thing, and I was at the North Gym. So with that, along with what you just told me, simply having access to class schedules is both highly unlikely and not enough information for them to act on. Barring the chance of them actually physically spying on all the people they are planning to rob, I really have no idea how they have been able to pull this off for this long.*

"It sounds as though you're looking to solve the case yourself," Kimberlee observed.

*When you have eliminated all which is impossible, then whatever remains, however improbable, must be the truth,* Trust offered.

Kimberlee smiled.

"Ahh, a Sir Arthur Conan Doyle fan. So, are you any closer to finding the truth?"

Trust shrugged.

*It's a good mystery.*

"And not just a fictional one," Kimberlee agreed.

Trust smiled, backing away from the desk.

*So, are you going to tell Kendell you kissed me, or shall I the next time I'm in Hollins?*

*You sure you want to play that game?* Kimberlee motioned back. *Are you planning to tell Mariana I kissed you?*

Still walking in reverse, Trust very nearly stumbled over his own feet.

"Merry Christmas!" Kimberlee called out, laughing and waving.

## 28.
## The Most Wonderful Time

COLD DAYS TURNED INTO FROSTY nights after the sun set. Yet, as the group drew closer to Centre Diamond, the usual queue of awaiting patrons snaking away from the entrance doors and lining the sidewalk illustrated that it was still not quite cold enough to prevent a night on the town.

Trust spotted Jayson the bouncer perform a double take when his eyes landed on their group. His voice was booming, animated, effortlessly traversing the distance separating them.

"Well, if it isn't the ol' gang, back again! Paxson, Trust, Marcie, and Kyler, the boy we always have to keep a camera on now. And a new face!"

Paxson looked at the rest of the group.

"Remember how I told you Marcie and I have been here a few times since...you know."

His eyes flitted briefly to Kyler, who arched an eyebrow.

"Anyway, we've tried to sneak around to get in line, but they've got cameras watching or something. They make an even bigger scene when they pull us out and usher us to the front."

Paxson and Marcie led the group toward the entrance. As Jayson split from the other security guard controlling the line to get in the club, Trust saw Allison glance to Kyler with a curious look. Kyler attempted to shrug it off innocently. Trust snickered.

"Let me guess," Jayson remarked, grinning, his voice back to a more suitable level so that the rest of the crowd wouldn't overhear. "Blowing off a little steam in between exam days?"

"Yep," Kyler said, stretching the word smugly as he extended his arms into the air. "Just a little change of pace before we hit the grindstone again tomorrow."

"He's actually the one amongst us that least needs a break," observed Marcie. "He's some sort of memory savant."

Jayson smirked at Kyler before turning to Allison.

"Now, for some reason, you look familiar. You've been here before, right?"

"Yes," Allison said, nodding. "My name is Allison. I came once before, just before the school started—"

"Oh, yeah!" Jayson exclaimed. "Same night!"

Allison looked confused.

"The same—"

"So, she's a part of your gang now?" Jayson asked, looking to the others. "Is this one"—he pointed to Trust—"going to punch another drunk in the throat who tries to hassle her?"

Paxson and Marcie nodded, grinning. Trust grimaced.

"What?" Allison began, glancing around at the group as well. "I don't—"

Jayson interrupted her.

"Well, I'll tell ya, Allison, straight up. You picked yourself a really fine group of friends here, and these guys get treated like Centre Diamond family when they come. I'll let them explain exactly what that entails, but let's just say that if we catch you standing in line out here, I may personally pick you up and carry you to the entrance myself."

"And PS," Marcie said, leaning toward Allison, "he's totally not joking. He nearly did it to me last time."

"But I still don't—" Allison started.

"A-Rock," Jayson called to the other hulking bouncer standing at the line of people waiting to gain access. "I'll hold the line. You take these guys in. Boss wants them on the upper level."

The group of freshmen looked at each other. Allison still looked out of sorts.

"You got it," A-Rock said, gesturing for the teenagers to follow him.

Trust, at the rear of the group, started forward, before Jayson halted him. He met the guard's gaze.

"I know you're deaf, but you can understand me, right?"

Trust nodded.

"Mariana didn't tell any of us the full story, but I know something happened. I remember your friend kept talking about being on 'the list' before. Technically, that list still doesn't really exist, but if it did, the boss has definitely put you on it."

Jayson extended his hand. Trust took it, his eyes still slightly curious, although, deep inside, he knew what the guard was referring to.

"Whatever you did, whenever you did it," Jayson said before chuckling softly, observing the deaf teen's face. "Yeah. Good job."


"I'M STILL WAITING," ALLISON DECLARED, looking at the others pointedly.

Inside from the cold, the five freshmen were on the second floor of Centre Diamond. The second floor was set farther back, which allowed those on the main level an unobstructed view up and through the glass-domed roof, where darkness presently lingered, buffeted by a light glow coming from the rest of the lights from downtown Centre City. In addition, the upper level carried with it a more laid-back, lounge-like feel relative to the excited chaos of the dance floors downstairs. The music played by the club DJ was buffered to allow for more relaxed conversation.

Tonight, Centre Diamond exhibited a Christmastime décor similar to what it had during the Disability Services dinner, though Trust saw it had been somewhat modified. At the dinner, the club did not have the look and ambiance of a nightclub at all, more resembling a grand ballroom.

Now, it was a nightclub again.

"I have a feeling you could be waiting a while," Paxson replied to Allison's comment, just before Marcie elbowed him in his side, nearly causing him to slosh the drink a waitress had just brought over.

"What does that mean?" Allison challenged. "Will someone please tell me what's going on here?"

Trust, who had brought along his stack of note cards, scribbled something down and then tossed it on the table between the plush benches they each sat on. Both Allison and Kyler reached for it—Kyler presumably already knowing what Trust had written—but Allison was more determined and slightly quicker.

As her hand landed on the note, Kyler's hand landed on hers. The two looked to each other.

"Well," Kyler voiced. "This is kinda awkward, huh?"

Marcie rolled her eyes.

"Not if you take your hand off, it won't be," Allison replied.

"This is oddly entertaining," Paxson said, leaning in. "I can't seem to tear my eyes away—not that I really want to."

"Kyler," Allison said in warning.

*Dude,* Trust motioned. *How long are you actually expecting to keep this up? I don't even think the story's a big deal, but it's unfair of you not to tell her.*

"Kyler," Marcie said, "let go, or I'm going to tickle you under your arm."

She slid closer to him.

"Okay, okay!" Kyler said, though he still did not loosen his hold on Allison's hand. "Let's not all fly off the deep end here."

The group watched as he looked across the table to Allison.

"You said you've been to Centre Diamond before," Kyler said. "Well, we were here, too."

Allison tilted her head slightly.

"We?"

"Pax, Marcie, Trust, and I."

Kyler breathed deeply.

"I saw your face for, like, a second, if that, and I saw how beaut—"

Trust's gaze shifted.

"So, I take it everyone's doing okay over here?"

It was Mariana.

At the brutal interruption, Kyler leaned back in his seat, inadvertently letting go of Allison's hand as he roughly combed through his hair. With everyone else watching, Allison swiftly snatched the card. Kyler's eyes snapped open as he realized what he had done.

"Wait—"

"'Is it just me,'" Allison read, "'or is anyone else getting hungry again?'"

She looked to Trust. The entire group did.

Trust was finding it extremely difficult to hold a straight face.

Kyler looked irate.

"Trustice!"

He lunged out of his seat, but Trust was quicker, nimbly leaping to his feet on the other side. Mariana, meanwhile, glanced toward the others.

"I just interrupted something important, didn't I?" she asked.

"Actually, I think you just made everything ten times funnier," Paxson replied.

Kyler reached for Trust again. Trust agilely hurdled over the back of the couch beside Allison. What should have been a cumbersome maneuver, and potentially disastrous if he had miscalculated and crashed into a neighboring couch full of club goers, Trust made look graceful, as though he had performed the move before.

He stepped behind Mariana, hiding, his hands on her shoulders, and thus did not see what was said next.

"Do you mind if I borrow him for a second?" Mariana asked, gesturing faintly to the boy behind her, Kyler taking his seat again.

"You probably should take him," Kyler answered, still fuming a little. "If I catch him, I'm probably going to wring his little neck until he—yeah, I see you hiding back there!"

Trust was peeking over Mariana's shoulder.

"And you guys don't need anything?" Mariana asked. "Anything to eat? Refills?"

Paxson raised his glass.

"I think our server forgot the shot of Dark Rose I asked f—umph."

He rubbed his side again as Marcie said, "We're fine, Mariana. Everything's great."

Trust started to step from behind Mariana, but she grabbed on to his hand. Trust looked at her.

"Your friends said I could borrow you for a second," she declared as she started to pull him away.

Trust looked quickly back to his table. He caught Kyler's gaze.

With one hand, Trust signed, *Tell her. For real.*

He then pointed fleetingly to Allison before he turned around again.

Mariana led Trust by the hand past the smaller bar that supplied the patrons on the upper level, Trust nearly having to break into a trot to keep up with Mariana's determined stride. They went through a door marked CLUB PERSONNEL ONLY, emerging into a much quieter hallway. The door closed behind them.

Trust watched as she lifted her wrist to her mouth, her eyes fixed on his.

"This is Mariana. I'm shutting down Hallway Two for a moment."

Then, without looking, she pointed a small remote to the cameras located in the upper corners of the hall. Trust, following her hand, didn't observe her other as she pushed him against the wall.

Trust's glance came back to her. He was currently not wearing his shades, and so his blue eyes glowed in the low-lit corridor.

"You're a freshman," she said, whispered.

Trust pulled out his phone.

*There's only a select few people I would allow to push me into*
*a wall.*

"I didn't tell Jayson or any of the other guys what you did that night. I only told them you're on the list, separate from just being Paxson's friend."

*So there's a list now?*

Mariana smiled.

"There's no *actual* list. It's just easier to call it that."

*You couldn't tell Jayson or the others what I did because you*
*don't know that I did anything. They were on the ground*
*when you came.*

"I saw the blood on your shirt, on your jacket. I saw all those boys sprawled out in the alley like an eighteen-wheeler ran through them."

*Why did you kiss me?*

"Why didn't you stop me?"

They looked at each other. Mariana started to lean in, but Trust swiftly spun her around, her back hitting the wall, a gasp coming from her lips. After closing them from the abrupt impact, Mariana slowly opened her eyes again.

Trust had one hand resting on the wall close to Mariana's head, the other manipulating his phone. He finally lifted it into her sightline again.

*Why didn't you stop ME?*

He then leaned in, taking her lips with his own.

As THEY CAME BACK TO their table, Trust instantly took note of the fact that two among their group were conspicuously absent.

"Dude, where did you go?" Paxson asked. "It looked like Mariana nearly broke your arm off pulling you away."

Marcie was eyeing him as well, smirking, her eyebrow arched.

Trust gestured to the two empty places as he sat down.

"Oh, no," Paxson said, chuckling. "I don't think so. You spill what just happened between you and *the owner of Centre Diamond*, and then we'll tell you where Kyler and Allison are. I will say this, though. After you left, the K-man totally spilled his guts out to Allison about how he saw her here at the club that night. 'Beautiful,' 'awesome,' and 'model' were some of the words used in his description. And then, inexplicably, Allison wanted to talk to him in private for a few moments. Safe to say, if they even talk at all, it will go much the same way as you and Mariana."

He then sat back, crossing his arms.

"But that's all you're getting out of me. Nothing else."

Trust looked to Marcie with a disbelieving expression.

"Before you deny anything," Marcie said, "you should know that you have some lip gloss on your mouth."

Trust frowned, looking at her mischievous grin, before lifting his glass, surreptitiously wiping at his lips as he took a swallow. When he lowered the cup again, he saw Mariana back at their table, a barely there smile on her lips. She was holding a new drink, with familiar coloring, though Trust was not quite able to place...

Mariana pointed, and Trust followed the gesture.

Wick, the viticulture major from the kitchen of the fraternity house party four months earlier, was manning the bar, pointing back excitedly in their direction. Trust could read the boy's lips even from that distance.

"Trust! You know I got you, dude! Mickey Mouse, no alcohol!"

Trust grinned, giving him a thumbs-up and accepting the drink. He smiled at Mariana, too.

*And you're sure I shouldn't be worried about whatever you're going to use these for?*

Huffing, Allison looked up to Trust again, who was standing in his boxer briefs...and nothing else.

"Give me one—*one*—logical reason why you should be worried."

Trust's response was quick.

*You're taking measurements of every single part of my body.*

Allison feigned a dazzling smile.

"Like, oh my gosh, Trust! You're just, like, so observant!"

The smile instantly evaporated.

"Now keep your legs still."

Trust wrote again.

*A Valley accent? Just because Kyler looks like a surfer boy doesn't mean he expects you to start talking like that.*

"Oww," Trust said dryly as Allison punched him in the thigh. She then looked up again, pointing at him.

"I am *not* Kyler's girlfriend," she stated in a deadly tone. "Let's get that straight right now."

Trust arched an eyebrow.

"Oww," he said again, as Allison delivered another punch.

The two were in Trust and Kyler's dorm room, the bright December sunlight streaming through the window with such intensity that all interior lighting was switched off. It was the last day of exams before the official start of Winter Break—Trust and Allison were done, and Kyler was presently in his final examination.

*Heard anything from police?*

Allison shook her head.

*Any more gifts?*

Another shake of the head.

*Are you afraid that Kyler's not serious?*

Allison froze.
A moment passed.
The girl's eyes moved, slowly, gradually meeting Trust's.
"Did..."
She glanced down, then back up to him.
"Did he tell you what happened yesterday?"
Trust looked at her for a moment.

*Honestly, no. But he didn't have to. I know him. I've been
around him my entire life. He's my brother. My twin.*

Allison looked down again. She moved to sit on Trust's bed, the
measuring tape now balled up in her grip. Trust kneeled in front of her
so he could see her face.

"After you left with Mariana, Kyler finished talking about that first
night at Centre Diamond. He..."

Allison looked at Trust directly, meeting his inquiring blue eyes.

"I think what I like best about both you and Kyler is your...humility.
Both of you put on a cocky act sometimes, of course, but it's so easy for
anyone else to see that it's just a joke. It's not really who you two are. It's
like neither of you actually realize how...attractive you are, I guess—and
I'm not just saying that. You should have heard how everyone was
talking about Kyler in a towel, all of those girls in the hallway. And even
now, with you, sitting here in just your underwear..."

She chuckled, shaking her head.

"You realize you have, like, a ten-pack, don't you?"

Trust jotted something down.

*Wait a minute. Is this about to get weird?*

Allison rolled her eyes.

"See? That's exactly what I'm talking about. I don't think you really
understand what would happen right now if I told the other girls on this
floor that you were in here with just your boxer shorts on. And with

Kyler...well, obviously you saw we weren't there when you came back."

Trust smiled faintly.

"We were in one of the stairwells, talking. He was tripping over his words, something I don't think I've ever heard him do as long as I've been around you guys. He told me about the fight with the drunk guy."

*Did he really call it a fight?*

Allison smiled.

"And he said you would respond in exactly that way."

*He knows me, though sometimes I wish he knew me a little less.*

"But we were just talking about that night and everything, and I...we...I kissed him."

*That I guessed. Though I'm sure he had no trouble kissing back.*

Allison looked at him.

"I wonder if it might have been a mistake."

Trust's smile slowly diminished.

*Your mistake, or his?*

He held the card toward Allison. She read it and shook her head.

"I don't...I wasn't there that day with the towel, but I've been around both of you more than enough to see how other girls look at you two around campus. Neither of you even notice. I don't know if you're just used to it by now, or you simply don't see it, but it happens. A lot. I don't—and I say this without meaning any disrespect and being completely ignorant to how the two of you were before I met you—but I don't see what Kyler could possibly see in me to make him say the things he said. To make him kiss me like that. Not with all the other girls who go to this school or are in the city. He could have any of them. I don't understand it. I think the kiss was a mistake for him, which makes it a mistake for me, because the last thing I want right now is for the friendship we have to change."

She had started to look down again, forcing Trust to follow her head with his own so he could maintain sight of her mouth. He now sat beside her on the bed, still only in his boxers. Ditching his cards, he reached for his notebook. He motioned for Allison to follow along as he wrote.

*You and Kyler are actually pretty similar. Smart, brilliant even...but still awfully dumb sometimes.*

Allison laughed quietly, nudging him.

*He told you about that night at the club. Did he tell you how he obsessed over the mysterious red-haired girl after that, driving me, Pax, and Marcie nuts?*

*Did he tell you why he was acting the way he was that first day in Honors Seminar? You know how much he likes to talk. Did he tell you why it seemed like he was the one who was deaf between the two of us that day, and for days and weeks after that whenever you were around? Did he tell you he didn't act that way when he first met Marcie? Or Paxson?*

*And I told you before that he was "strongly suggesting" I learn how to say your name. Typically, he doesn't make those suggestions—I go to him. Did he tell you why he did any of these things?*

*Actually, whether he did or didn't tell you these things, it doesn't really matter. And whether you want to admit it to yourself or not, I think you already know the answer. It's obvious to everyone else. Next time you talk to your Uncle Smith, you should ask him about it.*

*Something else obvious to me is, while you say Kyler and I aren't aware of girls looking at us, you're completely BLIND to the attention you get. You're only kidding yourself if you think all the words Kyler used to describe you don't apply. Everyone else knows it to be true. Everyone else knows it to be FACT—except for you. You had some drunk 30-year-old dude—who you had apparently never even seen—ready to beat up a couple of college kids because of you. You had a boy who saw your face for literally a second practically chase after you through the most packed club in the city, filled to the brim with pretty girls, and he nearly got punched for it.*

*So, if you could, please explain again why, in a gazillion years, Kyler would think kissing you would be a mistake, only this time if you could just speak slower and use visual aids, maybe this time I won't think you're being so ridiculous.*

Allison read through it again when he had finished. Then Trust wrote more.

*The note that I wrote in the police station? You think that was to make you feel better?*

Allison smiled.

"I hate you. And how do you write so fast and so legibly at the same time?"

*A lifetime of practice. So, I can put my pants back on now?*

"No! Wait. I haven't gotten all the measurements I need yet."

She beckoned Trust to stand again. As she pressed the tape to Trust's shoulder, Trust's eyes quickly flitted to the door. The knob was twisting.

"Yo yo yowhattha!"

In his winter coat and standard worn baseball cap, and fresh from outside, Kyler froze in the doorway.

Allison turned, approached. Kyler's surprised glance shifted to her. She pulled him into the room and closed the door behind him.

Kyler peeked around the girl to glance at his near-naked roommate fleetingly before his attention turned back to Allison—

—just before she kissed him, her hands cupping his face.

Kyler hesitated for only a moment—a split second—before embracing her as well.

"Allison."

Allison broke off from the kiss in surprise, Kyler still leaning forward, his eyes closed. She turned to Trust, beaming.

"Trust, you got it right! That was perfect!"

Smirking but shaking his head, Trust gestured to his body.

And then, to Kyler, who had finally opened his eyes, *Dude. You so owe me, it's not even funny. And tell Allison that when she measures to leave some additional space in the groin area. You know, to make sure it doesn't get too tight down there.*

Kyler stared at him.

Then he arched an eyebrow and scoffed.

## 29.
## Viper Skin

ON THE AFTERNOON BEFORE THE first day of second semester classes, Allison had gathered Trust and Kyler in her dorm room in Mueller Hall to show them what she had been working on for nearly a year, and working on aggressively in the last few months. It was why Trust's measurements had been taken before they left for Winter Break.

Knowing Allison's aptitude and interest in things high-tech, both boys were eagerly anticipating whatever it was Allison was retrieving from her suitcases, though they tried hard to conceal their childish excitement. Melody, Allison's elusive roommate, had apparently come and gone. Her belongings were back in the room, but she, as usual, was not.

*I know,* Trust signed in response to Kyler's question, *but I don't want to be a bother, and like you say, she has a whole nightclub to manage. I figure I should just take it one day at a time. Anyway, it gives me a chance to do my own thing.*

"I feel ya," Kyler said, sighing. "Dating an older woman can be...different. Especially when she has her own business. It's a whole different skill set, dude."

Trust looked to his best friend with a skeptical expression.

*First off, I'd rather not label it as anything, particularly "dating." And second, what on earth do you know about dating older women? I've met every single one of the girls you've gone out with, and absolutely zero of them were that kind of "older." Wasn't Elisa only a couple of months older than you?*

"A couple of days, a couple of months, a couple of years, a couple of decades. It's all relative, and it's all the same. Mariana is an exception, but older women generally want their guys to be dependable, stable, laid-back. In other words, boring. I think we both know you don't fit that title."

*And I think you're an idiot,* Trust motioned. *What slapdash relationship advice article did you pull that—*

His attention shifted.

"Okay," Allison said, finally emerging out of the closet with a closed box. "Here it is. Like I said, it's completely safe—I've done extensive testing. It's just a question now of how effective it is in the field."

*Does she realize that's the fifth time she's mentioned that it's safe?* Trust signed to Kyler, which Kyler then voiced aloud.

"Four of the times I said it were after you asked if it was safe," Allison replied with a laugh in her voice Trust was able to identify. "I said it now as a preemptive strike before you asked again."

She laid the box on her desk and removed the intricate seal, pulling out what, to Trust, appeared to be...

He and Kyler stood, looks of amazement coming across both of their faces.

"For right now, I'm calling it Viper Skin," Allison explained, holding up the sleek black bodysuit. "What it is supposed to do, and what it has done so far in my performance testing, is operate loosely based on the abilities of a pit viper—detecting movement, distance calculations, and proximity of other warm-blooded bodies, in this case, people."

She flipped the suit around, showing the backside, where there were a series of slightly raised ridges lining the spine, faintly resembling stegosaurus plates. They looked made of a glossy black rubber.

"The suit, or skin, if you will, is made of a number of materials, and you can see these tiny reflective flakes throughout. That is polyurethane glass."

Trust and Kyler glanced fleetingly to each other.

"Semiconducted polyurethane, actually," Allison went on, pointing, completely in her element. "It's not quite the same as what Trust used to get into the Thomas Building, but this adapted adhesive is able to conduct electricity more effectively."

Trust arched an eyebrow.

"It is safe," Allison declared again, meeting his gaze. "Direct body temperature powers the skin, delivering electric currents throughout the material. There is a thin layer on the inside that touches your skin. The outermost layer contains the adhesive, as well as the thermo-receptors in the material, both of which work together to specifically target nearby heat sources. This is then signaled by electrical current to the stanax ridges along the spinal column and then back again, producing a heated sensation in the suit in the area nearest to the opposing heat source. The effect is similar to if you were standing close to a fireplace. If your back is to the fire, you feel it on your back; if you hold your arm out, you feel it on the arm."

By then, Trust and Kyler were examining the Viper Skin close up, feeling along the outer layer of skin, along the stanax plates.

"Didn't really understand any of that," Kyler declared, "but with this on, I'm assuming the person wearing it will be aware of other people nearby without have to see or hear them. It's like hearing them, without hearing them."

Allison nodded.

*What caused you to even want to create this?* Trust raised. *And why are you showing it to us instead of—I don't know—the CIA, maybe?*

"You can show it to the CIA if it works," Allison replied, "but right now, even with all the testing and research I've done, it's just a glorified wetsuit. You will be the first and one person so far to wear the full suit— that is, if you're not too scared—so you'll—"

Trust was waving his arms.

"Uh oh," Kyler said, grinning. "I think somebody may have just said the magic word."

*I need you to verify right now that your girlfriend* did not *just imply that I was too scared to wear a bodysuit,* Trust directed to Kyler.

"Yes, she did say something like that," Kyler replied after interpreting for Allison, "though it's funny how her name changed so quickly from Allison to 'your girlfriend.'"

*Tell your girlfriend I'm not scared to wear it. I just want to understand the possible—*

"Trust, I can absolutely, without a doubt, assure you it is no more dangerous than wearing a normal bodysuit. Unless you have an allergic reaction to the material, which now you've already touched anyway, my only concern is whether or not it actually activates when you put it on. I've put it through every possible safety analysis I could think of, both here at the university and at home. The only reason I thought of you to wear it first instead of me or Kyler or someone else was the fact that I thought you would be the one—out of everyone I know—most capable of utilizing the suit's benefits most quickly. You're deaf, so you won't be able to rely on your sense of hearing at all, but from what I've learned from being around you this year, you have such an amazing...but, honestly, if you're afraid something might—"

Trust huffed in obvious annoyance, his eyes going from a seemingly innocent Allison to Kyler, who looked to be having difficultly keeping a straight face.

*I know you have something to do with this.*

Kyler was twisting his face in an unusual manner, somewhere between a smile and an open-mouthed grimace.

Trust then turned to Allison. He signaled for the suit. She handed it over.

After shooting both of them another glare, he immediately departed, the door shutting behind him.

Allison turned to Kyler.

"I thought you said he would think it was funny to say he was scared? I think he was leaning toward trying it on without me saying any of the stuff you suggested."

Kyler looked surprised.

"Oh, me?" he asked, pointing to himself. "Oh, no. What I meant was that *I* would think it was funny if you said he was scared. *He* just gets more determined...and sometimes, irrationally angry."

Allison put her hands on her hips, frowning. Kyler looked immediately contrite.

"But you know that means he's angry at me, right?" he tried to explain. "He's angry at me, not at you. And when he's angry at me, he's really not that angry."

"Maybe he should be that angry," Allison muttered under her breath.

A FEW MINUTES LATER, TRUST burst back into Allison's dorm room. Allison jumped as she turned toward the door. Kyler startled so much he fell out of his seat.

Trust's eyes were wide, sparkling. He grinned.

*I think it's working,* he signed swiftly.

He stepped inside the room fully and closed the door. He was wearing the same clothes he had been wearing all day, though the sleeves and neck of the Viper Skin bodysuit could be seen peeking out from underneath his shirt.

"Really?" asked Allison, her own eyes widening in excitement as she brought her hands together. "It's really working?"

"Can you feel anything now?" Kyler asked.

*I can feel the heat here,* Trust signed before gesturing to the left half of his chest and then down his left leg. *It feels weird. It's like heat, but not quite the same. It's different somehow.*

Allison was practically bouncing.

"Okay, okay!" she said. "Close your eyes and stand in the middle of the room here. I'll move around. Kyler, you translate."

"But why don't I get to—"

Allison swiftly kissed him on the cheek. Kyler grinned.

Trust made a face.

*I hate watching the honeymoon phase,* he gestured.

"Okay, okay, close your eyes!" Allison said again.

Trust closed his eyes, putting his shades on as well.

Shutting his eyes, and then firmly covering them with his hand or another object, was the only guaranteed way to rid Trust of his vision completely. Dark rooms, seemingly pitch-black to everyone else, were virtually never *completely* pitch-black—there was always even the faintest, most minute trace of illumination coming from somewhere, usually a crack located in the wall, perhaps near the door, or perhaps in some far corner of the ceiling. Even just shutting his eyes but failing to cover them up, a soft glow penetrated his lids in normally lit rooms...and he could see through them.

But now, with his eyes closed and covered and his world already enduringly silenced, his other senses—chiefly, his senses of touch and smell—were even more necessary. The smell in the room was already identifiable—the pleasant, almost soothing fragrance of Allison. Trust assumed it was some type of perfume, but had never asked. In addition to that was another sweet, softer fragrance he could not immediately attach a face to...presumably Allison's roommate, Melody, whom he had never met. Also present was the all-too-familiar scent of *Kyler Eau de Parfum*, along with Trust's own smell. If he had walked into the room at random with his eyes covered, he would have recognized the smells, though he would not have been as able to distinguish where they were in the room.

However, with the Viper Skin, he could pinpoint them exactly.

Trust sensed Allison step around him, the odd sensation of heat following her movements along the suit...*She's moving beside me, around my left*...the heat dipping, vanishing from his back but remaining strong along the backs of his legs...*Behind me, still close. She's bending down*...up again, covering his back, but the intensity fading, the heated sensation diminishing...*She's still behind me, moving away*...the flow of heat moving like a liquid, adjusting fluidly...*Back left, back right, back left. She's jumping around*...fading again, more, but still present...*She's moved farther away, back right, where the closet is*...and now gaining strength...*Closer, she's coming closer, back right. Slowly closer. Closer*...

Then...

Trust's eyes shot open.

A touch of ice, which then almost instantly dissipated again.

Trust turned to look at her.

"Cold?" Allison inquired, to which Trust nodded.

She came back in front of him. Her heat signature on the Viper Skin blended with Kyler's.

"Yeah, I'm still not completely sure why it does that," she said, examining Trust as though using x-ray vision to see the bodysuit underneath. "The temperature readings show an instant drop to below forty degrees, and then an immediate rebound to normal levels. I think it may have something to do with the thermal elasticity seeking the underlying electrical current, but I don't see—"

*Should I be worried about any kind of radiation from this?* Trust signed.

Even as she listened to Kyler voice Trust's question aloud, she appeared to still be lost in thought, though she shook her head.

"No, the mild-endorphin coating would prevent any radioactive abnormality interference with the adhesive flakes..."

"I'm going to take that as a...probably not?" Kyler said. "I really don't speak rocket surgeon."

Trust quirked an eyebrow.

"Wait, what?" Allison asked, snapping out of her ponderings and shifting her gaze between Trust and Kyler.

*And she returns,* Trust observed.

"Oh. Oh! No, no. No radiation. It's the same as you would get sitting under a light bulb."

Trust and Kyler reflexively glanced up toward the overhead lights in the room.

"Which is to say, there's nothing to worry about," Allison clarified as Trust's eyes lowered again. "Would you be willing to wear the suit for a couple of days, Trust? I'm really interested to know how it performs over the course of an extended period, at least a full twenty-four hours. You don't have to, of course. It would just provide me with some useful information."

Trust raised his shirtsleeve to get a better look at the Viper Skin.

*All day? What about when I take a shower? What about when I go to sleep? What if I want to take a midnight stroll across campus butt-naked?*

"You can take it off when you shower. I would actually like you to sleep in it, but you can take it off if it's too uncomfortable. And streaking across campus? Kyler, you want to take that one?"

Kyler shrugged.

"Well, technically, it wouldn't be streaking if you had—"

He stopped abruptly, his expression changing as he looked from Trust to Allison.

"Wait."

He looked back to Trust.

"Wait, you told her...wait. Wait. You told her about the time I went streaking in high school?"

Trust quirked an eyebrow.

*No.*

Allison looked at Kyler, and then burst out laughing.

## 30.
## Jezzie Tells Trust

TRUST KEPT THE VIPER SKIN bodysuit on for the rest of the day after leaving Allison's dorm. After receiving their required books for their second semester courses, the trio lounged about campus with Paxson and Marcie, who returned to the university from nearby Potomac Park later that evening. Paxson and Marcie soon learned about the suit as well, with Trust becoming a voluntary parlor trick off and on for the rest of the night.

He slept in the Viper Skin as well. Normally, he slept in as little clothing as possible, but Trust was content with the change. Strangely enough, he found himself pleased at being woken up in the middle of the night while Kyler rummaged about for something to drink, the bodysuit effortlessly relaying his roommate's drowsy trek to the small refrigerator and back. Excluding something extraordinary happening, like Kyler falling down, Trust would have typically slept through such an episode.

Out amongst the multitudes before and during his first class was a distinctive experience, though again, not quite as unpleasant as he had theorized. Allison had mentioned the previous night that the heated sensation would diminish when there was a large amount of moving heat sources in the surrounding vicinity, such as in busy hallways or out on the grounds immediately before or following class periods.

For Trust, the front side of the skin did dull with increased stimulus. The back, however, remained active until he turned around, whereupon what was previously behind him, now in front and within his field of vision, would ebb on the suit, and what was now behind him, previously in front, would intensify.

Apparently, Allison had thought of everything.

Coming out of the lecture hall, Trust was once more focusing on the activity behind him communicated by the suit when he sighted Jezzie sitting at a small, high table with another girl whom he did not recognize. Jezzie appeared to spot him at the same time through the crowd of students, and Trust watched as she quickly excused herself from her friend, gathering her belongings and starting in his direction. Trust slowed in the middle of the busy corridor, allowing the girl to reach him.

Trust saw the other girl still sitting at the table studying him with a curious eye.

"I'm glad I caught you," Jezzie said, Trust's eyes returning to her. "I heard you were here. I wanted to talk to you, if you have time."

Still standing in the middle of the hallway with students streaming past them in different directions, Trust directed a pointed glance to the table Jezzie had just left, his question obvious. Jezzie glanced back as well before returning to Trust.

"Oh, that's just Alyssa," Jezzie explained. "But what I want to talk about, I really don't want her to hear."

Trust motioned for her to lead the way, and she did, both of them moving down the hall and arriving at a study room. Designed to look like a cross between a library and a living area, complete with multiple tables and a TV built into a cabinet with books lining the shelves, the room was empty—and when Trust shut the door behind them, quiet, noticeably quieter compared to the hallway just outside.

Trust, of course, didn't notice, though the activity along the Viper Skin faded considerably, apart from Jezzie's signature. The two of them sat down on the couch in front of the television cabinet, Trust looking at Jezzie as he retrieved his notebook. He had last seen her in terrible shape, being carried up the front steps of the Millennium Complex by Jeremy Higgins before Winter Break. Looking at her now, Trust was hard-pressed to find even one sign of her ordeal.

"First," she said, "thank you. For everything."

Trust looked at her.

Waiting.

Jezzie combed a hand through her dirty-blond hair. She looked tired. She sighed.

"I haven't told Jeremy yet," she said. "I actually only remember a few of the faces...I'm pretty sure something was put in my drink. I've never been...out of it like that before. I think...I think Jeremy knows more than I've told him. I keep saying I don't remember, that I was drunk or high or whatever, but I think he knows. I...I think he suspects."

*Do you remember what you had that night? How much?*

Jezzie ran both hands through her hair this time, but Trust still caught her shaking slightly.

"I so don't do that. Every time I go out, there are only three or four things I drink, and even then, it's never enough to get drunk. Just enough to feel...loose, I guess. Just enough to feel a buzz."

*So you think you were drugged by Ror*

Jezzie's hand stopped Trust's writing.

"No. I mean, I...I don't know. I'm really not sure what happened. Jeremy had decided to stay in, and I was planning to meet up with him after. I went to the party at some warehouse-type deal downtown. A bunch of people I knew were there—my friends; Jeremy's friends; Alyssa, that girl you saw out there; Ror—I don't know. Before I knew what was going on, I'm outside and—"

Her eyes then shifted swiftly, meeting Trust's.

"The woman with you. Do you think she would say—"

Trust shook his head.

*I told her how I knew you. She won't say anything. She's not a student at UCC anyway.*

Jezzie read the comment, and then nodded.

*We're dancing around the important question right now.*

She looked away.

Trust reached up and gently turned her face back toward him, her eyes meeting his once more. He then wrote.

*You don't have to tell me, although I think you should. You don't have to tell Jeremy, although I REALLY think you should. But I do think you have to tell someone. This can't just stay some secret you—we—keep. You CAN'T let these guys get away with what they did.*

But she was shaking her head even as he finished writing.
"Trust."
Her voice was even quieter than before.
"You wouldn't understand."
Trust clenched his jaw, the only outward manifestation of his sudden flare of anger. If Kyler had been in the room, he would have been able to point out the "you wouldn't understand" problem.

*Make me understand. Force me to understand.*

Jezzie exhaled softly, looking down.
"You're a lot like him, you know that?" she mumbled.
Trust missed it. He used his hand to angle her head toward him again. They looked at each other. The seconds stretched.
"How much have you heard about the Freesef Society since you've been a student here?"
Trust's eyebrow arched infinitesimally before his eyes narrowed. He tilted his head to the side.
"I'm sure you've heard some of the stories by now, like what Jeremy mentioned at the party at the beginning of the year."

*What does that have to do with you?*

Jezzie looked at him, obviously debating with herself.

*Are Rory and those other guys a part of it?*

She opened her mouth, and then closed it again.
"Your friend. The girl with the red hair—sorry, I don't remember her name. She was...assaulted last semester, right?"
Trust angled his head again, leaning slightly closer. His eyes appeared to swirl in color, becoming slightly, subtly darker.
"I don't...Trust, I don't know for sure who did it," Jezzie said. "I swear it. But I've heard them talking about it before—"

*WHO?*

Jezzie was shaking her head again.

"Trust," she started, "I don't—"

*The same group who did it to you?*

More head shaking.

"I don't—"

A frustrated growl emerged from Trust's throat. He stood abruptly, throwing the notebook toward the closed cabinet, causing Jezzie to flinch back into the couch.

Jezzie then watched as his face almost instantly calmed, and he sat back down again. The anger seemed to roll off him in waves, though he had obviously—on the outside, at least—regained control. Instead of retrieving his notebook, he took out his phone.

*There seems to be the possibility that whoever attacked Allison also attacked you, along with potentially any number of other girls. I recognized Rory and two of the other boys. They hang around Jeremy. Allison remembers the voice of one of her attackers. Tell me why I don't want to look for Rory right now.*

Jezzie clutched his wrist, her expression frantic.

"Please, Trust, you can't. You don't understand..."

His eyes flashed again.

"It's not that simple," Jezzie continued. "Please, you have to believe me. You have to trust me. This, right here, this is the reason I can tell you this and I can't tell Jeremy. This is the exact reason."

The faintest trace of uncertainty came across Trust's face.

"The way you got mad just now? You're just like Jeremy, Trust; you're *just like* him—except where you can stop yourself, he can't. He *won't*. And they will hurt him, Trust. They will take him away from here, and they will *hurt him*. They know who he is. They understand him. They want him. And they know me. This is not just a group of frat boys running around campus after dark. It's so much bigger than that, Trust. Much bigger than everyone talks about, much bigger than anyone else knows."

Trust sat back, studying her a moment.

*How did you know I would be here?*

Her mouth moved, but Trust could not immediately read her response. His brow furrowed.

Jezzie said the word again. Trust still didn't catch it. He handed her his phone.

*Tigresa*

Trust's eyebrows creased even more.

"It's the new university app," Jezzie explained. "It tracks where people are. Someone types that they saw Trust and Jezzie in the study lounge on the second floor of the Bocholis Building at 12:15, and anyone who types our names in will know where we were last seen."

*I've never heard of it.*

"It was actually created just before school began in the fall. Everyone's using it now. It's pretty neat."

*And pretty illegal, I would think.*

Trust then motioned for Jezzie to pull her phone out.

*I'm giving you my number. I still think you should talk to Jeremy about this, and the police, too, but I'm not going to force you. But if something happens, or you want to talk again, text me. And know that we're not nearly done with this conversation. I'm not going to ignore or forget what happened to you in that alley. Jeremy won't either, even if you never tell him.*

## 31.
## Kobe and Oliver


THE FOLLOWING DAY MARKED THE start of Trust's martial arts class, taking place in the Tiger Dome in downtown Centre City.

The complex was enormous and state of the art, a joint venture between the city and the renowned university residing within it. It took up nearly a full city block by itself, the building a captivating blend of brick, concrete, and glass. It was a work of art without even taking a glance inside.

For inside, there lay an entirely different world, all its own.

The Tiger Dome, the workspace of the University of Centre City's sports teams, and housing any number of recreational or entertainment events the city wished to have, along with the associated vending, utilities, and fun-filled attractions of any modern-day sports super-arena. A seating capacity of 33,811, one of the largest such arenas in the country.

Adjoined to the Tiger Dome was the Centre City Fitness Venue, a nationally recognized fitness complex housed on four separate floors. UCC sports teams, and then university-enrolled students and faculty, possessed primary domain of the equipment and areas of play throughout the arena and fitness complex, though the place was so large, so vast, so varied and all-encompassing, that there was hardly ever a need to resort to any tiered system among the visitors, UCC-affiliated or not.

The martial arts class was being held in one of the many studio classrooms along one long hall of the fitness center. Trust passed by a spinning and yoga class, both already in progress, along with an empty room, before reaching the designated space. Several students had arrived before him.

The instructor, who wished to be addressed simply as Kobe, struck Trust as the quiet type—studious and observant, not gregariously interactive, but always around. Always watching. What Trust could hear was not too dissimilar from the actual sound in the room as the class stretched.

There was only movement. Slow movement. At intervals, there was the sound of workout attire rustling and rubbing against the floor, or other clothing.

Controlled breathing, though a few of the more out-of-shape were a little louder, more irregular, more erratic. But, overall, quiet.

Trust quiet.

Kobe circled the room, almost gliding as he moved, assisting or suggesting at varying intervals. A subtle nudge. A slight pull. A soft, quiet adjustment. Trust's eyes, everyone's eyes, following, one series of stretches leading seamlessly into another, seemingly without any direction from Kobe at all. Time itself seemed to stretch with them, as though also under the instructor's spell.

He passed in front of Trust. Kobe was black, his skin the color of mocha, very close to Trust's own complexion. His hair was closely cut, impeccable. He had a mustache, trimmed to an exacting specification. His eyes were light brown, almost hazel.

Trust, bending down to the floor, saw Kobe stop. He twisted his head to look up.

Kobe bent down, easily mirroring Trust's stretch.

The two stared at each other.

Kobe bent farther, his body extending to a sharper angle.

Trust mirrored the movement.

Kobe progressed even farther, his face remaining expressionless as he studied the boy in front of him.

Trust followed.

Kobe sat down fully.

Trust did as well.

The two faced each other in a full side split, their legs completely straight at a 180-degree angle, neither seeming to feel any exertion...because there was none.

Kobe squinted and nodded. His smile was present but barely there. A ghost, a hint.

Class continued.

"YOU DON'T REMEMBER ME, DO you."

Trust could tell Kobe's voice was soft, deliberate, calm, just like the mannerisms he had shown throughout class, just like his demeanor. The instructor was relaxing, his back against the front mirrored wall, his arms crossed, Trust standing just in front of him. The rest of the class had departed, the first day's session over, the room otherwise empty and hushed again.

Trust could typically identify when someone was asking a question based on facial expression alone—a slight widening of the eyes, a faint raise of the brow. Though the instructor's words conveyed a question, the way he expressed it however, made it declarative.

Now, after the question-turned-statement, Trust studied the man, leaning his head slightly to the side, before shaking it.

"We've met before. A long time ago. You were four, maybe five."

Trust looked at him.

"I trained under your grandfather."

Trust's eyes widened a little.

"I saw your name, and I recognized you from the moment you walked through the door. Admittedly, the blue eyes were a good hint, also."

Trust opened his mouth, but didn't attempt to speak. His eyes narrowed, as though still trying to place the martial arts teacher.

"You're not staying in this class."

Trust's mouth closed.

"We'll schedule one-on-one sessions. Presuming you chose this to fulfill your physical education requirements, I will keep you on the roster. Grading and everything else will remain the same."

One side of Trust's mouth edged upward into a smirk as he nodded.

*Grandfather?*

Kobe grinned his slight grin as well.

"You choose the time. We'll use the same days as these classes to begin with, and we can adjust as necessary."

*How late can you do?*

**375**

The instructor's eyes fell to the material showing from under Trust's sleeves.

"What is that you're wearing?" he asked.

The layer of heat up and down the Viper Skin pulsed steadily, monitoring the instructor's presence.

THAT NIGHT, TRUST AND KYLER were on their way to Holden's dorm room in Weaver Hall. Trust had more questions, and Holden would most likely have the answers—or, at least, know someone who would.

"I don't know how I feel about you just handing over the Viper Skin suit to Allison like that earlier," Kyler remarked as the two traversed the main lobby, heading for the elevators that would take them up to the seventh floor.

Trust gave a faint salute to a passing student.

*What?* he then signed. *What are you talking about? She told me she just wanted me to try it out for a few days. It's been a few days. You were there when she said it.*

They stepped into the elevator and turned around, Kyler pressing the seven.

"But you didn't even wash it or anything," he muttered. "And you practically threw it at her..."

Trust gave his friend a quizzical look.

*Since when did a throw and a handoff become the same thing? You know, a handoff like you generally do when you give something to someone? And what do you mean, "wash it"? She specifically said she had a particular way she was using—*

Trust stopped his signs and pointed at Kyler, his mouth open in an—

"Ahh."

The elevator doors opened at the same moment. In the common area of the seventh floor, Amanda, one of their floor mates sitting in one of the overstuffed chairs, heard him.

Her mouth dropped open.

"Oh my God. Trust, you can talk?"

"Huh?" Trust replied, grinning and stepping out of the elevator.

"Hey, Phyllisha," Kyler said. "Holden's in his room, right?"

Amanda scoffed, watching the boys as they headed toward the first

376

hall.

"You always say that! You know that's not my name!"

"Of course. It's Amanda Peters. How could I forget?"

Amanda smiled.

"I'm coming to your baseball game tomorrow," she declared.

"Huh?" Trust asked again, just as they disappeared from her view.

Trust immediately turned back to Kyler.

*You're feeling protective of her. Overly protective. Kyler, you do this every time.*

"Overprotective?" Kyler sucked his teeth. "What are you talking about? I have no idea what you're talking about. And you know what? I actually don't even want to know what you're talking about."

Trust gave him a knowing look.

*Oh, now I* know *you know what I'm talking about.*

"Whatever," Kyler said. "Just, you know, a little consideration is all I ask."

Arriving at the resident assistant's doorway, his attention still turned to Trust, Kyler raised his hand, about to knock...

...not realizing until after the fact that the door was already wide open. He nearly fell as he stumbled through the entrance.

Trust casually entered the room behind him.

Holden was in the room, and he had a guest.

"Now that was entirely predictable," Holden declared from a chair as Kyler lurched to a stop.

Oliver, in another chair that had been brought in, his sock-clad feet propped on Holden's bed—the only bed in the room—was holding his stomach as he laughed.

"Ha ha! You should probably think about hanging up a sign telling everybody the door's open."

Oliver. Trust recognized the boy's face, and then remembered where from.

A friend of Rory's, he had come with the other boy to the North Gym when Trust and Jezzie had been talking, seemingly so many months ago now.

A lot had happened since.

"Ollie," Holden said, "these are some of the guys who stay in my—"

"Aah! Wait!"

Oliver planted his feet on the ground.

"I *so* know who these guys are."

He started to point to Kyler, his finger lowering slowly as he thought, his tongue peeking out as he concentrated.

"Man, I know your fa—Kyler Brooks! You're on the baseball team, right? I saw your picture in the official program. You're supposed to be some type of hotshot freshman, eh?"

"Key word being 'freshman,'" Kyler replied. "And it's Kyler-Scott Brooks, actually. Kyler-Scott is my entire first name."

"Oh, yeah. With the hyphen. I remember that."

Oliver's eyes shifted to Trust.

"And I so know you—those blue eyes are killer, man. Wait, hold on, nobody say anything, nobody help me. I'm going to get it. Deaf, I know you're deaf...I recognize you from the...Trrrr...holy crap, I've got a name in my head right now, but if I'm wrong, I'm going to look like the biggest idiot..."

Trust glanced to Holden with an arched eyebrow. The RA shrugged.

"It's...Trust, right? Please tell me it's Trust."

"Argh, you were so close," Kyler said. "And Timothy gets so insulted when people don't know his name."

"I'm guessing you've met Trust before?" Holden asked, looking to Oliver.

Trust started to move his hands before Oliver could respond verbally, drawing everyone's attention.

"Yeah, I remember you," Kyler relayed, interpreting Trust's signs aloud. "You're friends with Rory. How's he doing? I heard he was in some kind of...altercation before Winter Break."

As he spoke, Kyler issued Trust a faintly questioning look.

"Oh, man, you heard about that?" Oliver said. "Dude, you have no idea. I don't even know what happened. He and a few of the other guys must have gotten jumped or something when they left the party—you should have seen them afterward. They had to go to the medic's. And get this: they won't even talk about it with anybody. But, I mean, they got jumped. That's nothing to be embarrassed about."

"He was probably asking for it," Holden said, motioning for Trust and Kyler to sit. "I don't like that guy. I've told you that, Ollie. He always acts so...entitled."

*That's an opinion I've heard more than once about him,* Trust observed.

"He's all right usually," said Oliver. "You just have to know him."

"I don't think I've ever met him," Kyler commented, settling into a nest chair. "But what could he have possibly done to get jumped? And with all his friends with him?"

His eyes flitted toward Trust.

"I mean, was it just random?"

Trust met his eyes for a moment before looking away.

"Seriously, dude, I don't even know," Oliver said, not noticing Kyler's wayward glance. "We were at a warehouse party downtown—you guys ever been to one of those? They're crazy!—and the drink is flowing, like usual, you know. One minute, Rory's there, and the next, he's split out. I didn't even see him until the next day, and that's when I saw how messed up they all were. Man...but I bet they got a couple of licks in, too. I mean, it was, like, five of them."

Both Trust and Holden scoffed, but for different reasons. Oliver snickered and shook his head.

"You guys really don't like him, huh? I'll have to remember not to bring up his name in conversation."

"What were you two talking about before we came in?" Kyler asked.

The junior RA grinned.

"You're the one who came in here," he said. "I should ask you what *you* wanted to talk about."

Kyler leaned forward in the nest chair, a somewhat awkward feat.

"Have you guys heard of this Tigresa app? What the heck is—"

"Gah," Trust gagged, before signaling, *He hasn't shut up about this since I mentioned it to him yesterday.*

Kyler translated.

"Yeah, I've seen it," Holden said. "I don't use it, but I've seen it. Apparently, it started getting super popular late last semester."

"Tigresa?" Oliver repeated. "What's that, some kind of girl superhero?"

"It's an app," Holden said. "Only UCC students can download it. You type in a student's name—Oliver Handley, for instance—and it'll tell you pretty much every footstep you've taken since the beginning of school. You can find out where someone lives, where and what time their classes are, when they go to Hollins or the library—and probably what they ate in Hollins and what book they checked out of the library. When someone sees you doing something or going somewhere, they can just upload the info onto the app, or you can upload yourself if you want. It's like Facebook or Twitter or anything else, times fifty. I guess since it's gotten so popular, the administration had to send an email to the RAs, and they'll probably be sending one to the rest of the students as well, just to inform everyone what it is and what type of information it carries. The rumor was that it was university-sanctioned, but this email says differently. I think they're going to try to shut it down."

*Basically, if someone's stalking you,* Trust motioned, *this program makes their work a million times easier.*

"And everybody's on here?" Oliver asked, pulling out his phone. "What's it called again? Tiger Shot?"

"Tigresa," Holden supplied, "and I can already tell you're going to get hooked. I don't know if everyone's on there, but that's probably not too far off by now. The popularity breeds its effectiveness. With so many students using it, more information gets uploaded, which causes more people to get curious and want to use it, which leads to more info being shared. From what I've heard, there weren't that many people on it at the beginning of the school year, but then it started to grow, and then it just exploded. The police are on it—they think it's a potential hazard. It's possible the Dorm Room Robbers have been using it to monitor people's comings and goings from their rooms."

*I think you're onto something there,* Trust signed.

"I know it's kind of creepy," Kyler intoned, fiddling with his phone as well, "but at the same time, it's oddly...addictive. You do everything you do in a day, and then you can actually see on here everything you've done without ever having put anything in yours—hey, I'm on here!"

*You were on there yesterday when I looked at it,* Trust directed to him. *You're high profile enough that I wouldn't be surprised if you've been on it the entire time. And dude, you've got some* serious *stalkers. This is your first time looking yourself up? Who were you looking at yesterday?*

"Everyone else! You, Pax, Marcie, Allison, Holden—dude! It says I'm in Holden's dorm room. Now that is crazy!"

"I'm on it, too," Oliver said. "It just says I'm in Weaver Hall."

*Don't look mine up,* Trust signed. *I don't even want to—*

"I'll look you up," Oliver said.

Trust rolled his eyes.

"Anything new with Allison?" Holden asked.

"It's a stalemate," Kyler replied. "I don't think they have anything."

*That's actually kind of what I came in here for,* Trust motioned. *You mentioned it before, but I've heard some stuff that made me think of it again. Out of all these alleged Freesef assaults that you've heard of, do you not remember even one time when the girl went to the police?*

He kept a fleeting eye on Oliver, as though waiting for a reaction as Kyler interpreted his words. There wasn't any. It was as if the boy wasn't even paying attention, enthralled in his phone.

"Ooh," Holden said, grinning and sitting back in his chair. "You couldn't have picked a better person to ask that question around."

Trust and Kyler watched the RA nod toward Oliver.

"Ollie here is even worse than me. He practically minors in Freesef Society Studies."

They all looked to Oliver.

"Yo, Handley!" Holden called.

"Man, it's like someone follows you everywhere, Trust. Did you know you were at the Centre Diamond nightclub the same night we were at that warehouse party—wait. Did somebody say something?"

Holden shook his head, smiling.

"You've got two inquiring minds about Freesef in the room, and you're looking up what Trust had for breakfast last week."

"Which day?" Kyler said, chuckling. "Ask me. I can tell you that one."

"Ooh, the Freesef Society," Oliver crooned. He glanced to Holden. "I told you about that new one I heard about the girl in Revere, didn't I?"

*You mean another assault?* Trust signed. *In Revere Hall?*

"I doubt it was actually *in* Revere," Oliver responded. "Just that the girl supposedly lives there. It happened a few days ago, so that information could be wrong; it usually takes a week or two for the story to sift itself out."

*You seem awfully unconcerned about it. I take it you're one who doesn't actually believe these stories.*

"Believe?" Oliver shrugged. "This stuff isn't exactly coming from Walter Cronkite, if you understand what I'm saying, but..."

The others leaned forward.

"But..." Kyler prompted.

"But, sometimes at least, I think the stories may not be too farfetched."

*So, some of them you do believe?* Trust posed.

"I mean, the girls seem like they're telling the truth."

"You've actually talked to some of these girls?" Kyler asked, his eyes widening in surprise.

"Sure. I've run into a couple of them."

"Run into them?" Holden said. "More like tracked them down like Sherlock Holmes. Like a bloodhound. Like a tracking beacon. Like a guided miss—"

"What?" Oliver cut in. "They're interesting stories, and I get bored. I'm just like you guys."

Oliver pointed to Trust and Kyler.

"You hear these kinds of stories—a secret group that goes around, targeting freshman girls—so, of course, you want to know more. You want to know if it's true. First off, it just sounds so bizarre—a secret society on campus whose only purpose seems to be finding 'obedient' freshmen, let's say, and performing what is basically a gang rape, only to learn that the girls—that's multiple girls on multiple occasions across multiple years—not only refuse to report it, but brag about it to their friends afterward. It's like those videos where you see someone's leg bone shooting out of their skin when they break it. It's disgusting, it's gruesome, but you can't turn away from it, either."

"Tell them what the girls say when you ask why they don't want to go to the police," Holden instructed.

"One told me it was none of the police's business, which...okay, I guess. You're the, quote unquote, 'victim' in the center of it all, I guess, in some kinda way, it's your choice, right? The other girls...it's kind of like I said before. It's something I still don't really understand, but apparently, being chosen by the Freesef Society in that way is like, I don't know, some kind of tribute or something. Like only a special type of girl attracts their attention, and if you're going to be one who actually complains about it and goes to the police, you're really not that special type of girl after all. It's twisted, but...I don't know, you know?"

"Hey, Ollie," Holden said, "what are the chances that there's money involved? Like the Freesef Society is paying these girls to keep quiet?"

He subtly waved off Trust and Kyler when they looked at him in question, since he was one of the few who would know of the attempts at bribing Allison.

Oliver frowned as he considered it. Then his eyebrow arched.

"That's actually not a terrible theory," he declared. "The bragging rights thing never really made much sense to me, and the girls I talked to never really went into it. I mean, is there some segment of the UCC population that I'm unaware of that would value the fact that you were attacked by this group of guys, but at the same time you don't want people to know your name? But if it's money or some type of gift that you're showing off, maybe you tell your friends just enough. Yeah, that makes some sense, actually. At least, it's better than anything else I've heard."

"And the money would keep the girl from going to the police or anyone else," Holden added.

*Not to mention the fact that they probably have help keeping it quiet,* Trust observed, thinking about his discussion with Jezzie from the day before.

He told the others about the instances in which he brought up the Freesef Society with Chancellor Beverly and Dr. Duncan and their lack of knowledge on the subject, along with Dr. Duncan's news on the Freesef Society's humble beginnings.

"And I'll do you one better than that," Oliver said. "Since the Freesef Society supposedly targets these girls beforehand, what would you think if I told you they didn't always pick the right one?"

Trust froze.

His gaze switched to Kyler. The blond was wide-eyed and staring back at him.

"What, as in made a mistake?" Holden questioned. "Like they mistook one girl for another?"

"Or they misjudged one girl and thought she would be more agreeable when she absolutely wasn't," Oliver replied.

"*Where* did you hear *that*?"

"Just little bits and pieces here and there," Oliver explained, "and it's not that much. Rumors again. But I'll tell you this—for some reason, I don't know, I believe it. I think it's true."

"What?" Kyler asked quickly, leaning in. "What? When?"

Oliver looked at him.

"Are you okay? This supposedly happened a few years ago."

Kyler closed his eyes, finally releasing a breath, before putting his head in his hands, combing his fingers through his hair.

"Uhm..."

Oliver looked to Trust inquiringly. Trust mimed a sleeping gesture, and then mimicked swinging a baseball bat.

"Oh, that's right," Oliver said, looking back to Kyler. "You do have a game tomorrow. You've gotta rest up. I can save the story for another time—"

"What?" Kyler exclaimed, quickly lifting his head. "What does that have to do with—oh, don't pay any attention to that one over there. It's not even late. Anyway, I can run perfectly fine on three hours of sleep most nights."

*And others, you need thirteen hours,* Trust rebutted.

"So," Oliver said, "should I keep going, or..."

"Yeah, go," Holden replied. "I've never heard this before."

"Well, it's like I said. This is years old now—before me and you got here, Holden, at least by a few years. I really don't know a lot of the specifics—I doubt anyone who's a student here now has even heard of this, if it's even true in the first place.

"The story goes that Freesef went after some girl—a freshman, obviously—who they thought would go along with the usual plan. If they're paying them, maybe they thought she would be one of the girls who would accept the payment and keep quiet. Apparently, the girl was exceptionally beautiful, just stunning. A real score for them. But this girl—and I don't know how they find these girls—but this girl was definitely *not* the submissive, obedient, cooperative type they thought she'd be. Apparently, she fought back, hard, but there were so many, she really didn't have much chance. But then, some passerby, maybe another student, seemingly out of nowhere, jumps right into the middle of it and completely wipes the whole gang out—I mean, *annihilates* them. I've never heard of him having any type of weapon, but I'm sure he had something. Heck, he may have even killed a couple of them for all I know."

Holden scoffed.

"Killed? And this is where the story goes off the rails."

"Yeah?" Kyler said. "And what happened after that?"

"What happened after that? End of story happened after that. That's all I've pieced together, and even then, I may have embellished the story a tiny bit to tell it to you guys—"

Holden scoffed again.

"Oh, no," Oliver said. "There is one more thing. A name, or maybe a nickname, or some type of symbol or something. I doubt anyone would have this as an actual name."

*A name?* Trust gestured. *What is it?*

"For some reason, I want to say it may have been a friend to the person who jumped into the fight," Oliver said.

"What's the name?" Holden asked.

The boy mumbled something, covering his mouth in the process.

The room seemed to still for a moment.

Then Holden burst into laughter.

*Wait. Wait,* Trust declared. *I missed it. I couldn't see.*

"And you pick this as one of the stories you believe?" Holden remarked, continuing to laugh. "I mean, the story's pretty far out in the first place, but then you drop *that* jewel in the middle of it—"

*What?* Trust signed urgently, looking at Kyler, and then to—

"It's Dolphin, okay?" Oliver exclaimed. "Dolphin. Dolphin. Look, I know—"

Trust started to laugh, but then his brow furrowed almost instantly. He looked to Kyler again.

Dolphin.

Dolphin.

Dolph—

Trust's eyes widened, his mouth parting slightly.

Kyler nodded.

Holden caught the motion.

"What?" he inquired, his amusement finally beginning to dampen. He glanced between the two freshmen. "What was that? What was that little thing there?"

Oliver looked to the two boys as well.

"It's a stretch," Kyler said, still holding Trust's gaze, "but with a name like that, we may just know who Dolphin is."

"Oh, you're kidding me," Holden said. "Who?"

Trust stood to shut the door.

"Oh, crap," Oliver said. "We're about to get whacked."

"This conversation can't leave this room," Kyler warned. "At least until we talk to some people. Holden, you're going to know who I'm talking about."

The junior RA raised an eyebrow.

Trust's phone pulsed. He held up a finger to Kyler while he reached into his pocket. As he was pulling it out, he noticed Holden reaching for his phone as well.

Trust tapped his screen.

It was a text.

From Allison.

> **Allison (9:01 PM):** Melody, my roommate, is at Arlington Memorial. I'm with her. I'm fine. Melody was beaten up pretty badly, don't know much else yet. To you and Kyler, DO NOT COME TO HOSPITAL. Again, I'm fine; wasn't with her when it happened. DO NOT COME. Kyler has first game tomorrow. I'll text again with updates.

Trust looked up quickly.

"Wow," he saw Holden saying. "Someone was—"

Trust cleared his throat loudly, drawing everyone's attention. He stood and approached the older boy. He pointed to his phone, and then did a speaking motion and pointed to Kyler. Holden read the message swiftly. Trust glanced toward his roommate.

"Hey, what's up?" Kyler said. "What's going on? Is that a—"

"It's a text from Allison," Holden said. He read it aloud, and then remarked, "And I just got a message from Sarah, Allison's RA, about this same—"

"Wait. What?" Kyler said. He was already standing and moving toward the—

"Trust, we've got to—"

Trust stepped in his path, blocking his exit. This was about to get out of control. Fast.

He took the phone and handed it to Kyler.

"No," Kyler said, shaking his head as he finished reading, attempting to move past Trust again. "She said almost the same thing when she called last time—"

Trust shifted, catching Kyler's eyes. He raised his eyebrows.

*Almost means there's a difference, Kyler. She's fine. Breathe. Relax, man.*

Kyler was breathing, but he was not relaxed. Trust was losing him.

"No, dude. Just get out of—"

He tried to rush quickly to the side, but Trust blocked him.

"Whoa. Okay, Kyler," Holden voiced, his arms out, seemingly ready to corral the boy. "Just chill—"

*Interpret for me. Ask Holden to ask Allison for a picture.*

"Ask Allison for a picture?" Kyler repeated without thinking, his expression contorted. "No! Trust, seriously, get out of the—"

Trust tossed his phone to Holden just as Kyler charged at him again.

"Trust!" Oliver shouted. "Watch out—"

Trust opened the door as Kyler rushed toward him, Kyler not expecting it and nearly sliding across the floor into the closed door on the other side of the dormitory hallway...

...but Trust was on him almost instantly, grabbing him before Kyler could fully regain his balance and pinning his back against the door, his forearm placed just under Kyler's throat.

"Kyler," Trust warned softly with just the slightest hint of exertion as he held on to the boy. "Kyler..."

Kyler was still struggling against him, trying to break free. Trust tightened his hold ever so slightly.

"Kyler..."

The two of them suddenly fell, the door opening behind Kyler, he and Trust tumbling to the carpeted floor of the room across the hall from Holden's.

"Holy sh—" the boy who had opened the door uttered, nearly falling himself in the tumble.

As Trust and Kyler hit the ground, Trust lost his hold, and Kyler took the opportunity to quickly roll away and scramble to his feet. Trust's original intention was to get Kyler out of Holden's room and into the open space of the hall—he knew exactly how Kyler was going to react to the news from Allison—and yet here they had fallen right into another room—

Trust remained still on the ground. Kyler hesitated.

"Trust? Are you—"

Trust swiftly secured his feet around Kyler's ankle and pulled.

Kyler, reacting instinctively to avoid snapping his ankle, immediately started to crumble to the ground.

"Umph!"

Trust was coming up as Kyler fell down, grabbing his dominant arm. He then—in the cramped space of the dorm room entryway—spun over Kyler's bowed back at the same moment that Kyler caught himself. The move was enough to yank Kyler back into the hall.

Trust had Kyler's arm in a threatening hold, and Kyler knew it. He immediately went to the ground again, Trust going with him.

"Okayokayokayokayokay!" cried Kyler, panicking and snapping out of his hysterical state.

But Trust wasn't looking in his direction, instead observing Holden rush out of the room. Holden's eyes widened as he noticed both boys wrestling on the ground.

"Trust, I've got it! She sent the picture!"

Trust indicated to Kyler, his other arm and the rest of his body in such a configuration as to put a particular amount of pressure on a particular area in Kyler's—

"Okay, okay!" Holden said, tapping Trust on the shoulder. "He's good! He's good!"

Trust immediately let go and corkscrewed himself to his feet, the clutch that he had on Kyler seamlessly transforming into a hand helping the other boy up, an "Oh God!" spewing from Kyler's lips at the sudden, forceful pull to an upright position. The tug caused the two boys to bump into each other.

Trust looked Kyler in the eye and then released him, taking his phone back from Kyler's other hand.

A picture of Allison, smiling faintly, filled the screen. Trust recognized the traditional, sterile surroundings of the hospital in the background.

He bowed, waving Kyler back into Holden's room. It was a graceful yet comical gesture given the circumstances, acting as though nothing had happened. As Kyler entered again, Trust turned to the room across the hall. The boy who had opened the door was staring back at him, still with a bewildered expression on his face. Ronnie was his name.

Trust bowed again, his hands clasped together in apology. He backed into Holden's room, delivering one more small bow in the process, before slowly shutting the door once again.

He then turned into the room. Everyone was standing, until Kyler settled back down into the hammock chair with a large exhalation of air.

"Sorry, guys," he started. "Kinda lost my head there for a—"

"What in the name of Hell's Highway was that?" Oliver all but shouted.

"Look, I'm definitely not proud—"

"You!" Oliver said, pointing to Trust. "You looked like you were about to break his arm!"

Trust performed a visceral snapping motion in the air as he saw Kyler reaching into his pocket for his phone. He knew it would be Allison.

"But...but he's your friend!" Oliver continued. "You were going to break his arm? Seriously? And he has a baseball game tomorrow! First of the season!"

Trust shrugged nonchalantly and performed the snapping motion again. Kyler was talking, the phone to his ear.

Oliver looked to Holden in disbelief. Holden was shaking his head in resignation.

"Dude," he said simply.

Trust gestured for something to write with, and Holden quickly collected a pen and a loose sheet of paper. Trust went to Holden's desk.

*Of course, that won't happen again.*

And then,

*Probably.*

And then,

*But you see what started it, right?*

"Allison in the hospital," Holden said after reading aloud for Oliver what Trust had been writing.

"Who's Allison?" Oliver asked.

"Girlfriend," Holden answered.

"Whoa!" Oliver said. "That was major! And just for a girl? First girlfriend?"

Holden looked to Trust. Trust shook his head.

"First *real* girlfriend," Holden observed.

"Uh, just because I'm on the phone, don't think I can't hear every word you guys say," Kyler remarked.

*Melody?* Trust signed to him.

"Melody's stable," Kyler replied, "but she's going to have to stay in the hospital for a few days."

"Who's Melody?" Oliver asked.

"Allison's roommate," Holden answered.

"Freshman?" Oliver asked.

Holden nodded.

Oliver's mouth did not move, so Trust missed the quiet "hmm" that emerged from the boy's throat.

Holden turned back to Trust.

"So, who's Dolphin? You said you think you know who it is."

Trust returned to the paper.

*We're going to have to talk to Paxson first. He knows. But tell Oliver not to say anything else about that story with the girl fighting back until Pax can confirm.*

"You know this Paxson guy pretty well?" Oliver asked after Holden read from the sheet. "You actually think he would know? I'm assuming he's a freshman, too, right?"

*He knows someone who goes by Dolphin, but we'll have to see if it's the SAME Dolphin. He's gone on some astronomy lab thing tonight, though; I'll catch him later, or sometime tomorrow...*

"...but here's another Freesef question in the meantime," Holden continued to read. "Have you ever heard any names of any possible members? Any idea what any of them look like?"

Oliver chuckled.

"That's a good one," he observed.

*Shot in the dark.*

Oliver continued, "They wear those balaclava things. You can't make out anyone in those."

## 32.
## Kyler at Work

"Strike!"

The weather in Centre City was cold, but not unbearably so on this day—it wasn't cold enough to postpone the first baseball game of the season, and it certainly wasn't cold enough to dissuade ardent fans and intrigued spectators from packing into Wood Field.

But there was snow in the forecast for later in the day.

Wood Field, home of the University of Centre City's baseball and softball teams, was located on a far end of the rural campus, bordering a wide swath of woodland and facing the university buildings, which rose in the near distance. At about eight thousand, attendance capacity was reasonably modest, especially compared to The Stadium at UCC and the Tiger Dome downtown, though there had been recent talks of an expansion. If current crowd attendance was any indication, those talks would need to be accelerated. The number present was beyond standing room only—even those areas amidst the presently dormant grass beyond the confines of the playing field were full of the watching audience.

And one reason for the large attendance—contrary to what he himself believed—was currently at the plate. From his seat, Trust closely observed as Kyler-Scott Brooks gathered himself again, his bat once more taking position over his shoulder, beginning its familiar bob back and forth as he waited for the next pitch. He was down in the count—zero balls, one strike.

The pitch came.

Kyler started—and then held back.

"Ball!" the umpire announced.

There was a loud applause. From the sound alone, it was as though

Kyler had gotten a hit. Obviously, his reputation preceded him.

Trust wrote in the notebook on his lap, and showed it to Paxson beside him.

*He's nervous. And probably still thinking about Allison, too.*

"Well, it is his first at-bat in college," Paxson returned loudly over the noise of the surrounding crowd as they settled down again. "First at-bat, bottom of the first inning, and he's in the three-hole—as a freshman. I feel nervous, too, and I'm not even playing."

"How do you know he's nervous?" Marcie asked as she leaned over Paxson to read the notebook as well. "It's not like he's doing bad. It's his first at-bat."

"Strike two!"

Trust spotted the ump's hand motion on the video display beside the scoreboard. He looked toward home plate, though the scoreboard showed the action just as clearly.

A groan arose from the crowd.

*If he were focused, he would be on base already—even against this pitcher, who's supposed to be pretty good.*

"Well, Allison definitely said she was coming here straight from the hospital," Marcie remarked. "I'm sure she's on her way."

*Should look on Tigresa. I'm sure someone's posted her whereabouts.*

Kyler checked his swing again. The umpire called a ball. The count was two balls, two strikes.

Marcie shot Trust a look at the Tigresa comment.

*What, no good? I've been waiting to use that.*

Kyler was gazing out into the outfield as he readjusted his batting gloves. His gold and black long-sleeved jersey and pants were still spotless; his appearance would most likely be far different by the end of the game.

"You can't hit 'em all," Paxson said wisely.

*You know who says that? People who can't actually hit 'em all.*

Paxson snorted as he laughed.

On the field, Kyler started to swing, but then caught himself yet again. The baseball sped by.

Frowning, Trust was already shaking his head as Kyler glanced back to the lead ump, waiting for the—

"Strike three! Out!"

Disappointed groans rained down from the seats overlooking the field of play. Kyler, however, looked like he was trying to hold back a smile. His glance flitted into the seats, to where Trust and the others were sitting. Trust met his gaze, and then watched as the boy began to walk back to the dugout, the inning over. The score was still 0-0.

*Yep, he's off. He hardly ever looks up to the seats while*

Out of the corner of his eye, he noticed someone beginning to make their way down the row. Trust turned his head completely to look, and Paxson turned as well, following his gaze.

Allison was moving toward them, bundled against the cold, complete with a scarf and a knit cap. Even though, to her, it was normal clothing, it did not—could not—conceal her beauty.

Trust grinned despite himself, standing and making room to allow her to pass in front of him, on the way to the empty seat on Trust's opposite side.

"Hey," Allison greeted. "I'm not too late, am I? Are we winning?"

She then looked toward the scoreboard.

"Oh, good. It's still 0-0. It hasn't even started yet."

Trust arched an eyebrow before turning to his notebook. An instant later he displayed to Paxson what he had written.

*The savior arrives. Let's see how Kyler plays now.*

He rose from his seat again, departing down the aisle that Allison had just entered from and making his way down, closer to the railing separating the spectators from the field.

The two teams were still preparing for the start of the second inning. With the anticipatory buzz of the opening day of the baseball season still hanging in the cool air, Trust arrived at the dividing railing just as Kyler was emerging from the UCC dugout with a few of his teammates, his baseball glove—the same one he constantly fiddled with in the dorm room—in his possession.

"Kyler!"

Judging by the general animation of the surrounding crowd, Trust assumed he wasn't the only one calling for a player's attention. Nevertheless, as had been true since tee-ball—and really, in whatever setting they were in—Kyler was able to pick out Trust's voice through the noise. He turned, locating Trust along the rail almost instantly.

Trust didn't move, only gazing out at him, his hands in his pockets.

*What?* Kyler signed. *I'm fine. I've struck out before. Let's not turn this into a thing.*

The spectators watching the interaction probably assumed Kyler was sending out baseball signals.

*So, you're admitting you struck out on purpose,* Trust sent back.

*That's not even close to what I just said,* Kyler motioned, beginning to back away moving farther out into the field.

Trust pointed back up into the seats, to where their friends were. To Paxson and Marcie.

And now, Allison.

She was smiling brightly, her scarf flopping smoothly with her motions as she waved when Kyler spotted her.

Kyler's eyes returned to Trust. He grinned slightly as well.

*Guess you can stop playing around now?* Trust gestured.

Kyler tipped his ball cap in playful fashion.


BOTTOM OF THE THIRD INNING. Centre City was ahead 1-0 off a solo home run from Trent Atkins, senior first baseman and Kyler's usual batting practice partner. It had been a towering hit, sending the ball over four hundred feet and deep into those taking residence in the open fields beyond the outfield wall and seats.

The gang had switched their seating arrangements—now Paxson, beside Trust, beside Allison, beside Marcie—to spare Marcie from having to listen to Paxson's baseball talk for a full nine innings, and to spare Paxson from being strangled by Marcie in the process. But with Kyler not scheduled to bat yet, discussion had veered away from the game anyway.

"So, she's going to be okay then?" Paxson inquired, referring to Allison's roommate.

Allison nodded.

"They're going to keep her in the hospital for another day or two," she explained. "Her parents got here really early this morning, and—"

She paused briefly as a UCC batter at the plate fouled another ball off into the left-field seats.

"—and I don't think they've decided for sure yet," she then went on, "but I think they're thinking about pulling her out of school and deferring the rest of this year, if not transferring altogether, neither of which Melody wants to do. I don't think she should either, nor should she be forced to, but if this is related to what happened to me...well, it is. That's a fact. But she shouldn't have to leave school because of my problem."

"Don't say that, Al," Marcie said, looking at the girl sternly. "I'm serious. You're right. She shouldn't be pressured to go home or to another school because of some group of sick thugs, but, at the same time, this definitely isn't your 'problem.'"

*You know you're not to blame for what happened to her, right?*

Trust showed her the message in his notebook. Allison grimaced visibly, hesitating.

*NOT YOUR FAULT*

"He's right, Allison," Paxson said over the din as the Tigers batter sent a high fly ball into shallow left field, where it fell snugly into the glove of the opposing team's fielder.

"Logically, of course, you're right," Allison declared. But she was shaking her head. "But we all know that if I had done things differently— if I had accepted the first gift, or even the second, or if I stopped talking to the police, then Melody wouldn't be where she is right now. Bruised ribs, a broken wrist, a concussion, a hairline fracture on her skull...if I had just—"

Trust reached up and covered her mouth with a finger. He shook his head as he gave her a grave look. He went back to his notebook.

*If you had done things differently, this situation would have*
*only turned out worse for someone else—probably you.*
*Believe it or not, you're winning; you're beating them right*
*now by not following their instructions, so they're lashing out*
*in desperation, trying to hurt you, trying to get your*
*attention. But this is probably something they never planned*
*on doing. This is a mistake on their part, and with the police*
*involved and able to connect both crimes so quickly, time is*
*running out until people are caught. This whole Freesef*
*Society thing would still just be some vague rumor if you had*
*stayed quiet.*

"Listen to him," Paxson advised, pointing to Trust's notebook. "He knocked a guy on his face with one punch and got in and out of the Thomas Building undetected."

Trust looked at the boy, and then,

*Please tell me he didn't just say all of that out loud when*
*people could hear.*

The batter currently at the plate, the ninth batter in the Tigers lineup, was down in the count, one ball and two strikes, in danger of striking out. It was shaping up to be the opposing school's pitcher's fourth strikeout of the game thus far, suggesting that he wasn't just some run-of-the-mill baseball player, but quite talented.

"My parents and Melody's have talked to each other on the phone, probably more than the one time I'm aware of," Allison told the group. "I know they're trying to persuade them to allow Melody to stay also, but it's of course their decision as to whether they think she will be safe"—the stadium groaned as the batter swung and missed, striking out—"and she may not be safe hanging around me."

"Nonsense," Marcie declared.

"Nonsense? She was assaulted, maybe by the same exact boys who came after me, wearing those same stupid masks. And it was all directed toward me as a warning. Argh! I'm so mad about all of this I could spit."

Trust vaguely pointed in Marcie's direction, though he wasn't slick enough, as the girl spotted the gesture.

"If she spits on me," Marcie warned, "I'm spitting right in your face, Trustice Jeffries."

*If you spit on me, I'll spit on Pax.*

"And if you spit on me," Paxson threatened, "I'm gonna spit right on this guy with the beer gut hanging out from under his jacket...Actually, he looks like he would just try to eat it. I'll have to choose someone else."

Trust turned back to Allison.

*Have you heard anything new from Chancellor Beverly?*

Allison shook her head.

"She called me that first time, but these last few calls have been from some other guy. Some aide, I think. I know my parents have talked to her, though. My dad likes her, but he said she doesn't seem to know a lot about what's going on. I don't know if that's intentional on her part or not."

*I think she's being deliberately shut out. What about from the police? Officer Ryan?*

"I like him. He calls regularly to give updates on what he knows of the investigation, though it's usually just to say that everyone is working hard to find out who did it. I just wish I had been able to give him and the detectives more to go on.

"He was there in Melody's hospital room earlier today with another officer. Officer Longley, I think? I told Officer Ryan what you had learned from Oliver about the Freesef Society and the balaclavas. Of course, it's only circumstantial evidence coming from him, but it is another piece of information to work off of."

Trust spotted the agitated body language from nearby fans as the third and final batter of the inning struck out, retiring the side. The fifth strikeout for the opposing team's pitcher, and the game was not even midway completed. UCC's 1-0 lead this early in the contest seemed a matter of luck more than anything else.

> *Slight change of subject. What about the Viper Skin? Did I*
> *give you the information you needed?*

"Oh!"

Allison grabbed his wrist in excitement.

"I wanted to ask you a question about that. I was going to bring it up later, but I can do it now, too, though I'll have to talk quieter. How do you think you would have been if you had worn the Viper Skin when you went into the Thomas Building that night? Do you think it would have helped?"

Trust arched an eyebrow.

> *Not sure it would have made much difference. Only saw that*
> *one boy, and I was facing him. He probably could have used it*
> *more than me that time.*

"Yeah," Allison said, "but I mean...say you were ever in any sort of situation, and...I guess what I'm asking is, if you or someone else were to get in some sort of situation like that again, do you think..."

Trust looked at her.

"Actually, I don't even know what I'm trying to say. I'll get back to you on that."

> *But it was okay the way I gave it back to you and everything,*
> *right? I didn't throw it at you? And you said not to wash it.*

Allison looked at him strangely and shrugged.

"Yeah, it was fine. When did you throw it? And it's waterproof, but I'm using a special cleaning solution I created. Why do you ask?"

> *Just curious.*

TOP OF THE SIXTH INNING. The Tigers were now behind 2-1. The temperature outside was in the mid- to upper-thirties, but apparently it was just cool enough for a few fluffy snowflakes to fall, though not enough to stick to any surface or disrupt the game.

The flakes were also not enough to disrupt a dozing Allison, who was now leaning against Trust's shoulder.

The various stirrings of the crowd must have served purely as ambient noise.

Trust glanced to Paxson, smirking.

"Do it! Do it!" Paxson whispered eagerly. Grinning. Nodding his head in anticipation.

Trust turned his head slowly toward Marcie. She was looking out onto the field, where Kyler and the rest of the UCC defense were going through their fielding warm-ups. The rest of the crowd also preoccupied during the short intermission between innings, conversing with one another and generally lounging about, waiting for the action to begin again.

Trust counted down in his head.

Three...

Two...

One...

He leapt to his feet, clapping excitedly—

—and immediately sat down as Allison sprang out of her seat as well, also clapping and cheering.

Wood Field appeared to turn as one, staring at her.

Allison's cheerfulness trailed off, her applause diminishing. She glanced down.

Paxson was cracking up, laughing hysterically.

Trust was looking out toward the field in an innocent, seemingly studious manner, moving his mouth as though mumbling to himself, although no sound emerged.

For a deaf person, it was an obvious tell.

Allison waved bashfully to the crowd of spectators still gaping at her.

"Hi," she said, before retaking her seat.

On the field, Kyler could be seen grinning, hands on hips, as he gazed in their direction.

Now, Trust glanced toward Allison, an amused smirk on his face.

Allison was facing the baseball field, apparently ignoring him. Without looking, she took hold of his notebook.

*I so completely hate you right now, anything I say will come out as a shout.*

Trust grinned.

*Mariana will be hearing about this.*

Trust's grin evaporated.

"And just what are you laughing at?" Marcie intoned, leaning over and shooting a searing gaze toward Paxson.

Paxson stopped snickering.

"Me? No, I wasn't laughing. I'm not even sitting here right now."

The first batter for the visiting team finally approached the plate.

TOP OF THE EIGHTH INNING. The score was now tied 2-2. Neither school's offense had been able to gain much of an advantage, which was mostly the result of good pitching and fielding from both sides.

The light flakes of snow had come and gone intermittently throughout the contest. Presently, they were absent, fleeting glimpses of the winter sun seen as it descended slowly below the horizon line, the bright stadium lights already on and shining.

Trust glanced to the baseball diamond again before returning to Paxson. There was a base runner on first, testing to see how far he could stretch the base without arousing too much suspicion from the Tigers pitcher on the mound. Kyler was crouched into a ready stance in his shortstop position, his glance hovering between the pitcher and the opposing base runner.

"He never mentioned anything to me," Paxson replied, referring to his brother, Randolph. "And this Oliver guy says Dolphin may have known the guy who jumped in? Beats me, but you definitely have me curious."

This time, both boys looked to the field, where the pitcher swung around quickly toward first base, faking a throw. The base runner dived back, Trent Atkins standing just in front of him, ready for the throw if it had come.

*Apparently not a lot of people even know anything about it,
since it happened years ago.*

The powerful lights in Wood Field might as well have been imitating a clear, sunny day, so for Paxson, the notebook paper was still easy to read.

*I'm sure since the girl was uncooperative, she wouldn't be the
kind to spread the story, and since it was surely embarrassing
to the boys, Freesef wouldn't circulate the rumor either.*

"I'm guessing Oliver wouldn't be able to describe this Dolphin or any of the other people involved," Paxson surmised.

Trust shrugged, then shook his head.

*All he knew was some guy jumping into the middle of the
assault and laying everyone out, and somebody called Dolphin
somehow connected to it. He also said something about
somebody dying, but he pretty much admitted he made that
part up.*

At the plate, the batter whiffed on a pitch. The count was 2-2, two balls and two strikes.

"He's in some type of special training program right now. They're really strict on the phone calls, but he can check email, though he sometimes can't reply immediately. I'll email him tonight. If he is the Dolphin Oliver is talking about, and he knows what happened between that girl and Freesef, do you think it would help with Allison's and Melody's cases? Dolphin graduated from UCC five years ago, so that means it would have been at least that long, if not longer, depending on how old the girl is now."

*Remember when we were talking about Allison's attack right
after it happened, and you asked if there was a chance they
picked the wrong girl?*

"Is this your way of saying I would make a good detective?" asked Paxson.

*Not really, no.*

The pitcher started his windup, and then threw hard.

*Crack!*

The baseball rocketed off the bat—

—Trust's gaze shifted immediately—

—Kyler's reactions were lightning fast, already high in the air, jumping straight up, his body fully extended, his glove high...

*Pffft!* The sound of the ball striking against leather was audible to everyone but Trust, though the deaf boy observed as the exertion spun Kyler around in the air so that he landed with his back turned toward the batter, a complete one-eighty. He braced himself as he landed, crouching, his free hand grazing the ground, his other hand holding his glove just above the surface, the glove then sweeping around behind him as he stumbled slightly.

Trust also could not hear the immense roar from the crowd, but he could feel it. He jumped up with Paxson and Allison and Marcie and everyone else, the sudden cheer at the spectacular catch like a wave that began in his chest and flowed quickly throughout his entire body. Or maybe it was just the adrenaline of watching his lifelong friend do something so impressive, so amazing, so...

Kyler tipped his baseball cap meekly at the applause, a humble, completely Kyler-like response. He slapped gloves with the third baseman as he jogged toward the dugout.

It was only the eighth inning. The game wasn't over quite yet.

BOTTOM OF THE NINTH INNING. The low-scoring game was still tied at 2-2. There was one Centre City runner on first base, with no outs.

After the current batter at the plate, Kyler was due up next. For now, he was in the on-deck circle, though he was not taking any practice swings. He stood, leaning on his bat like a cane, watching the pitcher. Studying.

A nudge from Allison brought Trust's attention to her, and then to Marcie on her other side.

"Did Allison tell you we saw that crazy custodian at the hospital again last night?" Marcie asked.

"That was my first time meeting him," Allison corrected. "*You* saw him again."

Trust looked momentarily confused before his expression reset.

The UCC batter at the plate fouled a pitch off. This was a critical at-bat for both teams, as a score from UCC in this, the final inning, would end the game.

Trust scribbled out his reply. By now, the sky was almost fully dark, the large, lofty stadium lights providing all of the illumination.

> *I remember. I could barely understand that guy with his accent. What was his name again?*

"Kian," Marcie answered. "Kian the custodian. I told Allison and Melody the same thing I told you when we first met him—there's something seriously off about that guy."

On the field, the Tigers batter swung mightily at a pitch and missed. A quick check toward the scoreboard display showed he was now down in the count 1-2. Even without the assistance of sound, Trust could see the crowd getting anxious again.

He wrote,

> *Something off in a bad way?*

Marcie shook her head.

"No, something off in...well, an *off* way. You saw him, Allison, and you agreed with me. And he accused me of being Irish. I mean, I think I would know."

"He's just...abrasive," Allison explained, Marcie nodding alongside her. "Not mean, necessarily; just like he doesn't really know how he comes across. But at the same time, he seems really smart, really quick—not that custodians can't be smart or anything—"

Trust nodded, scrunching his face up in understanding.

> *Some of the smartest people I know are custodians. My best friend is a custodian.*

"I'm serious, though," Allison intoned, grinning. "One minute he's yelling at someone about how he just mopped the floor in this thick Irish brogue you can barely make out, and then the next—"

The batter swung, making contact with the baseball and sending it darting down the left-field line, staying just fair and skirting past the diving third baseman. Trust and the others leaped from their seats as the crowd cheered wildly, the runner on first rounding second base and arriving at third before the ball was back to the infield. The player who had gotten the hit appeared to contemplate stretching his success into a double, but wisely thought better of it, returning to first. Trust's body vibrated with the applause.

Now there were runners on first and third, and still no outs in the inning.

And Kyler was heading to the plate. The opposing school's manager jogged out to the pitcher's mound, accompanied by the catcher and the rest of the infield.

A major team conference. A critical moment. With the Centre City runner on third, they were ninety feet away from losing the game.

Allison, still cheering, her face reflecting the excitement of the rest of the stadium, turned to Trust. Even without Trust's unique visual capabilities, Allison's eyes appeared to glimmer in the Wood Field lighting overhead.

"Kyler has to get a hit here, doesn't he?" she asked. "Is he going to be all right? Do you think he's nervous?"

Trust replied in his notebook.

*I keep forgetting this is your first time watching him play.*
*Don't worry; just keep watching.*

As the opposing university's coach and infield players moved away, leaving the pitcher alone on the mound again, Kyler stepped back into the batter's box. For all intents and purposes, Kyler—tufts of his blond hair shooting out from under his helmet—did not appear nervous. The thousands in the stands seemed nervous for him, virtually every single one of them sitting on their hands. Waiting.

Watching.

Trust could feel the hush. He smiled faintly, leaning forward.

Kyler rocked and swayed back and forth in a metronome, his body keeping time with his waving bat.

The pitcher shifted his weight. Raised his leg. Delivered.

Even in the cold air, the fastball was red hot.

Ninety-one miles per hour.

Trust watched the home plate umpire signal a strike.

The spectators let out a disappointed sigh, visible puffs of warm air appearing to emerge at once. Kyler did one slow revolution with the bat in front of his body, seemingly retuning, before going through his pre-pitch routine again.

Allison glanced toward Trust.

Trust felt her glance and looked at her. He smirked.

Kyler settled down, returning to the swaying oscillations, as the opposing pitcher readied again.

The slow, coiling windup.

The pitch. Breaking ball.

The crowd, anticipating for just an instant, before—

Kyler swung.

*Crack!*

Trust felt it.

"OHMYGODOHMYGODOHMYGODOHMYGOD, that was *amazing*! That was the most incredible thing I've ever seen in my life!"

In the corridor of the Tigers field house just before the locker room doors, Allison practically danced as she held on to Trust's shoulder, Trust looking at her with a bewildered smirk. The hallway was carpeted, looking almost like a plush office building, with framed photographs of past UCC baseball and softball games lining the walls. For the amount of people waiting—with permission to do so at the approval of the players—the hallway was relatively quiet, as though the setting requested a particular reverence, even with a college locker room mere feet away.

"Uh, Allison," Paxson voiced, drawing the excited girl's attention, "I know you're not any kind of sports expert, but you do know that not every game is going to turn out like that, right? We're probably going to lose some games, and Kyler is going to strike out and not play well at times. Heck, he struck out in his first at-bat before you arrived."

Trust nodded, pointing to Paxson.

"Wow," said another person who was waiting. "Way to try and snatch all the joy out of the room."

405

"I know, right?" a young girl agreed, most likely a girlfriend of one of the players. "Can't she be excited after such a good game? Why do you have to be such a downer, huh?"

Trust nodded, pointing to the two onlookers. Marcie snickered. Paxson glanced around.

"Wait," he said, the door to the UCC locker room opening, "it didn't just become weird in here, did it? Because I'm not accustomed to playing the bad—"

"I'm sure it was weird as soon as you walked through the door," Trent interrupted, the senior first baseman the first to emerge in casual clothing and an athletic bag hanging across his chest.

Paxson wheeled around.

"Trent Atkins!" he squealed, sounding a full twelve years younger than his actual age.

He started to run up to the older boy, but Trent quickly held his hand up as a girl—the one who had responded to Paxson's dampening comments—came to his side.

"Don't even think about doing what you're thinking about doing," he warned Paxson, resulting in more than a few chuckles as more players filtered out of the locker room.

Trent then looked to the girl alongside him.

"Scott wants us to make a stop first before we go get something to eat," he said to her.

Trust's gaze shifted to the doors as Kyler came out, his worn, familiar white cap once again in place as his hair hung down loosely. Kyler caught his roommate's glance first, grinning.

Trust bowed slightly in acknowledgement.

Kyler was caught off guard when Allison catapulted herself at him, and he stumbled back, bumping into some of his teammates behind him.

"Oomph! Wha—"

"That was fantastic!" Allison exclaimed. "I love baseball!"

She then kissed him on the lips. It lasted a few seconds.

There were cheers from some of the others looking on.

Trust snickered.

Allison released the blond-haired boy, her smile ecstatic, and Kyler's eyes flew open.

"Wow!"

"Mr. Brooks, if I could have a moment."

A woman in a suit advanced through the small crowd of players and supporters in the hall. She was accompanied by a small boy, no older than five or six. He was wearing a coat with an oversized replica Tigers baseball jersey over it, and he had a baseball in his hands.

"Mr. Brooks," the woman started, her voice and bearing Trust deemed as overly formal, "my name is Florence—"

"Flo-Jo!" Kyler said. "You don't have to introduce yourself every time. I have a pretty good memory. Hey, is that a baseball?"

He bent down to one knee in front of the boy, who stood, seemingly awestruck, as the woman glanced around almost sheepishly.

"Um, yes," she said. "Actually, I—"

"You can blame 'Flo-Jo' on Coach," Trent declared. "He let slip what your nickname used to be when you went to school here, like the sprinter, so that won't be going away anytime soon."

"Wow," Kyler remarked meanwhile, studying the ball still in the small boy's hands. "That's a nice one. Actually, it looks a little familiar. Where'd ya get it?"

"I caught it," the boy said faintly, the strong urge to smile tugging at the corners of his mouth, his shyness attempting to hold it off and mostly failing.

"Caught it?" Kyler echoed. "Dude, sweet! You caught that at the game tonight?"

"Yeah!" the boy said, Kyler's contagious enthusiasm rubbing off. "You hit a home run, and the ball was, like, *phewm!*"—he moved the ball with both hands through the air—"and it was coming right at me! I had to close my eyes at the last second, but I still caught it! It hurt my hands!"

"Wow! You caught it without a glove? That's amazing! You see, my buddy Trent over there has to wear a huge glove to catch baseballs, but you did it without one. I think he's a little scared."

The boy was beside himself with excitement now.

"Wow! Trent Atkins! He hit a home run, too!" he exclaimed, pointing to the senior nearly dropping his baseball in the—

"He—"

Then he did drop the ball, immediately scooping it up again, the other onlookers chuckling at the child's animated antics.

"He hit it *really* far!" the boy went on, demonstrating with the ball again. "I saw it go out of the stadium!"

The boy was escorted out of the clubhouse by Florence not long after, leaving with Kyler's game-winning three-run home-run baseball signed by those players who still lingered behind. Kyler stood again, turning to Allison.

"Oh," he said, "I should probably say now that I asked a couple of the guys if they wanted to go with us to visit Melody in the hospital. I know you said she's a fan of the baseball team, and—"

"Eh," Marcie piped up, shrugging. "More like just a fan of boys in baseball uniforms, or any type of uniform, or any type of shirt, or out of one..."

"The more the merrier," Allison said, looking around at Trent and the other players still standing in the corridor with their supporters. "She would be over the moon if you guys could come see her."

*Talented, thoughtful, good with kids,* Trust signed with Kyler looking at him. *Someone's turning out to be a pretty good boyfriend.*

Kyler grinned, sending Trust a casual salute.

# 33.
## One on One

TRUST AND KOBE MET IN the North Gym for their first one-on-one session. It was late, after nine in the evening. Still, there were a few playing basketball on a couple of the courts in the gymnasium.

The soft-spoken martial arts instructor leaned back against the boxing ropes in a sleeveless shirt and gym shorts with high-top basketball shoes, looking quite at home in the ring. He was watching Trust, who stood more toward the center of the ring in his usual workout clothes.

"Tell me what makes you angry."

Trust squinted faintly, his mouth hanging open a little.

"Obviously, your combat abilities are highly advanced. And no, that's not something your grandfather told me—it's obvious from the way you move, and from the way you moved in class to anyone who knows what to look for. What's also obvious is that you train regularly—you don't become as advanced as I suspect you are without constant, consistent practice. With that in mind, what I don't want is for these sessions to be us just going through the motions every time. We'll do that occasionally, but if your grandfather trained you as he did me, I'm sure you do a lot of that on your own. Instead, I want to home in on the nuance."

Kobe pushed himself off the ropes.

"So, tell me what makes you angry."

Even though Trust could not hear it, he could tell the instructor's voice was quiet, calm, composed.

Deliberate.

Trust lifted his note card.

*Doubt. Underestimation. Taunting.*

"Good. It's good you're aware of that. Now, what scares you?"
Trust's lips pursed slightly as he thought.

*Something happening to someone I know, and I'm not able to stop it.*

After reading, Kobe indicated Trust's previous answer.
"Your answer is the same; you just worded it differently."
He started to back away slowly.
"One of the things I want to discover while we are together is how you focus through fear and anger. Of course, we won't be able to get into that much tonight, but that can be one of our overall objectives. There is a level where skill and technique will no longer be the reason you fail—you may have already reached it. It will be from what's inside—your thoughts, your emotions. Fear and anger have claimed many more victims than improper technique ever will. And from what I've heard, you're no stranger to that battle."
Trust started to write again, stepping forward.

*You never told me how you knew my grandfather.*

Kobe smiled faintly.
"Actually, I did. I told you he was one of my instructors when I was younger."
Trust waited.
Kobe just stood there, his ghost of a smile barely present.
Trust raised an eyebrow.

*That's all I'm going to get from you tonight, isn't it?*

"We've got all semester. Maybe longer, if you choose to continue. We're going to need something to talk about, and I'm not much of a conversationalist."

*But you say we've met before?*

"You were really young. Three, four, five. I wouldn't expect you to remember that."

*Did you meet my friend Kyler?*

"Perhaps. Why?"

*He'll remember you if you did.*

"Don't count on it."

*You're doubting me.*

Kobe's eyes rose to meet Trust's again.
"Okay," he said, smiling after a moment. "Now, we stretch."
But Trust held up a finger.

*One more thing. How long have you been an instructor here?*

"Six years."

*Does the Freesef Society mean anything to you?*

Kobe shook his head. Trust bowed slightly, relinquishing the floor as he moved to put his cards off to the side.

THE NEXT DAY FOUND TRUST with an open block of time during the middle part of an outwardly dreary day, and he hopped on a Centre Line bus destined for downtown. The sky was gray, overcast; it seemed the perfect conditions for snow, but sprinkles of rain fell off and on instead, the atmosphere not quite frosty enough.

It was a good day to spend inside, but Trust had been anticipating the free time for a while.

Before long, he was standing in front of the Centre Diamond nightclub, a light, cold drizzle falling. For Trust, rain had a similar effect as snow—visually, at least. The surrounding wintry gray was highlighted and speckled with a kaleidoscope of color, each raindrop entirely distinct from the next until it splashed onto the ground.

Trust waited.

One of the heavy front entrance doors pushed open.

"Trust!"

Trust smiled, taking Mariana's appearance in. She was dressed casually, jeans and long sleeves, looking as unintentionally beautiful as ever. In fact, the relaxed look almost seemed to enhance it.

Mariana beckoned him in out of the rain, into the vestibule, Trust eyeing her slyly as he edged past. He did not venture too far in, however. When Mariana turned back around after closing the door again, Trust was standing directly in front of her.

Smirking.

Mariana returned the smirk with one of her own, before biting her bottom lip between her teeth.

Trust stepped forward.

Mariana took a half step back before coming into contact with the door. Trust placed his arm against the frame, leaning in closer, his eyes slightly hooded as they flicked between hers...and her lips. Mariana's gaze did the same.

Closer.

Closer still...

Trust held up his phone.

*Have you eaten lunch yet?*

The girl laughed before rolling her eyes.

*Now I feel like I'm taking advantage.*

Turing his gaze to her as she read his statement, Trust watched as she smiled, still chewing.

"How were you supposed to know we get first-rate gourmet sandwiches once a week?" she posed, her eyes sparkling even in the normal lighting of the club. "Now, if you came back *next* week with a bunch of your college friends with the express purpose of getting a free lunch again, *then* you would be taking advantage."

A few Centre Diamond staff that were present milled about, none of whom Trust recognized. The interior of the club itself was barely recognizable, different from how it appeared during the evening and night hours, with hundreds of people dancing to a pulsating beat, and different from Trust's visit during the Disability Services holiday dinner. Presently, the place looked almost like a warehouse, though some features, such as the towering display screens and more permanent nightlife décor, alluded to the space's true purpose.

The club seemed asleep, the rest before coming alive again when Centre Diamond opened to the public that night.

*I'm no sandwich aficionado, but these are addictively good. No wonder you call them first-rate gourmet. Also, no way you made them.*

Mariana shoved him playfully, feigning shock.

"Now what is that supposed to mean?" she asked. "What if I did make them?"

*Then I would be forced to strongly consider marrying you right now.*

Trust wrote as he took another bite.

*And I don't even have any money for a big wedding.*

Mariana tilted her head, smiling adorably.

"I'm a simple girl," she said.

Trust looked at her. It turned into a stare, his eyes widening. Mariana maintained a straight face for an extended moment, before she burst out laughing.

"If only you could have seen your face just now!" she cried. "Looks like someone's a little afraid of commitment, eh?"

*Commitment? Is that what the kids are calling it these days?*

"You are afraid!" Mariana asserted, giggling. "That was such a misdirection. You're a commitment-phobe!"

*If I didn't know the context of this suddenly terrifying
conversation, I would say you just made that last word up.
But that reminds me, have you heard about this Tigresa app
at UCC?*

"Oh, yeah!" Mariana said, gesturing to Trust with a portion of her sandwich. "Some of the people who work here and go to school are on it. You would *never* catch me on that thing; it just sounds creepy. Too invasive, like a stalker."

She then shrugged.

"But the guys here seem to find it interesting."

Mariana then watched as Trust pulled out his phone, quickly bringing up the program and handing it off to her.

*I don't know if you've heard, but we've had a series of
robberies on campus since the beginning of the school year.
Someone almost broke into our room, but Kyler scared him
off. Doesn't this seem like the perfect way to monitor when
people are going to be out of their rooms? Perfect time to walk
right in.*

Mariana looked from the paper Trust wrote on back to the phone, shaking her head.

"This is amazing, and not in a good way," she said. "Look. It says you got on the Red Centre Line at 11:52 a.m. I'm sure there's some kind of right-to-privacy argument to be had here. I would almost be too afraid to leave my room. But if those robberies are occurring, why...I mean, is Kyler in your room now? What if both of you have class at the same time and someone posts it?"

Trust smirked.

*Are you trying to come up with a reason to stop me from
coming to see you on Sandwich Day?*

"Oh, so you want to try to be big and bad now, but if I bring up our wedding—"

Trust held up his hands, shaking his head.

*Emails were sent out, and we had a hall meeting. Everyone knows what to look out for with these robberies; it's almost like a neighborhood watch thing. Can't assume someone carrying stuff is "returning it" or "going to get it fixed." But, of course, you can't go too far, or it would be an invasion of privacy going the other way.*

Mariana held Trust's phone up, grinning mischievously.
"I should put 'Trust got married at 12:37.'"
Trust cut his eyes at her.

*So, you graduated from UCC about twenty years ago, right? Or is it coming up on thirty now?*

Mariana gaped at him and threw a pickle wedge in his—
"Oh my God! I can't believe you just caught that in your mouth!"
Trust smirked again, chewing.

*Oh, that wasn't what you meant to do? What I was going to ask about, though, was if you have ever heard of the Freesef Society.*

He slid the paper over again, and reached for the last section of his sandwich...but he didn't make it. He did a double take, his hand freezing over his plate, his eyes on the girl.

Hesitation. An immediate tensing as her eyes stilled on a portion of the page...

...before her muscles relaxed again.

Trust shifted his head slightly, attempting to catch her—

Mariana looked up, shaking her head as she slid the paper back across. She started to smile.

"No, I don't think I remember any club called the Freesef Society, though since it's been twenty years..."

Trust looked at her quizzically, his brow furrowing. Mariana looked back at him, then swiftly glanced down and away.

Trust's eyes flitted about the club.

Nothing out of the ordinary.

Back to Mariana.

"You want another one?" she asked, gesturing to the platter of sandwich portions artfully arranged.

Trust continued to look at her, his head leaned slightly sideways. His hand started to move toward the paper, but then stopped...and then started, and then stopped again. His eyes darted to hers, and then to the side, and then down, quick, hurried as he thought, his mouth parted.

One thought in particular continued to pass through his mind...but...

"Mary-anna."

Her widened eyes met his again. His voice was nearly a whisper.

The name felt off. He tried again.

"Mari-ana. Mariana."

"Please..."

Trust could tell that she was whispering as well. Deep, in the pit of his stomach, he sensed the feeling he had been trained and taught to control, the feeling that—during individualized sessions with Kobe—he would be asked to unleash, and then restrain.

"...please don't..."

Fear.

It was thoroughly unsettling, as was the rest of the meal.

As was Mariana's parting peck on his cheek.


KYLER WAS LAUGHING, SPRAWLED ON Trust's bed as Trust walked in.

"Ha ha! Pax, I don't even—"

As his eyes shifted toward Trust in the archway, Kyler saw him for all of a second before immediately rising to his feet. He still had a grin on his face, and Trust could not yet see around the corner, but he could assume Paxson was sitting somewhere on the other—

"Here, man," Kyler said, tossing the television remote out of Trust's sightline while holding a hand up in Trust's direction. "Stay right there, T. I wanted to show you something really quick."

He jogged forward, ushering Trust back out of the room again. Trust did as instructed, not having moved deep enough into the dorm to greet—or even see—Paxson.

*To the bathroom,* Kyler signed quickly before turning back around again, leading them around the corner and into the bathroom on the boys' side of the floor. The door swung closed after they entered. They were the only two inside.

Trust glanced around before returning to Kyler.

*Dude,* Kyler motioned, standing directly in front of Trust. *That look. I know that look. I know it. I've seen that look exactly twice since we've been in Centre City. You probably had that same look when you read my text about Allison being in the hospital. You* know *I know that look. So here's how it's going to go. You don't leave this bathroom until you tell me what happened to put that look on your face—and I mean right now— or I swear I will not be friends with you anymore. I won't talk to you again. I'm seriously not joking.*

Trust's gaze shifted down slightly, past his roommate and lifelong friend.

He sighed.

*You act like you not talking to me anymore is some kind of punishment,* he signed.

Kyler did not take the bait.

*You wouldn't last two days,* Kyler returned. *And the first day would just be you being mad at me.*

Trust blew out another puff of air.

*I mentioned Freesef to Mariana.*

Kyler waited for him to continue.

*So?* he then prompted after a while.

*She...*Trust paused, collecting his thoughts. *I think...She didn't say anything, but I think something happened to her when she was a student here. I'm trying really hard not to jump to any conclusions, but...the way she acted when I mentioned it...*

*By the look on your face when you came in the room, T, I'd say you're already there,* Kyler signed. *You think she might have been assaulted by the Freesef Society?*

*I don't want to jump to any conclusions,* Trust motioned again.

*You were writing, right?* Kyler asked. *What did you say?*

*I just asked her if she had ever heard of the Freesef Society when she was—Kyler, you can't tell anyone about this. Not Paxson, not Marcie, not Holden. Not Allison. Not until I know what happened, if she ever tells me.*

*Of course,* Kyler signed, nodding. *But she scared you. You know that, right? Whatever her reaction was, it scared you. I know that look. The others probably aren't able to recognize it—yet—but I've known you my whole life. Your whole life.*

He continued to examine Trust.

*Before Christmas break,* Kyler started again. *When you came back from the Disability Services dinner with blood—*

He stopped, and both boys turned as the other bathroom door opened on the far side of the room. They watched as someone started to enter.

"—find it, and then you can—"

They saw Holden turn away from whomever he was speaking to and notice them.

"Oh!" he said, grinning. "If it isn't the two most notorious..."

The bathroom door closed behind the junior RA as he looked at his two freshman charges. His grin started to dissipate.

"Whoa. Am I interrupting something?"

"You're good," Kyler said, his own easy grin surfacing. "Me and Trust were just having a little tête-à-tête."

"Ooookay."

Holden shrugged and went to one of the urinals. Kyler turned back to Trust.

*When you came back from the Disability Services dinner late, without your coat and with someone else's blood on your shirt, you saw me cover for you with the others. But when you came through the door, you had that same look on your face. It's an expression that makes you look cold, detached, almost angry, and maybe you are feeling some of that, but you and I both know there's a certain level of concern behind it, too. It's not a face I see very often, fortunately.*

Trust's eyes switched to Holden, who was finishing up at the sinks. The RA turned to them again.

"So, everything's all right?" the boy asked, reaching for a hand towel. "I can put my RA hat on really quickly, you know. Like, instantly. I've been practicing."

"Nope, we're *mucho bueno,*" Kyler said, twirling to look at him again.

"All righty then," Holden said, moving toward the door. "I'm in John's if you need me."

"Got it," Kyler replied as Holden departed.

He started to turn back to Trust, but Holden stuck his head back in the bathroom doorway.

"Oh, and I'm pretty sure it's *muy bueno*. I wasn't going to say anything, but..."

Kyler chuckled smugly.

"Heh heh. Holden, I don't mean to brag but...you're talking to a guy who took three years of Spanish in high school. I'm *pretty* sure it's *mucho bueno*."

"Oh, wow. Three years?"

"That's a lot of Spanish," Kyler stated, grinning.

Holden grinned as well.

"I was born and raised in San Bernardino, California. My next-door neighbors on both sides are Latino. My mom is actually a professor at Cal State San Bernardino, and you'll never guess what she teaches. So, and I don't mean to brag, but...you're talking to a guy who's had way more than three years of Spanish in high school. I'm *pretty* sure you're wrong, but I'm also smart enough to be *pretty* sure that you already knew that."

Kyler turned toward Trust slightly, snapping his fingers.

"You know what?" he whispered, loud enough for Holden to hear at the door. "I think Holden just burned me."

Holden only laughed, his head disappearing once more. The bathroom became quiet and still again.

Trust and Kyler looked at each other.

*Well?* Kyler signed.

*Well what?* Trust replied. *I've already told you what happened that night. I've already told you what happened to Jezzie. And I've already told you I'm not going to tell you who it was. As far as I know, from the last time I saw her, she still hasn't told Jeremy exactly what happened.*

*And I still don't see how that's possible,* Kyler remarked. *Was she able to cover up her injuries?*

*She was in the hospital nearly a week,* Trust replied. *Jeremy knows that. He took her there in the first place. He suspects what happened, but Jezzie won't confirm it, nor will I, nor will the doctors without Jezzie's consent. That's what he was talking about when he came to batting practice that one time. What I'm saying is she doesn't want him to know who did it.*

*But why?* Kyler asked. *What does that mean? Jezzie knows the guys who attacked her. Why not say something?*

Trust just looked at him. Kyler exhaled.

"And now, Mariana," Kyler said aloud, quietly.

Trust nodded.

*I saw Jezzie at the start of the semester,* Trust signed slowly. *She said that the Freesef Society was bigger than everyone realizes. The story was more complicated. The group was more powerful. Not only does she* know *Freesef exists, she still won't go to the police or tell her boyfriend what she knows about what happened to her that night. You say I have a look? Jezzie was drugged that night, high on something when I found her in that alley. She was impaired, and she was reacting slowly. But the look on her face when she was huddled against that wall...she's not talking, not because she's ashamed or embarrassed, and not because she thinks she's gaining cool points. She's not talking because she's afraid. Even after what's happened to her, she's afraid of what comes next. To Jeremy. To me or anyone else who knows too much. She's afraid of something, and neither you nor I can say or do much of anything about it until we find out what that something is. These Freesef Society rumors have been coming up for years—there has to be a good reason why people haven't done anything about it.*

When the two of them finally returned to the dorm room, Paxson was playing Kyler's video game.

"Jeeza Louisa!" he exclaimed. "Where'd you guys go? The Sistine Chapel?"

"Well, I see that your Art History class is really going to your head," Kyler said, plopping back down on Trust's bed in much the same way he had been when Trust had entered the room the first time.

*Sistine Chapel?* Trust raised. *So I'll assume that the first part of what you said was Italian and not some gobbledygook?*

"Ha ha! You used the gobbledygook sign!" Kyler observed. "But actually, it was some gobbledygook he tried to turn *into* Italian."

"Jeeza Louisa!" Paxson exclaimed again, this time with an even more dramatic Italian inflection.

## 34.
## Crazy Marcie

WITH KYLER AND THE REST of the Tigers baseball team having not yet returned from an out-of-state road trip, and Paxson and Allison in evening labs, Trust found himself with what was becoming a familiar exercise partner. The steady series of bordering streetlights they walked under provided suitable illumination for the girl to read his notebook as they made their way to the North Gym, both of their classes concluded for the day as the early onset of twilight prevailed.

"So, how long have you been doing kung fu?" Marcie asked.

*Oh, is that what it's called? I just read up on it the night before our first time at the gym. Can't you tell?*

Marcie was unimpressed.

*It's not kung fu. Or, at least, it's not only kung fu. I started early. Four or five, I guess.*

"Fourteen years," Marcie intoned. "It shows. I was just talking to Pax about it today. I'm no fighting expert or anything, but just watching you—the way you move in the ring or when you're hitting the punching bags—have you ever thought about doing that MMA cage-fighting stuff?"

Trust held the door to the Sylvia J. Rose Fitness Center open, again writing in his notebook as Marcie passed through.

*Only when someone else brings it up.*

Marcie held the second door open.

"But why martial arts? What attracted you to it in the first place? Why keep doing it when you don't plan to compete?"

Both freshmen swiped their student IDs, allowing them through the turnstile and into the fitness center.

*You think that I should?*

"Actually, no. Just based on what I've seen when I come with you, and that guy at Centre Diamond at the beginning of the year, you would probably kill somebody."

Trust's eyebrows rose.

"Not on purpose," Marcie clarified. "Well, not *deliberately* on purpose."

Trust screwed his face into a bemused expression as they navigated through the fitness and exercise complex toward the large gymnasium at the rear. The number of people in the facility was moderate, the typical amount during a weeknight for those enthusiasts inclined to accomplish their workouts near the end of the day instead of at the beginning or during the afternoon. Although the North Gym possessed no view of the outside except for at the entrance, the atmosphere of the facility in the evening hours was different from at other times.

For Trust, the feel was intriguing, exciting, but tricky to identify.

More metropolitan, perhaps.

*You know, deliberately and on purpose mean the same thing.*

"I like when you get on my nerves before we start," Marcie remarked as Trust held the gymnasium door open. "Then I can just imagine your head on the dummy and it gives me a burst of adrenaline."

*And who said violence wasn't the answer...*

Marcie snickered.

The head count of those in the North Gym had been too quick. An intramural basketball tournament was in progress, with all four courts active, and spectators lining the playing area and the walls beyond. The persistent thumping of multiple basketballs reverberated through Trust's insides, a vigorous, staccato heartbeat.

Nevertheless, a flickering glance to his usual training area in and around the boxing ring displayed its usual availability, all attention turned to the basketball games.

"It's a little busy, huh?" Marcie asked. "I didn't even know there was some type of event going on today."

Trust grinned.

*Can you speak a little louder? I didn't quite catch that over the noise I can't hear.*

"I said it seems a little busy!" Marcie yelled, though she was laughing as well.

Trust began to turn to circumvent the crowd when another familiar face halted him. Jeremy, his familiar smirk readily present, was advancing toward them, wearing one of the thin mesh jerseys donned by the participants.

A sidelong look toward Marcie confirmed that she had spotted the older boy as well.

"Don't tell me you're playing in this tournament, too!" Jeremy proclaimed. "I'd say you're running a little late, though."

His eyes shifted.

"Marcie, right? Actually, I had a dig for you, too, but you look like you can play."

"I actually don't. I don't see the appeal. I'd rather hit things."

"And by things, you mean people? Yeah, you look like one of those types."

Trust tried to hide a laugh. He tried harder when Marcie aimed a glare in his direction.

"You probably liked starting fires when you were younger, didn't you?" Jeremy went on.

"Really?" Marcie said. "So I like to hit people, and I like to start fires. Why does it sound like you're describing a sociopath?"

*We're headed to the ring. Marcie's anger management classes. How's Jezzie?*

Jeremy turned slightly and indicated with his head. Trust and Marcie followed the motion, soon identifying her.

Trust's eyes immediately darted to the boy sitting alongside her as they both watched the action on the courts. He quickly identified other faces as well.

He was frowning when his attention turned back to Jeremy.

"What?" Jeremy asked, chuckling. "What's that look for? Is that sign language?"

*Rory's here.*

Jeremy glanced over again.

"Yeah..."

"Who's Rory?" Marcie asked. "Which one is she?"

Jeremy hooted.

"Oh, wow," he began. "I am so telling him you just said—"

Trust watched as the boy cut himself short, turning again toward the courts, looking in the direction of Jezzie and the others amidst the throng of students. Trust looked as well, and then turned quickly to Marcie.

"Jezzie's saying Jeremy's team is up next," Marcie explained smoothly.

Trust looked again.

Jezzie had caught sight of them, and was now staring in his direction, her eyes slightly widened. She then glanced over as Rory also stood...slowly.

Trust tilted his head ever so slightly.

Rory's face was unscathed.

Of course. Trust had never hit him in the face.

He was still favoring his midsection, however.

"You heard about that, too, didn't you?" Jeremy remarked. "Rory and a few of the other guys got totally railed by some gang or something—I don't even know. It actually happened the same night as...you know. Jez's thing."

Trust just nodded, a faint uptick of his head.

"NO. WAIT."

Trust saw Marcie's hand shoot up in a halting gesture, stopping his forward progress toward the ring edge. The girl's breathing was still slightly labored from the hour's worth of exercise she had just been put through, but she was holding her own.

"I waited until the games were done and almost everyone had left."

She waved around the now mostly empty gym, only a few people shooting at one of the basketball hoops.

"I waited until after we were done kicking this mannequin's butt all over the ring, which we are now. But now I'm through waiting. Tell me now why you're not a fan of this Rory guy."

Trust looked at her—more than a full head shorter than him but standing firm in the ring and acting as though she were several feet taller. He went to his notebook.

*I don't like him that much. Okay, time to go.*

"You know what you're not good at doing?" Marcie remarked. "Turning a big deal into a small deal. It would have been so easy for you to brush this whole thing under the rug if you had just told me when I first asked about him before we started. But no, you've been avoiding it and putting it off like all you macho guys do, somehow expecting the poor little girl to forget. Don't you know that just makes it harder for you? Now, I'm just going to poke"—she poked him in his side—"prod"—she prodded—"and needle you"—she needled—"and I'm just going to keep going and going until you tell me because I have absolutely nothing else to do. Just poking, and prodding, and needling, and poking—"

Trust danced away from her impending prod, holding his hands up. He then stood still.

The two stared each other down in the ring.

Marcie started to advance again.

"Nothing to do, Trust," she intoned, her finger prepared to needle again. "Absolutely nothing to do..."

Trust edged away once more, his attention shifting to his notebook.

*OK*. *But this is a serious question.*

After reading, Marcie plopped down onto the ring apron, placing her head in her hands, and appearing to all the world like a dedicated pupil waiting at the foot of the master.

Trust rolled his eyes before taking a seat as well.

*What I write next is NOT TRUE, just a hypothetical to get
your first reaction.*

Marcie nodded seriously.

*Rory's in the Freesef Society. He was one of the boys who
attacked Allison. I know for a fact another girl he and his
friends have assaulted, and he may have been involved in
Melody's assault as well.*

Trust, covering his words as he wrote, watched closely as he slid the notebook across the mat to Marcie.

Marcie's eyes widened.

"Rory's in Freesef?"

Trust sprang to his feet nimbly, instantly, glancing to the small group on the basketball court, but they seemed not to have heard anything as they continued playing. He gestured for Marcie to stand, obviously annoyed.

"No! I'm sorry, I'm sorry!" Marcie whispered frantically, holding on to Trust's shorts. "You said hypothetical. You said hypothetical."

Shaking his head and still standing, Trust wrote,

*Exactly what I thought! You really expect me to tell you now?
You're a bomb with the countdown clock turned off—I don't
know when you're going to explode.*

"Me?" Marcie raised, still whispering. "You're the one who punched a guy in the throat in the middle of a crowded nightclub!"

She poked him in his chest.

*I didn't punch him in the throat—directly, at least—and that
was, literally, last year! Let's move on, shall we? You're crazy!
Why can't I just tell you when we get back to the dorm?*

"Because you'll come up with another excuse by the time we get back to the dorm," she hissed.

She then stepped forward, standing very close to Trust and pointing a finger directly in his face.

"And don't you even think about calling me crazy again, Trustice Jeffries. I mean it. I'm not scared of you. You could probably rip my arm off in three seconds, but that's exactly what you would have to do to stop me from gouging out your eyes with my fingers."

Trust's eyes widened as he looked at her. She glowered back at him.

Trust relented, stepping back slightly.

*I think you could use another round with the fighting dummy.*

Marcie's tense posture loosened slightly as she relaxed.

"No," she said. "It's a long story, but I really, *really* don't like that word. I'll tell you all about it some other time."

Trust studied her.

*Are you all right?*

Marcie ran both hands through her hair—which, for once, was not in tiny pigtails but instead hanging freely to just below her jaw line. She then smiled faintly.

> *I THINK Rory is somehow connected to Freesef, along with some of his friends, but I definitely don't know that yet for sure. I have no idea if he was involved in Allison or Melody's attack, but I do know of one girl he did assault. I won't tell you who she is. I can't go to the police because she asked me not to. This girl says Freesef is real, and it's bigger than simply a group of students attacking freshman girls. I believe her, and I think Rory is a part of it—maybe a big part. DON'T TELL ANYONE. We'll tell the others when we're all together again, but it's important people don't know. It could get back to him or someone in Freesef. Promise me you won't tell anyone, Marcie, unless I'm there when you do it.*

Marcie's jaw tensed visibly as she read, but she nodded when she met Trust's level gaze again.

"I think...I think I will need another round with the dummy after all," she said.

Trust nodded.

*Yes, ma'am.*

# 35.
## Kyler's Fears

KYLER AND TRUST BURST INTO their dark dorm room, Kyler immediately flipping on the light and pulling off his shirt in the same motion, Trust closing the door behind him and then doing the same, keeping his attention on Kyler as the boy spoke.

"So you're going to call her, right?" Kyler said, his face turned toward his roommate just enough as he rushed to get out of his clothes.

Trust was unzipping his jeans.

*Call?* he motioned, pausing just briefly.

"Oh, don't play the naïve card now," Kyler intoned, hopping on one foot as he tried to shuck his second leg from his pants. "You know what I—argh!"

Trust, already down to his underwear and socks, saw Kyler fall, though the boy did finally manage to get his jeans off after a brief, and somewhat amusing, wrestling match on the floor. Kyler quickly threw his pants onto his bed in annoyance, as though it was entirely their fault, before springing to his feet again.

"You know what I mean," he finished.

*Are we going to act like you didn't just get body-slammed by your pants?* Trust asked, his shorts now nearly up to his waist.

"What? No. That didn't happen."

*I'll text her after we're done, but I don't know if it will matter. I haven't talked to her since that lunch.*

"Perfect, then. A baseball game is an excellent Valentine's Day gift."

Trust gave Kyler a look as he tied his shoes. Kyler pulled a shirt over his head.

"Hey, I still can't believe I missed you almost get punked by Marcie.

429

You can't give me that look."

*Almost punked?* Trust asked, fully clothed again and heading for the door. *It wasn't almost anything. I may have peed my pants a little. But I also seem to recall that in this very room, she choke-slammed you worse than those pants did just now.*

"But she went crazy!" Kyler exclaimed, looking up as he tied his own shoes. "I wasn't ready for that at all."

*I would advise you not to use the C-word around her,* Trust motioned, *or you also won't be ready when she kicks your—*

He flipped off the light, leaving Kyler in darkness as he opened the door again.

"How do you always change faster than me?" Kyler called after him. "You can't sign and take off your pants at the same time!"

Trust, of course, did not hear a thing.

LEANING NONCHALANTLY, HIS BACK AGAINST the ropes on the far side, Kobe watched as Trust smoothly stepped into the ring. He then watched as another boy tried to leap over the top rope in ridiculous style, barely making it over and nearly falling flat on his face. He smiled faintly.

Feeling the awkward movements, Trust glanced back to the stumbling Kyler before returning his gaze to the instructor.

"Cutting it close tonight," Kobe observed in his usual soft-spoken tone, before his eyes shifted briefly to the blond boy again.

Trust only nodded, finding it unnecessary to write down a response.

"And I see you've brought along a baseball player."

Trust followed Kobe's gaze to Kyler, who was still standing slightly behind him, though now he came forward.

"Kyler-Scott Brooks at your service, sir," Kyler said, extending his hand and bowing as he and Kobe shook. He quickly looked up again. "That's with a hyphen between Kyler and Scott. I don't want you to think I'm giving you my full first, middle, and last or anything."

*You don't have a middle name,* Trust supplied.

"That's right. I don't have a middle name."

"Ah, I do remember you now," Kobe said.

"And I remembered you as soon as I walked through those double doors," Kyler said, pointing back across the gym, currently devoid of any other students, the cavernous space quiet except for the hum of the air conditioning and the faint echo of Kyler's voice. "Actually, I remembered you when Trust told me your name, but I remembered that I remembered you just now."

Kobe stared at him.

Kyler translated Trust's signs.

"Don't worry. He really is like this all the time."

"Trust told you why I wanted you here tonight?"

"Yeah. Because this—this ring, this training—*this* is where we lay the *foundation*...for learning how to bust heads in."

"Not even close," Kobe answered instantly, quietly.

*I told him this is where we begin to discover the reaches of my emotional control,* Trust signed.

Kyler translated.

He then added, "And I had no idea what that meant, so I just said bust heads in because it sounds cooler."

Kobe already had the wooden man post positioned in the ring, and he went to retrieve it.

"What are you afraid of, Kyler?"

With Kobe's head tilted down as he examined the apparatus, Trust did not even realize the man had spoken until Kyler relayed the question.

"What am I afraid of? You."

Kyler moved closer to Kobe while still facing in Trust's general direction. As Kobe stooped, studying the lower half of the dummy, Kyler stooped as well.

"You know you speak really quietly, right?"

His voice came out a whisper, even softer than Kobe's usual tone.

Kobe smirked faintly as he wiped down an area with his hand.

"And what's the serious answer?" he asked Kyler.

Trust could now read his lips again.

Kyler looked at the instructor for a moment, and then turned again, nodding toward Trust.

"You want to know what scares me?" Kyler declared. "He does. Something happening to my family or the people I care about scares me, too, but he"—Kyler pointed at Trust—"he's a little extra. I'm afraid of what he would do—how far he would go—if he thought someone he cared about was in danger."

He paused briefly.

"I've seen glimpses of that fear coming true before," he added.

Kobe slowly stood again, and Kyler did as well. Kobe looked from Kyler to Trust. As he spoke, his words were still directed to Kyler, though his eyes locked on the deaf teen.

"Afraid of how far he would go? How far do you think? And why Trust in particular?"

Trust's eyes flitted swiftly to Kyler, who was looking at him as well.

"As you no doubt know already, Trust has certain...skills that allow him to do things others only dream of doing. That can be good...or bad. And as to how far he would go—that's the bad part."

Another pause.

"He would go as far as possible, and he wouldn't think about himself for one moment in the process. It's a one-way ticket. That's what scares me."

Kobe turned to the boy.

"You said you've seen glimpses."

Trust clenched his jaw.

"I've seen it," Kyler replied, still looking at Trust unwaveringly. "And I've seen the aftermath. And I know, if the circumstance arose, he would do it again, even if I and everyone else said not to. I'm afraid he wouldn't care if he survived."

"Thank you, Kyler. You have been helpful."

Kobe then shifted to Trust, moving from behind the apparatus.

"I must admit here, Trust, that I talked to Kyler before tonight. Yesterday, in fact. I told him not to tell you, and that I would explain it all tonight. After you said in our last meeting that he would be able to come, I called to confirm, and to tell him what I had planned, and to tell him what I would ask. It was very important that he be here, and that you hear what he said—the answer he gave just now—coming from his lips and his alone. He may have told you this before, I don't know. But I apologize for deceiving you."

Kobe was now close. He placed his hand on Trust's shoulder.

"But it's extremely important that you remember his answer. Not just for tonight, not just for this semester, but for the rest of your life. The feeling that you have right now, whatever thoughts are running through your head—I want you to remember those, too. Because those feelings, those thoughts, what your friend said—those make up the recipe for your downfall. You have it, right in front of you, in black and white.

That is your Achilles heel. And that is what we're going to work on. *This* is what we're going to explore. But it's important that you don't forget any of it, because that is what we will use to conquer it."

Trust exhaled deeply, not realizing he had been holding his breath, before nodding and glancing down to the ring floor. He looked up again as Kobe patted his shoulder.

"And now, we stretch."

"And then after that, since we've sucked all the fun out of the entire universe, we get to practice busting some heads in, right?" Kyler asked, also coming from around the wooden man post. "And what about my other fear that I told you about? You said you'd have an answer."

Kobe dropped lightly to the mat, his legs spread wide. He looked up to Kyler.

"I've thought about that," the instructor said, his calm, tranquil voice not even loud enough to resonate through the empty gym, but somehow still distinctly clear. "Besides seeking out a licensed therapist if that fear gets too severe, I would suggest building a house entirely of rat poison. That would work against genetically mutated rats, wouldn't it?"

Kyler sucked his teeth in disapproval.

"Obviously, if they're genetically mutated, they would be resistant to all known rat poisons. Thanks for nothin'."

Trust shook his head as he lowered himself to the floor as well.

## 36.
## Boy in Red Hat

*Glad you could make it.*

The Tigers were playing a midday game, on Valentine's Day of all days. While it was no official holiday for the university and classes went on as usual, the spectating crowd was impressively large, most likely owing to the popularity and potential of this year's squad, drawing even more casual fans at the chance to gain a glimpse of the team's play. That play had currently fueled a 5-1 lead thus far in the fourth inning, aided in large part by a mammoth three-run homer by Trent Atkins in the first. Only nearing the midway point of the contest, Kyler had already scored two runs, and stolen two bases.

Trust was lucky that his schedule for the day had a chunk of free time right when the game was scheduled—Marcie and Allison were not as fortunate. But Paxson had been enthusiastic in making the short trek to Wood Field, along with another acquaintance of his and Trust's.

The February air, even at midday, possessed the steady hand of chilled, wintry air, and the crowd watching the outdoor game was dressed accordingly. Even the players on the field wore their pants and long-sleeved jerseys, faintly recalling an otherwise bygone era of America's pastime.

"That is literally the ninth time you've written that down since I got here," Mariana remarked, laughing softly underneath her stylish woolen knit cap and coat.

Trust shrugged, smirking and giving her a sidelong glance.

*What can I say? I'm glad you could make it.*

435

Mariana shook her head, nudging him.

"That's ten," she observed.

Trust wrote again.

*I'm sorry also.*

"Don't, Trust. I'm serious. You have absolutely nothing to be sorry about. It's my thing, not yours."

Trust felt an enthused elbow from his other side as Paxson leaned over. As was becoming the norm, Trust had to adjust his gaze down from Paxson's gaudy, glittering gold UCC cap that he had recently acquired.

"Great day for a game, right?" he said, his grin nearly as bright as his cap in the midday sun. "Perfect baseball weather!"

"Perfect?" Mariana echoed. "I think the high is supposed to be in the lower fifties today."

*There's a reason baseball players are called the "boys of summer," Pax.*

Trust showed Paxson his comment.

"That's in the pros," Paxson returned, "and that's because they're weak! Baseball in the cold is an entirely different game. It takes more brain than brawn. Unless your name is Trent Atkins, that is."

*Really? I didn't even realize it was cold, since it looks like you're wearing the freaking sun on the top of your head.*

A Tigers batter hit a shallow fly ball into right field, an easy out for the opposing school's fielder.

"Marcie doesn't know about that hat, does she?" Mariana questioned.

Trust snorted. Paxson looked petulant, grasping the cap with one hand as though someone would even have the desire—much less the audacity—to take it.

"Well, I'll have you know, Miss Eldorado, that...no, she doesn't know about it. How could you possibly have known that?"

"Because I highly doubt Marcie would allow you to set foot out of your room with it on. Paxson, it's ridiculously, um, not good. I don't think even Dolphin would be brave enough—actually, you know what, he absolutely would. Now I see where you get it from."

*Marcie will definitely burn it, though, when she finds out. You can't hide it forever.*

"Oh, that reminds me," Paxson said, looking to Trust. "My brother's actually out of the country right now, but he did send me an email that he would be able to talk sometime in March. It'll probably be after we get back from Spring Break. You still want to talk to him, don't you?"

Trust nodded. On the field, the inning was over, the Tigers not having scored. The teams were switching sides, with UCC taking the field, and the rival university preparing to bat.

"How is Dolphin, anyway?" Mariana asked. "I got an email from him around Christmas. I always write, and I know to expect a delay, but I never know when it's a regular delay, or—"

Paxson dismissed her concern with a wave of his hand.

"No worries; he's perfectly fine. Some sort of super-secret training thing. I just got the email today. You should probably check your inbox. I'm sure you'll be hearing from him in the next few days, if you haven't gotten one already."

"You said he was going to call? Is there any chance I could talk to him?"

Trust and Paxson looked at each other. Mariana seemed to sense their hesitation.

"I mean, only if it is convenient," she swiftly amended. "I don't want to interrupt anything you have scheduled. You could even have the call at the club if you want. You can use one of the conference rooms. But I don't want to intrude."

*We're going to be talking about some guy stuff, but it's fine with me as long as it's okay with Pax.*

Mariana wrinkled her nose.

"Guy stuff?" she repeated. "Why would you possibly want to discuss guy stuff with—"

Something caught Trust's eye over Mariana's shoulder, and his gaze shifted, trying to find it again. For a second, he thought he saw—

Yes. There. Moving up the steps, one of thousands in attendance.

However, the red hat, similar to Paxson's monstrosity, was easy to spot in the crowd.

The boy was either Asian or white with Asian features. His hair was relatively long for a boy—though not nearly as lengthy as Kyler's—straight and black, long enough to escape from under his cap.

Mariana, noticing Trust's attention suddenly diverted, turned to look as well. Just as quickly, she turned back.

"What? What is it?"

*Boy in red hat.*

There was a shift in the crowd as the spectators seemed to groan as one. Trust noticed the change and shot a quick glance back to the field.

UCC had just given up a solo home run to the opposing batter. The score was now 5-2.

Paxson nudged him. His gaze was still directed toward the seats.

"I see him," he said. "You thinking what I'm thinking?"

Trust looked up again. He had to search for a moment before his eyes locked on him once more.

The boy was situated a fair distance away from them and had taken off his hat, a knit cap of black and gold now on top of his head. But Trust could pick his face out now. And so, apparently, could Paxson.

Trust wrote quickly.

*He switched hats. Did you see that?*

"I saw it," Paxson said after reading Trust's comments. "I think he's got a book bag with him, but he's almost too far away, I can't really tell. It looked like he put the red hat in there and took the other one out. You think that's the guy?"

All three of them turned back around, facing the action on the field again. The batter currently up against UCC's pitcher was at a full count, three balls and two strikes, but was keeping his chance alive by consistently fouling off pitches.

"Who is he?" Mariana asked, leaning in closer. Trust could tell she was speaking in a softer tone, though it probably didn't matter much in the middle of a baseball stadium. "Do you know him?"

"Did Trust tell you about the robberies on campus?" Paxson asked.

Mariana nodded.

Then a quick jerk of her head caused Trust to follow, looking toward the field as well.

The baseball was rocketing toward the gap between the shortstop and third-base positions. Kyler, at shortstop, was fast to react, turning and accelerating quickly in the dirt infield. He slid into a half-kneel, scooping up the skirting ball backhanded.

Still sliding, he was able to rise again, Trust watching it all, seemingly in slow motion...

...the moment Kyler moved the ball from his glove to his throwing hand...

...the moment he turned toward first base, his arm stretching back...

...the moment said arm shot forward with tremendous force and concentrated power, the baseball leaving his hand in a blur, racing toward the other side of the infield at the time that the batter who made the hit was doing the same, both seeking the same place...

At first base, Trent's glove was outstretched, waiting.

The first-base umpire punched the air emphatically as the batter's cleat touched the base.

"Out!"

The baseball was already secure in Trent's glove.

Trust, Paxson, Mariana, and the rest of the Centre City supporters came to their feet and shouted their approval. The UCC fielders began to jog back to the dugout amidst the applause. When Trent caught up to Kyler, the larger player pulled playfully at the freshman's ball cap. As it covered his eyes, Trust could see both Trent and Kyler, along with the other players who saw, laughing.

"That was a nice one!" Mariana exclaimed, clapping as she glanced toward Trust. Earlier, Trust had learned that Mariana was quite familiar with the sport of baseball, and, unlike Allison, could not be tricked into applauding at inopportune moments.

Trust grinned at her.

*Happy Valentine's Day, courtesy of Kyler-Scott Brooks and the UCC Tigers baseball team.*

Mariana pushed him again before kissing him on the cheek.

A nudge from his opposite side again redirected his attention.

"Check this out," Paxson said. He motioned to his phone.

On the screen was a boy centered amid a horde of screaming Tigers fans. He wore a black and gold UCC knit cap, his facial features clear.

Trust looked at Paxson, his mouth hanging open in surprise. It then transformed into a laugh and a smile. He held up his hand for a high five, which Paxson reciprocated.

"You never know. It may come in handy," he said. "Happy Valentine's Day, courtesy of Paxson Haynes and his superb covert photography skills!"

He then leaned in, puckering his lips to kiss Trust on his other cheek, and Trust shoving his face away, grimacing and laughing at the same time. Mariana, hearing Paxson's words, reached around Trust to shove Paxson as well.

"And take that hat off!" she said.

The baseball stadium's public address announcer came across the speakers as a grinning University of Centre City face appeared on the video scoreboard over the outfield seats.

"And now...up to the plate...number two...number two...Kyler-Scott Brooks!"

## 37.
## A Legal Search

WITHOUT QUESTION, TRUST SHOULD HAVE thought of this sooner. Instead, he blamed it on the others, though he didn't actually tell them that.

Cortez burst out laughing. Trust, Kyler, and Allison swiftly attempted to shush him while glancing toward the professor's desk at the front of the lab room. However, as usual, Professor Reid appeared completely oblivious, his concentration fixated wholly on the computer screen in front of him.

"You've been carrying this picture around since February and you're only now getting around to trying to find out who this guy is?"

*Is he talking loud?* Trust motioned to Kyler. *Of course, I can't tell exactly, but he seems to be talking loud.*

"Usually, I say no to that question," Kyler inserted after interpreting for the others, "but this time, yes, I will admit, he is speaking a tad bit louder than is otherwise necessary."

"Hey, I've been to some of your games," Cortez said out of nowhere, looking to Kyler. "You're awesome, dude. You could probably be in the majors right now."

Kyler beamed.

"Thanks, dude," he replied. "You play?"

"When I can find a game," Cortez said. "And when I can find the time. I stopped playing formally after my sophomore year in high school on account of I'm really not as good as I think I am, but I always—"

"Look, *dudes*," Allison interrupted. "Can we get back to the topic at hand, please?"

*Technically, the topic at hand now is baseball,* Trust observed.

Allison shot him a look, her eyebrows raised.

"She's just now beginning to learn about the game," Kyler whispered to Cortez, loudly. "I think it bothers her when I talk too much about baseball because she can't really follow along as she would like."

"She's also been working on some projects here at the lab," Cortez said, turning to Allison. "A couple of setbacks, I'd guess, based on how irritable she's been lately. How's that Vip—"

"Okay!"

Trust was certain Allison's interjection was loud that time, and a fleeting glance toward Professor Reid further confirmed it, as the instructor glanced sidelong in their direction...and then returned to his computer.

*Was she loud?* Trust signed.

"Yes, I know I said that loudly," Allison said before Kyler even had the chance to interpret, "and yes, I may have run into some...impediments the last few weeks, but I refuse to succumb to the pressure and give them voice."

"That's my girlfriend!" Kyler whispered excitedly to Cortez, who grinned, nodding.

"Furthermore," Allison said, rounding on Trust, who backed away slightly, "*you're* the one who brought this whole idea up in the first place, and now you want to get distracted by the golden retellings of two eighteen-year-olds who sound like they're sixty-five?"

She adopted a deeper, lazy drawl.

"Oooh, dude, I used to play baseball my sophomore year—which was actually only two years ago, but I'm going to make it sound like it was thirty. Oooh, dude, you think I can play in the majors? Thanks, dude. Dude, dude, thanks."

"Wow," Kyler said, looking at Cortez. "She totally nailed you, man."

"Me?" Cortez said. "I thought she was doing you?"

Trust took his phone out and placed it on the table, pushing it over to Cortez. He then signaled for Kyler to translate.

"Allison's right," Kyler voiced verbatim. "We're through playing around here. I want answers, Cortez, and I want them right now. I want to know if you can give us the identity of this guy and a way to find him. Spill it; we don't have all day."

After Kyler finished relaying Trust's message, all three of them turned to the deaf boy.

Trust pointed to Allison.

*It's her fault. She got me riled up.*

"Trust wanted to know if there was a legal method you could use to find out that information from just a picture," Allison said, "and the first person I thought of was you."

"Aww," Cortez said, touching his chest. "Now that just tugs at the heartstrings. Where's this picture, anyway?"

Trust pointed to his phone again. Cortez picked it up.

"It's locked."

*Can you unlock it?*

Cortez smirked.

"Did you steal it?"

Trust shook his head emphatically before glancing to Professor Reid again.

*It's just a question. I want to know if you can do it.*

"Do what?" Cortez asked.

"Oh, come on, Cortez. Trust, just open your phone and bring up the photo."

Trust hurried to do Allison's bidding.

"Seriously, Allison," Kyler said, looking concerned. "Are you okay?"

"Yeah, you know I'm just joking, right?" Cortez said as Trust handed him the phone again. "You know I'll try to help you if I—wait, this is from a baseball game? Valentine's Day, you said?"

Trust nodded, his brows pulling together faintly.

"I was at this game! In fact...no, but if you had taken this a little wider, I would be in this picture. I remember seeing some of these guys on my row."

Allison came around to the other side of the table, next to Cortez. Kyler followed.

"Do you know any of them in the photo?" Allison asked.

Cortez shook his head.

"No. I went with a friend of mine, but neither of us is in this picture. Which one of these people are you trying to identify? The one in the UCC beanie here?"

He pointed to the screen and Allison nodded.

"Who took this picture?" Cortez asked. "It's pretty good. You can tell it's from distance, but he"—he glanced to Allison—"or she zoomed in nicely. It was the perfect moment to get that shot."

"Is there any way to run it through the university's photo database?" Allison asked. "I'm sure you're more familiar with the different methods than I am for digital matching. Perhaps this guy is in a university club or on a sports team, or in a picture in the newspaper or on the website."

"Why not just look through the student ID listing?" Cortez asked. "You'd have your answer in ten minutes. Maybe less."

*You can try it,* Trust signed, *but we need a name, and he could be unlisted. I'm not in that listing.*

"I'm talking about the full listing, where they issue the student ID cards for everyone—students, faculty, staff, administration. You're in that one for sure. We all are."

*Students don't have access to that, do they?*

"Heh."

Cortez chuckled.

"Authorized access, Cortez. Come on," Allison admonished. Cortez shrugged, smirking again. "We don't have much to go on—nothing, really—except he was wearing a red hat at one point and he matches the general description. But he may be totally uninvolved—"

"Red hat...oh, you're talking about the Dorm Room Robbers thing?"

He glanced to the picture again.

"You think this is the lookout kid they're talking about?"

"Depends on how common red hats are," Kyler said.

"I would say they're not completely *un*common," Cortez returned.

*Exactly,* Trust added. *That's why this is just an inquiry. But he does match the Asian male description, however vague it may be. If he's in some type of club or something, those pictures are public anyway, and we could learn more about him and track him down that way.*

"That'll take longer, you know. So, let me get this straight. You're willing to bypass the quicker method that would pretty much guarantee you identifying this guy, for the more time-intensive method that may not even come up with the answers you're looking for. Do I have that right?"

"Fantastic," Allison remarked. "So, you'll look into it, then?"

"My question was rhetorical," Cortez said. "That was my subtle attempt to persuade you into doing it the easier way."

"Your way is unauthorized for a reason, Cortez. Do you have any idea how much trouble you could get in if somebody caught you? And my 'So, you'll look into it, then?' question was rhetorical, too, by the way."

"Trouble? Since when are you guys worried about getting in trouble?"

Trust arched an eyebrow.

"What is that supposed to mean?" Allison questioned.

Cortez handed the phone back to Trust. He gave him his number.

"Send the photo to me. I can start going through the directories tonight. Hang on, my phone's on the other table."

As he left, both Kyler and Trust turned to Allison.

"He'll do it our way, don't worry," she said. "Going through the card identification database like he suggests would be quicker, but it would also be a lot more challenging to not get caught, not to mention the fact that it is restricted—the two main reasons he wants to do it that way in the first place. Searching through the open university listings won't provide as much of a challenge. He's kind of a technological daredevil in that regard."

*Sounds familiar,* Trust motioned, grinning.

"What are you saying?" Allison returned.

Trust's grin vanished.

Kyler came closer to Allison, putting his arm around her shoulder.

"I know I'm repeating myself here," he started, "and I know I'm repeating myself here, but are you sure everything's okay? Cortez is right—you have seemed a little off the past couple of weeks, but today in particular has been...weird. Something happened. Have you heard anything from Officer Ryan?"

Before Allison could respond, Cortez was back at the workstation.

"Argh, stop worrying about the police already," he said. "We'll do it your way. I've got the picture here and I'll send it to my computer to work on it in my dorm. The good thing is that I probably won't have any trouble sleeping while I'm working on this. I just hope I don't mess up my keyboard when my head slams down on it as a result of a mind-numbing coma."

"I just remembered you owe me anyway for helping you with that smart walking cane prototype," Allison said.

"What are you, twisting the knife?" Cortez moaned. "I said I would do it. And that wasn't even my project; that's Raul's. He owes you, not me. I was just the intermediary."

"You still owe me," Allison asserted.

"For what?"

"Don't worry. I'll think of something."
"Well, just put it on my tab, all right?"

# 38.
## The Party Before Spring Break

MORE DAYS PASSED. SPRING BREAK was swiftly approaching, a welcome reprieve during a period of the academic year when the burden of a collegiate-level course load began to weigh slightly heavier. Encumbered by repetitive monotony, the break would do much to alleviate additional strain before the push toward the end of the year.

Another helpful inclusion was a pre-Spring Break party.

"Tigresa says that me, Marcie, Trust, and Allison are all 'probably' headed toward the party on Decatur Lane," Paxson observed, reading off his phone as the group walked along the edge of the street under clear, bright skies toward the now infamous—to them, at least—manor. "I'm checking yours, too, Kyler, but I think it's safe to say that—oops, and I spoke too soon. It seems Kyler is already at the party on Decatur. I wonder how that's possible?"

*Probably somebody saw a girl with blond hair,* Trust signed. *It's an easy mistake to make. I do it all the time.*

Kyler gave his roommate a dubious look as the rest laughed.

The party was an all-day, all-night event, students coming and going as they pleased, food and drinks constantly replenished by trips to and from the store. As it was a Friday, the last school day before the break officially began, a number of students attending the party would leave Decatur Lane to catch a ride back to the UCC campuses for a class or two, only to return again later. Some classes had even been canceled, their instructors seemingly just as ready to begin their break as the students they taught. Trust, Allison, Paxson, and Marcie were not that fortunate, though their classes each had met and dismissed before lunchtime.

Kyler was one who did have a free day, and had—like the exemplary

447

college student—slept in.

"Oh, Trust, before I forget," Allison said, turning fully toward him. "I was wondering if you would be up for another go with the suit. I finally worked a few things out and I would like another field test."

The large house was less than a hundred yards away. There were many more people partying outside than had been present during the group's last visit, though it was indeed daytime on this occasion rather than night.

"Why does Trust always get to wear the suit?" Kyler complained, pouting like a child. "I want to wear the Viper Skin, too."

"Well," Allison began, "it's mainly because you—"

"Too handsome?" Kyler finished, batting his eyelids. "I know. I get that a lot."

"Uh, no. It's because you—"

"Wouldn't look good in all that black? Yeah, I think I would want one in...oooh! Black and red!"

"Uh, no. Again. It's because—"

*It's because she would have to make a completely different suit,* Trust commented, *specifically because of the measurements in the general groin area.*

Paxson let loose a humored snort.

"I know," Kyler said, smirking. "Yep, she would probably have to let it out a little bit more on my suit, on account of I'm so—"

"Delusional?" Marcie finished, glaring. "I mean...eww. Now, can we please change the subject before—nah-uh!"

Paxson, grinning and about to chime in with what was most likely an off-color joke, was stopped by his girlfriend's hand over his mouth.

"Nope! No more!" she said. "You missed it. It's over."

*It's no problem,* Trust directed to Allison. *You want me to wear it over the break?*

"No," Allison replied. "Just in case there's some type of malfunction or something goes wrong—which I don't expect, and no, you still won't be electrocuted. But just in case something happens that I want to look at, I don't want to have to wait until we get back from break to examine it.

"And," she said, turning to Kyler, Kyler automatically signing for Trust, since Allison's back was now to him, "Trust is actually right, to answer your question. At least, the first part was right. It has to fit exactly so, and that suit matches Trust. But the main reason—and what I was going to say—is that you can hear someone coming up behind you, and Trust can't. Trust is better able to rely on the indicators of the suit without being distracted by what he hears."

"Okay, and that's a perfectly good reason," Kyler admitted, "but don't let him fool you for a minute. Just because he may not be able to hear someone coming doesn't mean he's unaware of it. I'm sure you've noticed you've never really snuck up on him before. I haven't either, and I've had eighteen years to try to do it."

"You know what? I have noticed that," Paxson said, looking at Trust.

Trust pointed to his own eyes, and then aimed his fingers at Paxson menacingly. The message was clear, and the others laughed.

*But, I will admit, the Viper Skin does make things much, much easier,* he signed.

After making their way through the partiers at the front of the house, the party of five went inside. The front and back doors were open, making for a near seamless transition between outside and in. The interior was not as jam-packed as their last visit—the partiers now taking the opportunity to spread out along the grounds—though the count was still high.

With Paxson taking the lead, their first stop was the kitchen. It was predictable, as the smells from the party were in evidence as soon as they had stepped off the Centre Line at the end of the street.

"Holy guacamole!" Paxson exclaimed, the first to lay eyes on the impressive spread lining the countertop. "Am I dead? Between walking in the front door and walking into the kitchen, did I have some sort of painless heart attack and die and not know it, and now I'm in heaven? I'm serious!"

Desserts. On seemingly every available surface. Pies, cakes, cookies, tarts, more pies, and more cakes.

*Nope, you're still alive,* Trust signed, taking in the sight as well. *Though you'll probably keel over pretty soon if you're planning what I think, judging by the look in your eyes.*

"Aww, but Spring Break's pretty much started already for us," Allison defended. "Pax at least deserves a little treat. Don't you think, Marcie?"

Kyler waved down a passing student.

"Dude, you know where all of this dessert came from? Did somebody here make it?"

The boy squinted at Kyler before taking a gulp from the drink in his grasp.

"You mean, as opposed to it tumbling down from Dessert Heaven?"

He then laughed.

"Nah, man. For real, I think someone said it came from Hollins. Catered, you know the deal."

*And I know who probably made it then,* Trust remarked. *We're going to have to get a straitjacket for Pax once he takes a bite.*

"Too late," Marcie said, motioning over to the counter where Paxson already had a plate in his hands, eating—inhaling—a piece of cake with his fingers.

"Oh. My. God. Guys," he said, still eating and swallowing. "The answer to all of the world's problems is right here. Cancer? AIDS? Poverty? Fuhgeddaboudit. I'm never leaving this house again."

Through Paxson's chewing, Trust could barely make the words out, particularly the one that didn't seem like much of a word at all. His gaze then flicked to the side as he spotted someone passing the kitchen doorway on the far end, most likely heading for the rear of the house and the backyard beyond.

He turned back to look at Kyler, who was contemplating the dessert choices as well.

*I'll be around,* Trust signed.

"If you hear an ambulance coming down the street, don't worry," Kyler replied. "It's probably just me and Pax going in with a sugar overdose."

Trust was already pulling out his note cards as he navigated through the kitchen and the rest of the large Victorian residence, dodging around a small group huddled around the back entrance, and emerging into the open air of the covered patio. The floorboards were a pale blue, matching the trimming of the house. Numerous chairs and a few hammocks were arranged facing out into the wide, sunny yard, with only a few of them currently occupied. Many more people were out on the lawn, where more tables were set up and more food was ready to be eaten. The grills being attended to were smoking.

Trust noticed her back was turned toward him as she looked out into the yard, leaning against the white wooden patio railing. Knowing from feel alone that his movements were quiet, he moved toward her, arriving alongside and resting against the rail as well.

He didn't turn to look at her immediately, instead watching the activities in the yard. He did detect her looking in his direction, however.

Without looking, he handed her the card at the top of his stack. He had written it out beforehand on the off chance of seeing her at the party.

*We meet again. Back at the scene of the crime.*

Trust had not seen Jeremy yet. He had not spotted Rory or any of the others either.

Perhaps she was at the party alone?

He felt a light tap on his arm as Jezzie poked him with the card. He finally turned his head to look at her, grinning faintly.

"Scene of the crime?" she asked. "I seem to recall it being in the kitchen, although I was slightly buzzed at the time."

Trust took the card back.

*I meant the general location.*

"I know. I was just kidding."

*Glad to see you're not with the usual faces.*

He watched as her eyes flashed toward the yard, and then behind them on the patio.

"They're here," she said, leaning slightly closer to him, her head tilted down lower, though Trust could still read her speech. "Or, at least, they were. They've probably gone upstairs."

*Jeremy, too?*

"He's with them."

She was avoiding his eyes.

*I guess that means you still haven't told him.*

She glanced behind them again.

"Trust, you have to believe me. This...this thing isn't...I know it looks bad, but you don't understand—"

Trust looked away, writing on the card again.

*Looks bad? I don't understand? Don't forget that I WAS THERE. I SAW YOU. I saw Rory, and I saw those other guys. And you're letting Jeremy pal around with them like nothing happened. He would murder them on the spot if he knew, and I wouldn't blame him for it.*

But Jezzie was shaking her head.
"Trust, we can't do this here—"

*Keep your voice low, and keep leaning against the rail. No one will know what we're talking about.*

"No, you don't understand. Someone could see us and—"
Trust flipped to a fresh card, ready to write again, but Jezzie grabbed his hand, making him pause.

"Look at me," she said. "I'm saying someone could see me talking to you. I've heard Rory and the rest of them talk about you, more when Jeremy isn't around now that they think you two are friends. Even before that, they were talking about you. I don't know how high...you have to believe me, Trust. There's a lot about this that you don't understand—or me, for that matter—and what happened to me that night is the least of it. The fact that they know who you are and don't like you already is bad enough. You could get seriously, *seriously* hurt, Trust. You, Jeremy, your friends, anyone if you get too close to this, and that includes continuing to talk to me. Please."

Trust tapped his note cards against the wooden railing, pondering as he looked out into the lawn again, and the heavy woodland beyond that. A dark chuckle escaped from his throat.

*How many Free*

It wasn't difficult to perceive the shift in Jezzie's body as she turned to look over her shoulder again. Even easier to recognize was the sudden jerk that made him stop writing immediately. He tucked the cards back into his pocket as he slowly turned, already guessing at the individuals who would be there to greet him.

Rory's eyes, which had been aimed at Jezzie, shifted when Trust turned.

Trust surveyed the situation in a split second.

Five. No, six. No Jeremy. All faces he recognized. Rory. Three others from the alleyway.

And two from the woods along the walking trail between the Thomas Building and Mueller Hall. His eyes lingered on them before they returned to Rory, who was speaking.

"...just looking for you," he said, his gaze moving back to Jezzie but continuing to dart frequently, fleetingly, to Trust. "Jeremy was heading back out to the store for another run, so I wanted to check and see where you were and if you wanted to hang out upstairs with us. You know how boring it gets up there. You wanna go?"

Trust looked to Jezzie and watched as she shook her head, looking down slightly and avoiding Rory's gaze.

He had noticed the change in her mannerisms around the boy at the basketball tournament. It was the first time he had seen both of them together since that night in the alley. In the North Gym, during the tournament, it had been subtle, and completely nonverbal, as Trust had never gotten close enough to either of them for them to speak. From the seconds-long stretches of time that he peeked over at them before they left, it had been mostly intuition on his part.

Now, even with Rory's seemingly innocent remarks and Jezzie's once again unspoken response, the transformed dynamic was even more apparent.

Jezzie's bravado, her confident tone and demeanor when facing down Rory when he and Trust had first been formally introduced to each other so many months ago, was now gone. It was as though it had never been there in the first place.

Replacing it was a dynamic that had Trust fighting against himself for control. Yet, on the outside, he maintained an air of detachment. Almost disinterest. It had taken him years of practice to reach that point.

Rory tilted his head down, as though attempting to catch Jezzie's eyes again. The smirk—similar to Jeremy's, yet containing a touch of something else—graced his features under his backward-facing baseball cap.

"You sure?" he pressed. "You sure you don't want to come—oh, hey. Truth, right?"

He looked to Trust as though it were the first time he had noticed him, though both boys knew that it wasn't. The eyes of the boys surrounding Rory had never ventured away from Trust anyway.

Trust smiled faintly. He looked to Jezzie, and then pointed to the other boys behind Rory. Jezzie looked at him with a trace of uncertainty.

"What?" she asked. "You want to know their names?"

Rory took a step forward, waving Trust's inquiry away.

"Nah, he doesn't need to know 'em."

He then reached out to Jezzie, who started to shrink back. Trust quickly stepped in, holding his finger up, grinning. Rory's confident smirk diminished as Trust reached into his pocket for his cards again.

"Oh, you're about to write me a love letter or something? Thanks, man, but I don't play for that team."

The other boys laughed on cue. Rory's smirk returned. Trust's eyebrow arched.

Then he chuckled.

"Heh."

"Oh, snap. You can speak? Say something else."

"No."

Though he couldn't actually tell, Trust's voice was cool, calm, measured. Even.

It was somewhat unsettling, given how little he used it.

He showed what he had written to Jezzie.

*Step off the porch.*

Jezzie looked at him.

"What did he write?" Rory asked. "Let me see."

He tried to snatch the card out of Jezzie's grasp, but Trust was much quicker, the note back in his own pocket in the blink of an eye.

Rory glared at him, his jaw tensing, before he returned to Jezzie.

"Okay. Let's go up."

He reached for her again, but Jezzie backed away. She stepped down the set of wooden steps to the grass below.

"No," she said. "I'm fine out here. Thanks."

Rory frowned.

"What are you doing? What, you're scared of hi—"

Kyler exploded through the entryway, obviously excited.

"Hey, Trust, you've gotta come in and see this—"

As the attention shifted, Trust stepped off the porch as well. He could no longer see what Rory was saying, as the boy's back was now turned toward him.

"Hey, if it isn't Kyler-Scott Brooks...the Natural," Rory welcomed, beaming, his arms outstretched. "I didn't even know you were coming. Dude, I've seen you play. You're awesome at shortstop. And the way you swing the bat, it's—"

In the yard, Jezzie looked to Trust.

"That's your friend, right? Why did he call out to you? He knows you're deaf."

Trust grinned.

Kyler looked at Rory, a confused look on his face, before he broke out into a grin.

"Oh, yeah! Tristan! Right. We've met before, haven't we?"

Rory shook his head.

"Uh, no. And my name's not Tristan, it's—"

"Oh, right! Billy Thumpkins! How could I forget?"

"What? Dude, Kyler, we haven't met before. I was just saying—"

"Hey, what are you doing?" one of the other boys in Rory's group called out loudly, looking down to Trust and Jezzie. He started to move toward them, but apparently forgot about the steps as he quickly lost his footing, plunging face-first to the ground. But he got back to his feet almost immediately, breathing hard through his nostrils and advancing toward Trust.

Outside, every eye was now focused on them. Trust stepped away from Jezzie, the other boy turning with him.


ON THE PATIO, KYLER STARTED to step forward, but Rory's arm halted him. Kyler gave him a curious look.

"You know your friend's about to get embarrassed, right?" Kyler said. "I know you remember what happened at the gym."

Rory looked at the freshman, his brow furrowed, before he looked toward the other boys. They started to move toward the steps as well.

"Uhh..."

Kyler's voice stopped them.

"Seriously, guys. I wouldn't."

As one, they looked to Rory again.

"YOU STAY AWAY FROM JEZZIE!"

Trust was allowing the other boy to close the distance between them quickly.

The boy swung.

For Trust, it was almost amusingly slow, and he avoided the punch by stepping back seemingly before the boy had even decided to cock his fist. The boy lunged off-balance.

Trust immediately regretted the decision, however, as the boy was now between Trust and Jezzie. He turned toward the porch, about to sign, before the glimpse at more familiar faces made him change his mind.

"Hey!" Jeremy called, his face absolute fury. "Hey!"

The boy who had thrown the punch had regained his footing and was now reaching out for Jezzie's arm.

If he touched her at all, it was only fleetingly, before he was rudely shoved away by Jeremy.

"What are you doing?" Jeremy yelled. "Who the heck are you?"

Trust could tell Jeremy's voice was booming from the reactions of others as he glanced around. His eyes quickly returned to Jezzie, who rushed to restrain her boyfriend.

The other boy was backing away, his face hardened, though it was no match for Jeremy's expression, which seemed nearly murderous. The boy pointed to Trust.

"He was messing with Jezzie."

"You're lying. When I came through the door, I saw you throw a punch at him and then try to grab my girlfriend! What's your problem?"

"J, calm down, dude," Rory said from the porch. "Donnie's right. I saw the whole thing."

Trust rolled his eyes.

PAXSON WAS GIGGLING HYSTERICALLY AS he came through the open door to the back patio, followed by Marcie, Allison, and Holden.

"Oh—heh, heh—hey, Kyler. Dude, look—ha!—look who we just ran into. And, I mean that lit—heh, heh—like, literally—"

He paused as he finally became aware of the unusual amount of attention trained in his direction and the tense atmosphere enveloping the patio. He squinted and shook his head.

"Argh. What-what happened now?"

"Kyler?" Allison called, stepping up, a worried look coming across her face. "Kyler? Where's Trust?"

Kyler, already turned to her, his back to the yard, held his hands up in a placating manner.

"It's all right, everybody. Trust is fine. It's all under contr—"

"Holy crap!" someone shouted. "He just clocked him!"

Kyler quickly turned back around as the crowd on the porch rushed forward.


"JEREMY!" JEZZIE CRIED OUT.

Trust didn't hear the exclamation as he blocked Jeremy from the front, quickly pushing the older boy away from the fallen Donnie, who was now sprawled on the grass, holding his mouth. He also didn't see what Jeremy was screaming at the boy.

"Whatever it is you're smoking, knock it off! You're high, you're throwing punches at guys who could smash your face in, and you grab my girl after she already told you not to! You're lucky I'm not detaching your head from the rest of your body right now! Get off! Get off me!"

Trust could sense Jeremy fighting against him now and gave the star athlete a final shove, which put some distance between him and Jeremy just in case he decided to come after Trust. Trust held his hands up, palms facing out.

Jeremy growled in frustration, his movements agitated and keyed up as he paced in a small circle like an anxious bull waiting for the gate to rise. Jezzie ran over to him.

"What was that, Jeremy?" Rory yelled, still not having come down off the back porch, though some of his friends had already descended to go to Donnie.

The party, at least in the backyard, had ground to a halt.

"Dude, Donnie was trying to help you!" Rory went on. "You want to go agro on somebody, do it to him!"

His finger pointed to Trust.

"He's been trying to get with Jezzie behind your back, just like I told you. He's been badmouthing you to her this entire time."

Trust stared at Rory.

He raised his hand, beckoning for him to come out into the yard.

KYLER LEANED IN CLOSER TO Rory.

"Ignore him, dude," he warned. "Seriously, don't go down there. You see that little smile on his face? Believe me, that is *not* a good sign. Look, I know he's kinda making you look like a punk right now, but you've gotta stay smart and keep your head here, or risk losing it. Whatever he did to you before Winter Break, this would be a lot worse."

Rory jerked away at the last remark, turning to look at Kyler with widened eyes. Kyler shook his head quickly, giving Rory an appeasing look that seemed genuine. He leaned closer again.

"Don't worry, man; Trust didn't tell me. I don't think he told anyone. But you just did."

TRUST COULD SEE KYLER WHISPERING something into Rory's ear, but his head was turned away just enough to prevent Trust from reading the words.

Knowing Kyler, it was probably intentional.

Trust's eyes returned to the yard. Oliver had come down off the porch and was now speaking as he approached Jeremy. Trust moved so he could keep up with what was being said.

"...only met him a few times, and he seems cool. I don't think Trust is a guy who would do that. Anyway, I heard he's already got a girlfriend. An older chick, in the city."

Both Jeremy and Jezzie's eyes widened. So did Trust's. He glared at Oliver.

"Oh, dang, dude," Oliver said, spotting Trust's expression. "That's my bad. You're trying to keep your girl on the low?"

"Oliver, you idiot!" Rory called out. "What are you even talking about? You and I saw both him and Jezzie talking at the gym that one time—"

"Shut up, Rory!" Jezzie exploded. "Just shut up! Oh my God, you're such a freaking douche! You're trying to start trouble and you forgot I already told him about all of that after you squealed like a little—"

"Okay," Jeremy said abruptly. "We're leaving."

Before she could react, Jeremy picked Jezzie up as though she weighed next to nothing, slinging her over his shoulder.

He started to walk off, carrying Jezzie, but only managed a few steps before turning back to Donnie. The boy was back to standing, still accompanied by a few of the gang who had finally ventured down from the patio.

"It's Donnie, right?"

"Yeah."

"Listen. I really don't know you that well. Only seen you around a few times. Sorry for hitting you like that."

"It's cool, m—"

"Wait, I'm not finished. It's really not cool. Because if I hear you're even thinking about laying a finger on my girlfriend again, I'm going to rip your finger off and shove it so far up your—"

"Jeremy!"

Jezzie thumped him on the back.

"Right. Donnie, I'll catch you later, man. Trust, Ollie, you guys are with me, right?"


As Trust, Oliver, and Jeremy—with Jezzie still over his shoulder and trying to wiggle her way off him with zero success—departed around the outside of the house, Rory turned quickly to head back inside, seething.

But he stopped short as he spotted the two girls near the door.

One girl looked dressed for a rave, her dark hair fashioned in tiny pigtails across her head. She looked vaguely familiar, and the girl next to her more so...

His eyes lingered on the red-haired girl a bit longer than was necessary. Kyler clapped him on the shoulder as he made to move past him.

"Yes, pretty ladies, aren't they?" he said. "But hey, please don't tell me Trust is trying to come after them, too. Pax and I really can't fight that well, so we'd have no shot."

He looked back to see Rory smirking at him.

"Whatever you say, superstar."

Turning back, Kyler saw Allison was now the only one of their friends who remained, the rest having quickly passed through into the house en route to the front entrance to catch up with Trust and the others.

"Hey, you okay?" he asked.

It was an extra moment before Allison snapped out of her daze. She had been staring at Rory.

"We can come back and pick it up later before we head out," Jeremy replied, answering Jezzie's question about their car as he set her down on her feet again. "Right now, I just want to take a walk and get a little space."

He then turned to the others as they all ambled up the road.

"So, anyone know of another place to hang out that's not here?"

Trust. Kyler. Paxson. Marcie. Allison. Jeremy. Jezzie. Oliver. Holden. They walked the same street Trust and the others had traveled down just a short while before from the Centre Line bus stop at the end of the lane, now moving away from the sounds, smells, and commotion instead of toward it. The sun remained high in the sky in almost the exact same position as before, as though mocking their outing thus far.

At the question, most of the eyes went to Holden.

"Hey," he said, "I got nothin'. But, uh, are we going to just act like what happened back there didn't really happen? I mean, I can do it; I just want to be on the same page as everyone else."

"For now, let's just say it didn't happen," Jeremy said. "It's not about any of you guys anyway."

His eyes found Trust.

"Well, almost any of you."

"Hey, Trust," Paxson called. "What do you think Mariana's doing right now?"

"Mariana?" Oliver said. "Is that the older chick?"

The entire group turned to him.

"Man! That's two times in a row!" he said, rolling his head up to the sky in exasperation.

Trust typed a message into his phone, which was easier to write with when he was walking. He held it up for Paxson to read.

*I'll text her. Maybe she'll let us stop by.*

Paxson read it for the rest of the group.

"You keep saying it," Jeremy directed to Oliver. "How much older are we talking here?"

Jezzie hit him in the chest, causing Jeremy to smirk.

"Oh, you have no idea," Paxson responded before Oliver had the chance. "And she's *smoking* hot—ahh!"

Marcie gave Paxson a similar shot to the chest, and the others laughed at Paxson's reaction.

After Trust finished typing his message to Mariana, he dropped back. Kyler and Allison were at the rear of the troupe. Trust had seen them talking quietly to each other, seemingly engrossed in a private conversation, which was why he had typed his response to Paxson in the first place instead of interrupting his roommate's exchange.

But now, he was curious.

*Dude,* Trust signed as Kyler glanced to him.

"Keep acting like I'm not about to tell you anything important," Kyler said. He was grinning.

*Wow, is that smile phony. Is this the start of some joke?*

Kyler snickered.

"I don't want the others to pay attention to what I'm saying, so just act like I'm telling you a joke."

*Okay. I'll make sure not to laugh so they won't get suspicious.*

Kyler leaned in closer, wrapping his arm around Trust's shoulder.

"I know Rory was part of the group that assaulted Jezzie."

Trust laughed loudly. Fortunately, it was at the same moment someone else said something funny at the front of the group, so no one picked him out.

*Nice try,* Trust signed. *You think you can use that move on me? I taught you that move.*

"Yeah, but apparently Rory doesn't know that move."

Trust looked at him. Trust's smile had diminished somewhat, but was still present.

*Did you get a look at those other guys who were with him?*

"I'll assume that was rhetorical," Kyler remarked. "Were they there, too?"

*A couple of them. And you remember the guys I told you about the night after Allison was attacked? You just saw them, also. One of them is the guy Jeremy hit. You can't tell anyone about Rory yet—especially Jeremy. You saw how he reacts. That's one reason why Jezzie hasn't told him anything. She thinks he's capable of reacting in a way that would get him in serious trouble, not that he would care at all. And after seeing that back there, I agree with her.*

Kyler chuckled again, and Trust mirrored him. The others must have been laughing at something.

"That's why I'm debating with myself over telling you something else," Kyler said. "As much as you try to convince me—and yourself—that it wouldn't happen, you and Jeremy are a lot alike in that way."

*Jezzie has said the same thing. But I don't think you understand. She thinks Jeremy would kill Rory.*

"Like I said, you and Jeremy are a lot alike."

Trust's smile dipped.

"You've got to keep smiling, Trust, or I'm not going to tell you."

*What happened?*

Kyler snickered again and then stepped in front of Trust, walking backward as Trust moved forward, placing both his hands on Trust's shoulders.

*I'm not talking now, I'm just mouthing the words,* Kyler mimed. *This is the first time Allison has met Rory. She recognized his voice. The smile in his voice. Remember? It's him.*

Trust looked as though he didn't know whether he should smile or grimace. His mouth opened and closed repeatedly, as though he were obnoxiously chewing on a piece of gum that did not exist. He glanced over to Allison, who was now beside him after Kyler's move. Her face was inscrutable, though she stared back at him as they continued to walk.

"I'm okay," she murmured, seemingly knowing the question Trust wanted to ask her.

A squeeze from Kyler on Trust's shoulder brought his attention to the front again.

"How about you?" Kyler queried. "Are you okay?"

Trust felt his phone vibrate. It was Mariana.

> **Mariana (12:48 PM):** Do you have some sort of sandwich radar? Hollins Caf brought over some extra sandwiches, and it's not even Sandwich Day! And your friends are more than welcome to come. Remember our talk about taking advantage?

He showed the text to Kyler.

"Looks like we're headed to Centre Diamond, everybody!" he announced jovially to the rest of the group as they neared the end of the street. "They've got sandwiches from Hollins, and Trust is buying!"

Trust, however, did not see what Kyler said. He looked to Allison again, and then back the way they had come, the large house now quite small in the distance.

## 39.
## Text Conversations

THE CLOCK WAS TICKING, THE situation developing further, the pieces beginning to fall into place.

Friday night, after Trust and Kyler had returned home to the Outer Banks, Trust sent Jezzie his first message.

*Friday*

**Trust (9:48 PM):** This is Trust. I'm going to text tomorrow. It's time to let me in. And I think you know what I'm talking about.

**Jezzie (9:50 PM):** It's better and safer for everyone if I don't tell you. Please, you have to trust me.

**Trust (9:51 PM):** You have to trust me now. More girls have been attacked, and I'm not just referring to you. Other people are involved. This is going to end.

**Jezzie (9:51 PM):** Girls you know? Or like the rumors?

**Trust (9:52 PM):** The first one.

**Trust (9:53 PM):** Allison identified Rory by his voice. Her roommate was assaulted and put into the hospital as retribution for Allison cooperating with the police.

**Trust (9:55 PM):** And I found you in an alley. I looked Rory in the face.

## *Saturday*

**Trust (2:14 PM):** Happy Saturday.

**Trust (2:16 PM):** Five guys in the alley. One was Rory. Names of the other four. No one will know I got the names from you. I saw all of them. They will think I figured it out.

**Jezzie (2:17 PM):** I'm with Jeremy.

**Trust (2:17 PM):** I'll be texting him soon.

**Jezzie (2:17 PM):** Don't tell him.

**Jezzie (2:18 PM):** I'll do it.

**Trust (2:20 PM):** I wasn't going to tell him. But I do need to talk to him. Give me the names. First and last.

**Jezzie (2:21 PM):** Why do you need their names?

**Trust (2:21 PM):** Give them to me.

**Jezzie (2:23 PM):** Are you okay? You're scaring me a little.

**Trust (2:24 PM):** Good.

**Trust (2:24 PM):** The names.

She gave them to Trust three minutes later.

**Trust (2:29 PM):** Thank you. I'll send a gift basket in the mail.

## *Sunday*

**Trust (3:01 PM):** Is Jeremy reading over your shoulder? I can only imagine what he would think if he saw my name on your screen.

**Jezzie (3:03 PM):** No. I'm with my parents. What did you need those names for?

**Trust (3:05 PM):** Knew their faces, didn't know their names. It would be impolite if I saw them again. You ready?

**Jezzie (3:07 PM):** Didn't really understand first part. Ready for what?

**Trust (3:08 PM):** Tell me why those five guys raped you.

**Trust (3:09 PM):** Assume I'll understand.

Ten minutes went by with no response.

**Trust (3:20 PM):** Imagine me staring at the side of your face as you go about your day.
**Trust (3:21 PM):** That's what's happening right now.
**Jezzie (3:23 PM):** I wasn't ignoring you.
**Jezzie (3:24 PM):** What are you planning to do with this info?
**Trust (3:25 PM):** What would you want me to do? Ideally.
**Jezzie (3:28 PM):** Stay out of it. I know it seems bad, but there's a lot you don't know. They would come after you if you tried anything.
**Trust (3:29 PM):** They? Rory & Co.?
**Jezzie (3:31 PM):** They meaning UCC. The entire city. What if the entire city turned its back on you?
**Trust (3:36 PM):** I'll text you later.

**Trust (10:13 PM):** What about you? Would you turn your back on me?
**Jezzie (10:16 PM):** I probably wouldn't have much choice. Jeremy's here.
**Trust (10:18 PM):** What if Jeremy were asking you these questions? Would you turn your back on him?
**Jezzie (10:19 PM):** Jeremy wouldn't ask the questions, and he would probably get hurt because he didn't listen to the warnings.
**Jezzie (10:20 PM):** For the record, I wouldn't turn my back on either of you. But I don't think that would make much difference.
**Trust (10:23 PM):** You have no idea the difference it makes. Sweet dreams.

### *Monday*

**Trust (1:39 PM):** I'm going to text Jeremy later. When are you going to be with him? I'll text when you're around.
**Jezzie (1:45 PM):** Don't tell him! Trust, please! It would kill

him, and I don't know what he would do.

**Trust (1:48 PM):** You should delete that message you just sent. Without context, he could get a very different idea about you and me.

**Trust (1:49 PM):** But you know you're going to have to tell him. Soon.

**Jezzie (1:50 PM):** Why? If you don't, and I don't, he will never know. Those other guys won't say anything.

**Trust (1:54 PM):** Of course they will. Eventually.

**Jezzie (1:55 PM):** How do you know?

**Trust (1:57 PM):** I could be there when you tell him if that would make it easier for you.

**Jezzie (1:59 PM):** You should delete that. He could get the wrong idea about you and me.

**Jezzie (1:59 PM):** Or Mariana.

**Trust (2:00 PM):** You're funny.

**Trust (2:00 PM):** The Mariana part wasn't funny at all. But I was serious about being with you when you tell him. Maybe we could meet after break?

**Jezzie (2:01 PM):** It was even funnier given your reaction. Just you and I meet?

**Trust (2:02 PM):** And Jeremy. Get him to promise not to do anything in retaliation.

**Trust (2:03 PM):** At least, not yet

**Jezzie (2:05 PM):** It's cryptic stuff like that that makes me not want to tell you or him anything.

**Trust (2:08 PM):** Have you ever seen Jeremy in an actual fight? I've sparred with him; he could definitely hold his own.

**Jezzie (2:11 PM):** It amazes me how alike you two are. This isn't some bully you go beat up. You beat up Rory and the others, and they were back in class after a week.

**Trust (2:14 PM):** First, I didn't beat them up. Second, I know Rory's not the entire problem. That's why I'm trying to get you to tell me.

**Trust (2:15 PM):** Third, a week is a long time. And fourth, you never told me why they attacked you.

**Trust (2:15 PM):** Your answer is important to me. And think about the meeting with Jeremy for when we get back to CC.

Trust obtained Jeremy's phone number from Kyler.

**Trust (6:03 PM):** What's up. This is Trust.
**Jeremy (6:07 PM):** Total waste of a text, bro.

Trust smiled. Typical Jeremy Higgins.

**Jezzie (6:08 PM):** Jeremy just told me you texted him.
**Trust (6:09 PM):** What were you expecting?
**Jezzie (6:09 PM):** I really wonder about you sometimes...

*Tuesday*

**Trust (11:47 AM):** Hey.
**Jezzie (11:48 AM):** Uh oh.
**Trust (11:50 AM):** Excluding Rory, three of the five guys hanging around him at that Spring Break party were in the alley. Who were the other two?
**Trust (11:51 AM):** One of them was Donnie, who Jeremy wiped out.
**Jezzie (11:53 AM):** They're both freshmen. I know Donnie, and I think the other one is named John or Jim or something.
**Trust (11:55 AM):** Are they in Freesef?

No response.

**Trust (12:26 PM):** Here's what happens when you go quiet. I do what I want anyway, only without the info I'm asking for. Your not telling me is not going to change what comes next; it just makes everything messier.
**Jezzie (12:28 PM):** What you want? What comes next? Please, Trust, I don't want to see you or anyone else get hurt.
**Trust (12:31 PM):** What about you? You were hurt. Allison was hurt. Her roommate was hurt. I don't like seeing people hurt either. Take it from me, the fact that I haven't done

anything for this long is remarkable. It disturbs me.

**Trust (12:32 PM):** And I won't let it go on much longer.

**Trust (12:34 PM):** Are they in Freesef?

**Jezzie (12:37 PM):** Ugh...kind of. I think it's sort of a probationary thing with them.

**Trust (12:39 PM):** Are you in Freesef?

**Jezzie (12:42 PM):** It's complicated.

**Trust (12:44 PM):** Cool. Is Jeremy?

**Jezzie (12:46 PM):** No, but they want him in. Badly. He doesn't take them seriously, another reason I don't tell him any of this.

**Trust (12:47 PM):** Why do they want him?

**Jezzie (12:49 PM):** Prestige. He may decide to go into the NFL draft next year. Freesef doesn't need his money, but his name will bring a lot of attention. It already does.

**Trust (12:50 PM):** I was wondering why he didn't enter this year...

**Jezzie (12:52 PM):** We all know how cocky he can be, but he really doesn't like all the glitz. He just likes to play football, and he likes UCC.

**Trust (12:54 PM):** You mentioned his name means something.

**Jezzie (12:55 PM):** People know his name already, just from college ball. But there's other stuff, too.

**Trust (12:56 PM):** Such as?

**Jezzie (12:57 PM):** His dad, but I'm not going to go into it. Jeremy doesn't like to talk about it.

**Trust (12:59 PM):** One more question and I'll let it go. Is his dad in Freesef?

**Jezzie (1:02 PM):** Used to be.

**Trust (1:03 PM):** Why did Rory and the others come after you if you're in Freesef?

**Jezzie (1:05 PM):** My association is...involuntary. What you saw was a reminder, I guess. A warning.

**Jezzie (1:05 PM):** I have to go.

**Trust: (7:11 PM):** How's our girl doing?

**Jeremy (7:13 PM):** You've got to be kidding.

**Trust (7:14 PM):** I am. But I'm serious about my question. From what happened before Christmas. I've only seen her a few times in passing.

**Jeremy (7:18 PM):** Honestly, she's still off. Scared sometimes. Still won't tell me what happened. I assume there's still not

**Jeremy (7:19 PM):** any chance you would tell me.

**Trust (7:20 PM):** She made me promise. But if she said I could tell you, nothing would make me happier. Why do you think she's afraid to tell you?

**Jeremy (7:21 PM):** Afraid?

**Trust (7:22 PM):** What other reason is there?

**Jeremy (7:25 PM):** Never really thought about it like that. Just knew she wasn't telling me for some reason.

**Trust (7:27 PM):** What would you do if she told you?

**Jeremy (7:28 PM):** Do to them what they did to her. Eye for an eye and everything.

**Jeremy (7:28 PM):** And then kill them.

**Trust (7:30 PM):** Maybe that's why she doesn't tell you.

**Trust (7:31 PM):** Because she knows you would say that, and mean it.

**Jeremy (7:34 PM):** Look who's talking. According to that coat I got cleaned for you, you would probably do the same thing, and it's not even your girlfriend. Imagine if it was that hot Mariana chick from Centre Diamond.

**Jeremy (7:35 PM):** And anyway, I would still call the police after. You didn't, I'm guessing.

**Trust (7:37 PM):** Point taken. I didn't kill anyone, though.

**Jeremy (7:40 PM):** You were with Mariana. She stopped you, or Jezzie did. Jez is the only person that could stop me.

*Wednesday*

**Trust (1:00 PM):** Hope you're having a good day.

**Jezzie (1:02 PM):** You're like the voice of death, but without the voice. I almost dread seeing your name come up.

**Trust (1:04 PM):** Well, now I just feel fantastic.

**Trust (1:05 PM):** How do the bribes work?

**Jezzie (1:07 PM):** Bribes?

**Trust (1:08 PM):** To stop the girls from going to the police. Allison was sent two gifts and asked to stop talking to police before her roommate was attacked.

**Jezzie (1:09 PM):** I didn't know. Hold on.

**Jezzie (1:14 PM):** I don't know anything about bribes. You know this is from Freesef for sure?

**Trust (1:16 PM):** Not for the other girls. Just Allison. But it makes sense.

**Trust (1:17 PM):** When did you find out they were actually doing what the rumors said?

**Jezzie (1:17 PM):** I've never even heard bribes mentioned.

**Jezzie (1:18 PM):** I've known about other girls, but I can't say anything.

**Trust (1:18 PM):** Can't? Or won't?

**Jezzie (1:20 PM):** Can't. People will get hurt.

**Trust (1:21 PM):** Where would they get money for bribes? The dollar amount was pretty high for Allison.

**Jezzie (1:23 PM):** You're still thinking this is just a college group. It's not. That's what I'm trying to tell you. Freesef is not just some club. It's mostly adults, grown men. Powerful men.

**Jezzie (1:24 PM):** It's more a corporation. Would be easy to get money and bribes, I just don't know how or where specifically.

**Trust (1:25 PM):** Endeavor Group.

**Jezzie (1:26 PM):** Downtown? I've seen the building but don't know anything about it. Looks like a bank.

**Trust (1:28 PM):** Very personal question coming. Feel free not to answer.

**Jezzie (1:29 PM):** You'll just bug me until I do.

**Trust (1:30 PM):** Had you been sexually assaulted before that time in the alley?

**Trust (6:49 PM):** Fair enough. Thanks for answering all my other questions, though.

**Jezzie (7:00 PM):** Trust...

**Trust (7:41 PM):** Yo. How much do you know about the Freesef Society?

**Jeremy (7:44 PM):** What the heck, dude? Enough to know it's usually the start of some bad joke.

**Trust (7:46 PM):** But it's a real group, right? Real members?

**Jeremy (7:48 PM):** You're talking about those rumors?

**Jeremy (7:49 PM):** Girls tell that stuff to their friends. Gets them into special parties, etc.

**Trust (7:50 PM):** So the stories aren't real?

**Jeremy (7:52 PM):** Don't know. Don't care, really, since they're always bragging about it. Doubt they're real. Police would be involved.

**Trust (7:55 PM):** Allison, my friend you apologized to in Hollins that one time. She went to the police.

**Jeremy (7:57 PM):** They found who did it? Someone saying they were in Freesef?

**Trust (7:58 PM):** Not yet. Just my theory.

**Jeremy (8:00 PM):** Waste of time, man. Freesef's a bunch of try-hards. Trying to be a gang or something. Guy's I've heard it from are all idiots.

**Trust (8:05 PM):** There was a point where I thought you were in it.

**Jeremy (8:09 PM):** They wish.

*Thursday*

**Jezzie (7:28 AM):** I'll answer your question if you answer one of mine.

**Trust (7:30 AM):** What are you texting at the butt crack of dawn for?

**Jezzie (7:32 AM):** Gross! But I've seen you working out in the North Gym this early. I do, too, sometimes. But if you don't want my answer...

**Trust (7:32 AM):** Wait.

**Trust (7:34 AM):** Now, don't be so hasty. It's a deal,

473

although I feel like I already know the answer to my question, with all due respect.

**Jezzie (7:35 AM):** Fine. I'll just ask you my question then.

**Trust (7:36 AM):** Okay, what's your answer? You don't have to answer it, you know. I know it's personal.

**Jezzie (7:37 AM):** Your assumption is probably right.

**Jezzie (7:37 AM):** My freshman year.

**Jezzie (7:38 AM):** You're the first person I've told about that. Not my parents. Not Jeremy.

**Trust (7:40 AM):** Sorry you have something to tell. You know who?

**Jezzie (7:41 AM):** Not for sure. Masks. But I think Rory may have been one. Maybe upperclassmen who have graduated by now.

**Trust (7:43 AM):** Is saying I'm sorry even appropriate?

**Jezzie (7:43 AM):** Thanks. I understand the sentiment. Now, my question.

**Jezzie (7:44 AM):** You're planning something, aren't you? You're going to go after these guys I'm telling you about?

**Trust (7:46 AM):** These guys?

**Jezzie (7:48 AM):** You know exactly who I mean.

**Trust (7:50 AM):** Every single one of them.

**Jezzie (7:55 AM):** Is there anything I can say—anything I can do—to change your mind?

**Trust (8:00 AM):** This feeling you have every time you try to warn me off, why you don't want to tell Jeremy. I want them—Freesef, the guys who attacked you and other girls and have gotten away with it for so long—I want them to know what you're feeling.

**Trust (8:04 AM):** And I want them to know what I'm feeling. But if you can get them to apologize to you and everyone else, I'll be quiet. But I think we both know that won't happen.

**Trust (8:09 AM):** Did Rory or any of those other guys ever apologize to you?

**Trust (11:38 AM):** Remember these talks we have. And know that I would never turn my back on you.

**Jezzie (11:39 AM):** Do you talk to Mariana like this?

**Trust (11:41 AM):** No comment.

**Jezzie (11:42 AM):** So much like Jeremy...

**Trust (8:03 PM):** Any thought to meeting when we're back on campus?

**Jezzie (8:06 PM):** God, I don't think that's a good idea.

**Trust (8:09 PM):** I talked to Jeremy the other night. I didn't tell him anything, but I think he'll listen to you. Tell him that you don't want him to do anything rash, and he won't. But it has to come from you.

**Trust (8:10 PM):** I know that Jeremy Higgins is the big man on campus, but where you point, he goes. I noticed it from that first party at the beginning of the year. I'm sure you know it.

**Jezzie (8:12 PM):** Not for stuff like this. Not if I tell him what happened to me.

**Trust (8:13 PM):** Yes, for stuff like this. Get in his face like you did at that first party. When he sees you're serious, he will listen to every word you say.

**Trust (9:49 PM):** Why don't your friends like me?

**Jeremy (9:50 PM):** You can't be serious. Are you drunk right now?

**Trust (9:51 PM):** I'm just curious.

**Jeremy (9:53 PM):** The heck? Half the time, I'm not sure I like you. How would I know about them? Why would I care? And who said they were my friends?

**Jeremy (9:54 PM):** Just showed Jezzie your texts, by the way. She laughed.

**Trust (9:57 PM):** Oliver seems cool, but I don't think Rory ever liked me.

**Jeremy (9:59 PM):** Seriously, are you drunk? You sound so much like a girl right now it's not even funny.

**Jeremy (10:01 PM):** Ollie's cool peoples, though. Known him since middle school.

**Trust (10:02 PM):** How long have you known Rory?

**Jeremy (10:03 PM):** Met him at orientation my freshman year. He's all right. Annoying sometimes. Had a crush on Jezzie. You know, like you.

**Trust (10:06 PM):** That's funny. You sure Jezzie's the one he had a crush on, though?

**Jeremy (10:08 PM):** Knock that off, bro. Seriously. Creeping me out right now. That's like the second or third time you've said something like that.

**Trust (10:09 PM):** You're right. It's not good to talk behind someone's back like that.

**Jeremy (10:10 PM):** Dude, was that some kind of gay joke? I can't tell. Knock it off.

**Trust (10:12 PM):** Huh? Someone's paranoid. Sounds like you've heard those things about Rory before.

### *Friday*

**Jezzie (3:16 PM):** I've solved you. You have commitment issues.

**Trust (3:20 PM):** Ah, thy name is preemptive strike. No, see, how this goes is, I'll start off with something cute, and then immediately go into my Freesef questions while you're still off-balance.

**Jezzie (3:22 PM):** Aw, you think Mariana is cute! Jeremy has them, too, you know. Commitment issues.

**Trust (3:24 PM):** Yes, I am aware Jeremy is a guy. How many Freesef members are at UCC right now, would you say? Do you have meetings?

**Jezzie (3:25 PM):** Are you saying all guys naturally have commitment issues?

**Trust (3:27 PM):** I'm saying I think the phrase "commitment issues" was coined by a girl. Freesef...does Rory own a gun or a weapon of some kind?

**Jezzie (3:29 PM):** Trust, you're terrible.

**Trust (3:30 PM):** You're talking about the Rory part, right?

**Jezzie (3:30 PM):** Yes.

**Trust (3:31 PM):** Just checking.

Jezzie (3:32 PM): The other part was pretty bad, too, though.

Jezzie (4:58 PM): No more questions?
Trust (4:59 PM): About our meeting...
Jezzie (5:00 PM): Besides that.
Trust (5:00 PM): I'll wait until we're all face-to-face again.
Trust (5:02 PM): Stay safe. Don't do anything I would.
Jezzie (5:04 PM): Ha ha ha

*Saturday*

Jezzie (10:59 PM): Can you meet at Jeremy's Thursday at 8? I can send you the address again.
Trust (11:03 PM): Why so early?
Jezzie (11:04 PM): 8 PM.
Trust (11:05 PM): Oh. That does make more sense.
Jezzie (11:05 PM): Oh my God! You're ridiculous!
Trust (11:07 PM): I think you're doing the right thing, Jezzie. And I think you're going to be surprised how Jeremy responds.
Trust (11:08 PM): If not, I'll put him down nice and easy before he gets to the door. He won't feel a thing.
Jezzie (11:10 PM): Absolutely without a doubt the Worst. Joke. Ever.
Trust (11:11 PM): Ouch. I'll admit it wasn't the best, but really? Worst?

Jeremy (11:38 PM): You get a message from Jez?
Trust (11:39 PM): Yeah.
Jeremy (11:40 PM): You know what she wants to talk about?
Trust (11:41 PM): I have an idea.
Trust (11:42 PM): So do you, if you think about it.
Jeremy (11:43 PM): Before Winter Break?
Trust (11:45 PM): That's what I'm thinking.
Jeremy (11:47 PM): Serious question. Should I be worried?
Trust (11:48 PM): You afraid of a girl?
Jeremy (11:49 PM): Shut the hell up.

**Trust (11:51 PM):** You trust her?

**Jeremy (11:52 PM):** You serious?

**Trust (11:53 PM):** Answer the question.

**Jeremy (11:54 PM):** She's about the only one.

**Trust (11:55 PM):** Then listen to what she says.

**Trust (11:56 PM):** Wait. You don't trust me? That's my name.

**Jeremy (11:57 PM):** Not so much when you're around Jez. But that goes for most guys, so don't feel bad.

**Trust (11:58 PM):** But I see Mariana.

**Jeremy (11:58 PM):** Dude, she is SMOKING hot.

### *Sunday*

"THAT'S ODD."

Trust stilled his movements as he stood in front of the wooden man post, his hands halted in their positions in midair. Abraham Jeffries, Trust's grandfather, stood just behind the apparatus, facing him. The elderly man's hands were behind his back, as they had been since Trust started. His gaze was pensive.

"Keep going," Abraham directed.

Trust's eyes lingered on him a split second longer before he resumed, his hands and arms blurring through a series of moves as they impacted the post, never twice striking the exact same spot in the exact same way. The sensation of his hits against the old, sturdy wood was familiar. Even when he used the post with Kobe during their sessions in Centre City, the feel reminded him of exactly where he was right now.

Home.

"It's just odd that you think, after all this time, that you can pull one over on me. As though I wouldn't be able to read it on your face."

Trust, watching the lip movements just off his straight-line vision, paused again.

*What are you going on about, old—*

"Keep. Going."

Abraham arched his brow.

Trust huffed out of his nose and continued.

"I don't know exactly what you have planned in that mind of yours, but I can see you're ready to risk something. Your life, perhaps?"

Trust, still able to read his grandfather's mouth as he worked, flitted his eyes toward him, his hands continuing to execute the progressions.

"No, not your life," Abraham said, shifting slightly so he was now standing on the other side of the post, on the left instead of the right, Trust's eyes continuing to track him. "You don't think it will come to that. But still, there's something."

He was quick, stepping forward and catching Trust's hand before he could strike out again. Trust looked at him.

"There's eighteen years old," Abraham intoned, "and then there's eighteen years old. Understand what it is you feel you must do, and understand that which you are capable of doing right now."

He let go of Trust's fist.

*And what am I capable of doing right now?* Trust signed.

Abraham smiled.

"You tell me."

He then struck out, lightning quick.

Trust avoided the hit just in time.

## 40.
## Jezzie Speaks

BY THURSDAY, THE MECHANISMS AND routines of daily life at the University of Centre City were back in order for students and staff alike. And by Thursday night, Trust was making his final approach toward the Millennium Complex, Jeremy Higgins' luxury condominium building, after traversing the very short route from the closest Centre Line bus stop. The streets were alive, the sidewalk full of evening pedestrians, many of them students but just as many not, bustling.

He skipped up the outside staircase nimbly and went into the golden-trimmed doors.

A dramatic change. The inside was startlingly calm as compared to outdoors.

The lobby of the Millennium Complex was just as striking and impressive as any five-star hotel Trust had ever seen in a movie or advertisement, a cavernous, open space with what were most likely expensive paintings hanging on the walls, a grand staircase climbing up to the second floor and beyond, a bank of elevators to one side, and a tall, classy, elegant doorman waiting behind a desk. The way he was standing, Trust almost felt he was expected...

"Mr. Trustice Jeffries, I presume?"

Trust's steps slowed as he approached, seeing the doorman's mouth form his name.

The man, dressed in a neat uniform, smiled gently, his hands positioned behind his back.

"My name is Montague. Mr. Higgins told me I should be expecting you," he explained. "He gave a very general description, but I see that it was all that was necessary. Your blue eyes are simply mesmerizing. Right this way, if you please."

Trust, already uncomfortable with the extreme deference the man was showing, glanced around the lobby again, making sure no one else was there to witness the scene. He then trailed after toward the elevators, which also appeared coated in gold. The doorman glanced to him again.

"Mr. Higgins is on the eighteenth floor. I will need to swipe a card to allow you access."

The elevator doors opened. Trust stepped in.

The doorman leaned in, as he had probably done so many times before, deftly swiping a card that Trust didn't even notice him retrieve, and keying in the eighteenth floor.

"You are very quiet," Montague remarked, stepping out of the path of the doors.

Trust's brow furrowed. He began to reach into his pocket, but the porter held up his hand as the doors started to close.

"Only a joke, Mr. Jeffries. Only a joke."

Thirty seconds later, the door opened to Jeremy's condo and Trust was beckoned in. He revealed to Jeremy what he had written in the elevator on the way up.

*Should I start calling you Your Royal Highness now?*

Jeremy shook his head.

"Seriously, don't mention it again," he said.

Trust immediately noted the cleanliness of the large front foyer, the hallway, the kitchen he passed by on the way to a dining area. Lines and angles were straight, the décor a pleasing blend of modern and classic, everything in its place.

Nothing like how one would expect a single male to live.

A college-aged single male.

A college-aged single male athlete.

*Nice digs.*

"Yeah?" Jeremy said. "Well, get your own."

Trust chuckled faintly.

Jezzie, waiting in the dining room, directed Trust toward a seat at the glass dining table. Jezzie and Jeremy then took seats on the other side. It was as though Jezzie knew to give Trust the easiest vantage point to see both their faces.

Trust noticed that it was also a great position in case Jeremy decided to bolt from his chair, though he wasn't sure if such a scenario went into her thinking at all.

"This is my parents' doing," Jeremy said in explanation. "I don't know...I was in the dorms my first year. It was actually pretty good. I liked it."

*So, what's stopping you from going back?*

Jeremy scratched at the scruff along his jaw before glancing to Jezzie beside him.

"I told you," she declared simply.

"Jesus Christ," Jeremy said, rolling his eyes. "Can we just get started now, finally? We had this meeting scheduled like it's the G8 Summit and nobody's telling me what it's about. It makes me nervous. I try to avoid that feeling if at all possible."

"Well, if it makes you feel any better," Jezzie said, her shoulders drooping slightly as she looked down, "I'm a little nervous, too."

"No. Actually, that makes me feel a tad bit worse," Jeremy said. "But thanks for the effort."

Trust sat back in his chair, his hands in his lap, his elbows resting on the armrests. His eyes shifted between the two across from him. Jeremy met his gaze.

"Man, those eyes are bluer than I remember," he commented. "You wear contacts?"

Trust looked to Jezzie and arched an eyebrow.

"Okay, so before I start, you have to promise me you're not going to do anything," Jezzie said.

Jeremy continued looking at Trust before he realized Jezzie had directed her words to—

"Me? What are you talking about?"

"Promise me," Jezzie said again.

"This about what happened to you before Christmas? 'Cause Trust already told me—"

Jezzie whipped her head in Trust's direction, her eyes suddenly widened.

"Tru—"

Trust shook his head.

"Wait," Jeremy said in a cautionary tone, holding up his hand. "What I was going to say was that Trust told me that's what you might want to talk about. He said you made him promise not to tell me anything, and he hasn't, despite multiple attempts by me to persuade him to do otherwise."

"Good," Jezzie remarked. "And now you're going to promise me."

Jeremy gave a nervous chuckle.

"Oh, come on already. Can we just get on—"

He stopped and watched Trust scribble in his notebook.

*What would you do if she told you?*

It was the same question Trust had raised during Spring Break, and it took a few moments for Jeremy to remember. He looked up, pushing the notebook back across the table before Jezzie could read it.

"That?" he said. "I was just kidding."

Trust looked at him for a moment, and then shook his head softly, his lips pursed.

*Apparently, there are a few people who think we're a lot alike in some ways. You called me out on what I might have done in that alley if Mariana wasn't there. I can show Jezzie the conversation. She will be able to tell if you were kidding or not.*

Jeremy flexed his jaw, seemingly a stress-relieving movement, as he eyed Trust again.

Trust remained unaffected. He glanced down to his phone in his other hand, the correct display already open. He then returned to his notebook one more time.

*You were with Mariana. She stopped you, or Jezzie did. Jez is the only person who could stop me.*

After giving him time to read, Trust motioned for the book again. He pointed to Jezzie before scribbling,

*She's stopping you now.*

Jeremy's eyes slowly rose from the words to Trust's calm face, his head still tilted slightly down, delivering a classic under-look.

After a moment, he nodded.

Trust stayed for nearly two hours.

# 41.
# Dolphin

THE WEEK FOLLOWING PASSED QUIETLY. Jeremy was keeping his promise to Jezzie by apparently staying as far away from Rory and the rest Jezzie had identified as much as possible. When they did interact, the exchange was stilted and fleeting.

According to Jezzie, Rory assumed Jeremy was still miffed about the events at the party just before Spring Break.

For his part, Trust had managed to avoid Rory and his friends as well, although that was easier for him to do, since he did not regularly cross paths with them anyway.

On Friday, a week and a day after the sit-down in Jeremy's condo, Trust was on the way to Centre Diamond. Even with the typical Friday night ambiance and festivities, the crew of freshmen that were coming with him were there for something different.

"Yo, A-Rock," Jayson said when the other bouncer showed up to the front entrance where Trust, Kyler, and the others were waiting, again separated from the long line queued to get into the club. "Take these guys to the second-floor conference room. Boss is expecting them."

Paxson was on his phone as they entered the club. Kyler interpreted his words for Trust, since he was looking down.

"Whether they're slowing down or not," Paxson was saying, continuing their conversation from the walk down to the club, "another robbery today means they've found a way around the new rules. Even with everyone looking out for them now, the Dorm Room Robbers are able to get through. And I still think we're all sitting ducks with this Tigresa app still online—there it is. Everyone on is going to know Kyler and Trust aren't currently in their rooms, but are in fact on the Green

Centre Line."

"Your stalkers are slacking," Marcie observed. "No one knows they're at Centre Diamond yet?"

*Patriots Hall may be slacking, too,* Trust signed. *And that's the new dorm. I don't think those robbers are going to be able to get anything out of Weaver anytime soon. Amanda has eagle eyes; she's taking the honorary title of Robber Catcher very seriously. Holden may have created a monster.*

"Has Cortez found anything on the boy in the red hat?" Kyler asked Allison.

She shook her head.

"I haven't had a chance to see him this week, but last I heard, he was coming up empty on the UCC website search, so he's opened it up to all university media platforms. Who knows how long that will take to sift through."

"And that's assuming we're not tracking the wrong guy anyway," Paxson added.

Having not ventured into the main club area, the group of freshmen were ushered into a room with a long table and chairs all around. It actually did have the appearance of a smaller-sized boardroom, not necessarily a setting one expected to find in a downtown nightclub. As they filed in, Trust turned to see A-Rock holding a finger to his ear.

"Boss'll be in in a minute," A-Rock told them. "Anybody need anything in the meantime?"

"Ye—"

"Anything non-alcoholic," he interrupted, looking at Kyler.

Kyler sat back in his plush office seat. He looked like someone who had stumbled across the CEO's chair and was now taking full advantage while the executive wasn't looking.

Paxson raised his hand.

"Do we have to call Mariana 'boss,' too? Or is that just for you guys?"

Laughing, Paxson and Kyler gave each other high fives. Marcie and Allison rolled their eyes.

"First off," A-Rock said, smirking, "this isn't a classroom, so you don't have to raise your hand."

"Oooh," Trust said, laughing and pointing. Allison and Marcie snickered.

"Second," A-Rock went on, "no, you don't call her boss. Well…"

His attention shifted to Trust.

"At least, the rest of you don't."

The room was silent. Trust looked at the large man.

Then came the guffaws.

It was now Trust's turn to roll his eyes.

*Why is everyone laughing so hard? It wasn't even that funny.*

"Not even a little bit?" Paxson questioned, still laughing, as A-Rock departed the room, shaking his head and smiling, pulling the door closed behind him.

Trust's expression illustrated his displeasure.

*I don't even understand what he meant by that.*

"Don't understand?" Kyler repeated after interpreting for the others, who were still chuckling as well. "Maybe this'll help. Wuh-psssh! Totally whipped, dude!"

He made the whipping motion with his hand. Trust arched an eyebrow.

*This, coming from the guy who still forgets how to speak every time a certain redhead kisses him.*

"...every time a certain redhead kisses—now that," Kyler said, interrupting himself and inducing another fit of giggles from Paxson, "that, sir, is not entirely accurate."

Trust turned to Paxson.

*And don't even get me started on you. Where's your sparkly hat?*

Paxson's chuckles died off fast.

"Aww, don't worry, boys," Marcie cooed. "Just because what Trust is saying is completely true, it doesn't mean you're completely emasculated or anything."

Trust leaned back in his chair, glancing under the conference table.

"What are you looking for?" Allison asked when his head popped up again.

*My masculinity,* he signed. *I swear I had it when I walked in...*

Trust then spotted the blinking lights on the phone in the middle of the table at the same time as the others heard its ring.

"Pax, the phone's ringing," Kyler announced.

"Really?" Paxson replied. "What gave it away?"

*Put it on speaker,* Trust signed.

"While I like your optimism, T," Kyler said, "I really don't think that's going to help you—"

Trust stood quickly, leaning over the table. Kyler stood as well, reaching out to stop him, but Trust was too quick. He tapped the phone display.

"No-hey!" Kyler greeted, suddenly displaying a smile but looking around at everyone in worry. "This is the Centre Diamond lounge and nightclub located in downtown Centre City. How may I direct your call?"

Trust's eyes flitted around the table. Everyone seemed to be waiting, holding their breath for the caller's reply.

There was a chuckle.

"You're not Pax, so I'm going to guess this is Kyler."

Paxson's face broke out into a grin as Kyler interpreted the words to Trust.

"Dolphin! Man, for some reason, I was so not expecting to hear *your* voice."

"Whose voice were you expecting, bro?" Randolph "Dolphin" Haynes replied. "The Easter Bunny? Since you're on the phone, too, I'm assuming I did in fact call the correct number at the correct time. Who's there with you?"

Marcie leaned forward in her chair.

"Hi, Dolph. This is Marcie. You're on speaker, so we can all hear you."

"It's always a relief to hear your voice, Marcie. Is our boy staying out of trouble in the big city?"

Marcie smirked, glancing toward Paxson.

"You know I rule with an iron fist to keep him in line," she declared.

"Sounds about right," Dolphin replied.

"Kyler-Scott Brooks, at your service, Captain Haynes," Kyler said next. "If you need any help on SEAL Team Six, just let me know. Pax has my number. He can give it to you."

"Well, I'm not a captain," Dolphin said, "SEAL Team Six is the Navy, which I'm not in, and from what my brother's told me about you, you would be either really, really good, or really, *really* terrible as a soldier, so nice to meet you, Kyler-Scott Brooks with a hyphen. I'll be sure to get your number from Pax later. Much later."

"This is Allison. Sorry, I really don't have anything funny to say, but thank you for your service, Mr. Haynes."

"Mr. Haynes? Pax, did you put Dad on this call, too? Call me Dolphin, or Randolph—either one, or any variation therein that you prefer. And it sounds like I should be thanking you for *your* service. Keeping tabs with that Kyler-Scott Brooks character should win you some sort of—oh, wait. Am I still on speaker? Can Kyler hear this?"

Kyler nodded slightly toward Trust, and the deaf teenager leaned forward.

"My name is Trust."

There was a pause. The others in the room looked toward him in astonishment, with Kyler grinning. He gave a thumbs-up.

"Ha," Dolphin chuckled. "That's funny. You're pulling my leg right now. Pax, who is that really?"

Paxson was still looking at Trust, astonishment painting his features.

"I'm just as surprised as you are, bro, although I really shouldn't be. Why do I always forget you can speak, Trust?"

*Probably because Kyler won't shut up,* Trust signed, and Kyler translated aloud.

Dolphin laughed.

"Well, Trust. I am honored that you have chosen to grace me with your voice. From what I hear from Pax, it doesn't happen often, for understandable reasons. I look forward to your questions—to everyone's questions."

*If everyone had that sort of response to my voice, I would try to talk more often,* Trust motioned. *It's such a pain to learn and practice, though.*

"You really should," Marcie intoned. "You have a fantastic voice. It actually gives me chills when I hear it."

Paxson glanced at her, his eyebrow arched.

"What the—"

He was interrupted by someone entering the conference room. Trust turned to look as he saw the others' attention diverted.

"Sorry, guys," Mariana said, hurrying in. "I got held up with a late shipment. They said they directed Dolphin's call up here. Did I miss him?"

Trust had to make the conscious decision to stop staring.

"Yep, you just missed me and Marcie drooling over Trust's voice," Dolphin explained jokingly.

Trust had to turn again as he noticed everyone once more looking at Mariana behind him.

She met his glance and smirked slyly.

"Oh, believe me, I am aware of his voice," she said.

This time, turning away was impossible. Mariana arched an eyebrow, still smirking. She then started to move, Trust following her with his eyes.

He watched as she spoke and then took a seat at the head of the table. Eventually, he was able to drag his attention back to the others as the conversation progressed along a casual thread, Dolphin entertaining them all with a few exploits that he explained "may or may not have happened." Trust could detect the similarity in humor between the two Haynes brothers, along with their ability to draw an audience into a story, even with one brother absent from the room. The fraternal camaraderie was clear.

But, judging by the way Kyler translated, complete with the general conveyance of Dolphin's vocal expression, the older brother possessed a certain glint of...something that Trust had thus far not seen from Paxson. Actually, he had met only a few people in a while that possessed a similar air.

Allison's Uncle Smith was one of them.

So was Kobe, the martial arts instructor.

And so was Jeremy Higgins.

Randolph Haynes was about to exhibit it again.

"So, Trust," Dolphin remarked, Kyler interpreting, "are we going to get into that stuff you wanted to talk about? Now is as good a time as any."

Trust nodded, looking at Kyler.

"He says he's ready," Kyler relayed.

"Before we start, then, I'd like to speak to Mariana alone."

Mariana smiled from her chair, looking around the table.

"Oh, is this the part where you guys kick me out? Just because I work here, don't forget that I was a UCC student a very short time ago—shorter than you, Randolph Haynes."

Nevertheless, Paxson motioned for them to leave Mariana alone, standing. Trust was somewhat confused, and he could tell that the others were the same, though Paxson seemed to know what was going—

"What's going on?" Mariana questioned, a crease of worry coming across her face. "Seriously, I was just joking. I can leave if—"

Kyler interpreted Dolphin's response for Trust even as they filtered out of the room.

492

*No. It's okay. You're fine. This has to do with you, actually. I just have to ask you something about what they want to ask me about...*

Trust turned his head quickly, his eyes wide as he caught just a glimpse of Mariana before Paxson pulled the door closed.

She was looking back at him.

Now, the group of them were huddled together in the hallway.

"Dolphin knows what we want to talk about," Paxson explained, "and he had mentioned he wanted to talk to Mariana about something before—"

*It's her.*

Trust rubbed his face before smacking himself on the head repeatedly.

*How the heck did I miss it? I should have known from the way she acted when I visited—*

"Wait, Trust. Calm down," Marcie said, placing a hand on his arm. "What do you mean, 'It's her'? What are you talking about?"

*It's her. It's Mariana. She's the girl in Oliver's story. Mariana's the one who Dolphin's friend saved.*

Marcie, Paxson, Kyler, and Allison all stared at Trust, before turning to look at each other.

"He's asking if it's all right to tell us what happened," Allison filled in. "She's like me, and the police probably never caught the guys who attacked her."

Trust stepped between Kyler and Paxson, reaching and pushing the door open before anyone could raise an objection. Bursting into the room again, he swiftly turned, heading for Mariana.

He saw the anguish in her face as she sat in the chair, listening to whatever Dolphin was saying. She glanced up with watery eyes at Trust's sudden entrance, and then stood as Trust rushed over.

"Trust, I—"

He did not get to see the rest of what she said as he quickly advanced, swiftly cradling her face in his hands, and, pushing her chair away with his foot, kissing her as he pinned her against the far wall. Her hesitation was only fleeting before she melted into the kiss, her lips moving in sync with his, her hands clutching and gripping at his shirt-sleeves.

After a moment, he slowly, slowly inched back. He reached into his back pocket, retrieving his spare note cards.

*I'm sorry. I should have realized it sooner. We don't have to
talk about this now.*

Mariana shook her head. Tears had begun to trail down her cheeks,
but she brushed them away, smiling faintly.

"No, you shouldn't have realized anything," she murmured, Trust
still standing close and looking down to her lips. "And, except for that
time at lunch, I've gotten pretty good at hiding it. But you shouldn't be
sorry. I'm sorry I didn't have the courage to tell you then."

Trust cupped her chin with his fingers, tilting her head up to meet
his eyes again. He then directed her gaze to one portion of the note card.

*I'm sorry.*

Mariana smiled, her eyes welling up again, and kissed him.

At the door, Kyler called to Dolphin, "Hang on a minute, Mr.
Lieutenant Dolphin, sir. We're having some technical difficulties on our
end, but we'll be back with you shortly."

"They're kissing, aren't they?" Dolphin said. "Jeez, this phone is
sensitive."

DOLPHIN AND MARIANA TOLD THEIR story. Kyler sat quietly, gripping
Allison's hand as she then told the account of her assault in November, of
the bribes, and the attack on her roommate, Melody. It was the first time
Trust and the others actually heard the full account.

The group had also learned that Dolphin was not simply friends with
the person who saved Mariana.

Dolphin was the one who had saved her.

The room was silent.

Trust looked up as Kyler signed again, interpreting Dolphin's words.

"I'm interested to hear how Trust feels about all of this."

Trust leaned back in his seat, tapping his fingers on the tabletop.

He then sat forward again.

*I was in a conversation similar to this last week. In Jeremy Higgins'
condo.*

Everyone's eyes got slightly wider at the news. At the time, Trust had not told anyone where he was going.

"This is Kyler again," Kyler directed to the phone. "I don't know what kind of news you guys get at CIA headquarters, but Jeremy Higgins is, like, *the* star athlete at this school. Heck, he was up for the Heisman this year."

"I see you're once again fishing for a location, Kyler, and once again, you've come up empty," Dolphin replied. "But let's just say I get my Centre City news just fine. I definitely know who Jeremy Higgins is, but I also hear the Tigers have some hotshot freshman shortstop on their baseball team. His name escapes me at the moment..."

*Jeremy's girlfriend was sexually assaulted just before the start of our Winter Break by members of this same group we're talking about—this Freesef Society. We know that one for certain, and perhaps even more, were also involved in Allison's attack. There may be an overlap with Melody's attack as well.*

"You're talking about Jezzie?" Marcie asked. "She told you she was attacked by Freesef?"

*She didn't have to tell me. I was there.*

He glanced to his left.

*Mariana was there, too.*

"The blood on your shirt," Paxson recalled. "You came back from that thing, that dinner you had, with blood on your shirt. I'm hoping that was..."

*Some other guy's.*

Paxson leaned back in his seat as well, exhaling deeply.

"Holy..."

"Sorry to cut in, Trust," Dolphin said. "Mariana, you were there when this happened?"

"Yeah," Mariana began, "but I wasn't...I didn't...Trust sent me back here, to the club, to get my car. We were around the block. I think he saw we would need it to get her out of there fast. The girl was in pretty bad shape—worse than I was when you found me. She was high on something, or drugged, or just really, really drunk. When I got back to the alley with my car, it was already over."

"What happened to the guys?" Dolphin asked.

*We got away,* Trust replied.

"How many were there?"

*I think we're losing the focus of the topic—*

"Mariana?" Dolphin interrupted.

"I—"

*Look,* Trust signed again. *You were one against six when you found Mariana. I know where you're going with this, but with all due respect, I—*

"While I appreciate the respect," Dolphin cut in again, "if you know where I'm going with this, then you know I'm going to get there whether you avoid answering my questions or not. Mariana, how many guys?"

*Don't answer,* Trust signed quickly, looking at her.

"There's a reason why I joined the military, Trust," Dolphin said, "and even if Mariana had a change of heart and wanted to tell others what happened to us that day, there's a reason why I still would be reluctant to have that information out there."

"Wait, wait," Paxson said, holding up his hand. "You two seem to have climbed to another level in this conversation, and now I'm confused."

"Kyler," Dolphin called, "you've known Trust a long time, right? Known him since forever, right? My guess on how many guys were in that alley is at least five, but you tell me—what is the highest number of guys you've seen Trust ready to face off against at one time?"

Kyler's mind immediately flitted to the near-brawl he had broken up on the first day he and Trust encountered Jeremy, Rory, and all their merry friends. Trust was gazing at him.

"You know what?" Dolphin said. "You don't even have to answer that. But please, let me ask this. Did you think, even for one second, that Trust was overmatched? Did you think he was in trouble?"

There was a moment's silence.

"There were five of them," Mariana said quietly.

"And they couldn't move when Trust was through with them," Dolphin finished. "Just like the guys who attacked you, Mariana."

Paxson shook his head.

"But I still don't—"

"Kyler," Dolphin said, "have you ever seen Trust get into a fight and you thought he went too far?"

Reading Kyler's translation, Trust's entire body tensed, his arm flexing on the table, his hand balled into a tight fist.

"Trust, listen," Dolphin said. "We've never met, and I don't know what Pax or Marcie or Mariana has told you about me, if anything. But

Pax has told me a little about you and the other friends he has in that room through our emails and phone calls. Normal conversations.

"He tells me you want to ask me some questions about the Freesef Society, and I ask him to tell me more about you. 'I know he's your friend, which means he's probably cool, but I need to know more about this Trust kid.' The little incident Pax told me from the start of the school year about some drunk in Centre Diamond—seemingly arbitrary at first—begins to make more sense.

"I'm not saying this is true for you, but I had a bit of a problem with my temper growing up. Some would say I still do at times. I was a good kid, don't get me wrong, but I got into more than my fair share of fights. Pax has seen some of them—some of them were *over* him. I've been arrested; I've been to jail. I joined the military—aside from wanting to do it—to hopefully prevent something worse from happening.

"From what little I know and have heard about you, and from this talk we've had so far, I can tell where you're going, because it's the exact same place I would go. You've faced down groups of guys ready to smash your head in without blinking, completely and utterly unafraid, because you know you're capable and you know how it's going to play out—it's just a matter of being able to control yourself and stop yourself from going too far. I don't know your background—Pax has mentioned 'kung fu stuff,' which I take to mean martial arts training—which means you're already light years ahead of where I was at your age in terms of learning how to channel that kind of energy. I wasn't sure how to do it, but I knew I needed to and I knew I couldn't do it on my own, hence the Army. I'm sure you've met people with that...darkness about them, that same energy that you have. So have I. The military's littered with them if you know where to look.

"All I'm saying is, I understand where your head is at, but tread very carefully. It sounds like you guys have dug into this Freesef thing more than I or anyone else ever even thought of doing. But now is the time to be smart, and to be super careful. Listen to the people in that room with you, Trust. I know I can't talk you out of anything you're thinking about doing concerning this—no one would be able to tell me anything either, and that's not necessarily a bad thing. But watch your step."

A few minutes later, the call ended, Mariana tapping a section on the phone console's interface before sitting back in her seat again. The small conference room was again quiet, the silence stretching. Eventually, all eyes drifted to Trust, whose head now rested on the table over folded arms, his brow furrowed, his gaze directed downward as he contemplated Dolphin's words.

## 42.
## Dorm Room Robbers

**Cortez (6:13 PM):** I got him!

The text came from Cortez a few hours before, along with a name and address.

The boy in the red hat. Perhaps *the* boy in the red hat.

"Now, are you absolutely sure you're okay with this?" Kyler asked, looking at Allison, who was sitting in the seat beside Trust on the Centre Line bus. "We can go to Plan B. If you're in any way uncomfortable with this, we can just scrap it and—"

"Are you sure *you're* okay with this?" Allison shot back, a smirk present on her lips. "I've been fine with this plan. You seem much more worried about it than I do. What, you think I can't pull it off?"

"No," said Kyler, "it's not that I don't think you can pull it off. I definitely think you can pull it off. It's just that—"

*Wait a minute,* Trust signed. *We have a Plan B? Nobody told me about a Plan B.*

Their destination was close, as the address Cortez had given them from a separate UCC directory—accessible to anyone, he had reminded them—after matching the face to a name was not far from the rural campus. Twilight was falling, the sky outside the bus windows cast in purples, pinks, and navy blues that ordinarily came with the sun's departure below the horizon. Inside the bus, the lights were on and shining.

"Plan B is the improvisation plan," Kyler told him. "'B' stands for 'Improvise.'"

Trust glanced to his seat neighbor.

*Uh, Allison, can you bring up a dictionary on your phone? Because, and correct me if I'm wrong, but I don't believe improvise starts with a—*

Kyler stuck a hand in his loosely hanging hair, burrowing it deeply.

"Argh, yes. Improvise doesn't start with a 'B,' hence the improvisational name of the plan. They also tell me x and y can add up to five, so I think we all have a right to make up our own rules with letters."

Trust, sitting sideways on his seat so he was able to see both Allison and Kyler without much effort, gazed at Kyler now.

*Are you sure you're okay with this?*

Kyler waved his concern away.

"My girlfriend's about to play the femme fatale to a possible criminal to try to get some information that he will be unlikely to part with so easily. Piece of cake."

The boy then watched as Trust signed a reply. Kyler interpreted aloud.

"You sound a little...jealous."

He then huffed.

"Nothing could be further from the truth," he said.

Allison made a face.

"What was that?" she asked.

*You mean the part where he practically jumped out of his seat after telling that gigantic lie?* Trust signed. *That, dear Allison, is called a tell. It's why I've always said he's terrible at lying to people he knows, and why he typically doesn't do it that often. Acting, good. Lying, terrible.*

"And moving on..." Kyler intoned.

"If it really bothers you that much," Allison said, "you can try flirting with him instead of me. You really are quite pretty."

"Oh, you think so?" Kyler said in a girlish tone, primping his hair. "Gee, I don't know—not funny!"

Allison and Trust laughed.

The bus rolled to a stop, the PA announcement and electronic scroll lining the bus's interior expressing the need for passengers to—as always—watch their step while disembarking. As the trio got off, Trust observed the address on a nearby mailbox, indicating that they were only a few houses down from their intended location. Seemingly as soon as Kyler's shoe touched the pavement, the rear exit doors of the Centre Line hissed closed, the bus soon rumbling quietly down the same street they were about to walk.

Not within the downtown limits of Centre City, the street, and the houses along both sides, looked almost suburban in appearance, as though quaint families dwelled inside each residence, most likely sitting down to after-dinner activities, if the present time was any indication.

However, that imagined scene was most unlikely, as the entire neighborhood, including the houses, was only intended to look so innocently residential. In fact, every single house along the street accommodated groups of renting college students. Occasional streetlights gave evidence to tidied front lawns.

*You go ahead,* Trust signed to Allison. *We'll hang back and try to get a look through the windows. When you're done, just head back here to the bus stop. We'll meet you.*

"And don't try to be a hero," Kyler said.

Allison grinned and pecked him on the cheek. The two boys let her get a head start before skulking across the lawns of the neighboring houses.

Both behaved as though such covert activities were not entirely unfamiliar to them.

Trust nudged his friend as they moved.

*Dude.*

Kyler seemed to know what Trust was referring to.

*Shut up*, Kyler signed back simply, silently.

Due to their swift movement across shadow-cast lawns in an effort to avoid incidental eyes peeking out of windows, the two boys arrived at the designated house before Allison did, positioning themselves just along the edge of the address with a clear view of the front entrance. Allison didn't look their way; it was hard to tell if she was even aware of their location at that point.

She rang the doorbell, and then casually glanced back toward the quiet street.

The door to 1374 Waldorf Avenue South opened, the illumination from inside cutting into the relative darkness not lit by the streetlamps outdoors. Trust peered through a side window, while Kyler remained at the corner, glancing around to the front.

Trust's vantage point looked through a kitchen and dining space into a central hallway and foyer, with what appeared to be a living room on the opposite side. The boy at the front door was clothed as though he were not expecting to go anywhere anytime soon—barefoot, with shorts and a T-shirt. His hair was longish, black and straight, and he was clean-shaven, though Trust could only observe him in profile at the moment as he talked with Allison, who was hidden from his view. Trust could not tell what the boy was saying.

Nevertheless, he was the boy from Paxson's picture. The boy they were looking for.

The red hat perched loosely atop his head was now only a final but unnecessary hint as to his identity.

The boy—Cortez had given his name as Idela—stepped back slightly and turned to the window as he let Allison inside. Trust slowly backed away in an attempt to avoid attracting attention with quick movements, stepping deeper into the shadow. Still, he maintained his view.

Now, which way were they going to go...into the kitchen...toward a back room...or into the...

*Other side,* Trust motioned quickly, his eyes following Allison's and Idela's movements, but knowing that Kyler was now watching him for their next course of action. *Other side. They're going to the living room.*

Kyler went around the front, while Trust went toward the rear of the house. Peeks into the other windows revealed no other housemates currently at home. Either Idela lived alone—which would be a steep monthly rent payment in this neighborhood—or his housemates were out.

*Could you hear what they were saying?* Trust asked Kyler when the two met on the other side of the house. They now stood away from the wall, back in the darkness where shine from the windows did not extend. The adjacent house behind them was dark and had blinds pulled closed.

*Dude, she totally just sweet-talked her way inside with a bunch of phony baloney,* Kyler replied, both he and Trust glancing fleetingly back and forth into the window. *You have to tell me if she ever does that to me.*

*If?* Trust signed. *You act as though it hasn't already happened.*

THEY WATCHED ALLISON AND IDELA for a few minutes before the boy rose from the couch again. Trust, able to read their lips clearly, had been relaying the conversation to Kyler, for once serving as his best friend's interpreter instead of the other way around.

*Stay with her,* Trust signed, nodding faintly toward the window. *I'm going to follow him.*

He then trotted toward the back of the house again, where Idela had disappeared to when he had turned left to walk down the hallway. Behind his tinted shades, Trust's eyes constantly shifted, always taking in his surroundings. The airborne particles floated lazily in the otherwise still air, disturbed only by his own movements. He turned the corner, keeping an acceptable berth with the wall, and stopped at the first dark window along the rear.

A text from Allison.

**Allison (8:26 PM):** Going somewhere. I think it's where the stolen items are.

Apparently, the light coming in from the hallway was all that was needed, as Idela sat on a bed in the darkness of the room, putting on his shoes. Trust watched as the boy reached for a jacket on the back of his desk chair, but he stopped short, turning toward his bed again. From outside, Trust could see the synchronized flashing that, for him, lit up the room.

For Idela, it was simply the flicker of a ringing cell phone.

The phone was turned away as Idela looked at it. Trust would have been able to read the screen otherwise. However, he didn't need to.

Another subtle vibration coming from his pocket.

**Kyler (8:28 PM):** Car pulling in.

The text from Kyler had Trust moving farther away from the window, edging toward the corner of the house again while still maintaining an eye into the dark room. Idela now had the phone up to his ear, talking.

Trust's eyes shifted slightly.

Kyler had also backed farther away from Idela's house and dropped into a crouch in the grass. Trust could distinguish the additional illumination coming from the car at the front of the house, though, aimed straight ahead, the cone of light did not reach Kyler's position along the side.

Trust's eyes shifted again.

Idela was leaving the bedroom, jacket in hand.

Trust went to his phone again, finding a name and sending off a quick message. He snuck back to Kyler.

Through the window, Idela had returned to the archway of the living room and was now motioning for Allison to follow him as he turned to the front door.

*We're going to lose her,* Kyler said. *I think this car is here to pick Idela up. Should I call someone? A taxi?*

*Wait a minute,* Trust returned, glancing into the window again. *I'm working on it.*

Allison and Idela had arrived at the door, Idela waiting courteously as Allison passed through. Trust and Kyler moved, now hugging the outer wall of the residence again as they peeked around...

An incoming text. Trust looked down.

> **Mr. Jackson (8:30 PM):** What a coincidence! I'm in that area, 3 min out. Good enough?

Trust responded.

> **Trust (8:30 PM):** Perfect.

Kyler nudged him.

*They're arguing,* he signed. *This new guy's mad our boy told Allison about the warehouse.*

Trust looked around the edge of the house again.

*That's the kid I saw in the Thomas Building.*

With innocent eyes and lingering touches that could be interpreted as either inadvertent or flirtatious, Allison was helping to steer the argument between the two boys in her favor.

*Dude, who the heck is that girl?* Kyler signed. *And what has she done with Allison Tyler? She's going to have them both eating out of her hand in thirty seconds. What about our ride?*

*He's coming,* Trust replied. *I just hope he doesn't show up while these guys are still here, though.*

Exactly thirty-two seconds later, Allison was getting into the backseat of the car, the boy Trust had first spotted still behind the wheel and Idela riding shotgun. They started to back out of the driveway.

"Can you believe this?" Kyler whispered, a hint of excitement in his voice. "She just infiltrated a criminal theft ring in, like, three minutes!"

The two boys slowly came out of their hiding spot as the car drove down the street. Trust had noted Allison leaning forward onto the backrests of the seats in front, laughing at something that was said.

*Well, she did say she could do it,* Trust observed.

"The plan was to see if this Idela kid was the Boy in the Red Hat and to see if we could get any information about the stolen stuff from him. She just convinced them to take her to their lair quicker than it took to actually get here!"

*I guess she's persuasive.*

Trust was surveying the street in both directions. The car Allison was in had turned a corner and was now out of sight.

"Now what?" Kyler asked. "We've lost Allison, and we don't have any way of finding her, and we don't have a ride out of here. Man...I knew we should have gone with Plan B."

*I think we're already in Plan B.*

Trust turned again. This time, his eyes locked on to a weak but rapidly growing diffusion of light that pierced through the air above the road, signaling an approaching vehicle currently out of sight around the corner. The displacement of said particles followed, the vehicle coming closer still.

*This may be our ride now,* Trust signed. Kyler came closer, following his gaze.

A few more moments...the light becoming brighter, the trillions of minuscule specks and particles in the air becoming more agitated, swirled and pushed about...

A long, sleek black limousine skidded around the corner, hardly slowing down as it turned but never weaving into the opposite lane. The sequence looked like something out of an action movie. Trust could feel the low rumble of acceleration as the limo approached the address, before decelerating and stopping smoothly, as though the vehicle had only been moving at ten miles an hour instead of much, much more than that on an otherwise quiet residential road.

A swift glance to Kyler found the boy with his mouth hanging open limply.

The driver leaped out of the limo.

"What's going on? Is everything all right? I got here as quick as I—

*what are you doing here?"*

Had Trust been able to hear, he would have heard Kyler ask the exact same question at the exact same time.

But he couldn't, and he was a moment late in turning to look at the boy beside him.

*You remember Mr. Jackson?* Trust asked.

"Remember him? It seems like I'm on one of his routes every week. I'm surprised you remember him. He's the driver who slammed on the brakes that one time and I fell out of my seat."

"One time?" Mr. Jackson said in disbelief. "What are you, eighteen years old and you're already going senile? It's happened a lot more than one time, and it wouldn't happen at all if you actually sat in a seat!"

"Senile?" Kyler shot back. "Well...you're bald!"

He then looked to Trust.

"How do you know his name is Mr. Jackson?" he asked.

*He was the driver in that bus holdup.*

Kyler's eyes widened as he looked from his deaf friend to the limousine-slash-bus driver.

"What's the emergency, Trust?" asked Mr. Jackson. "You want a quick getaway from the boy who parades around in a girl's wig?"

"Girl's wig?" Kyler echoed incredulously, pointing to his head. "This is one hundred percent—"

*We're wasting time,* Trust interrupted. He looked to Kyler, pointing to the driver. *Tell him that we have to go after Allison.*

"Well, let's go!" Mr. Jackson said. "Is she in trouble? All I need is an address, and you can fill me in on the way."

The boys started to hurry to the limo.

"Great," Kyler said. "An address—the one thing we don't have."

Reaching the rear door of the stretch limo, Trust tossed his phone across the roof of the vehicle to Mr. Jackson.

*Just follow the indicator.*

"Just follow the indicator..." Kyler relayed automatically. "Wait. Just follow the indicator?"

But Trust had already climbed into the limo.

THE LIMOUSINE TURNED ANOTHER STREET corner at an astonishing rate of speed, lightly pulling the passengers inside but still under the expert control of Reuben Jackson, before accelerating again as it came onto the entrance ramp to the expressway.

"It looks like they're heading uptown," Mr. Jackson called through the partition.

"What kind of limousine is this?" Kyler called back, righting himself in his seat again. Trust was situated on the bench seat facing him, though, with his seat belt fastened, he appeared quite composed. "This isn't like the limo we rode in to prom in high school. This feels like a race car!"

"Consider yourself lucky," Mr. Jackson said, "'cause not only is this not the limousine you or anyone else will ever take to prom, but this is probably also the last time you'll ever ride in one of these unless you're elected to public office, and I'm not talking about the mayor of Centre City, either."

Trust and Kyler glanced toward each other, leaning to the side as Mr. Jackson weaved through the evening traffic.

"What?" Kyler cried. "This is a *presidential limousine*?"

"Of course not!" Mr. Jackson returned. "I haven't installed all of the add-ons for the Secret Service yet. I was actually just out test-driving it when you texted me, Trust. And, with this little adventure we're on now, I think I can skip the usual road course tonight. She's handling like a dream."

*So, you're a bus driver who test-drives presidential limousines in his off time?* Trust signed, Kyler voicing aloud.

"Something like that," the driver said, "though, technically, I don't know if this would be considered off time, since I'm still getting paid...a lot. Your friend got off on the Debussy exit. I wonder if they're headed for the industrial district."

"First, I learn that my girlfriend is a secret agent and a tactical mastermind who planned for us—well, at least, *you,* Trust—to follow the GPS tracker on her phone. Then I learn that the bus driver who's as witty as a potato is rolling in dough from his side job as a presidential limousine builder. Do I have that right? Please, anyone, feel free to speak up."

The traffic scenery through the tinted limo windows zoomed by in a shimmering interstate blur. They had to be moving at well over the posted speed limit.

"I don't know anything about the first part," Mr. Jackson replied, "but the part about me is full of assumptions. About the only thing you got right is that I take on side jobs. And your face looks like a potato."

*How fast are we going?* Trust asked before Kyler could respond to the driver's words. *Why haven't we been pulled over yet?*

"Because I, Trust and Kyler, am a professional. And I taught every cop in this city how to drive. Another side job. Seriously, don't try this stuff at home."

"YOU'VE GOT TWENTY MINUTES BEFORE I call the police," Mr. Jackson said through the front window, both Trust and Kyler leaning in, Trust to see, Kyler to hear. "One second over and my finger's on the nine. I don't care if you're breaking bread in there or not."

Trust signed.

"You sure you want to stay?" asked Kyler, translating. "You can just point us to the nearest bus stop and we'll be good to go."

"Look," Mr. Jackson said, "you two are lucky I'm not calling the police right now, so don't push it. If these guys have actually been stealing from university dorm rooms all year, I'd much rather have the Centre City police on the scene instead of three college students, even if you know what you're doing."

His gaze was directed at Trust.

"You've got twenty minutes."

Allison's GPS indicator had led them to what Mr. Jackson described as an "abandoned industrial yard", acreage filled with leftover equipment, alongside empty buildings most likely waiting for repair and restoration.

The place seemed entirely uninhabited.

The tracker was so exact it could pinpoint a specific location amidst the abandoned buildings, toward one in the near distance from where Trust had instructed Mr. Jackson to drop them off, dousing his lights lest he alert anyone in the vicinity.

After advising the driver to wait somewhere that would not be so easily stumbled across by any other arriving vehicles, Trust and Kyler started to run toward their objective. Sporadically functioning lights only faintly aided the pale shine of the moon, casting shallow, faded off-white streaks across the ground and long-empty containers before being swallowed up by deep, wide swaths of shadow. Kyler was only able to hear their quick, fleeting footfalls and short bursts of breath as they hurried, the rest of the area silent.

They stopped at the nearest container to the building they were looking for.

*Another day at the office,* Trust signed, regulating his breathing. *You do that thing you do and try to find the circuit breakers, and then I'm in. It will probably be best if you and Allison are in a corner or standing along the wall or something. Watch out for guns. And don't do anything stupid like trying to hit someone; you have a game tomorrow night.*

Kyler rolled his eyes.

*All I need is five minutes to find Allison and the breakers. And you've known me for eighteen years. When have I ever voluntarily punched someone?*

*Well, I don't want you starting now,* Trust signed.

Kyler started to turn away, but Trust grabbed his shirt at the last moment.

*And keep an eye out for Perry's stuff. Maybe we can get it back to him.*

A FEW COLLEGE-AGED BOYS were lingering near the first table just inside the large warehouse doors. They glanced up, surprised, when Kyler hurried in, huffing as though out of breath.

"I just..."

He bent at the knees, wheezing.

"I just got the call...boss said get over here quick...what the heck did you guys do?"

"What?" one of the boys replied, looking at Kyler quizzically, a cell phone in his hand. "Who are you? Why are you breathing so hard?"

"Freakin' cigs," Kyler replied, standing upright once more, his hands on his hips, still attempting to gain control of his breathing. "Feels like I've run five miles in this humidity. Boss said there was an outage out here, something going haywire with the electrical. I saw some of those lights off in the yard. Wait, what are you guys standing around for? Where is everybody? You know the truck is coming in tonight, right?"

"Truck?" another of them said, his cut of red hair contrasting drastically with his pale skin. "Pierce said we weren't loading until tomorrow night."

Kyler was already moving farther into the building, glancing around.

"Shipment schedule got moved up. That's what I'm trying to tell you. I'm here to make sure nothin' goes offline while you're loading. That's already good to go?"

He was pointing to the large black van parked inside at the other end of the building—the same black van he and Paxson had sighted at the Thomas Building during the attempted robbery. It was backed up to one table, its rear loading doors open.

The warehouse itself was filled, tables lining the hard floor in long rows, every available inch of space and surface covered with what Kyler assumed was all stolen merchandise, sorted by product, brand name, and size. The amount visible was enough to stock a busy electronics store for a year.

However, it seemed far too much just to have been taken from the UCC thefts alone. Apparently, this was a much larger operation.

The huddle of boys was trailing Kyler as he walked purposefully down one of the rows.

"Yeah," the first boy with the phone said. "We just finished unloading the van a few minutes...Wait, but there's a shipment going out tonight? Do we even have enough people for that?"

Kyler stopped and turned. A fantastic assortment of portable music players lay on the table alongside him. He gave the boy who had spoken a skeptical look.

"How many people are we going to need?" he questioned. "We're not sending out a shipment to supply—hey, who's she?"

The other boys turned, following his point.

Allison had just emerged from a corner room, along with Idela, the boy who had driven them to the warehouse, and a few others he didn't recognize.

The boy with the phone turned back to Kyler and shrugged.

"Someone's girl, probably. Who care—"

"Hey! Idela!"

Kyler moved past the group that had been following him, returning up the aisle they were on. The others continued to tag along.

Allison and the gang around her turned at Kyler's shout. Kyler saw

Allison's eyes widen for an instant when she spotted him.

"Idela, who the heck is this? Is she with you? Dude, you can't just bring random people in here! You tryin' to get us caught?"

Idela looked at him, frowning.

"This is Pierce's girlfriend. She's supposed to meet him up here, so we thought we would just give her a ride and save her the trouble...Hey, aren't you on the baseball—"

"What?" Kyler interrupted. He then scoffed, walking briskly past Idela, Allison, and the others, moving toward the door of the office they had just come out of.

"You talking about that Brooks kid? Please! I get that all the time. Kyler-Scott Brooks wishes he could look like me on his best day on *my* worst day. And can someone *please* point me toward the circuit breakers in this place? I haven't been in here for months and now I'm all turned around. And what's everyone still standing around for like we don't have a truck coming in here in a few hours? I mean, seriously, is this how Pierce runs this place?"

One from the group of boys Kyler had first encountered glanced to the others, at last jumping into action.

"All right, you heard 'em, guys. We got an early shipment going out tonight, so let's get this stuff packed up and ready to go. Pierce can break it down further when he gets here."

He then looked to Kyler.

"The breakers are in the last office on the end. Don't electrocute yourself in there."

Kyler was already moving toward the indicated room but twisted around, now walking backward.

"Please," he returned. "You should have seen what I had to deal with last week. My hair was out to freakin' here."

He held his hands out. The final set of eyes he met were Allison's, and he lingered ever so slightly on her before turning and trotting away. Many of the others present had already started working, moving down the various packed aisles.

Allison turned to Idela, putting on an adorable smile.

"I want to watch and see if that guy *does* electrocute himself," she said. "He doesn't look like he really knows what he's doing. Tell Pierce where I am when he gets here, 'kay?"

Idela couldn't help but grin himself.

"Sure thing. But hey, don't touch that guy. If he gets shocked, you will, too."

Allison smiled again, touching the boy on the arm faintly, lightly, before departing the same way Kyler had gone.

Idela looked to the boy who had driven them in, smirking.

"Holy crap, dude. That chick is, like, an eleven, and she's totally into me."

"Yeah, and Pierce'll totally be into your face with that gun he always carries around if he catches you smiling at her like that," the other boy warned.

THERE WERE NEW ARRIVALS AT the warehouse a few minutes later. A man—a guess at his age would have put him somewhere approaching thirty—was laughing at something that was said by another who came in with him. The commotion from the work that greeted them was unexpected.

"Yeah? Well, you can tell Skeeter and whoever else what I said, and then he can go jump off a—yo, what's going on in here?"

Idela, sorting through a pile of new smart watches on an aisle close to the doors, glanced up.

"Yo, P. The electrical guy that you sent told us about the early shipment tonight. None of us knew about it. Oh, and your girl is here, back in the room."

Pierce was tall and lean, dressed in high-end street gear, which had always served as an unmentioned recruiting tool when hiring young local help for these types of long-term assignments. His youthful features lent the impression that he was not so far removed from his own college years, and with the light scruff on his face, along with a pristine ball cap that was seemingly always present, he was able to convincingly toe the line between cool and criminally experienced. The two characteristics attracted those looking to make fast, easy money—such as a number of the university students in Centre City—while still commanding a cautious respect.

He was part of the group, but, at the same time, he would always remain above it.

"What?" Pierce declared, stopping and giving Idela a strange look.

"There's no shipment going out tonight."

Idela's eyebrow arched as he glanced over to the corner room.

"Uh, but didn't you send some guy to look at the circuit break—"

The door to the office opened, voices emerging, drawing their attention. Kyler appeared first.

"All right, everyone. I'm about to run through a diagnostic check on the lights in here to make sure there aren't any prob—"

"Hey! Hey!" Pierce exclaimed, taking a step forward, his right hand already inching up to his waist. "Who the hell are you? I don't remember ever hiring you. How'd you get in here?"

"Me? Who the heck are you, man? Pierce told me to—"

Pierce pulled the gun out of his waistband. Kyler immediately put his hands in the air.

"I am Pierce. You want to try that again? Actually, just forget it. How about I just shoot you right now and save—"

"Hey, that's Kyler-Scott Brooks!" another college-aged boy spoke up just behind Pierce. "He's on the baseball team. Cortez sent me to hit his room, but—"

"But I got back early and almost caught you, you little turd," Kyler finished. "You didn't think I would remember your face, did ya? But here I am—"

"Hey! Kylie!" Pierce shouted.

Kyler frowned, his arms still raised.

"What, you really think I'm playing with you, kid? You think this is a game? You think I won't end you right now?"

He took another step forward. Kyler, his hands still up, remained silent.

Pierce took another step.

"Oh, yeah. You shut up real quick now, huh? So here's how this is gonna go. I can shoot you—"

"Anytime, please, Allison," Kyler called loudly. "You can shut the lights off at any time. No rush."

Pierce stopped his advance.

"What—"

There was an echoing *click* as all the lights in the warehouse shut off at once.

THE WAREHOUSE WAS OLD.

The entire structure would most likely have to be stripped down and renovated when the time came for it to become operational again, if not completely leveled and rebuilt altogether. With a quick glimpse inside the entrance as Kyler prepared to run across the short distance to go in, Trust had noted the lack of a proper second floor to the building. Instead, there were a series of catwalks, with metal staircases and numerous ladders leading down to the ground, along with wider, sturdier bars for, perhaps, cranes...

It really didn't matter what else was up there. The catwalks and stairs alone made the decision easy.

Even the climb up was simple, as if placed there for Trust's exact purposes. A long flight of steps affixed to the outside wall of the building, leading to a door at the top...to Trust, it seemed as though Kyler had the harder assignment by far. Ascending the steps, Trust's concentration went entirely into feel—the way the stairs responded to his footfalls was his only way of knowing if he was making any sound.

Also, it was his only way of knowing if the rickety steps could even hold his weight in the first place.

He need not have been concerned.

While Kyler was most likely weaving some tale that only just slightly hinted at any plausibility at all, Trust was carefully trying the door at the top of the—

Locked.

The entire episode would have been too easy otherwise.

The side of the warehouse he was on was shrouded in darkness, seemingly set in a deeper shadow than the rest of the dark recesses of the industrial park.

Trust almost preferred it to daylight.

The doorknob was old, both in age and make. Trust was not a doorknob expert, but it just seemed that way. Old.

He also did not have his lock-picking tools and was mentally punching himself in the face at the oversight.

Still, the doorknob *did* look quite old.

After a quick search of the grated landing he stood on and the door itself, he took up a stance, leaning in slightly, testing...

...a little...he could feel it...

He leaned more, pulling and twisting harder, exerting added force but still hanging on...

This was a risky move. The sounds now would certainly give him up.

A bit more force...it was loosening...careful...careful... lighter...*lighter*...

He could feel the doorknob begin to break off and he lessened the pressure at once. As the handle fell off into one hand, he immediately slipped the fingers of the other into the hole in the door, clutching the pieces inside, preventing them from falling on the other side of the door.

See? He knew it was old.

It only took a few moments for him to open the door enough to slip through, and he quickly assumed a low profile—on his stomach—as he slowly, carefully pulled the door shut again.

A second...two...three...completely still. Waiting to see if something happened.

No. He was clear.

He slowly crawled and peeked over the edge of the landing.

Well...they were definitely in the right place. The amount of retail merchandise in the so-called abandoned warehouse would supply the entire UCC student and staff population a few times over.

Which would not be much of a problem, since some of the items came from the UCC student population.

Trust settled in, bracing himself for a quick rise, or a swift drop if the circumstance arose.

He saw Kyler. That familiar blond mane was hard to miss.

Allison. Idela, with his red hat still on. The other boy he had encountered in the Thomas Building. A few more of the individuals on the ground looked somewhat familiar, though Trust couldn't quite place them.

Kyler and, soon after, Allison going into a room situated in the corner of the building along the opposite wall from Trust. From his particular vantage point, it was almost impossible to observe exactly what was being said, but the rest in the warehouse went to work, arranging and packing some of the products into boxes. More boxes were stacked along the wall near the loading doors, mostly likely already filled and ready to move.

Something at the entrance. More people arriving.

Trust spotted the gun tucked away almost as soon as the boy—man—carrying it stepped into view.

That...altered things a little, though it also should have been expected in a situation like this. In a warehouse full of stolen, expensive, high-end commodities, the fact that Trust had only spotted *one* gun so far should have been the more surprising note.

He was, however, having second thoughts regarding Allison's presence on the premises. Trust had faced firearms before, and Kyler had as well...but Allison?

Kyler came back out of the room. His head was tilted up just slightly as he spoke, as though he knew Trust was somewhere above him...

"All right, everyone. I'm about to run through a diagnostic check on the lights in here to make sure there aren't any prob—"

Then he turned. The man with the gun was taking a step toward him. He must have said something.

"Me? Who the heck are you, man? Pierce told me to—"

The gun was out. Kyler's hands were raised, and Trust tensed.

More words. Another boy, behind the one with the gun, pointing toward Kyler...

"But I got back early and almost caught you, you little turd," Kyler was saying. "You didn't think I would remember your face, did ya? But here I am—"

The man with the gun had a short fuse, Trust could tell. He seemed ready to shoot Kyler any second.

And Allison was still in the office.

Trust was very close to making a move, though showing himself now, with the lights on, provided a high likelihood of getting Kyler, and probably himself, shot almost immediately—

*Come on, Kyler. Do that thing you do...*

"Anytime, please, Allison. You can shut the lights off at any time. No rush."

Trust's eyes widened.

*What?*

Darkness suddenly enveloped him. His vision adapted effortlessly, and he sprang.

THE GUNSHOT REVERBERATED LOUDLY IN the dark warehouse just before pandemonium broke out.

"Hey!"

"Watch out!"

"Jeez, Pierce! What're you doing?"

"I can't see! I can't see anything!"

"Lights! I need lights! Where is he?"

"What was that? Did anyone hear that? Is there something on the roof?"

Without looking directly at them, Trust could see the flashlight function on numerous cell phones coming on, sending cones of light into the air as they waved around frantically. Trust was sliding down the railing of one of a series of connecting staircases leading down to the floor, but, still sliding, he turned and stood, now grinding the railing on his feet, before leaping out...

...still nearly forty feet above the concrete floor.

He felt like he was suspended in the air, the fall seemingly taking forever.

Moreover, it would surely be the last thing he ever did if he didn't already have a plan...

"Ugghh!"

Trust did not hear the strangled yelp as he landed on the boy's back with tremendous force, dropkicking the boy into a table full of televisions, sending him flying, sprawling, crashing, and then tumbling to the floor on the other side, the displays smashing to the floor all around him. Trust ricocheted in the other direction just enough, falling hard into a row of computer monitors on the next aisle over. The combined crash from both boys was thunderous, the lights from all the phones immediately swerving in their direction.

"Oh, man!"

"What the heck was that?"

Trust was rolling and sliding as he made hard contact with the ground, his downward energy further nullified as he remained out of view of the lights. He immediately felt the familiar twinge of a broken bone, perhaps more than one, in his wrist, but with his adrenaline now pumping freely, it was just as quickly overlooked and forgotten.

"Kenny! Are you—aaah!"

Trust swept the next boy's legs out from underneath him, the boy's phone flipping out of his grasp...

But Trust was already on his feet again and moving quickly, as he had seen the man with the gun racing toward where Kyler had been standing when he fired...

"ALLISON!" KYLER WHISPERED LOUDLY AS he flew into the corner office, bent into a crouch. He turned and quickly shut the door behind him, locking it.

"Get in the—"

There was another gunshot on the other side of the door, Kyler flinching instinctively as the bullet impacted the wall outside. Pierce was shooting blindly, not yet realizing that Kyler was no longer there.

"Corner. Get in the corner," Kyler said again, herding Allison quickly to the far area of the room, behind a desk. "Stay low."

With frantic movements, Allison tried to glance around the boy to the doors and windows, which illustrated nothing but the current blackness of the warehouse.

"Kyler! Where's Trust? We've got to get him out of there. Someone's shooting!"

"No! Stay down!" Kyler cried, yanking Allison's head back down behind the desk as he, too, ducked. "He's okay. Believe me, the safest place for us is right here. We've got to give him spa—"

"Hey!"

It was Pierce. He was close. At the door.

A loud blast, sounding almost like a shotgun round, as another bullet from Pierce's gun tore into the office doorknob and lock, wood splintering, metal flying.

Allison screamed out at the sudden noise.

"I hear you in there! You think you can come—aaah!"

Allison began to raise her head again, but Kyler quickly forced it down.

Trust was not paying any particular attention to the man's mouth, so he didn't know he was speaking.

He had, however, watched the man lower his gun slightly and fire into the closed door. Trust was in a full sprint as he reached him, his sights squarely on the target.

The discharge of a gun was an eerily beautiful sight through Trust's eyes, particularly when the shot was fired in the dark. A sudden and enormous kaleidoscope of color, the glimmers seeming to ride the accompanying sound wave in a sharp funnel that instantly expanded into a wide sphere spreading in every direction, an explosion that always appeared—to Trust—to be more uncontrolled than it actually was. It was one of the times he was actually able to see sound.

Also, when he was really concentrating, he was able to see the spiraling bullet as it exited the muzzle of the firearm—but only for an instant.

He didn't see and couldn't hear the agonized bark that leaped from Pierce's lips as he came around, behind the man's back, yanking his hand and head up and back at the same time, and spinning with him, almost like a dance, the gun falling from Pierce's grasp with the acute, painful angle of his wrist and slipping seamlessly into Trust's grasp, their bodies still turning, nearing a complete revolution, Pierce, in an effort to lessen the pressure on his hand and neck while not realizing that his hand was already free, Trust directing their movements, readjusting his hold ever so slightly, now gripping Pierce's neck as he slammed him—with momentum on his side—into the wall, the same wall Pierce had shot at— twice—aiming for Kyler moments before...

Pierce did not even have time to register his body and head slamming into the hard wall before the gun came sweeping across in Trust's hand, striking his temple.

He slumped limply to the floor.

Trust was disassembling the handgun without looking as he continued to move.

"Kyler!"

He shoved the destroyed door open, the doorknob already rendered useless—

"We're okay! We're okay!"

Kyler's head popped up from behind the desk. Trust wasn't sure exactly how much Kyler could see of him—he had learned that, excluding absolute darkness, the more enhanced his night-vision capabilities, the darker it was for everyone else—but the blond-haired boy had the astuteness to still face in Trust's general direction as he spoke so Trust could read his lip movements.

And, just as quickly, Trust was gone again.

A few of the theft ring were foolish enough to linger. Most had taken the opportunity to escape during the seconds Trust had been preoccupied with Pierce.

One was at a table, attempting to stuff as many items as he could into a backpack.

The boy quickly flashed his lit phone toward the corner, where he had seen...*whatever* was throwing Pierce into the wall.

Pierce was drooped over, but the dark figure was gone. The warehouse was quiet except for the hurried movements of a few others behind him, and Kenny's distressed groaning...

"Oh, crap," he muttered softly to himself, before voicing in a louder tone, "Uh, guys? Anyone see where that...that..."

Fumbling for a suitable descriptor, he felt the slightest tickle of breath on the back of his neck before his phone—his only source of light—was abruptly snatched away.

The boy froze, his eyes wide in the darkness.

More light breaths on the back of his neck.

Another boy, from a few rows behind, flipped his phone over.

"What'd you say, Le—holy crap!"

Sensing the light on him again, Trust shoved the boy one way and flipped in the other—a complete backflip. The other boy's light started to follow his friend, but quickly jerked back to try to get another look at...

...but the...thing? Person?...was gone just that quickly. Surely it was a person...it had been *standing* like a person, but the way it moved so quickly, so nimbly out of the light...

The illumination from his phone found his friend again.

"Leo, let's just forget this stuff and get out of here! Leo? Leo?"

Leo was still not moving, not responding to the light or his friend's voice, too scared to even budge. His friend began to come around the table toward him.

"Leo, snap out of—"

"Aah! He's here! He's got me! Help! Argh, it hurts!"

It was Kenny, still on the ground behind them. The other boy quickly swung the light. Kenny was writhing on the floor, clutching around his middle.

But he was alone.

"Kenny, are you—augh!"

Another cell phone was put in the boy's face just as his own phone was jerked from his possession.

> *Leave now, police catch you. Help your friend, tell EMS*
> *possible broken rib. Help friend, I don't hurt you.*

The boy seemed to be suddenly afflicted with the same feeling of terror that had affected Leo.

In the darkness, Trust stepped closer, breathing hard again so the boy could hear and feel it on his skin.

The boy nodded quickly.

"I'll...I'll stay. I'll stay."

A different phone dropped in front of his face.

> *Tell police everything you know. Including me.*

"O-o-okay. Just, please, d-don't hurt—"

Both phones were forced into the boy's chest, causing him to stumble back a bit. When he regained his footing and brought up the flashlight app again, the figure had vanished.


"IS IT OVER?" ASKED ALLISON, still crouching behind the desk alongside Kyler.

Kyler strained his ears.

"I can't hear anything," he said. "Can you hear anything? I can't hear anyth—"

"Kyler."

Trust's voice was quiet, a whisper. Kyler peeked over the desk. As soon as he did, he was blinded by the light shining at him, before Trust quickly turned it back to his face.

He was holding a finger to his lips. He then handed the phone to Kyler as he moved farther into the dark office, away from the door and windows.

*Turn the light off and follow me. Take my hand.*

Kyler switched off the light. Back in the shadows, he turned to Allison.

"Take my hand," he whispered. "We follow Trust from here. I think I forgot to mention he can see in the dark—like, really good."

The three friends formed a line, hands clasped, as Trust silently led them out of the room. No one could see their departure, even when they lit out into the spotty, pale illumination just outside the front entrance. Kyler and Allison could hear police sirens in the vicinity and quickly approaching. They ran to one of the abandoned containers.

Trust highlighted the number in his phone and then handed it to Kyler. Kyler pressed talk.

"Mr. Jackson, this is Kyler. Are you still around to give us a ride in the Air Force Limo thing?"

And, five minutes later, the trio was back in the limousine, heading out of the industrial complex on a side road at the same time the beginning of a steady string of police cars were streaming in along the main street. Kyler settled back into the cushiony seat.

"Ahh," he said, grinning and closing his eyes, "I could really get used to this."

Mr. Jackson hit the brakes hard, causing Kyler to topple out of his seat.

"What, are you allergic to seat belts or something?" Mr. Jackson asked. "I want an explanation from all of you *now*. I called the police as soon as I heard gunshots. Gunshots! I counted three. Was somebody trying to shoot all three of you?"

*No, just Kyler,* Trust motioned. He felt the twinge in his wrist again, the rush wearing off quickly as his mind registered he was no longer in fight mode.

"Yes, I would also like an explanation," Allison declared, crossing her arms. "From both of you, actually. What was all that stuff *you*"—she pointed to Kyler—"were talking about in there, like you owned the place, and then the way you seemed to know exactly what to do when I turned the lights off? And *you*"—pointing to Trust—"that guy had a gun! How...when did you come in? Where? *And you can see in the dark?* What does that even mean?"

"Oh, don't even try to play the innocent card now, little Miss Allison Tyler," Kyler declared. "You got into Idela's house in about ten seconds flat when you've never even met him before. Then you somehow convince two complete strangers to take you to the one place they're least likely to admit to anybody that they even know about, but you get in on the first meeting and have them eating out of your hand. You don't even know these guys, and it's all because you say that you're this Pierce guy's girlfriend—"

"Ow."

Everyone, including Mr. Jackson in the rearview, looked to Trust, who was twisting his wrist gingerly back and forth. He stopped when he sensed the others' attention on him. He moved his hands.

*I didn't say that out loud, did I?*

He then grimaced.

"What happened?" Kyler asked, his voice suddenly laced with concern as he leaned closer.

"Trust, are you all right?" Allison asked.

"Do we need to go to the hospital?" Mr. Jackson voiced from the front. "I can get to a hospital in five minutes from here."

*I'm fine,* Trust signed, taking his time. *I may have sprained my wrist on that fall back there.*

"Aha!" Kyler exclaimed, pointing at him. "I knew I saw you up there. Please, *please*, tell me you did not jump fifty feet down onto one of those tables—"

"Fifty feet?" Allison gasped. "Trust!"

"Fifty feet!" Mr. Jackson shouted. "Boy, are you crazy? Are you out of your mind? Whaddaya think, you're some type of superman or something? Fifty feet is just crazy! Just crazy!"

Trust rolled his eyes, lolling his head back into the headrest.

## 43.
## The Real Cortez

CORTEZ WAS WHISTLING AN OBSCURE tune as he entered his dorm room in Centre City Hall on the second floor. It was the oldest—and, with only two floors, the smallest—residence hall on the university grounds. At the late hour, his room was dark, his roommate absent.

Cortez had a banana in his hand. The whistling continued as he flicked on the light, pushing the door closed with his foot. He turned back into the room.

"Aah!"

Trust was standing in front of the window on the far side of the room, his arms crossed, his shades on. Motionless.

Holding a cell phone.

"Cortez, it's me."

Cortez looked around before he could stop himself, quickly realizing there was no possible way anyone else was in the room.

"Allison?" the boy called, looking back to the phone in Trust's grasp. Trust was looking down to something on his wrist.

"Take the phone from Trust, Cortez, and take it off speaker. What I'm going to say I will assume you don't want to be heard by anyone potentially passing by your door."

Trust tossed the phone over to the bewildered boy. Cortez juggled it and the banana momentarily before securing them both. He put the phone to his ear. Trust looked back down to his wrist.

> **Allison:** "I know what you've been doing, Cortez. I know about your involvement in the theft ring."

Trust glanced up from the display on his wrist, meeting Cortez's stunned gaze. Trust smirked, his eyes shaded behind his tinted glasses.

THE FOLLOWING MORNING, A SATURDAY, Cortez stood in front of the campus police station entrance, an envelope in his hands. He sighed.

"You really think this is the best idea?" he asked quietly, looking straight ahead.

"I do," Allison intoned, standing beside him, "and honestly, I think you know it, too. You've played the conceited, know-it-all computer whiz for so long that you think that's who you really are. But I know better. I've worked beside you all year in labs, and you were in one of my classes. You're not conceited; you're dedicated. You're not a know-it-all; you're desperate to learn. You're not a bad guy; you're...misguided, I guess."

Cortez smiled faintly, holding the sealed envelope up, still not looking at the girl.

"Is that what this says?"

"If I wanted you to know what that said, I would let you read it. Think of it like a letter of reference."

"I can still walk away."

He finally turned to her.

"These guys would never in a million years be able to prove I was involved."

"Well, I take back the conceited part," Allison said.

Cortez's smile grew a little wider, though it did not reach his eyes.

"You remember everything we talked about last night, right?" Allison asked.

Cortez sighed again.

"This is a colossal deal," Allison explained. "Chancellor Beverly's going to be at a news conference about it. Everyone's talking. And you know whoever else is in the group that knows your name is going to tell on you first thing. I'm sure you've covered your digital footprint—I still wouldn't know about your involvement if those guys at the warehouse hadn't mentioned your name and I recognized your program on the computer in that corner office—but it will still be your word against theirs, and they don't have any reason to even bring your name up in the first place unless you were actually involved. But if you go into the station now and confess—to all of it—I'm sure they'll take it into account, along with what's in that letter."

Cortez, who had been glancing down, jerked his head up quickly.

"Can you tell Trust and Kyler again that I'm—"

"They know," Allison said. "You said it last night, and Trust was right there in front of you. Remember?"

"How could I forget? He smiled and shook my hand, although I think he was ready to rip it off."

"Well, you don't need to be fluent in sign language to understand the overall sentiment. Now, go on. The sooner you go in, the better."

"What if this doesn't work—this confession and whatever you wrote in the letter?"

"You did commit a crime, Cortez. A major crime, and more than one. But, through whatever happens, know that there are at least three UCC students here—two who you even attempted to steal from—that will support you. Four if you count Raul, but that's just because he won't have anyone else to cheat off in Discrete Algorithms."

Cortez smiled and shook his head as he took another step toward the station entrance. He then paused again.

"I never asked this earlier. Why are you guys forgiving me so quickly? Why are you doing this? I mean, it's like you just said. I practically sent that guy to go steal from their room, and he would have gotten away with it if Kyler hadn't come back early."

"Because they trust me," replied Allison. "And I trust you."

"It's that simple, eh?"

"Believe me, it really is that simple. Otherwise, I'm sure Trust would have had no problems caving your face in with his fist last night."

"Yeah, I think I'll pass on that. But seriously, he actually jumped sixty feet to the ground and took out Pierce? That guy carries a gun, you know."

"I wouldn't know anything about that."

"Oh. Right. Sure."

Cortez moved again, reaching for the door.

"By the way," Allison said, Cortez turning a final time, "I don't actually know what's in that letter you're holding, either. I didn't write it."

Cortez arched an eyebrow, and then glanced down to the envelope.

"Who did?" he inquired.

"I wouldn't know anything about that, either," Allison replied, smiling softly.

As Cortez went through the door, Allison turned away.

Across the courtyard, past the snaking path that went by the picturesque—and now functioning—water fountain out front, waiting, almost hidden, under a tree, Trust and Kyler waved, Kyler giving a thumbs-up.

Inside the campus police station, Cortez looked around, noting the typical, casual hustle and bustle of law enforcement personnel and visitors as he slowly made his way to the front desk. The woman on the other side of it, not a sworn officer and in formal business attire instead of a police uniform, looked up and smiled graciously as the boy approached.

"Yes, sir. How may I help you today?"

Drumming the envelope on the chest-high counter, Cortez glanced around once more, almost as though he were thinking about bolting, before he returned his attention to the front. He mumbled something.

The woman leaned forward in her chair, her smile still on her face.

"I'm sorry, sir?"

"The—ahem—uh, this theft ring thing everyone's talking about? Yeah...uh, I kinda know everything about that. I know you're going to have to, uh, arrest me or whatever, but is Officer Mendez here? I'm really supposed to give this to her. It's a letter—what I mean is that it's not a bomb or anything, but...yeah. I did it."

The woman continued to look at him.

Smiling, her face, seemingly, frozen.

## 44.
## Theft Ring News Conference


WITH THE LATE MORNING NEWS conference being held outdoors, the springtime sun shone vibrantly, illuminating the media event with perfect natural lighting, aptly exhibiting the picture-perfect backdrop of the campus' rural scenery. The number of cameras, journalists, and reporters in front of the erected stage was surprisingly large. Students and other UCC constituents mostly went about their business—it was, after all, still a Monday—though some lingered along the outskirts of the production for moments or minutes at a time, taking in the affair.

On stage were a number of university administrators, as well as law enforcement personnel. As the public relations official spoke into the huddle of microphones situated on the podium, Chancellor Beverly, standing behind and to the side, slated to speak and answer questions next, leaned over slightly. Officer Amelia Mendez of the Centre City Metro Police Department was standing alongside her.

"The boy who came in," the chancellor said lowly, "the one who had all the information on this theft ring. What's your take on him?"

"I'm sorry, ma'am?" Mendez said, seemingly taken aback that the chancellor was even speaking to her.

"The boy who came in and confessed. I heard he would only talk to you, right? I want to know your impression of him—your gut instinct. Is he telling the truth about all of this? Can we rely on his story?"

"Yes, ma'am, I believe so," Mendez replied, also keeping her voice down so no one else would overhear. "All of the video and intel he has given us backs up everything he has told me."

"And the level of his own involvement. You think that's true as well?"

"Ma'am, I am in no way a computer expert, but from what he's shown us, just in the last two days...we have verification from the others also in custody that this was not his idea. He was not the mastermind, nor was he in any way the leader of this operation. He was recruited just like many of the other college kids who are involved, all by this Pierce Xavier. But I would daresay that this kid—Cortez Romero is his name—was not only the most critical part of this outfit, but had he not come in himself and confessed, I doubt we would have been able to pin any of this on him, even with the testimony of the others. It would have been his word against theirs. We would've needed the National Security Agency to be able to track down even a whiff of what he's given us so far."

The public relations admin was winding down his statement at the podium.

"Ma'am."

Chancellor Beverly looked to the cop again.

"Saturday, when the boy first came in, he gave me an envelope with a letter inside. He refused to give it to anyone else, and he said it was specifically addressed to me, which it was. I had never met this Cortez kid before Saturday. He said he didn't write the letter, nor did he know what it said—only that he was supposed to give it to me."

"I wasn't told about a letter," Beverly stated.

"You're now one of the few who know about it," Mendez informed her. "We're sitting on it right now. The letter has no special information regarding the particulars of what we're working on—this Cortez boy's evidence, along with what we're getting from the other individuals, is going to be more than enough to wrap this thing up with a bow on top. However, it does add credence to what some of them are saying about someone else being at the scene that night, someone we have not apprehended, or even identified, yet. I think that someone else may be the one who wrote this letter, and I think it may be something you need to be aware of moving forward."

Officer Mendez was removing a folded piece of paper from her shirt pocket as she spoke, handing it to the chancellor.

"I really think it would be best if no one else knows about this right now, ma'am."

"...and the chancellor of our university, Dr. April Beverly, will speak to you next and answer some of your questions. Following her will be the chief of the Centre City Metro Police, Robert Manuel."

"Do we have any idea who this person is?" Beverly inquired quietly as she started to step forward, looking back at the female officer. There was a smattering of applause from some of the students watching the proceedings, the circumstance notwithstanding.

"It's unsigned," Mendez stated.

Chancellor Beverly's gaze lingered on the officer for a moment longer before she turned fully and approached the open podium. She placed the speech folder that she had also been holding on the stand, unfolding the letter Mendez had handed her and setting it on the opposite side.

She slipped her glasses on.

"Before I read the short statement I prepared and answer some of your questions—many of which, I'm sure, I will be politely referring to Chief Manuel—I believe I heard some clapping from some of the students I see near the back. You are, of course, free to stay if your schedules permit. Nevertheless, I do see a young man named Jason Martz back there. Jason, I'm sure, didn't expect me to remember his name, or his face, or that he has a class that I visited exactly one week ago to the day. A class that begins in...yes, two minutes. You can go now, Jason."

The fully grown adults on stage attempted to conceal their smirks and snickers to maintain a sense of decorum. Those students in the back, off camera, did not hold the same concern, laughing loudly with amusement.

SITTING AT A TABLE IN the busy student union, Trust watched the press conference on the large television screen overhead, Chancellor April Beverly holding court and seemingly very much in her element on stage in front of the cameras.

"...but any specifics on that, I would certainly direct to Chief Manuel. Yes, in the front here."

She pointed to a journalist. There was a few seconds' delay with the switch in television cameras, so by the time the image of the reporter came on screen, he was already into his question.

"...some sort of letter as you were first walking up to the podium by Officer Mendez, and I noticed you had it open during your statement and through the opening question. Is there any chance that letter is related to our subject today, and if so, could you tell us the contents?"

The scene switched back to a genial chancellor.

"It's Bob, right?" she asked. "Bob McNeil of the *Tribune*?"

If Trust had been able to hear, or if the television had been displaying closed captions, he would have noted the "Yes, ma'am" response that came from the journalist.

"Well, Mr. McNeil, as to your first question, I will again refer you to Chief Manuel, as I know he will be able to answer in more depth than I can at this time. And, as to the piece of paper you saw, it was actually a recipe for spicy clam chowder that I have been trying to get my hands on for a while."

An amused smile.

Trust didn't see the "Are you lying, ma'am?" that came from McNeil.

"Yes, I am. However, if I felt the contents of the note I was handed seemed either relevant or appropriate to this news conference, I would have surely informed you of its contents already, but it isn't, and so I don't. Also, before I do get letters and messages on the subject, I am not, in fact, looking for a spicy clam chowder recipe. I don't eat clams.

"I have time for a few more questions, and then I want to hand it over to the chief, who I know also has a schedule to keep. Yes, the young man near the back. Nice shirt, by the way."

*That was Cortez's letter,* Trust signed. Kyler, beside him, interpreted for the rest of the table.

"How you figure that?" Paxson questioned just before he shoveled a section of syrup-laden waffle into his mouth.

*She and Officer Mendez were speaking in the background while that first guy was at the microphones.*

Cortez was also at the table.

"So?" he said.

Everyone looked at him, and it seemed to dawn on Cortez at that moment.

"Oh. Right. You can read lips. Man, that must be a useful skill to have."

"So is digitally orchestrating an illegal theft ring," Allison retorted, giving Cortez a look.

*Illegal theft ring?* Trust repeated, smirking. *That's a little redundant.*

Allison shot him the same look. Trust reached for his drink, looking away.

"But here's what I still don't understand," said Paxson, his mouth now partially full as he cut into his waffle again. "You"—he pointed the syrupy fork in Cortez's direction—"told us the name of the boy in the red hat. You probably already knew his name. Why bother to give him up when you were involved? You had to realize that would put you at risk—not to mention the entire operation. Are you some sort of psychopath with no sense of self-preservation?"

Cortez sighed, scratching his head.

"Well, that's...a theory, I guess," he said.

"Yeah, pretty terrible," said Kyler, looking to Paxson. "How about just sticking to eating waffles and taking pictures of suspicious-looking people."

"Yousth said it lasth nigh when youth tolth me!" Paxson exclaimed, his mouth now completely full.

Kyler's eyes flitted around the table.

"Uhh...no, I didn't."

"I think I may have some sort of competitive problem," Cortez said. "It could be ego, like Allison has said countless times, but that's honestly why I joined up with Pierce and those guys in the first place. I already told the police all of this, but I wasn't even getting paid like everyone else, although that was probably incredibly stupid of me looking back now—"

"Oh, so you think *that* was the stupid part of this whole mess," Allison said, rolling her eyes. "Glad to see you've learned your lesson."

"I should say a minor stupid part in an avalanche of massively stupid parts," Cortez tried again. "But I seriously did it just to see if I could—and to see if I could get away with it. And I did, to both of them. A terrible reason, I know, but I think it's the same reason any major accomplishment happens. You step off a cliff, right? You step past the fear of the unknown and run straight into the darkness. Why? Because you don't know what's on the other side and it's time for you to discover it. It's what we do. It's what I do, and it's what you guys do, too, every day, whether you realize it or not.

"Even though it was obviously, blatantly, highly illegal; even though it would negatively affect people I sat beside in lecture halls and labs, all of these kids going to the same school that I do...at the same time, it's kind of a challenge, you know? To see if I would be able to set everything up, no mistakes, and I'm sitting right there beside these guys. To know when students would be out of their rooms or apartments...and I created Tigresa and developed a system that worked to perfection. The police weren't close to solving it, at least with regard to all the stuff I was doing.

Only a few freak situations—Kyler coming back to his room early—had the capability of derailing what I had set up. And, even then, I had backups. Then you come up with an actual picture of Idela, the ultimate in freak situations.

"The others had told him over and over to stop wearing that red hat everywhere, especially after that campus alert about who to look out for. And he did stop wearing it—when he was being a lookout. But I do remember him wearing it at that Valentine's Day game—the other guys almost had a fit. And that's exactly when you all caught him.

"When you brought in that pic...I don't know. For some reason, it became another part of the challenge. I had a virtually foolproof setup on one side. If I was working it from the other direction, though—like from the police perspective, or you guys—how would I go about getting through the net I had created? I was playing against myself. The fact that you actually had a picture of Idela and could connect him to the red hat, and then came to me of all people, one of probably only a handful at this school who could have matched him digitally without going around door to door asking every person, 'Do you know this boy?'

"Truthfully, you guys had the whole thing solved as soon as Paxson snapped that picture. You also ruined the challenge for me a little bit by saying I couldn't find him my own way—that's why I tried so hard to get you to change your minds that day—but I knew all of you by then, and I knew Allison well enough from being lab partners all year, so I just decided to do it your way, by the book. If I found out Idela that way—and it was no guarantee that I would—then I would give him up. If not, I'm almost certain we wouldn't be having this conversation, unless you just ran into Idela randomly on campus somewhere and happened to remember him."

*What I want to know,* Trust gestured, *is what's stopping you from doing this again for the next smooth-talking lowlife who needs a computer genius for some complex job that you've never done before? What's stopping you then?*

Cortez thought about it for a moment.

"You," he said. "Well, all of you, really."

He looked back to Trust.

"You're the one who wrote that letter, aren't you?"

*What makes you say that?*

"I don't know," Cortez said, grinning. "A feeling. But...this goes to all of you. And Marcie, too, though she's in class, so she's not here to hear it.

"I'm used to doing stuff on my own. My parents were always too busy, and I don't have any siblings. I have friends...ephemerally. No one's ever...I don't know, paid this much attention to me like you have in such a laid-back, cool way. Not unless they wanted me to do something for them. Allison, I've never met...I mean, you're so *patient*, even when you get frustrated. And all of you, the way you hang out together and come to visit Allison in lab—"

"They come to visit you, too, Cortez," Allison reminded him.

"What's ephemerally mean?" Paxson asked.

"I know it's going to sound kind of weird," Cortez continued, "but I kind of look up to you guys or something, what you guys have."

"Just admit it," Paxson said. "Spending so much time in the police station this weekend scared you straight."

"That definitely doesn't hurt," Cortez said. "And I'm not even close to being done. Officer Mendez said they're going to be asking me questions for weeks, and I'll have to show exactly how I did *everything*—which programs I used, how I encrypted the records. And then, on top of that, I basically have to work in their intelligence division for the next two school years without pay, like community service. If I even think about doing something else—which I absolutely, positively will not—but if I do, the punishment that they would have given me for this will get added on to whatever I did."

"Which means they'll be sendin' ya up the river for a *long* stretch," offered Kyler.

Everyone looked at him.

"That's prison slang," he clarified. He leaned back in his chair, putting his hands behind his head. "Yep. Learned that from my stint in the pen."

*Field trip,* Trust corrected.

"Still counts," Kyler commented after interpreting.

He then brought his hands back quickly.

"Hey, it's Clark Kent! You're the one who broke up this theft ring, didn't you? Shouldn't you be at the news conference so you can write an article for the *Daily Planet*?"

An approaching Perry smirked, rolling his eyes. Cortez sat forward in his seat.

"Dude, you actually do look a lot like Super—"

"Shhh!" Kyler cut in. "It's Clark when he's trying to blend in."

"Well," Perry said, "excluding that routine—which never gets old, by the way—I'm actually glad I spotted you guys over here. I just got off the phone with the police a few minutes ago. They said they were able to find all of the things stolen from me and Rob's room—even the things that had already been transported out of town. Something to do with some digital records they now have access to. We should be getting our stuff back within the next couple of weeks."

There were "Hey!"s and "Wow!"s and "That's great news!" from the others. Cortez, who had remained quiet, stood to his feet.

"Those were my records."

Everyone turned to look at him. Perry raised his eyebrows in question.

"You don't know me, Clark, but my name is Cortez Romero, and I was—am—actually a major part of this whole Dorm Room Robbers thing, and not in a commendable way. I was the one who figured out when you and your roommate were going to be out of your dorm room, invading virtually every aspect of your digital privacy that you can possibly imagine in the process. I really, really do apologize for everything that you went through, from the moment those guys got to your door to steal your things, and I have no excuse that could possibly justify what I did. Again, I'm incredibly sorry, and I'm glad you're getting your stuff back."

Perry looked at Cortez for a moment. He began to smile, but then stopped himself as he realized the boy was not—

"Wait. You're not kidding?"

Cortez shook his head.

"Look, Clark. You have every right to be mad at me. I've already talked to the police and I'm in the process of telling them everything I know. And believe me, these guys will tell you that I'm facing pretty much every single punishment possible short of actually spending time in prison, which I'm incredibly thankful for. But if you want to hit me, and your name really is Clark Kent, I understand. I would only ask you to hold back on your punches as much as possible."

*His name's not Clark Kent,* Trust signed.

"It's Kal—" Kyler started, before the older boy interjected.

"My name's Perry," he said, extending his hand to Cortez, "and I accept your apology, Cortez Romero. I'm terrible at holding grudges, and it seems like everyone is going to get their stuff back safe and sound. I do appreciate the apology, though."

Perry and Cortez shook.

"Wow," Kyler remarked. "You really are a superman. I don't know if I would be able to accept an apology as quick as that."

*You did Saturday night when Cortez told you,* Trust signed.

"Hey, Perry," Paxson said. "Can I get a picture with me and you? My brother's a huge Superman fan. He's going to be so jealous."

Perry smirked, rolling his eyes.

## 45.
## Boom Baby

KOBE HELD TRUST'S WRIST CAREFULLY in his hands, examining it. Trust held the homemade wrap in his other hand. The two were down on the gymnasium floor beside the punching bag. The rest of the gym was deserted for the moment, a rarity. Typically, there were at least a few people running around the floors, even at the later hour that Trust and the martial arts instructor usually met.

"How long has your friend Kyler played baseball?" Kobe inquired in his quiet tone, not even looking up.

Trust, who had been observing the man's face, was able to read him. He waved vaguely with his other hand.

"As long as you've been doing this?"

Trust nodded faintly. Kobe's eyes dropped back to the wrist.

"I assumed so. He's really good."

Trust smirked, shaking his free hand in a so-so motion.

"When's the last time you saw him make his own baseball glove?"

Trust's grin faltered.

Kobe's eyes rose again.

"I want you to take that wrap you have in your other hand, and throw it into the biggest fire you can find. You need a doctor to look at this, and you're not a doctor."

Trust made a face.

"I'll assume, from that look, that you think this is only a minor injury. A sprain, perhaps."

Kobe flipped Trust's wrist over.

"Or maybe you knew it was broken and now you feel stupid thinking that wrap was going to do anything to help you. Don't try to diagnose

539

yourself. There's a Medical Services Department that's a five-minute walk from anywhere on this campus. Use it."

Trust looked at him.

"Your grandfather would tell you to burn that wrap, too."

Kobe ran his fingers over Trust's palm, still studying.

"They don't ask questions at Medical Services if they don't think it's necessary. They won't ask, for example, how far you fell to fracture your wrist like this."

Trust's eyes widened ever so slightly as Kobe glanced at him again.

"Fifteen feet? Twenty? Among other reasons, I can tell because your knuckles aren't bruised, but neither are your palms. But that is to be expected for someone who has trained extensively with their hands for as much and as long as you have. Kyler could probably hit a baseball with his eyes closed; you can withstand heightened trauma with significantly less effect. Therefore, perhaps the fall was even higher and you were somehow able to counteract the force. Twenty-five feet? Thirty? Thirty-five?"

The man was smirking as he finished. He let Trust's hand go free.

"It will be an abbreviated class tonight. We're going to take a field trip to Medical Services after this."

Trust went to retrieve his note card as he started to wrap his hand again.

"You'll do less damage if you leave that thing off," Kobe said.

Trust wrote with his uninjured left hand.

*And what do we do before the field trip?*

"In the meantime," replied Kobe, "we're back in the ring. I get to try to hit you as much as I want, and you don't get to hit me at all. We shall call it...advanced defensive technique."

THE NEXT DAY, TRUST ENTERED his dorm room, arriving back from class. He found Kyler and Allison already inside.

*I thought we already talked about this,* Trust signed. *Something about a sock, or a rubber band—*

"May I remind you, sir," Kyler said, cutting in after simultaneously interpreting for Allison what the deaf teenager was saying, "that there is a lady in the room."

He glanced over to Allison, who was sitting on Trust's bed, looking down at her phone.

"He's just kidding. We definitely did not have any sort of discussion about...uh, that."

Allison looked up.

"Oh. What? I actually wasn't even listening. Did you say something about a rubber band inside of a sock?"

"Hmm, no," Kyler replied. "What I actually said was I still can't believe how cool Trust's new wrist brace looks. And you said it was the nurse from Arlington Memorial who gave it to you? Nurse Hailey?"

*I know. I was surprised to see her there. She said the hospital staff bids for shifts on campus. Apparently, it's a very sought-after station. Why doctors and nurses would want to hang around a college—*

Trust was interrupted again, this time by a look from Allison, his hands freezing in mid-gesture. Trust looked at her. Then he looked at Kyler.

*Did I say something wrong, or...*

"Really?" Allison replied. "Did you really forget what we were going to try today?"

Confused, Trust started to turn back toward the door.

*So, I actually did miss the rubber band on the doorknob—*

He turned back quickly, catching the pillow Kyler had hurled toward him.

"Wow, T," Kyler said loudly. "It's *so* not your day to be funny."

"Rubber band on the doorknob?" Allison echoed, appearing confused. "I don't even understand that. Look, I asked Uncle Smith for the new number for my old phone. I guess the phone company is able to switch numbers, so of course you already knew I kept my old number for my new phone. I wanted to call my old phone again to see if anyone answered."

Trust's eyes warily flicked between Allison and Kyler.

*Anything from Officer Ryan?* he signed.

Allison glanced down, biting her lip. Kyler sighed.

"About thirty minutes ago," he replied. "They had Rory brought in after Allison talked to them. According to Ryan, they didn't mention anything to Rory specifically to make sure they didn't spook him or imply that Allison knows anything, but they weren't able to get anything out of him about that night and had to let him go. He's supposedly got an alibi, and there's no way to disprove it on the evidence—or lack thereof—that they have so far."

*But the police have been trying to find that cell phone since it first went missing, right? What's calling it now going to do?*

Allison dropped back forcefully onto the bed, the frustration evident in her body language. She had also apparently replied to Trust's question as she sprawled, but Trust missed it.

*Nothing,* Kyler relayed, signing back.

Allison sat up again.

"I just feel like I'm missing something. Like there's something else I can be doing—something I *should* be doing."

Her eyes focused on Trust.

"Is there any chance of convincing Jezzie to speak to the police about what happened to her? I mean, I know it's her decision, but maybe if she—"

But Trust was already signing.

*I think you're right, Allison, and you know I agree with you. In her defense, she has opened up a lot more about her involvement with Freesef. Telling it to Jeremy was a big deal. But she's still really afraid of something about them, what they would do to her, Jeremy, and perhaps others, if she went to the police. I'm still not sure exactly what that is.*

Allison's face took on a thoughtful expression, her brow furrowing slightly.

"How is Jeremy doing?" Kyler inquired.

*Staying away from Rory and the others as much as humanly possible to avoid committing a murder. Jezzie said they think he's still mad about the Spring Break party. Apparently, they've had rifts like this before, so it's nothing too unusual.*

Allison shook her head.

"She has to be so afraid, almost forced to continue hanging out with those guys. I can't imagine."

Trust remained still, looking at her.

"I want to talk to her," Allison declared.

Then the faintest hint of a smile crept across her lips.

"And I just realized who you should talk to about this stolen phone."

Trust's eyebrow rose slightly.

*Why me?* he asked.

"Because I think he really likes the way you make an entrance."

TRUST CONTINUED TO THINK ABOUT what Allison said, even as he stood waiting in the dark inside Cortez's dorm room. Behind him, the open window exhibited the campus nightscape outside, evening having fallen over Centre City.

He took out his phone.

> **Trust (8:42 PM):** My friend, Allison, wants to talk to you about Freesef. I don't think it's such a bad idea.

It was nearly a full minute before a response came through.

> **Jezzie (8:43 PM):** ?
>
> **Trust (8:44 PM):** She knows about what happened. Long story, but she hasn't told anyone, and she won't. But you already knew about what happened to her before Thanksgiving, and you had suspicions as to who was involved.
>
> **Jezzie (8:45 PM):** You told her because you thought it would make us even? Are you serious?
>
> **Trust (8:45 PM):** DEFINITELY NOT. I hope you know I wouldn't do that. Even though she knows, I still don't think I've betrayed you. She can explain it better if you talk to her.
>
> **Trust (8:46 PM):** She saw blood on my shirt that night and didn't ask questions after I said not to. I think she can help with this.

In his periphery, Trust noticed the slight change in lighting as someone stopped in front of the closed dorm room door, the crack of illumination underneath the doorframe broken. Trust put his phone back into his pocket.

Cortez was mumbling the same incomprehensible song under his breath as he unlocked the door with his key, another banana in his other hand.

"Watch out! You know you're gonna get it, you know I'm gonna find you—"

The door opened into darkness, which meant his roommate, Raul, was out, present whereabouts unknown. Probably in labs at the Thomas Building.

"—you know you won't make it back home tonight! Watch out!"

He shut the door and flipped on the light. He closed his eyes as he turned, getting into the guitar solo.

"Yeah! Dee-nee-neew-nee-nee-neewawahh!"

He jumped back as his eyes opened again. He fell into the door, and then fell, his butt hitting the floor.

Trust was smirking at him, his eyebrow arched.

"Again?" Cortez exclaimed. "What, is using the door outdated and nobody told me? What is it with you sneaking through the window when nobody's here?"

As the boy got to his feet again, Trust moved to Cortez's desk, note cards already in his hand.

*Are you going back to the Thomas Building tonight?*

"Once I recover from that near heart attack that you just gave me," Cortez replied. "Seriously, the last time you came to my room, you came through the window and you had just discovered that I was a part of a massive criminal conspiracy. Please don't tell me you're here because you found out I stole an extra piece of candy at a Halloween party in the third grade."

*Wow. So you have a history of stealing. Good to know.*
*Allison's going to meet us in the lab.*

Cortez was booting up his computer as he read.

"Us?" he questioned.

Trust nodded.

*Us.*

Cortez tapped Trust's card.

"You want to use this?"

He gestured to the laptop screen, where the TalkText program was already running, Cortez's dialogue already on the screen. Trust glanced at him, his eyebrow arched again, before he reached for the keyboard.

> **Unknown:** That was fast. And I guess this has a built-in microphone, since you're not wearing one.

> **Cortez:** "It's not exactly a cutting-edge feature anymore, trust. Virtually every laptop has a mic these days, but the professors use the wireless to make sure everything gets picked up no problem, even in a noisy class or at the opposite end of a room. My baby's not going to have any trouble picking up my voice in here, anyway. Natalie, change Unknown user to 'Trust.' Trust is typing."

Trust watched the interplay on screen between Cortez and the computer. It was almost as though he were talking to another person.

> **Natalie**: "Trust? Is this correct?"

> **Cortez:** "Boom, baby."

The **Unknown** designate instantly transformed, and the "trust" occurrences in the earlier dialogue turned to uppercase. Trust looked to Cortez, his eyebrow arched yet again.

"And yeah, this thing better be fast," Cortez continued, "considering I'm the one who built it."

> **Trust:** Boom, baby?

> **Cortez:** "I have some key phrases programmed in that give instructions to the operating system. So sue me. Boom, baby.

It also talks back, verbalizing what you type, but not in any of those ridiculous, generic mechanical voices that get on everyone's nerves. Mine sounds like a girl—totally hot. I don't have to see what you typed to know what you said. Boom, baby!"

**Trust:** So the words I'm typing now are coming out, sounding like a hot girl named Natalie?

**Cortez:** "Boom, baby!"

**Trust:** You're an idiot! How's that sound in sexy woman speak?

**Cortez:** "The first sentence, not so great. The second sentence was pretty awesome, though."

Cortez had since moved away from Trust and the laptop, gathering what he would need for the Thomas Building in his computer bag.

**Trust:** Allison was actually the one who recommended I come see you.

**Cortez:** "Oh? Did she recommend the Batman entrance also? That's breaking and entering, you know. I know that because I spent three and a half hours at the campus police station today."

**Trust:** Well, serves you right for turning into a criminal mastermind. You know Allison's phone was stolen earlier this year, just before Thanksgiving?

Cortez came over to the desk, beginning to rifle through a drawer.

**Cortez:** "Yeah. She had to re-upload the beta version of the TalkText program and she, quote unquote, 'accidently' downloaded my joke slang dictionary instead of the standard one. We laughed...well, I laughed. She said some bad words."

**Trust:** Do you know anything about finding missing or stolen phones?

**Cortez:** "Aren't the police supposed to be looking for it? Why bother anyway? That thing's probably long gone by now. She's got a new phone, and she kept all her data on her computer, so it's not like she needs that one back."

**Trust:** It's been over five months. You think the police are hot on the trail? Like you said, it could be long gone. But then again, I'm not so sure.

**Cortez:** "The Apsolon RX Chip in the SIM card was probably deactivated—that is, if the thieves know what they're doing. It's not the easiest thing to do, but the police won't be able to get a fix on it."

**Trust:** How would you know it was deactivated and not destroyed or turned off?

**Cortez:** "Pssh. How old are you? Phones from the earlier part of the twenty-first century may have worked that way, but not anymore. A destroyed card would still give off a residue signal. That's why phone companies deactivate the Apsolon Chip before they destroy or recycle the card. The police *maybe* would have located the residue signal if it was destroyed in the city, though I don't know if they have that kind of equipment. They would probably have to go to the phone company for help. And whether the phone's on or not doesn't make a difference."

**Trust:** So, would someone like you be able to find a stolen cell phone with a deactivated Apsolon Chip?

**Cortez:** "Yep."

**Trust:** Legally? I'm not trying to add time to your prison sentence here.

**Cortez:** "And the felon jokes keep rolling in. It's not illegal if you have permission from the owner of the phone as far as I know, although I may have just made that rule up in my head just now. It would still take some time to do, especially since I practically live at the police station at the moment."

**Trust:** We would owe you one if you could try.

Cortez stopped by the desk again, Trust looking at him.

"No," Cortez returned, "you really wouldn't. You snuck in here just for this, though? Couldn't Allison have just asked me in lab?"

**Trust:** She said you would appreciate my entrance.

**Cortez:** "Heh. Yeah. Hey, check this out. Natalie, load the TS800...TS8006 file in a separate window. I think that's the right one."

Trust watched the laptop display as another window opened. The TalkText window had minimized and shifted slightly to remain readable.

The new window contained a video. Trust recognized the footage instantly by the setting—nighttime outside of the Thomas Building, the surrounding grounds still and vacant. A sole, sneaky, shadowy figure stole swiftly across the open ground toward the rear of the building. The camera did not zoom in. Had Trust not already been intimately familiar with the event being played out on the screen, it would have been impossible to identify the individual.

Trust glanced over to Cortez.

The boy appeared mesmerized by the unfolding scene, but he seemed to feel Trust's eyes.

"Wait," he said, motioning back to the screen. "We haven't even reached the good part yet. Natalie, skip forward to 21:22."

The video leaped forward to an interior hallway of the building, conspicuously dark, the lights turned off.

**Trust:** I've seen this movie before. Not very exciting.

**Cortez:** "Not very exciting? Are you kidding me right now? If this isn't an action suspense movie come to life, I don't know what is. I was watching on this very laptop as it happened, and I could not believe my eyes—literally."

The video continued to play.

**Cortez:** "When you're running through the halls, checking the doors, sneaking up on Vince. That's his name, by the way...and there! Sprinting to catch that container. Did you even know—"

**Trust:** You must have shown this to Allison. That's what she meant by "appreciating the entrance." She's suddenly got jokes now, hanging around Marcie all the time...

**Cortez:** "Seriously, man, I had no idea this was even you until I showed it to Allison. I mean, holy crap! And then, at the industrial yard—"

**Trust:** Please don't tell me you have video of that, too.

**Cortez:** "Are you kidding? Of course! That had to be, like, a forty-foot drop. Boom, baby! And even then, after I saw that, I still didn't know it was you, though whatever you were doing with the phones should have been a clue, looking back on it. That was so sick! You've got to let me keep these!"

**Trust:** Police?

He looked over.

"Sorry, man," Cortez said. "I actually did think about not telling them about it before I went in Saturday morning, and that was, of course, before I knew it was you. But the video is time-stamped, and you guys said it would be best if I gave them everything I had. Even if I had cut those parts out, the police would have noticed the skip, and there wasn't enough time to alter it."

**Trust:** And I wouldn't want you to alter it. Kinda goes against the whole being honest thing you're trying to build back. And if you didn't realize it was me, no one else will.

**Cortez:** "Please, Trust. I'll get rid of them if you want, but please, please, *please* let me keep them."

Trust looked over again to see Cortez's hands clasped together. For a moment, he looked like a child begging his mother for something.
Trust shrugged.

**Trust:** What do I care? Just keep it to me, you, Allison, Kyler, Paxson, Marcie, and the Centre City Metro Police Department. Nobody else.

**Cortez:** "Woo-hoo! Boom, baby!"

**Trust:** Boom, baby. Should have seen that coming. By the way, do you still have entries from that Tigresa app?

Cortez was picking up his computer bag.

**Cortez:** "Yeah. But you know I had to shut that down, right? Yeah, a pretty blatant invasion of privacy, they said. But they also said I could publish it again if I wanted to...after I make some major adjustments."

**Trust:** I would be curious to see a few entries.

**Cortez:** "Eh, no problem. They were all public anyway while it was online, so it's not as if you'd be seeing something nobody else could have accessed. The drive is actually in Thomas, so you can look at it there. You ready to go? Or are you planning to sneak out through the window again like last time? I can't believe I fell for that."

Standing, Trust smiled as the other student closed the laptop, taking it and the power cord under his shoulder.
"I was thinking," Cortez intoned as he wrapped the cord, looking at

Trust. "I asked this in passing to Allison, and she mentioned you can actually talk—like, really good. That you have a good speaking voice. If you wanted—and only with your permission—I think I could use your voice for the TalkText program on your computer. Then it would be as though you were actually speaking instead of using the factory voice or having someone else reading your words for you."

Trust smiled again, gripping his note cards in one hand as he wrote.

*Is that what you did with "Natalie"?*

"Man, trust me, Trust. If you could just hear her voice, and then imagine the person it belongs to, you would realize I wouldn't have a shot of getting in the same building as her, much less being able to make a recording. No, this came off one of the boards online."

*Don't sell yourself short, kid.*

Cortez chuckled.

"Says the black guy with 'chocolate skin and blue eyes who has all the girls fighting over him.'"

He clasped his hands together and batted his eyes, Trust shooting him a peculiar look. Cortez continued.

"But seriously, just think about it. I don't need an answer now. I think it would be a neat thing to try, and a challenge. I don't know how many words you can actually say, but if I can get it to work for you, we may be able to bring it university-wide for whoever is using the program. So, we ready now? Allison's probably wondering if I got arrested again."

Trust wrote,

*Check the hall. It's going to seem weird if I walk out of here without anyone having seen me come in.*

Cortez read the note, and then looked to Trust—and then shrugged. He moved toward the door, with Trust following. Cortez switched off the light, his hand on the doorknob as he turned again.

"You know, what's really weird is—"

He stopped. The now dark room was empty. Cortez rushed toward the still-open window, sticking his head out.

Outside, in the darkness, there was no sign of him.

On the windowsill, propped against the other portion of the sliding window, rested a note card...and Cortez's still uneaten banana.

*Meet you in Thomas.*

Cortez picked up the banana.

"I don't even remember laying this down," he mumbled to himself. "Dude, this guy is *so awesome!*"

## 46.
## Allison and Jezzie Meet

A FEW DAYS LATER FOUND Trust and Kyler in Allison's dorm room. The meeting had been set.

Jezzie was on her way over.

And Melody, naturally, was absent. Allison would not say why.

*Including the time the baseball team visited her in the hospital,* Trust gestured, *I think I've met Melody exactly one time. She's like a ghost. I hear about her on occasion, but I never see her.*

"That's your fault," Kyler said. "I see her all the time. I've seen her exactly twice as many times as you have."

*What are you, some type of stalker? Give the girl some space already.*

They both laughed, and Kyler turned to Allison. The blond boy was sprawled on Allison's bed, playfully taking up as much space as possible, leaving Allison only the bottom corner to sit on. Persistent nudges from both of them exemplified the war still going on for bed space. The grins exchanged between both of them, however, conveyed their playful intentions.

"I know what the two of you are doing," Allison declared, "and it's not going to work. I told you she's fine, and that's really all you need to know."

Allison's head twisted between the two as she spoke. Trust had no difficulty following her words, even when her head was turned away, since Kyler continued to interpret. He seemingly had a knack for realizing when Trust would need his assistance, along with the complete selflessness to provide such assistance without hesitation or complaint.

*What, are you hearing voices now?* Trust signed, to which Allison laughed. *I don't think either of us even asked where Melody was. But,*

553

*speaking of that, Cortez let me look at some of the old entries from Tigresa.*

"Yes," Allison said. "Seeing as I was also there in the lab when you looked it up, I actually already knew that. You looked up Rory and some of those other names that I now can't remember. But what did you expect to find from that?"

*Exactly what I did. Those guys are pretty much unaccounted for at the times on those nights I looked up, and you know how precise some of those entries can get. It's completely circumstantial, but I find it highly telling they disappeared during those times. Actually, I was just thinking that I should have looked up Melody's name and—*

"Oh, for crying out loud, just shut the—" Allison began, before her eyes tracked to the door, Kyler's following in the same breath. "Come in!"

Trust turned his head as the door started to open, Jezzie materializing. Her curled, dark blond hair hung loosely, and she gave a faint smile as her eyes fell on Trust first before seeing the other two freshmen farther in the room. Trust turned to see Kyler chuckling.

"Wow. T, just put that little wager on my open tab of the things I owe you."

*I'm pretty sure I'm the one who's got the tab from all of your interpreting services through the years,* Trust signed as Allison stood to greet the new arrival. *If you could just deduct the five dollars from that, kind sir, I would be much obliged.*

"I hate entering in the middle of a joke," Jezzie said.

As Allison directed her to sit anywhere, Trust signed, *Definitely not a joke. How did you get in without a card? They're supposed to be pretty strict now with that, especially after all the Dorm Room Robbers stuff.*

Jezzie shrugged.

"Somebody let me in."

Trust put on an innocent look.

*Really? A girl let you in?*

Jezzie looked between the three of them, slightly confused.

"It...was a boy. Why? I don't understand."

"Five dollars has been deducted from your debt, my good man," Kyler said, looking over to Trust and laughing. "It was a pleasure doing business with you."

He then turned back to Jezzie.

"Jezzie, did this boy stare at you as you walked in? Perhaps his

554

tongue was hanging down to the floor?"

He and Kyler laughed again.

Allison rolled her eyes, explaining to Jezzie, "It's probably best to just ignore them right now. They had a bet to see if you would be able to get in without having to call us to come down. It's a new university policy to not let in anyone who doesn't have a card—you've probably gotten the email—and that policy is, supposedly, strictly enforced after all the robberies."

*In other words, I'm ninety-nine percent certain the reason you were let in here no problem is because you're hot.*

Trust then quickly turned to Allison, his hands already moving even as her mouth started to open in objection.

*And I know you and Marcie will say that is objectification or something else that I really have no idea about, so let me simply say...no, it isn't. It's just a fact and, hopefully, a compliment. The same thing would happen to you and Marcie if you tried to get into another dorm, and you know it. Don't shoot the messenger.*

Allison started to speak again, but Jezzie held up her hand, smiling.

"So you think if it was a group of girls at the door, they wouldn't be pushing each other out of the way to let either of you in a dorm you didn't live in? How did you two get in here?"

She looked between Trust and Kyler, her eyebrow arched. Allison crossed her arms, smiling brightly in that insincere way that expresses, "Now what?"

Trust pointed to the other boy in the room.

*He gets that all the time, but what did I do? You know, you're actually the second person who's given me a compliment like that recently. The other person is a boy who likes girls so much, his computer is named Natalie and apparently has a sensuous female voice that talks back to him. Is it my hair? I mean, I did get a haircut, but that was about a week ago—*

"Well, I am glad this rousing conversation has come to a close," Allison said, beginning to usher both boys out of their reclined positions, Kyler groaning as he was jostled.

"Actually..."

Trust, who happened to be looking at Jezzie as she began to speak, stopped as her hazel eyes fell on him. Kyler and Allison stopped and looked as well.

"This is going to sound a little random, but I was wondering if maybe you guys could stop by Jeremy's. If you have something else planned, by all means, forget that I even asked, but...it's just that he's been acting a little...off lately, I guess. I know it's about all of this Freesef business and what happened—"

Trust saw Kyler hold up his hand.

"Say no more," he replied. "Where is he? I haven't even seen him since the Spring Break jubilee."

"He's at his apartment."

She reached into her small purse for her keys.

"Here, you can take my car. It's in the parking lot across the stre—"

But Trust waved her off.

*Then how would you get back?* he gestured.

"If you're not back by the time we're finished talking, I can just take the Centre Line—"

But Trust waved her off again. The faces he made were almost comical.

"You know what?" Kyler said, glancing down to the clock on his phone before replacing it in his pocket. "I happen to know a certain bus driver who is working right now and will be able to take us. Jeremy lives somewhere downtown, right? I happened to look at this bus driver's schedule. Man, is he going to wish I didn't have such a good memory."

He was smirking.

"Fine," Allison said, waving toward the door again. "Whatever. Go."

Dodging her gesticulations, Kyler snuck in and landed a delicate kiss her on the cheek, causing her to grin despite herself.

Trust's eyes shifted to Jezzie when Kyler's attention was on him again.

*And you're okay? You're sure you're all right with this?*

A small grin came across Jezzie's face.

"Don't you guys have a bus to catch?" she asked.

Trust returned her grin.

The bus door hissed open.

"Oh, come on!" Mr. Jackson exclaimed. "What did I do to deserve this? I just saw you, what, four hours ago? I need a longer break than that!"

Kyler was grinning as he climbed the steps. Trust was chuckling behind him, able to see what the bus driver said.

"How about getting your friend to actually sit in the seat for once, Trustice?" Mr. Jackson said as the deaf boy passed him.

Trust nodded, giving a thumbs-up. In seconds, the Centre Line bus was easing away from the curb, moving again.

Unbidden by Trust, Kyler did sit properly in his seat. The bus was largely empty.

"How's Mariana?" Kyler asked.

The smirk on his face hinted at the implications of his words. Trust simply gave him a look.

"Always the commitment-phobe," said Kyler, shaking his head. "Hey, you ever notice we get to hang out with a lot of hot women? Allison, Marcie, Mariana, Jezzie's beautiful—"

*You know what I like about being deaf?* Trust motioned. *When I look away, it's like you don't even exist anymore.*

He watched as Kyler laughed.

*But really,* he went on as Kyler calmed down again, *I wonder how Jeremy's going to react when we show up at his front door—well, front desk.*

Kyler looked at him, tilting his head slightly to the side.

"Front desk?" he repeated.


"MR. TRUSTICE JEFFRIES AND MR. Kyler-Scott Brooks here to see you, sir," the doorman Trust remembered as Montague stated into the phone, smiling slightly as he took in the two boys, particularly Kyler. "Mr. Brooks requested that I remind you that is Kyler *hyphen* Scott."

Kyler was looking around the opulent entrance foyer, unabashedly impressed. He was tugging at his shirt as if he meant to button it at any moment.

Impossible, since it had no buttons.

"I feel like I need to straighten my tie in here," he said.

*You don't even know how to tie a tie, much less how to wear one,* Trust replied.

"Hey, clip-ons can be straightened, too," Kyler retorted.

"Indeed they can, Mr. Brooks," Montague said. "Mr. Higgins will see you both. I trust you remember the way, Mr. Jeffries?"

He started to chuckle lowly. Trust looked at him, shaking his head at the pun.

"Is that a clip-on?" Kyler asked, pointing to the doorman. "That's a nice one."

The doorman's smile vanished.

"Now that...is preposterous," he said stiffly.

"And what's with the Mr. Brooks and Mr. Jeffries stuff? Kyler and Trust are way better."

*Already tried that,* Trust observed as they both followed Montague to the elevators. *It's not going to work.*

Upstairs, Jeremy opened the door after Trust's knock. The upperclassman met Trust's gaze briefly before his eyes flitted to Kyler.

"Door's over here, smart guy."

Kyler had his back turned, continuing to take in the impressive surroundings of the building. He finally faced forward.

"So, the baseball superstar and the deaf kid who convinced me not to kill my so-called 'friends.' I'm guessing Jezzie asked you to check up on me."

*Kill?* Trust signed. *That's strong.*

"Is it? Rape's pretty strong, too, especially when it actually happened, and especially when you have classes with some of the people who did it and you know where they live."

Trust glanced down the hall to the closest door.

*Please tell me you're not yelling right now. What are the chances someone can hear?*

"Zero. That's Mrs. Lobowski. If you're a ten out of ten on the deafness scale, she's a 9.8. Still, I guess you should come in. My mom always told me it was impolite to talk in the halls."

Once they were inside and the door was closed, Kyler was looking around in amazement once again.

"Before we get to what you've guessed we're already here for, I just have to say, holy—"

"Put a sock in it, Brooks," Jeremy said, breezing past them toward the hall, leaving the two freshmen to follow behind and for Kyler to interpret for Trust. "You can come back another time and I can give you a grand tour. But I'm seriously, *seriously* not in the mood these days."

"Fair enough," said Kyler, "but I'm curious. Do people actually know you live here? I mean, I've been around you a handful of times now, but I had no idea you were this rich."

Jeremy looked back over his shoulder.

"I'm not ri—"

He stopped, turning fully, and looked at Trust.

"You didn't tell him where I lived?"

Trust shrugged.

*Why would I? Anyway, you didn't seem so fond of showing the place off the last time I was here.*

Jeremy looked at him for a moment before shaking his head and chuckling faintly. He led the two visitors into the den, an area of the luxury condo Trust had not seen on his previous trip. Like the rest of the apartment, it was large, tasteful, and almost startlingly tidy, given the fact that a college student resided there.

There was also an enormous television. A University of Centre City football game from the season that had just concluded a few months earlier was paused on the giant screen.

"Oh, cool. The game's on," Kyler said. He launched himself into a plush-looking recliner, before turning back and catching Jeremy's expression. "This isn't your usual seat, is it? 'Cause I can move."

"It's...fine?" Jeremy said, his inflection rising at the end. He glanced to Trust.

"Good, 'cause I was lying," Kyler said, laughing. "I wasn't really going to move."

Jeremy shook his head and chuckled again, sinking into a leather sofa, Trust doing the same a moment later.

"Look," Jeremy declared, "I know you came here to see if I wanted to talk about, you know, all of the nonsense that has gone down, but do you mind if we just watch the game for a while? I've been obsessing over this Freesef crap constantly, but I think, with you guys here, you'll be able to, I don't know, distract me or something, and I can just relax for a little bit."

Trust scoffed.

*You thought we were here to talk about Freesef? We came to watch the game. Which one is this, at Wisconsin? We lost this one, right?*

Jeremy gave him a look.

"Are you kidding?" he asked sarcastically. He reached for the remote control.

"Wait," Kyler said, jumping up from his seat. "Before you start it again, how about pointing me to the popcorn cabinet in this mansion of yours. I'm feeling popcorn right now."

Jeremy looked to Trust again.

*Oh, yeah. This is twenty-four-seven. Please, feel free to borrow him anytime you like.*

The Freesef Society never again arose in conversation the rest of the evening.

## 47.
## Abduction

"HE'S IN AN ADMINISTRATIVE MEETING," Kimberlee informed Trust the next afternoon as he stood in front of the receptionist's desk in Adams Hall. "It should only be a few more minutes. It was actually supposed to be over fifteen minutes ago."

Trust smiled and shrugged.

*I'm sure Dr. Duncan is the main reason the call is still going on,* he signed, *but don't tell him I said that.*

"Why?" the graduate student commented. "It's the truth and everyone knows it."

She then grinned playfully.

"So, how is Mrs. Jeffries—I mean, Mariana?"

Trust started to move past the desk.

*Well, I guess he's off the phone now...*

Kimberlee laughed.

"There you go again. She told me you would do that."

*You know, it's kind of annoying that you two actually know each other. Maybe I should hang out with Kendell and learn how to make desserts that have people lining up in the cafeteria at all hours of the night. Then we can gossip about you.*

"Who says we gossip? Anyway, Kendell would probably get a kick out of teaching you how to cook if you ask him. He loves teaching the culinary students."

She then glanced down to her computer.

"Dr. Duncan should be back in his office now."

Trust started to turn away before turning back again.

*Do you remember that group of guys I had that...altercation with last semester? I think you called us all kindergarten babies, if I remember correctly.*

"Oh, how could I forget?" Kimberlee said, rolling her eyes. "The unchecked testosterone that day nearly strangled me. And I believe I used the simple preschooler designate."

*Yeah, whatever. Do they still come in to volunteer?*

Kimberlee arched an eyebrow.

"'Yeah, whatever'? You want to have another shot at that?"

Trust grinned cheekily.

"Good-bye, Mr. Jeffries."

*I'm getting the weirdest sense of déjà vu here,* Trust signed.

"That's probably because you seem to have a knack for inserting something rude or cocky in an otherwise great conversation. But I'm done now."

"AMERICAN POLITICS, ABNORMAL PSYCHOLOGY – HONORS, Biomed II, Mathematics and Analytical Theory, Current Events Elective, and Martial Arts II," Dr. Duncan listed, "including two classes again with dear Mr. Brooks. Is that his name? Brooks? Brooks, Brooks...yes, Kyler Brooks—no, Kyler-*Scott* Brooks. Such a character, that boy! He was just in here constructing his own fall schedule a few days ago. Oh, but I'm sure he mentioned it to you. You see each other all the time—and how else would you have been able to coordinate your courses?"

Trust sat, waiting. He didn't even reach toward the keyboard.

"Oh! And I also wanted to raise the Freesef Society topic that I believe we discussed the last time you were here. What you told me in our last meeting disturbed me deeply—*deeply*. For stories such as those to be circulating on this campus, in this city—on any campus in any city, for that matter—simply unconscionable. I have broached the subject with others, both inside the university and out, and all of them seemingly have no idea. Moreover, these people I talked to, Trustice, I do believe them. However, I also believe you. So, I reached out to another group of contacts."

Trust gazed at him.

"You've heard the name Grayson Thomas?" Dr. Duncan posed, leaning forward in his chair, his elbows resting on the table between them.

Trust nodded.

Seemingly maintaining a permanent place at or near the top of the list of the world's richest people, virtually anyone who had heard any sort of financial or technological news was aware of the names of both Grayson Thomas and the Grayson Thomas Interface Corporation—GTI. The University of Centre City's fabled Thomas Building within the School of Engineering quadrant was named after him. The story went that, as he was arguably the university's most famous alumnus, it was the only building he finally relented to being named in honor of him.

"I was his academic advisor while he was a student here, believe it or not," the senior administrator remarked, "and I also taught in a few of his classes...or perhaps he taught me. We've kept in touch over the years. I actually mentioned this Freesef issue to him. Have you met Grayson Thomas before?"

Trust gave Dr. Duncan an amused look before shaking his head.

"Really?" the old man said. "Well, anyway, I mentioned it to him. And do you know what he said? *Do you know?* His exact words were, 'I have whispers of that as well, Dr. Duncan. But I think it best if you not worry yourself over it. I'm looking into it.' And yet what he said next was even more astounding to me."

Dr. Clarke Duncan and Trustice Jeffries looked at each other for a moment in silence.

"He asked...he asked if I knew a student currently enrolled at the university by the name of Trustice Jeffries."

Trust tilted his head slightly, his brow furrowing.

"Yes," Dr. Duncan said, nodding. "That's exactly what I said."


THE TEASINGLY MISNAMED "EXAM WEEK" had once again arrived, signaling the final two weeks of the school year. With his first exam completed on the first day of Exam Week, Trust was already on his phone as he departed the small lecture hall with a group of other students.

Even with the intentional spread of examinations over the two-week period, Trust, Allison, and Paxson each had an exam on the very first day, and at a similar time, though Trust had managed to finish his mercifully quickly, while Pax and Allison had been all but guaranteed a long and mind-numbing evaluation. Kyler was traveling with the baseball team, once more out of town for a series of road games.

> **Trust (12:02 PM):** Yo, yo, yo. You ready? I'm ready. You ready?
> **Marcie (12:02 PM):** Yo, I'm so ready, I'm already here, yo.
> **Marcie (12:02 PM):** And you and Grayson Thomas can pick up the check. How was your exam?

Trust rolled his eyes, smirking.

> **Trust (12:03 PM):** Piece of cake. And speaking of, be there in 4 minutes.
> **Trust (12:03 PM):** Oh, and not funny.

On exam days, the academic buildings themselves were not as active as they typically were, since a lesser number of classes were meeting than would be on a normal school day. Presently, the hallway Trust walked down was mostly—

His phone vibrated.

> **Cortez (12:04 PM):** Narrowed phone location to approx 5 sq miles along Decatur Lane and property. Guessing the phone was tampered with, if not destroyed. Residue readings are oddly weak.
> **Trust (12:04 PM):** Is 5 miles common? Can you narrow it down further? And why do you say the reading is odd?
> **Cortez (12:04 PM):** Range is common if you can't get good reading. If I try to get closer with the current condition of the phone, I'll lose it. Possible electronic interference or something else shielding the reading, like a vault so the signal can't get out.
> **Cortez (12:05 PM):** All this for a stolen phone?

Trust was already outside, now approaching the walkway leading up to Hollins Cafeteria. Passing through one of the campus's well-maintained and picturesque open courtyards, he saw numerous students lounging about, either under shady trees or out in the sunlight on top of blankets, taking advantage of the warm springtime weather. Most had their heads buried in textbooks and papers, though a few also found the time for more leisurely relaxation or more active recreational activities.

> **Trust (12:06 PM):** Allison's stolen phone. I think it's related to the Freesef Society, and I think I know who took it. I just want to be sure.

He let exiting diners pass before going through the entrance doors.

> **Cortez (12:06 PM):** If you know the guy's number or the number of anyone else in that area, I can use it to triangulate a location. But you seem like a stickler for the law, at least in some things, and this would be a gray area.

Another message came through as Trust was reading.

> **Jezzie (12:06 PM):** Trust, Jeremy is missing. I'm at his condo with police. Can you come?

Trust had already spotted Marcie sitting at a table and had been walking in her direction.

Jezzie's text halted him in his tracks.

To Cortez:

> **Trust (12:07 PM):** Stay on it. I'll get back to you.

And to Jezzie:

> **Trust (12:07 PM):** I'm on my way.

He hurried over to Marcie. Marcie, observing the sudden change in his demeanor, was now standing.

"What happened?"

Trust handed over the phone. Marcie looked at it quickly, then at him. Her emerald-green eyes were set.

"I'm coming with you."

Her voice, and for Trust, her expression, ended any arguing before it could start.

BOTH TRUST AND MARCIE LEAPED from the Centre Line bus as soon as the exit door eased open, drawing curious glances from others on the bus and those out on the sidewalk in front of the Millennium Complex.

There were three Centre City Metro police vehicles parked at the curb. The two students raced past, bounding up the steps and through the golden front doors.

The bus ride had taken them sixteen minutes.

Bursting into the lobby, Trust absorbed everything in an instant, his head whipping around swiftly and immediately noting two officers off to one corner of the hall, their backs turned away as they stood in front of a distraught-looking Jezzie Delaney. A fleeting look toward Marcie indicated that she should follow him, and the two hurried over.

Jezzie's eyes landed on him first before either of the cops had fully turned around.

"Oh, God, Trust!"

She lunged at him, Trust momentarily taken aback by the desperate embrace. Turning slightly, he glanced to the officers, recognizing them both.

Longley.

Ryan.

Trust patted Jezzie as she shuddered, her head coming just under his chin.

Marcie appeared in his field of vision then, facing the two officers.

"What happened here?" she asked brazenly.

Officer Ryan looked at her, his eyebrow arched.

"Excuse me?"

Jezzie pulled away from Trust.

"Jeremy's gone," she declared, looking into Trust's eyes before turning to Marcie, Trust shifting so he maintained a visual on her face. "Something happened. I *know* something happened. I haven't heard from him since early yesterday, and when I came today to check on him after I still hadn't heard anything, he didn't answer the door. I went in, and his condo is..."

She appeared as though she were about to break down, and Marcie reached out to console her. She gave a look to Trust.

Trust looked to the two policemen.

"You know Jeremy Higgins?" Officer Ryan asked, gazing back at him.

Trust nodded. He then pointed to the currently unmanned front desk.

"What?" Officer Longley asked, craning his head. "What is it?"

Trust took out his phone.

*Montague. The doorman at the front desk.*

"I completely forgot he was deaf," Longley mumbled. "I didn't make the connection when she said she was calling Trust."

"We found the doorman behind that door."

Trust followed Ryan's finger to a door behind the desk, under the large staircase.

"Looks like an assault," he continued. "Multiple attackers. I would guess he had only just regained consciousness when we arrived on scene. He's been transported to Arlington Memorial."

"There's signs of struggle in the condo," Longley picked up. "Miss Delaney here describes the apartment as always being organized. Now, things are broken and strewn all over the floor. Points of impact on the walls where something—or someone—was violently thrown around in the entrance foyer and in the hallway. More damage in the back living and bedroom areas. We were just asking Miss Delaney if it was possible Jeremy could have done all of that damage himself, if he had a violent temper—"

"That doesn't even make any sense," Marcie said, still holding Jezzie as the older girl sniffled. "You just got finished saying the doorman was beaten up and taken to the hospital. Would Jeremy have done that, too?"

Jezzie lifted her head away from Marcie, turning around again.

"That's just what I told them."

Her eyes found Trust again.

"I told them everything. The Freesef Society, what happened before Winter Break and at the Spring Break party, what I know about what happened to your friend Allison."

"We've already dispatched units to find and pick up the individuals Miss Delaney has named. Once they are located," Ryan remarked, "they'll be taken down to the station for questioning."

*One of them is named Rory?*

"I'm not at liberty to give out—"

Trust shifted in mid-sentence to Jezzie. He held up his phone to her. She nodded.

"It has to be him," she asserted, "and some of the other guys I told you about."

She exhaled, attempting to collect herself, running both hands through her hair.

"Trust, this is exactly what I was afraid would happen. What if...what if they hurt him?"

Back to Ryan.

*She told you I found her in the alley before Christmas?*

"You seem to be drawn toward these types of situations," Ryan observed.

*And you seem to be running out of chances to hold these guys. My turn is coming up soon.*

The officer looked down at the message typed out on the phone, and then back to Trust. He suddenly looked frustrated.

"What does that mean?" he asked lowly, his teeth clenched.

Trust stared back at him. Ryan turned to Longley, who had resumed questioning Jezzie, Marcie lending support by continuing to hug her lightly on the shoulder.

"If you don't mind, sir," Ryan said, "I need to speak to Trust for a moment."

Trust gave Marcie a fleeting nod before he walked with the young officer closer to the staircase. Officer Ryan turned on him as they stopped, the impressive foyer of the Millennium Complex silently observing their every action from all sides.

"Look—"

But Trust had already typed a message into his phone.

*Why is it you seem to be in contact with Allison Tyler more
than the detective supposedly assigned to her case?*

"You don't know what that detective has been doing concerning that
investigation, so you don't get to comment on it. Moreover, if—"

Trust looked down to start typing, but Ryan covered the phone with
his hand, causing Trust to look up again. Slowly.

"Moreover," Ryan resumed, his tone measured and with a slight
sharpness, "if you're insinuating an attempt to take the law into your
own hands like I think you just did a moment ago, I would highly, *highly*
advise against that plan of action. Questioning how we conduct an
investigation is bad enough. Threatening to turn yourself into a vigilante
is something else entirely. Do we understand each other?"

Trust typed.

*Nope. I'm not questioning how "we" conduct an investigation,
I'm questioning the detective. I don't think he's doing much of
anything, and I think you're covering for him for some reason.
How far along would the PD be with her case without the info
Allison has told you? She identified Rory by his voice. You let
him go after a couple of hours. Allison, Jezzie, Allison's
roommate, Melody—you're nowhere without the information
Allison gives you.*

*The question you should be asking yourself now is how she
gets this information. Then ask yourself if either of us would
be standing here if the detective actually did his job.*

Ryan's jaw tightened as he read.

"I understand your concern, and your loyalty to your friends," he said
slowly. "I've witnessed your devotion firsthand. But Officer Tubbs is
upstairs in Jeremy Higgins' apartment with Detective King as we speak,
and—"

Trust held up his hand.

*You've noticed the cameras. Have you checked the video yet?*

"Detective King is the lead officer on the scene. He wants to check the surveillance footage personally after—"

*After he stalls a little longer. I'll save him some time. Tell him it was a group, like you said, and they were wearing balaclavas. You can't miss them. They probably took them off when they got to Jeremy's door. Has anyone talked to Montague?*

Officer Ryan put a hand up to his blond hair, obviously agitated.

"I honestly don't know why I'm even bothering to answer these questions..."

Trust pointed again to his phone.

"The doorman was in the ambulance on the way to the hospital before the detective arrived. He is going there next after he's finished here."

*Did you talk to the doorman before he was taken to the hospital?*

"The detective wants to talk to him first in order to get the initial story."

"Heh."

Trust chuckled.

*Why doesn't he want you to get the first impression?*

Trust studied the quiet officer standing before him for a moment.

*You know something's off about this—about him—and you've known it from the beginning. It's why you continue to talk to Allison and Melody.*

Ryan's face was set, his expression unreadable.

*The Freesef Society has assaulted four girls that I am aware of for sure, not to mention the stories of dozens—hundreds—of others throughout the years. Now they've kidnapped a person who's turning into a friend of mine. You've now heard about me fighting in alleys, running through traffic, and facing off against a man with a gun. What do you think I'll do when you can't find these guys—and I do?*

As the young officer looked back at him after reading the text, Trust turned away, walking back to Marcie, Jezzie, and Officer Longley.

Trust was typing again.

*Is anyone else coming to meet you? That Alyssa girl who was looking at me weird that one time?*

For the first time since Trust had arrived, Jezzie cracked a faint smile.

"She thought you were hot," Jezzie said, "and that maybe I was cheating on Jeremy. That's why she was looking at you like that. She gets out of her exam in...fifteen minutes, and then I'm going to call her. I was supposed to meet her, but thank you—and you, Marcie—for coming. I don't know if I interrupted anything you had going on—"

Marcie shook her head.

"Trust had just gotten finished with his exam and was meeting me in Hollins. I don't have any exams this week, fortunately."

*You don't have to stay.*

Trust showed the text to Marcie, and she gave him a hard look.

"There's five seconds that you just wasted," she declared.

"You three stay here for a second," Officer Longley requested. "I need to speak with Ryan."

His gaze then settled on Trust.

"Let's not plan on doing anything rash, all right?"

Trust's eyes shifted back to Marcie as the officer walked away, joining Ryan, who was now speaking on his phone at the foot of the staircase.

*I still think you rigged your exam schedule on purpose, by the way.*

Marcie chuckled and showed the message to Jezzie, who smiled once more.

*Any idea where they could have taken him?*

"I told them about the house on Decatur and a few other places, but I...I don't think it will be that easy. I'm worried they took him somewhere that I don't know about. God, Trust, I know this is what I told you I was afraid of, but I...I don't know. Why? Why now? Did Allison say anything else to the police? Do you think they would really hurt Jeremy?"

"No way did Allison say anything if you asked her not to," Marcie asserted firmly. "And they will find Jeremy. I know it."

> *And I'm sure Jeremy wasn't taken out of here without a fight.*
> *I'll bet some, if not most, of the damage in his apartment was*
> *him giving it to someone else. I've been in the ring with him,*
> *and I saw that punch he threw before Spring Break. He*
> *wouldn't go down without others getting trampled in the*
> *process.*

"Jeremy's parents are on their way from Ohio, where we're from," Jezzie told them. "His dad has an office here in Centre City, but they don't live here."

> *Neither of you ever mentioned who his dad was. If you don't*
> *think Jeremy would want us to know, you don't have to say,*
> *but*

Jezzie got his attention, stopping him as she read along with his text.

"A few days ago, Jeremy and I were talking about you and Kyler—you especially. He really does trust you, you know—and, of course, he had to make a joke about trusting you that you've probably heard a thousand times before. But ever since what you did for me before Christmas, and then just coming over here to hang out with him lately...it's the most relaxed I've seen him since the night we met here. All of that is to say that out of anyone, you're probably at the very top of a very short list that he would tell."

"Should I step to the side or something?" Marcie inquired. "I don't mi—"

"No," Jezzie said. "That trust goes for Trust's friends, too. Has either of you heard the name Henry Higgins?"

Marcie shook her head.

Trust typed.

*No idea.*

"That's intentional," Jezzie said. "What about Cobalt Lincoln?"

"Definitely," Marcie said. "That's a law firm, right? They have offices all over the country, according to the commercials—including here in Centre City. They're supposed to be one of the best."

"Maybe *the* best," said Jezzie, "and that's not just in the United States—in the world. The founding attorney, Mr. Lincoln, died about eight years ago and left it to his successor, his protégé, Jeremy's dad, Mr. Higgins. Cobalt Lincoln is now a multinational, multibillion-dollar law firm, and Mr. Higgins is at the head of it, though he tries his best to stay out of the spotlight. He's also the best attorney you'll probably ever hear of, extremely wealthy, and he'll be in this lobby in less than two hours."

"Huh," Trust said.

"Well, we'll be here to greet him with you, if you're okay with that," Marcie said.

"Mr. Higgins used to be a member of the Freesef Society back in the day," Jezzie observed. "He did his undergrad at UCC. I'm almost positive he knows nothing about how they function these days."

## 48.
## Wheels In Motion

THAT EVENING, IN HOLDEN'S DORM room, Trust leaned over, displaying the text on his phone to Allison. With Kyler out of town for another few days, writing, either by hand or on his phone, was still the most efficient way for him to communicate.

*Heard anything on your bribe sender?*

Allison shook her head.

*I'm beginning to think my questions on the progress of this police investigation are meant to be rhetorical.*

Meanwhile, the resident assistant of Weaver Hall's seventh floor, central wing, was also shaking his head.

"I still can't believe this," Holden said. "But you said that the police caught who did it? Rory and his friends?"

"They can only hold them for twenty-four hours," Marcie said. "Technically, they haven't arrested them for anything, and I doubt they will. Apparently, they all have some sort of alibi, which has to be a lie. The police are checking it, but Officer Ryan said it's not looking good. They're going to have to let them go again if they can't find anything concrete."

"Something's so not right about any of this," Paxson intoned. "I'm with Trust. This entire thing is like a gigantic black hole. Whatever information or evidence the police get is taken in and then disappears. It's like we keep falling back to step one all over again. You said you met

575

the detective assigned to Allison's case this afternoon? What did you think?"

Marcie scoffed. Trust grinned.

"I never really understood the definition of an empty suit until I met this so-called Detective King," said Marcie. "He's obnoxious and completely ignorant at the same time. I mean, I don't even know how that's possible. He's patronizing—he spoke to Jezzie and me like we were two little girls in plaid skirts and pigtails, and he talked to Trust as though he were mentally handicapped. I was *this* close to wiping that smirk off his puny little face—"

"Fortunately, however," Holden cut in, "since you're here, you must have restrained yourself. Otherwise, you would be down at the station now with Rory and the others, and, from the sound of it, you would be worse off than they are."

"I only met him one time," Allison informed them, "right after I got back from Thanksgiving Break. He seemed...unconcerned, to say the least. Disinterested. But I don't know."

Trust typed as the others spoke, alternately glancing up and down.

> *Jezzie keeps saying this is bigger than some secret student organization, that it affects the entire city. There's a chance— and I think it's a pretty good one the more I think about it— that Rory and Co. are receiving help from higher places, maybe even from within the PD.*

Allison read the message aloud.

"Detective King being one of them, I'm sure," Marcie asserted. "The little snot."

"Scooby-Doo, where are you? We could use some help on this one."

Everyone looked to Paxson.

"I was just saying what I thought everyone else was thinking," he said.

"I'm almost certain no one else was thinking that," Marcie returned. "You know, since he's a fictional talking dog and everything."

Trust leaned forward, showing his phone to Holden.

> *What about Oliver? Could he possibly be involved in this?*

Holden pulled out his own phone.

"If you're asking if he was involved in abducting Jeremy Higgins, I would bet all the money I've ever seen in my life against it. But if you're asking if he knows anything, that's a good question. He may know something and not even know that he knows it."

"Hmm," Marcie hummed, glancing pointedly toward her boyfriend. "That sounds like a familiar trait."

Paxson wasn't even paying attention, glancing down at his own phone as well.

*Why do I get the feeling this is going to turn into the Dorm Room Robbers, Part II?*

Trust showed the text to Allison.

"Didn't you say you went back to the trail behind Mueller the night after what happened to me?" she asked. "In this year I've gotten to know you, Trustice Jeffries, I'm not sure I would expect any differently. But then again, I'm not sure that's not the preferable choice. We have to find Jeremy, and we have to stop a group that thinks they have so much power that they can get away with it. Now tell me, who do you think can best get to the bottom of this? Us, or them?"

THE NEXT DAY, IN THE UCC library, amidst a sea of other tables filled with students, Trust saw his phone flash alongside the book he was reading.

The text message was from Holden.

> **Holden (10:17 AM):** Ollie was with them when the police came. He was shocked. Police didn't take him in since Jezzie Delaney didn't name him. He said Rory and the others were making jokes, didn't seem very concerned.
> **Holden (10:17 AM):** Ollie didn't even know Jeremy was missing until police showed up. Has trouble believing Rory, others could be involved. Told me he guessed they would hold Jeremy at the house like you guys, but
> **Holden (10:17 AM):** that's where he and the others were

when police came. Police searched, found nothing.

Trust brought up another name from his contacts list.

> **Trust (10:18 AM):** Yo, Cortez. Any update?

He then sent another text.

> **Trust (10:19 AM):** Jezzie, any news? I heard they let Rory
> and the others go this morning.

A response came in from Cortez.

> **Cortez (10:19 AM):** I had a slightly stronger signal when you
> gave me that Rory guy's number from Jezzie Delaney, down
> to 3 square miles when he was at the address you mentioned.
> But the phone is not in the house. If he were closer,
> **Cortez (10:20 AM):** the reading would have pinpointed to
> within a few feet.
> **Trust (10:20 AM):** Are you tracking him now? Is that legal?
> **Cortez (10:20 AM):** Technically, I'm not. I'm at the police
> station right now on a break.
> **Trust (10:21 AM):** Technically?
> **Cortez (10:21 AM):** Oops. Suddenly got busy with this thing.
> Gotta go.

It wasn't hard to spot that lie, even through text messaging. Trust shook his head, putting the phone to the side again, and went back to his reading.

"YOU KNOW, YOU COULD TEST out of the physical education requirement completely if you wanted," Kobe intoned, his breathing barely labored, as he faced the deaf student. "I would sign off on it."

Trust looked at him coolly, his posture unwavering.

The slightest flicker from behind the instructor's eyes indicated that he understood, and the man quickly shifted his center of gravity, twisting and unleashing a powerful kick—a kick he would have never performed on a first-year martial arts student.

Trust caught his foot, cradling it into his body.

Unlike most of their thrice-weekly meetings, the two of them were in one of the private aerobic studios for Trust's final exam. Trust remembered the cushioned flooring and wall-length mirrors, though he had not set foot in a similar room since the beginning of the spring semester.

He liked the old boxing ring at the North Gym better.

Trust pushed Kobe's foot away at the same moment the instructor turned again, this time in the opposite direction, his second kick aimed higher, shooting directly for Trust's head. Trust ducked under—and ducked again as the kick cycled back. The duo's movements were alarmingly, terrifyingly quick, and nearly silent in the padded room.

As Kobe's foot came to the floor, Trust shot forward with his right hand, and then his left, and then his right again. Kobe bobbed around all three, and then went to the ground.

Leg sweep. Trust jumped forward, deftly avoiding Kobe's leg and aiming a dropkick at Kobe's head. Kobe was almost too quick, catching Trust's feet and propelling him up and over like a trampoline toward the mirrored wall at the front of the room.

Trust contorted his body in the air, his socked feet making contact with the topmost portion of the mirror. For a fleeting instant, he was parallel to the ground nearly ten feet below, facing up toward the ceiling. Faster than a blink, he bounded off again, flipping backward and landing on his feet.

Now facing the mirror, he could see Kobe standing as well, observing him from behind.

A barely there smirk graced the instructor's face.

"Your spatial ability is uncanny," Trust watched the reflection say. "That's something even your grandfather wouldn't be able to teach."

Trust moved over to his notebook. Impromptu breaks in their sessions were quite common, mostly because Trust was not able to communicate on the fly as a speaking person would. In any case, it was hardly a hindrance, as neither Trust nor Kobe fought purely to increase their cardio fitness.

Had either of them been involved in an actual fight against any other opponent, the "fight" would have probably been over long before, negating the need for much cardio anyway.

Trust maintained deep, controlled breathing through his nose as he wrote.

> *We always talk about fear. How do you manage to keep your*
> *fears from making you lose control?*

Kobe looked Trust in the eye.

"By understanding you can never completely rid yourself of the fear in the first place—nor should you ever want to. Fear is not what makes you lose control; it is what reminds you to regain it."

> *There have been a number of rapes and assaults that have*
> *gone on in secret at this university for years, perpetrated by a*
> *single group. Most of them go unreported, and the few victims*
> *who do go to the police are swept under the rug by people*
> *who have enormous reach and influence. A prominent, highly*
> *visible UCC student was kidnapped recently, and no one*
> *seems to even know about it, and the probable culprits were*
> *just released from police custody.*

After he read, Kobe looked at Trust. Silent. Unwavering.

"So tell me," he finally uttered softly. "What do *you* expect to do about it?"

Trust's jaw clenched as he thought. Soon, the two were sparring again, lightning fast and with near-lethal force.

It was practice.

## 49.
## Second Abduction

OUT BEYOND THE OUTFIELD WALL, Kyler's player profile appeared on the scoreboard video display, the sun shining brightly overhead. A loud cheer arose from the crowd.

Similar to the athlete profiles shown at the football stadium and the basketball arena, Kyler-Scott Brook's number, height, year, and assorted information materialized artistically on the screen, alongside a dynamic Kyler mugging for the camera, making a series of amusing faces, before the scene switched again to various highlight plays he had made over the course of the season. As the real-life Kyler settled into his stance in the batter's box, the text overlay on the scoreboard transformed once more.

*Collegiate Baseball Freshman Player of the Year*

*Collegiate Baseball Player of the Year Nominee*

Trust shrugged, seemingly to himself, as he read the accolades. Show-off.

"Kyler's going to be running the school next year," Paxson declared as the crowd finally began to settle, Kyler waiting for the first pitch. "I'm calling it right now. He's going to be in Jeremy Higgins territory, if he isn't already."

The mention of Jeremy caused Trust to glance at his phone again.

"You still haven't heard from Jezzie?" Allison asked, spotting his movement.

Trust shook his head. On the field, Kyler wisely let a pitch sail by for a ball.

"She could be in an exam," Marcie tried. "Or she could have gotten out of one and forgotten to turn her phone back on."

Trust looked at her, arching an eyebrow.

"Hey, don't give me that look! It could happen! It has happened! To me! More than once!"

Trust smirked as he typed.

> *Suffice it to say, Jezzie's more of a girly-girl than you are. She wouldn't forget to turn on her phone.*

"And thank the heavens for that," Marcie said. "I think I would drown in my own puke if I turned into a girly-girl."

> *If you keep using phrases like "drown in my own puke," I don't think you'll have much to worry about.*

Kyler drew a walk. The opposing pitcher seemed to be suddenly having difficulty locating the strike zone, so afraid was he to actually give Kyler something to hit.

Moreover, it wouldn't get any easier with the Tigers' next batter, the country's top home-run hitter and the winner of the Player of the Year award, Trent Atkins.

THE TIGERS HAD TAKEN TO the outfield. On this, a Friday, in a Super Regional game of the collegiate playoff tournament, the score was tied 2-2. Kyler could be seen lollygagging in his shortstop position as they waited for the next batter to step up.

> *Why do Rory and the others let Oliver hang around if he's not actually in the Freesef Society? I've been trying to figure that out.*

"They were hanging around Jeremy all the time, and Jeremy's not in Freesef," Allison observed beside him.

> *But apparently, they have been trying to get him to join for a*

*while. For prestige. What does Oliver give them?*

The batter hit the ball on a soft grounder back to the pitcher, who threw him out easily. Trust continued to type, more to get his thoughts down than to show anyone else.

*But they had to know how Jeremy felt about Freesef, and they still were trying to get him to join, even when Jeremy questioned whether the group actually existed. Before Jezzie told him, he thought the stories were a myth. But his dad...but they weren't pressuring Oliver to join.*

*Who's in control? Why do they need Jeremy so badly?*

His phone vibrated in his hands.

**Cortez (2:33 PM):** ½ sq mile area, either in house or somewhere in backwoods. Probably as close a reading as we're going to get. Major interference. Fortified room in the house or
**Cortez (2:33 PM):** shelter in the woods, perhaps? You think it's possible they may be hiding Jeremy Higgins somewhere out there, too?
**Trust (2:34 PM):** Police apparently looked through house, didn't find anything. I've never been in woods. Only one way to find out.

Out on the field, the opposing school's player on first base was running as his teammate at bat swung at a pitch, hitting a sharp shot into the area between first and second base. The Tigers second baseman nearly turned the wrong way, anticipating where the ball would be going as soon as it struck the bat, but he recovered quickly, diving onto his knees and scooping up the ball before it was completely out of reach. He had to torque his body while in the dirt to fire toward second base, where both Kyler and the base runner were converging. It was going to be close...

...but the timing was perfect. Kyler snagged the toss out of the air in a dead run, tapping the base with his cleat and stepping over just as the opposing base runner slid in, his legs high. Still running, and now past the base, Kyler took another step before twisting and firing a rocket toward Trent at first.

Trent was in a full stretch, his glove extended far in front of him, ready for the throw.

The sound of the ball smacking into his glove was audible to those who could hear. The first-base umpire made a hard fist and pumped it dramatically. Even if he didn't know the gesture, Trust could read the ump's mouth, even from his present distance. The simple phrase wasn't difficult to comprehend.

"Outta there!"

Kyler was only just slowing to a stop in the deep infield when the cheer arose from the seats. Standing again, Trust checked his phone.

> **Cortez (2:35 PM):** Oh, yeah, and just so you know, what we're doing is technically maybe probably most likely illegal. But it's for a good cause so it cancels out. Like the Boston Tea Party or the sit-ins during the Civil Rights Movement.
> **Trust (2:37 PM):** Yeah, because this is exactly the same as those things.

Kyler and his teammates were jogging off the field, heading toward their dugout to prepare for the bottom of the inning amidst a sustained applause from the Centre City faithful. On the large video screen, time turned back on itself as the double play transpired once again.

Trust turned to Allison, displaying for her the new message he had just typed into his phone.

> *I'm going to Jeremy's place. Jezzie's supposed to be staying there.*

Allison started to reach down to pick up her things.

"Is there a way to signal to Kyler that we're leaving, or—"

Trust waved her off.

> *You're not going. Stay and watch Kyler.*

Allison looked at him for a moment.

"Can I hold this for a sec?" she asked.

Before Trust could respond, she turned, displaying the screen to Marcie.

"Look at this," Allison said. "Look what Trust just wrote."

"What is it? Let me see," requested Paxson, leaning over.

Marcie read the words quickly and then looked up.

"Chauvinistic much, Mr. Jeffries?" she raised, arching an eyebrow at the same time. "If Allison wants to go, I don't see why—"

"Wait," Paxson cut in. "I don't get it, though. That doesn't sound like anything bad."

Marcie turned to glare at him.

Paxson turned away as though he had heard something. Meanwhile, Trust received his phone back.

*What happened? I don't understand. I spelled all the words correctly.*

"'You're not going'?" Allison repeated. "'Stay and watch Kyler'? Is that an order, sir?"

Trust stilled his movements, looking at Allison, and then Marcie. He tilted his head slightly to the side.

*I've obviously fallen blindly into some type of men-are-pigs vortex, so I will blindly apologize. Anyone and their mother can come with me, but I think someone should stay and watch the game.*

"Are we all still going to the party later?" Allison inquired.

*You can bet your lipstick on it.*

Allison, and then Marcie, frowned.

*Wow, that was such an obvious and corny joke! Really? That merits a frown?*

A short while later, Trust was at the bottom of the steps in front of the railing protecting against the short drop to the playing field.

Trust whistled as the opposing team's manager stepped out of his dugout to head to the pitcher's mound. His whistle was loud, sharp, shrill—or so he had been told. It was also distinctive.

In the Tigers dugout, Kyler turned around, his eyes finding the boy. He grinned.

*I'm headed out,* Trust signed. *Jezzie's still not answering her phone.*

*What about tonight?* Kyler replied.

*No change. I'll be there.*

*Take someone with you.*

*You worried about me?*

*More worried about the other guy. But you, too, though.*

Their exchange was rapid-fire, even with the goings-on of a collegiate playoff game all around them. Trust gestured to the person standing alongside him.

*I tried to convince her there was no need,* Trust signed, *and now I think I've been labeled sexist.*

*There's a statement that could be easily misconstrued if you had said it out loud,* Kyler returned. *But dude, seriously. Stay cool. Remember, Allison is with you, so you can't try to do anything stupid.*

*Why do you think I'm letting her come? Don't make any highlight-reel plays while I'm gone.*

Trust saw Kyler laugh.

*Letting her come? Maybe you are a little sexist.*

The game continued.

*Are you okay?*

Trust nudged Allison on the seat beside him. They were on the Centre Line, destined for downtown. Allison hesitated for a moment, as though bringing herself out of her reverie. She shook her head.

"I mean, yes, I'm fine. I was just thinking, and I only just now realized what it is you must be thinking. What is the worst-case scenario when we arrive at Jeremy's apartment building?"

Trust had an instant answer.

*Bodies on the floor.*

Allison looked at him, not even close to cracking a smile at the distasteful joke. Trust tried again.

*Two options, really. One, she's there, or someone has seen her recently. Two, she's not there and no one has seen her recently. Unfortunately, I think we're going to find it's the latter. I just have a bad feeling.*

"And you think Rory and the others may have taken her, too?"

*If she's actually gone, they would be at the top of my list.*

He pulled the phone back, typing again.

*They would be the only ones on my list right now.*

She nodded, and then looked down. Trust watched as her body swayed gently with the rocking of the moving bus.

*You know, once we get to Jeremy's, you can stay on the bus if you want. Or in the lobby. I honestly don't expect to find anything there.*

"I was thinking again about what you said in Holden's room," Allison started, still looking down but with her head tilted just enough for Trust to see. "Did you, at the beginning of the year, in your wildest, craziest dreams, expect us to be here, now, in this situation? If we were anyone else, or we went to a different school, or did any number of things differently, how different would this year have been? Surely we wouldn't be running around, worrying about some secret organization where it's some type of ritual for a group of male students to sexually assault freshman girls and everyone looks the other way, or that they kidnap people who disagree with them. Is this really a normal college experience? Was this what we were trying to reach every time someone asked us what we planned on doing after high school?"

Trust looked at her until she met his eyes again. Then he went to his phone, Allison able to follow along as he typed.

*No, I didn't expect it, but excluding what you and Jezzie and Melody have been through this year, I wouldn't have it any other way. It's probably terrible to say, and I would certainly never wish it to happen to anyone, but we—and the university—could have been worse off. You went straight to the police after it happened and have kept in contact with Officer Ryan while money has been thrown at you to do otherwise. How many girls before you, perhaps in the exact same situation, if not worse, have done differently?*

*Jezzie, even with how afraid she was to tell ANYONE about what she knows, chose us to confide in.*

*Melody went to the police and wanted to stay at UCC—the same location where her attack took place, the same school as her attackers—even when her parents gave her the perfect out to leave.*

*Talk about courage. That's all of you.*

*The Freesef Society would be operating as normal if none of us were here, or if it had happened to different people. Why did they hurt Melody and Jezzie? Why did they abduct Jeremy? Why did they attempt to bribe you twice? They're facing something they've never faced before—people willing to fight back. Now they're afraid. They're panicking and they don't know what to do because they're not sure what happens next. They don't get to decide what happens next. We do. We're in control.*

*Fear is not what makes you lose control; it is what reminds you to regain it.*

*No, I didn't see any of us in this situation at the beginning of the year. But like you said in Holden's room, I'm glad it's us, because we can do something about it.*

After reading, Allison looked at Trust for a long time. Silent.

At last, a smile appeared.

"'If there was even a second that he thought you were in trouble, he would be the first one out the door, no matter how dark it was. I would be right behind him,'" she recited.

Trust smiled as well.

*For a girl, you have a pretty good memory.*

Allison huffed, rolling her eyes, though she couldn't erase the grin on her face.

"And you were doing so well."

*I blame your boyfriend. I've been around him for too long.*

"We're not together anymore."

The bus slowed down, but Trust, not paying any attention, nearly slammed his head into the seat in front of him. His gaze shifted to his phone, but Allison grabbed his wrist before he had a chance to start typing.

"We're fine," she assured him. "Nothing's wrong. Let's just concentrate on Jezzie right now."

AT THE MILLENNIUM COMPLEX, MONTAGUE was once again manning the front desk, as though he were never absent. Officer Ryan had later told Trust that the doorman's most egregious injury was to the back of the head, but Trust could see that the older man's face was still faintly showing signs of the assault.

"I'm afraid that if it is Mr. Higgins you are here to visit, Mr. Jeffries, he is otherwise...unaccounted for."

Trust flipped his phone around, displaying it to the old doorman. The message transcribed was a simple one.

*Are you okay?*

Montague nodded gravely. His overall bearing was more somber than on Trust's previous visits, giving the man, with the aid of his uniform, the appearance of an undertaker more than the gentlemanly and softly amusing courtesy officer.

"I will assume you have heard the misfortune that has come to our door," Montague said, his eyes shifting between Trust and Allison. "Reprehensible is a word I am apt to use. In all of my dealings with Mr. Higgins, he has been nothing but cordial to myself and the other residents of this condominium."

*This is my friend, Allison. We actually came to check on Jezzie Delaney. I understand that she is staying here, at least temporarily, while Jeremy is missing.*

Montague greeted Allison and said, "It was my understanding that Miss Delaney would be staying here as well, but I have, surprisingly enough, not seen or heard any word of her. Indeed, the records of the other officers who have been on duty since then show the same. Unfortunately, she left us with no way to contact her, only that she would be back."

*Be back? When was this? Did she say where she was going?*

Montague thought for only a moment.

"I do believe she was headed to the university. This was about...yes, a day and a half ago now. I understand the end-of-the-year exams are presently taking place, and she had her satchel with her. She also mentioned that she would be stopping by her own residence before returning. Perhaps she only decided she would rather stay there after all?"

*Perhaps, but I think that is unlikely. You wouldn't happen to know her address, would you?*

Montague shook his head. Trust nodded and looked toward—

"I've got it," Allison declared. "She's in the student directory."

She was reading from her phone. Then she closed her eyes, as though calculating in her head.

Her eyelids lifted.

"I know where this is. It's on the Purple route. I pass it every time I'm coming back from the salon."

Trust looked at her, his eyebrows raised ever so slightly. He then turned back to the doorman.

*Have you ever met a boy named Rory? He may have come to visit Jeremy before.*

With Montague attempting to maintain his professional demeanor, the reaction was very faint. Had Trust not been looking toward his mouth, waiting for a response, the lip curl could have just as easily gone unnoticed.

"Yes, I've met the...young man."

*What did you think about him? Seem okay?*

"Honestly, Mr. Jeffries, I'd rather not even discuss *him*, if you don't mind."

"He does seem to have that effect on people, doesn't he?" Allison said.

*The guys who attacked you, they were wearing ski masks? Balaclavas?*

"Balaclavas, yes, as a matter of fact, they were. How did you know that? The detective I spoke with told me they were going to attempt to prevent that information from becoming public knowledge in order to prevent copycats. I really don't understand why there would be a copycat of an assault on an old doorman, but..."

Trust shook his head as well.

*Yeah. Thanks for talking with us, Montague. Glad to see you're okay.*

"Wait."

Trust and Allison had started to turn away, but the unanticipated movement from Montague captured Trust's attention. The old, tall doorman looked between the two young students.

"In the last few weeks before Jeremy—excuse me, Mr. Higgins—was abducted by those savages, you and your friend...Mr. Brooks, yes. You were the only people Mr. Higgins allowed to visit besides Miss Delaney. I am not privy to the what or the why of this fact, but I can only assume that there is a very good reason for it, just as I assume there is a reason he did not let in those...others. They came a few times about a month or so ago, but he did not wish to permit them, and I was only too happy to show them the door.

"Whatever it is that you're doing, Mr. Jeffries, whatever it is that you are onto, I only ask that you be extremely careful. Boys like these...they simply do not care."

Trust nodded.

AFTER CATCHING A CENTRE LINE bus traveling on the Purple route, Trust and Allison arrived at Jezzie's apartment a short time later.

Though it would certainly not be confused with the luxury apartments of the Millennium Complex, Greenpark Estates was nevertheless nice, a tidy community of apartment buildings catering to the collegiate clientele. The grass and foliage in evidence were well cared for, the buildings themselves seemingly newly washed, if not just built. The two freshmen walked past the buildings leading up to Building 484. The adjoining parking lot was only sparsely filled. Trust's eyes surveyed their surroundings as they walked.

The neighborhood appeared quiet.

"This seems nice," Allison remarked.

Trust typed.

> *Nice and open. If we had more time, we could probably go door to door and question her neighbors. Someone might have seen her.*

They entered under the awning of Building 484 and soon arrived at the appropriate door. Trust knocked.

> *Hear anything? Any movement at all?*

After a few seconds, Allison shook her head. Trust tried the doorknob.

Locked.

*Tap me on the shoulder if you hear anyone coming.*

"What are you about to—"

But Trust was already looking away, bending down slightly in front of the door, his familiar set of lock-picking tools already out and in his hands. He glanced back, and then typed quickly into his phone.

*Don't watch what I'm doing. If anyone catches you, you need plausible deniability.*

Allison just looked at him, her skepticism evident.

*Yeah, that sounded stupid as I was writing it.*

Sooner than she would have expected, Allison heard the lock click. Trust started to turn the doorknob again. He looked to Allison.

She shook her head.

Trust held a finger to his lips. He then slowly pushed the door open. He didn't step inside until it was fully ajar.

ALLISON, WITH TRUST POSITIONED SLIGHTLY behind and to the side of her, knocked at apartment number 484-9, which stood diagonally across and a short distance away along the open corridor from Jezzie's 484-8.

Trust had slipped on his tinted shades, a rarity when the sun was still out.

Allison had already indicated that there was loud music coming from inside.

After multiple knocks, the door to the loud apartment opened to an older man, most likely in his thirties or early forties, significantly overweight, balding, wearing a tank top, flimsy shorts, and flip-flops. The closed door had actually done a superb job at suppressing the music that emerged from inside the apartment, as the sound now crashed into Trust in thumping waves.

Trust's brow furrowed.

Feeding a cluster of chips into his mouth, the man surveyed Allison and Trust quickly.

"I don't know you. You don't live in Greenpark. I know everyone who lives in this complex by face, and I know you don't live here."

Allison leaned forward. Being behind her, Trust could not see what she was—

"I said I don't know you!" the man bellowed. "I know everyone who lives in Greenpark, and—"

Trust made a motion, lowering his hand slightly, which got the man's attention. He cursed and hurried back inside, leaving the door open.

There was an unappetizing smell seeping from the doorway.

Allison turned back to Trust, screwing her face up in an amusing expression. The man returned, snack bag still in hand.

"So, like I said, I don't know either of you, which means—"

"We're so sorry for interrupting you," Allison said, smiling brightly and clasping her hands in front of her. "We were actually just looking for the girl who lives just across the hall from you in 484-8. Jez—"

"Jezzie Delaney," the man finished, nodding, stuffing more food into the hole in his face. "Nice girl. Hot. Good tenant. Pays the rent on time, every time. No problems. I think she's dating some football player."

"That's her," Allison bubbled. "Has she been around the last few days? She's not answering her phone. All the girls are supposed to work a group number tonight, but we still need to pract—"

"Wait," the large man said, his obnoxious chewing halting immediately. He studied Allison.

"You're..."

His eyes flitted again to Trust.

"And he's...oooh."

The man smiled lecherously.

"So, have you seen Jez around?" Allison asked again. She was twisting slightly back and forth on her feet, the epitome of veiled innocence.

"Oh, no, I haven't seen her since—what was that—the day before yesterday, I guess? After that, not a peep, Scout's honor. You may want to try her boyfriend's, if you know him. She spends a lot of time at his apartment, apparently."

The man looked from Allison's head to her feet, and back up again.

He started to lean forward.

"So tell me, babe. What's a guy gotta do to get a little private da—hey, whoa, whoa. Okay, okay."

Trust had quickly stepped forward as soon as the man started to reach his hand out toward Allison. The man retracted it quickly, as though he had been scalded.

Trust smiled faintly.

"Sorry," Allison sang, smiling and dancing away slightly. "No dances outside the club. Strict policy."

"So I can tell," the man mumbled, still eyeing Trust warily.

"Well, if you do run into Jez again, just tell her that I came around and to pick up her darn phone! 'Kay?"

"Uh...yeah, su-sure. Wait, what's your name?"

"It's Alice. Jez'll know. See ya!"

Trust continued to observe with an unwavering gaze as the overweight man slowly shut his door again. He then moved to catch up to Allison.

"So, I'm thinking that was a gigantic and displeasing waste of a conversation," she said as they retraced their steps toward the awning of the building again.

Trust shrugged.

*It solidifies what we assumed. While that guy probably wouldn't miss an opportunity to see Jezzie in the hallway, and he remembers he saw her about two days ago, if he plays his music that loud regularly, the UCC marching band could come through here and he wouldn't know it, much less Rory and his friends—if that's what happened.*

The two of them emerged into the daylight. Trust removed his shades.

"What happens now?" asked Allison. "Should we call the police?"

*Not the police, although we'll be calling Officer Ryan later. I want to see what we find at the party first, before Detective King and whoever else can mess this up, too.*

## 50.
## Shut It Down

*SO, YOU JUST HAD TO do it, huh,* Trust motioned.

In the dorm room, Kyler rolled his eyes playfully and smirked, tossing the baseball to himself.

*You're just so selfish, doing that for the team. It makes me sick,* Trust continued. *What about me? Did you even think, for one second, that I might want to see you hit* a grand slam *in a playoff game? But no, you save it for when I'm not there. By the way, when were you going to tell me you and Allison broke up?*

Kyler froze, looking at him. The baseball hit him in the head, though he didn't appear to feel it.

At that moment, Trust detected movement in the open doorway to their room and turned his head as Allison entered with a book bag and a box. She shut the door behind her.

"Okay, so I have everything here—the Viper Skin, the wrist holder for your phone, the new mask. But I want to go over Raul's baton one more time before we...what? What happened?"

Trust followed her gaze to Kyler.

"You told Trust we...we broke up?" the boy said, swallowing.

Kyler and Allison looked at each other. Allison's gaze had turned questioning, while Kyler's was slightly pained. Trust's gaze shifted between them both, before he clapped his hands.

The other two startled, turning to look at him.

*Yeah, that's what I thought. But forget about it for now; we'll definitely revisit the subject at a later time. I'll look stupid in the mask, and you've already explained the stick. Three times. I know how to use a stick.*

"Well," Allison intoned, coming out of her fog, "it's obvious why you need to wear the mask, as we've been over it just as many times as the baton. And the fact that you keep calling it a stick makes me think you do need it explained to you again. The only thing I'm really worried about is the grappling spring-hook. It's passed all the strength and capability screenings Cortez's roommate, Raul, has put it through, and I can't imagine any circumstance for which you would need to use it tonight, but for the way it's meant to be used—for the way you would use it—we haven't—"

*So, it's another field test,* Trust signed. *Like the Viper Skin was. I can handle it, Mommy. I'm sure I'm in good hands.*

"I don't know about this, T," Kyler put in. "I agree with Allison. You and I both like to experiment with new things, but you should really do everything in your power to hold off on this one. I'm sure Raul will let you test-drive the grappling thingamajig personally, but in a controlled environment, not somewhere where you could be falling fifty feet—"

"And I still can't believe you did *that*, by the way," Allison cut in, looking at Trust crossly. "I'm serious, don't ever do that again. Would it have been so bad to use the stairs and at least get closer to the ground first?"

Trust started to sign, but—

"For me, man," Kyler went on, "just hold off on using the grappling thing and avoid any high jumps tonight. Okay? Just...hold off on it. And that mask is so cool! You look awesome! All you need now is some kind of cape."

Trust looked at Allison, and then shifted to Kyler again.

*You hit a grand slam—*

"Dude!" Kyler exclaimed, throwing himself back on his bed and— "Ow! I hit my head on the baseball!"

*You guys should grab Pax and Marcie and head over there,* he then signed when Kyler was looking at him again, still rubbing the back of his head. *I'm going to make a stop in the woods first for Cortez to see if anything's out there.*

**Trust (8:02 PM):** On the way.
**Cortez (8:02 PM):** Dude, this is SO AWESOME. I can't

believe we're actually doing this.

**Kyler (8:02 PM):** Keep your pants on, C. Ha.

**Allison (8:02 PM):** Be careful, Trust.

**Paxson (8:03 PM):** I know, right? This is like some superhero secret mission. No real names. My code name on this assignment is Shaggy.

**Marcie (8:04 PM):** You seem more a Daphne type to me.

**Cortez (8:04 PM):** Ha!

On the Centre Line bus, Trust rolled his eyes at the group exchange.

At least it meant everyone was paying attention.

The bus drove toward the outskirts of Centre City and Trust's eventual disembarking point, where the others had already arrived minutes before.

Decatur Lane.

"EVERYBODY JUST ACT NATURAL," MARCIE directed as she, Paxson, Kyler, and Allison crossed the already crowded front yard toward the large house. "And by everyone, I mean you two, Kyler and Paxson."

Paxson avoided a boy spinning around in the yard with an amusing novelty drinking hat on his head.

"Are you kidding?" he returned. "Need I remind you, Marcie-Bear, that it was Mr. Brooks and me who crept silently through the shadows, keeping a sharp lookout while Trust was inside the Thomas Building dodging laser beams? We both have covert experience under our belts—it's you and Allison I have questions about. Where's your dossier?"

Marcie gave him a doubtful look.

"We're all going to be fine," Allison remarked. The group climbed the short set of steps leading up to the porch and front door. Kyler was already beginning to be recognized by pockets of the partygoers and was given steady streams of congratulations.

"Just remember," Allison continued, "stay close to your phones, and when the lights go out, stay close to the wall, just in case we get separated."

"Hey, it's Kyler-Scott Brooks, the man of the hour!" a familiar voice boomed over the general hubbub just as they reached the doorway. "Get your grand-slammin' butt in here, young man!"

There was a roar amongst the crowd of people inside as Kyler and the others crossed the threshold. Big Trent Atkins, another hero of the Tigers playoff win earlier in the day and the one who had announced Kyler's presence, was standing at the forefront. Allison, Paxson, and Marcie each received similar—and thus, unexpected—adulation as well, seemingly anointed as party celebrities for being the ones privileged enough to come in with the baseball star.

Trent grabbed the bemused freshman shortstop as he came near.

"Here he is, ladies and gentlemen!" he proclaimed. "And ladies, please, *please*! Just wait your turn!"

He then leaned forward, speaking in a lower voice that did not carry above the partygoers.

"Don't get used to this treatment, bro," he said. "Don't let it go to your head—that's the key. Tonight, we can celebrate. But tomorrow, you're back to being Scott. Cool?"

Kyler smirked, shrugging.

"It always sounds weird when you're not calling me Scott anyway," Kyler replied, to which Trent laughed. With one burly arm around Kyler's shoulders, his other arm went into the air.

"Kyler-Scott Brooks, everybody!"

Another surge from the party grouped around them.

AMID THE HEAVY WOODLAND AT the rear of the properties facing Decatur Lane, Trust lowered his backpack to the ground and leaned it against a tree. He studied the location for a moment, and then looked around again, examining the setting.

In the fading vestiges of nightfall, the woods were, by now, almost completely in the dark, with only the faint, smoky hint of dark blue visible, broken up by the thick tree line. However, Trust could see everything, his eyes perfectly adapted to the ambient night, better even than the nocturnal creatures that came alive after the sun set.

In spite of this, there was nothing much to see. Just the trees.

Trust looked to his phone.

**Trust (8:47 PM):** I'm still on it, right? I'm not seeing

anything.

**Cortez (8:47 PM):** You're in the center of the area I've narrowed it down to. May not be exactly where it is, but close. No secret buildings or shelters?

Trust moved through the brush and woodland debris, fallen trees and branches, keeping a close eye for any signs of activity, but observing nothing out of the ordinary. The Viper Skin clung to his body, but he didn't need its lack of sensation to know there was no one close by. No hidden shelters. No secret buildings. No nothing.

The forest was still. Trust could see the party he would eventually be crashing in the distance, well out of the Viper Skin's range.

**Cortez (8:49 PM):** Still could be in the house. Or maybe buried in the ground?

Trust was moving in the general direction of the festivities, though he was still hundreds of yards away. His shades were on, as was the mask Allison had found time to fabricate, with a black hoodie also secure over his head. The cell phone holder secured to his forearm allowed him to glance down and read quickly as he moved, or to pull the phone out without difficulty so he could type.

**Trust (8:50 PM):** Definitely not going to waste time digging for it if it's out here. Just wanted to see if there was somewhere to hide Jeremy and Jezzie, which there isn't.
**Cortez (8:50 PM):** Understood. Long shot anyway. But we know the phone is on that property somewhere, and Rory and the others don't know that we know.

Trust continued. He could feel the silence, and each careful, efficient step maintained the stillness. A shadow.

**Cortez (8:51 PM):** I'm watching you move toward the house now.

Trust picked up his pace. More familiar with his surroundings with each step, more confident in being able to stay quiet at a near-running pace, he began covering ground swiftly.

The party came closer.

He slowed, and then stopped suddenly, still in the woods. The edge of the tree line was a hundred yards away.

**Trust (8:53 PM):** Serious question, and I know I'm going into gray territory now. Exactly how much can you do on that computer of yours?

He glanced up again. With the large number of people he could see even in the backyard, his entry into the house was going to be...interesting.

Crouching now, he looked back to the phone in his hands.

**Cortez (8:53 PM):** The answer would scare you, but I like the sound of this. What do you have in mind? Illegal, smillegal.

**Cortez (8:59 PM):** All right, check one, two. Everybody got that? Your phone signal will go down with the lights, but restarting your phone will bring it back up. Everybody say okay when ready.

Kyler looked up from his phone. Even with the chaotic partying going on around him, he was able to spot Allison and Marcie a short distance away, directly in his sightline. He held his phone up.

Both girls already had theirs out. They nodded.

*Where's Pax?* Kyler mouthed.

Marcie pointed into the kitchen.

"Oh, there he is! Kyler! Kyler-Scott!"

Kyler turned at the sound of his name to see two attractive girls making their way toward him. Their attire was thin, sensuous, sparse— hinting suggestively at what it hid and accentuating beautifully what it didn't.

"We *need* a picture with you, Kyler," one of them, a brunette with lightly tanned skin and smoky eyes, said.

He glanced toward the kitchen archway again.

Allison was watching him with an unreadable expression on her face.

TRUST SAW THE FOURTH CONFIRMATION come in from Paxson.

**Paxson (9:01 PM):** I'm good. Just how dark is this going to get, though? Ha ha.
**Trust (9:01 PM):** I'm going to need about ten seconds to reset my phone before I make a move. I don't know if I'll get another chance to stand around and wait for it.

He watched as one boy in the backyard chased another after being doused with a cup of beer.

**Cortez (9:01 PM):** I can do it remotely if you want, no sweat. Technically, I can do them all since I have everyone's numbers. Everybody okay with that?
**Trust (9:02 PM):** Fine.
**Paxson (9:02 PM):** Cool.
**Marcie (9:02 PM):** Yeah.
**Kyler (9:02 PM):** That's good.
**Allison (9:03 PM):** Okay. But I haven't seen Rory or any of the others since we've been here. Are they even at this party?
**Cortez (9:03 PM):** I've got a lock on Rory, so his phone is there at least. And it's moving.
**Paxson (9:03 PM):** I just saw him going upstairs like 5-10 mins ago.
**Trust (9:04 PM):** I've got one who will know in the backyard. I'm bringing him inside, then heading upstairs. Countdown from 30 sec, Cortez, then shut it down.

The boy's name was Nikko. With Cortez's assistance, Trust knew all of their names now.

KEEPING A SMILE ON HIS face but very nearly having to forcibly wrestle himself away from the group of intoxicated girls who had begun to crowd him, Kyler skirted around other partiers as he made his way into the kitchen.

"I think we should get to this back wall," Kyler remarked, indicating. "Better chance of avoiding any potential bodies flying around."

"Were you having fun over there with your new friends?" Allison charged, crossing her arms.

Marcie and Paxson approached from the side.

"We've got thirty seconds," Marcie observed. "Are we okay here, or...What's wrong, Al?"

Allison was still looking in Kyler's direction, her gaze slightly frosty.

"Uh oh," said Paxson. "I know that stare."

He shifted quickly to Kyler.

"Dude, what'd you do?"

"What? I just came over here and—"

"Kyler and I broke up," Allison stated flatly.

Three pairs of eyes widened, Kyler's for the second time on the subject.

"What?" Marcie whispered urgently, her voice barely audible, but her expression quite clear. "You mean, just n—"

"Oh, Kyler," a distinctly feminine voice crooned from behind as a slender arm clutched the boy. "Come back in here! We want you to dance with us—"

Suddenly, the lights, the music, and the power switched off with an audible *pop*. The interior of the house was now, abruptly, almost pitch-black.

TRUST WAS MOVING AS SOON as the blackness descended over the house and back lawn, now nimbly sprinting through the woodland, his steps light—still quiet, but now much, much faster. He burst out of the forested tree line with an almost unnatural ease.

And, apparently, almost completely soundless.

He saw most of the partiers turn toward the house when the lights went out, some with their hands raised, as though blaming someone inside for the sudden lack of power on the back porch and portable position lights, most not yet realizing that, even with the stoppage of music, all electrical power had been affected.

And even more not yet realizing the shadowy, dark-clothed figure already in their midst.

The boy Trust targeted was apparently tipsy and not as aware of the sudden change in his environment as he would have been otherwise, as he was raising his cup to his mouth again even as others around him started to complain.

*Where are they?*

A cell phone picture of Jeremy Higgins and Jezzie Delaney was unexpectedly staring Nikko in the face, the words a caption in the foreground of the picture.

Nikko didn't—couldn't—notice that the phone was on and recording his response.

"What? I—"

As Trust watched the words forming, he kicked at the back of the boy's leg, jerking him backward at the same moment. Nikko fell to the grass hard, flat on his back, his cup and the alcoholic beverage contained within flying out of his grasp. The air in his lungs was forced out in a painful gasp on impact.

With the violent, attention-grabbing maneuver, Trust's internal clock automatically accelerated. Only seconds now...

He flashed the phone into Nikko's face again. Then, glancing up and looking behind him as he did so, somehow feeling—seemingly at the same moment as the sensors on the Viper Skin suit he wore under his clothes—movement from behind.

The crowd was beginning to notice what was going on in the darkness.

"Hey, what are you—oomph!"

Trust shot to his feet, shooting a palm forward and sending an advancing boy stumbling a few steps back. He then crouched swiftly again.

*Where are they?* the phone read.

He jerked the boy on the ground, Nikko's head bouncing off the—

This time the Viper Skin beat his own natural senses, the increase in heat along his side compelling him into action once more. Trust's sudden aggressive movement caused those in the crowd venturing closer to immediately jump back, like a pack encircling a wild, dangerous animal.

In the darkness, the figure was in complete deep shadow. They couldn't make it out...and it was all so sudden...

Trust pulled Nikko to his feet with one hand—"Ahh!" Nikko cried in surprise—and shoved him, hard. Trust swiftly turned yet again, taking a hard step forward.

The crowd again kept its distance.

Trust's movements were so fast that he was back on Nikko before he had a chance to fully regain his balance. He pushed Nikko back quickly with one hand, continuing to keep him just slightly off kilter, shuffling him back toward the large, dark residence, Trust's phone still up and close to the boy's face, the light from the phone illuminating Nikko's frightened expression...

Trust's back was warming considerably. He gave Nikko another forceful shove, sending him to the ground again, and spun—

—his fist turning with him.

Solid, bone-rapping contact. Just under the side of the jaw. Trust could feel the boy's teeth clicking together.

The boy—who had been coming toward him—was flung to the side with the force of Trust's punch, stumbling into the procession now following Trust and Nikko. Trust quickly turned back again, yanking his target up by the shirt and forcing him, backward, up the set of steps toward the open back door, still moving quickly. Nikko and Trust crossed the porch and hurtled through the doorway, Nikko falling to the ground yet again. There were gasps and cries of surprise that Trust, of course, did not hear. He fell on top of Nikko, and then rolled over him fully, transitioning nimbly to his feet in one fluid motion.

Trust could see the people in the dark house just as distinctly, if not more so, than if the residence had been brightly lit. A few were already bringing their phones out—and rebooting them after noticing that they had inexplicably shut off.

Not getting the immediate answer he was only somewhat hopeful he would get in the first place, and wanting to move upstairs, Trust began to leave the boy behind, on the ground, storming his way through the packed house...

"Hey! What—"

He pushed another partier back onto a couch as he traversed the large living room area. With some phones now pointed in his direction, they were able to finally see a...shadow...

Trust whirled quickly, turning one hundred and eighty degrees to look directly behind him.

As though reacting to a snarling predator, the crowd retreated quickly again. Trust scanned the faces in an instant, and then continued.

Around the corner. Beginning up the staircase. Someone at the top was just starting to come down...

...and, spotting the dark figure coming up, the boy at the top turned and retreated.

The Viper Skin was alive, adjusting to the shift in surroundings accordingly. Trust's movements were controlled and surprisingly unhurried, his eyes constantly surveying...

...in hindsight, he probably should have moved more quickly.

Top of the staircase. An empty hallway extended along both sides, with a railing protecting an overlook back down onto the staircase. On one end, the hallway turned a blind corner, shielded by the wall. All of the doors presently visible were closed.

One at a time. Trust tried the first door at the end...

...and then kicked it in.

A second-long survey of the interior.

Nothing.

The next closed door.

And then the next.

It only took a few minutes to realize something was wrong. He knew the boy went this way...

More doors were either unlocked or kicked in. A bedroom. A hall closet.

Quicker.

A bathroom. Another bedroom.

The Viper Skin was not detecting any heat signatures. Neither were his eyes. He had missed something...

A glance down to his phone. He had been upstairs for thirty-five seconds. He could see the group text conversation as Kyler relayed to Cortez what was going on from the ground floor, the splintering of wood that could be heard, coming from upstairs—

Trust sprinted down the steps again.

"I-I DON'T KNOW," NIKKO babbled, still down but now sitting up on the floor just inside the doorway that led out to the back porch. "I couldn't...I didn't even see him. He was moving...it was all so fast—"

There were gasps and a short, sharp scream coming from somewhere in the living room, an increased, agitated commotion.

"Watch out!" someone called. The voice sounded like it could have been from Trent Atkins, the baseball player. "Just get out of his way!"

Nikko pushed away from those crouching around him, desperate to get up and avoid another encounter with...whatever *that* was.

"Move, move!" he hissed urgently. "Watch out! That's him! He's coming back!"

He pushed his way past people into the kitchen in an attempt to outwit the figure. It was still too dark to make much out. Even with more people with their cell phones, eerie, uneven shadows were all that played in the light—

A phone was thrust into his face again.

*Remember what you did to her?*

The caption overlaid a picture of Jezzie Delaney.

"Look," Nikko started, "I didn't do anything—argh!"

His head was wrenched back by the hair. He started to reach for the hand grabbing it, but the figure abruptly stepped forward, his face now only inches away.

Sunglasses? Nikko could not move his head to get a more complete view. The hand yanked hard again, forcing him to shut his eyes briefly with the pain. He then opened them again, his vision watery.

*Where are they?*

It was the same picture and message as before.

Nikko gritted against the pull along the back of his head.

"I...I don't—argh!"

The shadowy figure was dragging him standing up, now cutting a path through the kitchen. In the dark. By his hair.

In a last-ditch effort, Nikko swung.

Trust, his gaze swinging quickly between the crowd of people and back to Nikko, saw the attempt coming. He let go of Nikko's scalp.

The punch came...and went.

Trust struck quick, straight, full-on.

Nikko's head recoiled, as though he had been hit with an uppercut.

"Ahh!"

Trust could see the yelp just before Nikko's hands rose to cover his face.

The blood would begin to flow freely from his nose in a few seconds.

Trust turned him and pushed him ahead. Nikko, now tilting his head back voluntarily, and holding his hands against his face, cooperated.

More cell phones were on. Bright. Recording. Able to distinguish a little bit more of what was transpiring. But still, no one had a signal or a way to communicate out.

Directing a now compliant Nikko to the stairs, Trust could sense— and see—the horde trailing behind them, keeping a short separation of space.

Nikko began to climb.

Trust turned around, his phone already out of his wrist holder. He held it up, moving it slowly so everyone could see.

*Anyone seen Trent Atkins?*

THEY WERE BACK UPSTAIRS IN the first room Trust had checked. Still shrouded in darkness, collegiate baseball's national Player of the Year gripped his phone in his meaty hand as it emitted Cortez's voice.

"First, quickly, I just have to say that I'm a big fan of—"

Able to read along to the conversation on his phone, Trust pressed send on the message he already had prepared. With Cortez, he had a feeling he would need to use it—and he did.

**Trust (9:09 PM):** Don't have time for this.

"Okay, okay," Cortez voiced. "Trent, you don't know me, but you're going to have to trust me right now. I'm looking for Jeremy Higgins and

Jezzie Delaney. You know them. I have reason to believe they were abducted by members of the Freesef Society, members who are throwing the party you are currently attending. Why they did it, I'm not completely sure, and it would take too long to explain, but suffice it to say that the guy in the room with you right now—the one with the broken nose—not only knows where they are, he participated in a gang rape of Jezzie just before Winter Break."

"What?" Nikko cried. "Whoa! Now, wait just a minute—"

Trust took a step toward him. Nikko, stepping back, tripped over a laundry basket on the floor and fell.

"Look," Trent said, his eyes roving as he spoke, shifting between Trust and Nikko, "I don't know about any of this 'missing' stuff, but if what you're talking about is true, I don't know what I can do to help you."

His eyes halted on Trust's shadowy figure again.

"And I don't know who this dude in the superhero mask is."

Trust rolled his eyes, though Trent could not see it.

"He's my eyes and ears," Cortez said. "Well, maybe not ear...yeah. Anyway, he does the things I can't do. And he's going to be the one who finds Jeremy and Jezzie—with your assistance."

"But what am I supposed to do?"

"It's simple. You ask Nikko here where they are, and if he doesn't answer, the guy in the mask gets to beat the living snot out of him. See, that guy—the one in the mask—he got burned on his face in a freak accident years ago. Completely fried his vocal cords, too, so he doesn't like to talk too much. I do the talking for him. But he fights...like, awesomely."

Behind his shades, and in the dark where no one could see, Trust's eyes rolled yet again.

"You and Jeremy Higgins are two of the most recognizable faces at UCC," Cortez went on. "When you talk, people listen. People listen so hard, they take your jokes seriously, dude. So when you tell people that Nikko Anderson of Des Moines, Iowa, raped at least one female student and was probably complicit in a number of other assaults, that he was aware of, if not directly involved in, the abduction of a nationally known college athlete and his incredibly photogenic girlfriend who news channels will want plastered all over their broadcasts twenty-four-seven, Nikko's life will be all but over before it ever really got started."

"Wait!" Nikko interjected into the dark room.

"Oh, hold on a second, Trent," Cortez said through the phone. "Our friend Nikko just saw his life flash before his eyes after realizing every single thing that I just said is true. Go ahead, Nikko. We're all listening. And I'm afraid we don't have that much time."

> **Cortez (9:13 PM):** Got it. Secret staircase from upstairs room. Trust, Trent are going down now.

Each with their phones on, Kyler, Allison, Paxson, and Marcie were huddled close enough together to see each other's faces in the soft artificial light. They looked at each other.

"Should we go up there? Should we call the police?" Paxson whispered.

"Yes, we should, and yes, we should, in about five minutes," Kyler replied. "We need to give T some time to do his thing. But whoever he runs into at the bottom of that secret staircase is probably going to need them. And a stretcher."

The group then started to move. The other partiers around them were still wondering why the electricity, and, much more importantly, their phone signals, remained out of service.

It was a conundrum that could be solved instantly with a simple command from a UCC freshman's laptop—a freshman by the name of Cortez Romero.

TRUST ARRIVED AT ANOTHER SHALLOW turn in the stonewalled underground passageway, which then led him to a sharp corner. It had crossed his mind that he was already a good distance away from the house, but not having paid any attention to the general direction he was running...

The Viper Skin gave him his warning.

He turned the corner.

And then stopped immediately, gauging.

Thirty feet away. Two men standing near a closed door. Both were large, muscular, meant to intimidate, meant to impose.

Meant to be guarding something. Way too obvious.

Trust looked at the two men. The two men turned their heads, looking back toward him. One raised a phone to his mouth.

"We've got company down here...Some freak with a mask...No, don't send anyone else. We'll take care of it."

Trust held his own phone up, taking a picture of the men, who were gazing back at him, but had not moved from their positions. He sent the picture to Cortez.

**Trust (9:16 PM):** I like these odds.

Then he moved. Trotting the first few steps, and then picking up speed.

The two brawny men finally stepped away from the door, readying themselves.

A few strides away from them, Trust sidestepped slightly and jumped. Briefly, it seemed as though he were able to run horizontally along the wall, shocking the two men...

One step...

Two...

Trust's foot came up hard and lightning quick, catching the first man along the side of his head before he even considered reacting. Powerful impact. The man tumbled sideways toward the other side of the passageway, but Trust was still moving, already back on the ground, ducking under a violent swing from the second man, and then another from the opposite hand. Trust kicked low, aiming at the man's kneecap, and connected, the leg buckling, the man swaying forward. Trust then hit him with a swinging right hand, and then swiftly grabbed the man's head, shoving it brutally into the closed door just behind him.

Trust turned instantly, fully homed in on the fight and ultra-aware of every single movement and action around him, delivering a flying knee to the head of the first man, who was still struggling to get back to his feet after Trust's kick. The man's head smashed into the stone wall, completely unprotected.

In seemingly the same moment, never stopping, Trust spun and leaped to the other side of the underground corridor. The second man was leaning groggily against the door, holding on to his face...

Trust jumped into the air, his feet coming forward, dropkicking the man in his stomach and sending him into the door again.

Apparently, it was hard enough to upset the man's stomach, as some recently consumed contents made a sudden reappearance.

The man fell, clutching his abdomen, vomiting again. Trust was upright once more. He looked back.

The first man on the other side of the passageway, opposite the door, was slumped down into an awkward crouch, hugging the stone wall but with his arms hanging limply.

Unconscious.

Trust returned to the second man. He grabbed him, the man dazed and in obvious discomfort but not completely out of it, snatching his head up by his closely cut hair.

Another picture, which was quickly sent to Cortez.

Shoving the man's head back into the dirt floor, just avoiding the mess that he had upchucked, Trust stood and tried the door.

Unlocked.

He stepped into a barren room, completely empty. The walls looked to be made out of concrete, if not a smoothed-out, even composition of the stone found along the walls of the underground tunnel. Trust moved to the sole door in the far corner of the empty room. There were slits along the top portion of the steel door, too high for Trust to see through.

The Viper Skin was able to sense what he couldn't through the thick door, however.

Locked. He hurried back out into the tunnel.

The man Trust had left conscious was writhing around on the ground, seemingly unable to make any attempt to crawl as he held his midsection with both hands. Trust bent down and felt him for keys. A few seconds later, he was back in front of the door in the empty room again.

He guessed the correct key on the second try. The reinforced door was heavy.

"OKAY. LET'S JUST STAY CLOSE together, just to be sure. We don't need any mummies or mutated rats popping up on us down here."

The others shook their heads at Kyler's observation, which was apparently serious on his part. Marcie looked ahead into the stone tunnel as they arrived at the bottom of the secret staircase found deep inside a large closet in one of the upstairs bedrooms.

"Seriously, Kyler," she said. "What movie scarred you so much as a kid that you think there are genetically mutated rats hiding behind every dark corner?"

"Do you guys hear anything?" Allison asked as they walked. "I don't like how quiet it is down here."

"It's like a dungeon," agreed Kyler.

His phone rang, echoing loudly.

"At least we know we still have service," Paxson intoned, beginning to chuckle but curtailing it swiftly as Marcie hit him on the arm.

"Hello—"

Kyler, in mid-step, abruptly stopped, nearly tripping over himself as he held the phone to his ear. He looked toward the others in confusion.

"Wait! Okay, I can barely hear you. Say that again?"

"What's going—"

Kyler held up his hand, stopping Allison.

"Did you call the—wait, hello? Hello? Mariana? Mariana, can you hear me? Is anyone there?"

Kyler brought the phone down quickly, tapping and swiping the screen.

"Kyler, what happened?" Allison said urgently. "What did Mariana say? You're scaring me."

"I'm texting Trust," Kyler told them. "Something's happening at Centre Diamond. Mariana said something about Freesef. I think she said at least one of the bouncers is dead, and something about a fire, and then I lost the connection. It sounded like someone took her phone away."

"What?" Marcie gasped. "Are you serious?"

Allison covered her mouth, stifling her own sharp breath. Paxson started to turn back.

"Should we go?" he asked.

"I need to see what Trust is doing," Kyler said. "If he's read my text already, and he hasn't already found another route out of here, he's going to come back this way. We still don't know if he found Jeremy or Jezzie or Rory or anybody else. He could be—"

At that moment, all four of their phones went off at the same time with text message alerts.

Kyler's phone started ringing again.

DEEPER IN THE UNDERGROUND PASSAGE, Trust was severing the cord around Jeremy Higgins' wrists with a small tactical knife. He silently chastised himself for not bringing something of his own to secure the two large men down near the doorway.

Presently, however, there was no need for it, as both were still on the ground—particularly after a retaliatory kick to the face from Jeremy to the man Trust had left conscious.

"Jesus, Holy Joseph, and Mary," Trent breathed, having finally caught up to Trust as the deaf teen helped Jeremy and Jezzie out of the back room. "I mean, how was this kept a secret? I saw you weren't in the Civ exam, but I wouldn't have even imagined...oh, man..."

"That? What you're feeling right now?" Jeremy intoned, his voice carrying a flinty edge as Trust cut loose the last binding. "I'm feeling it multiplied by a fact or a million. Oooh, I can't *wait* until I lay my hands on Rory and those other—"

A pleasant string of curses shot from his mouth. He then looked to Jezzie.

"And you're sure you're all right, Jez? We're gonna be out of here soon, and—"

Trust felt the pulse on his wrist and glanced down to his attached phone.

**Kyler (9:19 PM):** Trouble at Centre Diamond. Bouncer possibly dead. Fire. Freesef.

Trust read the message three times. He removed the phone from its slot.

*I need to go. Trent knows the way out. Is everyone okay?*

He held the phone up, showing the display to Jeremy, Jezzie, and Trent.

"We'll be fine as soon as we get the hell out of this place," Jeremy declared, still rubbing his wrists. "This is a—"

He stopped, looking to Trust again.

"Hold up. The way you use your phone like that. I know someone else who—"

Trust gave a quick salute and turned away, trotting back through the passageway in the direction he had come.

In the other direction, the tunnel didn't stop at the door where the two men had been standing. It led deeper, to somewhere, but he didn't have time to—

"Hey!" Jeremy shouted after him. "Where are you going? I'm talking to you!"

Trust was not aware he was even speaking, already having turned the corner and now out of sight.

Jeremy reached forward, grabbing Trent's hand, which still held on to his phone.

"Hey, mysterious kid on the phone. This is Jeremy Higgins. Tell me the one in the mask wasn't Trustice Jeffries."

"Trustice Jeffries?" Trent repeated, his eyebrows rising. "The deaf dude? Kyler's friend?"

"The one in the mask wasn't Trustice Jeffries," Cortez said.

"He's just repeating what you said to say," Jezzie said, rolling her eyes as she stepped forward, before turning and directing her voice toward the phone. "Was that Trust? I know you know, whoever you are."

TRUST RACED AS FAST AS he could through the winding passageway, kicking up dirt behind him, the lights lining the stone walls streaming by.

Mariana...Freesef...fire...someone's dead...

The Viper Skin warmed quickly.

Turning another corner, Trust put the brakes on, barely avoiding barreling into Kyler, Allison, Marcie, and Paxson.

"Wow!" Paxson said, his eyes widening as he took in Trust's appearance. "I couldn't really see you upstairs because it was dark and all the people, but you seriously look like some sort of superhero right now."

*Is everyone okay?* Trust asked, looking to Kyler, who nodded.

"We're fine," he said quickly. "Did you want us to go with you to Centre Diamond?"

Trust shook his head.

*Trent, Jeremy, and Jezzie are coming. Watch out for any...any people on the...*

Trust's breathing was beginning to labor quickly, his arms becoming sluggish.

"Come on, keep moving," Kyler instructed knowingly, beginning to run in place. "Keep breathing."

Trust mirrored Kyler's actions.

*Watch out for any bodies on the ground. They're not dead. Tell Cortez to call Mr. Jackson to pick me up at the point I went into the woods. He's off today; I already checked. I'm officially cashing in the favor on the bus holdup.*

Kyler nodded.

"I'll call Cortez now. You go."

*I didn't find Rory or any of the others.*

"You found who we were looking for. Go. Centre Diamond. Mariana."

Trust spun quickly, sprinting again toward the tunnel entrance.

Paxson turned to Kyler.

"What was that? He looked like he was starting to lose his breath or something after he stopped running."

"He was," Kyler answered, tapping his phone screen. "Cortez? You need to make a phone call. Now. T is going to need a ride."

"Gosh, he's fast," Marcie said, still looking the way Trust had fled.

"Maybe faster than you, even," Allison added, glancing back to Kyler.

Kyler just looked at her.



TRUST HAD REACHED THE HIDDEN staircase. He continued to sprint, two steps at a time, then three, up, up, up, ascending steadily, quickly, swiftly, his breathing even and controlled again, almost as though he were not moving at all...

He burst into the bedroom. Nikko was gone—not that it mattered now. Out of the room, into the hall, steps again, leaping down the final ones...

The party had thinned, but only slightly, the power in the house still out. The many who remained were startled by Trust's abrupt return...and then his just as sudden disappearance as he dashed through the house.

More phones, and now a few flashlights. Still, they managed barely a glimpse as Trust rushed, dodged, and nimbly skirted past.

Out the door, onto the porch, and—

The boy Trust had hit earlier was being tended to on one of the couches outside. Trust stopped.

Those near the boy immediately abandoned him as Trust approached. The boy shrank back. He seemed a few years older than Trust, almost certainly an upperclassman, and he looked relatively fit. But still, he all but cowered in the mysterious figure's presence.

Trust extended his gloved hand.

The young man, his face conveying a look of pure amazement, looked from the hand, to Trust's masked face.

Trust could feel his breathing beginning to change again, but he held on.

A moment passed...

The boy reached out, slowly.

The two shook.

And Trust was gone again, hightailing it across the lawn, passing through the crowd still in the backyard, and vanishing into the dark woodland. He finally glanced down to his phone again, still running.

> **Cortez (9:24 PM):** That Mr. Jackson guy is on the way to the
> spot. Should be there by the time you show up. I told him to
> look out for a crazy dude in a mask.

Using the map on his phone—a similar map to the one Cortez was probably watching at that very same moment as he tracked Trust's movements—Trust was quickly able to locate where he had placed his book bag. He reached the spot and picked it up in one motion, not stopping, but now slowing down, trying to pace himself for Mr. Jackson's pickup.

Running or exerting himself for longer periods of time had always been unusually easy for Trust, but without a proper cooldown period afterward, it was also highly dangerous...

He typed as he ran, dodging and hopping around the natural obstacles of the forestry.

> **Trust (9:26 PM):** Police?

He decelerated further, his pace now resembling a moderate jog.

**Cortez (9:26 PM):** Called it in as soon as you made it into woods. Closest car is 5 mins out. Should get to house as you're being picked up.
**Cortez (9:27 PM):** Power's back up at the house also. Something odd with the police, though. I'm looking at their live patrol map and listening to radio. Major call across town—fire, ambulance, and PD. No one's even responded to Centre Diamond yet.
**Trust (9:27 PM):** Call it in, and pinpoint the number I'm about to send. Mariana's location.

Approaching the site where he had originally ventured into the woods, Trust continued to jog but remained hidden from view of the road.

"DISPATCH TO BRAVO 31. GO to channel five."

As she drove, Officer Amelia Mendez keyed her radio.

"Bravo 31, going to five."

She switched over, her eyes remaining on the road, so used to the action that she could perform it without looking.

"Bravo 31, go ahead, Dispatch."

"Bravo 31, we're receiving a flood of phone calls now from 1844 Decatur Lane. Be on the lookout for a—I don't even know how to say this—a masked individual somewhere on the premises, possibly having fled into the wooded area behind the property. Reports are this masked figure is dangerous but apparently unarmed. Callers are saying this individual is dressed like some sort of hooded superhero or something. I don't know what's going on here."

"Superhero?" Mendez repeated, taking the turn onto Pecan Lane and passing a sleek, dark vehicle driving in the opposite direction. She gave the car a backward glance through her rearview mirror, but that was all.

"You mean like at the old shipment yard uptown with the theft ring?" she continued.

"That's what it sounds like, 31."

The skepticism in the dispatcher's voice was obvious even through the radio.

"But I'll let you connect those dots, not me. I never saw the video that kid brought in, but I heard the stories."

"Yeah," Mendez drew out. "Look, I'm on scene, and I can smell the alcohol from here. I'll stay on five to keep channels one and two open for whatever's going on in Deerbourne. But I could probably use some backup for crowd control."

"Copy that, 31."

TRUST'S BREATHING WAS ONLY FAINTLY arduous as he rode in the front passenger seat of the Maserati GranTurismo SP, the suburban night scene streaking past through the windows as Mr. Jackson sped toward downtown.

> **Trust (9:35 PM):** Tell him to let me off somewhere near
> back of club. I'll find a way in.

Mr. Jackson was still talking.

"...but I can't believe—you know, seeing as I'm the one who actually *teaches* the Vehicular Technique and Tactics for the police academy, I still keep in touch with many of those officers. That one we just passed back there? Amelia Mendez. I can only hope she didn't recognize this car, because I'm not lying for you. I'm not lying, you hear me? It's just that simple."

Trust typed quickly again.

"Uh, Mr. Jackson, sir," Cortez said, his voice coming through the speakers of the car while simultaneously being transcribed into text on Trust's phone. "Trust said you can let him off somewhere in the back of the club and he'll find a—"

"Back of the club?" Mr. Jackson interjected. "If there's trouble at Centre Diamond, we shouldn't be going anywhere near it—"

"And he also said you already lied for him, during the bus holdup."

The driver fell silent, the flickering illumination from passing streetlamps flashing quickly across his face through the glass.

He then exhaled loudly, making a face.

"Okay, you got me on that one. And I do owe you."

"He said that after this, you'll be even," Cortez relayed.

Mr. Jackson scoffed, making a quick turn.

"Yeah, not even close to being close," he said. "That guy had a freakin' gun and you disarmed him like you were taking a toy from a child. He was holding the entire bus hostage, and it could have ended bad. Real bad. I figure about thirty or forty more of these pickups, then I'll be approaching the realm of even."

**Trust (9:37 PM):** This is the last pickup.

"CALL IT IN, RYAN," LIEUTENANT Wallace O'Patrick directed, the gaggle of officers glancing around the quiet neighborhood, engines from the Fire Department of Centre City and EMT trucks standing by also, their respective emergency lights flashing brightly, illuminating the scene. "We can't locate the freakin' caller and nothing seems out of place out here. This has got to be one heck of a prank call."

"Adam 3 to Dispatch," Ryan intoned, speaking into his wrist.

"Adam 3, go ahead."

"I'm in the Oak Meadows neighborhood in Deerbourne with practically everyone else. You may want to check for some hidden cameras, because I think the city's entire public safety sector just got taken for a ride. We're ready to call a 10-18 on this—"

A sudden, blaring tone came from his radio and those of the other officers on scene, followed a second later by a slightly different, but equally as urgent tone coming from the firefighters and medics in the cul-de-sac. The message sounding from all of them was the same.

"This is a Code 1. All available units respond to 15689 East End Avenue, the Centre Diamond nightclub..."

The patrol lieutenant cursed loudly as everyone started to scramble, sirens sounding, thoroughly piercing the quiet of the neighborhood for the second time.

"We got set up. Got us lookin' like the Keystone flippin' Cops out here...Rodrigo, you and Parker stay here and verify everything checks out. Everyone else, move! Tubbs, get your fat butt in gear!"

Frowning, Ryan glanced toward Sergeant Longley for just an instant, meeting his eyes.

"Yep, we just got taken for a ride, all right," Longley said as they raced back to their respective patrol cars. "That's what you call a grand misdirection."

SOME HAD HEARD THE GUNSHOTS. Most, if not all, had heard the fire alarm, so people were continuing to stream out of the front entrance to Centre Diamond as Mr. Jackson's vehicle came to a quick stop at the back.

Trust typed out a quick message before opening his door.

*Thanks for the ride.*

"Don't think you're gettin' rid of me," Mr. Jackson remarked, looking at him. "I'm not moving from this spot until you're back in this car again, and if you're not back in this car, I'm telling everybody what you did on the bus, and about this little outfit you've got going on right now."

*Seems fair.*

Trust shut the door behind him. Moving closer to the club, which appeared as nondescript as any building from its rear, Trust looked up as he advanced, his eyes searching, seeking, examining.

He shuffled sideways. He did it again, still looking up, pulling Raul's baton from the sleeve Allison had fashioned on the back of the bodysuit.

He stopped. He glanced down at the baton, and then up to the roof again. He then raised the device, aiming it toward the roof ledge

The end of the baton shot out quickly, like an arrow, the grappling hook instantly expanding, zipping up into the night air and trailing a thin—but, according to Allison and Cortez, incredibly sturdy—wire behind it in a straight-line path.

Trust touched the small indention again when the grappling hook shot past the roof. He could feel the sudden change in tension as the rope immediately reversed course, retracting back at him.

It caught on the ledge, the wire immediately and automatically locking its tautness.

Trust tried pulling it. It would not budge.

He was losing time. Mariana was inside, and at least one of the club's bouncers was dead already.

And Freesef was involved.

Time for a field test. He would have to apologize to Allison later.

He touched the next indention on the baton handle. A handle to hang on to instantly emerged from the bottom near his hand, and Trust was tugged into the air at the same time, astonishingly, unexpectedly quickly, air whizzing past the mask he wore. In a few short seconds, he flipped over the ledge of the rooftop, barely staying on his feet as he landed. Another touch of the baton retracted both the grip handle and the grappling hook again, the hook's talons automatically snapping back into place and smoothly sliding into the top of the baton, delivering a slight kick in Trust's hand in the process.

He moved forward on the roof, toward the glassed dome that looked down onto the main dance floor. Ducking his head and peeking in, he saw the floor empty, a highly unusual sight at this time of night.

Also, there was smoke.

Trust swung the baton at the glass, shattering a large section of it. Through his eyes, the flying shards captured all the colors of the rainbow at once, sparkling brilliantly in glittery display.

He only glanced briefly at it, already moving again. The grappling hook came to life once more.

This time, he knew what to expect.

Down through the dome he went, free-falling until he touched the button to slow his descent.

On second thought, this method of entering was a terrible idea. He should have thought of another way. He was way too exposed.

Fortunately, the entire room looked deserted. No one in sight.

Trust reached the ground and retracted the hook.

**Trust (9:42 PM):** I'm in. Main floor empty. Fire somewhere. Smoke.

He began to cross the dance floor, heading for the—

Spotting someone, he changed direction quickly, hurrying toward the main doors.

A body.

A-Rock.

He was still. His eyes, open.

Trust checked for a pulse. Then, he glanced up again, to one spot in particular.

**Trust (9:43 PM):** Cut power to Centre Diamond.

"WHY ARE WE STILL HERE?" the man in the club's control room mumbled to the other, who was sitting at the panel, gazing at the numerous monitors positioned on the wall in front of him. "We're hanging around too long. Those guys are trying to be dramatic. We need to do what we came here to do and get out."

"It's not going to take the police long to figure out the Deerbourne call is a hoax," the seated man agreed, looking up.

"Why are we even leaving the Eldorado girl here?" the first man continued, beginning an agitated pacing around the small room. "We should just take her and get out. We should just—"

"Wait," the other man said abruptly. "Wait. Something just happened. Crap, I missed something."

"What is it?"

The pacing man paused, leaning down to look over the other's shoulder.

"What happened?"

"I don't know. Where is it, where is it, come on...I know I saw some—there! Something happened. There's something on the floor out there. Is that..."

"Zoom in. Can you get closer?"

"It almost looks like...glass, maybe?"

At that moment, an audible *clack* was heard as the monitors suddenly switched off at once, as did the lights and everything else running under electrical power in the room...as did the air coming through the ventilation. The space was suddenly alarmingly quiet, and nearly pitch-black.

"What the..." the standing man started.

The second man raised his phone, but quickly saw that it had been automatically disabled.

"ETA, ADAM 3."

Ryan keyed his radio, one hand remaining on the steering wheel.

"Adam 3 to Dispatch. ETA two minutes."

"Copy that. Notice to all units. Possible power outage in the 15600 block, including the Centre Diamond nightclub. Looks to be connected to emergency call, over."

CENTRE DIAMOND'S INTERIOR WAS DARK now, all lights shut off. Trust had moved to the second-floor lounge area by use of the grappling hook, his new favorite toy. Now, he ventured farther into the hallways and corridors of the club. The smoke present so far, originating from a still-undetectable source, was becoming thicker.

For Trust, the smoke, and certainly the fire, would pose more than just the obvious problems.

He was already slowing his pace, the Viper Skin coming alive on his body. Nearing the corner, he crouched slightly, anticipating, his fingers flexing in his gloves.

A few seconds...

He sprang just as the man appeared, too swift and too quiet for him to react in time.

TRUST WAS MOVING QUICKLY DOWN the hallway, checking every door and room he came across and finding nothing. Now along the same hall the control room—

"Hey, who's out there?"

The Viper Skin was aware of the company, but it was a moderately weak signature. Trust slowed, and then stopped completely in the middle of the dark hall as a man emerged from what he knew was the control room, where the views from all the club's security cameras were relayed. Centre Diamond's security staff rotated in and out of the room every night during operating hours, typically leaving no less than two bouncers monitoring the cameras at any one time.

Trust had met—or at least seen—nearly all of Centre Diamond's staff. He had certainly met the entire security team.

He had never come across the man now standing in the hallway in his life.

And with A-Rock lying lifeless downstairs, there was a high chance this was a man he would never have the desire to see again.

The man raised a gun as he attempted to see through the darkness of the hall. He had his phone in his other hand, attempting to provide some light, though it didn't carry to Trust's position.

Trust could see him just fine.

He smoothly pulled the baton out of the sheath on his back. He knew his actions were quiet, as the man failed to react.

Still positioned just outside the doorway, the man glanced back into the room.

"You did hear something, right? It wasn't just m—"

Trust had already closed the distance between him and the man by half as one section of the baton struck the man hard on his temple, sending him careening into the side wall, his gun and phone flying out of his hands. He had not even fallen over as Trust came to the open door of the control room, pivoting and hurling the other half of the baton on sight, nailing the second man square in the face, even while his eyes swiftly surveyed the rest of small room for additional targets.

The second man had not even managed to pull his weapon before he crashed back into the control panels.

Trust retrieved the two halves of Raul's baton and moved on.

The entire encounter from the moment he saw the man emerge from the doorway?

Eight seconds.

New world record.

"WHATEVER THIS OUTAGE IS, IT'S also knocked our radios off the grid, so we're doing this the old-fashioned way," Wallace barked loudly, the phalanx of other officers who had also arrived at Centre Diamond crowding around him, awaiting instructions. "As soon as I say your name, get on it. Everyone reports back to me, here. I want Thomas and

Dillon back on Cherry for crowd control and reestablishing contact with Dispatch. Trivett, Boykins, down to Thruway. Tubbs, you lead Nixon, Williams, Shoemaker, Yoder and work this crowd. From this point forward, no one leaves until we've talked to them first. I want everything they saw tonight and everything they know about what's going on. Longley, Yancy, Manuel, Zeigler, Ryan—inside the club. We've got at least one possible shooting victim down, maybe more, which means we've got a shooter. This has gone fubar, and we've jumped in the middle of it. Avoid fire areas or places with too much smoke that you can't see, and if the FD says it isn't safe in there anymore, get the heck out. Go.

"And Sanchez, you're on me; don't leave my side unless I say so. You're my connect to the boys talking to Dispatch. And one of the first things I want—besides the shooter—is an explanation of how in the heck our radios are down in this block. What is this, some made-up electromagnetic hullabaloo?"

In every direction emergency lights flashed as the lead firefighter, a battalion chief on scene, finished giving his own orders to the team of firefighters and emergency medical service personnel on hand.

> **Cortez (9:49 PM):** PD, FD, EMS at the club and starting to come in. You're going to have company shortly.

Trust was reading the message upside down.

"WHAT THE HECK ARE WE supposed to do now? We're losin' time here."

Below Trust, the dark room held four people. Three of them, all adult men, were standing. Each had their phone in hand, attempting repeatedly, and unsuccessfully, to establish contact with their associates—either inside the club or out.

The fourth person in the dark was sitting in a chair, bound, her mouth covered.

"We're going to have to do something," one of the men said, "and I mean right now. She's obviously not going to give us anything, and we need to go, and now we can't communicate with the rest of the team. Who knows if they're even still in this dump. They may have gotten out of here already."

"Well, it sounds like the decision's been made, then," another one said, reaching into the inside of his jacket. He pulled out a pistol. "Leave no stone unturned and all that."

He leveled the weapon at Mariana.

Movement from above.

A crash. A shot rang out wildly, impacting a wall.

Trust was already engaged with the second man.

A kick to the kneecap. An elbow to the face, just under his nose and directed upward.

Spinning off him and onto the third. As it was dark, Trust delivered a forceful shot to the side of the man's face with the same arm used to elbow the previous man, landing it on his cheekbone, crushing inward. It was a quick, compact, powerful movement specially adapted for close quarters. The man, who had been reaching to his waist for his own weapon, went crashing onto the table...

...without even looking, Trust drove another elbow—same arm again—to the head of the stooped second man...

...and then, rolling over the second man's back, launched a flying strike straight into the first man's face just as he was trying to rise again onto unsteady footing, the back of his head crashing hard against the back wall, leaving an indentation. He crumbled down.

All three men seemed to hit the floor at the exact same time...and all without knowing exactly who or what had attacked them so abruptly.

Trust only registered it then, his mind slipping out of fight mode.

Smoke. Coming into the room in a continual stream. From the air-conditioning vents.

And from the door.

Mariana was frantic, looking around in the darkness, squirming against her bindings. It was obvious she was not able to see him.

But surely, she could smell the smoke. It was unmistakable now.

**Trust (9:51 PM):** With Mariana. Send message to FD/PD
more people in building, unconscious. 2nd floor.

Slipping the phone into his wrist holder, he moved toward the girl. The light from his phone remained, bathing him in a very pale, very faint, but visible glow.

Mariana was able to see him. Vaguely.

He carefully removed the strips of tape from over her mouth. Her eyes were squinting, either from the smoke or in an effort to better distinguish the masked figure in front of her.

"What...who are—"

A sudden flash of heat at Trust's back changed his more deliberate plans instantly. The Viper Skin, other than detecting Mariana's close proximity in front, and the men lying prone on the ground, remained dormant.

No, this was *actual* heat.

Trust turned to look over his shoulder, and then back to Mariana, having to narrow his eyes, even behind his shades, against the contrasting glare.

He picked up Mariana, her body still tied, turning back toward the harsh light—

A firefighter was now in the doorway in full turnout gear, the light on his helmet turned on to a bright setting. His body blocked the overwhelming glare from the nearby flames, allowing Trust to see again.

The firefighter's mask blocked his mouth.

Without waiting, Trust handed Mariana over to him.

Mariana began to cough. Trust was beginning to have some difficulty as well.

*Three.*

He gestured back into the room.

*Three.*

He then gestured back down the hall, presumably the way the firefighter had arrived. Not being able to fully recognize the firefighter's face, he could only hope the message got across.

Cradling Mariana in his arms, the firefighter departed.

His coughing becoming more frequent, Trust dragged the three incapacitated men into a heap near the door, and then shut it.

The fire was a short distance away. Trust turned immediately in the other direction, away from the glare...crouching to avoid the worst of the smoke, one hand on the warm wall as he moved down the hall...more firefighters advancing toward him, he shrugged them off, pointing them back the way he had come...back toward the room...

"I'VE GOT ONE! I'VE GOT...I've got one!"

The firefighter materialized from the smoke spewing out of the front of Centre Diamond, ripping his mask off with one hand while still supporting Mariana in the other, as the battalion chief ordered in two more firefighters to take his place. The nearby area immediately surrounding the club was in a state of semi-organized pandemonium—law enforcement, fire department, and various other emergency service personnel swarming, hurrying this way and that, each with a job to do and rushing to fulfill it, dodging between an intricate labyrinth of patrol cars, fire trucks, ambulances, emergency lights bursting, illuminating the block that would otherwise lie in shadow due to the still unexplained electrical blackout.

Two paramedics rushed over with a stretcher. The scene was loud and hectic, voices shouting over a constant clamor, a siren intermittently sounding to add punctuation to the chaos.

"She just lost consciousness as we were nearing the door," the firefighter explained. "She's breathing, though. She's breathing."

As the medics put a respiratory mask over her face and rolled her toward one of the waiting ambulances, the fireman removed his helmet and went over to the chief. Though the lights were still off the length of the city block, radio communication had been restored, and the senior firefighter held a portable walkie-talkie in his hands. It was an obsolete piece of equipment, but one the chief seemed fond of.

"Chief, there's somebody else in there."

His attention still largely on the information coming through the radio, the senior chief nodded absently without looking in his direction.

"Yeah, we're getting them out now, Pete. And good work with the girl—no, I'm not letting any more in after my guys get clear. It's getting too—no, you need to get the district chief to a phone so he can call the commissioner. I don't care if he's having a late dinner—"

"No," Pete interrupted loudly, still trying to catch his breath. "There's someone else. Black clothes, wearing some type of mask. He handed me the girl."

This got the chief's attention.

TRUST COUGHED HARD, NEARLY CHOKING. He was very low to the floor now, practically crawling, thick, sooty smoke billowing in waves over his head but also beginning to swirl and encompass the entire hallway. The smoke affected his vision in much the same way the flames had, the miniscule flecks producing a ruthless brilliance that almost blinded him.

He arrived at the door leading out to the lounge area above the dance floor, and pushed it open.

The painful intensity of the shine halted him, causing him to fall completely and cover his head, still coughing. Whether it was fire or more smoke, he wasn't even able to differentiate anymore—even with his eyes shut and covered, all he could see now was a bright, blinding white, as though it had instantly seared his retinas.

Deaf, and now blind. And fighting to breathe. He could still feel the heat from the encroaching fire, still smell the all-too-recognizable stench of the world around him burning.

Even the air seemed to be on fire now.

Clawing the floor, he started to push himself back into the hall...

He felt someone grab at him from behind. He tried fighting them off, but he was wildly disoriented, his lungs burning, ready to slash their way out of his body—

But a corner of his mind registered the oddly familiar squeeze on the back of his neck before he blacked out...

...MOVING...HIS FACE...SOMEONE, SOMETHING was grabbing at his face, his mask—

He clutched the offending hand in a crushing grip, his eyes snapping open.

Kyler.

"Ow, ow, ow, ow, ow—"

Trust glanced down, realizing he was holding on to Kyler's wrist, and released it.

Wait...

Kyler.

He could see again.

But his chest was still burning. He realized he was gasping for air.

Wait...

Kyler?

"We're going to Arlington Memorial," Kyler explained, reaching for Trust's mask again, and this time succeeding. "We're two minutes away. We have to get this mask and suit off before you go in. You're okay. Just keep breathing."

His mask and shades now off, Trust looked down. He was sprawled along the backseat of Mr. Jackson's GranTurismo, his bodysuit already open and tugged down to his torso, his chest bare, rising up and down rapidly as he gasped.

He looked up to Kyler again, who was in the backseat with him.

"I know it's kinda difficult right now, but I think you're the one who's going to have to pull the suit down the rest of the way and put some underwear on. I mean, if your life actually depended on me having to pull the suit down right this minute, I would do it...I think...but...yeah. I'll hand you the shorts, though. They're in your bag, right?"

Trust leaned back in the buttery-soft seat again, his breaths coming in hard, steady pants as he tried to manage it. He wrestled with the Viper Skin as Kyler grimaced and looked away...

...NOW UNDER THE EMERGENCY BAY of Arlington Memorial Hospital. Kyler practically kicked open the door of the car, leaping out and turning back, holding out his hand as Trust slid himself over. With an arm slung over his shoulder, Kyler was carrying the majority of his weight, Trust appearing as though he were going to topple over at any moment. The automatic doors of the hospital slid open. Before they could reach the second set, a nurse—Hailey—was hurrying toward them.

"Kyler, Trust, what happened?"

"My crazy friend here had to go and get himself mixed up in that Centre Diamond fire."

Hailey turned back into the lobby as they both helped Trust inside.

"Dr. Andrews?" she called. "Dr. Andrews?"

A man backed from around a corner, as though he had just departed the lobby a moment earlier.

"Good God, boy! What in the name of Tallaght happened to your clothes?"

Still breathing hard and drooping slightly, Trust could only squint at the familiar face...who, strangely enough, was wearing a white coat.

Kyler struggled to keep Trust upright.

"What are you—umph—impersonating doctors now, Kian? Can't you see my friend's in the midst of acute inter-lapse respiratory failure? We need a real doctor over here, like Dr. Andrews."

Hailey leaned in.

"Kian is Dr. Andrews."

Kyler's face contorted into one of pure bewilderment.

"But I thought—"

"Oi!" the Irish doctor shouted down the hall. "Bring that stretcher this way. This one's about to hit the dirt!"

Kyler looked back.

"What are you talking—"

"I'm actually surprised he's stayed up this long," Dr. Andrews said.

"But I don't underst—Trust? Trust!"

Trust lost consciousness again.

And almost instantly thereafter, his breathing began to even out.

THE SAME BLINDING, PAINFUL BRIGHTNESS...and then, it disappeared.

Welcome darkness.

Trust jerked. He attempted to move his arm, but he felt something tugging back...

Even with his eyes closed, he detected the approaching movement. His hand shot up, his eyes opening at the same moment.

His clutch on the slender wrist immediately softened. His eyes grew wide.

"Mari-ana."

Trust had never seen a more beautiful girl than at that exact moment. Mariana's glossy lips stretched into a smile, her silky, jet-black hair hanging down freely, perfectly framing her olive-toned face, the faintest pattering of freckles touched lightly, delicately, across her softly rounded cheeks under chocolate-kissed eyes. She was a vision, a mirage, a dream.

The hand touching Mariana's wrist slowly slid down until their fingers touched, and then intertwined.

"The others went to get something to eat."

Trust's fingers curled ever so slightly, briefly gripping her hand even harder as he smiled.

"Mariana," he said again, his voice crystal clear and shockingly soft.

Mariana smiled that smile again.

"It was you, wasn't it?" she asked, leaning forward slightly as though it actually mattered to Trust whether or not she was whispering. "That was you, in the ma—"

Movement at the door caught his eye.

"Okay, Mariana. So, remember when you said you didn't want anything? Well, I actually didn't believe—Trust! Yes! You're awake!"

With a pile of unhealthy-looking snacks cradled in his hands, Kyler rushed back to the doorway.

"Hey! Everybody! Everyone within hearing range of my voice! Trust is awake! I repeat, Trustice Jeffries is awake!"

Trust frowned, able to see what Kyler shouted into the hall. He started to sit up, but Mariana stopped him with a soft hand to his bare shoulder. She shook her head, her grin turning slightly playful.

"Uh-uh," she said. "We're under strict orders from the doctor not to let you sit up yet."

With Kyler approaching the hospital bed again, unceremoniously dumping all of the assorted munchies on the lower half of Trust's bed, Trust signed, *But you're up and moving. You're dressed and walking around. Weren't you in the fire?*

Mariana smiled, rolling her eyes.

"Dude, you won't believe this story," Kyler said. "She was saved from the fire by some nutjob in a mask. I mean, seriously? A nutjob in a mask? What a nutjob."

Trust just looked at him as others began to filter into the room, all familiar faces. His parents—Tyson and Sonja Jeffries; Kyler's parents—Tom and Sherry Brooks—and his sister—Michelle; Paxson, Marcie, Allison, Cortez, Nurse Hailey; Mariana's uncle and the owner of Centre Diamond, Pablo Eldorado; Dr. Kian Andrews—

"Excuse me, excuse me," the doctor called out, jostling his way into the hospital room. No one appeared to mind his otherwise brusque behavior. In fact, everyone else seemed used to it.

Trust was the only one who looked at him with some wariness, stopping him in his tracks. Kian huffed.

"Yes, surprise, surprise, Trustice Jeffries. I really am your doctor. Can I actually do a wee bit o' work now, or should I go retrieve my medical diploma from the janitorial cabinet?"

Trust glanced to Kyler.

*Is he actually speaking English right now? Who even is this guy?*

"Oh, that's very funny," Kian intoned after Kyler translated, glancing through Trust's medical folder. "You had no problem believing me as a custodian, but when I have a stethoscope around my neck, oh, all of a sudden I get a 'who is this guy'? That's hilarious."

Trust feigned a grin and started to sit up again.

"Ah, ah, ah," the doctor said, holding up his hand. "Not quite yet. Now, I'm sorry to be the one to have to tell you this, but the effects from a fire have caused you to suffer complete hearing loss. You are deaf, Mr. Jeffries."

Just behind him, Tyson Jeffries nudged his wife.

"I love this guy," he whispered, leaning closer to her ear.

Trust gestured to the nurse, Kyler continuing to interpret.

*Okay, excluding the fact I can only understand every third word that he says, can we please bring in a real doctor so I can get out of here? Or are you allowed to release me? I'm fine either way.*

Before Hailey could reply, Kian asked, "Do you know what non-auditory inner ear dizziness is?"

Trust settled back into bed once more, sighing.

"Of course you do," Kian said, "because you didn't go deaf last night—you've been deaf for quite some time. Your entire life, in fact. So you know what would happen if you tried to stand up right now."

"Wait, what'll happen?" Paxson said.

"He'll fall flat on his face," Michelle Brooks supplied, snickering.

"Michelle!" Sherry Brooks admonished.

"I actually couldn't have said it better myself, Mrs. Brooks," Kian said. He then scanned Trust's chart again.

"But, other than that, you're as healthy as an Irish setter. The smoke's out of your lungs, no damage caused as far as I can see here. You can go back to wrestling bears—or whatever it is that you do to gain that physique—in no time."

Kian then glanced to Hailey, who had moved to the other side of the bed to the nurse's station in the room.

"I thought we were going to get some sort of sheet or something to cover his...upper body area," he muttered, attempting to keep his voice low.

Hailey shrugged, smiling faintly.

"We did, but he kept shrugging it off in his sleep," she replied. "Too hot, I guess."

"You can say that again," Mariana said, grinning.

Both Sonja Jeffries' and Pablo Eldorado's eyebrows rose.

"I'll second that," Michelle added. "Even though he is kind of stupid and my brother's friend, Trust is pretty hot."

"Well, then," Tom Brooks said, exhaling loudly.

"First it's Kyler running naked through the dorm halls," Marcie observed, shaking her head and smirking, "and now this."

Everyone looked at her.

Then everyone looked at Kyler.

"Kyler-Scott?" his father said. "Anything you want to share with the rest of the room?"

Kyler's face turned contemplative.

"Well, the only thing I can think of is that the baseball team does have a pretty big game tonight. It's the Super Regionals, so one more win and we go to the College World Series. Everyone is welcome to come."

"Uhm, pretty sure Dad meant the story about you streaking through the halls—" Michelle started.

"Okay," Sherry Brooks cut in, shooting her daughter a look and causing everyone else to laugh.

# 51.
# Changes

THE CONTINUED DISCOVERIES AT 1844 Decatur Lane and the Centre Diamond nightclub spawned a flurry of investigations over the weekend, already uncovering a great deal of information about the mythical Freesef Society that had long been suppressed. Another press conference was scheduled for the following Monday in a large courtyard on the rural campus of the University of Centre City, under pleasant skies. Speaking were the governor of the state, the mayor of Centre City, the CCMPD chief of police, and Chancellor April Beverly. Many more students were in attendance as compared to the Dorm Room Robbers event, as were many more members of the news media—local, regional, and national. Broadcast cameras stood sentinel along the sides and rear of the courtyard, capturing nearly every conceivable angle.

It was certainly a spectacle, particularly at the beginning of the second and final week of exams.

Trust, Kyler, Allison, Paxson, Marcie, and Cortez were also on hand, watching as the chancellor of their school approached the podium, the last official speaker before the news conference would be opened to questions.

Trust, none the worse for wear after his brief stay under the care of Nurse Hailey and Dr. Kian Andrews, looked to Kyler as Beverly began speaking.

*Officer Ryan has been looking over at us the entire time we've been here,* Trust signed.

*Hmmm...I don't think it's us,* Kyler replied. *I think it's mainly just you.*

"Pssst," Paxson hissed, leaning over. "What are you guys talking

637

about?"

"...a cover-up of massive proportions," April Beverly announced into the microphones in front of her, "and with substantial implications. This cannot and will not be ignored any longer, on any level, in any setting. I am relieved that the governor of our great state, along with Mayor Perkins, have come here today to..."

*Rory's gone,* Trust signed, Kyler now translating for the others. *No one's seen him; no one's heard from him. Pax is apparently the last person on Earth to have seen him. Or, at least, the last person to admit to it.*

"He had to have gone farther in that tunnel," Paxson noted, "past wherever you found Jeremy and Jezzie. I'm positive I didn't see him come back downstairs. And who knows where those tunnels go, how many there are, or who else went with him."

"The important thing, though," Marcie observed, "was finding Jeremy and Jezzie. If Freesef had known people were actively looking for them, they might have moved them before Trust could get down there, and then who knows where they would be right now."

"I think we should also thank Cortez for that," Allison remarked, to which Cortez grinned.

*Yeah,* Trust motioned. *Thanks for being so willing—eager even—to break the law again. Surely, this news conference wouldn't be happening right now without you.*

"Hey, I think punching people's brains in until they're spewing their own gray matter on the ground is pretty illegal, too," Cortez replied. "And from what I've seen and heard about you, you've kinda developed a habit for it."

"Burn," Paxson coughed.

Trust eyed both of them.

"...and as such," Chancellor Beverly went on, "there will be some changes taking place—some immediately—in various city agencies and within our own university.

"But, with that, I would like to take this brief moment to recognize, along with Chief Manuel, a few Centre City officers who have been quietly investigating the Freesef Society even before the events of this weekend, against pushback from within their own department—and even from some within my administration.

"May I present former Patrol Officer First Class Ben Ryan, former

Patrol Sergeant Armstrong Longley, former Patrol Sergeant Clifford Tubbs, and former Patrol Lieutenant Wallace O'Patrick. I say former, not because they are leaving the force, but on the contrary, they are being promoted to investigator, patrol lieutenant, patrol lieutenant, and commander, respectively."

Trust tried to conceal a grin as Officer Ben Ryan—who had been looking once more in Trust's direction from his location on stage—glanced quickly to the chancellor, and then to the police chief, a look of surprise coming across his face. He was nudged forward to join the other three officers now standing to the forefront, an applause ascending from the crowd.

"Look at Ryan," Kyler said, laughing. "He *so* doesn't even know what the heck is going on."

"He deserves it," Allison declared. "It's like he's one of the very few who took this whole thing seriously, and Lieutenant O'Patrick was the first officer to respond to Melody's assault. You should have seen him at the hospital. If he had the people who had attacked her in front of him..."

"And Longley was with Jezzie when Jeremy first went missing," Marcie added. "He seemed nice."

*Tubbs chased me through downtown on foot and through crowds,* Trust signed. *He didn't come close to catching me, of course, and I thought he was going to fall over and die at the hospital, but he never stopped running as far as I know. That deserves a promotion right there.*

After a short statement of recognition and the promise of a more formal ceremony at a later time, the chancellor faced the crowd again.

"With the emergence of these dreadful acts from an enigmatic organization residing within this very university, what also emerges is the painful evidence of a systematic failure from the very entity most trusted with the overall wellbeing and safety of the students and faculty— my administration. This starts at the top, with me. As such, I would like to announce, here and now, that I will be resigning my position as chancellor of the University of Centre City, effective at the end of the—"

Trust watched as Beverly had to stop speaking, not hearing the collective objections from the crowd that caused her to pause.

"That—that is the end of my statement," the chancellor announced, still fighting against the sounds of protest coming from the audience. "I'll open this conference to any questions at this t—"

"Excuse me. I'm sorry, excuse me, ma'am."

At the podium, Chancellor Beverly turned. All eyes shifted.

Officer—soon to be Investigator—Ben Ryan stepped forward again, this time of his own volition. Beverly stepped away from the microphones.

"I'm sorry for interrupting, ma'am," Ryan said, leaning somewhat awkwardly into the huddle of microphones, as though he really didn't want to be in front of them at all. He turned slightly, looking out into the crowd.

"I've been with Centre City Metro for just over three years now, which is as long as I've lived in this area. I'm not from here. But in these three years, I've interacted with a lot of UCC students. I've heard a lot about this school. I've heard a lot about you, Chancellor Beverly.

"From what has recently come to light over the weekend, I know now that you are not aware of the multiple requests I had in to talk to you. Those requests were apparently intercepted by at least one of the aides no longer holding a position with the university, and it is my opinion that they were intercepted for a reason—the reason being that you would have disrupted this entire operation from the start.

"I've been closely following with an assault investigation involving a UCC student that took place in late November of last year. Since I'm not—or, at least, was not at the time—an investigating detective, there was only so much I could do without overstepping my bounds. But this girl—just hearing and seeing her determination for finding the people who attacked her—people we have significant cause to believe are members of this Freesef Society—it exemplifies exactly why we are all here today. I know that this young woman has spoken to you, Chancellor; that her parents have spoken with you on more than one occasion; that her friends have spoken with you; that they all heard the same resolute drive and determination this young woman has in finding her assaulters.

"My chief believes in you, Chancellor Beverly. My fellow officers believe in you. The young girl we both have spoken to believes in you. I believe in you. A majority of the boys suspected in that assault I just mentioned are presently unaccounted for. We still have so many more questions than answers about this Freesef organization. I can think of no one else more suited to lead this university at a time when it needs a leader the most.

"That's...that's all I had to say. Sorry for interrupting."

The courtyard burst into cheers and applause. Ryan began to step back, but he did not get far before Chancellor Beverly approached him, extending her hand. They were far enough from the podium that those relying on the microphones to hear could not make out what they were saying.

Trust, however...

*Thank you,* Beverly said, *but I have to take responsibility for this.*

*Leaders don't take responsibility and then walk away,* Ryan replied. *They take responsibility, they learn from it, they get better, and they lead more effectively.*

AFTER THE MOST IMMEDIATE QUESTIONS WERE answered or deferred until a later date, the news conference began to break up. Much of the crowd remained as the noteworthy figures on stage came down. Trust and the gang went to Officer Ryan, Allison leading the way through the crowd of people.

"Congratulations on the promotion, Officer Ryan," she said, "and thanks for all that you did. I'm sure if you had been in charge of the investigation from the beginning, things wouldn't have turned out the way they have."

"It's not over," Ryan assured her determinedly. "We'll find those boys. All of them."

More praise came from Paxson, Marcie, and Cortez, the last of which made Ryan pause.

"From the theft ring."

Cortez shrugged sheepishly and nodded.

"I'm surprised they let a convicted felon get this close to the—oh, that's right. You received a plea deal, so you weren't actually convicted of those charges. I've heard you've been doing good work with the Intelligence Division. You're leaving for the summer soon, right?"

"Yeah, my last exam was on Friday," Cortez replied. "I'm scheduled to go to the station for a few more hours later today, and then I'm absconding—I mean, going back to Jersey."

"Yeah, one word of advice, kid," Ryan intoned. "Don't joke about absconding in front of an officer. It just makes me want to arrest you."

Kyler was next.

The two looked at each other, Kyler smirking, Ryan glaring.

The moment stretching...

Ryan cracked the faintest hint of a smile. Kyler laughed and stepped away slightly, allowing Trust to come forward.

"Heard you had to spend the night in the hospital Saturday. Smoke inhalation."

Trust looked at him.

"I also heard some talk of some kind of dark-clothed, masked figure. First sightings were at that house on Decatur Lane, and then at Centre Diamond during the fire. There's video from inside the Decatur house, numerous videos shot by the students there. Multiple individuals beaten unconscious at both locations. And you know what? It looks like it could be the same individual who was reported at that abandoned warehouse used by the theft ring."

"Oh, man," Kyler said, joining the thus far one-sided dialogue. "I saw that guy at that party, Officer Ryan—I was there. Dude, he was moving so fast, but he—or she, I guess—seemed to be looking for someone in particular. He didn't mess with other people as long as you stayed out of his way."

Ryan looked to Kyler again.

"What are you saying?"

Kyler grinned in the easy, playful way that he did so well.

"I'm not saying anything. I was just saying what I said—that I saw him there."

"Ahh. And do you think we'll see him again? Or does this dangerous and highly illegal vigilante spree end now before someone—namely the vigilante—gets hurt?"

Trust was shaking his head at Kyler, though he quickly stopped when Ryan glanced in his direction again. Kyler, meanwhile, shrugged, still smiling.

"Before someone really gets hurt? I think plenty of people already have. You said so in your speech up there. But I wouldn't worry about this 'vigilante' too much. And we've got to come up with a better name."

Trust held up his hand before looking to the officer again.

*The boys who escaped know their way out of that secret tunnel.*

"How do you know about the tunnel?"

*Come on, everyone knows about the tunnel. The ones the police had to let go—for the second time—are now gone. The fact that they even had access to something like that secret tunnel, the fact that it even exists, along with all of the other stuff we've learned about the Freesef Society this year...it tells me this is a big deal, and it's not going to go away so easily. But it looks like, this year, things are finally beginning to change. These promotions are a part of that. I think this so-called "masked vigilante" is, too.*

Ryan's jaw tensed after Kyler's translation.

"So, do you really expect me to pretend that I don't know what's really going on here?" he posed. "You expect me to allow you to keep doing what you're doing?"

Trust looked to Kyler, a befuddled expression on his face.

*What am I doing? Do you know what he's talking about right now?*

Kyler shrugged again.

"Heck if I know. Allison?"

Allison shook her head, though her face displayed a knowing smile.

"Marcie?" she asked.

"Half the time, I don't understand what any of you are talking about," Marcie stated. "For the other half, I usually just ignore it. Pax?"

"Yeah?"

Marcie looked at him.

"Oh, were we talking about something?" he asked. "I wasn't paying attention. Hey, doesn't that girl standing over there look a lot like Velma from Scooby-Doo?"

"As an honorary member of the Centre City Metro Police Department," Cortez stated, "I would just like to say that I will do everything in my power to find and apprehend this dastardly masked marauder and bring him to—"

"Yeah," Ryan drew out. "This coming from the kid who, for all intents and purposes, orchestrated the largest theft ring this city's seen in the last fifty years—and all from his laptop computer. And speaking of that...Saturday night, there were some still-unexplained electrical blackouts that occurred at both the Decatur Lane address and Centre Diamond—both, coincidentally, around the same time this so-called 'masked marauder' was spotted. You wouldn't happen to know anything about that, would you, Romero?"

"Well," Cortez started, "as an honorary member of the Centre City—"

"You do realize that you are *not* an honorary member, right? People go to prison for *years* for the same thing you—you know what, I really don't know why I'm still standing here having this conversation. You can go away now, all of you. And stay out of trouble."

Everyone laughed. Trust extended his hand toward the officer. The two shook.

"Stay out of trouble," Ryan repeated, looking at him.

Trust and the others then departed.

"Hey," Cortez said to Trust when they were away from the people who had attended the news conference, the group now walking along one of the many brick-laden paths that connected the buildings of the rural campus, "you're still going to let me record your voice for TalkText, right? You gotta let me do it, man. It's going to be so awesome, and I don't think anyone's even thought to use the voice of a deaf person before. I could have it done by the time we get back in the fall so you can use it."

"Whatevah."

Kyler interpreted Trust's shrug in a New York accent, setting off laughs from the others.


"YOUR SHIFT BEGINS SOON, DOESN'T it, son?" Chief Manuel asked as he and Ryan headed for their respective department-issued vehicles—Ryan in his usual patrol cruiser, Gregory in a black, new model Dodge Enterprise.

"Yes, sir."

Ryan checked his watch.

"In about thirty minutes. Sergeant—well, Lieutenant Longley is my CO, so he allowed me extra time because I had to be here, but I think I can still make it in at my usual time."

"It would be wise to get used to these conferences, Ryan. You're a detect—investigator, I've got to get used to that—you're an investigator now, or will be by the end of the week. Judging by your work so far, especially on this Freesef thing, I have a feeling you're going to be attending a lot more."

Both men stopped in front of the chief's car. Chief Manuel, looking distinguished in his suit, neatly concealing the experienced, hard-nosed cop underneath, turned to look at the young officer.

"It was a good thing, what you said up there about the chancellor."

Ryan nodded.

"You're around Longley, Tubbs, and O'Patrick a lot, aren't you?"

"Yes, sir?"

"Keep doing it. They're good cops. They sweat out more knowledge about policing in this city than most learn in their career."

"Yes, sir."

Manuel studied him for a moment.

"That your only suit?"

"I have one more."

The chief smiled knowingly.

"You may want to get one more to start off with. And more dress shirts and ties. Mix and match so it looks like you have ten different suits. Doesn't even have to be a suit, really, but something you can walk into a corporate environment in and not be given a second glance. Something that disguises the fact that you look like you should be finishing your sophomore year at UCC instead of one of my investigators sworn to protect it."

Ryan nodded firmly.

"Yes, sir."

"You're doing good, Ryan. Keep doing that, too."

"I'll do my best."

Manuel opened his door.

"Good," he declared, "because I really expect nothing less."

Ryan walked to his own CCMPD car, parked farther in the lot, his hand in his pocket. Thinking.

He felt something.

A slip of paper that had not been there before.

He pulled it out, opening it.

*See you in the fall, investigator.*

*-T*

## 52.
## Chasing Fear Into Darkness

THE STAGGERED EXAM SCHEDULE HAD the students of the University of Centre City leaving campus in small, manageable waves each day. Jezzie Delaney completed the last of her exams on a drizzly Tuesday in the early afternoon. Jeremy Higgins' exams would also be completed that day, but at a later time.

Jezzie was leaving early. Trust and Jeremy were hauling the final box to the moving truck.

"She's going to transfer to OSU for next year," Jeremy explained, Trust able to see the boy's mouth over the box they were moving. "It's, like, twenty minutes away from our hometown, so she'll be close to home, close to family. After all the stuff that's gone down this year—all the stuff that's happened since we started here as freshmen that I didn't even know about—I think it's the smart thing to do. She needs to get out of here, away from this city. Away from...people we thought we knew."

Trust just nodded, his hands full. They made it across the sidewalk, lifting the box up to the movers already in the back of the truck. Meanwhile, another car provided by the university was waiting to take Jezzie to the airport. Trust returned to his note cards.

*I hate everything that's happened. I hate she has to transfer,*
*but you're probably right.*

"Oh, yeah. I'm sure *you* hate she has to leave," Jeremy replied as Jezzie walked up to them. Jeremy's characteristic smirk was present, but a bit subdued, not as cocky as it usually was.

"I'll be sure to let you see some of the pictures she sends," he

647

continued. "Some of them. Not all of them."

Trust rolled his eyes.

"You do know I have Trust's number, right?" Jezzie said. "I can text him whenever I want."

"Trust, lose my girlfriend's number," Jeremy instructed.

Jezzie shifted to give Trust a hug.

"Thanks," she said, leaning back again so Trust could read her speech. "For everything. For...everything."

*I'm sorry to see you go like this. Who will keep Jeremy in line next year with you not here?*

Jezzie smiled.

"Oh, don't worry about him. I can keep him under control even if I'm a million miles away."

She then made a gesture.

*Wrapped around my finger,* she mouthed.

Jeremy, able to witness Jezzie's hand movements, scoffed.

"Anyway," she went on, "I have you and Kyler and your friends here to look out for him, too. I just knew you two would become friends, even with the somewhat rocky start at that first party. You have too much in common with each other."

She then paused briefly, grinning.

"And then there's always that mysterious masked guy who people have been talking about. I think he'll do a good job of keeping Jeremy Higgins safe next year."

Trust wrote,

*I wouldn't rely on that masked guy too much. Seems unstable.*

"Yeah, I think we already sussed that out," Jeremy said. "For instance, speaking in third person is usually a pretty good giveaway."

Trust stood by as Jezzie and Jeremy said their good-byes, Jezzie promising to call when she was about to board her flight, and then again when she landed. Jeremy walked her to the car, taking her and her carry-on luggage to the airport, telling her he would see her tonight after he caught his own flight home.

The moving truck transporting the rest of Jezzie's belongings from her apartment left. Trust gave a mock salute, and Jeremy a cool wave, as Jezzie's car departed the parking area in front of building 484.

Trust glanced around the tidy community of apartment buildings. Other students were seen preparing to leave as well.

The light rain falling from the sky was nearly indiscernible. The sky was overcast.

Trust looked to Jeremy, who was also looking around at the apartments, taking the scene in.

"Hearing Jez just now reminded me," Jeremy said, still looking away, but at an angle where Trust could read him. "We've been dealing with the police so much these last few days, I never said thanks. You know, for Saturday night."

Trust shook his head, raising his shoulders and looking confused.

"Yeah, whatever," Jeremy said, scoffing again. "It wasn't you. Got it. But seriously, thanks. Those idiots taking me is one thing—and for what, I still don't understand—but when they threw Jezzie in there with me, I..."

He shook his head, his brow wrinkling. Then he turned to look at Trust directly.

"I already owe you a ton for how you saved Jezzie before Christmas, and then just hanging out with me when I was going through...whatever. And now this stuff. So, whatever you need, whenever you need it, hit me up."

Trust smirked, nodding.

> *Maybe an autographed football or jersey wouldn't be so bad for my dad. And I'll make sure to pass along your thanks to that masked bandit whenever I see him.*

Jeremy threw his hands in the air, laughing.

"Oh, will you please knock it off already? I know you're him!"

Trust made an agitated face, shushing Jeremy while peeking around the Greenpark Estates complex again.

The two fell quiet.

After a minute or so, Trust jerked his thumb back behind them.

> *You ever meet the housing manager here?*

"Yeah. He's a fat perv. I think he's afraid of me, too."

THURSDAY BROUGHT ALLISON'S DEPARTURE.

And another visit from Uncle Smith.

"What's in this one?" he asked, holding up a box and shaking it.

The box contained the Viper Skin bodysuit Trust had worn, along with the accompanying mask, both of which Allison planned to improve over the summer break.

Trust arched an eyebrow at Smith's behavior, already knowing what was inside. Allison took it out of Smith's hands.

"Do you really need to ask that for every single box and package we've brought down?" she asked.

Trust saw Kyler glance again to what had been Melody's half of the dorm room. It had been cleaned out since before Trust and Kyler had even arrived to help Allison finish packing. It should have been no surprise, since Allison had already said that her roommate had left for home the previous Friday.

And now, Allison's side of the room was just as bare as Melody's.

"Seriously, she's like a ghost," Kyler declared. "How many times did I see her this year? Once? Twice? Oh, who am I kidding, acting like I don't remember? It was twice."

"Well, if she had been your roommate, I'm sure you would have seen her more often, like I did," Allison replied. "I actually know for a fact she saw you plenty of times—you just saw *her* twice. You, too, Trust."

She then looked around the room one last time.

"Okay, so that's everything. Nothing in the drawers, nothing in the closet...I guess we're ready to go, then?"

*Has Melody heard anything about what's happened since she left?* Trust signed.

"She messaged me either Sunday or Monday saying she saw some of the videos from the party on Decatur Lane."

Allison smiled as she moved toward the open door. Trust and Kyler looked to each other. And then shrugged.

"Videos?" Smith repeated, waiting for everyone else to pass through before shutting the door.

Kyler bounded ahead of the group and turned, walking backward as

Trust, Allison, and Smith moved ahead.

"Allison didn't tell you?" he exclaimed. "Oh, dude! It was amazing! All right, so, we're there—not drinking, of course. It was a party, mostly to celebrate our first win in Super Regionals, but really, it was just a party, because who knows what it would have been for if we had lost—"

"Someone in dark clothes and a mask came through the house during a power outage," Allison cut in as Kyler threatened to spill off into a tangent. "I'm pretty sure he was looking for someone in particular, though. We were in the kitchen when it happened, and he went by us so quickly, barely even looking. He was dragging some kid along with him, and he kept showing the kid something on his phone. I think it might have been a picture of someone."

The group was in the elevator, heading down.

"You're all right, though?" Smith inquired. "Did anyone get hurt?"

"Eh," Kyler said casually, waving him off. "A couple of guys got punched in the face, but really, that happens at practically every college party from what I can tell. Most high school parties, too. And I heard there were some guys who got *completely* knocked out in the secret tunnel they found Jeremy Higgins and Jezzie Delaney in. These were some, like, fully grown, bodybuilder-henchmen-type dudes...boom! Out like a light! They were like that when the police found them. Everyone thinks the Mask did it, but by the time the police got there, that dude was long gone."

Trust looked toward his friend.

*The Mask?* he repeated, and Kyler interpreted for the others.

"You're right," Kyler said. "We're really going to have to come up with some type of name for him. He's popped up more than once now. He could be, like, a superhero or something!"

As Allison was finishing the exit paperwork and turning over her keys and other Mueller Hall supplies, Kyler, Trust, and Smith were outside, standing on the sidewalk just beside the steps leading up to the dorm entrance. After days of cloudy skies, the sun was out again, illuminating the campus in its springtime grandeur. With only one and a half days of exams to go, the UCC campus held only a small fraction of its usual capacity, the grounds now mostly devoid of the strolling and sprawling students that it had held for the previous nine months. It reminded Trust of what the campus had looked like at the beginning of the year, before classes had officially started.

It seemed like only yesterday.

"Before Al comes back out and ruins this moment," Smith spoke up, looking to the boys, "I just wanted to thank you both again—on behalf of both myself and Allison's parents. They're sorry they couldn't make it; they really want to meet you. But from all Allison's told us, the way you have conducted yourselves—while still being eighteen-year-old boys, at that—I guess it just restores my faith once again in this sometimes crazy world we live in. My career typically has me wallowing in the full-tilt-crazy part. You two remind me of who I'm doing it for."

"Well," Kyler breathed in haughtily, tugging his pants up. If he had been wearing suspenders, the charade would have worked better. "Al's a good kid, so it's no problem. A little precocious, maybe, but she's a scrapper, she's a fighter, and by golly, she's got heart. When me and my associate Mr. Jeffries here spotted her walking into our freshman seminar class last fall, I said, I say I said, 'Trustice, my boy, you better watch out for this one, because this girl's got a good head on her shoulders. I tell ya, she's going places.' That's what I said."

*You were speechless when she walked into that classroom,* Trust signed.

Kyler chuckled nervously, shaking his head.

"Eh...that's not *quite* how I remember it—"

"So I guess that little Viper Skin project she's been working on paid off pretty good, eh?" Smith asked.

Allison exited Mueller Hall, skipping down the steps. She halted, spotting Trust's and Kyler's stunned expressions—and Smith's amused one.

"What'd I miss?" she asked, looking from one side to the other.

"Just another one of my dirty jokes you don't like," Smith said without hesitation, causing Allison to roll her eyes. "Apparently, your wholesome friends here have never heard them in the Outer Banks of North Carolina."

"And I'm sure they don't want to hear any more."

She turned to look at the two boys again.

"Sorry. I really shouldn't leave you guys around him unsupervised."

She then went to embrace Kyler.

"I don't like to say good—"

Trust watched as she stopped speaking, still holding on to Kyler. Her eyes drew closed. Kyler may have been whispering something into her ear, but Trust couldn't tell from his present angle.

He glanced to Smith, who arched an eyebrow.

Kyler and Allison slowly separated, eye contact lingering...

Smith started to clear his throat, and then started coughing. Allison shot him a glare before moving to Trust. She put her hands on his shoulders, looking at him. Smiling.

Trust smiled back.

"Allison."

She beamed. Smith's eyes widened.

AFTER ALLISON LEFT, THE TWO walked slowly back toward Weaver Hall. Kyler was back to signing, seemingly to bask in what Trust presumed was the quiet of an almost-empty campus. They would be staying until Kyler's baseball season was officially over.

With a talented team that could make it to the championship series, that could mean a few more weeks.

*Is it weird that Allison hardly ever seems to mention her parents?* Kyler asked.

*Is it weird that just before she left, you two looked like you were back together?* Trust returned.

*Is it weird that for someone who can see practically everything, you can't see my fist about to slam into your face?* Kyler asked.

*Is it weird that for someone with an impeccable memory, you somehow still conveniently forgot to tell me what the heck happened between you two?* Trust replied.

*Is it weird that you haven't talked about Mariana leaving for Miami while the club is being rebuilt?* Kyler asked.

Trust stopped walking.

*Allison mentioned her parents. And we've met her "uncle" a few times now. She's never met our uncles, but she's met our parents. Hey, is it weird that he seems to know about everything that we do up here? He knew about the bus holdup, he knows about the Viper Skin...*

*Did you just put uncle in quotes?* Kyler asked.

*He's interesting,* Trust signed.

Kyler shrugged.

*I guess it doesn't really matter. I mean, we'll meet her parents when we meet them, right?*

*If nothing else, we'll meet them at the wedding,* Trust replied, grinning, to which Kyler shoved him. *And we're still talking about all of this later, so just pencil it in to your mental schedule.*

*Fine,* Kyler said. *I'll pencil it in right beside Mariana.*

*Nothing to talk about.*

*Oooh, can I use that excuse, too?*

They walked more.

*Pax and Marcie say they will come in from Potomac Park to hang out later,* Trust gestured.

*What was that piece of paper Allison gave you before she left?* Kyler asked.

The deaf boy dug into his pocket, coming up with the slip.

*The same piece of paper that I gave her at the police station after she came back from Thanksgiving Break,* Trust signed. *The one that, at the time, I didn't want you to read.*

He held it up now, offering it to Kyler. The blond-haired boy, his hair hanging loosely from under his white cap, opened the folded paper.

> *Don't let Kyler read this, but if there was even a second that he thought you were in trouble, he would be the first one out the door, no matter how dark it was. I would be right behind him.*

*Chasing fear into darkness,* Trust signed, grinning.

# Author's Note

Thanks to Arran at Editing 720, Amy at Blue Otter Editing, and Najla at Najla Qamber Designs for their usual wizardry cleverly disguised as talent and hard work.

And, as always, thanks to YOU for reading this far.

On to the next one.

## About the Author

*Fear Into Darkness* is the third novel written by Taylor Dye and the first in the Trustice Jeffries series. He is also the author of *The Intermediaries: Beat & Case* and *The Intermediaries: Redemption*.

You can find the author, along with the latest news, books, and upcoming release info from Samanedna Publishers, at our website

Samanedna.com

www.ingramcontent.com/pod-product-compliance
Lightning Source LLC
Chambersburg PA
CBHW020819030726
47496CB00001B/6